TWO CLASSIC VOLUMES FROM

ROBERT R. McCAMMON

BOY'S LIFE

GONE SOUTH

POCKET BOOKS

New York London Toronto Sydney Tokyo Singapore

"I Get Around." Words and Music by Brian Wilson. Copyright © 1964 Irving Music, Inc. (BMI). All Rights Reserved. International Copyright Secured.

 POCKET BOOKS, a division of Simon & Schuster Inc.
1230 Avenue of the Americas, New York, NY 10020

Library of Congress Cataloging-in-Publication Data

McCammon, Robert R.
  [Boy's life]
  Two classic volumes from Robert R. McCammon.
     p.   cm.
  Contents: Boy's life—Gone south.
  ISBN 0-671-01883-3
    I. McCammon, Robert R. Gone south. II. Title. III. Title: Boy's life.
  IV. Title: Gone south.
  PS3563.C3345B6   1998
  813'.54—dc21   97-36491
                                                          CIP

First Pocket Books hardcover printing January 1998

10 9 8 7 6 5 4 3 2 1

POCKET and colophon are registered trademarks of
Simon & Schuster Inc.

Printed in the U.S.A.

Books by Robert R. McCammon

Baal
Bethany's Sin
Blue World
Boy's Life
Gone South
Mine
Mystery Walk
The Night Boat
Stinger
Swan Song
They Thirst
Usher's Passing
The Wolf's Hour

Published by POCKET BOOKS

CONTENTS

BOY'S
LIFE

We ran like young wild furies,
where angels feared to tread.
The woods were dark and deep.
Before us demons fled.
We checked Coke bottle bottoms
to see how far was far.
Our worlds of magic wonder
were never reached by car.
We loved our dogs like brothers,
our bikes like rocket ships.
We were going to the stars,
to Mars we'd make round trips.
We swung on vines like Tarzan,
and flashed Zorro's keen blade.
We were James Bond in his Aston,
we were Hercules unchained.
We looked upon the future
and we saw a distant land,
where our folks were always ageless,
and time was shifting sand.
We filled up life with living,
with grins, scabbed knees, and noise.
In glass I see an older man,
but this book's for the boys.

I want to tell you some important things before we start our journey.

I lived through it all. That's one problem about relating events in first person. The reader knows the narrator didn't get killed. So whatever might happen to me—whatever *did* happen to me—you can be sure I lived through it all, though I might be a little better or worse for the experience, and you can make up your own mind which.

There might be some places where you'll say, "Hey, how come he knows this event right here happened or this person said or did this or that if he wasn't even there?" The answer to that question is that I found out enough later on to fill in the blanks, or in some cases I made up what happened, or in other cases I figured it ought to have happened that way even if it didn't.

I was born in July of 1952. I am approaching my fortieth birthday. Gosh, that's some number, isn't it? I am no longer, as my reviews used to say, a "promising young talent." I am what I am. I have been writing since I was in grammar school, and thinking up stories long before I understood exactly what it was I was doing. I have been a published writer since 1978. Or is it "author"? Paperback writer, as the Beatles said. Hardback author? One thing's for sure: I certainly have developed a hard back. I have suffered kicks and smiled at kindnesses just like any other brother or sister on our spinning home. I have been blessed, to be able to create characters and worlds out of whole cloth. Writer? Author?

How about storyteller?

I wanted to set my memories down on paper, where I can hold them. You know, I do believe in magic. I was born and raised in a magic time, in a magic town, among magicians. Oh, most every-body else didn't realize we lived in that web of magic, connected by the silver filaments of chance and circumstance. But I knew it all along. When I was twelve years old, the world was my magic

1

lantern, and by its green spirit glow I saw the past, the present, and into the future. You probably did too; you just don't recall it. See, this is my opinion: we all start out knowing magic. We are born with whirlwinds, forest fires, and comets inside us. We are born able to sing to birds and read the clouds and see our destiny in grains of sand. But then we get the magic educated right out of our souls. We get it churched out, spanked out, washed out, and combed out. We get put on the straight and narrow and told to be responsible. Told to act our age. Told to grow up, for God's sake. And you know why we were told that? Because the people doing the telling were afraid of our wildness and youth, and because the magic we knew made them ashamed and sad of what they'd allowed to wither in themselves.

After you go so far away from it, though, you can't really get it back. You can have seconds of it. Just seconds of knowing and remembering. When people get weepy at movies, it's because in that dark theater the golden pool of magic is touched, just briefly. Then they come out into the hard sun of logic and reason again and it dries up, and they're left feeling a little heartsad and not knowing why. When a song stirs a memory, when motes of dust turning in a shaft of light takes your attention from the world, when you listen to a train passing on a track at night in the distance and wonder where it might be going, you step beyond who you are and where you are. For the briefest of instants, you have stepped into the magic realm.

That's what I believe.

The truth of life is that every year we get farther away from the essence that is born within us. We get shouldered with burdens, some of them good, some of them not so good. Things happen to us. Loved ones die. People get in wrecks and get crippled. People lose their way, for one reason or another. It's not hard to do, in this world of crazy mazes. Life itself does its best to take that memory of magic away from us. You don't know it's happening until one day you feel you've lost something but you're not sure what it is. It's like smiling at a pretty girl and she calls you "sir." It just happens.

These memories of who I was and where I lived are important to me. They make up a large part of who I'm going to be when my journey winds down. I need the memory of magic if I am ever going to conjure magic again. I need to know and remember, and I want to tell you.

My name is Cory Jay Mackenson. My hometown was a place called Zephyr, in south Alabama. It never got too cold there, or too hot. Its streets were shaded with water oaks, and its houses had front porches and screens on the windows. There was a park with two baseball fields, one for the kids and one for the grown-ups.

There was a public swimming pool where the water was blue and clear and children plumbed the deep end for pennies. On the Fourth of July there was a barbecue, and at the end of summer a writing contest. When I was twelve years old, in 1964, Zephyr held about fifteen hundred people. There was the Bright Star Cafe, a Woolworth's, and a little Piggly-Wiggly grocery store. There was a house where bad girls lived out on Route Ten. Not every family had a television set. The county was dry, which meant that bootleggers thrived. The roads went south, north, east, and west, and at night a freight train passed through on its way to Birmingham and left the smell of scorched iron in its wake. Zephyr had four churches and an elementary school, and a cemetery stood on Poulter Hill. There was a lake nearby so deep it might as well have been bottomless. My hometown was full of heroes and villains, honest people who knew the beauty of truth and others whose beauty was a lie. My hometown was probably a lot like yours.

But Zephyr was a magic place. Spirits walked in the moonlight. They came out of the grassy graveyard and stood on the hill and talked about old times when Coca-Cola really had a bite and you could tell a Democrat from a Republican. I know. I've heard them. The breeze in Zephyr blew through the screens, bringing the incense of honeysuckle and awakening love, and jagged blue lightning crashed down upon the earth and awakened hate. We had windstorms and droughts and the river that lay alongside my town had the bad habit of flooding. In the spring of my fifth year, a flood brought snakes to the streets. Then hawks came down by the hundreds in a dark tornado and lifted up the snakes in their killing beaks, and the river slinked back to its banks like a whipped dog. Then the sun came out like a trumpet call, and steam swirled up from the blood-specked roofs of my hometown.

We had a dark queen who was one hundred and six years old. We had a gunfighter who saved the life of Wyatt Earp at the O.K. Corral. We had a monster in the river, and a secret in the lake. We had a ghost that haunted the road behind the wheel of a black dragster with flames on the hood. We had a Gabriel and a Lucifer, and a rebel that rose from the dead. We had an alien invader, a boy with a perfect arm, and we had a dinosaur loose on Merchants Street.

It was a magic place.

In me are the memories of a boy's life, spent in that realm of enchantments.

I remember.

These are the things I want to tell you.

3

ONE
The
Shades of Spring

———————

Before the Sun—Down in the Dark— The Invader—Wasps at Easter—The Death of a Bike—Old Moses Comes to Call—A Summons from the Lady

1

Before the Sun

"**C**ory? Wake up, son. It's time."

I let him pull me up from the dark cavern of sleep, and I opened my eyes and looked up at him. He was already dressed, in his dark brown uniform with his name—Tom—written in white letters across his breast pocket. I smelled bacon and eggs, and the radio was playing softly in the kitchen. A pan rattled and glasses clinked; Mom was at work in her element as surely as a trout rides a current. "It's time," my father said, and he switched on the lamp beside my bed and left me squinting with the last images of a dream fading in my brain.

The sun wasn't up yet. It was mid-March, and a chill wind blew through the trees beyond my window. I could feel the wind by putting my hand against the glass. Mom, realizing that I was awake when my dad went in for his cup of coffee, turned the radio up a little louder to catch the weather report. Spring had sprung a couple of days before, but this year winter had sharp teeth and nails and he clung to the South like a white cat. We hadn't had snow, we never had snow, but the wind was chill and it blew hard from the lungs of the Pole.

"Heavy sweater!" Mom called. "Hear?"

"I hear!" I answered back, and I got my green heavy sweater from my dresser. Here is my room, in the yellow lamplight and the space heater rumbling: Indian rug red as Cochise's blood, a desk with seven mystic drawers, a chair covered in material as velvety blue-black as Batman's cape, an aquarium holding tiny fish so pale you could see their hearts beat, the aforementioned dresser covered with decals from Revell model airplane kits, a bed with a quilt sewn by a relative of Jefferson Davis's, a closet, and the shelves. Oh, yes, the shelves. The troves of treasure. On those shelves are stacks of me: hundreds of comic books—Justice League, Flash, Green Lantern, Batman, the Spirit, Blackhawk, Sgt. Rock and Easy Company,

Aquaman, and the Fantastic Four. There are *Boy's Life* magazines, dozens of issues of *Famous Monsters of Filmland, Screen Thrills*, and *Popular Mechanics.* There is a yellow wall of *National Geographic*s, and I have to blush and say I know where all the African pictures are.

The shelves go on for miles and miles. My collection of marbles gleams in a mason jar. My dried cicada waits to sing again in summer. My Duncan yo-yo that whistles except the string is broken and Dad's got to fix it. My little book of suit cloth samples that I got from Mr. Parlowe at the Stagg Shop for Men. I use those pieces of cloth as carpet inside my airplane models, along with seats cut from cardboard. My silver bullet, forged by the Lone Ranger for a werewolf hunter. My Civil War button that fell from a butternut uniform when the storm swept Shiloh. My rubber knife for stalking killer crocodiles in the bathtub. My Canadian coins, smooth as the northern plains. I am rich beyond measure.

"Breakfast's on!" Mom called. I zipped up my sweater, which was the same hue as Sgt. Rock's ripped shirt. My blue jeans had patches on the knees, like badges of courage marking encounters with barbed wire and gravel. My flannel shirt was red enough to stagger a bull. My socks were white as dove wings and my Keds midnight black. My mom was color-blind, and my dad thought checks went with plaid. I was all right.

It's funny, sometimes, when you look at the people who brought you into this world and you see yourself so clearly in them. You realize that every person in the world is a compromise of nature. I had my mother's small-boned frame and her wavy, dark brown hair, but my father had given me his blue eyes and his sharp-bridged nose. I had my mother's long-fingered hands—an "artist's hands," she used to tell me when I fretted that my fingers were so skinny—and my dad's thick eyebrows and the small cleft in his chin. I wished that some nights I would go to sleep and awaken resembling a man's man like Stuart Whitman in *Cimarron Strip* or Clint Walker in *Cheyenne,* but the truth of it was that I was a skinny, gawky kid of average height and looks, and I could blend into wallpaper by closing my eyes and holding my breath. In my fantasies, though, I tracked lawbreakers along with the cowboys and detectives who paraded past us nightly on our television set, and out in the woods that came up behind our house I helped Tarzan call the lions and shot Nazis down in a solitary war. I had a small group of friends, guys like Johnny Wilson, Davy Ray Callan, and Ben Sears, but I wasn't what you might call popular. Sometimes

I got nervous talking to people and my tongue got tangled, so I stayed quiet. My friends and I were about the same in size, age, and temperament; we avoided what we could not fight, and we were all pitiful fighters.

This is where I think the writing started. The "righting," if you will. The righting of circumstances, the shaping of the world the way it should have been, had God not had crossed eyes and buck teeth. In the real world I had no power; in my world I was Hercules unchained.

One thing I do know I got from my granddaddy Jaybird, my dad's father: his curiosity about the world. He was seventy-six years old and as tough as beef jerky, and he had a foul mouth and an even fouler disposition, but he was always prowling the woods around his farm. He brought home things that made Grandmomma Sarah swoon: snakeskins, empty hornets' nests, even animals he'd found dead. He liked to cut things open with a penknife and look at their insides, arranging all their bloody guts out on newspapers. One time he hung up a dead toad from a tree and invited me to watch the flies eat it with him. He brought home a burlap sack full of leaves, dumped them in the front room, and examined each of them with a magnifying glass, writing down their differences in one of his hundreds of Nifty notebooks. He collected cigar butts and dried spits of chewing tobacco, which he kept in glass vials. He could sit for hours in the dark and look at the moon.

Maybe he was crazy. Maybe crazy is what they call anybody who's got magic in them after they're no longer a child. But Granddaddy Jaybird read the Sunday comics to me, and he told me stories about the haunted house in the small hamlet of his birth. Granddaddy Jaybird could be mean and stupid and petty, but he lit a candle of wonder in me and by that light I could see a long way beyond Zephyr.

On that morning before the sun, as I sat eating my breakfast with my dad and mom in our house on Hilltop Street, the year was 1964. There were great changes in the winds of earth, things of which I was unaware. All I knew at that moment was that I needed another glass of orange juice, and that I was going to help my dad on his route before he took me to school. So when breakfast was over and the dishes were cleared, after I had gone out into the cold to say good morning to Rebel and feed him his Gravy Train, Mom kissed both Dad and me, I put on my fleece-lined jacket and got my schoolbooks and off we went in the coughy old pickup truck. Freed from his backyard pen, Rebel followed us a distance, but at the corner of Hilltop and Shawson streets he crossed into the territory of Bodog, the Doberman pinscher that belonged to the Ramseys, and he beat a diplomatic retreat to a drumroll of barks.

And there was Zephyr before us, the town quiet in its dreaming, the moon a white sickle in the sky.

A few lights were on. Not many. It wasn't five o'clock yet. The sickle moon glittered in the slow curve of the Tecumseh River, and if Old Moses swam there he swam with his leathery belly kissing mud. The trees along Zephyr's streets were still without leaves, and their branches moved with the wind. The traffic lights—all four of them at what might be called major intersections—blinked yellow in a steady accord. To the east, a stone bridge with brooding gargoyles crossed the wide hollow where the river ran. Some said the faces of the gargoyles, carved in the early twenties, were representations of various Confederate generals, fallen angels, as it were. To the west, the highway wound into the wooded hills and on toward other towns. A railroad track cut across Zephyr to the north, right through the Bruton area, where all the black people lived. In the south was the public park where a bandshell stood and a couple of baseball diamonds had been cut into the earth. The park was named for Clifford Gray Haines, who founded Zephyr, and there was a statue of him sitting on a rock with his chin resting on his hand. My dad said it looked as if Clifford was perpetually constipated and could neither do his business nor get off the pot. Farther south, Route Ten left Zephyr's limits and wound like a black cottonmouth past swampy woods, a trailer park, and Saxon's Lake, which shelved into unknown depths.

Dad turned us onto Merchants Street, and we drove through the center of Zephyr, where the stores were. There was Dollar's Barbershop, the Stagg Shop for Men, the Zephyr Feeds and Hardware Store, the Piggly-Wiggly grocery, the Woolworth's store, the Lyric theater, and other attractions along the sidewalked thoroughfare. It wasn't much, though; if you blinked a few times, you were past it. Then Dad crossed the railroad track, drove another two miles, and turned into a gate that had a sign above it: GREEN MEADOWS DAIRY. The milk trucks were at the loading dock, getting filled up. Here there was a lot of activity, because Green Meadows Dairy opened early and the milkmen had their appointed rounds.

Sometimes when my father had an especially busy schedule, he asked me to help him with his deliveries. I liked the silence and stillness of the mornings. I liked the world before the sun. I liked finding out what different people ordered from the dairy. I don't know why; maybe that was my granddaddy Jaybird's curiosity in me.

My dad went over a checklist with the foreman, a big crew-cut man named Mr. Bowers, and then Dad and I started loading our truck. Here came the bottles of milk, the cartons of fresh eggs, buckets of cottage cheese and Green Meadows' special potato and bean salads. Everything was still cold from the ice room, and the milk bottles sparkled with frost under the loading dock's lights. Their paper caps bore the face of a smiling milkman and the words "Good for You!" As we were working, Mr. Bowers came up and watched with his clipboard at his side and his pen behind his ear. "You think you'd like to be a milkman, Cory?" he asked me, and I said I might. "The world'll always need milkmen," Mr. Bowers went on. "Isn't that right, Tom?"

"Right as rain," my dad said; this was an all-purpose phrase he used when he was only half listening.

"You come apply when you turn eighteen," Mr. Bowers told me. "We'll fix you up." He gave me a clap on the shoulder that almost rattled my teeth and did rattle the bottles in the tray I was carrying.

Then Dad climbed behind the big-spoked wheel, I got into the seat next to him, he turned the key, and the engine started and we backed away from the loading dock with our creamy cargo. Ahead of us, the moon was sinking down and the last of the stars hung on the lip of night. "What about that?" Dad asked. "Being a milkman, I mean. That appeal to you?"

"It'd be fun," I said.

"Not really. Oh, it's okay, but no job's fun every day. I guess we've never talked about what you want to do, have we?"

"No sir."

"Well, I don't think you ought to be a milkman just because that's what I do. See, I didn't start out to be a milkman. Granddaddy Jaybird wanted me to be a farmer like him. Grandmomma Sarah wanted me to be a doctor. Can you imagine that?" He glanced at me and grinned. "Me, a doctor! Doctor Tom! No sir, that wasn't for me."

"What'd you start out to be?" I asked.

My dad was quiet for a while. He seemed to be thinking this question over, in a deep place. It occurred to me that maybe no one had ever asked him this before. He gripped the spoked wheel with his grown-up hands and negotiated the road that unwound before us in the headlights, and then he said, "First man on Venus. Or a rodeo rider. Or a man who can look at an empty space and see in his mind the house he wants to build there right down to the last nail

11

and shingle. Or a detective." My dad made a little laughing noise in his throat. "But the dairy needed another milkman, so here I am."

"I wouldn't mind bein' a race car driver," I said. My dad sometimes took me to the stock car races at the track near Barnesboro, and we sat there eating hot dogs and watching sparks fly in the collision of banged-up metal. "Bein' a detective would be okay, too. I'd get to solve mysteries and stuff, like the Hardy Boys."

"Yeah, that'd be good," my dad agreed. "You never know how things are gonna turn out, though, and that's the truth. You aim for one place, sure as an arrow, but before you hit the mark, the wind gets you. I don't believe I ever met one person who became what they wanted to be when they were your age."

"I'd like to be everybody in the world," I said. "I'd like to live a million times."

"Well"—and here my father gave one of his sagely nods—"that would be a fine piece of magic, wouldn't it?" He pointed. "Here's our first stop."

That first house must've had children in it, because they got two quarts of chocolate milk to go along with their two quarts of plain milk. Then we were off again, driving through the streets where the only sounds were the wind and the barking of early dogs, and we stopped on Shantuck Street to deliver buttermilk and cottage cheese to somebody who must've liked things sour. We left bottles glistening on the steps of most of the houses on Bevard Lane, and my dad worked fast as I checked off the list and got the next items ready from the chilly back of the truck; we were a good team.

Dad said he had some customers down south near Saxon's Lake and then he'd swing back up so we could finish the rest of the street deliveries before my school bell rang. He drove us past the park and out of Zephyr, and the forest closed in on either side of the road.

It was getting on toward six o'clock. To the east, over the hills of pine and kudzu, the sky was beginning to lighten. The wind shoved its way through the trees like the fist of a bully. We passed a car going north, and its driver blinked the lights and Dad waved. "Marty Barklee deliverin' the newspapers," Dad told me. I thought about the fact that there was a whole world going about its business before the sun, and people who were just waking up weren't part of it. We turned off Route Ten and drove up a dirt drive to deliver milk, buttermilk, and potato salad to a small house nestled in the woods, and then we went south toward the lake again. "College," my dad said. "You ought to go to college, it seems to me."

"I guess so," I answered, but that sounded like an awful long

12

distance from where I was now. All I knew about college was Auburn and Alabama football, and the fact that some people praised Bear Bryant and others worshipped Shug Jordan. It seemed to me that you chose which college to go to according to which coach you liked best.

"Gotta have good grades to get into college," Dad said. "Gotta study your lessons."

"Do detectives have to go to college?"

"I reckon they do if they want to be professional about it. If I'd gone to college, I might've turned out to be that man who builds a house in empty space. You never know what's ahead for you, and that's the—"

Truth, he was about to say, but he never finished it because we came around a wooded bend and a brown car jumped out of the forest right in front of us and Dad yelped like he was hornet-stung as his foot punched the brake.

The brown car went past us as Dad whipped the wheel to the left, and I saw that car go off Route Ten and down the embankment on my right. Its lights weren't on but there was somebody sitting behind the wheel. The car's tires tore through the underbrush and then it went over a little cliff of red rock and down into the dark. Water splashed up, and I realized the car had just plunged into Saxon's Lake.

"He went in the water!" I shouted, and Dad stopped the milk truck, pulled up the hand brake, and jumped out into the roadside weeds. As I climbed out, Dad was already running toward the lake. The wind whipped and whirled around us, and Dad stood there on the red rock cliff. By the faint pinkish light we could see the car wallowing in the water, huge bubbles bursting around its trunk. "Hey!" Dad shouted with his hands cupped around his mouth. "Get out of there!" Everybody knew Saxon's Lake was as deep as sin, and when that car went down into the inky depths it was gone for good and ever. "Hey, get out!" Dad shouted again, but whoever was behind the wheel didn't answer. "I think he's been knocked cold!" Dad told me as he took off his shoes. The car was starting to turn onto its passenger side, and there was an awful howling sound coming from it that must've been the rush of water pouring into the car. Dad said, "Stand back." I did, and he leaped into the lake.

He was a strong swimmer. He reached the car in a few powerful strokes, and he saw that the driver's window was open. He could feel the suction of water moving around his legs, drawing the car down into the unfathomed deep. "Get out!" he hollered, but the driver just sat there. Dad clung to the door, reached in, and grabbed the driver's shoulder. It was a man, and he wore no shirt. The flesh was white and cold, and my dad felt his own skin crawl. The man's head lolled back, his mouth open. He had short-cropped blond hair, his eyes sealed shut with black bruises, his face swollen and malformed from the pressures of a savage beating. Around his throat was knotted a copper piano wire, the thin metal pulled so tightly that the flesh had split open.

"Oh Jesus," my dad whispered, treading water.

The car lurched and hissed. The head lolled forward over the chest again, as if in an attitude of prayer. Water was rising up over the driver's bare knees. My dad realized the driver was naked, not a stitch on him. Something glinted on the steering wheel, and he saw handcuffs that secured the man's right wrist to the inner spoke.

My dad had lived thirty-four years. He'd seen dead men before. Hodge Klemson, one of his best friends, had drowned in the Tecumseh River when they were both fifteen years old, and the body had been found after three days bloated and covered with yellow bottom mud like a crusty ancient mummy. He'd seen what remained of Walter and Jeanine Traynor after the head-on collision six years ago between Walter's Buick and a logging truck driven by a kid eating pep pills. He'd seen the dark shiny mass of Little Stevie Cauley after firemen doused the flames of the crumpled black dragster named Midnight Mona. He had looked upon the grinning rictus of death several times, had taken that sight like a man, but this one was different.

This one wore the face of murder.

The car was going down. As its hood sank, its tail fins started rising. The body behind the wheel shifted again, and my father saw something on the man's shoulder. A blue patch, there against the white. Not a bruise, no; a tattoo. It was a skull with wings swept back from the bony temples.

A great burst of bubbles blew out of the car as more water rushed in. The lake would not be denied; it was going to claim its toy and tuck it away in a secret drawer. As the car began to slide down into the murk, the suction grabbed my father's legs and pulled him under, and standing on the red rock cliff I saw his head disappear and I shouted *"Dad!"* as panic seized my guts.

Underwater, he fought the lake's muscles. The car fell away beneath him, and as his legs thrashed for a hold in the liquid tomb, more bubbles rushed up and broke him loose and he climbed up their silver staircase toward the attic of air.

I saw his head break the surface. "Dad!" I shouted again. "Come on back, Dad!"

"I'm all right!" he answered, but his voice was shaky. "I'm comin' in!" He began dog-paddling toward shore, his body suddenly as weak as a squeezed-out rag. The lake continued to erupt where the car disturbed its innards, like something bad being digested. Dad couldn't get up the red rock cliff, so he swam to a place where he could clamber up on kudzu vines and stones. "I'm all right!" he said again as he came out of the lake and his legs sank to the knees in mud. A turtle the size of a dinner plate skittered past him and submerged with a perplexed snort. I glanced back toward the milk truck; I don't know why, but I did.

And I saw a figure standing in the woods across the road.

Just standing there, wearing a long dark coat. Its folds moved with the wind. Maybe I'd felt the eyes of whoever was watching me as I'd watched my father swim to the sinking car. I shivered a little, bone cold, and then I blinked a couple of times and where the figure had been was just windswept woods again.

"Cory?" my dad called. "Gimme a hand up, son!"

I went down to the muddy shore and gave him as much help as a cold, scared child could. Then his feet found solid earth and he pushed the wet hair back from his forehead. "Gotta get to a phone," he said urgently. "There was a man in that car. Went straight down to the bottom!"

"I saw . . . I saw . . ." I pointed toward the woods on the other side of Route Ten. "Somebody was—"

"Come on, let's go!" My father was already crossing the road with his sturdy, soggy legs, his shoes in his hand. I jump-started my own legs and followed him as close as a shadow, and my gaze returned to where I'd seen that figure but nobody was there, nobody, nobody at all.

Dad started the milk truck's engine and switched on the heater. His teeth were chattering, and in the gray twilight his face looked as pale as candle wax. "Damnedest thing," he said, and this shocked me because he never cursed in front of me. "Handcuffed to the wheel, he was. Handcuffed. My God, that fella's face was all beat up!"

"Who was it?"

"I don't know." He turned the heater up, and then he started driving south toward the nearest house. "Somebody did a job on him, that's for sure! Lord, I'm cold!"

A dirt road turned to the right, and my father followed it. Fifty yards off Route Ten stood a small white house with a screened-in front porch. A rose garden stood off to one side. Parked under a green plastic awning were two cars, one a red Mustang and the other an old Cadillac splotched with rust. My dad pulled up in front of the house and said, "Wait here," and he walked to the door in his wet socks and rang the bell. He had to ring it two more times before the door opened with a tinkle of chimes, and a red-haired woman who made three of my mom stood there wearing a blue robe with black flowers on it.

Dad said, "Miss Grace, I need to use your telephone real quick."

"You're all *wet!*" Miss Grace's voice sounded like the rasp of a rusty saw blade. She gripped a cigarette in one hand, and rings sparkled on her fingers.

"Somethin' bad's happened," Dad told her, and she sighed like a redheaded raincloud and said, "All right, come on in, then. Watch the carpet." Dad entered the house, the chimey door closed, and I sat in the milk truck as the first orange rays of sunlight started breaking over the eastern hills. I could smell the lake in the truck with me, a puddle of water on the floorboard beneath my father's seat. I had seen somebody standing in the woods. I knew I had. Hadn't I? Why hadn't he come over to see about the man in the car? And who had the man in the car been?

I was puzzling over these questions when the door opened again and Miss Grace came out, this time wearing a floppy white sweater over her blue gown. She had on sneakers, her ankles and calves thick as young trees. She had a box of Lorna Doone cookies in one hand and the burning cigarette in the other, and she walked to the milk truck and smiled at me. "Hey there," she said. "You're Cory."

"Yes'm," I answered.

Miss Grace didn't have much of a smile. Her lips were thin and her nose was broad and flat and her brows were black-penciled streaks above deep-set blue eyes. She thrust the Lorna Doones at me. "Want a cookie?"

I wasn't hungry, but my folks had always taught me never to refuse a gift. I took one.

"Have two," Miss Grace offered, and I took a second cookie. She ate a cookie herself and then sucked on the cigarette and blew smoke through her nostrils. "Your daddy's our milkman," she said. "I believe you've got us on your list. Six quarts of milk, two buttermilks, two chocolates, and three pints of cream."

I checked the list. There was her name—Grace Stafford—and the order, just as she'd said. I told her I'd get everything for her, and I started putting the order together. "How old are you?" Miss Grace asked as I worked. "Twelve?"

"No, ma'am. Not until July."

"I've got a son." Miss Grace knocked ashes from her cigarette. She chewed on another cookie. "Turned twenty in December. He lives in San Antonio. Know where that is?"

"Yes ma'am. Texas. Where the Alamo is."

"That's right. Turned twenty, which makes me thirty-eight. I'm an old fossil, ain't I?"

This was a trick question, I thought. "No ma'am," I decided to say.

"Well, you're a little diplomat, ain't you?" She smiled again, and this time the smile was in her eyes. "Have another cookie." She left me the box and walked to the door, and she hollered into the house: "Lainie! Lainie, get your butt up and come out here!"

My dad emerged first. He looked old in the hard light of morning, and there were dark circles under his eyes. "Called the sheriff's office," he told me as he sat in his wet seat and squeezed his feet into his shoes. "Somebody's gonna meet us where the car went in."

"Who the hell was it?" Miss Grace asked.

"I couldn't tell. His face was . . ." He glanced quickly at me, then back to the woman. "He was beat up pretty bad."

"Must've been drunk. Moonshinin', most likely."

"I don't think so." Dad hadn't said anything over the phone about the car's driver being naked, strangled with a piano wire, and handcuffed to the wheel. That was for the sheriff and not for Miss Grace's or anybody else's ears. "You ever see a fella with a tattoo on his left shoulder? Looked like a skull with wings growin' out of its head?"

"I've seen more tattoos than the Navy," Miss Grace said, "but I can't recall anything like that around here. Why? Fella have his shirt off or somethin'?"

"Yeah, he did. Had that skull with wings tattooed right about here." He touched his left shoulder. Dad shivered again, and rubbed his hands together. "They'll never bring that car up. Never. Saxon's Lake is three hundred feet deep if it's an inch."

The chimes sounded. I looked toward the door with the tray of milk quarts in my arms.

A girl with sleep-swollen eyes stumbled out. She was wearing a long plaid bathrobe and her feet were bare. Her hair was the color of cornsilk and hung around her shoulders, and as she neared the milk truck she blinked in the light and said, "I'm all fucked up."

17

I think I must've almost fallen down, because never in my life had I heard a female use a word that dirty before. Oh, I knew what the word meant and all, but its casual use from a pretty mouth shocked the fool out of me.

"There's a young man on the premises, Lainie," Miss Grace said in a voice that could curl an iron nail. "Watch your language, please."

Lainie looked at me, and her cool stare made me recall the time I'd put a fork in an electric socket. Lainie's eyes were chocolate brown and her lips seemed to wear a half smile, half sneer. Something about her face looked tough and wary, as if she'd run out of trust. There was a small red mark in the hollow of her throat. "Who's the kid?" she asked.

"Mr. Mackenson's son. Show some class, hear?"

I swallowed hard and averted my eyes from Lainie's. Her robe was creeping open. It hit me what kind of girl used bad words, and what kind of place this was. I had heard from both Johnny Wilson and Ben Sears that there was a house full of whores somewhere near Zephyr. It was common knowledge at the elementary school. When you told somebody to "go suck a whore," you were standing right on the razor's edge of violence. I'd always imagined the whorehouse to be a mansion, though, with drooping willow trees and black servants who fetched the customers mint juleps on the front porch; the reality, however, was that the whorehouse wasn't much of a step up from a broken-down trailer. Still and all, here it was right in front of me, and the girl with cornsilk hair and a dirty mouth earned her living by the pleasures of the flesh. I felt goose bumps ripple up my back, and I can't tell you the kind of scenes that moved like a slow, dangerous storm through my head.

"Take that milk and stuff to the kitchen," Miss Grace told her.

The sneer won out over the smile, and those brown eyes turned black. "I ain't got kitchen duty! It's Donna Ann's week!"

"It's whose week I say it is, missy, and you know why I ought to put you in the kitchen for a whole *month*, too! Now, you do what I tell you and keep your smart mouth shut!"

Lainie's lips drew up into a puckered, practiced pout. But her eyes did not register the chastisement so falsely; they held cold centers of anger. She took the tray from me, and standing with her back to my dad and Miss Grace, she stuck out her wet pink tongue in my face and curled it up into a funnel. Then the tongue slicked back into her mouth, she turned away from me, and dismissed all of us with a buttstrut that was as wicked as a sword slash. She swayed on into the house, and after Lainie was gone Miss Grace grunted and said, "She's as rough as a cob."

"Aren't they all?" Dad asked, and Miss Grace blew a smoke ring and answered, "Yeah, but she don't even *pretend* she's got manners." Her gaze settled on me. "Cory, why don't you keep the cookies. All right?"

I looked at Dad. He shrugged. "Yes, ma'am," I said.

"Good. It was a real pleasure to meet you." Miss Grace returned her attention to my father and the cigarette to the corner of her mouth. "Let me know how everything turns out."

"I will, and thanks for lettin' me use the phone." He slid behind the wheel again. "I'll pick up the milk tray next trip."

"Ya'll be careful," Miss Grace said, and she went into the white-painted whorehouse as Dad started the engine and let off the hand brake.

We drove back to where the car had gone in. Saxon's Lake was streaked with blue and purple in the morning light. Dad pulled the milk truck off onto a dirt road; the road, both of us realized, was where the car had come from. Then we sat and waited for the sheriff as the sunlight strengthened and the sky turned azure.

Sitting there, my mind was split: one part was thinking about the car and the figure I thought I'd seen, and the other part was wondering how my dad knew Miss Grace at the whorehouse so well. But Dad knew all of his customers; he talked about them to Mom at the dinner table. I never recalled him mentioning Miss Grace or the whorehouse, however. Well, it wasn't a proper subject for the dinner table, was it? And anyway, they wouldn't talk about such things when I was around, even though all my friends and everybody else at school from the fourth grade up knew there was a house full of bad girls somewhere around Zephyr.

I had been there. I had actually seen a bad girl. I had seen her curled tongue and her butt move in the folds of her robe.

That, I figured, was going to make me one heck of a celebrity.

"Cory?" my father said quietly. "Do you know what kind of business Miss Grace runs in that house?"

"I . . ." Even a third-grader could've figured it out. "Yes sir."

"Any other day, I would've just left the order by the front door." He was staring at the lake, as if seeing the car still tumbling slowly down through the depths with a handcuffed corpse at the wheel. "Miss Grace has been on my delivery route for two years. Every Monday and Thursday, like clockwork. In case it's crossed your mind, your mother *does* know I come out here."

I didn't answer, but I felt a whole lot lighter.

19

"I don't want you to tell anybody about Miss Grace or that house," my father went on. "I want you to forget you were there, and what you saw and heard. Can you do that?"

"Why?" I had to ask.

"Because Miss Grace might be a lot different than you, me, or your mother, and she might be tough and mean and her line of work might not be a preacher's dream, but she's a good lady. I just don't want talk gettin' stirred up. The less said about Miss Grace and that house, the better. Do you see?"

"I guess I do."

"Good." He flexed his fingers on the steering wheel. The subject was closed.

I was true to my word. My celebrityhood took flight, and that was that.

I was about to open my mouth to tell him about the figure I'd seen in the woods when a black and white Ford with a bubble light on top and the town seal of Zephyr on the driver's door rounded the corner and slowed to a stop near the milk truck. Sheriff Amory, whose first name was J.T., standing for Junior Talmadge, got out and Dad walked over to meet him.

Sheriff Amory was a thin, tall man whose long-jawed face made me think of a picture I'd seen: Ichabod Crane trying to outrace the Headless Horseman. He had big hands and feet and a pair of ears that might've shamed Dumbo. If his nose had been any larger, he would've made a dandy weathervane. He wore his sheriff's star pinned to the front of his hat, and underneath it his dome was almost bald except for a wreath of dark brown hair. He pushed his hat back up on his shiny forehead as he and my dad talked at the lake's edge and I watched my father's hand motions as he showed Sheriff Amory where the car had come from and where it had gone. Then they both looked out toward the lake's still surface, and I knew what they were thinking.

That car might've sunken to the center of the earth. Even the snapping turtles that lived along the lakeshore couldn't get far enough down to ever see that car again. Whoever the driver had been, he was sitting in the dark right now with mud in his teeth.

"Handcuffed," Sheriff Amory said, in his quiet voice. He had thick dark eyebrows over deep-set eyes the color of coal, and the pallor of his flesh suggested he had an affinity to the night. "You're sure about that, Tom? And about the wire, too?"

"I'm sure. Whoever strangled that fella did a hell of a job. Near about took his head off."

"Handcuffed," the sheriff said again. "That was so he wouldn't float out, I reckon." He tapped his lower lip with a forefinger. "Well," he said at last, "I believe we've got a murder on our hands, don't you?"

"If it wasn't, I don't know what murder is."

As they talked, I got out of the milk truck and wandered over to where I thought I'd seen that person watching me. There was nothing but weeds, rocks, and dirt where he'd been standing. If it had been a man, I thought. Could it have been a woman? I hadn't seen long hair, but then again I hadn't seen much of anything but a coat swirling in the wind. I walked back and forth along the line of trees. Beyond it, the woods deepened and swampy ground took over. I found nothing.

"Better come on to the office and let me write it up," the sheriff told my father. "If you want to go home and get some dry clothes on, that'd be fine."

My dad nodded. "I've got to finish my deliveries and get Cory to school, too."

"Okay. Seems to me we can't do much for that fella at the bottom, anyhow." He grunted, his hands in his pockets. "A murder. Last murder we had in Zephyr was in 1961. You remember when Bo Kallagan beat his wife to death with a bowlin' trophy?"

I returned to the milk truck and waited for my dad. The sun was up good and proper now, lighting the world. Or, at least, the world I knew. But things weighed heavy on my mind. It seemed to me that there were two worlds: one before the sun, and one after. And if that were true, then maybe there were people who were citizens of those different worlds as well. Some moved easily through the landscape of night, and others clung to the bright hours. Maybe I had seen one of those darktime citizens, in the world before the sun. And—a chilling thought—maybe he had seen *me* seeing him, too.

I realized I had brought mud back into the milk truck. It was smeared all over my Keds.

I looked at the soles, and the earth I had collected.

On the bottom of my left Ked was a small green feather.

2

Down in the Dark

The green feather went into my pocket. From there it found its way into a White Owl cigar box in my room, along with my collection of old keys and dried-up insects. I closed the box lid, placed the box in one of the seven mystic drawers, and slid the drawer shut.

And that was how I forgot about it.

The more I thought about seeing that figure at the edge of the woods, the more I thought I'd been wrong, that my eyes had been scared from seeing Dad sink underwater as the car went down. Several times I started to tell Dad about it, but something else got in the way. Mom threw a gut-busting fit when she found out he'd jumped into the lake. She was so mad at him she sobbed as she yelled, and Dad had to sit her down at the kitchen table and explain to her calmly why he had done it. "There was a man at the wheel," Dad said. "I didn't know he was already dead, I thought he was knocked cold. If I'd stood there without doing anything, what would I have thought of myself after it was over?"

"You could've drowned!" she fired at him, tears on her cheeks. "You could've hit your head on a rock and drowned!"

"I didn't drown. I didn't hit my head on a rock. I did what I had to do." He gave her a paper napkin, and she used it to blot her eyes. A last salvo came out of her: "That lake's full of cottonmouths! You could've swum right into a nest of 'em!"

"I didn't," he said, and she sighed and shook her head as if she lived with the craziest fool ever born.

"You'd better get out of those damp clothes," she told him at last, and her voice was under control again. "I just thank God it's not your body down at the bottom of the lake, too." She stood up and helped him unbutton his soggy shirt. "Do you know who it was?"

"Never saw him before."

"Who would do such a thing to another human being?"

22

"That's for J.T. to find out." He peeled his shirt off, and Mom took it from him with two fingers as if the lake's water carried leprosy. "I've got to go over to his office to help him write it up. I'll tell you, Rebecca, when I looked into that dead man's face my heart almost stopped. I've never seen anything like that before, and I hope to God I never see such a thing again, either."

"Lord," Mom said. "What if you'd had a heart attack? Who would've saved *you?*"

Worrying was my mother's way. She fretted about the weather, the cost of groceries, the washing machine breaking down, the Tecumseh River being dirtied by the paper mill in Adams Valley, the price of new clothes, and everything under the sun. To my mother, the world was a vast quilt whose stitches were always coming undone. Her worrying somehow worked like a needle, tightening those dangerous seams. If she could imagine events through to their worst tragedy, then she seemed to have some kind of control over them. As I said, it was her way. My father could throw up a fistful of dice to make a decision, but my mother had an agony for every hour. I guess they balanced, as two people who love each other should.

My mother's parents, Grand Austin and Nana Alice, lived about twelve miles south in a town called Waxahatchee, on the edge of Robbins Air Force Base. Nana Alice was even worse a worrier than Mom; something in her soul craved tragic manna, whereas Grand Austin—who had been a logger and had a wooden leg to show for the slip of a band saw—warned her he would unscrew his leg and whop her upside the head with it if she didn't pipe down and give him peace. He called his wooden leg his "peace pipe," but as far as I know he never used it for any purpose except that for which it was carved. My mother had an older brother and sister, but my father was an only child.

Anyway, I went to school that day and at the first opportunity told Davy Ray Callan, Johnny Wilson, and Ben Sears what had happened. By the time the school bell rang and I walked home, the news was moving across Zephyr like a crackling wildfire. *Murder* was the word of the hour. My parents were fighting off the phone calls. Everybody wanted to know the grisly details. I went outside to ride my rusted old bike and lead Rebel for a chase in the woods, and it came to me that maybe one of those people who called already knew the details. Maybe one of them was just trying to find out if he'd been seen, or what Sheriff Amory knew.

I realized then, as I pedaled my bike through the forest and Rebel ran at my heels, that somebody in my hometown might be a killer.

The days passed, warming into the heart of spring. A week after Dad had jumped into Saxon's Lake, this was the story: Sheriff Amory had found no one missing from Zephyr or from any of the surrounding communities. A front-page article in the weekly Adams Valley *Journal* brought forth no new information. Sheriff Amory and two of his deputies, some of the firemen, and a half dozen volunteers got out on the lake in rowboats and dragged nets back and forth, but they only came up with an angry catch of snapping turtles and cottonmouths.

Saxon's Lake used to be Saxon's Quarry back in the twenties, before the steam shovels had broken into an underground river that would not be capped or shunted aside. Estimates of its depth ranged from three hundred to five hundred feet. There wasn't a net on earth that could scoop that sunken car back to the surface.

The sheriff came by one evening for a talk with Dad and Mom, and they let me sit in on it. "Whoever did it," Sheriff Amory explained, his hat in his lap and his nose throwing a shadow, "must've backed that car onto the dirt road facin' the lake. We found the tire marks, but the footprints were all scuffed over. The killer must've had somethin' wedged against the gas pedal. Just before you rounded the bend, he released the hand brake, slammed the door, and jumped back, and the car took off across Route Ten. He didn't know you were gonna be there, of course. If you hadn't been, the car would've gone on into the lake, sunk, and nobody would ever have known it happened." He shrugged. "That's the best I can come up with."

"You talked to Marty Barklee?"

"Yeah, I did. Marty didn't see anything. The way that dirt road sits, you can drive right past it at a reasonable clip and never even know it's there."

"So where does that leave us?"

The sheriff pondered my dad's question, the silver star on his hat catching the lamplight. Outside, Rebel was barking and other dogs picked up the tribal call across Zephyr. The sheriff spread his big hands out and looked at his fingers. "Tom," he said, "we have a real strange situation here. We've got tire marks but no car. You say you saw a dead man handcuffed to the wheel and a wire around his throat, but we don't have a body and we're not likely to recover one. Nobody's missin' from town. Nobody's missin' in the whole area, except a teenaged girl whose mother thinks she ran off with her boyfriend to Nashville. And the boy don't have a tattoo, by the way. I can't find anybody who's seen a fella with a tattoo like the one you described." Sheriff Amory looked at me, then my mother, and then back to my dad with his coal-black eyes. "You know that riddle, Tom? The one about a tree fallin' in the woods, and if there's nobody around to hear it, does it make a noise? Well, if there's no body and no one's missin' anywhere that I can tell, was there a murder or not?"

"I know what I saw," Dad said. "Are you doubtin' my word, J.T.?"

"No, I didn't say that. I'm only sayin' I can't do anything more until we get a murder victim. I need a name, Tom. I need a face. Without an identification, I don't even know where to start."

"So in the meantime somebody who killed another man is walkin' around as free as you please and doesn't have to be scared of gettin' caught anytime soon. Is that it?"

"Yep," the sheriff admitted. "That about sums it up."

Of course Sheriff Amory promised he'd keep working on it, and that he'd call around the state for information on missing persons. Sooner or later, he said, somebody would have to ask after the man who had gone down in the lake. When the sheriff had gone, my father went out to sit on the front porch by himself with the light off, and he sat there alone past the time Mom told me to get ready for bed.

That was the night my father's cry awakened me in the dark.

I sat up in bed, my nerves jangled. I could hear Mom talking to Dad through the wall. "It's all right," she was saying. "It was a bad dream, just a bad dream, everything's all right."

Dad was quiet for a long time. I heard water running in the bathroom. Then the squeak of their bedsprings. "You want to tell me about it?" Mom asked him.

"No. God, no."

"It was just a bad dream."

"I don't care. It was real enough."

"Can you get back to sleep?"

He sighed. I could imagine him there in the darkened bedroom, his hands pressed to his face. "I don't know," he said.

"Let me rub your back."

The bedsprings squeaked again, as the weight of their bodies shifted. "You're awful tight," Mom said. "All up in your neck, too."

"That hurts like hell. Right there, where your thumb is."

"It's a crick. You must've pulled a muscle."

Silence. My neck and shoulders, too, had been comforted by my mother's supple hands. Every so often the springs spoke, announcing a movement. Then my father's voice came back. "I had another nightmare about that man in the car."

"I figured so."

"I was lookin' at him in that car, with his face beat all to pulp and his throat strangled with a wire. I saw the handcuff on his wrist, and the tattoo on his shoulder. The car was goin' down, and then . . . then his eyes opened."

I shivered. I could see it myself, and my father's voice was almost a gasp.

"He looked at me. Right at me. Water poured out of his eyeholes. He opened his mouth, and his tongue was as black as a snake's head. And then he said, 'Come with me.'"

"Don't think about it," Mom interrupted. "Just close your eyes and rest."

"I can't rest. I can't." I pictured my father's body, lying like a question mark on the bed as Mom kneaded the iron-tight muscles of his back. "My nightmare," he went on. "The man in the car reached out and grabbed my wrist. His fingernails were blue. His fingers bit hard into my skin, and he said, 'Come with me, down in the dark.' The car . . . the car started sinkin', faster and faster, and I tried to break loose but he wouldn't let me go, and he said, 'Come with me, come with me, down in the dark.' And then the lake closed over my head and I couldn't get away from it and I opened my mouth to scream but the water filled it up. Oh Jesus, Rebecca. Oh, Jesus."

"It wasn't real. Listen to me! It was only a bad dream, and everythin's all right now."

"No," Dad answered. "It's not. This thing is eatin' at me, and it's only gettin' worse. I thought I could put it behind me. I mean, my God, I've seen a dead person before. Up close. But this . . . this is different. That wire around his throat, the handcuff, the face that somebody had pounded into putty . . . it's different. And not knowin' who he was, or anythin' about him . . . it's eatin' at me, day and night."

"It'll pass," Mom said. "That's what you tell me whenever I want to worry the warts off a frog. Hang on, you tell me. It'll pass."

"Maybe it will. I hope to God it will. But for right now, it's in my head and I can't shake it loose for the life of me. And this is the worst thing, Rebecca; this is what's grindin' inside of me. Whoever did it had to be a local. Had to be. Whoever did it knew how deep the lake is. He knew when that car went in there, the body was gone. Rebecca . . . whoever did this thing might be somebody I deliver milk to. It might be somebody who sits on our pew at church. Somebody we buy groceries or clothes from. Somebody we've known all our lives . . . or *thought* we knew. That scares me like I've never been scared before. You know why?" He was silent for a moment, and I could imagine the way the pulse throbbed at his temple. "Because if it's not safe here, it's not safe anywhere in this world." His voice cracked a little on the last word. I was glad I wasn't in that room, and that I couldn't see his face.

Two or three minutes passed. I think my father was just lying there, letting Mom rub his back. "Do you think you can sleep now?" she finally asked him, and he said, "I'll try."

The springs spoke a few times. I heard my mother murmur something close to his ear. He said, "I hope so," and then they were silent. Sometimes my dad snored; tonight he did not. I wondered if he lay awake after Mom had drifted off, and if he saw the corpse in the car reaching for him to drag him under. What he'd said haunted me: *if it's not safe here, it's not safe anywhere in this world.* This thing had hurt my father, in a place deeper than the bottom of Saxon's Lake. Maybe it was the suddenness of what had happened, or the violence, or the cold-bloodedness of it. Maybe it was the knowledge that there were terrible secrets behind closed doors, even in the kindest of towns.

I think my father had always believed all people were good, even in their secret souls. This thing had cracked his foundations, and it occurred to me that the murderer had handcuffed my father to that awful moment in time just as the victim had been handcuffed to the wheel. I closed my eyes and prayed for Dad, that he could find his way up out of the dark.

March went out like a lamb, but the murderer's work was unfinished.

3

The Invader

Things settled down, as things will.

On the first Saturday afternoon in April, with the trees budding and flowers pushing up from the warming earth, I sat between Ben Sears and Johnny Wilson surrounded by the screaming hordes as Tarzan—Gordon Scott, the best Tarzan there ever was—plunged his knife into a crocodile's belly and blood spurted in scarlet Eastman color.

"Did you see that? Did you see that?" Ben kept saying, elbowing me in the ribs. Of course I saw it. I had eyes, didn't I? My ribs weren't going to last until the Three Stooges short between the double features, that was for certain.

The Lyric was the only movie theater in Zephyr. It had been built in 1945, after the Second World War, when Zephyr's sons marched or limped back home and they wanted entertainment to chase away the nightmares of swastika and rising sun. Some fine town father dug into his pockets and bought a construction man from Birmingham who drew a blueprint and marked off squares on a vacant lot where a tobacco barn used to be. I wasn't there at the time, of course, but Mr. Dollar could tell you the whole story. Up went a palace of stucco angels, and on Saturday afternoons we devils of the common clay hunkered down in those seats with our popcorn, candy, and Yoo-Hoos and for a few hours our parents had breathing space again.

Anyway, my two buddies and me were sitting watching Tarzan on a Saturday afternoon. I forget why Davy Ray wasn't there; I think he was grounded for hitting Molly Lujack in the head with a pine cone. But satellites could go up and spit sparks in outer space. A man with a beard and a cigar could jabber in Spanish on an island off the coast of Florida while blood reddened a bay for pigs. That bald-headed Russian could bang his shoe. Soldiers could be packing their gear for a trip to a jungle called Vietnam. Atom bombs could go off in the desert and blow dummies out of tract-house living rooms. We didn't care about any of that. It wasn't magic. Magic was inside the Lyric on Saturday afternoons, at the double feature, and we took full advantage of getting ourselves lost in the spell.

I recall watching a TV show—"77 Sunset Strip"—where the hero walked into a theater named the Lyric, and I got to thinking about that word. I looked it up in my massive two-thousand-four-hundred-and-eighty-three-page dictionary Granddaddy Jaybird had given me for my tenth birthday. "Lyric," it said: "Melodic. Suitable for singing. A lyric poem. Of the lyre." That didn't seem to make much sense in regards to a movie theater, until I continued following *lyre* in my dictionary. *Lyre* took me into the story-poems sung by traveling minstrels back when there were castles and kings. Which took me back to that wonderful word: *story*. It seemed to me at an early age that all human communication—whether it's TV, movies, or books—begins with somebody wanting to tell a story. That need to tell, to plug into a universal socket, is probably one of our grandest desires. And the need to hear stories, to live lives other than our own for even the briefest moment, is the key to the magic that was born in our bones.

The Lyric.

"Stab it, Tarzan! Stab it!" Ben yelled, and that elbow was working overtime. Ben Sears was a plump boy with brown hair cropped close to his skull, and he had a high, girlish voice and wore horn-rimmed glasses. The shirt wasn't made that could stay tucked into his jeans. He was so clumsy his shoelaces could strangle him. He had a broad chin and fat cheeks and he would never grow up to resemble Tarzan in any girl's dream, but he was my friend. By contrast to Ben's chubby exuberance, Johnny Wilson was slim, quiet, and bookish. He had some Indian blood in him that showed in his black, luminous eyes. Under the summer sun his skin turned brown as a pine nut. His hair was almost black, too, and slicked back with Vitalis except for a cowlick that shot up like a wild onion at the crease of his part. His father, who was a foreman at the sheet rock plant between Zephyr and Union Town, wore his hair exactly the same way. Johnny's mother was the library teacher at Zephyr Elementary, so I suppose that's how he got his affinity for reading. Johnny ate encyclopedias like any other kid might eat Red Hots or Lemonheads. He had a nose like a Cherokee hatchet and a small scar warped his right eyebrow where his cousin Philbo had hit him with a stick when we were all playing soldiers back in 1960. Johnny Wilson endured schoolyard taunts about being a "squawboy," or having "nigger blood," and he'd been born with a clubfoot to boot, which only doubled the abuse directed at him. He was a stoic before I knew the meaning of the word.

The movie meandered to its conclusion like a jungle river to the sea. Tarzan defeated the evil elephant poachers, returned the Star of Solomon to its tribe, and swung into the sunset. The Three Stooges short subject came on, in which Moe wrenched out Larry's hair by the handfuls and Curly sat in a bathtub full of lobsters. We all had a grand old time.

And then, without fanfare, the second feature began.

It was in black and white, which caused immediate groans from the audience. Everybody knew that color was real life. The title came up on the screen: *Invaders from Mars*. The movie looked old, like it had been made in the fifties. "I'm goin' for popcorn," Ben announced. "Anybody want anythin'?" We said no, and he negotiated the raucous aisle alone.

The credits ended, and the story started.

Ben returned with his bucket of buttered popcorn in time to see

what the young hero saw through his telescope, aimed at the stormy
night sky: a flying saucer, descending into a sand hill behind his
house. Usually the Saturday-afternoon crowd hollered and laughed
at the screen when there was no fighting going on, but this time the
stark sight of that ominous saucer coming down silenced the house.

I believe that for the next hour and a half the concession stand did
no business, though there were kids leaving their seats and running
for a view of daylight. The boy in the movie couldn't make anybody
believe he'd seen a flying saucer come down, and he watched
through his telescope as a policeman was sucked down into a vortex
of sand as if by a grotesque, otherworldly vacuum cleaner. Then the
policeman came to visit the house and assure the boy that no, of
course no flying saucer had landed. Nobody else had seen this
flying saucer land, had they? But the policeman acted . . . funny.
Like he was a robot, his eyes dead in a pasty face. The boy had
noticed a weird X-shaped wound on the back of the policeman's
neck. The policeman, a jolly gent before his walk to the sand hill,
did not smile. He was changed.

The X-shaped wound began to show up on the backs of other
necks. No one believed the boy, who tried to make his parents
understand there was a nest of Martians in the earth behind his
house. Then his parents went out to see for themselves.

Ben had forgotten about the bucket of popcorn in his lap. Johnny
sat with his knees pulled up to his chest. I couldn't seem to draw a
breath.

Oh, you are such a silly boy, the grim, unsmiling parents told him
when they returned from their walk. There is nothing to be afraid
of. Nothing. Everything is fine. Come with us, let us go up to where
you say you saw this saucer descend. Let us show you what a silly,
silly boy you are.

"Don't go," Ben whispered. "Don't go don't go!" I heard his
fingernails scrape against the armrests.

The boy ran. Away from home, away from the unsmiling strangers. Everywhere he looked, he saw the X-shaped wound. The chief
of police had one on the back of his neck. People the boy had always
known were suddenly changed, and they wanted to hold him until
his parents could come pick him up. Silly, silly boy, they said.
Martians in the ground, about to take over the world. Who would
ever believe a story like that?

At the end of this horror, the army got down in a honeycomb of
tunnels the Martians had burrowed in the ground. The Martians
had a machine down there that cut into the back of your neck and
turned you into one of them. The leader of the Martians, a head

30

with tentacles in a glass bowl, looked like something that had backed up out of a septic tank. The boy and the army fought against the Martians, who shambled through the tunnels as if fighting the weight of gravity. At the collision of Martian machines and army tanks, with the earth hanging in the balance . . .

. . . the boy awakened.

A dream, his father said. His mother smiled at him. A dream. Nothing to fear. Go to sleep, we'll see you in the morning.

Just a bad, bad dream.

And then the boy got up in the dark, peered through his telescope, and saw a flying saucer descending from the stormy night sky into a sand hill behind his house.

The End?

The lights came up. Saturday afternoon at the movies was over.

"What's wrong with them?" I heard Mr. Stellko, the Lyric's manager, say to one of the ushers as we filed out. "Why're they so darned *quiet?*"

Sheer terror has no voice.

Somehow we managed to get on our bikes and start pedaling. Some kids walked home, some waited for their parents to pick them up. All of us were linked by what we had just witnessed, and when Ben, Johnny, and I stopped at the gas station on Ridgeton Street to get air put in Johnny's front tire, I caught Ben staring at the back of Mr. White's neck, where the sunburned skin folded up.

We parted ways at the corner of Bonner and Hilltop streets. Johnny flew for home, Ben cranked his bike with his stumpy legs, and I fought the rusted chain every foot of the distance. My bike had seen its best days. It was ancient when it came to me, by way of a flea market. I kept asking for a new one, but my father said I would have to do with what I had or do without. Money was tight some months; going to the movies on Saturday was a luxury. I found out, sometime later, that Saturday afternoon was the only time the springs in my parents' bedroom could sing a symphony without me wondering what was going on.

"You have fun?" my mother asked when I came in from playing with Rebel.

"Yes ma'am," I said. "The Tarzan movie was neat."

"Double feature, wasn't it?" Dad inquired, sitting on the sofa with his feet up. The television was tuned to an exhibition baseball game; it was getting to be that time of year.

"Yes sir." I walked on past them, en route to the kitchen and an apple.

"Well, what was the other movie about?"

"Oh . . . nothin'," I answered.

Parents can smell a mouse quicker than a starving cat. They let me get my apple, wash it under the faucet, polish it, and then bring it back into the front room. They let me sink my teeth into it, and then my dad looked up from the Zenith and said, "What's the matter with you?"

I crunched the apple. Mom sat down next to Dad, and their eyes were on me. "Sir?" I asked.

"Every other Saturday you burst in here like gangbusters wantin' to tell us all about the movies. We can't hardly stop you from actin' 'em out scene by scene. So what's the matter with you today?"

"Uh . . . I guess I . . . don't know, exactly."

"Come here," Mom said. When I did, her hand flew to my forehead. "Not runnin' a fever. Cory, you feel all right?"

"I'm fine."

"So one movie was about Tarzan," my father plowed on, bulldog stubborn. "What was the other movie about?"

I supposed I could tell them the title. But how could I tell them what it was *really* about? How could I tell them that the movie I had just seen tapped the primal fear of every child alive: that their parents would, in an instant of irreversible time, be forever swept away and replaced by cold, unsmiling aliens? "It was . . . a monster movie," I decided to say.

"That must've been right up your alley, then." Dad's attention veered back to the baseball game as a bat cracked like a pistol shot. "Whoa! Run for it, Mickey!"

The telephone rang. I hurried to answer it before my folks could ask me any more questions. "Cory? Hi, this is Mrs. Sears. Can I speak to your mother, please?"

"Just a minute. Mom?" I called. "Phone for you!"

Mom took the receiver, and I had to go to the bathroom. Number one, thankfully. I wasn't sure I was ready to sit on the toilet with the memory of that tentacled Martian head in my mind.

"Rebecca?" Mrs. Sears said. "How are you?"

"Doin' fine, Lizbeth. You get your raffle tickets?"

"I sure did. Four of them, and I hope at least one is lucky."

"That's good."

"Well, the reason I'm callin' is, Ben got back from the movies just a little while ago and I was wonderin' how Cory is."

"Cory? He's—" She paused, and in her mind she was considering my strange state. "He says he's fine."

"So does Ben, but he acts a little . . . I don't know, maybe 'bothered' is the word I'm lookin' for. Usually he hounds the heck

32

out of Sim and me wantin' to tell us about the movies, but today we can't get him to talk. He's out back right now. Said he wants to make sure about somethin', but he won't tell us what."

"Cory's in the bathroom," my mother said, as if that, too, was a piece of the puzzle. She cast her voice lower, in case I could hear over my waterfall. "He does act a little funny. You think somethin' happened between 'em at the movies?"

"I thought of it. Maybe they had a fallin'-out."

"Well, they've been friends for a long time, but it does happen."

"Happened with me and Amy Lynn McGraw. We were fast friends for six years and then we didn't speak for a whole year over a lost packet of sewin' needles. But I was thinkin', maybe the boys ought to get together. If they've had an argument, maybe they ought to work it out right off."

"Makes sense."

"I was gonna ask Ben if he'd like Cory to spend the night. Would that be all right with you?"

"I don't mind, but I'll have to ask Tom and Cory."

"Wait a minute," Mrs. Sears said, "Ben's comin' in." My mother heard a screen door slam. "Ben? I've got Cory's mother on the phone. Would you like Cory to spend the night here tonight?" My mother listened, but she couldn't make out what Ben was saying over the flush of our toilet. "He says he'd like that," Mrs. Sears told her.

I emerged from the bathroom, into the well-meaning complicity. "Cory, would you like to spend the night at Ben's house?"

I thought about it. "I don't know," I said, but I couldn't tell her why. The last time I'd spent the night over there, back in February, Mr. Sears hadn't come home all night and Mrs. Sears had walked the floor fretting about where he might be. Ben told me his father took a lot of overnight trips and he asked me not to say anything.

"Ben wants you to come," Mom prodded, mistaking my reluctance.

I shrugged. "Okay. I guess."

"Go make sure it's all right with your father." While I went to the front room to ask, my mother said to Mrs. Sears, "I know how important friendship is. We'll get 'em patched up if there's any problem."

"Dad says okay," I told her when I returned. If my father was watching a baseball game, he would be agreeable to flossing his teeth with barbed wire.

"Lizbeth? He'll be there. 'Round six o'clock?" She put her hand over the mouthpiece and said to me, "They're havin' fried chicken for dinner."

I nodded and tried to summon a smile, but my thoughts were in the tunnels where the Martians plotted the destruction of the human race, town by town.

"Rebecca? How're things goin'?" Mrs. Sears asked. "You know what I mean."

"Run on, Cory," she told me, and I did even though I knew important things were about to be discussed. "Well," she said to Lizbeth Sears, "Tom's sleepin' a little better now, but he still has the nightmares. I wish I could do somethin' to help, but I think he just has to work it out for himself."

"I hear the sheriff's about given it up."

"It's been three weeks without any kind of lead. J.T. told Tom on Friday that he sent word out all over the state, Georgia and Mississippi, too, but he hasn't come up with a thing. It's like the man in that car came from another planet."

"Now, there's a chilly thought."

"Somethin' else," my mother said, and she sighed heavily. "Tom's . . . changed. It's more than the nightmares, Lizbeth." She turned toward the kitchen pantry and stretched the cord as far as it would go so there was no chance of Dad hearing. "He's careful to lock all the doors and windows, where before he didn't care about locks. Up until it happened, we left our doors unlocked most of the time, like everybody else does. Now Tom gets up two or three times in the night to check the bolts. And last week he came home from his route with red mud on his shoes, when it hadn't rained. I think he went back to the lake."

"What on earth for?"

"I don't know. To walk and think, I suppose. I remember when I was nine years old I had a yellow cat that got run over by a truck in front of our house. Calico's blood stayed on the pavement for a long time. That place pulled me. I hated it, but I had to go there and see where Calico died. I always thought that there was somethin' I could've done to keep him alive. Or maybe up until it happened, I thought everythin' lived forever." She paused, staring at pencil marks on the back door that showed the steady progress of my growth. "I think Tom's got a lot on his mind right now."

Their conversation rolled on into the realm of this and that, though at the center of it was the incident at Saxon's Lake. I watched the baseball game with Dad, and I noticed that he kept closing and opening his right hand as if he were either trying to grasp something or free himself from a grip. Then it got time to get ready to go, and I gathered up my pajamas, my toothbrush, and another set of socks and underwear and shoved everything down in my army surplus knapsack. Dad told me to be careful and Mom told me to have fun, but to be back in the morning in time for Sunday school. I rubbed Rebel's head and threw a stick for him to chase, and then I climbed on my bike and pedaled away.

Ben didn't live very far, only a half mile or so from my house at the dead end of Deerman Street. On Deerman Street I pedaled quietly, because guarding the corner of Deerman and Shantuck was the somber gray stone house where the notorious Branlin brothers lived. The Branlins, thirteen and fourteen years of age, had peroxided blond hair and delighted in destruction. Oftentimes they roamed the neighborhood on their matching black bicycles like vultures searching for fresh meat. I had heard from Davy Ray Callan that the Branlins sometimes tried to run cars off the street with their speeding black bikes, and that he'd actually witnessed Gotha Branlin, the oldest, tell his own mother to go to the bad place. Gotha and Gordo were like the Black Plague; you hoped they wouldn't get you, but once they laid a hand on you, there was no escape.

So far I had been insignificant to their careening meanness. I planned for it to stay that way.

Ben's house was much like my own. Ben had a brown dog named Tumper, who got up from his belly on the front porch to bark my arrival. Ben came out to meet me, and Mrs. Sears said hello and asked if I wanted a glass of root beer. She was dark-haired and had a pretty face, but she had hips as big as watermelons. Inside the house, Mr. Sears came up from his woodshop in the basement to speak to me. He was large and round, too, his heavy-jowled face ruddy under crew-cut brown hair. Mr. Sears was a happy man with a buck-toothed grin, woodshavings clinging to his striped shirt, and he told me a joke about a Baptist preacher and an outhouse that I didn't really understand, but he laughed to cue me and Ben said, "Aw, Daddy!" as if he'd heard that dumb joke a dozen times.

I unpacked my knapsack in Ben's room, where he had nifty collections of baseball cards, bottle caps, and wasps' nests. As I got squared away, Ben sat down on his Superman bedspread and said, "Did you tell your folks about the movie?"

"No. Did you?"

"Uh-uh." He picked at a loose thread on Superman's face. "How come you didn't?"

"I don't know. How come *you* didn't?"

Ben shrugged, but thoughts were working in his head. "I guess," he said, "it was too awful to tell."

35

"Yeah."

"I went out back," Ben said. "No sand. Just rock."

We both agreed the Martians would have a tough time drilling through all the red rock in the hills around Zephyr, if they were to come calling. Then Ben opened a cardboard box and showed me his Civil War bubble gum cards that had gory paintings of guys getting shot, bayoneted, and clobbered by cannon balls, and we sat making up a story for each card until his mother rang a bell to say it was time for fried chicken.

After dinner—and Mrs. Sears's wonderful black bottom pie washed down with a glass of cold Green Meadows milk—we all played a game of Scrabble. Ben's parents were partners, and Mr. Sears kept trying to pass made-up words that even I knew weren't in the dictionary, like "kafloom" and "goganus." Mrs. Sears said he was as crazy as a monkey in itching powder, but she grinned at his antics just like I did. "Cory?" he said. "Didja hear the one about the three preachers tryin' to get into heaven?" and before I could say "No" he was off on a joke-telling jaunt. He seemed to favor the preacher jokes, and I had to wonder what Reverend Lovoy at the Methodist church would think of them.

It was past eight o'clock and we'd started our second game when Tumper barked on the front porch and a few seconds later there was a knock on the door. "I'll get it," Mr. Sears said. He opened the door to a wiry, craggy-faced man wearing jeans and a red-checked shirt. "Hey, Donny!" Mr. Sears greeted him. "Come on in, you buzzard!"

Mrs. Sears was watching her husband and the man named Donny. I saw her jaw tense.

Donny said something in a low voice to Mr. Sears, and Mr. Sears called to us, "Me and Donny are gonna sit on the porch for a while. Y'all go on and play."

"Hon?" Mrs. Sears drew up a smile, but I could tell it was in danger of slipping. "I need a partner."

The screen door closed at his back.

Mrs. Sears sat very still for a long moment, staring at the door. Her smile had gone.

"Mom?" Ben said. "It's your turn."

"All right." She tried to pull her attention to the Scrabble tiles. I could tell she was trying as hard as she could, but her gaze kept slipping back to the screen door. Out on the porch, Mr. Sears and the wiry man named Donny were sitting in folding chairs, their conversation quiet and serious. "All right," Ben's mother said again. "Let me think now, just give me a minute."

More than a minute passed. Off in the distance, a dog began

barking. Then two more. Tumper took up the call. Mrs. Sears was still choosing her tiles when the door flew open again.

"Hey, Lizbeth! Ben! Come out here, and hurry!"

"What is it, Sim? What's—"

"Just come *out* here!" he hollered, and of course we all got up from the table to see.

Donny was standing in the yard, looking toward the west. The neighborhood dogs were really whooping it up. Lights burned in windows, and other people were emerging to find out what the uproar was about. Mr. Sears pointed in the direction Donny was looking. "You ever seen anythin' like *that* before?"

I looked up. So did Ben, and I heard him gasp as if he'd been stomach-punched.

It was coming down from the night sky, descending from the canopy of stars. It was a glowing red thing, purple spears of fire trailing behind it, and it left a white trail of smoke against the darkness.

In that instant my heart almost exploded. Ben took a backward step, and he might have fallen had he not collided with one of his mother's hips. I knew in my hammering, rioting heart that everywhere across Zephyr kids who had been in the Lyric theater that afternoon were looking up at the sky and feeling terror peel the lips back from their teeth.

I came very close to wetting my pants. Somehow I held my water, but it was a near thing.

Ben blubbered. He made mangled sounds. He wheezed, "It's . . . it's . . . it's . . ."

"A comet!" Mr. Sears shouted. "Look at that thing fall!"

Donny grunted and slid a toothpick into the corner of his mouth. I glanced at him and by the porch light saw his dirty fingernails.

It was falling in a long, slow spiral, ribbons of sparks flaying out in its wake. It made no noise, but people were shouting for other people to look and some of the dogs had started that kind of howling that makes your backbone quiver.

"Comin' down between here and Union Town," Donny observed. His head was cocked to one side, his face gaunt and his dark hair slick with brilliantine. "Comin' down like a sonofabitch."

Between Zephyr and Union Town lay eight miles of hills, woods, and swamp cut by the Tecumseh River. It was Martian territory if there ever was, I thought, and I felt all the circuits in my brain jangle like fire alarms going off. I looked at Ben. His eyes seemed to be bulging outward by the cranial pressure of pure fear. The only thing I could think of when I stared at the fireball again was the tentacled head in the glass bowl, its face serenely evil and slightly Oriental. I could hardly stand up, my legs were so weak.

"Hey, Sim?" Donny's voice was low and slow, and he was chewing on the toothpick. "How about we go chase that bugger down?" His face turned toward Mr. Sears. His nose was flat, as if it had been busted by a big fist. "What do you say, Sim?"

"Yeah!" he answered. "Yeah, we'll go chase it down! Find out where it falls!"

"No, Sim!" Mrs. Sears said. In her voice was a note of pleading. "Stay with me and the boys tonight!"

"It's a comet, Lizbeth!" he explained, grinning. "How many times in your life do you get to chase a comet?"

"Please, Sim." She grasped his forearm. "Stay with us. All right?" I saw her fingers tighten.

"About to hit." Donny's jaw muscles clenched as he chewed. "Time's wastin'."

"Yeah! Time's wastin', Lizbeth!" Mr. Sears pulled away. "I'll get my jacket!" He rushed up the porch steps and into the house. Before the screen door could slam, Ben was running after his father.

Mr. Sears went back to the bedroom he shared with his wife. He opened the closet, got his brown poplin jacket, and shrugged into it. Then he reached up onto the closet's top shelf, his hand winnowing under a red blanket. As Mr. Sears's hand emerged, Ben walked into the room behind him and caught a glint of metal between his father's fingers.

Ben knew what it was. He knew what it was for.

"Daddy?" he said. "Please stay home."

"Hey, boy!" His father turned toward him, grin in place, and he slid the metal object down into his jacket and zipped the jacket up. "I'm gonna go see where the comet comes down with Mr. Blaylock. I won't be but a little while."

Ben stood in the doorway, between his father and the outside world. His eyes were wet and scared. "Can I go with you, Daddy?"

"No, Ben. Not this time. I gotta go now."

"Let me go with you. Okay? I won't make any noise. Okay?"

"No, son." Mr. Sears's hand clamped down on Ben's shoulder. "You have to stay here with your mother and Cory." Though Ben stiffly resisted, his father's hand moved him aside. "You be a good boy, now," Mr. Sears said as his big shoes carried him toward the door.

Ben made one more attempt by grasping his father's fingers and trying to hold him. "Don't go, Daddy!" he said. "Don't go! Please don't go!"

"Ben, don't act like a baby. Let me go, son."

"No, sir," Ben answered. The wetness of his eyes had overflowed onto his pudgy cheeks. "I won't."

"I'm just goin' out to see where the comet falls. I won't be gone but a little while."

"If you go . . . if you go . . ." Ben's throat was clogging up with emotion, and he could hardly squeeze the words out. "You'll come back *changed*."

"Let's hit the road, Sim!" Donny Blaylock urged from the front porch.

"Ben?" Mr. Sears said sternly. "I'm goin' with Mr. Blaylock. Act like a man, now." He worked his fingers free, and Ben stood there looking up at him with an expression of agony. His father scraped a hand through Ben's cropped hair. "I'll bring you back a piece of it, all right, Tiger?"

"Don't go," the weeping tiger croaked.

His father turned his back on him, and strode out the screen door to where Donny Blaylock waited. I was still standing with Mrs. Sears in the yard, watching the fiery thing in its last few seconds of descent. Mrs. Sears said, "Sim? Don't do it," but her voice was so weak it didn't carry. Mr. Sears did not speak to his wife, and he followed the other man to a dark blue Chevy parked at the curb. Red foam dice hung from the radio antenna, and the right rear side was smashed in. Donny Blaylock slid behind the wheel and Mr. Sears got in the other side. The Chevy started up like a cannon going off, shooting black exhaust. As the car pulled away, I heard Mr. Sears laugh as if he'd just told another preacher joke. Donny Blaylock must've stomped the gas pedal, because the rear tires shrieked as the Chevy tore away up Deerman Street.

I looked toward the west again, and saw the fiery thing disappear over the wooded hills. Its glow pulsed against the dark like a beating heart. It had come to earth somewhere in the wilderness.

There was no sand anywhere out there. The Martians, I thought, were going to have to slog through a lot of mud and waterweeds.

I heard the screen door slam, and I turned around and saw Ben standing on the front porch. He wiped his eyes with the back of his hand. He stared along Deerman Street, as if he were tracking the Chevy's progress, but by that time the car had turned right on Shantuck and was out of sight.

In the distance, probably up in Bruton, dogs were still baying. Mrs. Sears released a long, strengthless sigh. "Let's go in," she said.

Ben's eyes were swollen, but his crying was done. No one seemed to want to finish the game of Scrabble. Mrs. Sears said, "Why don't you boys go play in your room, Ben?" and he nodded slowly, his eyes glazed as if he'd taken a heavy blow to the skull. Mrs. Sears went back to the kitchen, where she turned on the water. In Ben's room, I sat on the floor with the Civil War cards while Ben stood at the window.

I could tell he was suffering. I'd never seen him like this before, and I had to say something. "Don't worry," I told him. "It's not Martians. It was a meteor, that's all."

He didn't answer.

"A meteor's just a big hot rock," I said. "There're no Martians inside it."

Ben was silent; his thoughts had him.

"Your dad'll be okay," I said.

Ben spoke, in a voice terrible in its quiet: "He'll come back changed."

"No, he won't. Listen . . . that was just a movie. It was made up." I realized that as I said this I was letting go of something, and it felt both painful and good at the same time. "See, there's not really a machine that cuts into the backs of people's necks. There's not really a big Martian head in a glass bowl. It's all made up. You don't have to be scared. See?"

"He'll come back changed," Ben repeated.

I tried, but nothing I could say would make him believe any differently. Mrs. Sears came in, and her eyes looked swollen, too. But she managed a brave smile that hurt my heart, and she said, "Cory? Do you want to take the first bath?"

Mr. Sears was not home by ten o'clock, when his wife switched off the light in Ben's bedroom. I lay under the crisp white sheet beside Ben, listening to the night. A couple of dogs still conversed back and forth, and every once in a while Tumper offered a muttered opinion. "Ben?" I whispered. "You awake?" He didn't answer, but the way he was breathing told me he wasn't sleeping. "Don't worry," I said. "Okay?"

He turned over, and pressed his face against his pillow.

Eventually I drifted off. I did not, surprisingly, dream of Martians and X-shaped wounds on the backs of loved ones' necks. In my dream my father swam for the sinking car, and when his head went under, it did not come back up. I stood on the red rock cliff, calling for him, until Lainie came to me like a white mist and took my hand in a damp grip. As she led me away from the lake, I could hear my mother calling to me from the distance, and a figure stood at the edge of the woods wearing a long overcoat that flapped in the wind.

An earthquake woke me up.

I opened my eyes, my heart pounding. Something had crashed; the sound was trapped inside my head. The lights were still off, and the night still reigned. I reached out and touched Ben beside me. He drew in a sharp breath, as if my touch had scared the wits out of him. I heard an engine boom, and I looked out the window toward Deerman Street to see a Chevy's taillights as Donny Blaylock pulled away.

The screen door, I realized. The sound of the screen door slamming had jolted me awake.

"Ben?" I rasped, my mouth thick with sleep. "Your dad's come home!"

Something else crashed down in the front room. The whole house seemed to shake.

"Sim?" It was Mrs. Sears's voice, high-pitched. *"Sim?"*

I got out of bed, but Ben just lay there. I think he was staring at the ceiling. I walked through the hallway in the dark, my feet squeaking the boards. I bumped into Mrs. Sears, standing where the hall met the front room, no lights on anywhere.

I heard a hoarse, terrible breathing.

It was, I thought, the sound a Martian might make as its alien lungs strained on earthly air.

"Sim?" Mrs. Sears said. "I'm right here."

"Right here," a voice answered. "Right . . . here. Right . . . fuckin' . . . here."

It was Mr. Sears's voice, yes. But it was different. Changed. There was no humor in it, no fun, no hint of a preacher joke. It was as heavy as doom, and just as mean.

"Sim, I'm going to turn on the light now."

Click.

And there he was.

Mr. Sears was on the floor on his hands and knees, his head bowed and one cheek mashed against the rug. His face looked bloated and wet, his eyes sunken in fleshy folds. The right shoulder of his jacket was dirty, and dirt was smeared on his jeans as if he'd taken a fall in the woods. He blinked in the light, a silver thread of saliva hanging from his lower lip. "Where is it?" he said. "You see it?"

"It's . . . beside your right hand."

His left hand groped. "You're a goddamned liar," he said.

"Your other hand, Sim," she told him wearily.

His right hand moved toward the metal object lying there. It was a whiskey flask, and his fingers gripped it and pulled it to him.

He sat up on his knees and stared at his wife. A fierceness passed over his face, ugly in its swiftness. "Don't you smart-mouth me," he said. "Don't you open that big fat smart mouth."

I stepped back then, into the hallway. I was seeing a monster that had slipped from its skin.

Mr. Sears struggled to stand. He grabbed hold of the table that held the Scrabble tiles, and it went over in an explosion of vowels and consonants. Then he made it to his feet, and he unscrewed the cap off the flask and licked the bottle neck.

"Come on to bed, Sim," she said; it was spoken without strength, as if she knew full well what the outcome of this would be.

"Come on to bed!" he mocked. "Come on to bed!" His lip curled. "I don't *wanna* come to bed, you fat-assed cow!"

I saw Mrs. Sears tremble as if she'd been stung by a whip. A hand pressed to her mouth. "Oh . . . *Sim*," she moaned, and it was an awful sound to hear.

I backed away some more. And then Ben walked past me in his yellow pajamas, his face blank of expression but tear tracks glistening on his cheeks.

There are things much worse than monster movies. There are horrors that burst the bounds of screen and page, and come home all twisted up and grinning behind the face of somebody you love. At that moment I knew Ben would have gladly looked into that glass bowl at the tentacled Martian head rather than into his father's drunk-red eyes.

"Hey, Benny boy!" Mr. Sears said. He staggered and caught himself against a chair. "Hey, you know what happened to you? You know what? The best part of you stayed in that busted rubber, that's what happened."

Ben stopped beside his mother. Whatever emotion tortured him inside, it did not show on his face. He must've known this was going to happen, I realized. Ben had known when his father went with Donny Blaylock, he would come home changed not by the Martians but by the home brew in that flask.

"You're a real sight. The both of you." Mr. Sears tried to screw the cap back on, but he couldn't make it fit. "Standin' there with your smart mouths. You think this is funny, don't you, boy?"

"No sir."

"Yes you do! You can't wait to go laugh and tell everybody, can you? Where's that Mackenson boy? Hey, you!" He spotted me, back in the hall, and I flinched. "You can tell that goddamned milkman daddy of yours to go straight to hell. Hear me?"

I nodded, and his attention wandered away from me. This was not Mr. Sears talking, not really; this was the voice of what the flask flayed raw and bloody inside his soul, what it stomped and kicked and tortured until the voice had to scream for release.

"What'd you say?" He stared at Mrs. Sears, his eyelids swollen and heavy. "What'd you *say?*"

"I . . . didn't say—"

He was on her like a charging bull. Mrs. Sears cried out and retreated but he grabbed the front of her gown with one hand and reared his other hand back, the flask gripped in it, as if to smash her across the face. *"Yes you did!"* he shouted. *"Don't you backtalk me!"*

"Daddy, don't!" Ben pleaded, and he flung both arms around one of his father's thighs and hung tight. The moment stretched, Mr. Sears about to strike his wife, me standing in a state of shock in the hallway, Ben holding on to his father's leg.

Mrs. Sears's lips trembled. With the flask poised to strike her face, she spoke: "I . . . said . . . that we both love you, and that . . . we want you to be happy. That's all." Tears welled up and trickled. "Just happy."

He didn't speak. His eyes closed, and he opened them again with an effort.

"Happy," he whispered. Ben was sobbing now, his face pressed against his father's thigh, his knuckles white at the twining of his fingers. Mr. Sears lowered his hand, and he let go of his wife's gown. "Happy. See, I'm happy. Look at me smile."

His face didn't change.

He stood there, breathing roughly, his hand with the flask in it hanging at his side. He started to step one way and then another, but he couldn't seem to decide which way to go.

"Why don't you sit down, Sim?" Mrs. Sears asked. She sniffled and wiped her dripping nose. "Want me to help you?"

He nodded. "Yeah. Help."

Ben let him go, and Mrs. Sears guided her husband to his chair. He collapsed into it, like a large pile of dirty laundry. He stared at the opposite wall, his mouth hanging open. She drew up another chair close beside him. There was a feeling in the room as if a storm had passed. It might come again, some other night, but for now it was gone.

"I don't think—" He stopped, as if he'd lost what he was about to say. He blinked, searching for it. "I don't think I'm doin' so good," he said.

Mrs. Sears leaned his head gently on her shoulder. He squeezed

43

his eyes shut, his chest heaved, and he began to cry, and I walked out of the house into the cool night air in my pajamas because it didn't seem right for me to be in there, a stranger at a private pain.

I sat down on the porch steps. Tumper plodded over, sat beside me, and licked my hand. I felt an awful long way from home.

Ben had known. What courage it must have taken for him to lie in that bed, pretending to sleep. He had known that when the screen door slammed, long after midnight, the invader who wore his father's flesh would be in the house. The knowing and the waiting must've been a desperate torment.

After a while, Ben came outside and sat on the steps, too. He asked me if I was all right, and I said I was. I asked him if he was all right. He said yeah. I believed him. He had learned to live with this, and though it was a horrible thing, he was grappling with it the best he could.

"My daddy has spells," Ben explained. "He says bad things sometimes, but he can't help it."

I nodded.

"He didn't mean what he said about your daddy. You don't hate him, do you?"

"No," I said. "I don't."

"You don't hate *me*, do you?"

"No," I told him. "I don't hate anybody."

"You're a real good buddy," Ben said, and he put his arm around my shoulders.

Mrs. Sears came out and brought us a blanket. It was red. We sat there as the stars slowly wheeled their course, and soon the birds of morning began to peep.

At the breakfast table, we had bowls of hot oatmeal and blueberry muffins. Mrs. Sears told us that Mr. Sears was sleeping, that he would sleep most of the day, and that if I wanted to I could ask my mother to call her and they'd have a long talk. After I got dressed and packed all my belongings into the knapsack, I thanked Mrs. Sears for having me over, and Ben said he'd see me at school tomorrow. He walked me out to my bike, and we talked for a few minutes about our Little League baseball team that would soon start practicing. It was getting to be that time of year.

Never again would we mention to each other the movie where Martians plotted to conquer the earth, town by town, father by mother by child. We had both seen the face of the invader.

It was Sunday morning. I pedaled for home, and when I looked back at the house at the dead end of Deerman Street, my friend waved so long.

44

4

Wasps at Easter

The meteor, as it turned out, must've burned itself to cinders as it flamed down from outer space. A few pine trees had caught fire, but it started raining on Sunday night and the fire hissed away. It was still raining on Monday morning, when the school bell rang, and the rain fell all through that long, gray day. The following Sunday was Easter, and Mom said she hoped the rain—forecast to fall intermittently all week long—didn't spoil the Merchants Street Easter parade on Saturday.

Early on the morning of Good Friday, starting around six o'clock or so, there was always another parade of sorts in Zephyr. It began in Bruton, at a small frame house painted purple, orange, red, and sunburst yellow. A procession of black men in black suits, white shirts, and ties made their way from this house, with a number of women and children in somber clothing following behind. Two of the men carried drums, and beat a slow, steady rhythm to time the paces. The procession wound its way across the railroad track and along Merchants Street, the center of town, and no one spoke to each other. Since this was an annual event, many of Zephyr's white population emerged from their houses to stand along the street and watch. My mother was one of them, though my dad was already at work by that time of the morning. I usually went with her, because I grasped the significance of this event just as everyone else did.

The three black men who led the way carried burlap bags. Around their necks, dangling down over their ties, were necklaces of amber beads, chicken bones, and the shells of small river mussels. On this particular Good Friday, the streets were wet and the rain drizzled down, but the members of the black parade carried no umbrellas. They spoke to no one on the sidewalks, nor to anyone who happened to be so rude as to speak to them. I saw Mr. Lightfoot walking near the parade's center, and though he knew every white face in town he looked neither right nor left but straight ahead at the back of the man who walked before him. An invaluable asset to the interlocked communities of Bruton and Zephyr, Marcus Lightfoot was a handyman who could repair any object ever devised by the human mind though he might work at the pace of grass growing. I saw Mr. Dennis, who was a custodian at the elementary school. I saw Mrs. Velvadine, who worked in the kitchen at our church, and I saw Mrs. Pearl, who was always laughing and cheerful at the Merchants Street Bake Shoppe. Today, though, she was nothing but serious, and she wore a clear plastic rain hat.

Bringing up the very rear of the procession, even behind the women and children, was a spindly man wearing a black tuxedo and a top hat. He carried a small drum, and his black-gloved hand beat it to mark the rhythm. It was this man and his wife whom many had come out on the chilly, rainy morning to see. The wife would arrive later; he walked alone, his face downcast.

We called him the Moon Man, because we didn't know his real name. He was very old, but exactly how old it was impossible to say. He was very rarely seen outside of Bruton, except on this occasion, as was his wife. Either a birth defect or a skin malady had affected one side of his long, narrow face, turning it pale yellow while the other side remained deep ebony, the two halves merging in a war of splotches down his forehead, the bridge of his elegant nose, and his white-bearded chin. The Moon Man, an enigma, had two watches on each wrist and a gilded crucifix the size of a ham hock hanging on a chain around his neck. He was, we presumed, the parade's official timekeeper as well as one of its royal personages.

The parade continued, step by steady step, through Zephyr to the gargoyle bridge over the Tecumseh River. It might take a while, but it was worth being late to school to see, and because of it school never really got into session until around ten o'clock on Good Fridays.

Once the three men with the burlap bags reached the center of the bridge, they stopped and stood like black statues. The rest of the procession got as close as possible without blocking the bridge, though Sheriff Amory had set up sawhorses with blinking lights along the route.

In a moment a Pontiac Bonneville covered hood to trunk with gleaming plastic rhinestones was driven slowly along Merchants Street from Bruton, following the parade's path. When it arrived at the center of the gargoyle bridge, the driver got out and opened the rear door, and the Moon Man took his wife's wrinkled hand and helped her to her feet.

The Lady had arrived.

She was as thin as a shadow, and just as dark. She had a cotton-cloud of white hair, her neck long and regal, her shoulders frail but unbowed. She wore not a costume of outlandish color and design, but a simple black dress with a silver belt, white shoes, and a white pillbox hat with a veil. She wore white gloves to her bony elbows. As the Moon Man helped her from the car, the driver opened an umbrella and held it over her royal, ancient head.

The Lady, it was said, had been born in the year 1858. That made her one hundred and six years old. My mom said the Lady had been a slave in Louisiana, and had run away with her momma into the swamp before the Civil War. The Lady had grown up in a colony of lepers, escaped convicts, and slaves in the bayou below New Orleans, and that was where she'd learned everything she knew.

The Lady was a queen, and Bruton was her kingdom. No one outside Bruton—and no one inside Bruton, as far as I understood—knew her by any name but "the Lady." It suited her; she was elegance, through and through.

Someone gave her a bell. She stood looking down at the sluggish brown river, and she began to slowly swing the bell back and forth.

I knew what she was doing. My mom did, too. Everyone who watched did.

The Lady was calling the river's monster up from its mansion of mud.

I had never seen the beast that was called Old Moses. One night when I was nine years of age, I did think I heard Old Moses calling after a heavy rain, when the air itself was as thick as water. It was a low rumble, like the deepest bass note from a church's pipe organ, so deep your bones hear it before your ears do. It went up into a hoarse roar that made the town's dogs go crazy, and then the noise was gone. It hadn't lasted but maybe five or six seconds. The next day, that noise was the talk of the school. Train's whistle, was Ben's and Davy Ray's opinion. Johnny didn't say what he thought. At home, my folks said it must've been the train passing through, but we didn't find out until later that the rain had washed away a section of track more than twenty miles from Zephyr and the freight to Birmingham hadn't even run that night.

Such things make you wonder.

A mangled cow washed up, once, under the gargoyle bridge. Missing its head and guts, Mr. Dollar told my father when he and I went to get scalped. Two men netting crayfish along the riverbank just beyond Zephyr spread the story that a human corpse had floated past on the current, the body's chest peeled open like a sardine can and its arms and legs ripped off at the roots, but no

47

corpse was ever found downriver. One October night, something hit a submerged piling of the gargoyle bridge and left cracks in the support columns that had to be filled with concrete. "A big tree trunk" was Mayor Swope's official explanation in the Adams Valley *Journal.*

The Lady rang the bell, her arm working like a metronome. She began to chant and sing, in a voice surprisingly clear and loud. The chant was all African words, which I understood about as much as I grasped nuclear physics. She would stop for a while, her head slightly cocked to one side as if watching or listening for something, and then she'd swing the bell again. She never once said the name "Old Moses." She kept saying "Damballah, Damballah, Damballah," and then her voice would sail upward in an African song again.

At last she ceased ringing the bell, and she lowered it to her side. She nodded, and the Moon Man took it from her. She was staring fixedly at the river, but what she was seeing there I don't know. Then she stepped back and the three men with the burlap bags stood at the edge of the gargoyle bridge. They opened the bags and brought out objects wrapped up in butcher's paper and tape. Some of the paper was bloody, and you could smell the coppery odor of fresh meat. They began to unwrap the gory feast, and as they did they threw the steaks, briskets, and beef ribs down into the swirling brown water. A whole plucked chicken went into the river, too, along with chicken intestines poured from a plastic jar. Calf brains slid out of a green Tupperware bowl, and wet red beef kidneys and liver came out of one of the damp packages. A bottle of pickled pigs' feet was opened, its contents splashing down into the water. A pig's snout and ears followed the feet. The last thing in was a beef heart bigger than a wrestler's fist. It splashed in like a red stone, and then the three men folded up their burlap bags and the Lady stepped forward again, watching her footing on the blood that had dripped onto the pavement.

It occurred to me that an awful lot of Sunday dinners had just gone into the drink.

"Damballah, Damballah, Damballah!" the Lady chanted once more. She stood there for maybe four or five minutes, motionless as she watched the river move beneath the bridge. Then she breathed a long sigh and I saw her face behind the veil as she turned toward her rhinestone Pontiac again. She was frowning; whatever she had seen or had not seen, she wasn't too happy about it. She got into the car, the Moon Man climbed in after her, the driver closed the door and slid behind the wheel. The Pontiac backed up to a place where it

could turn around and then started toward Bruton. The procession
began to go back the route it had come. Usually by this time there
was a lot of laughing and talking, and people would stop to speak to
the white faces along the way. On this particular Good Friday,
however, the Lady's somber mood had carried and no one seemed
to feel much like laughing.

I knew exactly what the ritual was all about. Everybody in town
did. The Lady was feeding Old Moses his annual banquet. When
this had started, I didn't know; it had been going on long before I
was born. You might think, as Reverend Blessett at the Freedom
Baptist Church did, that it was pagan and of the devil and should be
outlawed by the mayor and town council, but enough white people
believed in Old Moses to override the preacher's objections. It was
like carrying a rabbit's foot or throwing salt over your shoulder if
you happened to spill any; these things were part of the grain and
texture of life, and better to do them than not, just in case God's
ways were more mysterious than we Christians could grasp.

On the following day the rain fell harder, and thunderclouds
rolled over Zephyr. The Merchants Street Easter parade was canceled, much to the dismay of the Arts Council and the Commerce
Club. Mr. Vandercamp Junior, whose family owned the hardware
and feeds store, had been dressing up as the Easter bunny and
riding in the parade's last car for six years, having inherited the task
from Mr. Vandercamp Senior, who got too old to hop. This Easter
the rain doused all hopes of catching candy eggs thrown by the
various merchants and their families from their cars, the ladies of
the Sunshine Club couldn't show off their Easter dresses, husbands,
and children, the members of Zephyr's VFW unit couldn't march
behind the flag, and the Confederate Sweethearts—girls who
attended Adams Valley High School—couldn't wear their hoop
skirts and spin their parasols.

Easter morning arrived, cloaked in gloom. My dad and I were
compatriots in grousing about getting slicked up, putting on
starched white shirts, suits, and polished shoes. Mom had an all-
purpose answer to our grumbles, much the same as Dad's "Right as
rain." She said, "It's only one day," as if this made the stiff collar
and the necktie knot more comfortable. Easter was a family day, and
Mom phoned Grand Austin and Nana Alice and then Dad picked
up the telephone to call Granddaddy Jaybird and Grandmomma
Sarah. We would all, as we did every Easter, converge on the Zephyr
First Methodist church to hear about the empty tomb.

The white church on Cedarvine Street, between Bonner and
Shantuck, was filling up by the time we parked our pickup truck.

We walked through the sloppy mist toward the light that streamed through the church's stained-glass windows, all the polish getting soaked off our shoes. People were shedding their raincoats and closing their umbrellas at the front door, beneath the overhanging eaves. It was an old church, built in 1939, the whitewash coming off and leaving gray patches. Usually the church was primed to its finest on Easter day, but this year the rain had defeated the paintbrush and lawn mower so weeds were winning in the front yard.

"Come in, Handsome! Come in, Flowers! Watch your step there, Noodles! Good Easter morning to you, Sunshine!" That was Dr. Lezander, who served as the church's greeter. He had never missed a Sunday, as far as I knew. Dr. Frans Lezander was the veterinarian in Zephyr, and it was he who had cured Rebel of the worms last year. He was a Dutchman, and though he still had a heavy accent he and his wife Veronica, Dad had told me, had come from Holland long before I was born. He was in his mid-fifties, stood about five eight, was broad-shouldered and baldheaded and had a neatly trimmed gray beard. He wore natty three-piece suits, always with a bow tie and a lapel carnation, and he made up names for people as they entered the church. "Good morning, Peach Pie!" he said to my smiling mother. To my father, with a knuckle-popping handshake: "Raining hard enough for you, Thunderbird?" And to me, with a squeeze of the shoulder and a grin that shot light off a silver front tooth: "Step right in, Bronco!"

"Hear what Dr. Lezander called me?" I asked Dad once we were inside. *"Bronco!"* Getting a new christening for a day was always a highlight of church.

The sanctuary was steamy, though the wooden ceiling fans revolved. The Glass sisters were up front, playing a piano and organ duet. They were the perfect definition of the word strange. While not identical twins, the two spinster sisters were close enough to be slightly skewed mirrors. They were both long and bony, Sonia with piled-high whitish-blond hair and Katharina with piled-high blondish-white hair. They both wore thick black-framed glasses. Sonia played the piano and not the organ, while Katharina did vice versa. Depending on who you asked, the Glass sisters—who seemed to always be nagging each other but lived together on Shantuck Street in a house that looked like gingerbread—were either fifty-eight, sixty-two, or sixty-five. The strangeness was completed by their wardrobes: Sonia wore only blue in all its varying shades, while Katharina was a slave to green. Which brought about the inevitable. Sonia was referred to by us kids as Miss Blue Glass, and

Katharina was called . . . you guessed it. But, strange or not, they sure could play up a storm.

The pews were packed almost solid. The place looked and felt like a hothouse where exotic hats had bloomed. Other people were trying to find seats, and one of the ushers—Mr. Horace Kaylor, who had a white mustache and a cocked left eye that gave you the creeps when you stared at it—came up the aisle to help us.

"Tom! Over here! For God's sake, are you blind?"

In the whole wide world there was only one person who would holler like a bull moose in church.

He was standing up, waving his arms over the milling hats. I could feel my mother cringe, and my dad put his arm around her as if to steady her from falling down of shame. Granddaddy Jaybird always did something to, as Dad said when he thought I wasn't listening, "show his butt," and today would be no exception.

"We saved you seats!" my grandfather bellowed, and he caused the Glasses to falter, one to go sharp and the other flat. *"Come on before somebody steals 'em!"*

Grand Austin and Nana Alice were in the same row, too. Grand Austin was wearing a seersucker suit that looked as if the rain had drawn it up two sizes, his wrinkled neck clenched by a starched white collar and a blue bow tie, his thin white hair slicked back and his eyes full of misery as he sat with his wooden leg stuck out straight below the pew in front of him. He was sitting beside Granddaddy Jaybird, which had compounded his agitation: the two got along like mud and biscuits. Nana Alice, however, was a vision of happiness. She was wearing a hat covered with small white flowers, her gloves white and her dress the glossy green of a sunlit sea. Her lovely oval face was radiant; she was sitting beside Grandmomma Sarah, and they got along like daisies in the same bouquet. Right now, though, Grandmomma Sarah was tugging at Granddaddy Jaybird's suit jacket—the same black suit he wore rain or shine, Easter or funeral—to try to get him to sit down and stop directing traffic. He was telling people in the rows to move in tighter and then he would holler, *"Room for two more over here!"*

"Sit down, Jay! Sit down!" She had to resort to pinching his bony butt, and then he scowled at her and took his seat.

My parents and I squenched in. Grand Austin said to Dad, "Good to see you, Tom," and they shook hands. "That is, if I *could* see you." His spectacles were fogged up, and he took them off and cleaned the lenses with a handkerchief. "I'd say this is the biggest crowd in a half-dozen Eas—"

"Place is packed as the whorehouse on payday, ain't it, Tom?"

Granddaddy Jaybird interrupted, and Grandmomma Sarah elbowed him in the ribs so hard his false teeth clicked.

"I sure wish you'd let me finish a single sentence," Grand Austin told him, the red rising in his cheeks. "Ever since I've been sittin' here, I've yet to get a word in edgewi—"

"Boy, you're lookin' good!" Granddaddy Jaybird plowed on, and he reached across Grand Austin to slap my knee. "Rebecca, you feedin' this boy his meat, ain't you? You know, a growin' boy's got to have meat for his muscles!"

"Can't you hear?" Grand Austin asked him, the red now pulsing in his cheeks.

"Hear what?" Granddaddy Jaybird retorted.

"Turn up your hearin' aid, Jay," Grandmomma Sarah said.

"What?" he asked her.

"Hearin' aid!" she shouted, at her rope's end. *"Turn it up!"*

It was going to be an Easter to remember.

Everybody said hello to everybody, and still wet people were coming into the church as rain started to hammer on the roof. Granddaddy Jaybird, his face long and gaunt and his hair a white bristle-brush, wanted to talk to Dad about the murder, but Dad shook his head and wouldn't go into it. Grandmomma Sarah asked me if I was playing baseball this year, and I said I was. She had a fat-cheeked, kind face and pale blue eyes in nests of wrinkles, but I knew that oftentimes Granddaddy Jaybird's ways made her spit with anger.

Because of the rain, the windows were shut tight and the air was really getting muggy. The floorboards were wet, the walls leaked, and the fans groaned as they turned. The church smelled of a hundred different kinds of perfume, shaving lotion, and hair tonic, plus the sweet aromas of blossoms adorning lapels and hats. The choir filed in, wearing their purple robes. Before the first song was finished, I was sweating under my shirt. We stood up, sang a hymn, and sat down. Two overstuffed women—Mrs. Garrison and Mrs. Prathmore—came up to the front to talk about the donation fund for the poverty-stricken families of Adams Valley. Then we stood up, sang another hymn, and sat down. Both of my grandfathers had voices like bullfrogs battling in a swamp pond.

Plump, round-faced Reverend Richmond Lovoy stepped behind the pulpit and began to talk about what a glorious day it was, with Jesus risen from the dead and all. Reverend Lovoy had a comma of brown hair over his left eye, the sides of his hair gone gray, and every Sunday without fail his brushed-back hair pulled loose from its shellacked moorings and slid down over his face like a brown flood as he preached and gestured. His wife was named Esther, their three children Matthew, Luke, and Joni.

As Reverend Lovoy spoke, his voice competing with the thunder of heaven, I realized who was sitting directly in front of me.

The Demon.

She could read minds. That much was an accepted fact. And just as it dawned on me that she was there, her head swiveled and she stared at me with those black eyes that could freeze a witch at midnight. The Demon's name was Brenda Sutley. She was ten years old, and she had stringy red hair and a pallid face splashed with brown freckles. Her eyebrows were as thick as caterpillars, and the untidy arrangement of her features looked like somebody had tried to beat out a fire on her face with the flat side of a shovel. Her right eye looked larger than the left, her nose was a beak with two gaping holes in it, and her thin-lipped mouth seemed to wander from one side of her face to the other. She couldn't help her heritage, though; her mother was a fire hydrant with red hair and a brown mustache, and her red-bearded father would've made a fence post look brawny. With all those red kinks in her background, it was no wonder Brenda Sutley was spooky.

The Demon had earned her name because she had once drawn a picture of her father with horns and a forked tail in art class, and had told Mrs. Dixon, the art teacher, and her classmates that her pappy kept at the back of his closet a big stack of magazines that showed boy demons sticking their tails in the holes of girl demons. But the Demon did more than spill her family's closeted secrets: she had brought a dead cat to school in a shoebox with pennies taped to its eyeballs for show-and-tell; she had made a graveyard out of green and white Play-Doh for her art class project, with the names of her classmates and the dates of their deaths on the headstones, which caused more than one child to go into hysterics when they realized they would not live to see sixteen; she had a fondness for bizarre practical jokes that involved dog manure pressed between sandwich bread; and it was widely rumored that she was behind the explosion of pipes in the girls' bathroom at Zephyr Elementary last November, when every toilet was clogged with notebook paper.

She was, in a word, weird.

And now her royal weirdness was staring at *me*.

A slow smile spread across her crooked mouth. I couldn't look away from those piercing black eyes, and I thought *She's got me.* The thing about adults is, when you want them to pay attention to you and intervene, their minds are worlds away; when you want them to be worlds away, they're sitting on the back of your neck. I wanted my dad or mom or anybody to tell Brenda Sutley to turn around and listen to Reverend Lovoy, but of course it was as if the Demon had willed herself to be invisible. No one could see her but me, her victim of the moment.

Her right hand rose up like the head of a small white snake with dirty fangs. Slowly, with evil grace, she extended the index finger and aimed it toward one of her gaping nose holes. The finger winnowed deep into that nostril, and I thought she was going to keep pushing it in until her whole finger was gone. Then the finger was withdrawn, and on the tip of it was a glistening green mass as big as a corn kernel.

Her black eyes were unblinking. Her mouth began to open.

No, I begged her, mind to mind. *No, please don't do it!*

The Demon slid her green-capped finger toward her wet pink tongue.

I could do nothing but stare as my stomach drew up into a hard little knot.

Green against pink. Dirty fingernail. A sticky strand, hanging down.

The Demon licked her finger, where the green thing had been. I think I must've squirmed violently, because Dad gripped my knee and whispered, "Pay attention!" but of course he never saw the invisible Demon or her act of prickly torment. The Demon smiled at me, her black eyes sated, and then she turned her head away and the ordeal was over. Her mother lifted up a hand with hairy knuckles and stroked the Demon's fiery locks as if she were the sweetest little girl who ever drew God's breath.

Reverend Lovoy asked everyone to pray. I lowered my head and squeezed my eyes shut.

And about five seconds into the prayer, something thumped hard against the back of my skull.

I looked around.

Horror choked me. Sitting directly behind me, their pewter-colored eyes the hue of sharpened blades, were Gotha and Gordo Branlin. On either side of them, their parents were deep in prayer. I imagined they prayed for deliverance from their brood. Both Branlin boys wore dark blue suits, white shirts, and their ties were similar except Gotha's had black stripes on white and Gordo's had red. Gotha, the oldest by one year, had the whitest hair; Gordo's was a little on the yellow side. Their faces looked like mean carvings in brown rock, and even their bones—lower jaws jutting forward, cheekbones about to tear through flesh, foreheads like slabs of granite—suggested coiled rage. In the fleeting seconds that I dared to look upon those cunning visages, Gordo thrust an upraised middle finger in my face and Gotha loaded a straw with another hard black-eyed pea.

"Cory, turn around!" my mother whispered, and she tugged at me. "Close your eyes and pray!"

I did. The second pea bounced off the back of my head. Those things could sting the whine out of you. All during the rest of that prayer, I could hear the Branlins back there, whispering and giggling like evil trolls. My head was their target for the day.

After the prayer was over, we sang another hymn. Announcements were made, and visitors welcomed. The offering plate was passed around. I put in the dollar Dad had given me for this purpose. The choir sang, with the Glasses playing piano and organ. Behind me, the Branlins giggled. Then Reverend Lovoy stood up again to deliver his Easter sermon, and that was when the wasp landed on my hand.

My hand was resting on my knee. I didn't move it, even as fear shot up my spine like a lightning bolt. The wasp wedged itself between my first and second fingers and sat there, its blue-black stinger twitching.

Now let me say a few things about wasps.

They are not like bees. Bees are fat and happy and they float around from flower to flower without a care for human flesh. Yellowjackets are curious and have mood swings, but they, too, are usually predictable and can be avoided. A wasp, however, particularly the dark, slim kind of wasp that looks like a dagger with a head on it, was born to plunge that stinger into mortal epidermis and draw forth a scream like a connoisseur uncorking a vintage wine. Brushing your head against a wasps' nest can result in a sensation akin to, as I have heard, being peppered with shotgun pellets. I have seen the face of a boy who was stung on the lips and eyelids when he explored an old house in the middle of summer; such a swollen torture I wouldn't even wish on the Branlins. Wasps are insane; they have no rhyme or reason to their stingings. They would sting you to the marrow of your bones if they could drive their stingers in that deeply. They are full of rage, like the Branlins. If the devil indeed ever had a familiar, it was not a black cat or monkey or leather-skinned lizard; it was, and always will be, the wasp.

A third pea got me in the back of the head. It hurt a lot. But I stared at the wasp wedged between my first and second fingers, my heart beating hard, my skin crawling. Something flew past my face, and I looked up to watch a second wasp circle the Demon's head and land on her crown. The Demon must've felt a tickle. She reached back and flicked the wasp off without knowing what she was flicking, and the wasp rose up with an angry whir of black wings. I thought sure the Demon was about to be stung, but the wasp must've sensed its brethren because it flew on up to the ceiling.

Reverend Lovoy was really preaching now, about crucified Jesus and weeping Mary and the stone that had been rolled away.

I looked up at the church's ceiling.

Near one of the revolving fans was a small hole, no bigger than a quarter. As I watched, three wasps emerged from it and descended down into the congregation. A few seconds later, two more came out and swirled in the muggy, saccharine air.

Thunder boomed over the church. The noise of the rain almost drowned out Reverend Lovoy's rising and falling voice. What he was saying I didn't know; I looked at the wasp between my fingers again, then back to the hole in the ceiling.

More were coming out, spiraling down into the steamy, closed-up, rain-damp church. I counted them. Eight. . . nine . . . ten . . . eleven. Some of them clung to the fan's slow blades and rode them like a merry-go-round. Fourteen . . . fifteen . . . sixteen . . . seventeen. A dark, twitching fist of wasps pushed through the hole. Twenty . . . twenty-one . . . twenty-two. I stopped counting at twenty-five.

There must be a nest of them up there in the attic, I thought. Must be a nest the size of a football, pulsing in the damp dark. As I watched, transfixed at the sight as Mary must have been when a stranger on the road showed her his wounded side, a dozen more wasps boiled out of the hole. No one else seemed to notice; were they invisible, as the Demon had been when she picked a nose grape? The wasps spun slowly around and around the ceiling, in emulation of the fans. There were enough now to form a dark cloud, as if the outside storm had found a way in.

The wasp between my fingers was moving. I looked at it, and winced as another pea stung the back of my neck where the hair was stubbled. The wasp crawled along my index finger and stopped on the knuckle. Its stinger lay against my flesh, and I felt the tiny little jagged edge of it like a grain of broken glass.

Reverend Lovoy was in his element now, his arms gesturing and his hair starting to slide forward. Thunder crashed outside and rain beat on the roof. It sounded like Judgment Day out there, time to hew some wood and call the animals together two by two. All but the wasps, I thought; this time around we could fix Noah's mistake. I kept watching that hole in the ceiling with a mixture of fascination and dread. It occurred to me that Satan had found a way to slip into the Easter service, and there he was circling above our heads, looking for flesh.

Two things happened at once.

Reverend Lovoy lifted his hands and said, in his loud preacher's cadence, "And on that *glorious* mornin' after the *darkest* day the angels came down and *gakkkk!*" He had raised his hands to the angels, and suddenly he found them crawling with little wings.

My mom put her hand on mine, where my own wasp was, and squeezed in a loving grip.

It got her at the same instant the wasps decided Reverend Lovoy's sermon had gone on long enough.

She screamed. He screamed. It was the signal the wasps had been waiting for.

The blue-black cloud of them, over a hundred stingers strong, dropped down like a net on the heads of trapped beasts.

I heard Granddaddy Jaybird bellow, *"Shitfire!"* as he was pierced. Nana Alice let out an operatic, quavering high note. The Demon's mother wailed, wasps attacking the back of her neck. The Demon's father flailed at the air with his skinny arms. The Demon started laughing. Behind me, the Branlins croaked with pain, the peashooter forgotten. All across the church there were screams and hollers and people in Easter suits and dresses were jumping up and fighting the air as if grappling the devils of the invisible dimension. Reverend Lovoy was dancing in a paroxysm of agony, shaking his multiple-stung hands as if to disconnect them from the wrists. The whole choir was up and singing, not hymns this time but cries of pain as the wasps stung cheeks, chins, and noses. The air was full of dark, swirling currents that flew into people's faces and wound around their heads like thorny crowns. "Get out! Get out!" somebody was shouting. "Run for it!" somebody else hollered, behind me. The Glasses broke, running for the exit with wasps in their hair. All at once everybody was up, and what had been a peaceful congregation barely ten seconds before was now a stampede of terror-struck cattle.

Wasps will do that to you.

"My damn leg's stuck!" Grand Austin shouted.

"Jay! Help him!" Grandmomma Sarah yelled, but Granddaddy Jaybird was already fighting his way out into the clogged, thrashing mass of people in the aisle.

Dad pulled me up. I heard an evil hum in my left ear, and the next instant I took a sting at the edge of my ear that caused the tears to jump from my eyes. *"Ow!"* I heard myself shout, though with all the screaming and hollering one little *ow* was of no consequence. Two more wasps, however, heard me. One of them got me in my right shoulder, stinging through my suit coat and shirt; the other darted at my face like an African lance and impaled my upper lip. I gave a garbled shout— owgollywowwow—of the kind that speaks volumes of pain but no syllable of sense, and I, too, fought the churning air. A voice squealed with laughter, and when I looked at the Demon through my watering eyes I saw her jumping up and down on the pew, her mouth split in a grin and red whelps all over her face.

"Everyone *out!*" Dr. Lezander hollered. Three wasps clung, pulsing and stinging, to his bald skull, and his gray-haired, stern-faced wife was behind him, her blue-blossomed Easter hat knocked awry and wasps crawling on her wide shoulders. She gripped her Bible in one hand and her purse with the other and swung tremendous blows at the attacking swarms, her teeth gritted with righteous anger.

People were fighting through the door, ignoring raincoats and umbrellas in their struggle to escape from torment into deluge. Coming into church, the Easter crowd had been the model of polite Christian civilization; going out, they were barbarians to the core. Women and children went down in the muddy yard, and the men tripped over them and fell facefirst into rain-beaten puddles. Easter hats spun away and rolled like soggy wheels until the torrent slammed them flat.

I helped Dad pry Grand Austin's wooden leg loose from under the pew. Wasps were jabbing at my father's hands, and every time one would sting I could hear his breath hiss. Mom, Nana Alice, and Grandmomma Sarah were trying to get out into the aisle, where people were falling down and tangling up with each other. Reverend Lovoy, his fingers swollen like link sausages, was trying to shield his children's faces between himself and sobbing Esther. The choir had disintegrated, and some of them had left their empty purple robes behind. Dad and I got Grand Austin out into the aisle. Wasps were attacking the back of his neck, and his cheeks were wet. Dad brushed the wasps off, but more swarmed around us in a vengeful circle like Comanches around a wagon train. Children were crying and women were shrieking, and still the wasps darted and stung. "Out! Out!" Dr. Lezander was shouting at the door, shoving people through as they knotted up. His wife, Veronica, a husky Dutch bear, grabbed a struggling soul and all but flung the man through the doorway.

We were almost out. Grand Austin staggered, but Dad held him up. My mother was plucking the wasps out of Grandmomma Sarah's hair like living nettles. Two hot pins jabbed into the back of my neck, one a split second after the other, and the pain felt like my head was going to blow off. Then Dad took hold of my arm and pulled and the rain pounded on my skull. We all got through the door, but Dad slipped in a puddle and went down on his knees in the muck. I grasped the back of my neck and ran around in circles, crying with the pain, and after a while my feet slipped out from under me and my Easter suit met Zephyr's mud, too.

Reverend Lovoy was the last one out. He slammed the church door shut and stood with his back against it, as if to contain the evil within.

Thunder boomed and rolled. The rain came down like hammers and nails, beating us all senseless. Some people sat in the mud; others wandered around, dazed; others just stood there letting the rain pour over them to help cool the hot suffering.

I was hurting, too. And I imagined, in my delirium of pain, that behind the church's closed door the wasps were rejoicing. After all, it was Easter for them, too. They had risen from the dead of winter, the season that dries up wasps' nests and mummifies their sleeping infants. They had rolled away their own stone and emerged reborn into a new spring, and they had delivered to us a stinging sermon on the tenacity of life that would stay with us far longer than anything Reverend Lovoy could have said. We had, all of us, experienced the thorns and nails in a most personal way.

Someone bent down beside me. I felt cool mud being pressed against the stings on the back of my neck. I looked into Granddaddy Jaybird's rain-soaked face, his hair standing up as if he'd been electric-shocked.

"You all right, boy?" he asked me.

He had turned his back on the rest of us and fled for his own skin. He had been a coward and a Judas, and there was no satisfaction in his offering of mud.

I didn't answer him. I looked right through him. He said, "You'll be all right," and he stood up and went to see about Grandmomma Sarah, who huddled with Mom and Nana Alice. He looked to me like a half-drowned, scrawny rat.

I might've punched him if I'd been my father's size. I couldn't help but be ashamed of him, a deep, stinging shame. And I couldn't help but wonder, as well, if some of Granddaddy Jaybird's cowardice might be inside *me*, too. I didn't know it then, but I was going to find out real soon.

Somewhere across Zephyr the bells of another church rang, the sound coming to us through the rain as if heard in a dream. I stood up, my lower lip and shoulder and the back of my neck throbbing. The thing about pain is, it teaches you humility. Even the Branlins were blubbering like babies. I never saw anybody act cocky after they got a hide full of stingers, have you?

The Easter bells rang across the watery town.

Church was over.

Hallelujah.

5

The Death of a Bike

The rain kept falling.

Gray clouds hung over Zephyr, and from their swollen bellies came the deluge. I went to sleep with rain slamming the roof, and I awoke to the crash of thunder. Rebel shivered and moaned in his doghouse. I knew how he felt. My wasp stings had diminished to red welts, but for day upon day no ray of sunshine fell upon my hometown; only the incessant rain came down, and when I wasn't doing homework I sat in my room rereading old *Famous Monsters* magazines and my stock of comic books.

The house got that rainy smell in it, an odor of damp boards and wet dirt wafting up from the basement. The downpour caused the cancellation of the Saturday matinee at the Lyric, because the theater's roof had sprung leaks. The very air itself felt slick, like green mold growing on damp stones. At the dinner table a week after Easter, Dad put down his knife and fork and looked at the steamy wet windows and said, "We're gonna have to grow gills if this keeps up."

It did keep up. The air was heavy with water, the clouds cutting all light to a dim, swampy murk. Yards became ponds, and the streets turned into streams. School started letting out early, so everyone could get home, and on Wednesday afternoon at seventeen minutes before three o'clock my old bike gave up the ghost.

One second I was trying to pedal through a torrent on Deerman

Street. The next second my bike's front wheel sank into a crater where the pavement had broken and the shock thrummed through the rust-eaten frame. Several things happened at once: the handlebars collapsed, the front wheel's spokes snapped, the seat broke, the frame gave way at its tired old seams, and suddenly I was lying on my belly in water that flooded into my yellow rain slicker. I lay there, stunned, trying to figure out how the earth had knocked me down. Then I sat up, wiped the water out of my eyes, and looked at my bike, and just like that I knew it was dead.

My bike, old in the ways of a boy's life long before it had reached my hands by merit of a flea market, was no longer a living thing. I felt it, as I sat there in the pouring rain. Whatever it is that gives a soul to an object made by the tools of man, it had cracked open and flown to the watery heavens. The frame had bent and snapped, the handlebars hanging by a single screw, the seat turned around like a head on a broken neck. The chain was off its sprockets, the front tire warped from its rim, and the snapped spokes sticking up. I almost cried at the sight of such carnage, but even though my heart hurt, I knew crying wouldn't help. My bike had simply worn out; it had come to the end of its days, pure and simple. I was not its first owner, and maybe that made a difference, too. Maybe a bike, once discarded, pines away year after year for the first hand that steered it, and as it grows old it dreams, in its bike way, of the young roads. It was never really mine, then; it traveled with me, but its pedals and handlebars held the memory of another master. Maybe, on that rainy Wednesday, it killed itself because it knew I yearned for a bike built for me and me alone. Maybe. All I knew for sure at that moment was that I had to walk the rest of the way home, and I couldn't drag the carcass with me.

I pulled it up onto somebody's yard and left it under a dripping oak tree, and I went on with my drenched knapsack on my back and my shoes squeaking with water.

When my father, who was home from the dairy, found out about the bike, he packed me into the pickup truck, and off we went to fetch the carcass on Deerman Street. "It can be fixed," he told me as the wipers slogged back and forth across the windshield. "We'll get somebody to weld it together or somethin'. That'll be cheaper than a new bike, for sure."

"Okay," I answered, but I knew the bike was dead. No amount of welding was going to revive it. "The front wheel was messed up, too," I added, but Dad was concentrating on his driving.

We reached the place where I'd pulled the carcass up under the oak tree. "Where is it?" Dad asked. "Was this the place?"

61

It was, though the carcass was gone. Dad stopped the truck, got out, and knocked on the front door of the house we sat before. I saw the door open, and a white-haired woman peered out. She and Dad talked for a minute or so, and I saw the woman point toward the street. Then my dad came back, his cap dripping water and his shoulders hunched in his wet milkman's jacket. He slid behind the wheel, closed the door, and said, "Well, she walked out to get her mail, she saw the bike lyin' there under her tree, and she called Mr. Sculley to come pick it up." Mr. Emmett Sculley was Zephyr's junkman, and he drove around in a bright green truck with SCULLEY'S ANTIQUES and a telephone number painted on the sides in red. My dad started the engine and looked at me. I knew that look; it was hard and angry, and I could read a grim future in it. "Why didn't you go to that woman's door and tell her you were gonna come back for your bike? Didn't you think of that?"

"No, sir," I had to admit. "I didn't."

Well, my dad pulled the truck away from the curb and we started off again. Not toward home, but heading west. I knew where we were going. Mr. Sculley's junk shop lay to the west, past the wooded edge of town. On the way, I had to endure my father's tale, the one that began like this: "When I was your age, I had to walk if I wanted to get somewhere. I wish I'd had a bike back then, even a *used* one. Heck, if my buddies and me had to walk two or three miles, we didn't think a thing about it. And we were healthier for it, too. Sun, wind, or rain, it didn't matter. We got where we were going on our own two le—" And so on, you know the kind of speech I mean, the generational paean of childhood.

We left the town limits behind us, and the glistening road wound through the wet green forest. The rain was still coming down, pieces of fog snagged on the treetops and drifting across the road. Dad had to drive slowly because the road around here was dangerous even when the pavement was dry. My dad was still going on about the dubious joys of not having a bike, which I was beginning to realize was his way of telling me I'd better get used to walking if my old ride was unfixable. Thunder boomed off beyond the hazy hills, the road deserted before us as it curved beneath the tires like a wild horse fights a saddle. I don't know why I chose that moment to turn my head and look back, but I did.

And I saw the car that was coming up fast behind us.

The hair on the back of my neck stood up, and the skin beneath it tingled like the scurrying of ants. The car was a black, low-slung, mean-looking panther with gleaming chrome teeth, and it rocketed around the long curve my father had just negotiated with an uneasy alliance of brake and accelerator. The pickup truck's engine was sputtery, but I could hear no sound from the black car that closed on us. I could see a shape and a pale face behind the wheel. I could see red and orange flames painted on the slope of the ebony hood, and then the car was on our tail and showed no sign of slowing or swerving and I looked at my father and shouted, *"Dad!"*

He jumped in his seat and jerked the wheel. The truck's tires slewed to the left, over the faded centerline, and my father fought to keep us from going into the woods. Then the tires got a grip again, the truck straightened out, and Dad had fire in his eyes when he swung his face in my direction. "Are you crazy?" he snapped. "You want to get us killed?"

I looked back.

The black car was gone.

It hadn't passed us. It hadn't turned off anywhere. It was just gone.

"I saw . . . I saw . . ."

"Saw *what? Where?*" he demanded.

"I . . . thought I saw . . . a car," I told him. "It was . . . about to hit us, I thought."

He peered into the rearview mirror. Of course he saw only the same rain and empty road I was seeing. He reached out, put his hand against my forehead, and said, "You feelin' all right?"

"Yes sir." I didn't have a fever. Of that, at least, I was certain. My father, satisfied that I was not building up heat, pulled his hand away and refastened it to the steering wheel. "Just sit still," he said, and I obeyed him. He fixed his attention on the tricky road again, but his jaw muscle clenched every few seconds and I figured he was trying to decide whether I needed to go see Dr. Parrish or get my butt busted.

I didn't say anything more about the black car, because I knew Dad wouldn't believe me. But I had seen that car before, on the streets of Zephyr. It had announced itself with a rumble and growl as it roamed the streets, and when it had passed you could smell the heat and see the pavement shimmer. "Fastest car in town," Davy Ray had told me as he and I and the other guys had lounged around in front of the ice house on Merchants Street, catching cool breezes from the ice blocks on a sultry August day. "My dad," Davy Ray had confided, "says nobody can outrace Midnight Mona."

Midnight Mona. That was the car's name. The guy who owned it was named Stevie Cauley. "Little Stevie," he was called, because he stood only a few inches over five feet tall though he was twenty years old. He chain-smoked Chesterfield cigarettes, and maybe those had stunted his growth.

But the reason I didn't tell my dad about Midnight Mona streaking up behind us on that rain-slick road was that I remembered what had happened on a night last October. My dad, who used to be a volunteer fireman, got a telephone call. It was Chief Marchette, he'd told Mom. A car had wrecked on Route Sixteen, and it was on fire in the woods. My dad had hurried out to help, and he'd come home a couple of hours later with ashes in his hair and his clothes smelling of burnt timber. After that night, and what he'd seen, he hadn't wanted to be a fireman anymore.

We were on Route Sixteen right now. And the car that had wrecked and burned was Midnight Mona, with Little Stevie Cauley behind the wheel.

Little Stevie Cauley's body—what was left of it, I mean—lay in a coffin in the cemetery on Poulter Hill. Midnight Mona was gone, too, to wherever burned-up cars go.

But I had seen it, racing up behind us out of the mist. I had seen someone sitting behind the wheel.

I kept my mouth shut. I was in enough trouble already.

Dad turned off Route Sixteen and eased the truck onto a muddy side road that wound through the woods. We reached a place where rusted old metal signs of all descriptions had been nailed to the trees; there were at least a hundred of them, advertisements for everything from Green Spot Orange Soda to B.C. Headache Powders to the Grand Ole Opry. Beyond the signpost forest the road led to a house of gray wood with a sagging front porch and in the front yard—and here I mean "sea of weeds" instead of yard as ordinary people might know it—a motley collection of rust-eaten clothes wringers, kitchen stoves, lamps, bedframes, electric fans, iceboxes, and other smaller appliances was lying about in untidy piles. There were coils of wire as tall as my father and bushel baskets full of bottles, and amid the junk stood the metal sign of a smiling policeman with the red letters STOP DON'T STEAL painted across his chest. In his head there were three bullet holes.

I don't think stealing was a problem for Mr. Sculley, because as soon as my dad stopped the truck and opened his door two red hound dogs jumped up from their bellies on the porch and began baying to beat the band. A few seconds later, the screen door banged open and a frail-looking little woman with a white braid and a rifle came out of the house.

"Who is it?" she hollered in a voice like a lumberjack's. "Whadda ye want?"

My father lifted his hands. "It's Tom Mackenson, Mrs. Sculley. From Zephyr."

"Tom *who?*"

"Mackenson!" He had to shout over the hound dogs. "From Zephyr!"

Mrs. Sculley roared, *"Shaddup!"* and she plucked a fly swatter from a hook on the porch and swung a few times at the dogs' rumps, which quieted them down considerably.

I got out of the truck and stood close to my dad, our shoes mired in the boggy weeds. "I need to see your husband, Mrs. Sculley," Dad told her. "He picked up my boy's bike by mistake."

"Uh-uh," she replied. "Emmett don't make no mistakes."

"Is he around, please?"

"Back of the house," she said, and she motioned with the rifle. "One of them sheds back there."

"Thank you." He started off and I followed him, and we'd taken maybe a half-dozen steps when Mrs. Sculley said, "Hey! You trip over somethin' and break your legs, we ain't liable for it, hear?"

If what lay in front of the house was a mess, what lay behind it was nightmarish. The two "sheds" were corrugated metal buildings the size of tobacco warehouses. To get to them, you had to follow a rutted trail that meandered between mountains of castaway things: record players, broken statuary, garden hose, chairs, lawn mowers, doors, fireplace mantels, pots and pans, old bricks, roof shingles, irons, radiators, and washbasins to name a few. "Have mercy," Dad said, mostly to himself, as we walked through the valley between the looming hills. The rain spilled and spattered over all these items, in some places running down from the metallic mountaintops in gurgling little streams. And then we came to a big twisted and tangled heap of things that made me stop in my tracks because I knew I had found a truly mystical place.

Before me were hundreds of bicycle frames, locked together with vines of rust, their tires gone, their backs broken.

They say that somewhere in Africa the elephants have a secret grave where they go to lie down, unburden their wrinkled gray bodies, and soar away, light spirits at the end. I believed at that moment in time that I had found the grave of the bicycles, where the carcasses flake away year after year under rain and baking sun, long after the spirits of their wandering lives have gone. In some places on that huge pile the bicycles had melted away until they resembled nothing more than red and copper leaves waiting to be burned on an autumn afternoon. In some places shattered headlights poked up, sightless but defiant, in a dead way. Warped handlebars still held rubber grips, and from some of the grips dangled strips of colored vinyl like faded flames. I had a vision of all these bikes, vibrant in their new paint, with new tires and new pedals and chains that snuggled up to their sprockets in beds of clean new grease. It made me sad, in a way I couldn't understand, because I saw how there is an end to all things, no matter how much we want to hold on to them.

"Howdy, there!" somebody said. "Thought I heard the alarms go off."

My dad and I looked at a man who pushed a large handcart before him through the muck. He wore overalls and muddy boots, and he had a big belly and a liver-spotted head with a tuft of white at its peak. Mr. Sculley had a wrinkled face and a bulbous nose with small broken veins showing purple at its tip, and he wore round-lensed glasses over gray eyes. He was grinning a square grin, his teeth dark brown, and on his grizzled chin was a mole that had sprouted three white hairs. "What can I do for you?"

"I'm Tom Mackenson," my dad said, and offered his hand. "Jay's son."

"Oh, yeah! Sorry I didn't recognize you right off!" Mr. Sculley wore dirty canvas gloves, and he took one of them off to shake my father's hand. "This Jay's grandson?"

"Yep. Cory's his name."

"Seen you around, I believe," Mr. Sculley said to me. "I remember when your daddy was your age. Me and your grandpa go back a piece."

"Mr. Sculley, I believe you picked up a bike this afternoon," Dad told him. "In front of a house on Deerman Street?"

"Sure did. Wasn't much to it, though. All busted up."

"Well, it was Cory's bike. I think I can get it fixed, if we can have it back."

"Oops," Mr. Sculley said. His square grin faltered. "Tom, I don't think I can do that."

"Why not? It *is* here, isn't it?"

"Yeah, it's here. *Was* here, I mean." Mr. Sculley motioned toward one of the sheds. "I took it in there just a few minutes ago."

"So we can get it and take it back, can't we?"

Mr. Sculley sucked on his lower lip, looked at me, and then back to Dad. "I don't believe so, Tom." He pushed the handcart aside, next to the mound of dead bikes, and he said, "Come on and have a look." We followed him. He walked with a limp, as if his hip worked on a hinge instead of a ball-and-socket.

"See, here's the story," he said. "Been meanin' to get rid of those old bikes for over a year. Tryin' to clean the place up, ya see. Got to make room for more stuff comin' in. So I said to Belle—that's my wife—I said, 'Belle, when I pick up one more bike I'm gonna do it. Just one more.'" He led us into an open doorway, into the building's cool interior. Light bulbs hanging on cords threw shadows between more mounds of junk. Here and there larger things rose up from the gloom like Martian machines and presented a glimpse of mysterious curves and edges. Something squeaked and skittered; whether mice or bats, I don't know. The place sure looked like a cavern, where Injun Joe would feel right at home.

"Watch your step here," Mr. Sculley cautioned us as we went through another doorway. Then he stopped beside a big rectangular machine with gears and levers on it and he said, "This here crusher just ate your bike about fifteen minutes ago. It was the first one in." He prodded a barrel full of twisted and crumpled metal pieces. Other barrels were waiting to be filled. "See, I can sell this as scrap metal. I was waitin' for one more bike to start breakin' 'em up, and yours was the one." He looked at me, the overhead bulb shining on his rain-wet dome, and his eyes were not unkind. "Sorry, Cory. If I'd known anybody was gonna come claim it, I'd have held on to it, but it was dead."

"Dead?" my father asked.

"Sure. Everythin' dies. It wears out and can't be fixed for love nor money. That's how the bike was. That's how they all are by the time somebody brings 'em here, or somebody calls me to come pick 'em up. You know your bike was dead long before I put it in that crusher, don't you, Cory?"

"Yes sir," I said. "I do."

"It didn't suffer none," Mr. Sculley told me, and I nodded.

It seemed to me that Mr. Sculley understood the very nucleus of existence, that he had kept his young eyes and young heart even though his body had grown old. He saw straight through to the cosmic order of things, and he knew that life is not held only in flesh and bone, but also in those objects—a good, faithful pair of shoes; a reliable car; a pen that always works; a bike that has taken you many a mile—into which we put our trust and which give us back the security and joy of memories.

Here the ancient hearts of stone may chortle and say, "That's *ridiculous!*" But let me ask a question of them: don't you ever wish— even for just a fleeting moment—that you could have your first bike again? You remember what it looked like. You remember. Did you name it Trigger, or Buttermilk, or Flicka, or Lightning? Who took that bike away, and where did it go? Don't you ever, ever wonder?

"Like to show you somethin', Cory," Mr. Sculley said, and he touched my shoulder. "This way."

My dad and I both followed him, away from the bike-crushing machine into another chamber. A window with dirty glass let in a little greenish light to add to the overhead bulb's glare. In this room was Mr. Sculley's desk and a filing cabinet. He opened a closet and reached up onto a high shelf. "I don't show this to just anybody," he told us, "but I figure you fellas might like to see it." He rummaged around, moving boxes, and then he said, "Found it," and his hand emerged from dark into light again.

He was holding a chunk of wood, its bark bleached and dried mollusks still gripping its surface. What looked like a slim ivory dagger, about five inches long, had been driven into the wood. Mr. Sculley held it up to the light, his eyes sparkling behind his glasses. "See it? What do you make of it?"

"No idea," Dad said. I shook my head, too.

"Look close." He held the wood chunk with its embedded ivory dagger in front of my face. I could see pits and scars on the ivory's surface, and its edges were serrated like a fishing knife.

"It's a tooth," Mr. Sculley said. "Or a fang, most likely."

"A *fang*?" Dad frowned, his gaze jumping back and forth between Mr. Sculley and the wood chunk. "Must've been a mighty big snake!"

"No snake, Tom. I cut this piece out of a log I found washed up along the river when I was huntin' bottles three summers ago. See the shells? It must be from an old tree, probably laid on the bottom for quite a while. I figure that last flood we had pulled it up from the mud." He gingerly ran a gloved finger along the serrated edge. "I do believe I've got the only evidence there is."

"You don't mean . . ." Dad began, but I already knew.

"Yep. This here's a fang from the mouth of Old Moses." He held it in front of me once more, but I drew back. "Maybe his eyesight ain't so good anymore," Mr. Sculley mused. "Maybe he went after that log thinkin' it was a big turtle. Maybe he was just mean that day, and he snapped at everythin' his snout bumped up against." His finger tapped the fang's broken rim. "Hate to think what this thing could do to a human bein'. Wouldn't be pretty, would it?"

"Can I see that?" Dad asked, and Mr. Sculley let him hold it. Mr. Sculley went to the window and peered out as Dad examined what he held, and after another moment Dad said, "I swear, I believe you're right! It *is* a tooth!"

"Said it was," Mr. Sculley reminded him. "I don't lie."

"You need to show this to somebody! Sheriff Amory or Mayor Swope! Heck, the *governor* needs to see it!"

"Swope's already seen it," Mr. Sculley said. "He's the one advised me to put it in my closet and keep the door shut."

"Why? Somethin' like this is front-page news!"

"Not accordin' to Mayor Swope." He turned away from the window, and I saw that his eyes had darkened. "At first Swope thought it was a fake. He had Doc Parrish look at it, and Doc Parrish called Doc Lezander. Both of them agreed it's a fang from some kind of reptile. Then we all had a sit-down talk in the mayor's office, with the doors closed. Swope said he'd decided to put a lid on the whole thing. Said it might be a fang or it might be a fraud, but it wasn't worth gettin' folks upset over." He took the pierced wood chunk back from my father's hands. "I said, 'Luther Swope, don't you think people would want to see real evidence that there's a monster in the Tecumseh River?' And he looked at me with that damn pipe in his mouth and he says, 'People already know it. Evidence would just scare 'em. Anyway,' Swope says, 'if there's a monster in the river, it's *our* monster, and we don't want to share it with nobody.' And that's how it ended up." Mr. Sculley offered it to me. "Want to touch it, Cory? Just so you can say you did?"

I did, with a tentative index finger. The fang was cool, as I imagined the muddy bottom of the river must be.

Mr. Sculley put the piece of wood and the fang back up on the closet shelf, and he closed the door. The rain was coming down hard again outside, banging on the metal roof. "All this water pourin' down," Mr. Sculley said, "must make Old Moses mighty happy."

"I still think you ought to show somebody else," Dad told him. "Like somebody from the newspaper in Birmingham."

"I would, Tom, but maybe Swope's got a point. Maybe Old Moses *is* our monster. Maybe if we let everybody else know about him, they'd come try to take him away from us. Catch him up in a net, put him in a big glass tank somewhere like an overgrown mudcat." Mr. Sculley frowned and shook his head. "Nah, I wouldn't want that to happen. Neither would the Lady, I reckon. She's been feedin' him on Good Friday for as long as I can remember. This was the first year he didn't like his food."

"Didn't like his food?" Dad asked. "Meanin' what?"

"Didn't you see the parade this year?" Mr. Sculley waited for Dad to say no, and then he went on. "This was the first year Old Moses didn't give the bridge a smack with his tail, same to say 'Thanks for the grub.' It's a quick thing, it passes fast, but you get to know the sound of it when you've heard it so many years. This year it didn't happen."

I recalled how troubled the Lady looked when she left the gargoyle bridge that day, and how the whole procession had been so somber on the march back to Bruton. That must have been because the Lady hadn't heard Old Moses smack the bridge with his tail. But what did such a lack of table manners mean?

"Hard to say what it means," Mr. Sculley said as if reading my mind. "The Lady didn't like it, that's for sure."

It was starting to get dark outside. Dad said we'd better be getting home, and he thanked Mr. Sculley for taking the time to show us where the bike had gone. "Wasn't your fault," Dad said as Mr. Sculley limped in front of us to show us the way out. "You were just doin' your job."

"Yep. Waitin' for one more bike, I was. Like I said, that bike couldn't have been fixed anyhow."

I could've told my dad that. In fact, I did tell him, but one sorry thing about being a kid is that grown-ups listen to you with half an ear.

"Heard about the car in the lake," Mr. Sculley said as we neared the doorway. His voice echoed in the cavernous room, and I sensed my father tightening up. "Bad way for a man to die, without a Christian burial," Mr. Sculley continued. "Sheriff Amory got any clues?"

"None that I know of." My father's voice was a little shaky. I was sure that he saw that sinking car and the body handcuffed to the wheel every time he lay down in bed and closed his eyes.

"Got my own ideas about who it was, and who killed him," Mr. Sculley offered. We reached the way out, but the rain was still falling hard onto the mountains of old dead things and the last of the sunlight had turned green. Mr. Sculley looked at my father and leaned against the door frame. "It was somebody who'd crossed the Blaylock clan. Must've been a fella who wasn't from around here, 'cause everybody else in their right mind knows Wade, Bodean, and Donny Blaylock are meaner'n horny rattlers. They got stills hidden all up in the woods around here. And that daddy of theirs, Biggun, could teach the devil some tricks. Yessir, the Blaylocks are the cause of that fella bein' down at the bottom of the lake, and you can count on it."

"I figure the sheriff thought of that already."

"Probably did. Only trouble is, nobody knows where the Blay-locks hide out. They show up now and again, on some errand of meanness, but trackin' 'em to their snakehole is another thing entirely." Mr. Sculley looked out the door. "Rain's easin' up some. Reckon you don't mind gettin' wet."

We trudged through the mud toward my dad's truck. I looked again at the mound of bikes as we passed, and I saw something I hadn't noticed before: honeysuckle vines were growing in the midst of the tangled metal, and the little sweet white cups were sprouting amid the rust.

My father's attention was snagged by something else that lay over beyond the bikes, something we had not seen on the way in. He stopped, staring at it, and I stopped, too, and Mr. Sculley, limping ahead, sensed our stopping and turned around.

"I wondered where they brought it," Dad said.

"Yeah, gonna haul it off one of these days. Gotta make room for more stuff, y'know."

You couldn't tell much about it, really. It was just a rusted mass of crumpled metal, but some of the metal still held the original black paint. The windshield was gone, the roof smashed flat. Part of the hood remained, though, and on it was a ripple of painted flames.

This one had suffered.

Dad turned away from it, and I followed him to the pickup. Real close, I might add.

"Come back anytime!" Mr. Sculley told us. The hound dogs bayed and Mrs. Sculley came out on the porch, this time without her rifle, and Dad and I drove home along the haunted road.

6

Old Moses Comes to Call

Mom had picked up the phone when it rang, past ten o'clock at night about a week after our visit to Mr. Sculley's place.

"Tom!" she said, and her voice carried a frantic edge. "J.T. says the dam's burst at Lake Holman! They're callin' everybody together at the courthouse!"

"Oh, Lord!" Dad sprang up from the sofa, where he'd been

watching the news on television, and he slid his feet into his shoes. "It'll be a flood for sure! Cory!" he called. "Get your clothes on!"

I knew from his tone that I'd better move quick. I put aside the story I was trying to write about a black dragster with a ghost at the wheel and I fairly jumped into my jeans. When your parents get scared, your heart starts pounding ninety miles a minute. I had heard Dad use the word *flood*. The last one had been when I was five, and it hadn't done a whole lot of damage except stir up the swamp snakes. I knew, though, from my reading about Zephyr that in 1938 the river had flooded the streets to the depth of four feet, and in 1930 the spring flood had risen almost to the rooftops of some of the houses in Bruton. So my town had a history of being waterlogged, and with all the rain we and the rest of the South had been getting since the beginning of April, there was no telling what might happen this year.

The Tecumseh River fed out of Lake Holman, which lay about forty miles north of us. So, being as it is that all rivers flow to the sea, we were in for it.

I made sure Rebel would be all right in his dog run behind the house, and then my mom, dad, and I jammed into the pickup truck and headed for the courthouse, an old gothic structure that stood at the terminus of Merchants Street. Most everybody's lights were on; the message network was in full operation. It was just drizzling right now, but the water was up to the pickup's wheel rims because of the overloaded drainpipes and some people's basements had already flooded. My friend Johnny Wilson and his folks had had to go live with relatives in Union Town for that very reason.

Cars and pickup trucks were filling up the courthouse's parking lot. Off in the distance, lightning streaked across the heavens and the low clouds lit up. People were being herded into the courthouse's main meeting room, a large chamber with a mural painted on the ceiling that showed angels flying around carrying bales of cotton; it was a holdover from when cotton crop auctions used to be held here, twenty years ago, before the cotton gin and warehouse were moved to floodproof Union Town. We found seats on one of the splintery bleachers, which was fortunate because the way other folks were coming in, there soon wasn't going to be room enough to breathe. Somebody had the good sense to turn on the fans, but the hot air emanating from people's mouths seemed inexhaustible. Mrs. Kattie Yarbrough, one of the biggest chatterboxes in town, squeezed in next to Mom and started jabbering excitedly while her husband, who was also a milkman at Green Meadows, trapped my father. I saw Ben come in with Mr. and Mrs. Sears, but they sat down across the room from us. The Demon, whose hair looked as if it had just been combed with grease, entered trailing her monstrous mother and spindly pop. They found places near us, and I shuddered when the Demon caught my repulsed gaze and grinned at me. Reverend Lovoy came in with his family, Sheriff Amory and his wife and daughters entered, the Branlins came in, and so did Mr. Parlowe, Mr. Dollar, Davy Ray and his folks, Miss Blue Glass and Miss Green Glass, and plenty more people I didn't know so well. The place got jammed.

"Quiet, everybody! Quiet!" Mr. Wynn Gillie, the assistant mayor, had stepped up to the podium where the cotton auctioneer used to stand, and behind him at a table sat Mayor Luther Swope and Fire Chief Jack Marchette, who was also the head of Civil Defense. "*Quiet!*" Mr. Gillie hollered, the veins standing out on his stringy neck. The talking died down, and Mayor Swope stood up to speak. He was tall and slim, about fifty years old, and he had a long-jawed, somber face and gray hair combed back from a widow's peak. He was always puffing on a briar pipe, like a locomotive burning coal up a long, steep haul, and he wore perfectly creased trousers and shirts with his initials on the breast pocket. He had the air of a successful businessman, which he was: he owned both the Stagg Shop for Men and the Zephyr Ice House, which had been in his family for years. His wife, Lana Jean, was sitting with Dr. Curtis Parrish and the doctor's wife, Brightie.

"Guess everybody's heard the bad news by now," Mayor Swope began. He had a mayorly appearance, but he spoke as if his mouth was full of oatmeal mush. "We ain't got a whole lot of time, folks. Chief Marchette tells me the river's already at flood stage. When that water from Lake Holman gets here, we're gonna have us a real problem. Could be the worst flood we've ever had. Which means Bruton'll get swamped first, it bein' closest to the river. Vandy, where are you?" The mayor looked around, and Mr. Vandercamp Senior raised his rickety hand. "Mr. Vandercamp is openin' up the hardware store," Mayor Swope told us. "He's got shovels and sandbags we can use to start buildin' our own dam between Bruton and the river, maybe we can hold the worst of the flood back. Which means everybody's gonna have to work: men, women, and children, too. I've called Robbins Air Force Base, and they're sendin' some men to help us. Folks are comin' over from Union Town, too. So everybody who can work oughta get over to Bruton and be ready to move some dirt."

"Hold on just one damn minute, Luther!"

The man who'd spoken stood up. You couldn't miss him. I think a book about a white whale was named after him. Mr. Dick Moultry had a florid, puffed face and wore his hair in a crew cut that resembled a brown pincushion. He had on a tent-sized T-shirt and blue jeans that might've fit my dad, Chief Marchette, and Mayor Swope all at the same time. He lifted a blubbery arm and aimed his finger at the mayor. "What you're tellin' us to do, it seems to me, is to forget about our own homes! Yessir! Forget about our own homes and go to work to save a bunch of niggers!"

This comment was a crack in the common clay. Some hollered that Mr. Moultry was wrong, and some hollered he was right.

"Dick," Mayor Swope said as he pushed his pipe into his mouth, "you know that if the river's going to flood, it always starts in Bruton. That's the lowland. If we can hold it back there, we can—"

"So where are the Bruton people?" Mr. Moultry asked, and his big square head ratcheted to right and left. "I don't see no dark faces in here! Where are they? How come they ain't in here beggin' us for help?"

"Because they *never* ask for help." The mayor spouted a plume of blue smoke; the locomotive's engine was starting to stoke. "I guarantee you they're out on the riverbank right now, tryin' to build a dam, but they wouldn't ask for help if the water came up to their roofs. The Lady wouldn't stand for it. But they do need our help, Dick. Just like last time."

"If they had any sense, they'd move out of there!" Mr. Moultry insisted. "Hell, I'm sick and tired of that damn Lady, too! Who does she think she is, a damn *queen?*"

"Sit down, Dick," Chief Marchette told him. The fire chief was a big-boned man with a chiseled face and piercing blue eyes. "There's no time to argue this thing."

"The hell you say!" Mr. Moultry had decided to be stubborn. His face was getting as red as a fireplug. "Let the Lady come over here to white man's land and *ask* us for help!" That brought a storm of assenting and dissenting shouts. Mr. Moultry's wife, Feather, stood up beside him and hollered, "Hell, yes!" She had platinum-blond hair and was more anvil than feather. Mr. Moultry bellowed over the noise, "I ain't breakin' my ass for no niggers!"

"But, Dick," Mayor Swope said in a bewildered way, "they're *our* niggers."

The shouting and hollering went on, some people saying it was the Christian thing to keep Bruton from being flooded and others saying they hoped the flood was a jimdandy so it would wash

Bruton away once and for all. My folks kept quiet, as most of the others did; this was a war of the loudmouths.

Suddenly a quiet began to spread. It began from the back of the chamber, where people were clustered around the doorway. Somebody laughed, but the laugh was choked off almost at once. A few people mumbled and muttered. And then a man made his way into the chamber and you'd have thought the Red Sea was parting as folks shrank back to give him room.

The man was smiling. He had a boyish face and light brown hair cresting a high forehead.

"What's all this yelling about?" he asked. He had a Southern accent, but you could tell he was an educated man. "Any problem here, Mayor Swope?"

"Uh . . . no, Vernon. No problem. Is there, Dick?"

Mr. Moultry looked like he was about to spit and scowl. His wife's face was red as a Christmas beet under her platinum locks. I heard the Branlins giggle, but somebody hushed them up.

"I hope there's no problem," Vernon said, still smiling. "You know how Daddy hates problems."

"Sit *down*," Mayor Swope told the Moultrys, and they did. Their asses almost busted the bleacher.

"I sense some . . . disunity here," Vernon said. I felt a giggle about to break from my throat, but my father grasped my wrist and squeezed so hard it went away. Other people shifted uneasily in their seats, especially some of the older widow women. "Mayor Swope, can I come up to the podium?"

"God save us," my father whispered, and Mom shivered with a silent laugh beating at her ribs.

"Uh . . . I . . . suppose so, Vernon. Sure. Come on up." Mayor Swope stepped back, pipe smoke swirling around his head.

Vernon Thaxter stepped up to the podium and faced the assembly. He was very pale under the lights. All of him was pale.

He was stark naked. Not a stitch on him.

His doodad and balls hung out in full view. He was a skinny thing, probably because he walked so much. The soles of his feet must've been as hard as dried leather. Rain glistened on his white flesh and his hair was slick with it. He looked like a picture of a dark Hindu mystic I'd seen in one of my *National Geographics*, though, of course, he was neither dark nor Hindu. I'd have to say he was no mystic, either. Vernon Thaxter was downright, around-the-bend-and-through-the-woods crazy.

Of course, walking around town in his birthday suit was nothing new for Vernon Thaxter. He did it all the time, once the weather started warming up. You didn't see him very much in late autumn or winter, though. When he first appeared in spring, it was always a start; by July nobody gave him a second glance; by October the falling leaves were more interesting. Then it came spring again, and there was Vernon Thaxter with his private parts on public display.

You might wonder why Sheriff Amory didn't stand up right then and there and haul Vernon off to jail for indecent exposure. The reason he did not was because of Moorwood Thaxter, Vernon's father. Moorwood Thaxter owned the bank. He also owned Green Meadows Dairy and the Zephyr Real Estate Company. Just about every house in Zephyr was mortgaged through Moorwood Thaxter's bank. He owned the land the Lyric theater stood on, and the land where this courthouse had been built. He owned every crack in Merchants Street. He owned the shotgun shacks of Bruton, and his own twenty-eight-room mansion at the height of Temple Street. The fear of Moorwood Thaxter, who was in his seventies and rarely seen, was what kept Sheriff Amory in his seat and had kept forty-year-old Vernon naked on the streets of my hometown. It had been this way as long as I remembered.

Mom told me that Vernon used to be all right, but he'd written a book and gone to New York with it and a year later he was back home wandering around nude and nutty.

"Gentlemen and ladies," Vernon began. "And children, too, of course." He reached out his frail arms and grasped the podium's edges. "We have here a very serious situation."

"Momma!" the Demon suddenly squalled. "I can see that feller's dingdo—"

A hand with hairy knuckles clamped over her mouth. I guess the elder Thaxter owned their house, too.

"A very serious situation," Vernon repeated, oblivious to everything but his own voice. "Daddy sent me here with a message. He says he expects the people of this town to show true brotherhood and Christian values in this time of trouble. Mr. Vandercamp Senior, sir?"

"Yes, Vernon?" the old man answered.

"Will you kindly keep a record of the names of those able-bodied and good-thinking men who borrow digging utensils from you for the purpose of helping the residents of Bruton? My daddy would appreciate it."

"Be glad to," Mr. Vandercamp Senior said; he was rich, but not rich enough to say no to Moorwood Thaxter.

"Thank you. That way my daddy can have a list at hand when interest rates go up, as they are bound to do in this unsettled age. My daddy has always felt that those men—and women—who aren't loath to work for their neighbors are deserving of extra considerations." He smiled, gazing out at his audience. "Anyone else have anything to say?"

No one did. It's kind of difficult to talk to a naked man about anything but why he won't wear clothes, and nobody would dare bring up such a sensitive subject.

"I think our mission is clear, then," Vernon said. "Good luck to all." He thanked Mayor Swope for letting him speak, and then he stepped down from the podium and walked out of the chamber the way he'd come. The Red Sea parted for him again, and closed at his back.

For a minute or so everybody sat in silence; maybe we were waiting to make sure Vernon Thaxter was out of earshot. Then somebody started laughing and somebody else picked it up, and the Demon started screaming with laughter and jumping up and down, but other people were hollering for the laughers to shut up and the whole place was like a merry glimpse of hell. "Settle down! Settle down, everybody!" Mayor Swope was yelling, and Chief Marchette stood up and bellowed like a foghorn for quiet.

"It's damn blackmail!" Mr. Moultry was on his feet again. "Nothin' but damn blackmail!" A few others agreed with him, but Dad was one of the men who stood up and told Mr. Moultry to shut his mouth and pay attention to the fire chief.

This is how it got sorted out: Chief Marchette said that everybody who wanted to work should get on over to Bruton, where the river flowed against the edge of town on its way to the gargoyle bridge, and he'd have some volunteers load the shovels, pickaxes, and other stuff into a truck at Mr. Vandercamp's hardware store. The power of Moorwood Thaxter was never more evident when Chief Marchette finished his instructions: everybody went to Bruton, even Mr. Moultry.

Bruton's narrow streets were already awash. Chickens flapped in the water, and dogs were swimming. The rain had started falling hard again, slamming on the tin roofs like rough music. Dark people were pulling their belongings out of the wood-frame houses and trying to get to higher ground. The cars and trucks coming over from Zephyr made waves that rolled across submerged yards to crash foam against the foundations. "This," Dad said, "is gonna be a bad one."

On the wooded riverbank, most of the residents of Bruton were already laboring in knee-deep water. A wall of mud was going up, but the river was hungry. We left the pickup near a public basketball court at the Bruton Recreation Center, where a lot of other vehicles were parked, then we slogged toward the river. Fog swirled over the rising water, and flashlight beams crisscrossed in the night. Lightning flashed and thunder boomed. I heard the urgent cries of people to work faster and harder. My mother's hand gripped mine, and held on tightly while Dad went on ahead to join a group of Bruton men. Someone had backed a dump truck full of sand to the riverbank, and a Bruton man pulled Dad up into it and they started filling little burlap bags and tossing them down to other rain-soaked men. "Over here! Over here!" somebody yelled. "It ain't gonna hold!" someone else shouted. Voices crisscrossed and merged like the flashlight beams. They were scared voices. I was scared, too.

There is something about nature out of control that touches a primal terror. We are used to believing that we're the masters of our domain, and that God has given us this earth to rule over. We need this illusion like a good night-light. The truth is more fearsome: we are as frail as young trees in tornadoes, and our beloved homes are one flood away from driftwood. We plant our roots in trembling earth, we live where mountains rose and fell and prehistoric seas burned away in mist. We and the towns we have built are not permanent; the earth itself is a passing train. When you stand in muddy water that is rising toward your waist and you hear people shouting against the darkness and see their figures struggling to hold back the currents that will not be denied, you realize the truth of it: we will not win, but we cannot give up. No one on that disappearing riverbank, there in the pouring rain, thought the Tecumseh was going to be turned aside. It had never been so. Still, the work went on. The truck full of tools came from the hardware store, and Mr. Vandercamp Junior had a clipboard where people signed their names as they accepted a shovel. Walls of mud and sandbags were built up, and the river surged through the barricade like brown soup through a mouthful of weak teeth. The water rose. My belt buckle submerged.

Lightning zigzagged down from the heavens, followed by a crash of thunder so loud you couldn't hear the women scream. "That hit somethin' close!" said Reverend Lovoy, who held a shovel and resembled a mud man. "Lights are goin' out!" a black woman shouted a few seconds later, and indeed the power was failing all over Bruton and Zephyr. I watched the lights flicker and disappear from the windows. Then my hometown lay in darkness, and you couldn't tell sky from water. In the distance I saw what looked like a candle glowing in the window of a house about as far from Bruton as you could get and still be within Zephyr's boundaries. As I watched, the light moved from window to window. I realized I was looking at Mr. Moorwood Thaxter's mansion up at the high point of Temple Street.

I sensed it before I saw it.

A figure stood to my left, watching me. Whoever it was wore a long raincoat, his hands in his pockets. The wind shrilled in off the thunderstorm and moved the wet folds of the coat, and I almost choked on my heart because I remembered the figure in the woods opposite Saxon's Lake.

Then whoever it was started wading past my mother and me toward the laborers. It was a tall figure—a man, I presumed—and he moved with purposeful strength. Two flashlight beams seemed to fence in the air for a few seconds, and the man in the raincoat walked into their conflict. The battling lights did not reveal the man's face, but did reveal something else.

The man wore a drenched and dripping fedora. The band of that hat was secured by a silver disc the size of a half-dollar, and a small decorative feather stuck up from it.

A feather, dark with wet, but a feather with a definite glint of green.

Like the green feather I'd found on the bottom of my sneaker that morning.

My mind raced. Might there have been *two* green feathers in that hatband, before the wind had plucked one out?

One of the beams, defeated, drew back. The other pranced away. The man walked in darkness.

"Mom?" I said. "Mom?"

The figure was wading away from us, and had passed no more than eight feet from me. He reached up with a white hand to hold the hat on his head. "Mom?" I said again, and she finally heard me over the noise and answered, "What is it?"

"I think . . . I think . . ." But I didn't know what I thought. I couldn't tell if that was the person I'd seen across the road, or not.

The figure was moving off through the brown water, step after step.

I pulled my hand free from my mother's, and I went after him.

"Cory!" she said. "Cory, take my hand!"

I heard, but I didn't listen. The water swirled around me. I kept going.

"*Cory!*" Mom shouted.

I had to see his face.

"Mister!" I called. It was too noisy, what with the rain and the river and the working; he couldn't hear. Even if he did, he wouldn't turn around. I felt the Tecumseh's currents pulling at my shoes. I was sunken waist-deep in cold murk. The man was heading toward the riverbank, where my dad was. Flashlights bobbed and weaved, and a shimmering reflection danced up and struck the man's right hand as he pulled it from his pocket.

Something metallic glinted in it.

Something with a sharp edge.

My heart stuttered.

The man in the green-feathered hat was on his way to the riverbank for an appointment with my father. It was an appointment, perhaps, that he'd been planning ever since Dad dove in after the sinking car. With all this commotion, all this noise, and in all this watery dark, might not the man in the green-feathered hat find a chance to drive that blade into my father's back? I couldn't see my dad; I couldn't make out anyone for sure, just glistening figures straining against the inevitable.

He was stronger against the current than I. He was pulling away from me. I lunged forward, fighting the river, and that was when my feet slipped out from under me and I went down, the muddy water closing over my head. I reached up, trying to grab something to hold on to. There was nothing solid, and I couldn't get my feet planted. My mind screamed that I'd never be able to draw a breath again. I splashed and wallowed, and then somebody had gripped me and was lifting me up as the muddy water oozed from my face and hair.

"I've got you," a man said. "You're all right."

"Cory! What's wrong with you, boy?" That was my mother's voice, rising to new heights of terror. "Are you *crazy*?"

"I believe he stepped in a hole, Rebecca." The man set me down. I was still standing in waist-deep water but at least my feet were touching earth. I wiped clots of mud from my eyes and looked up at Dr. Curtis Parrish, who wore a gray raincoat and a rainhat. The hat had no band, therefore it had no silver disc and no green feather. I turned around, looking for the figure I'd been trying to reach, but he had merged with the other people nearer the river's edge. He and the knife he'd drawn from his pocket.

"Where's Dad?" I said, working up to another fever pitch. "I've gotta find Dad!"

"Whoa, whoa, settle down." Dr. Parrish took hold of my shoulders. In one hand he held a flashlight. "Tom's right over there." He pointed the flashlight's beam toward a group of muddied men. The direction he indicated was not the direction in which the man with the green-feathered hat had gone. But I saw my father over there, working between a black man and Mr. Yarbrough. "See him?"

"Yes sir." Again I searched for the mysterious figure. Vanished.

"Cory, don't you run away from me like that!" Mom scolded. "You scared me almost to death!" She took my hand again in a grip of iron.

Dr. Parrish was a heavyset man, about forty-eight or forty-nine years old, with a firm, square jaw and a flattened nose that reminded everyone he'd been a champion boxer when he was a sergeant in the army. With the same hands that had scooped me from the hole at my feet, Dr. Parrish had delivered me from my mother's womb. He had thick dark eyebrows over eyes the color of steel, and beneath his rainhat his dark brown hair was gray on the sides. Dr. Parrish said to Mom, "I heard from Chief Marchette a little while ago that they've opened up the school gym. They're puttin' in oil lamps and bringin' in some cots and blankets. Most of the women and children are goin' over there to stay, since the water's gettin' so high."

"Is that where we ought to go, then?"

"I think it'd be the wise thing. There's no use you and Cory standin' out here in this mess." He pointed with the flashlight again, this time away from the river and toward the swampy basketball court where we'd parked. "They're pickin' up whoever wants to go to the shelter over that way. Probably be another truck along in a few minutes."

"Dad won't know where we are!" I protested, still thinking of the green feather and the knife.

"I'll let him know. Tom would want you both in a safe place, and I'll tell you the truth, Rebecca: the way this is goin', we'll be catchin' catfish in attics before mornin'."

We didn't need much prodding. "Brightie's already over there," Dr. Parrish said. "You ought to go catch the next truck. Here, take this." He gave Mom the flashlight, and we turned away from the swollen Tecumseh and started toward the basketball court. "Keep hold of my hand!" Mom cautioned as the floodwaters swept around us. I looked back, could see only the lights moving in the darkness and glittering off the roiling water. "Watch your step!" Mom said. Farther along the riverbank, past where my father was working, voices rose in a chorus of shouts. I did not know it then, but a frothy wave had just swamped over the highest part of the earthen dam and the water churned and foamed and men suddenly found themselves up to their elbows in trouble as the river burst through. A flashlight's beam caught a glimpse of brown-mottled scales in the muddied foam, and somebody hollered, "Snakes!" In the next second, the men were bowled over by the twisting currents, and Mr. Stellko, the Lyric's manager, aged by ten years when he put his hand out to seize a grip and felt a log-sized, scaly shape moving past him in the turbulence. Mr. Stellko was struck dumb and peed in his pants at the same time, and when he could find his voice to scream, the monstrous reptile was gone, following the flood into the streets of Bruton.

"Help me! Somebody help me!"

We heard the voice of a woman from nearby, and Mom said, "Wait."

Someone carrying an oil lamp was splashing toward us. Rain hissed on the lamp's hot glass and steamed away. "Please help me!" the woman cried.

"What is it?" Mom turned the light onto the panic-stricken face of a young black woman. I didn't know her, but Mom said, "Nila Castile? Is that you?"

"Yes ma'am, it's Nila! Who's that?"

"Rebecca Mackenson. I used to read books to your mother."

This was before I was born, I presumed.

"It's my daddy, Miz Rebecca!" Nila Castile said. "I think his heart's give out!"

"Where is he?"

"At the house! Over there!" She pointed into the darkness, water swirling around her waist. I was about chest-deep by now. "He can't stand up!"

"All right, Nila. Settle down." My mother, a framework of little terrors with skin stretched over it, was amazingly calm when someone else needed calming. This, as I understood it, was part of being a grown-up. When it was truly needed, my mother could reveal something that was sorely lacking in Granddaddy Jaybird: courage. "You lead the way," she said.

Water was rushing into the houses of Bruton. Nila Castile's house, like so many others, was a narrow gray shotgun shack. She led us in, the river surging around us, and she shouted in the first room, "Gavin! I'm back!"

Her light, and Mom's light, too, fell on an old black man sitting in a chair, the water up around his knees and newspapers and magazines swirling in the current. He was clutching his hand to his wet shirt over his heart, his ebony face seamed with pain and his eyes squeezed shut. Standing next to him, holding his other hand, was a little boy maybe seven or eight years old.

"Grandpap's cryin', Momma," the little boy said.

"I know he is, Gavin. Daddy, I've brought some help." Nila Castile set the lamp down on a tabletop. "Can you hear me, Daddy?"

"Ohhhhh," the old man groaned. "Hurtin' mighty bad this time."

"We're gonna help you stand up. Gonna get you out of here."

"No, honey." He shook his head. "Old legs . . . gone."

"What're we gonna *do*?" Nila looked at my mother, and I saw the bright tears in her eyes.

The river was shoving its way in. Thunder spoke outside and the lightning flared. If this had been a television show, it would've been time for a commercial.

But real life takes no pauses. "Wheelbarrow," my mother said. "Have you got one?"

Nila said no, but that they'd borrowed a neighbor's wheelbarrow before and she thought it might be up on their back porch. Mom said to me, "You stay here," and she gave me the oil lamp. Now I was going to have to be courageous, whether I liked it or not. Mom and Nila left with the flashlight, and I stood in the flooding front room with the little boy and the old man.

"I'm Gavin Castile," the little boy said.

"I'm Cory Mackenson," I told him.

Hard to be sociable when you're hip-deep in brown water and the flickering light doesn't fill up the room.

"This here's my grandpap, Mr. Booker Thornberry," Gavin went on, his hand locked with the old man's. "He ain't feelin' good."

"How come you didn't get out when everybody else did?"

"Because," Mr. Thornberry said, rousing himself, "this is my *home*, boy. My home. I ain't scared of no damned river."

"Everybody else is," I said. *Everybody with sense*, is what I meant.

"Then everybody else can go on and run." Mr. Thornberry, whom I was beginning to realize shared a stubborn streak with Granddaddy Jaybird, winced as a fresh pain hit him. He blinked slowly, his dark eyes staring at me from a bony face. "My Rubynelle passed on in this house. Right here. I ain't gonna die in no white man's hospital."

"Do you *want* to die?" I asked him.

He seemed to think about this. "Gonna die in my own home," he answered.

"Water's gettin' deep," I said. "Everybody might get drowned."

The old man scowled. Then he turned his head and looked at the small black hand he was clutching.

"My grandpap took me to the movies!" Gavin said, attached to the thin dark arm as the water rose toward his throat. "We seen a Looney Tune!"

"Bugs Bunny," the old man said. "We seen ol' Bugs Bunny and that stutterin' fella looks like a pig. Didn't we, boy?"

"Yes sir!" Gavin answered, and he grinned. "We gone go see another one real soon, ain't we, Grandpap?"

Mr. Thornberry didn't answer. Gavin didn't let go.

I understood then what courage is all about. It is loving someone else more than you love yourself.

My mother and Nila Castile returned, lugging a wheelbarrow. "Gonna put you in this, Daddy," Nila told him. "We can push you to where Miz Rebecca says they're pickin' up people in trucks."

Mr. Thornberry took a long, deep breath, held it for a few seconds, and then let it go. "Damn," he whispered. "Damn old heart in a damn old fool." His voice cracked a little bit on that last word.

"Let us help you up," Mom offered.

He nodded. "All right," he said. "It's time to go, ain't it?"

They got him in the wheelbarrow, but real soon Mom and Nila realized that even though Mr. Thornberry was a skinny thing, they were both going to have a struggle pushing him and keeping his head above water. I saw the predicament: out beyond the house on the underwater street, Gavin's head would be submerged. A current might whisk him away like a cornhusk. Who was going to hold him up?

"We'll have to come back for the boys," Mom decided. "Cory, you take the lamp and you and Gavin stand up on that table." The tabletop was awash, but it would keep us above the flood. I did as Mom told me, and Gavin pulled himself up, too. We stood together, me holding the lamp, a small pinewood island beneath our feet. "All right," Mom said. "Cory, don't move from there. If you move, I'll give you a whippin' you'll remember for the rest of your life. Understand?"

"Yes ma'am."

"Gavin, we'll be back directly," Nila Castile said. "We've got to get Grandpap to where people can help him. Hear?"

"Yes ma'am," Gavin answered.

"You boys mind your mothers." Mr. Thornberry spoke up, his voice raspy with pain. "I'll whip both your butts if you don't."

"Yes sir," we both said. I figured Mr. Thornberry had decided he wanted to live.

Mom and Nila Castile began the labor of pushing Mr. Thornberry in the wheelbarrow against the brown water, each supporting one handle and Mom holding the light. They tilted the wheelbarrow up as high as they could, and Mr. Thornberry lifted his head up, the veins standing out in his scrawny neck. I heard my mother grunt with the effort. But the wheelbarrow was moving, and they pushed it through the water that was swirling around the open doorway and across the flooded porch. At the foot of the two cinderblock steps, the water came up to Mr. Thornberry's neck and splashed into his face. They moved away, the current at their backs helping them push the wheelbarrow. I had never thought of my mother as being physically strong before. I guess you never know what a person can do until that person has to do it.

"Cory?" Gavin said after a minute or so.

"Yeah, Gavin?"

"I cain't swim," he said.

He was pressed up against my side. He was starting to shiver now that he didn't have to be so brave for his grandpap. "That's okay," I told him. "You won't have to."

I hoped.

We waited. Surely they'd be back soon. The water was lapping up over our soggy shoes. I asked Gavin if he knew any songs, and he said he knew "On Top of Old Smoky," which he began to sing in a high, quavering yet not unpleasant voice.

His singing—more of a yodel, actually—attracted something that suddenly came paddling through the doorway, and I caught my breath at the noise and swung the light onto it.

It was a brown dog, matted with mud. Its eyes gleamed wildly in the light, its breathing harsh as it swam across the room toward us, through the flotsam of papers and other trash. "Come on, boy!" I said. Whether it was a boy or girl was incidental; the dog looked like it needed a perch. "Come on!" I gave Gavin the lamp, and the dog whimpered and yelped as a slow wave slipped through the door and lifted the animal up and down again. Water smacked the walls.

"Come on, boy!" I leaned down to get the struggling dog. I grasped its front paws. It looked up into my face, its pink tongue hanging out in the dank yellow light, as a born-again Christian might appeal to the Savior.

I was lifting the dog out by its paws, and I felt it shudder.

Something went *crunch.*

As fast as that.

And then its head and shoulders were coming out of the dark water and suddenly there was no more of the dog beyond the middle of its back, no hindquarters, no tail, no hind legs, nothing but a gaping hole that started spilling a torrent of black blood and steaming guts.

The dog made a little whining sound. That's all. But its paws twitched and its eyes were on me, and the agony I saw in them will last in my mind forever.

I cried out—and what I said I will never know—and dropped the mess that had once been a dog. It splashed in, went under, came back up, and the paws were still trying to paddle. I heard Gavin shout something; *wannawaterMars?* it sounded like. And then the water thrashed around the half of a carcass, the entrails streaming behind it like a hideous tail, and I saw the skin of something break the surface.

It was covered with diamond-shaped scales the colors of autumn leaves: pale brown, shimmering purple, deep gold, and tawny russet. All the shades of the river were there, too, from swirls of muddy ocher to moonlight pink. I saw a forest of mussels leeched to its flesh, gray canyons of scars and fishhooks scarlet with rust. I saw a body as thick as an ancient oak twist slowly around in the water, taking its own sweet time. I was transfixed by the spectacle, even as Gavin wailed with terror. I knew what I was looking at, and though my heart pounded and I could hardly draw a breath, I thought it was as beautiful as anything in God's creation.

Then I recalled the jagged fang driven like a blade into the chunk of wood at Mr. Sculley's. Beautiful or not, Old Moses had just torn a dog in half.

He was still hungry. This happened so fast, my mind hardly had time to see it: a pair of jaws opened, fangs glistened, and an old boot was in there impaled on one of them along with a flopping silver fish. The jaws sucked the remaining half of the dog's carcass in with a snarling rush of water and then closed delicately, as one might savor a lemonhead candy at the Lyric theater. I caught a quick glimpse of a narrow, pale green cat's-eye the size of a baseball, shielded with a gelatinous film. Then Gavin fell back off the table into the water, and the lamp he was holding hissed out.

I didn't think about being brave. I didn't think about being scared. *I cain't swim.*

That's what I thought about.

I jumped off the table to where Gavin had gone in. The water was heavy with mud, and up to my shoulders, which meant Gavin was nostrils-deep. He was flailing and kicking, and when I grabbed him around the waist he must've thought it was Old Moses because he almost jerked my arms off. I shouted, "Gavin! Stop kickin'!" and I got his face up out of the water. "Humma hobba humma," he was babbling, like a rain-soaked engine trying to fire its plugs.

I heard a noise behind me, in that dark and soggy room. The noise of something rising from the water.

I turned around. Gavin yelped and grabbed hold with both arms around my neck, all but throttling me.

I saw the shape of Old Moses—huge, horrible, and breathtaking—coming up from the water like a living swamp log. Its head was flat and triangular, like a snake's, but I think it was not just a snake because it seemed to have two small arms with spindly claws just below what would have been the neck. I heard what must have been its tail thwacking against a wall so hard the house shook. Its head bumped the ceiling. Gavin's grip was making my face balloon with blood.

I knew without seeing that Old Moses was looking at us, with eyes that could spot a catfish through murky water at midnight. I felt its appraisal of us, like a cold knife blade pressed against my forehead. I hoped we didn't look much like dogs.

Old Moses smelled like the river at noon: swampy, steaming, and pungent with life. To say I respected that awesome beast would be quite an understatement. But right at that moment I wished I was anywhere else on earth, even in school. But I didn't have much time for thinking, because Old Moses's snaky head began to descend toward us like the front end of a steam shovel and I heard the hiss of its jaws opening. I backed up, hollering at Gavin to let go, but he would not. If I'd been him, I wouldn't have let go, either. The head came at us, but just then I backed out of the front room into a narrow corridor—which I certainly didn't know was there—and Old Moses's jaws slammed against the door frame on either side of us. This seemed to make him mad. He drew back and drove forward again, with the same result, except this time the door frame splintered. Gavin was crying, making a *whoop whoop whoop* sound, and a frothy wave from Old Moses's agitations splashed into my face and over my head. Something jabbed my right shoulder, scaring a ripple up my spine. I reached for it, and found a broom floating in the debris.

Old Moses made a noise like a locomotive about to blow its gaskets. I saw the awful shape of its head coming at the corridor's entrance, and I thought of Gordon Scott's Tarzan, spear in hand, fighting against a giant python. I picked up the broomstick, and when Old Moses hit the doorway again I jammed that broom right down its gaping, dog-swallowing throat.

You know what happens when you touch your finger to the back of your throat, don't you? Well, the same thing happens, evidently, to monsters. Old Moses made a gagging noise as loud as thunder in a barrel. The head drew back and the broom went with it, cornstraw bristles jammed in the gullet. Then, and this is the only way I can describe it, Old Moses puked. I mean it. I heard the rush of liquid and gruesome things flooding from its mouth. Fish, some still flopping and some long dead, went flying all around us along with stinking crayfish, turtle shells, mussels, slimy stones, mud, and bones. The smell was . . . well, you can imagine it. It was a hundred times worse than when the kid in school throws up his morning oatmeal on the desk in front of you. I dunked my head underwater to get away from it, and of course Gavin had to go, too, whether he liked it or not. Underneath there, I thought that Old Moses ought to be more particular about what he scooped off the Tecumseh's bottom.

Currents thrashed around us. I came up again, and Gavin took a gasping breath and yelled his head off. At that point I started yelling, too. "Help!" I shouted. "Somebody help us!"

A light speared through the front door, over the choppy water, and hit me in the face.

"Cory!" came the sound of judgment. "I told you not to move, didn't I?"

"Gavin? Gavin?"

"Lord God!" my mother said. "What's that smell?"

The water was settling down. I realized Old Moses was no longer between the two mothers and their sons. Dead fish floated in a slimy brown sludge on the surface, but Mom's attention was on me. "I'm gonna tan your hide, Cory Mackenson!" she shouted as she waded in with Nila Castile behind her.

Then they walked right into the floating monster disgorgement, and from the sound she made I don't believe my mother was thinking about whipping me anymore.

Lucky me.

7

A Summons from the Lady

None of my friends believed me, of course.

Davy Ray Callan just laughed and shook his head, and he said he couldn't have made up a better story if he'd tried. Ben Sears looked at me like I had seen one too many monster movies at the Lyric. Johnny Wilson thought about it awhile, in that slow, deliberating way of his, and then he gave his opinion: "Nope. Didn't happen."

"It did!" I told them as we sat on the porch of my house in the shade under a clear blue sky. "It really did, I swear it!"

"Oh yeah?" Davy Ray, the feisty one of our group and the one who was most likely to make up astounding tales, cocked his brown-haired head and stared at me through pale blue eyes that always held a hint of wild laughter. "Then how come Old Moses didn't just eat you up? How come a monster ran from a kid with a *broom?*"

"Because," I answered, flustered and angry, "I didn't have my monster-killin' ray gun with me, that's why! I don't know! But it happened, and you can ask—"

"Cory," my mother said quietly from the doorway, "I think you'd better stop talkin' about this now."

So I did. And I understood what she meant. There was no use trying to make anybody believe it. My mom herself couldn't quite grasp it, though Gavin Castile had sputtered the whole story to his mother. Mr. Thornberry, incidentally, was all right. He was alive and getting stronger day by day, and I understand he wanted to get well so he could take Gavin to see more Looney Tunes.

My friends would have believed it, though, if they could've smelled my clothes before Mom threw them in the garbage. She threw her own tainted clothes away, too. Dad listened to the tale, and he nodded and sat there with his hands folded before him, bandages on his palms and fingers covering huge blisters that had been raised by the shoveling.

89

"Well," Dad said, "all I can say is, there're stranger things on this earth than we can ever figure out if we had a hundred lifetimes. I thank God the both of you are all right, and that nobody drowned in the flood. Now: what's for dinner?"

Two weeks passed. We left April and moved through the sunny days of May. The Tecumseh River, having reminded us who was boss, returned to its banks. A quarter of the houses in Bruton weren't worth living in anymore, including Nila Castile's, so the sound of sawing and hammering in Bruton was almost around the clock. There was one benefit of the rain and the flood, though; under the sunshine, the earth exploded in flowers and Zephyr blazed with color. Lawns were deep emerald, honeysuckle grew like mad passion, and kudzu blanketed the hills. Summer was almost upon us.

I turned my attention to studying for final exams. Math was never my strongest subject, and I was going to have to make a high grade so I wouldn't have to go to—and the mere thought of this made me choke—summer school.

In my quiet hours, I did wonder how I'd managed to beat Old Moses away with a bristle-brush broom. I had been lucky in jamming it down the monster's throat, that was for sure. But I figured it might have been something else, too. Old Moses, for all his size and fury, was like Granddaddy Jaybird; he could holler a good game, but at the first sting he took off running. Or swimming, as the case might be. Old Moses was a coward. Maybe Old Moses had gotten used to eating things that didn't fight back, like catfish and turtles and scared dogs paddling for their lives. With that broomstick in his throat, Old Moses might have figured there was easier prey where he came from, down at the bottom of the river in that cool, muddy banquet hall where nothing bites back.

At least, that's my theory. I don't ever want to have to test it again, though.

I had a dream about the man in the long coat and the green-feathered hat. I dreamed I was wading toward him, and when I grasped his arm he turned his face toward me and it was a man with not human skin but diamond-shaped scales the color of autumn leaves. He had fangs like daggers and blood dripping down his chin, and I realized I had interrupted him in the process of eating a small brown dog, the upper half of which he held struggling in his left hand.

It was not a pleasant dream.

But maybe there was some truth in it. Somewhere.

I was a walker in these days, bereft of two wheels to call my own. I enjoyed walking to and from school, but all my friends had bikes and I definitely had lost a step or two of status. One afternoon I was pitching a stick to Rebel and rolling around in the green grass with him when I heard a clankety sound. I looked up, Rebel looked up, and there was a pickup truck approaching our house.

I knew the truck. It was splotchy with rust and its suspension sagged, and the noise it made caused dogs to bay in its wake. Rebel started barking, and I had a time getting him quiet. The truck had a metal frame thing bolted in the bed from which hung, clattering like asylum inmates, a bewildering array of tools, most of which looked as antique and worthless as the truck. On the driver's door was stenciled, not very neatly, LIGHTFOOT'S FIX-IT.

The truck stopped in front of the house. Mom came out on the porch, alerted by the clamor, but Dad wouldn't be home from work for another hour or so. The truck's door opened, and a long, skinny black man wearing dusty gray overalls got out, so slowly it seemed that movement might be painful for him. He wore a gray cap, and his dark skin was smoky with dust. He came slowly toward the porch, and I have to say that even if a bull had suddenly come charging up behind him, Mr. Marcus Lightfoot probably wouldn't have hurried his pace.

"Good afternoon, Mr. Lightfoot," Mom said, her apron on. She had been working in the kitchen, and she wiped her hands on a paper towel. "How are you?"

Mr. Lightfoot smiled. His small, square teeth were very white, and gray hair boiled up from under his cap. This is how he spoke, in a voice like a slow leak from a clogged pipe: "Good   after-noon   to   you,   too,   Miz   Mackenson.   Hey there,   Cory."

This was a good-paced conversational clip for Mr. Lightfoot, who had been a handyman in Zephyr and Bruton for more than thirty years, picking up the task from his father. Mr. Lightfoot was renowned for his skill with appliances, and though he was slow as a toothache, he always got the job done no matter how baffling the problem. "Mighty fine." He stopped, looking up at the blue sky. The seconds ticked past. Rebel barked, and I put my hand over his muzzle.

"Day," Mr. Lightfoot decided.

"Yes, it is." Mom waited for him to speak again, but Mr. Lightfoot just stood there, this time looking at our house. He reached into one of his many pockets, brought out a handful of penny nails, and clicked them around, as if he were waiting, too. "Uh . . ." Mom cleared her throat. "Can I help you with anythin'?"

"Jus' passin'," he replied, slow as warm molasses. "Wonderin' if you"—and here he paused to study the nails in his hand for a few seconds—"might need somethin' fixed?"

"Well, no, not really. I can't think of—" She stopped, and her expression told me she *had* thought of something. "The toaster. It went out on me day before yesterday. I was gonna call you, but—"

"Yes'm, I know." Mr. Lightfoot nodded sagely. "Time sure does fly."

He went back to the truck to get his toolbox, an old metal fascination filled with drawers and every kind of nut and bolt, it seemed, under the workman's sun. He strapped on his tool belt, from which hung several different kinds of hammers, screwdrivers, and arcane-looking wrenches. Mom held the door open for Mr. Lightfoot, and when he walked into the house she looked at me and shrugged, her statement being: *I don't know why he's here, either.* I left Rebel the gnawed stick and went into the house, too, and in the cool of the kitchen I drank a glass of iced tea and watched Mr. Lightfoot stare down the toaster.

"Mr. Lightfoot, would you care for somethin' to drink?" Mom asked.

"Nome."

"I've got some oatmeal cookies."

"Nome, thank you kindly." He took a clean white square of cloth from another pocket and unfolded it. He draped the cloth over the seat of one of the chairs to the kitchen table. Then he unplugged the toaster, set it on the table alongside his toolbox, and sat down on the white cloth. All this had been done at an underwater pace.

Mr. Lightfoot chose a screwdriver. He had the long, graceful fingers of a surgeon, or an artist. Watching him work was a form of torture for the patience, but no one can say he didn't know what he was doing. He opened the toaster right up, and sat staring at the naked grills. "Uh-huh," he said after a long moment of silence. "Uh-huh."

"What is it?" Mom peered over his shoulder. "Can it be fixed?"

"See there? Little ol' red wire?" He tapped it with the screwdriver's edge. "Done come a'loose."

"Is that all that's wrong? Just that little wire?"

"Yes'm, that's." He began to carefully rewind the wire around its connection, and watching him do this was like a strange kind of hypnosis. "All," he finally finished. Then he put the toaster back

92

together again, plugged it in, pushed down the timer prongs, and we all saw the coils start to redden. "Sometimes," Mr. Lightfoot said.

We waited. I think I could hear my hair growing.

"Just the."

The world turned beneath us.

"Little things." He began to refold the white cloth. We waited, but this particular line of thought had either derailed or reached its dead end. Mr. Lightfoot looked around the kitchen. "Anythin' else need fixin'?"

"No, I think we're in good shape now."

Mr. Lightfoot nodded, but I could tell that he was searching for problems like a bird dog sniffing game. He made a slow circle of the kitchen, during which he delicately placed his hands on the icebox, the four-eyed stove, and the sink's faucet as if divining the health of the machinery through his touch. Mom and I looked at each other, puzzled; Mr. Lightfoot was certainly acting peculiar.

"Icebox kinda stutterin'," he said. "Want me to take a peek?"

"No, don't bother with it," Mom told him. "Mr. Lightfoot, are you feelin' all right today?"

"Surely, Miz Mackenson. Surely." He opened a cupboard and listened to the slight squeak of the hinges. A screwdriver was withdrawn from his tool belt, and he tightened the screws in both that cupboard door and the next one, too. Mom cleared her throat again, nervously this time, and she said, "Uh . . . Mr. Lightfoot, how much do I owe you for fixin' the toaster?"

"It's," he said. He tested the hinges of the kitchen door, and then he went to my mother's MixMaster blender on the countertop and started examining that. "Done paid," he finished.

"*Paid?* But . . . I don't understand." Mom had already reached up on a shelf and brought down the mason jar full of dollar bills and change.

"Yes'm. Paid."

"But I haven't given you any money yet."

Mr. Lightfoot's fingers dug into another pocket, and this time emerged with a white envelope. He gave it to Mom, and I saw that it had The Mackenson Family written across its front in blue ink. On the back, sealing it, was a blob of white wax. "Well," he said at last, "I 'spect I'm done for." He picked up his toolbox. "Today."

"*Today?*" Mom asked.

93

"Yes'm. You know." Mr. Lightfoot now started looking at the light fixtures, as if he longed to get into their electrical depths. "My number," he said. "Anythin'   needs fixin', you." He smiled at us. "Jus' call."

We saw Mr. Lightfoot off. He waved as he drove away in the clankety old pickup, the tools jangling on their hooks and the neighborhood dogs going crazy. Mom said, mostly to herself, "Tom's not gonna believe this." Then she opened the envelope, took a letter from it, and read it. "Huh," she said. "Want to hear?"

"Yes ma'am."

She read it to me: " 'I'd be honored if you would come to my house at seven o'clock this Friday evening. Please bring your son.' And look who it's from." Mom handed the letter to me, and I saw the signature.

The Lady.

When Dad got home, Mom told him about Mr. Lightfoot and showed him the letter almost before he could get his milkman's cap off. "What do you think she wants with *us?*" Dad asked.

"I don't know, but I think she's decided to pay Mr. Lightfoot to be our personal handyman."

Dad regarded the letter again. "She's got nice handwritin', to be so old. I would've thought it'd be crimped up." He chewed on his bottom lip, and just watching him I could tell he was getting edgy. "You know, I've never seen the Lady close up before. Seen her on the street, but . . ." He shook his head. "No. I don't believe I want to go."

"What're you *sayin'?*" Mom asked incredulously. "The Lady wants us to come to her *house!*"

"I don't care." Dad gave her back the letter. "I'm not goin'."

"Why, Tom? Give me one good reason."

"Phillies are playin' the Pirates on radio Friday night," he said as he retired to the comfort of his easy chair. "That's reason enough."

"I don't think so," Mom told him, setting her jaw.

Here we came to a rare fact of life: my parents, though I believe they got along better than ninety-nine percent of the married couples in Zephyr, did have their go-rounds. Just as no one person is perfect, no marriage of two imperfects is going to be without a scrape of friction here and there. I have seen my father blow his top over a missing sock when in fact he was mad he didn't get a raise at the dairy. I have seen my usually placid mother steam with anger over a muddy bootmark on the clean floor when in fact the root of her discontent lay in a rude remark from a neighbor. So, in this tangled web of civilities and rage riots that we know as life, such things will happen as now began to take shape in my parents' house.

"It's because she's colored, isn't it?" Mom threw the first punch. "That's the real reason."

"No, it's not."

"You're as bad as your daddy about that. I swear, Tom—"

"Hush!" he hollered. Even I staggered. The comment about Granddaddy Jaybird, who was to racism as crabgrass is to weeds, had been a very low blow. Dad did not hate colored people, and this I knew for sure, but please remember that Dad had been raised by a man who saluted the Confederate flag every morning of his life and who considered black skin to be the mark of the devil. It was a terrible burden my father was carrying, because he loved Granddaddy Jaybird but he believed in his heart, as he taught me to believe, that hating any other man—for any reason—was a sin against God. So this next statement of his had more to do with pride than anything else: "And I'm not takin' charity from that woman, either!"

"Cory," Mom said, "I believe you have some math homework to do?"

I went to my room, but that didn't mean I couldn't hear them.

They weren't really loud, just intense. I suspected this had been brewing awhile, and came from a lot of different places: the car in the lake, the wasps at Easter, the fact that Dad couldn't afford to buy me a new bike, the dangers of the flood. Listening to Dad tell Mom that she couldn't put a rope around his neck and drag him into the Lady's house, I got the feeling that it all boiled down to this: the Lady scared him.

"No way!" he said. "I'm not goin' to see somebody who fools with bones and old dead animals and—" He stopped, and I figured he'd realized he was describing Granddaddy Jaybird. "I'm just not," he finished on a lame note.

Mom had decided she had run this horse to death. I could hear it in her sigh. "I'd like to go find out what she has to say. Is that all right with you?"

Silence. Then, in a quiet voice: "Yeah, it's all right."

"I'd like to take Cory, too."

This started another flare-up. "Why? You want him to see the skeletons hangin' in that woman's closet? Rebecca, I don't know what she wants and I don't *care!* But that woman plays with conjure dolls and black cats and God knows what all! I don't think it's right to take Cory into her house!"

"She asks, right here in the letter, that we bring Cory. See?"

"I see it. And I don't understand it, either, but I'm tellin' you: the Lady is not to be messed with. You remember Burk Hatcher? Used to be assistant foreman at the dairy back in 'fifty-eight?''

"Yes."

"Burk Hatcher used to chew tobacco. Chewed gobs of it, and he was always spittin'. Got to be a bad habit he hardly even knew he had, and—don't you dare tell anybody this—but a couple of times he forgot himself and spat right in a milk vat.''

"Oh, Tom! You don't mean it!''

"Right as rain, I do. Now, Burk Hatcher was walkin' down Merchants Street one day, had just got his hair cut at Mr. Dollars's—and he had a full, thick head of hair he could hardly pull a comb through—and he forgot himself and spat on the sidewalk. Only the tobacco wattle never hit the sidewalk, 'cause it got on the Moon Man's shoes. Smack dab all over 'em. Wasn't on purpose, as I understand it. The Moon Man was just walkin' past. Well, Burk had a weird sense of humor, and this thing struck him as funny. He started laughin', right there in the Moon Man's face. And you know what?''

"What?'' Mom asked.

"A week later Burk's hair started to fall out.''

"Oh, I don't believe it!''

"It's true!'' The adamance of my father's voice indicated that he, at least, believed it. "Within one month after Burk Hatcher spat tobacco juice on the Moon Man's shoes, he was balder'n a cue ball! He started wearin' a wig! Yes ma'am, he did! He almost went crazy because of it!'' I could imagine my father leaning forward in his chair, his face so grim my mother was having to struggle to keep from laughing. "If you don't think the Lady had somethin' to do with that, you're crazy!''

"Tom, I swear I never knew you put so much faith in the occult.''

"Faith, smaith! I saw Burk's bald head! Heck, I can tell you a lot of things I've heard about that woman! Like frogs jumpin' out of people's throats and snakes in the soup bowl and . . . uh-uh, no! I'm not settin' foot in that house!''

"But what if she gets mad at us if we *don't* go there?'' Mom asked. The question hung.

"Mightn't she put a spell on us if I don't take Cory to see her?''

I could tell Mom was jiving my dad a little, from her tone of voice. Still, Dad didn't answer and he was probably mulling over the potential disasters of snubbing the Lady.

"I think I'd better go and take Cory, too,'' Mom went on. "To show that we respect her. Anyway, aren't you the least bit curious why she wants to see us?"

"No!"

"Not the tiniest least bit?"

"Lord," Dad said after another bout of thinking. "You could argue the warts off a toad. And the Lady's probably got bottles full of those, too, to go along with her mummy dust and bat wings!"

The result of all this was that on Friday evening, as the sun began to slide down across the darkening earth and a cool wind blew through the streets of Zephyr, my mother and I got in the pickup truck and left our house. Dad stayed behind, his radio tuned to the baseball game he'd been awaiting, but I believe he was with us in spirit. He just didn't want to make a mistake and offend the Lady, in manner or speech. I have to say I was no solid rock myself; under my white shirt and the clip-on tie Mom had made me wear, my nerves were frazzling mighty fast.

Work was still going on in Bruton, the dark people sawing and hammering their houses back together. We passed through Bruton's business center, a little area with a barbershop, grocery store, shoe and clothing store, and other establishments run by the locals. Mom turned us onto Jessamyn Street, and at the end of that street she stopped in front of a house from which lights glowed through every window.

The small frame house, as I've already mentioned, was painted in a blaze of orange, purple, red, and yellow. A garage was set off to the side, where I figured the rhinestone-covered Pontiac was stored. The yard was neatly trimmed, and a sidewalk led from the curb to the porch steps. The house appeared neither scary nor the residence of royalty; it was just a house and, except for its coat of many colors, very much like every other house on the street.

Still, I balked when Mom came around and opened my door.

"Come on," she said. Her voice had tightened, though her nervousness didn't show in her face. She was wearing one of her best Sunday dresses, and her nice Sunday shoes. "It's almost seven."

Seven, I thought. Wasn't that supposed to be a voodoo number? "Maybe Dad was right," I told her. "Maybe we ought not to do this."

"It's all right. Look at all the lights on."

If this was supposed to make me feel at ease, it didn't work.

"There's nothin' to be afraid of," Mom said. This, from a woman who fretted that the gray insulation they'd recently sprayed above the ceiling of the elementary school might be bad for your breathing.

Somehow I got up the porch steps to the door. The porch light was painted yellow, to keep bugs away. I'd imagined the door's knocker might be a skull and crossbones. It was, instead, a little silver hand. Mom said, "Here goes," and she rapped on the door.

We heard muffled talking and footsteps. It occurred to me that our time to flee was running out. Mom put her arm around me, and I thought I could feel her pulse beating. Then the door's knob turned, the door opened, and the Lady's house offered entry. A tall, broad-shouldered black man wearing a dark blue suit, a white shirt, and a tie filled up the doorway. To me he looked as tall and burly as a black oak. He had hands that looked as if they could crush bowling balls. Part of his nose appeared to have been sliced off with a razor. His eyebrows merged together, thick as a werewolf's pelt.

In seven mystic words: he scared the crap out of me.

"Uh . . ." Mom began, and faltered. "Uh . . ."

"Come right in, Miz Mackenson." He smiled. With that smile his face became less fearsome and more welcome. But his voice was as deep as a kettledrum and it vibrated in my bones. He stepped aside, and Mom grasped my hand and pulled me across the threshold.

The door closed at our backs.

A young woman with skin the hue of chocolate milk was there to greet us. She had a heart-shaped face and tawny eyes, and she took my mother's hand and said with a smile, "I'm Amelia Damaronde, and I'm so verra pleased to meet you." She had bangle bracelets covering her forearms and five gold pins up the edges of each of her ears.

"Thank you. This is my son, Cory."

"Oh, this is the young man!" Amelia Damaronde turned her attention to me. She had an electricity about her that made me feel as if the air between us was charged. "A pleasure to meet you, too. This is my husband, Charles." The big man nodded at us. Amelia stood about up to his armpits. "We take care of things for the Lady," Amelia said.

"I see." Mom was still holding on to my hand, while I was busy looking around. The mind is a strange thing, isn't it? The mind concocts spiderwebs where there are no spiders, and darkness where the lights are bright. The living room of the Lady's house was no temple to the devil, no repository of black cats and bubbling cauldrons. It was just a room with chairs, a sofa, a little table on which knickknacks rested, and there were shelves with books and framed, vividly colored paintings on the walls. One of the paintings caught me: it showed the face of a bearded black man, his eyes closed in either suffering or ecstasy, and on his head was a crown of thorns.

I had never seen a black Jesus before, and this sight both knocked me for a loop and opened up a space in my mind that I'd never known needed light.

The Moon Man suddenly walked through a hallway into the room. Seeing him so close caused a start for both my mother and me. The Moon Man wore a light blue shirt with the sleeves rolled up, a pair of black trousers, and suspenders. Tonight he had only one wristwatch on, and the white rim of a T-shirt showed instead of his chain and huge gilded crucifix. He wasn't wearing his top hat; the splotchy division of pale yellow and ebony flesh continued up his high forehead and ended in a cap of white wool. The white beard on his chin was pointed, and curled slightly upward. His dark, wrinkle-edged eyes rested on first my mother and then me, and he smiled faintly and nodded. He lifted a thin finger and motioned us into the hallway.

It was time to meet the Lady.

"She's not been feelin' well," Amelia told us. "Dr. Parrish's been loadin' her up with vitamins."

"It's not anythin' serious, is it?" Mom asked.

"The rain got in her lungs. She doesn't get along so good in damp weather, but she's doin' better now that the sun's been out."

We came to a door. The Moon Man opened it, his shoulders frail and stooped. I smelled dusty violets.

Amelia peered in first. "Ma'am? Your callers are here."

Sheets rustled within the room. "Please," said the shaky voice of an old woman, "send them in."

My mother took a breath and walked into the room. I had to follow, because she gripped my hand. The Moon Man stayed outside, and Amelia said, "If you need anythin', just call," before she gently closed the door.

And there she was.

She lay in a bed with a white metal frame, her back supported by a brocaded pillow, and the top sheet pulled up over her chest. The walls of her bedroom were painted with green fronds and foliage, and but for the polite drone of a box fan, we might have been standing in an equatorial jungle. An electric lamp burned on the bedside table, where magazines and books were stacked, and within her reach was a pair of wire-rimmed glasses.

The Lady just stared at us for a moment, and we at her. She was almost bluish-black against the white bed, and not an inch of her face looked unwrinkled. She reminded me of one of those apple dolls whose faces shrivel up in the hard noonday sun. I had seen handfuls of fresh snow scraped off the Ice House's pipes; the Lady's soft cloud of hair was whiter. She was wearing a blue gown, the straps up around her bony shoulders, and her collarbone jutted in such clear relief against her skin that it appeared painful. So, too, did her cheekbones; they seemed sharp enough to slice a peach. To tell the truth, though, except for one feature the Lady wouldn't have looked like much but an ancient, reed-thin black woman whose head trembled with a little palsy.

But her eyes were green.

I don't mean any old green. I mean the color of pale emeralds, the kind of jewels Tarzan might have been searching for in one of the lost cities of Africa. They were luminous, full of trapped and burning light, and looking into them you felt as if your secret self might be jimmied open like a sardine can and something stolen from you. And you might not even mind it, either; you might *want* it to be so. I had never seen eyes like that before, and I never have since. They scared me, but I could not turn away because their beauty was like that of a fierce wild animal who must be carefully watched at all times.

The Lady blinked, and a smile winnowed up over her wrinkled mouth. If she didn't have her own teeth, they were good fakes. "Don't you both look nice," she said in her palsied voice.

"Thank you, ma'am," Mom managed to answer.

"Your husband didn't want to come."

"Uh . . . no, he's . . . listenin' to the baseball game on the radio."

"Was that his excuse, Miz Mackenson?" She lifted her white brows.

"I . . . don't know what you mean."

"Some people," the Lady said, "are scared of me. Can you beat that? Scared of an old woman in her one hundred and sixth year! And me layin' here can't even keep no supper down! You love your husband, Miz Mackenson?"

"Yes, I do. Very much."

"That's good. Love strong and true can get you through a lot of dookey. And I'm here to tell you, honey, you got to walk through many fields of dookey to get to be my age." Those green, wonderful, and frightening eyes in that wrinkled ebony face turned full blaze on me. "Hello, young man," she said. "You help your momma do chores?"

"Yes'm." It was a whisper. My throat felt parched.

"You dry the dishes? Keep your room neat? You sweep the front porch?"

"Yes'm."

"That's fine. But I bet you never had call to use a broom like you used one at Nila Castile's house, did you?"

I swallowed hard. Now I and my mother knew what this was about.

The Lady grinned. "I wish I'd been there. I swanee I do!"

"Did Nila Castile tell you?" Mom asked.

"She did. I had a long talk with little Gavin, too." Her eyes stayed fixed on me. "You saved Gavin's life, young man. You know what that means to me?" I shook my head. "Nila's mother, God keep her, was a good friend of mine. I kind of adopted Nila. I always thought of Gavin as a great-grandchild. Gavin has a good life ahead of him. You made sure he'll get there."

"I was just . . . keepin' from gettin' eaten up myself," I said.

She chuckled; it was a gaspy sound. "Run him off with a broomstick! Lawd, Lawd! He thought he was such a mean ole thing, thought he could swim right up out of that river and snatch him a feast! But you gave him a mouthful, didn't you?"

"He ate a dog," I told her.

"Yeah, he *would*," the Lady said, and her chuckling died down. Her thin fingers intertwined over her stomach. She looked at my mother. "You did a kindness for Nila and her daddy. That's why whenever you need somethin' fixed, you call Mr. Lightfoot and it's done. Your boy saved Gavin's life. That's why I want to give him somethin', if I have your permit."

"It's not necessary."

"Ain't nothin' *necessary*," the Lady said, and she showed a little flare of irritation that made me think she would've been plenty tough when she was young. "That's why I'm gone do it."

"All right," Mom said, thoroughly cowed.

"Young man?" The Lady's gaze moved to me again. "What would you like?"

I thought about it. "*Anything?*" I asked.

"Within reason," Mom prodded.

"Anythin'," the Lady said.

I thought some more, but the decision wasn't very difficult. "A bike. A new bike that's never belonged to anybody before."

"A new bicycle." She nodded. "One with a lamp on it?"

"Yes'm."

"Want a horn?"

"That'd be fine," I said.

"Want it to be a fast one? Faster'n a cat up a tree?"

"Yes'm." I was getting excited now. "I sure do!"

"Then you'll have it! Soon as I can get my old self up from here."

"That's awfully nice of you," Mom said. "We sure appreciate it. But Cory's father and I can go pick up a bike from the store, if that's—"

"Won't come from a store," the Lady interrupted.

"Pardon?" Mom asked.

"Won't come from a store." She paused, to make sure my mother understood. "Store-bought's not good enough. Not *special* enough. Young man, you want a real special bicycle, don't you?"

"I . . . guess I'll take what I can get, ma'am."

At this, she laughed again. "Well, you're a little gentleman! Yessir, Mr. Lightfoot and I are gone put our heads together and see what we can come up with. Does that suit you?"

I said it did, but in truth I didn't quite understand how this was going to bring me a brand-new bicycle.

"Step closer," the Lady told me. "Come around here real close."

Mom let me go. I walked to the side of the bed, and those green eyes were right there in front of me like spirit lamps.

"What do you like to do besides ride a bicycle?"

"I like to play baseball. I like to read. I like to write stories."

"Write *stories*?" Her eyebrows went up again. "Lawd, Lawd! We gots us a *writer* here?"

"Cory's always liked books," Mom offered. "He writes little stories about cowboys, and detectives, and—"

"Monsters," I said. "Sometimes."

"Monsters," the Lady repeated. "You gone write about Old Moses?"

"I might."

"You gone write a book someday? Maybe about this town and everybody in it?"

I shrugged. "I don't know."

"Look at me," she said. I did. "Deep," she said.

I did.

And then something strange happened. She began to speak, and as she spoke, the air seemed to shimmer between us with a pearly iridescence. Her eyes had captured mine; I could not look away. "I've been called a monster," the Lady said. "Been called worse than a monster. I saw my momma killed when I wasn't much older than you. Woman jealous of her gift killed her. I swore I was gone find that woman. She wore a red dress, and she carried a monkey on her shoulder that told her things. Woman's name was LaRouge.

Took me all my life to find her. I've been to Lepersville, and I've rowed a boat through the flooded mansions." Her face, through that shimmering haze, had begun to shed its wrinkles. She was getting younger as I stared at her. "I've seen the dead walkin', and my best friend had scales and crawled on her belly." Her face was younger still. Its beauty began to scorch my face. "I've seen the maskmaker. I've spat in Satan's eye, and I've danced in the halls of the Dark Society." She was a girl with long black hair, her cheekbones high and proud, her chin sharp, her eyes fearsome with memories. "I have *lived*," she said in her clear, strong voice, "a hundred lifetimes, and I'm not dead yet. Can you see me, young man?"

"Yes'm," I answered, and I heard myself as if from a vast distance. "I can."

The spell broke, quick as a heartbeat. One second I was looking at a beautiful young woman, and the next there was the Lady as she really was, one hundred and six years old. Her eyes had cooled some, but I felt feverish.

"Maybe someday you'll write my life story," the Lady told me. It sounded more like a command than a comment. "Now, why don't you go on out and visit with Amelia and Charles while I talk to your momma?"

I said I would. My legs were rubbery as I walked past Mom to the door. Sweat had crept around my collar. At the door, a thought hit me and I turned back to the bed. " 'Scuse me, ma'am?" I ventured. "Do you . . . like . . . have anythin' that would help me pass math? I mean like a magic drink or somethin'?"

"*Cory!*" Mom scolded me.

But the Lady just smiled. She said, "Young man, I do. You tell Amelia to get you a drink of Potion Number Ten. Then you go home and you study *hard*, harder'n you ever did before. So hard you can do them 'rithmatics in your sleep." She lifted a finger. "That ought to do the trick."

I left the room and closed the door behind me, eager for magic.

"Potion Number Ten?" Mom asked.

"Glass of milk with some nutmeg flavorin' in it," the Lady said. "Amelia and me got a whole list of potions worked out for folks who need a little extra courage or confidence or what have you."

"Is that how all your magic's done?"

"Most all. You just give folks a key, and they can rightly open their own locks." The Lady's head cocked to one side. "But there's other kinds of magic, too. That's why I need to talk to you."

My mother was silent, not understanding what was about to come.

"Been dreamin'," the Lady said. "Been dreamin' asleep and awake. Things ain't right here no more. Things are tore up on the other side, too."

"The other side?"

"Where the dead go," she said. "Across the river. Not the Tecumseh. The broad, dark river where I'm gonna be goin' before too much longer. Then I'll look back and laugh and I'll say, 'So *that's* what it's all about!'"

Mom shook her head, uncomprehending.

"Things are tore up," the Lady went on. "In the land of the livin' and the world of the dead. I knew somethin' was wrong when Damballah denied his food. Jenna Velvadine told me what happened at your church Easter mornin'. That was the spirit world at work, too."

"It was *wasps*," Mom said.

"To you, wasps. To me, a message. Somebody's in terrible pain on the other side."

"I don't—"

"Understand," the Lady finished for her. "I know you don't. Sometimes I don't either. But I know the language of pain, Miz Mackenson. I grew up speakin' it." The Lady reached over to her bedside table, opened a drawer, and took out a piece of lined notebook paper. She gave it to my mother. "You recognize this?"

Mom stared at it. On the paper was the pencil sketch of a head: a skull, it looked to be, with wings swept back from its temples.

"In my dream I see a man with that tattoo on his shoulder. I see a pair of hands, and in one hand there's a billy club wrapped up with black tape—we call it a crackerknocker—and in the other there's a wire. I can hear voices, but I can't tell what's bein' said. Somebody's yellin', and there's music bein' played real loud."

"Music?" Mom was cold inside; she had recognized the winged skull from what Dad had told her about the corpse in the car.

"Either a record," the Lady said, "or somebody's beatin' hell out of a piano. I told Charles. He recalled me a story I read in the *Journal* back in March. Your husband was the one who saw a dead man go down in Saxon's Lake, ain't that right?"

"Yes."

"Might this have anythin' to do with it?"

Mom took a deep breath, held it, and then let it out. "Yes," she said.

"I thought so. Your husband sleepin' all right?"

"No. He . . . has bad dreams. About the lake, and . . . the man in it."

"Tryin' to reach your husband," the Lady said. "Tryin' to get his attention. I'm just pickin' up the message, like a party line on a telephone."

"Message?" Mom asked. "What message?"

"I don't know," the Lady admitted, "but that kind of pain can sure 'nuff drive a man out of his mind."

Tears began to blur my mother's vision. "I . . . can't . . . I don't . . ." She faltered, and a tear streaked down her left cheek like quicksilver.

"You show him that picture. Tell him to come see me if he wants to talk about it. Tell him he knows where I live."

"He won't come. He's afraid of you."

"You tell him," the Lady said, "this thing could tear him to pieces if he don't set it right. You tell him I could be the best friend he ever had."

Mom nodded. She folded the notebook paper into a square and clenched it in her hand.

"Wipe your eyes," the Lady told her. "Don't want the young man gettin' upset." When my mother had gotten herself fairly composed, the Lady gave a grunt of satisfaction. "There you go. Lookin' pretty again. Now, you go tell the young man he'll have his new bicycle soon as I can manage it. You make sure he studies his lessons, too. Potion Number Ten don't work without a momma or daddy layin' down the law."

My mother thanked the Lady for her kindness. She said she'd talk to my father about coming to see her, but she couldn't promise anything. "I'll expect him when I see him," the Lady said. "You take care of yourself and your family."

Mom and I left the house and walked to the truck. The corners of my mouth still had a little Potion Number Ten in them. I felt ready to tear that math book up.

We left Bruton. The river flowed gently between its banks. The night's breeze blew softly through the trees, and the lights glowed from windows as people finished their dinners. I had two things on my mind: the hauntingly beautiful face of a young woman with green eyes, and a new bike with a horn and headlight.

My mother was thinking about a dead man whose corpse lay down at the bottom of the lake but whose spirit haunted my father's dreams and now the Lady's dreams as well.

Summer was close upon us, its scent of honeysuckle and violets perfuming the land.

Somewhere in Zephyr, a piano was being played.

T W O
Summer of Devils
and Angels

———————

Last Day of School—Barbershop
Talk—A Boy and a Ball—I Get
Around—Welcome, Lucifer—Nemo's
Mother & A Week with the Jaybird—
My Camping Trip—Chile Willow—
Summer Winds Up

1

Last Day of School

*T*ick . . . *tick* . . . *tick.*

In spite of what the calendar says, I have always counted the last day of school as the first day of summer. The sun had grown steadily hotter and hung longer in the sky, the earth had greened and the sky had cleared of all but the fleeciest of clouds, the heat panted for attention like a dog who knows his day is coming, the baseball field had been mowed and white-lined and the swimming pool newly painted and filled, and as our homeroom teacher, Mrs. Selma Neville, intoned about what a good year this had been and how much we'd learned, we students who had passed through the ordeal of final exams sat with one eye fixed to the clock.

Tick . . . tick . . . tick.

In my desk, alphabetically positioned between Ricky Lembeck and Dinah Macurdy, half of me listened to the teacher's speech while the other half longed for an end to it. My head was full up with words. I needed to shake some of them out in the bright summer air. But we were Mrs. Neville's property until the last bell rang, and we had to sit and suffer until time rescued us like Roy Rogers riding over the hill.

Tick . . . tick . . . tick.

Have mercy.

The world was out there, waiting beyond the square metal-rimmed windows. What adventures my friends and I would find this summer of 1964, I had no way of knowing, but I did know that summer's days were long and lazy, and when the sun finally gave up its hold on the sky the cicadas sang and the lightning bugs whirled their dance and there was no homework to be done and oh, it was a wonderful time. I had passed my math exam, and escaped—with a C-minus average, if truth must be known—the snarling trap of summer school. As my friends and I went about our pleasures, running amuck in the land of freedom, we would pause every so often to think of the inmates of summer school—a prison Ben Sears had been sentenced to last year—and wish them well, because time was moving on without them and they weren't getting any younger.

Tick . . . tick . . . tick.

Time, the king of cruelty.

From the hallway we heard a stirring and rustling, followed by laughter and shouts of pure, bubbling joy. Some other teacher had decided to let her class go early. My insides quaked at the injustice of it. Still, Mrs. Neville, who wore a hearing aid and had orange hair though she was at least sixty years old, talked on, as if there were no noise of escape beyond the door at all. It hit me, then; she didn't want to let us go. She wanted to hold us as long as she possibly could, not out of sheer teacher spite but maybe because she didn't have anybody to go home to, and summer alone is no summer at all.

"I hope you boys and girls remember to use the library during recess." Mrs. Neville was speaking in her kindly voice right now, but when she was upset she could spit sparks that made that falling meteor look like a dud. "You mustn't stop reading just because school is out. Your minds are made to be used. So don't forget how to think by the time September comes around a—"

RINGGGGGGG!

We all jumped up, like parts of the same squirming insect.

"One moment," Mrs. Neville said. "One moment. You're not excused yet."

Oh, this was torture! Mrs. Neville, I thought at that instant, must have had a secret life in which she tore the wings off flies.

"You will leave my room," she announced, "like young ladies and gentlemen. In single file, by rows. Mr. Alcott, you may lead the way."

Well, at least we were moving. But then, as the classroom emptied and I could hear the wild hollering echoing along the hallway, Mrs. Neville said, "Cory Mackenson? Step to my desk, please."

I did, under silent protest. Mrs. Neville offered me a smile from a mouth that looked like a red-rimmed string bag. "Now, aren't you glad you decided to apply yourself to your math?" she asked.

"Yes ma'am."

"If you'd studied as hard all year, you might've made the honor roll."

"Yes ma'am." Too bad I hadn't gotten a drink of Potion Number Ten back in the autumn, I was thinking.

The classroom was empty. I could hear the echoes fading. I

smelled chalk dust, lunchroom chili, and pencil-sharpener shavings; the ghosts were already beginning to gather.

"You enjoy writing, don't you?" Mrs. Neville asked me, peering over her bifocals.

"I guess."

"You wrote the best essays in class and you made the highest grade in spelling. I was wondering if you were going to enter the contest this year."

"The contest?"

"The writing contest," she said. "You know. The Arts Council sponsors it every August."

I hadn't thought about it. The Arts Council, headed by Mr. Grover Dean and Mrs. Evelyn Prathmore, sponsored an essay and story-writing contest. The winners got a plaque and were expected to read their entries during a luncheon at the library. I shrugged. Stories about ghosts, cowboys, detectives, and monsters from outer space didn't seem much like contest-winning material; it was just something I did for me.

"You should consider it," Mrs. Neville continued. "You have a way with words."

I shrugged again. Having your teacher talk to you like a regular person is a disconcerting feeling.

"Have a good summer," Mrs. Neville said, and I realized suddenly that I was free.

My heart was a frog leaping out of murky water into clear sunlight. I said, "Thanks!" and I ran for the door. Before I got out, though, I looked back at Mrs. Neville. She sat at a desk with no papers on it that needed grading, no books holding lessons that needed to be taught. The only thing on her desk, besides her blotter and her pencil sharpener that would do no more chewing for a while, was a red apple Paula Erskine had brought her. I saw Mrs. Neville, framed in a spill of sunlight, reach for the apple and pick it up as if in slow motion. Then Mrs. Neville stared out at the room of empty desks, carved with the initials of generations who had passed through this place like a tide rolling into the future. Mrs. Neville suddenly looked awfully old.

"Have a good summer, Mrs. Neville!" I told her from the doorway.

"Good-bye," she said, and she smiled.

I ran out along the corridor, my arms unencumbered by books, my mind unencumbered by facts and figures, quotations and dates. I ran out into the golden sunlight, and my summer had begun.

I was still without a bike. It had been almost three weeks since Mom and I had gone to visit the Lady. I kept bugging Mom to call her, but Mom said for me to be patient, that I'd get the new bike when it arrived and not a minute before. Mom and Dad had a long talk about the Lady, as they sat on the porch in the blue twilight, and I guess I wasn't supposed to be listening but I heard Dad say, "I don't care what she dreams. I'm *not* goin'." Sometimes at night I awakened to hear my father crying out in his sleep, and then I'd hear Mom trying to calm him down. I'd hear him say something like ". . . in the lake . . ." or ". . . down in the dark . . ." and I knew what had gotten into his mind like a black leech. Dad had started pushing his plate away at dinner when it was still half full, which was in direct violation of his "clean your plate, Cory, because there are youngsters starvin' in India" speech. He'd started losing weight, and he'd had to pull the belt in tight on his milkman trousers. His face had begun changing, too; his cheekbones were getting sharper, his eyes sinking back in their sockets. He listened to a lot of baseball on the radio and watched the games on television, and as often as not he went to sleep in his easy chair with his mouth open. In his sleep, his face flinched.

I was getting scared for him.

I believe I understand what was gnawing at my father. It was not simply the fact that he'd seen a dead man. It was not the fact that the dead man had been murdered, because there had been murders—though, thank goodness, relatively few—in Zephyr before. I think the meanness of the act, the brutal cold-bloodedness of it, was what had eaten into my father's soul. Dad was smart about a lot of things; he was commonsense smart, and he knew right from wrong and he was a man of his word, but he was naive about the world in many ways. I don't think he'd ever believed that evil could exist in Zephyr. The idea that a fellow human being could be beaten and strangled, handcuffed to a wheel and denied a Christian burial in God's earth—and that this terrible thing had happened right in his own hometown where he'd been born and raised—had hurt something deep inside him. Broken something, maybe, that he couldn't fix by himself. Maybe it was also because the murdered man seemed to have no past, and that no one had responded to Sheriff Amory's inquiries.

"He had to be *somebody*," I'd heard Dad telling Mom one night, through the wall. "Didn't he have a wife, or children, or brothers or sisters? Didn't he have folks of his own? My God, Rebecca, he had to have a *name!* Who was he? And where did he come from?"

"That's for the sheriff to find out."

"J.T. *can't* find out anythin'! He's given it up!"

"I think you ought to go see the Lady, Tom."

"No."

"Why not? You saw the drawin'. You know it's the same tattoo. Why won't you at least go talk to her?"

"Because—" He paused, and I could tell he was searching inside himself for an answer. "Because I don't believe in her kind of magic, that's why. It's false trickery. She must've read about that tattoo in the *Journal*."

"It wasn't described in such detail in the paper. You know that. And she said she heard voices and piano music, and she saw a pair of hands. Go talk to her, Tom. Please go."

"She doesn't have anythin' to tell me," Dad said firmly. "At least not anythin' I want to hear."

And that was where it stood, as my father's sleep was haunted by a drowned phantom with no name.

On this first day of summer, though, I wasn't thinking about any of that. I wasn't thinking about Old Moses, or Midnight Mona, or the man with the green-feathered hat. I was thinking of joining my friends in what had become our ritual of celebration.

I ran home from school. Rebel was waiting for me on the front porch. I told Mom I'd be back after a while, and then I ran into the woods behind our house with Rebel at my heels. The forest was green and glorious, a warm breeze stirring through the foliage and trees and the bright sun slanting down. I reached the forest trail and followed it deeper into the woods, and Rebel veered off to chase a squirrel up a tree before he came on. It took me about ten minutes to break through the forest and reach the wide green clearing that stood on a rolling hillside with Zephyr stretched out below. My friends, who'd come on their bikes, were already there with their dogs: Johnny Wilson with his big red Chief, Ben Sears with Tumper, and Davy Ray Callan with his brown-and-white-spotted Buddy.

The wind was stronger up here. It whirled around and around in the clearing, a happy circle of summer air. "We made it!" Davy Ray shouted. "School's out!"

"School's out!" Ben yelled, and jumped around like a pure idiot with Tumper barking at his side.

Johnny just grinned, and he stood staring down at our hometown with the sun hot on his face.

"You ready?" Ben asked me.

"Ready," I told him, my heart starting to beat hard.

"Everybody ready?" Ben shouted.

We were.

"Let's go, then! Summer's started!" Ben began to run around the edges of the clearing in a wide circle, with Tumper loping along behind. I followed him, Rebel weaving in and out of my track. Johnny and Davy Ray started running behind me, their dogs racing back and forth across the clearing and tusseling with each other.

We ran faster and faster. The wind was first in our faces and then at our backs. We ran around the clearing on our sturdy young legs, the wind speaking through the pines and oaks that rimmed our playground. "Faster!" Johnny shouted, limping just a little on his clubfoot. "Gotta go faster!"

We kept going, fighting the wind and then flying before it. The dogs ran beside us, barking with the sheer happiness of movement. The sun sparkled on the Tecumseh River, the sky was clear azure, and summer's heat bloomed in our lungs.

It was time. Everyone knew it was time.

"Ben's goin' up first!" I shouted. "He's gettin' ready! He's gettin'—"

Ben gave a holler. Wings tore through the back of his shirt as they grew from his shoulder blades.

"His wings are gettin' bigger!" I said. "They're the same color as his hair, and they're lazy from not bein' used for so long, but now they're startin' to beat! Look at 'em! Just look!"

Ben's feet lifted off the earth, and his wings began to take him upward.

"Tumper's goin', too!" I said. "Wait for him, Ben!"

Tumper's wings unfurled. Yapping nervously, the dog ascended beneath his master's heels. "Come on, Tumper!" Ben cried out. "Let's go!"

"Davy Ray!" I said. "Do you feel it?"

He wanted to. He really did, but I could tell he wasn't ready. "Johnny!" I said. "You're about to go!"

Johnny's wings, when they exploded from his shoulder blades, were shimmering black. He went up with big red Chief flapping at his side. I looked up at Ben, who was already fifty feet above the earth and flying like a pudgy eagle. "Ben's leavin' you, Davy Ray! Look up there at him! Hey, Ben! Call Davy Ray!"

"Come on up, Davy Ray!" Ben shouted, and he turned a barrel roll. "The air's just fine!"

"I'm ready!" Davy Ray said, his teeth clenched. "I'm ready! Talk me up, Cory!"

"You can feel your wings startin' to grow, can't you? Yeah, I see 'em! They're gettin' ready to bust free! Here they come! They're loose!"

114

"I feel 'em! I feel 'em!" Davy Ray grinned, sweat on his face. His sleek auburn-colored wings began to flap, and he ascended with a swimming motion. I knew that Davy Ray was not afraid of flying; he never had been in the summers we'd been coming here. He was only afraid of that first leap of faith when you left the ground. "Buddy's comin' after you!" I shouted as the dog's brown-and-white-spotted wings caught the air. Buddy dog-paddled upward.

My own wings suddenly burst from my shoulder blades, unfurling like brown flags. They ripped through my shirt, hungry for wind. I felt the delirium of freedom lighten my bones. As I began to rise, I had a few seconds of panic akin to the summer's first jump into the cold waters of the public pool. My wings had been tight and dormant under my flesh since the end of August, and though they might have twitched every once in a while around Halloween, Thanksgiving, Christmas vacation, and Easter break, they had been asleep and only dreaming of this day. They felt heavy and ungainly, and I wondered—as I did every summer since our ritual had begun—how such things could read the air almost of their own accord. And then my wings filled up with wind and I felt their awesome muscular might. They gave a jerking motion, like the reaction after a sneeze. The second flap was more controlled and powerful; the third was as pretty as poetry. My wings began to beat in the current of air. "I'm doin' it!" I shouted as I rose after my friends and their dogs in the bright sky.

I heard a familiar barking, close behind. I looked back. Rebel's white wings had grown, and he was following me. I flapped upward, following the others who followed Ben. "Not so fast, Ben!" I cautioned, but he was soaring toward seventy feet. He deserved to fly, I thought, for what he had endured on the ground. Tumper and Buddy swooped around and around in a long lazy circle and Rebel barked to be allowed in the game. Chief, like his master, was more of a loner. Then Rebel swooped over toward me again and licked my face, and I put my arm around his neck and together we soared above the treetops.

Davy Ray had conquered his fears. He made a caw-caw-cawing sound and he put his head straight down with his arms rigid at his sides and he dove at the earth, laughing. His wings were smoothed back along his shoulders, his face contorted by the rush of air. "Pull up, Davy Ray!" I shouted as he streaked past me with Buddy in dogged pursuit. "Pull up!"

But Davy kept going down toward the green forest. When it seemed he was doomed to crash like a meteor, his wings suddenly spread out like a beautiful fan and he jackknifed his body upward.

He could've chewed on pine needles if he'd wanted. Davy flew across the treetops, yelling with delight, but Buddy crashed through a few thin branches before he got himself straightened out again. The dog came up from the trees spitting and growling, leaving shell-shocked squirrels in his wake.

I kept rising toward Ben. Off by himself, Johnny was executing slow figure-eights. Rebel and Tumper began playing chase sixty feet above the ground. Ben grinned at me, his face and shirt damp with sweat, his shirttail hanging out. "Cory!" he said. "Watch this!" Then he closed his arms over his belly and pulled his knees up tightly and he whooped as he cannonballed down. As Davy had done, Ben opened his wings large to catch the wind when he wanted to slow his speed, but here something went wrong. One of his wings didn't open full. Ben yelped, knowing he was in trouble. He cartwheeled, his arms flailing. "I'm goin' dowwwnnnn!" Ben wailed on a wing and a prayer.

He slammed into the treetops, belly first.

"You okay?" Davy Ray asked him.

"You all right?" I asked.

Johnny stopped running, too, and Tumper ran over to his master and licked Ben's face. Ben sat up and showed us a skinned elbow. "Wow," he said. "That stung a little bit." Blood was showing.

"Well, you shouldn't have gone so fast!" Davy Ray told him. "Numb nuts!"

"I'm okay, really I am." Ben stood up. "We're not through flyin' yet, are we, Cory?"

He was ready to go again. I started running, my arms spread out at my sides. The others sped around me in all directions, their arms out, too, and the wind buffeting us. "Now Davy Ray's up to seventy feet," I said, "and Buddy's right there with him. Johnny's doin' a figure-eight at fifty feet. Come on, Ben! Get out of those trees!"

He came up, pine needles in his hair, his mouth split by a grin.

The first day of summer was always a wonderful time.

"This way, fellas!" Davy Ray shouted as he began flying toward Zephyr. I followed him. My wings knew the blue roads.

The sun was hot on our backs. The houses of Zephyr lay below us like toys on gum-stick streets. The cars looked like little windups you might buy at the five and dime. We flew on over the Tecumseh's sparkling brown snake, over the gargoyle bridge and the old railroad trestle. I could see some fishermen in a rowboat down there. If Old Moses decided to grab their bait, they wouldn't be sitting so calmly waiting for a mudcat.

Our small shadows, and those of our dogs, moved across the

earth like secret writing. We flew over the dark brown, oblong stain of Saxon's Lake. I didn't like it, even as I caught a warm current and zoomed up to seventy feet. I didn't like what was lying in it like a seed in a rotten apple. Davy dove down and flew less than ten feet over the lake's surface. I figured he'd better be careful; if his wings got wet, he was through flying until they dried out. Then he ascended again, and all of us flew over the forest and farmland that lay beyond Saxon's Lake like a patchwork quilt of wild green and burnished brown.

"Where are we now, Cory?" Davy Ray asked.

I said, "We're almost to . . ."

Robbins Air Force Base, a huge flat clearing amid an ocean of woods. I pointed out a silver jet fighter heading in for a landing. Beyond the base, and off limits to everybody including boys with wings, was a testing ground where the fighter pilots shot at dummy ground targets and bombers occasionally dropped a real payload that rattled the windows of Zephyr. The airfield was the boundary of our jaunt, and we turned around in the hot blue and began flying back the way we'd come: over fields and forest, lake, river, and rooftops.

With Rebel at my side, I circled above my house. The other guys were swooping around their own houses, their dogs barking happily. I realized how small my house was compared to the great world that stretched off in all directions. From my height I could see roads going off to the horizon, and cars and trucks on those roads heading to destinations unknown. Wanderlust is part of summer, too; I was feeling it, and wondering if I would ever travel those roads, and if I did where I would be going. I wondered, as well, what might happen if Mom or Dad suddenly walked out of the house, saw my shadow and Rebel's on the yard, and looked up. I doubt if they ever knew their son could fly.

I made a circle of the chimneytops and turrets of the Thaxter mansion, at the top of Temple Street. Then I rejoined my friends, and we reached the clearing on tired wings.

We made a few circles, descending one after the other like graceful leaves. The ground was a jolt under my heels, and I kept running as my wings and body adjusted again to earth's grasp. Then we were all on the ground, running around the clearing with our dogs, first pushing the wind and then being pushed by it. Our wings folded up and returned to their hidden sheaths in our hollow shoulder blades; the dogs' wings slid down into the flesh and sealed over with a rippling of hair—white, brown, red, brown and white spotted. Our torn shirts mended themselves, and no mother would ever know what had burst through them. We were drenched with sweat, our faces and arms shining with it, and as we became earthbound again we ceased our running and dropped exhausted to the grass.

The dogs were upon us at once, licking our faces. Our ritual flight had ended for another summer.

We sat around for a while, talking once our hearts and minds had settled down. We talked about all the things we were going to do this summer; there were so many things, the days wouldn't be long enough. But we all decided we wanted to go camping, and that was for sure.

Then it was time to go home. "See you guys!" Ben said as he wheeled away on his bike with Tumper in pursuit. "Catch ya later!" Davy Ray told us as he departed on his bike and Buddy sprinted after a cottontail rabbit. "See you later!" Johnny said as he pedaled away with faithful Chief loping at his side. I waved. "Alligator!" I said.

I walked home, pausing to throw a few pine cones for Rebel to chase. He barked furiously at a snake hole he'd discovered, but I pulled him away from it before whatever was inside came sliding out. It was a mighty big snake hole.

At home, Mom looked at me aghast when I strolled into the kitchen. "You're drippin' wet!" she said. "What've you been *doin'?*"

I shrugged as I reached for the pitcher of cold lemonade.

"Nothin' much," I answered.

2

Barbershop Talk

"Little bit off the top and thin the sides out, Tom?"

"That'll do me, I believe."

"You got it, my friend."

This was how Mr. Perry Dollar, the owner of Dollar's Barbershop on Merchants Street, began every haircut. It never mattered how a fellow requested his hair cut; he always walked out with a little bit off the top and the sides thinned out. Of course, we're talking about a real haircut here, none of that "hair-styling" stuff. For one dollar and fifty cents, you got the treatment: wrapped to the neck under a crisp blue-striped barber towel, scissors-trimmed and clippers-raked, hot lather applied to the back of your neck and the fine hairs there scraped off with a freshly stropped straight razor, followed by a liberal dousing from one of the mystery bottles of Wildroot, Vitalis, or Brylcreem hair dressings. I say "mystery bottles" because every time I got my hair cut at Mr. Dollar's, those bottles, on a shelf above the barber chair, were exactly half full and never seemed to go up or down an inch. When the haircutting was done—"the scalping" was much the better term for it—and Mr. Dollar unpinned the barber towel from around your neck and swept the dead hairs out of your collar with a brush that felt like whiskers from a boar's snout, the adults got to reach into the peanut-brittle jar and the kids got their choice of lime, lemon, grape, or cherry suckers.

"Hot day," Mr. Dollar commented as he lifted up Dad's hair with a comb and snipped the ends with scissors.

"Sure is."

"Known it hotter, though. One hundred and three degrees this day in 1936."

"One hundred and *four* degrees this day in 1927!" said Mr. Owen Cathcoate, an aged specimen who was playing checkers with Mr. Gabriel "Jazzman" Jackson at the back of the barbershop, where the overhead fan kept the place the coolest. Mr. Cathcoate's wrinkled face was dotted with liver spots, like a map of some strange and foreign country. He had narrow-slit eyes and long-fingered hands, and his scraggly yellowish-white hair hung down around his shoulders, which must have been torture for Mr. Dollar to have to look at. Mr. Jackson was a big-bellied black man with iron-gray hair and a small, neat mustache, and he shined and repaired shoes for people who brought them in, his workshop being at the rear of Mr. Dollar's place. Mr. Jackson got his nickname because, as Dad told me, he could "blow butterflies and hornets out of that clarinet of his." The clarinet, in a well-seasoned black case, was never far from Mr. Jackson's side.

"Be a whole lot hotter 'fore July gets here," Mr. Jackson said as he pondered the pieces. He started to make a move and then thought better of it. "Owen, I do believe you're tryin' to put me between a rock and a hard place, ain't you?"

"I wouldn't dream of such a thing, Mr. Jackson."

"Oh, you sly old fox you!" the Jazzman said when he saw the simple but deadly trap Mr. Cathcoate had laid open for him. "Gonna skin me up and serve me for dinner, huh? Well, I'd be mighty tough to chew on!" He made a move that for the moment got him out of danger.

Mr. Dollar was short and stocky and had a face like a contented bulldog. His gray eyebrows stuck out everywhichway like wild weeds, and his hair was shaved to the sandy scalp. He could make the neatest parts of anybody I've ever seen. He knew all there was to know about the history of Zephyr. Because he had been the only barber in town for over twenty years, he had his finger on the roaring pulse of gossip and he could tell you everything that was going on, if you had an afternoon to sit and listen. He also had a nifty collection of tattered comic books, *Field & Stream*s, and *Sports Illustrated*s, and I had heard from Davy Ray that Mr. Dollar kept a box of *Stag, Confidential,* and *Argosy* magazines in the back for adults only.

"Cory?" Mr. Dollar said as he cut my father's hair. "You met the new boy yet?"

"No sir?" I didn't know there *was* a new boy.

"Came in here yesterday with his dad to get a haircut. Got good hair, but that cowlick about blunted my scissors." *Snip, snip,* they sang. "He just moved here last week."

"New family rentin' that house on the corner of Greenhowe and Shantuck?" Dad asked.

"Yeah, that's them. The Curliss family. Nice people. All of 'em got good hair."

"What's Mr. Curliss do?"

"Salesman," Mr. Dollar said. "Sells shirts for some company in Atlanta. The boy's a couple of years younger than Cory. I set him up on the horse and he didn't squirm a bit."

The horse was a carved golden palomino that had been salvaged from a doomed merry-go-round somewhere; now it was bolted to the floor next to the regular barber's chair. Only babies got their hair cut while sitting on the horse, even though there were times when I wished I might be able to sit on that horse again and put my feet in the stirrups while my hair was being snipped. Still, the fact that the Curliss boy—at nine or ten years of age, say—wanted to sit on the horse told me he must be a pansy.

"Mr. Curliss seems like a decent fella," Mr. Dollar went on, following the scissors across my father's scalp. "Quiet, though. Kinda timid for a salesman, I'd say. That's a hard row to hoe."

"I'll bet," Dad said.

"I got the impression Mr. Curliss has moved around quite a bit. He told me all the places he and the family have lived. I guess, bein' a salesman, you'd have to be prepared to go where the company says go."

"I couldn't do that," Dad said. "I've gotta have roots."

Mr. Dollar nodded. He left that topic and wandered through others like a man through high grass, not seeing anything but the next step. "Yessir," he said. "If them Beatle boys came in here, they'd sure 'nuff leave lookin' like men 'stead of women." His eyebrows squeezed together as he wandered on in a new direction. "Communists say they're gonna bury us. Gotta stop 'em while we can, 'fore they get to our country. Send our boys to bust their tails in that place over there . . . y'know, where they grow all the bamboo."

"Vietnam," Dad supplied.

"Right. That's the place. Kill 'em there and we won't have to worry no more." Mr. Dollar's scissors were getting up to speed. A new thought was being born somewhere between Mr. Dollar's ears. "J.T. ever figure out who went down in Saxon's Lake, Tom?"

I watched my father's face. No expression registered there, but I knew this question must be stabbing him. "No, Perry. He never did."

"He was a federal man, is what I think," the Jazzman ventured. "Must've been lookin' for stills. I think the Blaylocks killed him."

"That's what Mr. Sculley believes, too," Dad said.

"The Blaylocks are bad news, that's the truth." Mr. Dollar switched on his clipper and worked on Dad's sideburns. "Wouldn't be the first man they've killed."

"Why do you say that?"

"Sim Sears used to buy whiskey from the youngest boy, Donny. Oh—" Mr. Dollar looked at me. "I'm not talkin' out of school, am I?"

"It's all right," Dad told him. "Go ahead."

"Well, this is from Sim's mouth, so I guess he's come to grips with it. Anyway, Donny Blaylock used to sell moonshine to Sim, and Sim told me Donny and him got drunk up in the woods one night—the night that meteor fell up there near Union Town—and Donny told him things."

"Things?" Dad prodded. "What things?"

"Donny told Sim he'd killed a man," Mr. Dollar said. "Didn't tell him the why, the when, or the who. Just that he'd killed a man and he was glad of it."

"Does J.T. know about this?"

"Nope. And he won't hear it from me, either. I don't want to get J.T. killed. You ever see Biggun Blaylock?"

"No."

"Big as a moose and full of the devil. If I told J.T. what Sim had told me, he'd have to go out and find the Blaylocks. If he *did* find 'em, which I doubt he could, that bunch would hang him up by his heels and cut his throat open like a—" Again Mr. Dollar looked at me, sitting there, all eyes and ears, behind a Hawkman comic book. "Well, I kinda figure that'd be the last of our sheriff," Mr. Dollar finished.

"The Blaylocks don't own the county!" Dad said. "If they committed a murder, they ought to pay for it!"

"That's right, they should," Mr. Dollar agreed as he returned to his clipping. "Biggun came in here last November to pick up a pair of boots he was havin' resoled. Remember that, Jazzman?"

"Shore do. Fine, expensive boots. I was scared to death of gettin' a scuff on 'em."

"You know what Biggun said as he was payin' for his boots?" Mr. Dollar asked my father. "He said they were his stompin' boots, and anybody who got under 'em wouldn't be standin' up again. I figured that to mean he didn't want anybody messin' in his business. So who's gonna be fool enough to go lookin' to get killed by the Blaylocks?"

"That's what happened to that fella at the bottom of the lake," the Jazzman said. "He was messin' in the Blaylocks' business." *Bidness*, he pronounced it.

"I don't care if they brew up 'shine and sell it outta the back of their trucks," Mr. Dollar went on. "No harm done to *me*. I don't care if they fix the stock car races, because I'm not a gambler. I don't care what they do to them fallen angels at Grace Stafford's, because I'm a family man."

"Hold on," Dad said. "What about Grace Stafford's place?"

"Ain't her place. She just manages it. The Blaylocks own it, lock, stock, and hair curlers."

Dad grunted softly. "I didn't know that."

"Oh, yeah!" Mr. Dollar applied lather to the back of Dad's neck and worked a straight razor along the leather strop. "The Blaylocks are rakin' it in, that's for sure. Makin' a killin' off the Air Force fellas." With a steady hand, he began shaving my father's neck. "The Blaylocks are too much for J.T. to handle. It'd take Edgar Hoover himself to throw 'em in jail."

"Wyatt Earp could do it." Mr. Cathcoate spoke up now. "If he was still alive, I mean."

"I reckon he could at that, Owen." Mr. Dollar glanced at me, gauging my interest, and then back to the old man. "Hey, Owen! I don't think young Cory here knows about you and Wyatt Earp!" Mr. Dollar winked at me conspiratorially. "Tell him the tale, why don't you?"

Mr. Cathcoate didn't answer for a moment, but it was his turn and he didn't move any of the checkers pieces. "Naw," he replied at last. "I'll let it rest."

"Come on, Owen! Tell the boy! You want to hear it, don't you, Cory?" Before I could say yes or no, Mr. Dollar plowed on. "See there? He wants to hear it!"

"Long time gone," Mr. Cathcoate said quietly.

"Eighteen hundred and eighty-one, wasn't it? October twenty-sixth at Tombstone, Arizona? You were all of nine years old?"

"That's right." Mr. Cathcoate nodded. "I was nine years old."

"And tell the boy what you did on that day."

Mr. Cathcoate sat staring at the checkers board. "Go on, Owen," the Jazzman urged in a gentle voice. "You tell him."

"I . . . killed a man on that day," Mr. Cathcoate said. "And I saved the life of Wyatt Earp at the O.K. Corral."

"There you go, Cory!" Mr. Dollar grinned. "Bet you didn't know you were sittin' in here with a real live *gunfighter*, did you?" The way Mr. Dollar said that, though, made me think he didn't believe a word of it, and that he enjoyed goading Mr. Cathcoate about it.

Of course I'd heard about the O.K. Corral. Every boy with even a passing interest in cowboys and the Wild West knew that story, about the day the Earp brothers—Wyatt, Virgil, and Morgan—and cardsharp Doc Holliday faced down the rustling Clantons and McLowerys in the hot dust of Tombstone. "Is that for real, Mr. Cathcoate?" I asked.

"For real. I was lucky that day. I was just a kid, didn't know nothin' about guns. Almost shot my foot off."

"Tell him how you saved ol' Wyatt," Mr. Dollar urged as he blotted the last of the lather off the back of Dad's neck with a steaming towel.

Mr. Cathcoate frowned. I figured he didn't like remembering it, or else he was trying to put the details together again. A ninety-two-year-old man has to open a lot of locks to recall a day when he was nine years old. But I suppose that particular day was worth remembering.

Mr. Cathcoate finally said, "Wasn't supposed to be anybody on the street. Everybody knew the Earps, Doc Holliday, the McLowerys, and the Clantons were gonna spill blood. It had been a long time brewin'. But I was there, hidin' behind a shack. Little fool, me." He pushed his chair back from the checkers board, and he sat with his long-fingered hands twined together and the fan's breeze stirring his hair. "I heard all the shoutin', and all the guns goin' off. I heard bullets hittin' flesh. That's a sound you don't forget if you live to be a hundred and ninety-two." His slitted eyes stared at me, but I could tell he was looking toward the past, where dust clouds rose from the bloodstained earth and shadows aimed their six-guns. "A terrible lot of shootin'," he said. "A bullet went through the shack next to my head. I heard it whine. Then I got down low and I stayed there. Pretty soon a man came staggerin' past me and fell to his knees. It was Billy Clanton. He was all shot up, but he had a gun in his hand. He looked at me. Right at me. And then he coughed and blood spurted out of his mouth and nose and he fell on his face right next to me."

"Wow!" I said, my arms chillbumped.

"Oh, there's more!" Mr. Dollar announced. "Tell him, Owen!"

"A shadow fell on me," Mr. Cathcoate said, his voice raspy. "I looked up, and I saw Wyatt Earp. His face was covered with dust, and he seemed ten feet tall. He said, 'Run home, boy.' I can hear him say that, clear as a bell. But I was scared and I stayed where I was, and Wyatt Earp walked on around to the other side of the shed. The fight was over. Clantons and McLowerys were lyin' on the ground shot to pieces. Then it happened."

"What happened?" I asked when Mr. Cathcoate paused to breathe.

"The fella who'd been hidin' in an empty rain barrel raised up and took aim with his pistol at Wyatt Earp's back. I'd never seen him before. But he was right there, as close to me as you are. He took aim, and I heard him click the trigger back."

"This here's the good part," Mr. Dollar said. "Then what, Owen?"

"Then . . . I picked up Billy Clanton's pistol. Thing was as heavy as a cannon, and it had blood all over the grip. I could hardly hold it." Mr. Cathcoate was silent; his eyes closed. He went on: "Wasn't time to call out. Wasn't time to do a thing except what I did. I was just meanin' to scare the fella by firin' into the sky, and to get Mr. Earp's attention. But the gun went off. Just like that: *boom*." His eyes opened at the memory of the shot. "Knocked me down, 'bout busted my shoulder. I heard the bullet ricochet off a rock about six inches from my right foot. That bullet went straight through the fella's gunhand wrist. Blew the pistol out of his hand, broke his wrist open so the edge of a bone was stickin' out. He bled like a fountain. And as he was bleedin' to death I was sayin', 'I'm sorry, I'm sorry, I'm sorry.' 'Cause I didn't mean to kill anybody. I just meant to keep Mr. Earp from gettin' killed." He sighed, long and softly; it was like the sound of wind blowing dust over the graves on Boot Hill. "I was standin' over the body, holdin' Billy Clanton's gun. Doc Holliday came up to me, and he gave me a four-bit piece and he said, 'Go buy yourself a candy stick, kid.' That's how I got the name."

"What name?" I asked.

"The Candystick Kid," Mr. Cathcoate answered. "Mr. Earp came to my house to have dinner. My dad was a farmer. We didn't have much, but we fed Mr. Earp as best we could. He gave me Billy Clanton's gun and holster as a gift for savin' his life." Mr. Cathcoate shook his scraggly-maned head. "I should've thrown that damn gun down the well, like my momma wanted me to."

"Why?"

"'Cause," he said, and here he seemed to get irritable and agitated, "I *liked* it too much, that's why! I started learnin' how to *use* it! Started likin' its smell, and its weight, and how it felt warm in my hand after it had just gone off, and how that bottle I was aimin' at flew all to pieces in a heartbeat, that's why." He scowled as if he'd just had a taste of bitter fruit. "Started shootin' birds out of the sky, and believin' I was a quick-draw artist. Then it started workin' on my mind, wonderin' how fast I could be against some other boy with a gun. I kept practicin', kept slappin' that leather and pullin' that hogleg out time and again. And when I was sixteen years old I went to Yuma in a stagecoach and I killed a gunslinger there name of Edward Bonteel, and that's when I put a foot in hell."

"Ol' Owen here got to be quite a name," Mr. Dollar said as he brushed the clipped hairs from Dad's shoulders. "The Candystick Kid, I mean. How many fellas did you send to meet their Maker, Owen?" Mr. Dollar looked at me and quickly winked.

"I killed fourteen men," Mr. Cathcoate said. There was no pride in his voice. "Fourteen men." He stared at the red and black squares of the checkerboard. "Youngest was nineteen. Oldest was forty-two. Maybe some of 'em deserved to die. Maybe that's not for me to say. I killed 'em, every one, in fair fights. But I was lookin' to kill 'em. I was lookin' to make a big name for myself, be a big man. The day I got shot by a younger, faster fella, I decided I was livin' on borrowed time. I cleared out."

"You got shot?" I asked. "Where'd it hit you?"

"Left side. But I aimed better. Shot that fella through the forehead, smack dab. My gunfightin' days were over, though. I headed east. Wound up here. That's my story."

"Still got that gun and holster, don't you, Candystick?" Mr. Dollar inquired.

Mr. Cathcoate didn't reply. He sat there, motionless. I thought he'd gone to sleep, though his heavy-lidded eyes were still open. Then, abruptly, he stood up from his chair and walked on stiffened legs to where Mr. Dollar was standing. He pushed his face toward Mr. Dollar's, and I saw his expression in the mirror; Mr. Cathcoate's age-spotted face was grim and thin-lipped, like a skull bound up with brown leather. Mr. Cathcoate's mouth split open in a smile, but it was not a happy smile. It was a terrible smile, and I saw Mr. Dollar shrink back from it.

"Perry," Mr. Cathcoate said, "I know you think I'm an old fool half out of my head. I accept the fact that you laugh at me when you think I'm not lookin'. But if I didn't have eyes in the back of my head, Perry, I wouldn't be alive right now."

"Uh . . . uh . . . why, no, Owen!" Mr. Dollar blubbered. "I'm not laughin' at you! Honest!"

"Now you're either lyin', or callin' me a liar," the old man said, and something about the soft way he said that made my bones grow cold.

"I'm . . . sorry if you think I'm—"

"Yes, I still have the gun and holster," Mr. Cathcoate interrupted him. "I kept 'em for old time's sake. Now, you understand this, Perry." He leaned in closer, and Mr. Dollar tried to smile but he only summoned up a weak grin. "You can call me Owen, or Mr. Cathcoate. You can call me Hey, you or Old Man. But you're not to call me by my gunfighter name. Not today, not tomorrow, not ever. Do we see eye to eye on that, Perry?"

"Owen, there's no call to be—"

"Do we see eye to eye?" Mr. Cathcoate repeated.

"Uh . . . yeah. We do. Sure." Mr. Dollar nodded. "Whatever you say, Owen."

"No, not whatever I say. Just this."

"Okay. No problem."

Mr. Cathcoate stared into Mr. Dollar's eyes for another few seconds, as if looking for the truth there. Then he said, "I'll be leavin' now," and he walked to the door.

"What about our game, Owen?" the Jazzman asked.

Mr. Cathcoate paused. "I don't want to play anymore," he said, and then he pushed through the door and out into the hot June afternoon. A wave of heat rolled in as the door settled shut. I stood up, went to the plate-glass window, and watched Mr. Cathcoate walking slowly up the sidewalk of Merchants Street, his hands in his pockets.

"Well, what do you think about that?" Mr. Dollar asked. "What do you suppose set him off?"

"He knows you don't believe none of that story," the Jazzman said as he began to put away the checkers pieces and the board.

"Is it true, or not?" Dad stood up from the chair. His ears had been lowered considerably, the back of his neck ruddy where it had been shaved and scrubbed.

"'Course it's not true!" Mr. Dollar laughed with a snort. "Owen's crazy! Been out of his head for years!"

"It didn't happen like he said it did?" I kept watching Mr. Cathcoate move away up the sidewalk.

"No. He made the whole thing up."

"How do you know that for sure?" Dad asked.

"Come on, Tom! What would a Wild West gunfighter be doin' in Zephyr? And don't you think it'd be in the history books if a kid saved Wyatt Earp's life at the O.K. Corral? I went to the library and looked it up. Ain't no mention of any kid savin' Wyatt Earp's life, and in this book I found about gunfighters there's nobody called the Candystick Kid, either." Mr. Dollar brushed hair out of the chair with furious strokes. "Your turn, Cory. Get on up here."

I started to move away from the window, but I saw Mr. Cathcoate wave to someone. Vernon Thaxter, naked as innocence, was walking on the other side of Merchants Street. Vernon was walking fast, as if he had somewhere important to go, but he lifted his hand in greeting to Mr. Cathcoate.

The two crazy men passed each other, going their separate ways.

I didn't laugh. I wondered what it was that had made Mr. Cathcoate want to believe so badly that he'd been a gunfighter, just as Vernon Thaxter believed he really had somewhere to go.

I got up in the chair. Mr. Dollar pinned the barber towel around my neck, and he combed through my hair a few times as Dad sat down to read a *Sports Illustrated*.

"Little bit off the top and thin the sides out?" Mr. Dollar asked.

"Yes sir," I said. "That'd be fine."

The scissors sang, and little dead parts of me flew off.

127

3

A Boy and a Ball

It was on the front porch when we got home from Mr. Dollar's. Right there, on its kickstand.

A brand new bicycle.

"Gosh," I said as I got out of the pickup. That's all I could say. I walked up the porch steps in a trance, and I touched it.

It was not a dream. It was real, and it was beautiful.

Dad whistled in appreciation. He knew a good-looking bike when he saw it. "That's some piece of work, huh?"

"Yes sir." I still couldn't believe it. Here was something I had desired in my heart for a long, long time. It belonged to me now, and I felt like the king of the world.

In later years I would think that no woman's lips had ever been as red as that bike. No low-slung foreign sports car with wire wheels and purring engine would ever look as powerful or as capable as that bike. No chrome would ever gleam with such purity, like the silver moon on a summer's night. It had a big round headlight and a horn with a rubber bulb, and its frame looked as strong and solid as the biceps of Hercules. But it looked *fast*, too; its handlebars sloped forward like an invitation to taste the wind, its black rubber pedals unscuffed by any foot before mine. Dad ran his fingers along the headlight, and then he picked the bike up with one hand. "Boy, it hardly weighs anything!" he marveled. "Lightest metal I've ever felt!" He put it down again, and it settled on its kickstand like an obedient but barely tamed animal.

I was on that seat in two seconds. I had a little trouble at first, because the way both the handlebars and the seat tilted forward I felt like my balance was off. My head was thrust over the front wheel, my back pressed down in a straight line in emulation of the bike's spine. I had the feeling of being on a machine that could easily get out of my control if I wasn't careful; there was something about it that both thrilled and scared me.

Mom came out of the house. The bike had arrived about an hour before, she told us. Mr. Lightfoot had brought it in the back of his truck. "He said the Lady wants you to ride easy on it until it gets used to you," she said. She looked at Dad, who was walking in a circle around the new bike. "He *can* keep it, can't he?"

"I don't like us acceptin' charity. You know that."

"It's not charity. It's a reward for a good deed."

Dad continued his circling. He stopped and prodded his shoe at the front tire. "This must've cost her an awful lot of money. It's a fine bike, that's for sure."

"Can I keep it, Dad?" I asked.

He stood there, his hands on his hips. He chewed on his bottom lip for a moment, and then he looked at Mom. "It's not charity?"

"No."

Dad's gaze found me. "Yeah," he said, and no word was ever more welcome. "It's yours."

"Thanks! Thanks a million times!"

"So now that you've got a new bike, what're you gonna name it?" Dad asked.

I hadn't thought about this yet. I shook my head, still trying to get used to the way it held my body forward like a spear.

"Might as well take it out for a spin, don't you think?" He slid an arm around Mom's waist, and he grinned at me.

"Yes sir," I said, but I got off to chop the kickstand up and guide it down the porch steps. It seemed an indignity to jar the bike before we'd gotten to know each other. Either that, or I feared waking it up just yet. I sat on the seat again, my feet on the ground.

"Go ahead," Dad told me. "Just don't burn up the street."

I nodded, but I didn't move. I swear I thought I felt the bike tremble, as if with anticipation. Maybe it was just me.

"Crank 'er up," Dad said.

This was the moment of truth. I took a breath, put one foot on a pedal, and pushed off with the other. Then both feet were on the pedals, and I aimed the bike toward the street. The wheels turned with hardly any noise, just a quiet *tick . . . tick . . . tick* like a bomb about to go off.

"Have fun!" my mother called as she opened the porch door.

I looked back and took a hand off the handlebars to wave, and the bike suddenly lurched out of my control and zigzagged wildly. I almost went down in my first crash, but I grasped hold again and the bike straightened out. The pedals were smooth as ice cream, the wheels spinning faster across the hot pavement. This was a bike, I realized, that could get away from you like a rocket. I tore away along the street, the wind hissing through my newly cut hair, and to tell the truth, I felt as if I was hanging on for dear life. I was used to an old, sluggish chain and sprocket that needed a lot of leg muscle, but this bike demanded a lighter touch. When I put on the brakes the first time, I almost flew off the seat. I spun it around in a wide circle and gave it more speed again, and I got going so fast so quickly, the back of my neck started sweating. I felt one pedal-push away from leaving the ground, but the front wheel responded to my grip on the handlebars seemingly even as I *thought* what direction I wanted to turn. Like a rocket, the bike sped me through the tree-shaded streets of my hometown, and as we carved the wind together I decided that would be its name.

"Rocket," I said, the word whirling away behind me in the slipstream. "That sound all right to you?"

It didn't throw me off. It didn't veer for the nearest tree. I took that as a yes.

I started getting bolder. I sideslipped and figure-eighted and curb-jumped, and Rocket obeyed me without hesitation. I leaned over those handlebars and pumped the pedals with all my strength and Rocket shot along Shantuck Street, the pools of shadow and sunlight opening up before me. I zipped up onto the sidewalk, where the tires barely registered the passing cracks. The air was hot in my lungs and cool on my face, and the houses and trees were whipping past in a sublime blur. At this instant I felt at one with Rocket, as if we were of the same skin and grease, and when I grinned, a bug flew into my teeth. I didn't care; I swallowed it because I was invincible.

And such ideas inevitably lead to what next occurred.

I hit a patch of broken sidewalk without slowing down or trying to miss it, and I felt Rocket shudder from fender to fender. A noise like a grunt ran through the frame. The jolt knocked one of my hands loose from the handlebars, and Rocket's front tire hit an edge of concrete and the bike bucked up and twisted like an angry stallion. My feet left the pedals and my butt left the seat, and as I went off into the air I thought of something Mom had said: *The Lady wants you to ride easy on it until it gets used to you.*

I didn't have much time to ponder it. In the next second I crashed into a hedge in somebody's yard and my breath left me in a *whoosh* and the green leaves took me down. I had nearly ripped a hole clear through the hedge. My arms and cheeks were scratched up some, but nothing seemed to be skinned up and bleeding. I got out of the hedge, shaking off leaves, and I saw Rocket lying on its side in the grass. Terror gripped me; if this new bike was busted up, Dad's spanking hand would be finding work. I knelt beside Rocket, checking the bike for damage. The front tire was scuffed and the fender crimped, but the chain was still on and the handlebars straight. The headlight was unbroken, the frame unbent. Rocket had been bruised but was amazingly healthy for such a nasty spill. I righted the bike, thanking whatever angel had been riding on my shoulder, and as I ran my fingers over the dented fender I saw the eye in the headlamp.

It was a golden orb with a dark pupil, and it stared at me with what might have been a brooding tolerance.

I blinked, startled.

The golden eye was gone. Now the headlight was just a plain bulb behind a circle of glass again.

I kept staring at the headlight. There was no eye in it. I rolled Rocket around, from sun to shadow and back again, but the image did not return.

I felt my head, searching for a lump. I found none.

It's crazy, the things a boy can imagine.

I got back on the seat and started pedaling along the sidewalk again. This time I took it slow and easy, and I hadn't gone twenty feet before I saw all the glass from a broken Yoo-Hoo bottle scattered across the sidewalk in front of me. I swerved Rocket over the curb and onto the street, missing the glass fragments and saving Rocket's tires. I hated to think what might have happened if I'd gone over that glass at high speed; a few scratches from a leafy hedge were mild compared to what could have been.

We had been very lucky, Rocket and me.

Davy Ray Callan lived nearby. I stopped at his house, but his mother said Davy Ray had gone to the ball field with Johnny Wilson to practice. Our Little League team—the Indians, for whom I played second base—had lost our first four games and we needed all the practice we could get. I thanked Mrs. Callan and I aimed Rocket toward the field.

It wasn't far. Davy Ray and Johnny were standing out in the sunshine and the red dust, pitching a ball back and forth. I rode Rocket onto the field and circled them, and their mouths dropped open at the sight of my new bike. Of course they had to touch it, too, had to sit on it and pedal it around a little. Next to Rocket, their bikes looked like dusty antiques. Still, this was Davy Ray's opinion of Rocket: "It don't handle so good, though, does it?" And Johnny's: "It sure is pretty, but the pedals are stiff." I realized they were not saying this simply to rain on my parade; they were good friends, and they rejoiced in my happiness. The fact of the matter is that they preferred their own bikes. Rocket had been made for me and me alone.

I rested Rocket on its kickstand and watched while Davy Ray threw high fly balls to Johnny. Yellow butterflies flew from the grass, and overhead the sky was blue and cloudless. I looked toward the brown-painted bleachers, under the signs advertising different Merchants Street stores, and I saw a figure sitting at the top.

"Hey, Davy!" I said. "Who's that?"

Davy glanced over and then lifted his glove to snare Johnny's return pitch. "I don't know. Just some kid, been sittin' there since we got here."

I watched the guy. He was hunkered forward, watching us, with one elbow on a knee and his chin propped on his palm. I turned away from Davy and walked toward the bleachers, and the kid at the top suddenly stood up as if he meant to run.

"What're you doin' up there?" I called to him.

He didn't answer. He just stood there, and I could tell he was trying to decide whether to take to his heels or not.

I got closer. I didn't recognize him; he had short-cropped dark brown hair with a wiry cowlick sticking up from the left side of his head, and he wore glasses that seemed too big for his face. He was maybe nine or ten years old, I figured, and he was a real beanpole, with gawky arms and legs. He wore blue jeans with patched knees and a white T-shirt, and the buttermilk pallor of his skin told me he didn't get outside very much. "What's your name?" I asked him as I reached the fence between the field and the bleachers.

He didn't reply.

"Can you *talk?*"

I saw him tremble. He looked as scared as a deer caught in a hunter's flashlight.

"I'm Cory Mackenson," I said. I stood there, waiting, with my fingers grasping the fence's mesh. "Don't you have a name?"

"Yeth," the boy answered.

I thought he'd said *Seth* at first, and then it dawned on me that he had a lisp. "What is it?"

"Nemo," he said.

"Nemo? Like Captain Nemo?"

"Huh?"

A student of Jules Verne he was not. "What's your last name?"

"Curlith," he said.

132

Curlith. It took me a few seconds to decipher it. Not Curlith, but Curliss. The new boy in town, the one who had a traveling salesman as a father. The boy who sat on the horse to get his hair cut at Mr. Dollar's. The pansy.

Nemo Curliss. Well, the name suited him. He looked like something a net might drag up from twenty thousand leagues. But my parents had taught me that everybody deserved respect, no matter if they were pansies or not, and to tell the truth, I was nothing to write home about in the physical looks department. "You're new in town," I offered.

He nodded.

"Mr. Dollar told me about you."

"He did?"

"Yeah. Said"—*you sat on the horse*, I almost told him "you got a haircut."

"Uh-huh. 'Bout thaved me baldheaded," Nemo said, and he scratched the top of his scalp with a thin-fingered hand attached to a white, bony wrist.

"Heads up, Cory!" I heard Davy shout. I looked up. Johnny had put all his strength into a fly ball that not only overshot Davy's glove, but cleared the fence, banged against the second row of bleachers, and rolled down to the bottom.

"Little help!" Davy said, smacking his glove with his fist.

Nemo Curliss walked down from the top and picked up the ball. He was the littlest runt I think I'd ever seen. My own arms were skinny, but his were all bones and veins. He looked at me, his dark brown eyes magnified owlish by his glasses. "Can I throw it back?" he asked.

I shrugged. "I don't care." I turned toward Davy, and maybe it was mean but I couldn't suppress a wicked smile. "Comin' at you, Davy."

"Oh, wow!" Davy started backing up in mock terror. "Don't scorch me, kid!"

Nemo walked up to the top bleacher again. He squinted toward the field. "You ready?" he yelled.

"I'm ready! Throw it, big hoss!" Davy answered.

"No, not you," Nemo corrected him. "That other guy out there." And then he reared back, swung his arm in a circle that was impossible for the eye to follow, and the ball left his hand in a white blur.

I heard the ball hiss as it rose into the sky, like a firecracker on a short fuse.

Davy cried out, "Hey!" and backpedaled to get it, but the ball was over him and gone. Beyond Davy, Johnny looked up at the falling sphere and took three steps forward. Then two steps back. One more step back, to where he'd been standing when the ball was thrown. Johnny lifted his hand and held his glove out in front of his face.

There was a sweet, solid *pop* as the ball kissed leather.

"Right in the *pocket!*" Davy shouted. "Man, did you see that thing fly?"

Out toward first base, Johnny removed his glove and wrang his catching hand, his fingers stinging with the impact.

I looked at Nemo, my mouth agape. I couldn't believe anybody as little and skinny as him could throw a baseball over the bleachers fence, much less half the width of the field and into an outstretched glove. What's more, Nemo didn't even act as if it had hurt his arm, and a heave like that would've left my shoulder sore for a week, even if I could've gotten that kind of distance out of it. It was a major league throw if I'd ever seen one. "Nemo!" I said. "Where'd you learn to throw a ball like that?"

He blinked at me behind his glasses. "Like what?" he asked.

"Come down here. Okay?"

"Why?" Nemo looked scared again. I had the feeling that he was well acquainted with the bad end of the stick. There are three things every town in the country has in common: a church, a secret, and a bully ready to tear the head off a skinny kid who couldn't fight his way out of a paper bag. I imagined that Nemo Curliss, in following his salesman daddy from town to town, had seen his share of those. I felt ashamed for my wicked smile. "It's all right," I said. "Just come on down."

"Man, what a throw!" Davy Ray Callan, having retrieved the ball from Johnny, jogged up to where Nemo was entering the field through the players' gate. "You really nailed it in there, kid! How *old* are you?"

"Nine," was the answer. "Almost nine and a half."

I could tell Davy was as puzzled as I was about Nemo's size; there should have been no way on earth for a runt like that to drill a baseball into a mitt as he had. "Go stand on second base, Johnny!" I shouted, and Johnny waved and ran over to take the position. "You want to throw some, Nemo?"

"I don't know. I'm thaposed to be gettin' home thoon."

"It won't take long. I'd kinda like to see what you can do. Davy, can he wear your glove?"

Davy took it off. The glove swallowed Nemo's left hand like a brown whale. "Why don't you stand on the pitcher's mound and throw Johnny a few?" I suggested.

Nemo looked at the pitcher's mound, at second base, and then at home plate. "I'll thand right there," he said, and he walked to the batter's box while Davy and I stood dumbfounded. From home plate to second base was quite a toss for guys our age, much less anybody nine-and-a-half years old. "You sure, Nemo?" I asked, and he said, "Thure."

Nemo took the ball out of the glove with what might have been reverence. I watched his long fingers work around it, find a grip on the seams, and fasten themselves. "Ready?" he called.

"Yeah, I'm ready! Let 'er ri—"

Smack!

If we hadn't seen such a thing with our own eyes, none of us would ever have believed it. Nemo had wound up and pitched in a heartbeat, and if Johnny hadn't been extra quick, the ball would've caught him right in the center of his chest and knocked him flat. As it was, the sheer power of the pitch made Johnny stagger back off second base, dust smoking from the ball in his clenched glove. Johnny began to walk around in a circle, his face pinched with pain.

"You okay?" Davy shouted.

"Hurts a little," Johnny answered. Davy and I knew it must be bad for Johnny to admit it. "I can take another one." We were too far away to hear him say, under his breath, *"I hope."* He threw the ball back in a high arc to Nemo, who stepped forward six paces, watched the ball speed downward toward his face, and plucked it out of the air at the very last second. The kid knew what economy of movement was all about, but I swear he'd been an instant away from a smashed nose.

Nemo returned to the plate. He wiped dust off the tops of his brown loafers by rubbing them on the backs of his jeans legs. He started to wind up, and Johnny braced for the throw. Nemo unwound and put the ball back in his glove. "Throwin' ain't nothin'," he told us, as if all this attention embarrassed him. "Anybody with an arm can do it."

"Not like that!" Davy Ray said.

"You guyth think thith is a *big deal* or thomethin'?"

"It's fast," I said. "Real fast, Nemo. The pitcher on our team's not even as fast, and he's twice your size."

"Thith ith eathy thuff." Nemo looked out at Johnny. "Run for turd bayth!"

"What?"

"Run for turd bayth!" Nemo repeated. "Hold your glove anywhere, just keep it open and where I can thee it!"

"Huh?"

"Run as fath as you can!" Nemo urged. "You don't have to look at me, jutht keep your glove open!"

"Go ahead, Johnny!" Davy called. "Do it!"

Johnny was a brave fellow. He showed it right then, as he started pounding the dirt between second and third bases. He didn't look toward home, but his head and shoulders were pulled in tight and his glove was down in front of his chest, the pocket open and facing Nemo Curliss.

Nemo pulled in a quick breath. He drew back, his white arm flashed, and the ball went like a bullet.

Johnny was going full out, his gaze fixed on third base. The ball popped into his glove when he was still a half-dozen steps from third, and the feel of it wedging solidly into the pocket was so startling that Johnny lost his balance and went down on the ground in a slide that boiled up yellow dust. When the dust began to clear, Johnny was sitting on third base staring at the ball in his glove. "Wow," he said, stunned. "Wow."

I had never in my life seen a baseball thrown with such amazing accuracy. Johnny hadn't even had to reach an inch for it; in fact, he hadn't even known the ball was coming until it hit him in the glove. "Nemo?" I said. "You ever pitched on a Little League team before?"

"Nope."

"But you've played ball before, haven't you?" Davy Ray asked.

"Nope." He frowned and pushed his glasses up with a finger because the bridge of his nose was getting slick with sweat. "My mom won't let me. Thays I might get hurt."

"You've *never* played ball on a team?"

"Well, I've got a ball and glove at home. Thometimeth I practith catchin' fly ballth. Thometimeth I thee how far I can throw. I thet up bottleth on a fence potht and knock 'em down. Thuff like that."

"Doesn't your dad want you to play ball?" I asked.

Nemo shrugged and scuffed the dust with the toe of his loafer. "He don't have much to thay about it."

I was struck with wonder. Standing before me, in the shape of a skinny little runt with thick glasses and a lisp, was a natural. "Will you pitch me a few?" I asked, and he said he would. I got Johnny's glove—which he gave up gladly from his sore hand—and I tossed the ball to Nemo. I ran to second base and planted myself. "Put it right here, Nemo!" I told him, and I extended my arm and held the mitt level with my shoulder. Nemo nodded, wound up, and let fly. I never had to move my hand. The ball smacked into the glove with a force that jangled the nerves all the way from my fingertips to my collarbone. When I threw it back, Nemo had to run forward and dart and weave to catch it. Then I backed up some more, out toward center field, where the weeds were sprouting. I lifted the mitt up over my head. "Right here, Nemo!"

Nemo crouched down, almost on his knees. His head was bent forward, as if he were trying to squeeze himself into a tight knot. He stayed that way for a few seconds, the sunlight glinting off his glasses, and then he exploded.

He flew up from his crouch like Superman bursting out of a phone booth. His throwing arm whipped back and then forward. If anybody's jaw had been caught by that flashing, bony elbow they'd have been spitting out a mouthful of broken teeth. The ball left Nemo's hand and it came at me like gangbusters.

It was a low ball, and it almost skimmed the dust between the batter's box and the pitcher's mound. But it was rising as it passed over the mound, and it seemed to be picking up speed, too. It was still rising as it zipped over second base. I heard Davy yelling at me, but I don't know what he was saying. My attention was riveted to that flying white sphere. I kept the glove up over my head, exactly where it had been when the ball was thrown, but I was prepared to duck to keep from getting plastered. The ball entered the outfield, and I could hear its hissing, full of steam and menace. I didn't move my feet. I had time to swallow—*gulp*—and then the ball was upon me.

It popped into the mitt's pocket, its impact strong enough to make me step back a couple of paces. I closed my hand around the ball, trapping it, and I could feel its heat throbbing like a pulse through the cowhide.

"Cory!" Davy Ray was shouting, his hands up to bracket his mouth. "Cory!"

I didn't know what Davy was hollering about, and I didn't care. I was in a trance. Nemo Curliss had an unearthly arm. How much of this had been a gift and how much he had trained himself to do, I didn't know, but one thing was clear: Nemo Curliss possessed that rare combination of arm and eye that elevated him above mere mortals. In other words, he was a humdinger.

"Cory!" This time it was Johnny yelling. "Look out!"

"What?" I called.

"Behind you!" Johnny screamed.

I heard a sound like scythes at work, slicing wheat. I turned around, and there they were.

Gotha and Gordo Branlin, grinning astride their black bicycles, their peroxided-yellow hair aflame with sunlight. They were coming at me through the knee-high grass beyond the mowed outfield, their legs pumping the pedals. Green grasshoppers and black field crickets leaped for their lives under the grinding wheels. I wanted to run, but my legs were locked up. The Branlins stopped with me between them, Gotha on my right and Gordo on my left. Sweat glistened on their angular faces, their eyes cutting into me. I heard a crow cawing somewhere, like the devil's laughter.

Gotha, the oldest at fourteen, reached out and prodded the baseball mitt with his index finger. "You playin' *ball,* Cory?" The way he said it, it sounded dirty.

"He's playin' *with* his balls," Gordo snickered. He was thirteen, and just a shade smaller than Gotha. Neither one of them were very big, but they were wiry and fast as whippets. Gordo had a little scar between his eyebrows and another on his chin that said he was no stranger to either pain or bloodshed. He looked toward home plate, where Davy, Johnny, and Nemo stood. "Who the *fuck* is that?"

"New kid," I said. "His name's Nemo."

"Asshole?" Gotha stared at Nemo, too, and I could see the wolfishness in the Branlins' faces. They smelled sheep's blood. "Let's go see Asshole," he said to Gordo, and started pedaling. Gordo hit the bottom of my mitt with his hand and made the ball jump out. As I bent over to pick it up, he spat a wad into my hair. Then he pedaled away after his brother.

I knew what was going to happen. It was bad enough that Nemo was so small and skinny, but when the Branlins heard that lisp, it was going to be all she wrote. I held my breath as the Branlins approached Rocket. As they passed, Gotha kicked Rocket to the ground with supreme indifference. I swallowed my rage like a bitter seed, not knowing that it would bear fruit.

The Branlins pulled their black bikes to a halt, with the three boys between them. "You guys playin' a game?" Gotha asked, and he smiled like the snake in the Garden of Eden.

"Just throwin' the ball around some," Davy Ray told him.

"Hey, niggerblood," Gordo said to Johnny. "What're you lookin' at?"

Johnny shrugged and stared at the ground.

"You smell like shit, you know that?" Gordo taunted.

"We don't want any trouble," Davy said. "Okay?"

"Who said anythin' about trouble?" Gotha uncoiled from his bike and stood up. He rested the bike on its kickstand and leaned against it. "We didn't say anythin' about trouble. Gimme a cigarette."

Gordo reached into a back pocket and gave his brother a pack of Chesterfields. Gotha produced a matchbook that had Zephyr Hardware & Feeds across the front. He put a cigarette into his mouth and held the matchbook out to Nemo Curliss. "Light one."

Nemo took it. His hands were trembling. It took him three scrapes to make the match flare.

"Light my cigarette," Gotha ordered.

Nemo, who perhaps had seen many other Gothas and Gordos in many other towns, did as he was told. Gotha drew in smoke and exhaled it through flared nostrils. "Your name's Asshole, ain't it?"

"My . . . name ith . . . Nemo."

"*Ith?*" Gordo sprayed spittle. "*Ith?* What's the matter with your mouth, Asshole?"

I was picking up Rocket from the grass. Here I faced a decision. I could get on Rocket and ride away, leaving my friends and Nemo Curliss to their fates, or I could join them. I was no hero, that's for sure. My fighting ability was a fantasy. But I knew that if I rode away from that place and point in time, I would be forever disgraced. Not that I didn't want to, and not that every fiber of good sense wasn't telling me to haul ass.

But some good sense you listen to, and some good sense you can't live with.

I walked toward a beating, my heart pounding on its root.

"You look like a queer," Gordo said to Nemo Curliss. "Is that what you are?"

"Hey . . . listen, guys." Davy Ray managed a frail smile. "Why don't you guys—"

Gotha whirled on him, took two strides, planted a hand on Davy's chest, and shoved him hard, knocking him to the ground by hooking a sneakered foot around Davy's ankle. Davy grunted as he hit, dust pluming up around him. Gotha stood over him, smoking the Chesterfield. "You," he said. "Just. Shut. Up."

"I've gotta get home." Nemo started to walk away, but Gordo grabbed his arm and held him.

"C'mere," Gordo said. "You don't wanna go nowhere."

"Yeah, I do, 'cauth my mom thays I've gotta—"

Gordo howled with laughter, the sound startling birds out of the trees around the field. "Listen to him, Gotha! He's got shit in his mouth!"

"I think he's been suckin' too many cocks," was Gotha's opinion. "Is that right?" He aimed his hard stare at Nemo. "You been suckin' too many cocks?"

What made the Branlins the way they were was anybody's guess. Maybe the meanness had been born in them; maybe it had developed, like the pus around a wound that will not heal. In any case, the Branlins knew no law but their own, and this situation was rapidly spiraling into the danger zone.

Gordo shook Nemo. "That right? You like to suck cocks?"

"No." Nemo's voice was choked.

"Yes he does," Gotha said, his shadow heavy across Davy Ray. "He likes to suck big fat donkey cocks."

"No, I don't." Nemo's chest shook, and the first sob squeezed out.

"Oh, momma's little baby's gonna cry now!" Gordo said, grinning.

"I . . . wanna go . . . home . . ." Nemo began to sob, the tears flooding up behind his glasses.

There is nothing more cruel in this world than a young savage with a chip on his shoulder and anger in his soul. It is worse still when there is a yellow stripe down his back, as evidenced by the fact that the Branlins never went after boys their age or older.

I looked around. A car was passing the field, but its driver paid us no notice. We were on our own out here, under the scorching sun.

"Put the baby down, Gordo," Gotha said. His brother shoved Nemo to the ground. "Feed the baby, Gordo," Gotha said, and Gordo unzipped his blue jeans.

"Hey, come on!" Johnny protested. "Don't!"

Gordo, holding his exposed penis, stood over Nemo Curliss. "Shut up, niggerblood, if you don't want some rain in your face, too."

I couldn't take any more of this. I looked at the baseball in my hand. Nemo was crying. Gordo was waiting for the water to flow. I just couldn't take it.

I thought of Rocket being kicked over. I thought of the tears on Nemo's face. I threw the baseball at Gordo from about ten feet.

It didn't really have a lot on it, but it made a solid *thunk* as it hit his right shoulder. He wailed like a bobcat and staggered away from Nemo just as his fountain arced. The urine wet the front of his jeans and ran down his legs, but Gordo was grasping his shoulder and his face was all screwed up and he was yelling and sobbing at the same time. Gotha Branlin turned toward me, the cigarette clenched between his teeth and smoke whirling from his mouth. His cheeks flamed, and he propelled himself at me. Before I could think to dodge, he rammed me full force. The next thing I knew I was flat on my back with Gotha sitting on top of me, his weight crushing my chest. "I . . . can't . . . I can't . . . breathe . . ." I said.

"Good," he said, and he hit me in the face with his right fist.

The first two punches hurt. Real bad. The next two about knocked me cold, but I was squirming and yelling and trying to get away, and the scarlet blood was all over Gotha's knuckles. "Ohhhhh shit, my arm's broke!" Gordo moaned, on his knees in the grass.

A hand grabbed Gotha's peroxided hair. Gotha's head was jerked back, the cigarette fell from his mouth, and I saw Johnny standing over him. Then Davy Ray said, "Hold him!" and he smashed his fist into Gotha's nose.

The lump of flesh burst open. Blood streamed from Gotha's nostrils, and Gotha roared like a beast and got off me. He attacked Davy Ray, hammering at him with his fists. Johnny went after him, trying to grab Gotha's arms, but Gotha twisted around and swung a blow that crunched against the side of Johnny's head. Then Gordo was up again, his face a blotched rictus of pure rage, and he ran in kicking at Johnny's legs. Johnny went down, and I saw a fist bust him right in the eye. Davy Ray shouted, "You bastards!" and flung himself at Gotha, but the older boy grabbed him by the collar and swung him around like a laundry bag before throwing him to the ground. I was sitting up, blood in my mouth. Nemo was up and running for his life, but he tripped over his own tangled legs and fell headlong into the grass.

What followed in the next thirty seconds I don't like to think about. First Gotha and Gordo left Davy Ray crumpled up and crying, and then they pounced on Johnny and worked him over with brutal precision. When Johnny was gasping for air, the blood bubbling from his nostrils, the Branlins advanced on me again.

"You little piece o' shit," Gotha said, his nose dripping. He put his foot on my chest and slammed me down on my back again. Gordo, still holding his shoulder, said, "Lemme have him."

I was too dazed to fight back. Even if I hadn't been dazed, I couldn't have done very much against those two without a spiked mace and a broadsword and fifty more pounds on my bones.

"Stomp his ass, Gordo," Gotha urged.

Gordo grabbed the front of my shirt and started to haul me to my feet. My shirt ripped, and I remember thinking that Mom was going to tear me up.

"I'll kill you," somebody said.

Gotha laughed like a bark. "Put it down, kid."

"I'll kill you, I thwear I will!"

I blinked, spat blood, and looked at Nemo Curliss, who stood fifteen feet away. The baseball was in his hand, his skinny arm cocked back.

Now, this was an interesting situation. I'd been lucky in hitting Gordo's shoulder; in Nemo's hand, however, that hard round sphere was a lethal weapon. I had no doubt that Nemo could hit either one of the Branlins right between the eyes and knock their brains out. I had no doubt, either, that he *would*. Because I saw his eyes magnified behind those glasses. The fury trapped in them, like a distant conflagration, was terrible to behold. He was no longer crying or trembling. With that baseball in his grip, he was the master of the universe. I really think he was ready to kill somebody. Maybe it was the rage at being born a runt, of having a lisp, of attracting bullies like a weak calf makes a predator's mouth water. Maybe he was full to the gullet with being shoved and taunted. Whatever it was, it was there like a deadly resolve in his eyes.

Gordo let me go. Lip-ripped and shirt-ripped, I sat in the grass.

"Look at me shake," Gotha said silkily as he took a step toward Nemo.

Gordo fanned out a few paces from his brother. His penis was still hanging out of his jeans. I wondered if that would make a good target. "Throw it, chickenshit," Gordo said.

A Branlin was very close to death.

"Hey, you boys! Hey, there!"

The voice came across the field at us, from the road that ran along its edge. "Hey, you boys all right?"

I turned my head, my face as heavy as a bag of stones. Parked on the roadside was a mailman's truck. The mailman himself was walking toward us, a pith helmet shading his face. He wore shorts with black socks, and sweat stains darkened his blue shirt.

Like any animals, the Branlins knew the sound of the hinge on a cage's lid. Without a word to each other, they turned away from the carnage they had created and ran to their bikes. Gordo hurriedly pushed his penis back in and zipped up his fly, then he swung himself up in the seat. Gotha paused to kick Rocket over again; I suppose the temptation to ruin was just too great. Then he got on his bike and the two brothers started pedaling frantically back the way they'd come. "Wait a minute!" the mailman shouted, but the Branlins listened only to their inner demons. They raced across the field, dust swirling up behind them, and then they hit the trails they'd carved through the brushy grass and were gone into the patch of woods that stood beyond. Some ravens screamed in there: scavengers, welcoming their own.

It was all over but the cleaning up.

Mr. Gerald Hargison, our mailman who delivered my monthly issue of *Famous Monsters* magazine in a plain brown envelope, reached me and stopped when he saw my face. "Good God!" he said, which told me it was bad. "*Cory?*"

I nodded. My lower lip felt as big as a goosedown pillow, and my left eye was swelling up.

"You okay, boy?"

I didn't feel like twirling a Hula Hoop, that's for sure. But I could stand up, and all my teeth were still in their sockets. Davy Ray was all right, too, except his face was a mass of bruises and one of the Branlins had stepped on his fingers. Johnny Wilson, however, had been the hardest hit. Mr. Hargison, who had a fleshy, ruddy-cheeked face and smoked plastic-tipped cheroots when he was walking his route, winced as he helped Johnny sit up. Johnny's Cherokee hatchet of a nose was broken, no doubt about it. The blood was dark red and thick, and Johnny's swollen eyes couldn't hold a focus. "Boy?" Mr. Hargison said to him. "How many fingers am I holdin' up?" He held up three, right in front of Johnny's face.

"Six," Johnny said.

"I believe he's got a—"

And here was a word that never failed to frighten, giving images of brain-damaged drooling.

"—concussion. I'm gonna take him to Doc Parrish. Can you two get home?"

Us *two?* I saw Davy Ray, but where was Nemo? The ball was lying on the ground next to home plate. The boy with the perfect arm was gone.

"Those were the Branlin brothers, weren't they?" Mr. Hargison helped Johnny stand, and he took a handkerchief from his shorts pocket and held it against Johnny's nostrils. In no time, the white was spotted with blood. "Those fellas need their butts kicked."

"You're gonna be all right, Johnny," I told him, but Johnny didn't answer me and he walked rubber-legged as Mr. Hargison led him to the truck. Davy and I stood watching as Mr. Hargison got him in and then went around and started the engine. Johnny leaned back in the seat, his head lolling. He'd been hurt bad.

After Mr. Hargison had turned the mail truck around and sped off in the direction of Dr. Parrish's office, Davy and I rolled Johnny's bike up under the bleachers, where it wouldn't be readily seen. The Branlins might come back and tear it to pieces before Johnny's dad could come get it, but it was the best we could do. Then it dawned on our foggy minds that the Branlins might be in the patch of woods still, where they'd been waiting for Mr. Hargison to leave.

That thought hurried us up some. Davy retrieved his baseball and got on his bike and I picked Rocket up again. I saw, for a brief instant, the golden eye in the headlight. It seemed to regard me with cool pity, same to say, *"You're* my new master? You're gonna need all the help you can get!" Rocket had had a rough first day, but I hoped we'd get along all right.

Davy and I pedaled away from the field, both of us hurting. We knew what was to come: horror from our parents, indignation at the Branlins, angry phone calls, probably a visit by the sheriff, an empty promise from Mr. and Mrs. Branlin that their boys would never, ever do anything like this again.

We knew better.

We had escaped the Branlins for now, but Gotha and Gordo held grudges. At any moment, they might swoop at us on their black bikes and finish what they'd started. Or what *I* had started, by throwing that danged baseball.

Summer had suddenly been poisoned by the Branlin touch. With July and August still ahead, we were not likely to have all our teeth by September.

4

I Get Around

Our predictions of the future were correct.

After the parental horror and the angry phone calls, Sheriff Amory made a call on the Branlins. He did not, as he told my dad, find Gotha and Gordo at home. But he told their parents that the boys had broken Johnny Wilson's nose and come close to fracturing his skull, and this was what Mr. Branlin replied, with a shrug: "Well, Sheriff, I kinda figure boys will be boys. Might as well learn 'em when they're young that it's a tough old world."

Sheriff Amory had clamped his anger down tight and stuck his finger in Mr. Branlin's rheumy-eyed face. "Now, you listen to me! You control those boys of yours before they end up in reform school! Either you do it or I will!"

"Don't matter none," Mr. Branlin had said as he sat in front of the television in a room where dirty shirts and socks were scattered around and Mrs. Branlin moaned about her bad back from the bedroom. "They ain't scared of me. Ain't scared of nobody on earth. They'd burn a reform school smack to the ground."

"You tell 'em to come see me, or I'll come here and get 'em!"

Mr. Branlin, probing his molars with a toothpick, had just grunted and shaken his head. "You ever try to catch the wind, J.T.? Them boys are free spirits." He had lifted his gaze from the Calling-for-Cash afternoon movie and stared up at the sheriff, the toothpick between his teeth. "Say my two sons beat the asses of *four* other boys? Sounds to me like Gotha and Gordo were fightin' in self-defense. They'd have to be crazy to pick a fight with four boys at once, don't you figure?"

"It wasn't self-defense, from what I've heard."

"From what I've heard"—Mr. Branlin paused to examine a brown glob on the end of his toothpick—"that Mackenson boy threw a baseball at Gordo and came near breakin' his shoulder. Gordo showed me the bruise, and it's as black as the ace of spades. Those people want to push this thing, I reckon I might have to press charges against that Mackenson kid." The toothpick and the brown glob went back into his mouth. He returned his attention to the movie, which starred Errol Flynn as Robin Hood. "Yeah, those Mackensons go to church all high-and-mighty, and they teach their kid to throw a baseball at one of my boys and then whimper and whine when he gets his clock cleaned." He snorted. "Some *Christians!*"

In this matter, though, Sheriff Amory prevailed. Mr. Branlin agreed to pay Dr. Parrish's bill and for the medicine Johnny was going to need. Gotha and Gordo had to sweep and mop the jail and couldn't go to the swimming pool for a week by order of the sheriff, which I knew, of course, simply stoked their rage at Davy Ray and me. I had to have six stitches to seal the gash on my lower lip—an experience almost as bad as getting the lip split in the first place—but Mr. Branlin refused to pay for it on account of my throwing the baseball at Gordo. My mother pitched a fury, but my father let it go. Davy Ray went to bed with an ice pack, his violet-bruised face looking like two miles of bad road. As I learned from my dad, Johnny's concussion was severe enough to put him on his back until Dr. Parrish gave him the green light, which might be a couple of weeks or more. Even when Johnny was back on his feet, he was not to do any running or roughhousing and he couldn't even ride his bike, which his father had rescued intact from beneath the bleachers. So the Branlins had done something even worse than beating us up: they'd stolen part of Johnny Wilson's summer away from him, and he would never again be twelve years old in June.

It was about this time that, sitting on my bed with my eyes puffed up and the curtains drawn against the stinging light, I put my stack of *Famous Monsters* magazines in my lap and began to cut out some of the pictures with scissors. Then I got a roll of Scotch tape and started taping the pictures up on my walls, on my desk, on my closet door, and just about anywhere that would hold adhesive. When I finished, my room was a monster museum. Staring down at me were Lon Chaney's Phantom of the Opera, Bela Lugosi's Dracula, Boris Karloff's Frankenstein and Mummy. My bed was surrounded by moody black and white scenes from *Metropolis, London after Midnight, Freaks, The Black Cat,* and *The House on Haunted Hill.* My closet door was a collage of beasts: Ray Harryhausen's Ymir battling an elephant, the monster spider stalking the Incredible Shrinking Man, Gorgo wading across the Thames, the scar-faced Colossal Man, the leathery Creature from the Black Lagoon, and Rodan in full flight. I had a special place above my desk—a place of honor, if you will—for Vincent Price's suave, white-haired Roderick Usher and Christopher Lee's lean and thirsty Dracula. My mother came in, saw what I had done, and had to hold on to the door's edge to keep from falling down. "Cory!" she said. "Take these awful pictures off the walls!"

"Why?" I asked her, my lower lip straining against its stitches. "It's my room, isn't it?"

"Yes, but you'll have nightmares with these things starin' at you all the time!"

"No I won't," I said. "Honest."

She retreated graciously, and the pictures stayed up.

I had nightmares about the Branlins, but not about the creatures who adorned my walls. I took comfort in the belief that they were my watchdogs. They would not allow the Branlins to crawl through my window after me, and they spoke to me in the quiet hours of strength and endurance against a world that fears what it does not understand.

I was never afraid of my monsters. I controlled them. I slept with them in the dark, and they never stepped beyond their boundaries. My monsters had never asked to be born with bolts in their necks, scaly wings, blood hunger in their veins, or deformed faces from which beautiful girls shrank back in horror. My monsters were not evil; they were simply trying to survive in a tough old world. They reminded me of myself and my friends: ungainly, unlovely, beaten but not conquered. They were the outsiders searching for a place to belong in a cataclysm of villagers' torches, amulets, crucifixes, silver bullets, radiation bombs, air force jets, and flamethrowers. They were imperfect, and heroic in their suffering.

I'll tell you what scared me.

One afternoon I picked up an old copy of *Life* from a stack of magazines Mom was about to throw out, and I sat on the porch and looked through it with Rebel sprawled beside me, the cicadas droning from the trees and the sky as still as a painting. In this magazine were photographs of what had happened in Dallas, Texas, in November of 1963. There were sunny pictures of the president and his wife in a long black convertible, and he was smiling and waving to the crowd. Then, in a blur, it all changed. Of course I had seen that guy Oswald get killed on television, and what I remembered about that was how small the shot had sounded, just a *pop* and not at all like the cannon booms of Matt Dillon's six-shooter on "Gunsmoke." I remembered how Oswald had cried out as he fell. I made a louder noise than that stubbing my toe on a rock.

As I looked at the photographs of President Kennedy's funeral— the riderless horse, the dead man's little boy saluting, rows of people standing to watch the coffin go past—I realized what to me was a peculiar and scary thing. In those pictures, you can see black pools spreading. Maybe it was just the light, or the film, or something, but those pictures seemed to me to be filling up with darkness. Black shadows hang in the corners; they spread tendrils across men in suits and weeping women, and they connect cars and buildings and manicured lawns with long fingers of shadow. Faces are shrouded with darkness, and it has gathered around people's shoes like ponds of tar. The darkness seems like a living thing in those pictures, something growing among the people like a virus and hungrily stretching right off the frame.

Then, on another page, there was a photograph of a man on fire. He is baldheaded and Oriental, and he wears the flames like a cloak as he sits cross-legged in the street. His eyes are closed, and though the fire is eating up his face he is as serene as my dad listening to Roy Orbison on the radio. The caption said this had happened in a city called Saigon, and the Oriental man was a monk who poured gasoline on himself, sat down, and lit a match.

And there was a third picture that haunts me yet. It shows a burned-out church, the stained-glass windows shattered and firemen picking through the ruins. A few black people are standing around, their expressions dull with shock. The trees in front of the church have no leaves on them, though the caption said this event happened on September fifteenth of 1963, before summer's end. The caption said this was what was left of the 16th Street Baptist Church in Birmingham, after somebody planted a bomb that went off as Sunday school was just letting out and four girls died in the blast.

I looked out, across my hometown. I looked at the green hills and the blue sky, and the distant roofs of Bruton. Beside me, Rebel whimpered in a dog's dream.

I never knew what hate really was until I thought of somebody wrapping up a bomb and putting it in a church on a Sunday morning to kill little girls.

I wasn't feeling very well. My head, still lumpy from Gotha Branlin's fist, was hurting. I went to my room and lay down, and there amid my monsters I fell asleep.

This was early summer in Zephyr: an awakening to hazy morning heat, the sun gradually burning the haze off and the air getting so humid your shirt stuck to your skin by the time you'd walked to the mailbox and back. At noon the world seemed to pause on its axis, and not a bird dared to wing through the steaming blue. As afternoon rambled on, a few clouds rimmed with purple might build up from the northwest. You could sit on the porch, a glass of lemonade at your side and the radio tuned to a baseball game, and watch the clouds slowly roll toward you. After a while you might hear distant thunder, and a zigzag of lightning would make the radio crackle. It might shower for thirty minutes or so, but most times the clouds just marched past with a rumble and grunt and not a drop of rain. As evening cooled the earth, the cicadas droned in their hundreds from the woods and lightning bugs rose from the grass. They got up in the trees and blinked, and they lit up the branches like Christmas decorations here on the edge of July. The stars came out, and some phase of the moon. If I played my cards right, I could talk my folks into letting me stay up late, like until eleven or so, and I would sit in the front yard watching the lights of Zephyr go out. When enough lights were extinguished, the stars became much brighter. You could look up into the heart of the universe, and see the swirls of glowing stars. A soft breeze blew, bringing with it the sweet perfume of the earth, and the trees rustled quietly in its passage. It was very hard, at times like this, not to think that the world was as well-ordered and precise as the Cartwright ranch on "Bonanza," or that in every house lived a "My Three

148

Sons" family. I wished it were so, but I had seen pictures of a spreading dark, a burning man, and a bomb-wrecked church, and I was beginning to know the truth.

I got to know Rocket better, when my folks would let me ride again. My mom told it to me straight: "You fall down and bust that lip open again, it's back to Dr. Parrish's and this time it'll be fifteen or *twenty* stitches!" I knew better than to push my luck. I stayed close to the house, and I pedaled Rocket around as gingerly as riding one of those swaybacked ponies that plods in circles at the county fair. Sometimes I thought I caught a glimpse of the golden eye in the headlamp, but it was never there when I looked directly at it. Rocket accepted my careful touch, though I sensed in the smoothness of the pedals and chain and the snap of the turns that Rocket, like any high-strung Thoroughbred, wanted to run. I had the feeling that I had a lot to learn yet about Rocket.

My lip healed. So did my head. My pride stayed bruised, though, and my confidence was fractured. Those injuries, the ones that didn't show, I would have to live with.

One Saturday my folks and I went to the public swimming pool, which was crowded with high-school kids. I have to tell you that it was for whites only. Mom jumped eagerly into the choppy blue water, but Dad took a seat and refused to leave it even when we both begged him to come in. I didn't think until later that the last time Dad had been swimming, he'd seen a dead man sink into Saxon's Lake. So I sat with him for a while as Mom swam around, and I had the opportunity to tell him for the third or fourth time about Nemo Curliss's throwing ability. This time, though, I had his undivided attention, because there was no television or radio nearby and he wanted to focus on something beside the water, which he seemed not to want to look at. He told me I ought to tell Coach Murdock about Nemo, that maybe Coach Murdock could talk Nemo's mother into letting him play Little League. I filed that suggestion away for later.

Davy Ray Callan, his six-year-old brother, Andy, and their mom and dad showed up at the pool in the afternoon. Most of the bruises had vanished from Davy's face. The Callans sat with my folks, and their talk turned to what ought to be done about the Branlin boys, that we weren't the only ones who'd been beaten up by that brood. Davy and I didn't especially want to relive our defeat, so we asked our folks for money to go get a milk shake at the Spinnin' Wheel and, armed with dollar bills, we headed off in our flipflops and sunburns while Andy squalled and had to be restrained from tagging after us by Mrs. Callan.

The Spinnin' Wheel was just across the street from the pool. It was a white-painted stucco building with white stucco icicles hanging from the roof's edge. A statue of a polar bear stood in front of it, adorned with such spray-painted messages as "Nobody Else Will Beat Our Score, We're The Seniors '64" and "Louie, Louie!" and "Debbie Loves Goober" among other declarations of independence. Davy and I guessed Mr. Sumpter Womack, who owned and managed the Spinnin' Wheel, thought that "Goober" was some guy's name. Nobody told him differently. The Spinnin' Wheel was what might be called a teen hangout. The lure of hamburgers, hot dogs, fries, and thirty different flavors of milk shakes—from root beer to peach—kept the parking lot full of high school guys and girls in their daddy's cars or pickups. This particular Saturday was no exception. The cars and trucks were packed in tight, their windows open and the radio music drifting out over the lot like sultry smoke. I recalled that I had once seen Little Stevie Cauley, in Midnight Mona, parked here with a blond girl who leaned her head against his shoulder, and Little Stevie had glanced at me, his hair coal black and his eyes as blue as swimming-pool water, as I'd walked past. I had not seen the girl's face. I wondered if that girl, whoever she had been, knew that Little Stevie and Midnight Mona now haunted the road between Zephyr and Union Town.

Davy, ever the daring one, bought a jumbo peppermint milk shake and got fifty cents back. He talked me out of getting plain vanilla. "You can get plain vanilla anytime!" he said. "Try . . ." He scanned the chalkboard that listed all the flavors. "Try peanut butter!"

I did. I have never been sorry, because it was the best milk shake I ever tasted, like a melted and frozen Reese's cup. And then it happened.

We were walking across the parking lot, under the burning sun, with our shakes freezing our hands in the big white paper cups that had Spinnin' Wheel in red across the sides. A sound began: music, first from a few car radios and then others as teenaged fingers turned the dial to that station. The volume dials were cranked up, and the music flooded out from the tinny speakers into the bright summer air. In a few seconds the same song was being played from every radio on the lot, and as it played, some of the car engines started and revved up and young laughter flew like sparks.

I stopped. Just couldn't walk anymore. That music was unlike anything I'd ever heard: guys' voices, intertwining, breaking apart, merging again in fantastic, otherworldly harmony. The voices soared up and up like happy birds, and underneath the harmony was a driving drumbeat and a twanging, gritty guitar that made cold chills skitter up and down my sunburned back.

"What's that, Davy?" I said. "What's that song?"

. . . Round . . . round . . . get around . . . wha wha whaoooooo. . . .

"What's that *song?*" I asked him, close to panic that I might never know.

"Haven't you heard that yet? All the high-school guys are singin' it."

. . . Gettin' bugged drivin' up and down the same ol' strip . . . I gotta find a new place where the kids are hip . . .

"What's the *name* of it?" I demanded, standing at the center of ecstasy.

"It's on the radio all the time. It's called—"

Right then the high-school kids in the lot started singing along with the music, some of them rocking their cars back and forth, and I stood with a peanut butter milk shake in my hand and the sun on my face and the clean chlorine smell of the swimming pool coming to me from across the street.

"—by the Beach Boys," Davy Ray finished.

"What?"

"The Beach Boys. That's who's singin' it."

"Man!" I said. "That sounds . . . that sounds . . ."

What would describe it? What word in the English language would speak of youth and hope and freedom and desire, of sweet wanderlust and burning blood? What word describes the brotherhood of buddies, and the feeling that as long as the music plays, you are part of that tough, rambling breed who will inherit the earth?

"Cool," Davy Ray supplied.

It would have to do.

. . . Yeah the bad guys know us and they leave us alone . . . I get arounnnnddddd . . .

I was amazed. I was transported. Those soaring voices lifted me off the hot pavement, and I flew with them to a land unknown. I had never been to the beach before. I'd never seen the ocean, except for pictures in magazines and on TV and movies. The Beach Boys. Those harmonies thrilled my soul, and for a moment I wore a letter jacket and owned a red hotrod and had beautiful blondes begging for my attention and I got around.

The song faded. The voices went back into the speakers. Then I was just Cory Mackenson again, a son of Zephyr, but I had felt the warmth of a different sun.

"I think I'm gonna ask my folks if I can take guitar lessons," Davy Ray said as we crossed the street. Git-tar, he pronounced it.

I thought that when I got home I would sit down at my desk and try to scratch out a story in Ticonderoga #2 about where music went when it got into the air. Some of it had gotten into Davy Ray, and he was humming that song as we returned to the pool and our parents.

The Fourth of July sizzled in. There was a big barbecue picnic in the park, and the men's team—the Quails—lost to the Union Town Fireballs by seven to three. I saw Nemo Curliss watching the game as he sat crushed between a brunette woman in a red-flowered dress and a gangly man who wore thick glasses and was sweating through his once-crisp white shirt. Nemo's father didn't spend much time with his son and wife. He got up after the second inning and walked off, and I later saw him prowling through the picnic crowd with a book full of shirt swatches and a desperate look on his face.

I had not forgotten about the man in the green-feathered hat. As I sat with my folks at a picnic table in the shade, munching barbecued ribs as the elderly men threw horseshoes and the teenaged guys heaved footballs, I scanned the crowd for that elusive feather. It dawned on me, as I searched, that the hats of winter had been put away, and every hat in evidence was made of straw. Mayor Swope wore a straw fedora as he moved through the throngs, puffing his pipe and glad-handing barbecue-sauced palms. Straw hats adorned the heads of Fire Chief Marchette and Mr. Dollar. A straw boater with a bright red band was perched on the bald skull of Dr. Lezander, who came over to our table to examine the scar's pale line on my lower lip. He had cool fingers, and his eyes peered into mine with steely intensity. "Those fellows ever cause you any more trouble," he said in his Dutch dialect, "you just let me know. I'll introduce them to my gelding clippers. Eh?" He nudged me with an elbow and grinned, showing his silver tooth. Then his heavyset wife, Veronica, who was also Dutch and whose long-jawed face reminded me of a horse, came up with a paper plate piled high with ribs and pulled Dr. Lezander away. Mrs. Lezander was a cool sort; she didn't have a lot to do with any of the other women, and Mom told me that she understood Mrs. Lezander's older brother and his family had been killed fighting the Nazis in Holland. I figured something like that could hurt your trust in people. The Lezanders had escaped from Holland before the country had fallen, and Dr. Lezander himself had shot a Nazi soldier with a pistol as the man burst through the door of his house. This was a subject that fascinated me, since Davy Ray, Ben, Johnny, and I played army out in the woods, and I wanted to ask Dr. Lezander what war was really like but Dad said I was not to bring it up, that such things were best left alone.

Vernon Thaxter made an appearance at the picnic, which caused the faces of women to bloom red and men to pretend to be examining their barbecue with fierce concentration. Most people, though, acted as if Moorwood Thaxter's son was invisible. Vernon got a plate of barbecue and sat under a tree at the edge of the baseball field; he wasn't totally naked on this occasion, however. He was wearing a floppy straw hat that made him look like a happily deranged Huckleberry Finn. I believe Vernon was the only man Mr. Curliss didn't approach with his shirt sample book.

During the afternoon I heard the Beach Boys' song several times from transistor radios, and every time it seemed better than the last. Dad heard it and wrinkled his nose as if he'd smelled sour milk and Mom said it made her ears hurt, but I thought it was great. The teenagers sure went wild over it. Then, as it was playing for about the fifth time, we heard a big commotion over where some high school guys were throwing a football not far from us. Somebody was bellowing like a mad bull, and Dad and I pushed through the gawkers to see what it was all about.

And there he was. All six-foot-six of him, his curly red hair flying around his head and his long, narrow face pinched even tighter with righteous rage. He wore a pale blue suit with an American flag pin on his lapel and a small cross above it, and his polished black size-fourteen wingtips were stomping the devil out of a little scarlet radio. "This. Has. Got. To. Cease!" he bellowed in time with his stomps. The guys who'd been playing football just stared at the Reverend Angus Blessett in open-mouthed amazement, and the sixteen-year-old girl whose radio had just been busted to splinters was starting to cry. The Beach Boys had been silenced under the boot, or, in this case, the wingtip. "This Satan's squallin' has got to cease!" Reverend Blessett of the Freedom Baptist Church hollered to the assembled throng. "Day and night I hear this trash, and the Lord has moved me to strike it down!" He gave the offending radio a last stomp, and wires and batteries flew from the wreckage. Then Reverend Blessett looked at the sobbing girl, his cheeks flushed and sweat glistening on his face, and he held out his arms and approached her. "I love you!" he yelled. "The Lord loves you!"

She turned and fled. I didn't blame her. If I'd had a nifty radio smashed right in front of me, I wouldn't feel like hugging anybody either.

Reverend Blessett, who'd been embroiled last year in a campaign to ban the Lady's Good Friday ritual at the gargoyle bridge, now turned his attention to the onlookers. "Did you see that? The poor child's so confused she can't recognize saint from sinner! You know why? 'Cause she was listenin' to that wailin', unholy *trash!*" He aimed a finger at the dead radio. "Have any of you bothered to listen to what's fillin' our children's ears this summer? Have you?"

"Sounds like bees swarmin' on a donkey to me!" somebody said, and people laughed. I looked over and saw Mr. Dick Moultry's sweat-wet bloat, the front of his shirt splotched with barbecue sauce.

"Laugh if you want to, but before God it's no laughin' matter!" Reverend Blessett raged. I don't think I ever heard him speak in a normal voice. "You give that song one listen, and the very hairs will rise up on the back of your necks just like it did on mine!"

"Aw, come on, Reverend!" My father was smiling. "It's just a song!"

"Just a *song?*" Reverend Blessett's shiny face was suddenly up in my dad's, and his ash-colored eyes were wild under eyebrows so red they looked painted on. "Just a *song*, did you say, Tom Mackenson? What if I was to tell you this 'just a song' was makin' our young people itch with immorality? What if I was to tell you it preaches illicit sexual desires, hotrod racin' in the streets, and big-city evil? What would you say then, Mr. Tom Mackenson?"

Dad shrugged. "I'd say that if you heard all that in one listen, you must have ears like a hound dog. I couldn't understand a single word of it."

"Ah-ha! Yes! See, that's Satan's trick!" Reverend Blessett stabbed my father's chest with an index finger that had barbecue sauce under the nail. "It gets into our children's heads without them even knowin' what they're hearin'!"

"Huh?" Dad asked. By this time Mom had come up beside us and was holding on to Dad's arm. Dad had never cared much for the reverend, and maybe she was afraid he might blow his top and take a swing.

Reverend Blessett retreated from my father and surveyed the crowd again. If there's anything that pulls people in, it's a loud-mouth and the smell of Satan in the air like charred meat on a griddle. "You good folks come to the Freedom Baptist Church at seven o'clock on Wednesday night and you'll hear for yourselves exactly what I'm talkin' about!" His gaze skittered from face to face. "If you love the Lord, this town, and your children, you'll break any radio that plays that Satan-squallin' garbage!" To my dismay, several people with dazed eyes hollered that they would. "Praise God, brothers and sisters! Praise God!" Reverend Blessett waded through the crowd, slapping backs and shoulders and finding hands to shake.

"He got sauce on my shirt," Dad said, looking down at the stain.

"Come on, fellas." Mom pulled at him. "Let's get under some shade."

I followed them, but I looked back to watch Reverend Blessett striding away. A knot of people had closed around him, all of them jabbering. Their faces seemed swollen, and a dark sweat stain the shape of a watermelon wedge had grown on the back of the reverend's coat. I couldn't figure this out; the same song I'd first heard that day in the Spinnin' Wheel's parking lot was *unholy?* I didn't know very much about big-city evil, but I didn't itch with immorality. It was just a cool song, and it made me feel . . . well, cool. Even after all the listenings, I still couldn't decipher what the chorus was after the *I get around* part, and neither could Ben, Davy Ray, or Johnny, who still had a wrapping of bandages across his beak and couldn't yet leave his house. I was curious; what had Reverend Blessett heard in the song that I had not?

I decided I wanted to find out.

That night fireworks blossomed red, white, and blue over Zephyr.

And sometime after midnight, a cross was set afire in front of the Lady's house.

5

Welcome, Lucifer

I awakened with the smell of burning in my nostrils.

Birds were singing and the sun was up, but I was reminded of a terrible thing. Three years ago, a house two blocks south of us had caught fire. It had been a hot, dry summer, and the house had gone up quick as pineknot kindling in the middle of an August night. The Bellwood family had lived there: Mr. and Mrs. Bellwood, their ten-year-old daughter Emmie, and their eight-year-old son Carl. The fire, which had started from a bad electrical connection, had consumed Carl in his bed before the Bellwoods could get to him. Carl died a few days later, and was buried on Poulter Hill. His tombstone had Our Loving Son carved on it. The Bellwoods had moved away soon after, leaving their son in Zephyr earth. I remember Carl clearly, because his mother was allergic to animals and wouldn't allow him to have a dog, so he sometimes came up to my house to play with Rebel. He was a slight boy with curly, sandy-colored hair and he liked the banana Popsicles the Good Humor man sold from his truck. He told me once that he wished he could have a dog more than anything in the world. Then the fire took him away, and Dad sat down with me and said God has a plan but sometimes it's awfully hard to decipher.

On this particular morning, the fifth of July, Dad had gone to work and Mom was left to tell me what that burning smell was. She'd been on the phone most of the morning, wired into Zephyr's amazingly accurate information network: the society of women who circled gossip like hawks for the meat of truth. As I ate my breakfast of scrambled eggs and grits, Mom sat with me at the table. "You know what the Ku Klux Klan is, don't you?" she asked.

I nodded. I had seen Klansmen on the TV news, dressed in their white robes and conical hoods and walking around a fiery cross while they cradled shotguns and rifles. Their spokesman, a gent who had pulled his hood back to expose a face like a chunk of suet, had been talking about keeping your heart in Dixie or getting your ass out and "not lettin' no Washington politician say I gotta kiss a colored boy's shoes." The rage in the man's face had swollen his cheeks and puffed his eyelids, and behind him the fire had gnawed at the cross as the white-robed figures continued their grim parade.

"The Klan burned a cross in the Lady's yard last night," Mom said. "They must be warnin' her to get out of town."

"The Lady? *Why?*"

"Your father says some people are afraid of her. He says some people think she's got too much say-so about what goes on in Bruton."

"She *lives* in Bruton," I said.

"Yes, but some people are scared she wants to have say-so about what goes on in Zephyr, too. Last summer she asked Mayor Swope to open the swimmin' pool to the Bruton folks. This year she's been askin' him about it again."

"Dad's afraid of her, isn't he?"

Mom said, "Yes, but that's different. He's not afraid of her because of her skin color. He's afraid because . . ." She shrugged. "Because of what he doesn't understand."

I swirled my fork around in my grits, thinking this point over. "How come Mayor Swope won't open up the pool to them?"

"They're *black*," Mom answered. "White people don't like to be in the water with black people."

"We were in the flood water with them," I said.

"That was river water," Mom said. "The swimmin' pool's never been open to them. The Lady's gotten a petition up that says she either wants a pool built in Bruton or the Zephyr pool open for black people. That must be why the Klan wants her gone."

"She's always lived there. Where would she go?"

"I don't know. I don't think the people who set that cross on fire care much, either." Mom frowned, the little lines surfacing around her eyes. "I didn't know the Klan was even anywhere around Zephyr. Your father says they're a bunch of scared men who want to turn time backward. He says things are gonna get a lot worse before they get better."

"What'll happen if the Lady won't leave?" I asked. "Would those men hurt her?"

"Maybe. They might try, at least."

"She won't go," I said, remembering the cool green-eyed beauty I'd seen looking back at me from behind the Lady's wrinkled face. "Those men can't make her leave."

"You're right about that." Mom got up from her chair. "I'd hate to get on her wrong side, that's for sure. You want another glass of orange juice?"

I told her no. As Mom was pouring one for herself, I finished off my eggs and then said something that caused her to look at me as if I'd just requested money for a trip to the moon. "I want to go hear what Reverend Blessett has to say." She remained speechless. "About that song," I continued. "I want to know why he hates it so much."

"Angus Blessett hates *everything*," Mom said when she had recovered her voice. "He can see the end of the world in a pair of penny loafers."

"That's my favorite song. I want to find out what he can hear in it that I don't."

"That's easy. He's got old ears." She offered a faint smile. "Like me, I guess. I can't abide that song, either, but I don't think there's anythin' evil about it."

"I want to know," I persisted.

For me this was a first. I had never been so adamant about attending church before, and it wasn't even our congregation. When Dad got home, he tried his best to talk me out of it, by saying that

157

Reverend Blessett was so full of hot air he could blow up a blimp, that he wouldn't even think about crossing the threshold of Reverend Blessett's church, and so on, but, at last—after a hushed conference with Mom in which I overheard the words "curiosity" and "let him find out for himself"—Dad grudgingly agreed to go with us on Wednesday night.

And so it was that we found ourselves sitting with about a hundred other people in the sweltering hotbox of the Freedom Baptist Church on Shawson Street near the gargoyle bridge. Neither Dad nor I wore a coat and tie, as this was not a Sunday service, and some of the other men even wore their field-stained overalls. We saw a lot of people we knew, and before the service began the place was standing room only, including a lot of sullen teenagers who looked as if they'd been dragged into the church on nooses by their cheerless parents. I guess the reverend's urgent hollering had gotten his message across, as had the signs he'd posted all over town that proclaimed he would be "wrestling with the devil on Wednesday night—our children are worth the fight." A record player and speakers had been set up at the front of the church, and at long last Reverend Blessett—flush-faced and sweating in a white suit and a rose-colored shirt—strode out onto the podium with the offending 45 rpm disc of black vinyl in one hand. In the other he held the leather grip of a wooden box with small holes on its sides, which he placed on the floor out of the way. Then he grinned at his audience and hollered, "Are we ready to fight Satan tonight, brothers and sisters?"

Amen! they shouted back. *Amen!* and *Amen!*

They were ready, all right.

Reverend Blessett began with an impassioned sermon about how the evils of the big city were creeping into Zephyr, how Satan wanted to drag all the young people into hell and how the citizens had to fight the devil every minute of their lives to keep from being fried in fire. Reverend Blessett's face sweated and his arms flew this way and that and he paced back and forth before the congregation like a man possessed. I have to say, he put on a great show and I was more than half convinced Satan was hiding under my bed waiting for me to open a *National Geographic* to one of the naked-bosom pictures.

He stopped pacing and grinned out at us with his glistening face. The doors had been propped open, but the heat was stifling and the sweat was sticking my shirt to my skin. In the hazy golden light, Reverend Blessett was steaming. He held up the record. "You came to hear it," he said. "And hear it you shall."

He switched on the record player, put the disc down on its thick spindle, and held the needle over the first groove. "Listen," he said, "to the voices of the demons." Then he lowered the needle, and a static of scratches clicked through the speakers.

Those voices. Demons or angels? Oh, those voices! *Round round get around I get around. Way out of town. I get around.*

"Did you hear it?" He jerked the needle up. "Right there! Tellin' our children that the grass is greener on the other side of the fence? That they're not to be satisfied livin' in their own hometown anymore? It's devil's wanderlust they're singin' about!" Again the needle went down. When the song reached the part about having a car that's never been beat and never missing yet with the girls we meet, Reverend Blessett was almost dancing with delirious rage. "Hear it? Doesn't that tell our young people to race their cars in the streets? Doesn't it tell them to indulge in free and easy pleasures of the *flesh?*" He said it like a sneer. "Think of it, folks! Your sons and daughters inflamed by this garbage, and Satan just a-laughin' at us all! Picture our streets runnin' red with the blood of our children in wrecked hotrods, and your pregnant daughters and sex-mad sons! You think such things happen only in the big city? You think we here in Zephyr are *safe* from the prince of darkness? You listen to some more of this so-called 'music' and you'll find out how wrong you are!" He let the needle play some more. The sound wasn't very good. I think Reverend Blessett himself had listened to the song a few dozen times, judging from all the scratches. I don't care what he said; the music was about freedom and happiness, not about crashing cars in the streets. I didn't hear the song like Reverend Blessett did. To me it was the sound of summer, a slice of heaven on earth; to him it was all stinking brimstone and the devil's leer. I had to wonder how a man of God like he was could hear Satan's voice in every word. Wasn't God in control of everything, like the Bible said? If God was, then why was Reverend Blessett so scared of the devil?

"Heathen trash!" he roared at the part of the record where the Beach Boys sang about not leaving their best girl home on a Saturday night. "Sex garbage! God help our daughters!"

"The man," my father said as he leaned toward Mom, "is as crazy as a one-legged toad-frog."

As the song played, Reverend Blessett raged on about disrespect for the law and the destruction of the family, about Eve's sin and the serpent in the Garden of Eden. He was spouting spittle and flinging sweat, and his face got so red I feared he was going to explode at the seams. "The Beach Boys!" he said with another ferocious sneer. "You know what those are? They're bums who wouldn't know a good day's work if you handed 'em a hoe and paid 'em fifty dollars! They lay around all day out there in California and fornicate in the sand like wild beasts! And *this* is what our young people are listenin' to day and night? God help this world!"

"Amen!" somebody shouted. The crowd was getting worked up. "Amen, brother!" another voice yelled.

"You ain't heard nothin' yet, my friends!" Reverend Blessett hollered. He picked up the needle, put his hand flat against the record to keep it from turning, and as the player's gears whined in protest, he searched for a groove on the disc. "Listen to this!" He disengaged the gears, and he lowered the needle while his other hand rotated the record backward.

What came out, in a slow groan, was: *Daaadeelsmaaastraaabaaaa.*

"Hear it? Hear it?" The reverend's eyes glittered with triumph; he had unlocked the mystery at the music's heart. "The devil is my strawberry! That's what they said! Clear as a bell! They're singin' a song in praise of Satan and they don't care who knows it! And this thing is goin' out on the radio waves all over the country right at this very minute! It's bein' played by our children and they won't even know what they're hearin' until it's too late and there's no turnin' back! It's the devil's plan to snare their souls!"

"I think they said the same thing about the Charleston," Dad said to Mom, but his was a small voice in the fevered chorus of amens.

This is the way the world spins: people want to believe the best, but they're always ready to fear the worst. I imagine you could take the most innocent song ever written and hear the devil speaking in it, if that's what your mind told you to listen for. Songs that say something about the world and about the people in it—people who are fraught with sins and complications just like the best of us—can be especially cursed, because to some folks truth is a hurtful thing. I sat in that church and heard the reverend rage and holler. I saw his face redden and his eyes gleam and the spittle spray from his mouth. I saw that he was a terrified man, and he was stoking the hot coals of terror in his congregation. He skipped the needle around, playing more snippets backward that to me sounded like gibberish but to him held satanic messages. It occurred to me that he must've spent an awfully long time huddled over that record player, scratching the needle back and forth in search of an evil thought. I wasn't sure he was trying to protect people as much as he was trying to direct them. In this latter area he was highly successful; soon he had most everybody yelling amens like the cheerleaders at Adams Valley High yelled for touchdowns. Dad just shook his head and crossed his arms, and I don't think Mom knew what to make of all this commotion.

Then, with sweat dripping from his chin and his eyes wild, Reverend Blessett announced, "Now we'll make the devil dance to his own tune, won't we?" He snapped the wooden box open, and from it jerked something that was alive and kicking. As the Beach Boys continued to croon, Reverend Blessett gripped a leash and made the creature on its other end start dancing crazily to the music.

It was a little spider monkey, all gangly arms and legs, its face spitting with fury as the reverend jerked its chain this way and that. "Dance, Lucifer!" the reverend shouted, his voice carrying over even those of the Californicators. "Dance to your music!" Lucifer, who had been cooped up in that cramped box for Lord knew how long, did not look too pleased. The thing hissed and snapped at the air, its tail flailing like a furry gray whip, and Reverend Blessett kept shouting, "Dance, Lucifer! Go on and dance!" as he wrenched the monkey back and forth on the end of its tether. Some people got up and started clapping and writhing in the aisle. A woman whose stomach looked as big as a sofa pillow got up on her tree-trunk legs and staggered around sobbing and calling for Jesus as if He were a lost puppy. "Dance, Lucifer!" the reverend yelled. I thought he was going to start swinging that poor monkey round and round his head like a rabbit's foot on a key chain. A man in the row in front of us spread his arms wide and started shouting something with *God* and *praise be* and *destroy the heathens* in it, and I found myself staring at the back of his sun-browned neck to see if I might find an alien X whittled there.

The place had turned into a madhouse. Dad reached for Mom's hand and said, "We're gettin' out of here!" People were gyrating and jiggling in rapturous ecstasies, and all this time I'd thought Baptists couldn't dance.

Reverend Blessett gave the monkey a ferocious shake. "Dance, Lucifer!" he commanded as the music thundered on. "Show 'em what's in you!"

And then, quite abruptly, Lucifer did just that.

The monkey shrieked and, obviously fed up with the shaking and jerking, sprang for the reverend's head. Those spidery arms and legs wrapped around the reverend's skull, and Reverend Blessett squalled with terror as Lucifer sank his sharp little fangs into the reverend's right ear. At the same time, Lucifer displayed exactly what he'd been fed up *on*, as from his rear end spewed a stream of foul matter as brown as Bosco all over the reverend's white suit. It was a sight that caused all rapture and speaking in tongues to immediately cease. The reverend was staggering around, trying to get that monkey off his head as Lucifer's bowels sprayed his suit with runny brown patterns. The woman with a sofa-pillow belly screamed. Some men in the front row ran to help the reverend, whose ear was being chewed ragged. As the men reached the struggling reverend and the gnawing monkey, Lucifer suddenly turned his head and saw the hands about to grab him, a bit of bloody ear gripped in his teeth. He released his grip from Reverend Blessett's skull and with a chattering screech he sprang over the men's heads, making them holler and duck as more Bosco streamed down upon them. The leash came loose from Reverend Blessett's hand, and Lucifer was free.

Like his nasty namesake, the monkey jumped from person to person, snapping at their ears and spraying their clothes. I don't know what the reverend had been feeding him, but it must have disagreed with Lucifer's stomach. Mom screamed and Dad dodged as Lucifer sprang past us, and we barely missed getting splashed. Lucifer leaped from the edge of a pew, swung on the light fixture, and then landed on a woman's blue hat, where he fertilized a false carnation. Then he was on the move again, paws and claws and whipping tail, snapping teeth, a shriek, a splatter. The smell of rotten bananas was enough to knock you to your knees. A brave Christian soldier made a try at grabbing the leash, but he got a wet brown face for his efforts and Lucifer made a noise like a laugh as the man staggered back, temporarily blinded, and his own wife fled from him. Lucifer sank his teeth into a woman's nose, anointed a teenaged boy's hair with brown slickum, and leaped from pew to pew like a demonic little version of Fred Astaire.

"Get him!" Reverend Blessett shouted, holding his bleeding ear. "Get that damn thing!"

A man did get a hand on Lucifer, but he jerked it back a second later with a fang-stung knuckle. The monkey was quick, and as mean as hell. Most everybody was too busy dodging the flying streams to think about catching Lucifer. I was belly-down on a pew, and Dad and Mom crouched in the aisle. Reverend Blessett yelled, "The doors! Somebody shut the doors!"

It was a good idea, but it came much too late. Lucifer was already in motion toward the way out, his beady little eyes glittering with delight. Behind him, he left his signature on the walls. "Stop him!" the reverend hollered, but Lucifer danced over a man's shoulder and swan-dived off a woman's head and with a screech of triumph he bounded through the open doorway into the night.

A few men ran out after him. Everybody else started breathing a lot easier, though the air wasn't fit to breathe. Dad helped Mom to her feet, and then he helped another two men pick up the fat lady, who had fainted and fallen like an oak tree. "Everybody stay calm!" the reverend said shakily. "It's all right now! Everything's all right!"

I wondered about a man who could say that when his ear was half chewed off and his white suit covered with monkey mess.

The sinful song we had all gathered to hear was forgotten. That seemed a minor thing now, in perspective. People started to get over their shock, and what took its place was indignation. Somebody hollered at Reverend Blessett that he shouldn't have let that monkey get loose, and somebody else said that he was sending his cleaning bill over first thing in the morning. The woman with the bitten nose squawked that she was going to sue. The voices rose and clamored, and I saw Reverend Blessett shrink back from them, all the power sucked out of him. He looked confused and miserable, just like everybody else.

The men who'd chased out after Lucifer returned, sweating and breathless. The monkey had scrambled up a tree and gone, they said. Maybe he'd turn up somewhere when it got light, they said. Then maybe they could snare him in a net.

People trying to snare Lucifer instead of Lucifer snaring people. That struck me as peculiar and funny at the same time, but Dad put a voice to the thought. "Dream on," he said.

Reverend Blessett sat down on the podium. He stayed there, in his fouled white suit, and he looked at his hands as his congregation left him. On the record player, the needle ticked . . . ticked . . . ticked.

We went home, through the humid summer night. The streets were quiet, but the symphony of insects droned and keened from the treetops. I couldn't help but think that from one of those trees Lucifer was watching. Now that he had gotten free, who could put him back in his box again?

I imagined I smelled the burning cross again, wafting its taint over my hometown. I decided it must be somebody cooking hot dogs over an open fire.

6

Nemo's Mother & A Week with the Jaybird

The summer moved on, as summers will.

Reverend Blessett tried to keep the furor going, but except for a few people who wrote to the *Journal* demanding that the song be banned from sale, the steam was gone from the reverend's engine. Maybe it had something to do with the long, lazy days of July; maybe it concerned the mystery of who had set that cross afire in the Lady's yard; maybe people had listened to that song for themselves and made up their own minds. Whatever the reason, folks in Zephyr seemed to have decided that Reverend Blessett's campaign was nothing but hot air. It ended with a slam when Mayor Swope visited his house and told him to stop scaring people into seeing demons that weren't anywhere but in the reverend's mind.

As for Lucifer, he was seen traveling in the trees by a half-dozen people. A banana cream pie cooling on a shady windowsill at the house of Sonia and Katharina Glass was utterly destroyed, and at any other time I'd have said the Branlins did it but the Branlins were lying low. Lucifer, on the other hand, was swinging high. An attempt was made by Chief Marchette and some of the volunteer firemen to snag Lucifer in a net, but what they got for their trouble was monkey business all over their clothes. Lucifer evidently had a sure aim and a steady spout, both front and rear. Dad said that was a pretty good defense mechanism, and he laughed about it, but Mom said the thought of that monkey loose in our town made her sick.

Lucifer stayed pretty much to himself during the day, but sometimes when night fell he shrieked and screamed loud enough to wake up the sleepers on Poulter Hill. On more than one occasion I heard the crack of gunshots as someone, roused from sleep by Lucifer's racket, tried to put a hole through him, but Lucifer was never there to catch a bullet. But the gunfire would wake up all the dogs and their barking would awaken the entire town and therefore the Zephyr council passed an emergency ordinance forbidding gunshots in the town limits after eight o'clock at night. Soon afterward, Lucifer learned how to clang sticks against trash cans, which he liked to do between three and six A.M. He avoided a bunch of poisoned bananas Mayor Swope laid out for him, and he shunned a trip-wire trap. He started leaving his brown mark on newly washed cars, and he swung down from a tree one afternoon and bit a plug out of Mr. Gerald Hargison's ear when the mailman was walking his route. Mr. Hargison told my dad about it as he sat for a moment on the porch and puffed a plastic-tipped cheroot, a bandage on his diminished left ear.

"Would've shot that little bastard if I'd had my gun on me," Mr. Hargison said. "He was a fast thing, I'll give him that. Bit me and took off and I swear I hardly saw him." He grunted and shook his head. "Hell of a note when you can't walk on a street in the daylight without gettin' attacked by a damn monkey."

"Maybe they'll catch him pretty soon," Dad offered.

"Maybe." Mr. Hargison puffed blue smoke and watched it drift away. "Know what I think, Tom?"

"What's that?"

"There's more to that damn monkey than meets the eye, that's what I think."

"How do you mean?"

"Well, consider this. How come that damn monkey stays around here in Zephyr? How come he don't go over into Bruton and cause trouble?"

"I don't know," Dad said. "I haven't thought about it."

"I think that woman's got somethin' to do with it."

"What woman, Gerald?"

"You know." He cocked his head toward Bruton. "*Her.* The queen over there."

"You mean the Lady?"

"Yeah. Her. I think she's whipped up some kind of spell and put it on us, because of . . . you know . . . the trouble."

"The burnin' cross, you mean."

"Uh-huh." Mr. Hargison shifted into the shadows, because the sun was hitting his leg. "She's workin' some of that hoodoo on us, is what I think. It's spooky, how come nobody can catch that damn monkey. Thing screamed like a banshee one night outside my bedroom window and Linda Lou about had a heart attack!"

"That monkey gettin' loose was Reverend Blessett's fault," Dad reminded him. "The Lady didn't have anythin' to do with it."

"We don't know that for sure, do we?" Mr. Hargison tapped ashes onto the grass, and then the cheroot's tip returned to his teeth. "We don't know what kind of powers she has. I swear, I believe the Klan's got the right idea. We don't need that woman around here. Her and her petitions."

"I don't side with the Klan, Gerald," Dad told him. "I don't go in for cross burnin's. That seems to me like a cowardly thing."

Mr. Hargison grunted quietly, a little plume of smoke leaking from his lips. "I didn't know the Klan was even active around here," he said. "But I've been hearin' things lately."

"Like what?"

"Oh . . . just talk. In my profession, you hear a lot of lips flap. Some folks around here think the Klan's mighty brave for sendin' a warnin' to that woman. Some folks think it's high time she got sent on her way before she ruins this town."

"She's lived here a long time. She hasn't ruined Zephyr yet, has she?"

"Up until the last few years she's kept her mouth shut. Now she's tryin' to stir things up. Colored people and white people in the same swimmin' pool! And you know what? Mayor Swope's just fool enough to give her what she wants!"

"Well," Dad said, "times are changin'."

"My Lord!" Mr. Hargison stared at my father. "Are you takin' *her* side, Tom?"

"I'm not takin' anybody's side. All I'm sayin' is, we don't need attack dogs and fire hoses and bombs goin' off here in Zephyr. Bull Connor's days are done. It seems to me that times are changin' and that's the way of the world." Dad shrugged. "Can't hold back the future, Gerald. That's a fact."

"I believe those Klan boys might argue the point with you."

"Maybe. But their days are done, too. All hate does is breed more hate."

Mr. Hargison sat in silence for a moment. He was looking toward the roofs of Bruton, but what he was seeing there was difficult to say. At last he stood up, picked up his mail satchel, and slung it over his shoulder. "You used to be a sane fella," he said, and then he began walking back to his truck.

"Gerald? Wait a minute! Come on back, all right?" Dad called, but Mr. Hargison kept going. My father and Mr. Hargison had gradu-ated in the same class from Adams Valley High, and though they weren't close friends, they had traveled the same road of youth together. Mr. Hargison, Dad had told me, used to quarterback the football team and his name was on a silver plaque on the high school's Honor Wall. "Hey, Big Bear!" Dad called, using Mr. Hargison's high school nickname. But Mr. Hargison flipped his cheroot stub into the gutter and drove away.

My birthday arrived. I had Davy Ray, Ben, and Johnny over for ice cream and cake. On that cake were twelve candles. And sometime during the cake-eating, Dad put my birthday present on my desk in my room.

Before I found it, Johnny had to go home. His head still hurt him sometimes, and he had dizzy spells. He had brought me two fine white arrowheads from his collection. Davy Ray had brought me an Aurora model of the Mummy, and Ben's gift was a bagful of little plastic dinosaurs.

But on my desk, with a clean sheet of white paper gripped in its roller, was a Royal typewriter as gray as a battleship.

It had some miles on it. The keys showed wear, and Z.P.L. was scratched on its side. The Zephyr Public Library, I later learned, had been selling some of their older equipment. The E key stuck, and the lower-case i was missing its dot. But I sat at my desk in the deepening twilight of my birthday, and I pushed aside my tin can full of Ticonderoga pencils and, heart pounding, laboriously typed out my name on the paper.

I had entered the technological age.

Soon enough I realized typing was going to be no simple task. My fingers were rebellious. I would have to discipline them. I kept practicing, long after the night had thickened and Mom said I ought to go to sleep. COERY JAT MACKEMAON. DAVY RSU CALKAN. JIHNMY QULSON. BEM SEARS. REBEL. OLF MOSES. THE LADT. BURNUNG CROSD. BRAMKINS. GREEN-FEATHRED HAT. ZEPHIR. ZEPHTR. ZEPHYR.

I had a long way to go, but I sensed the excitement of the cowboy heroes, Indian braves, army troops, detective legions, and monster squads within me, eager to be born.

One afternoon I was riding Rocket around, enjoying the steam that rose from a passing shower, and I found myself near the house where Nemo Curliss lived. He was out front, a small figure throwing a baseball up in the air and catching it as it hurtled down again. I eased Rocket onto its kickstand, and offered to throw him a few. What I really wanted was to see Nemo in action once more. A boy with a perfect arm, no matter how frail that arm might look, surely had been touched by God. Soon I was encouraging Nemo to aim for the knothole in an oak tree across the street, and when he zoomed that ball right in and made it stick not once but three times, I almost fell to my knees and worshipped him.

Then the front door of his house opened with the ringing of chimes and his mother came out onto the porch. I saw Nemo's eyes flinch behind his glasses, as if he were about to be struck. "Nemo!" she shouted in a voice that reminded me of the stinging wasp. "I told you not to throw that ball, didn't I? I've been watchin' you out the window, young man!"

Nemo's mother descended the porch steps and approached us like a storm. She had long, dark brown hair, and maybe she'd been pretty once but now there was something hard about her face. She had piercing brown eyes with deep lines radiating out from their corners, and her pancake makeup was tinted orange. She wore a tight pair of black pedal-pushers, a white blouse with big red polka dots, and on her hands were a pair of yellow rubber gloves. Her mouth was daubed crimson, which I found peculiar. She was all fancied up to do housework. "Wait'll your father hears about this!" she said.

Hears about *what?* I wondered. All Nemo was doing was playing outside.

"I didn't fall down," Nemo said.

"But you *could've!*" his mother snapped. "You know how fragile you are! If you broke a bone, what would we do? How would we pay for it? I swear, you're not right in the head!" Her eyes swept toward me like prison searchlights. "Who're *you?*"

"Coryth my friend," Nemo said.

"Friend. Uh-huh." Mrs. Curliss looked me over from head to foot. I could tell by the set of her mouth and the way her nose wrinkled that she thought I might be carrying leprosy. "Cory what?"

"Mackenson," I told her.

"Your father buy any shirts from us?"

"No, ma'am."

"*Friend,*" she said, and her hard gaze returned to Nemo. "I told you not to get overheated out here, didn't I? I told you not to throw that ball, didn't I?"

"I didn't get overheated. I wuth jutht—"

"Disobeyin' me," she interrupted. "My God, there's got to be some order in this family! There's got to be some *rules!* Your father gone all day and when he comes home he's spent more money than he's made and you're out here tryin' to hurt yourself and cause me more worry!'' The bones seemed to be straining against the taut flesh of her face, and her eyes had a bright and awful shine in them. ''Don't you know you're *sickly?*'' she demanded. ''Don't you know your wrists could snap in a hard breeze?''

''I'm all right, Momma,'' Nemo said. His voice was small. Sweat glistened on the back of his neck. ''Honetht.''

''You'd say that until you passed out with heatstroke, wouldn't you? And then you'd fall down and knock your teeth out and would your good friend's father pay for the dentist's bill?'' Again, she glared at me. ''Doesn't anybody wear nice shirts in this town? Doesn't anybody wear nice tailored white shirts?''

''No, ma'am,'' I had to say in all honesty. ''I don't think so.''

''Well, isn't that just *dandy?*'' She grinned, but there was no humor in it. Her grin was as hot as the sun and terrible to look upon. ''Isn't that just so very *civilized?*'' She grasped Nemo's shoulder with one of her yellow-gloved hands. ''Get in the house!'' she told him. ''This minute!'' She began to haul him toward the porch, and he looked back at me with an expression of longing and regret.

I had to ask. I just had to. ''Mrs. Curliss? How come you won't let Nemo play Little League?''

I thought she was going to go on in without answering. But suddenly she stopped just short of the porch steps and spun around and her eyes were slitted with rage. ''What did you say?''

''I . . . was askin' . . . how come you won't let Nemo play Little League. I mean . . . he's got a perfect ar—''

''My son is fragile, in case you didn't know! Do you understand what that word means?'' She plowed on before I could tell her I did. ''It means he's got weak bones! It means he can't run and rough-house like other boys! It means he's not a *savage!*''

''Yes ma'am, but—''

''Nemo's not like the rest of you! He's not a member of your tribe, do you understand that? He's a cultured boy, and he doesn't get down and wallow in the dirt like a wild beast!''

''I . . . just thought he might like—''

''Listen, here!'' she said, her voice rising. ''Don't you stand on my lawn and tell me what's right or wrong for my son! You didn't worry yourself crazy when he was three years old and he almost died of pneumonia! And where was his father? His father was on the road tryin' to sell enough shirts to keep us from bankruptcy! But we lost that house, that pretty house with the window boxes, we lost that house anyway! And would anybody help us? Would any of those churchgoin' people help us? Not a one! So we lost that house, where my pretty dog is buried in the backyard!" Her face seemed to shatter for an instant, and behind its brittle mask of anger I caught a glimpse of a heartbreaking fear and sadness. Her grip never left Nemo's shoulder. Then the mask sealed up again, and Mrs. Curliss sneered. "Oh, I know the kind of boy you are! I've seen plenty of you, in every town we've lived in! All you want to do is hurt my son, and laugh at him behind his back! You want to see him fall down and scrape his knees, and you want to hear his lisp because you think it's funny! Well, you can find somebody else to pick on, because my son's not having anythin' to do with you!"

"I don't want to pick on—"

"*Get in the house!*" she shouted at Nemo as she pushed him up the steps.

"I've gotta go!" Nemo called to me, trying desperately to keep his dignity. "I'm thorry!"

The screen door slammed behind them. The inner door closed, too, with a *thunk* of finality.

The birds were singing, stupid in their happiness. I stood on the green grass, my shadow like a long scorch mark. I saw the blinds on the front windows close. There was nothing more to be said, nothing more to be done. I turned around, got on Rocket, and started pedaling for home.

On that ride to my house, as the summer-scented air hit me in the face and gnats spun in the whirlwinds of my passage, I realized all prisons were not buildings of gray rock bordered by guard towers and barbed wire. Some prisons were houses whose closed blinds let no sunlight enter. Some prisons were cages of fragile bones, and some prisons had bars of red polka dots. In fact, you could never tell what might be a prison until you'd had a glimpse of what was seized and bound inside. I was thinking this over when Rocket suddenly veered to one side, narrowly missing Vernon Thaxter walking on the sidewalk. I figured even Rocket's golden eye had blinked at the sight of Vernon strolling in the sun.

July passed like a midsummer's dream. I spent these days doing, in the vernacular of my hometown, "much of nothin'." Johnny Wilson was getting better, his dizzy spells abating, and he was allowed to join Ben, Davy Ray, and me on our jaunts around town. Still and all, he had to take things easy, because Dr. Parrish had told Johnny's folks that a head injury had to be watched for a long time. Johnny himself was just as quiet and reserved as ever, but I noticed that he'd slowed down some. He was always lagging behind us on his bike, slower even than tubby Ben. He seemed to have aged since

170

that day the Branlins had beaten him senseless; he seemed to be apart from us now, in a way that was hard to explain. I think it was because he had tasted the bitter fruit of pain, and some of the magic carefree view that separates children from adults had fallen away from him, gone forever no matter how hard he tried to pedal his bike in pursuit of it again. Johnny had, at that early age, looked into the dark hole of extinction and seen—much more than any of us ever could—that someday the summer sun would not throw his shadow.

We talked about death as we sat in the cooling breezes from the ice house and listened to the laboring lungs of the frosty machines within. Our conversation began with Davy Ray telling us that his dad had hit a cat the day before, and when they got home part of the cat's insides were smeared all over the right front tire. Dogs and cats, we agreed, had their own kinds of heaven. Was there a hell for them, too? we wondered. No, Ben said, because they don't sin. But what happens if a dog goes mad and kills somebody and has to be put to sleep? Davy Ray asked. Wouldn't that be a hell-bound sin? For these questions, of course, we only had more questions.

"Sometimes," Johnny said, his back against a tree, "I get out my arrowheads and look at 'em and I wonder who made 'em. I wonder if their ghosts are still around, tryin' to find where the arrow fell."

"Naw!" Ben scoffed. "There's no such thing as ghosts! Is there, Cory?"

I shrugged. I had never told the guys about Midnight Mona. If they hadn't believed I'd shoved a broomstick down Old Moses's gullet, how would they believe a ghost car and driver?

"Dad says Snowdown's a ghost," Davy offered. "Says that's why nobody can shoot him, because he's already dead."

"No such thing as ghosts," Ben said. "No such thing as Snowdown, either."

"Yes there is!" Davy was ready to defend his father's beliefs. "My dad said Grandpap saw him one time, when he was a little kid! And just last year Dad said a guy at the paper mill knew a guy who saw him! Said he was standin' right there in the woods as big as you please! Said this guy took a shot at him, but Snowdown was runnin' before the bullet got there and then he was gone!"

"No. Such. Thing," Ben said.

"Is too!"

"Is not!"

"Is too!"

171

"Is not!"

This line of discussion could go on all afternoon. I picked up a pine cone and popped Ben in the belly with it, and after Ben howled in indignation, everybody laughed. Snowdown was a hope and mystery for the community of hunters in Zephyr. In the deep forest between Zephyr and Union Town, the story went, lived a massive white stag with antlers so big and twisted you could swing on them as on the branches of an oak. Snowdown was usually seen at least once every deer season, by a hunter who swore the stag had leaped into the air and disappeared in the gnarly foliage of its kingdom. Men went out with rifles to track Snowdown, and they invariably returned talking about finding the prints of huge hooves and scars on trees where Snowdown had scraped his antlers, but the white stag was impossible to catch. I think that if a massive white stag really did roam the gloomy woods, no hunter really wanted to shoot him, because Snowdown was for them the symbol of everything mysterious and unattainable about life itself. Snowdown was what lay beyond the thickness of the woods, in the next autumn-dappled clearing. Snowdown was eternal youth, a link between grandfather and father and son, the great expectations of future hunts, a wildness that could never be confined. My dad wasn't a hunter, so I wasn't as involved in the legend of Snowdown as Davy Ray, whose father was ready with his Remington on the first chilly dawning of the season.

"My dad's gonna take me with him this year," Davy Ray said. "He promised. So you'll be laughin' through your teeth when we bring Snowdown back from the woods."

I doubted that if Davy Ray and his father saw Snowdown, either one of them would pull a trigger. Davy had a boy-sized rifle that he sometimes fired at squirrels, but he never could hit anything with it.

Ben chewed on a weed and offered his throat to an ice house breeze. "One thing I sure would like to know," he said. "Who's that dead guy down at the bottom of Saxon's Lake?"

I pulled my knees into my chest and watched two ravens circling overhead.

"Ain't it *weird?*" Ben asked me. "That your dad saw the guy go under, and now the guy's down there in his car gettin' all mossy and eat up by turtles?"

"I don't know," I said.

"You think about it, don't you? I mean, you were *there.*"

"Yeah. I think about it some." I didn't tell him that hardly a day went by when I didn't think of the car speeding in front of the milk truck, or my dad jumping into the water, or the figure I'd seen standing in the woods, or the man with the green-feathered hat and a knife in his hand.

"It's spooky, for sure," Davy Ray said. "How come nobody knew the guy? How come nobody ever missed him?"

"Because he must not have been from here," Johnny commented.

"Sheriff thought of that," I said. "He called around other places."

"Yeah," Ben went on, "but he didn't call everywhere, did he? He didn't call California or Alaska, did he?"

"What would a guy from California or Alaska be doin' in *Zephyr*, dope?" Davy Ray challenged him.

"He could've been! You don't know everythin', Mr. Smart!"

"I know a big dope when I see one!"

Ben was about to fire a reply back, but Johnny said, "Maybe he was a spy," and that halted Ben's tongue.

"A spy?" I asked. "There's nothin' around here to spy on!"

"Yes there is. Robbins Air Force Base." Johnny systematically began to crack his knuckles. "Maybe he was a Russian spy. Maybe he was watchin' the planes drop bombs, or maybe there's somethin' goin' on over there that nobody's supposed to know about."

We were silent. A Russian spy killed in Zephyr. The thought gave all of us delicious creeps.

"So who killed him, then?" Davy Ray asked. "Another spy?"

"Maybe." Johnny contemplated this for a moment, his head slightly cocked to one side. The lid of his left eye had begun to tic a bit, another result of his injury. "Or maybe," he said, "the guy at the bottom of the lake is an American spy, and the Russian spy killed him because the dead guy found out about him."

"Oh, yeah!" Ben laughed. "So somebody around here might be a Russian spy?"

"Maybe," Johnny said, and Ben stopped laughing. Johnny looked at me. "Your dad said the guy was stripped naked, right?" I nodded. "Know why that might be?" I shook my head. "Because," Johnny said, "whoever killed him was smart enough to take the dead guy's clothes off so nothin' would float up to the top. And whoever killed him had to be from around here, because he knew how deep the lake is. And the dead guy knew a secret, too."

"A secret?" Davy Ray was all ears now. "Like what?"

"I don't know what," Johnny answered. "Just a secret." His dark Indian eyes returned to me. "Didn't your dad say the guy was all beat up, like somebody had really worked him over? How come whoever killed him beat him up so bad first?"

"How come?" I asked.

" 'Cause the killer was tryin' to make him talk, that's why. Like in the movies when the bad guy's got the good guy tied to a chair and he wants to know the secret code."

"What secret code?" Davy Ray asked.

"That's just for instance," Johnny explained. "But it seems to me like if a guy was gonna kill somebody, he wouldn't beat him up for no reason."

"Yeah, but maybe the dead guy was just plain beat to death," Ben said.

"No," I told him. "There was a wire around the guy's neck, chokin' him. If he'd been beat to death, why would he get choked, too?"

"Man!" Ben plucked up a weed and chewed on it. Overhead, the two ravens cawed and flapped. "A killer right here in Zephyr! Maybe even a Russian spy!" He stopped chewing all of a sudden. "Hey," he said, and he blinked as a new thought jabbed his mind like a lightning bolt. "What's to keep him from killin' again?"

I decided it was time. I cleared my throat, and I began to tell my friends about the figure I'd seen, the green feather, and the man in the green-feathered hat. "I didn't see his face," I said. "But I saw that hat and the feather, and I saw him pull a knife out of his coat. I thought he was gonna sneak up behind my dad and stab him. Maybe he tried to, but he figured he couldn't get away with it. Maybe he's steamed 'cause my dad saw the car go down and told Sheriff Amory about it. Maybe he saw *me* lookin' at him, too. But I didn't see his face. Not a bit of it."

When I'd finished, they didn't say anything for a few seconds. Then Ben spoke up: "How come you didn't tell us this before? Didn't you want us to know?"

"I was gonna tell you, but after what happened with Old Moses—"

"Don't start that bull again!" Davy Ray warned.

"I don't know who the man in the green-feathered hat is," I said. "He could be anybody. Even . . . somebody we all know real well, somebody you wouldn't think could do such a thing. Dad says you never know people through and through, and that everybody's got a part they don't show. So it could be anybody at all."

My friends, excited by this new information, flung themselves eagerly into the roles of detectives. They would agree to be on the lookout for a man in a green-feathered hat, but we also agreed to keep this knowledge to ourselves and not spread it to our parents, in case one of them happened to tell the killer without knowing it. I felt better for having relieved myself of this burden, yet I was still troubled. Who was the man Mr. Dollar said Donny Blaylock had killed? And what was the meaning of the piano music in the dream the Lady had told my mom about? Dad still refused to visit the Lady, and I still sometimes heard him cry out in his sleep. So I knew that even though that ugly dawn was long behind us, the memory of the event—and of what he'd seen handcuffed to the wheel— haunted him. If Dad went out walking at Saxon's Lake, he didn't tell me, but I suspected this might be true because of the crusty red dirt he left scraped on the porch steps on more than one afternoon.

August came upon us, riding a wave of sultry heat. One morning I awakened to the realization that in a few days I would be spending a week with Granddaddy Jaybird, and I immediately pulled the sheet over my head.

But there was no turning back the clock. The monsters on my walls could not help me. Every summer, I spent a week with Granddaddy Jaybird and Grandmomma Sarah whether I wanted to or not. Granddaddy Jaybird demanded it, and whereas I spent several weekends throughout the year with Grand Austin and Nana Alice, the visit with Granddaddy Jaybird was one lump sum of frenetic bizarrity.

This year, though, I was determined to strike a bargain with my folks. If I had to go to that farmhouse where Granddaddy Jaybird jerked the covers off me at five in the morning and had me mowing grass at six, could I at least go on an overnight camping trip with Davy Ray, Ben, and Johnny? Dad said he'd think about it, and that was about the best I could hope for. So it happened that I said good- bye to Rebel for a week, Dad and Mom drove me out from Zephyr into the country, my suitcase in the back of the truck, and Dad turned off onto the bumpy dirt road that led across a corn field to my grandparents' house.

Grandmomma Sarah was a sweet woman, of that there was no doubt. I imagine the Jaybird had been a rounder in his youth, full of vim and vigor and earthy charm. Every year, however, his bolts had gotten a little looser. Dad would say it right out: Jaybird was out of his mind. Mom said he was "eccentric." I say he was a dumb, mean man who thought the world revolved around him, but I have to say this as well: if it wasn't for the Jaybird, I would never have written my first story.

I never saw Granddaddy Jaybird perform an act of kindness. I never heard him praise his wife or his son. I never felt, when I was around him, that I was anything but a—thankfully temporary—

possession. His moods were as fleeting as the faces of the moon. But he was a born storyteller, and when he focused his mind on tales of haunted houses, demon-possessed scarecrows, Indian burial grounds, and phantom dogs, you had no choice but to willingly follow wherever he led.

The macabre, it may be said, was his territory. He was grave smart and life stupid, as he'd never gotten past the fourth grade. Sometimes I wondered how my dad had turned out as he had, having lived seventeen years in the Jaybird's strange shadow. As I've said, though, my grandfather didn't really start going crazy until after I was born, and I guess there were sensible genes on my grandmother's side of the family. I never knew what might happen during that week of suffering, but I knew it would be an experience.

The house was comfortable, but really nothing special. The land around it was, except for the stunted corn field, a garden and a small plot of grass, mostly forest; it was where the Jaybird stalked his prey. Grandmomma Sarah was genuinely glad to see us when we arrived, and she ushered us all into the front room, where electric fans stirred the heat. Then the Jaybird made his appearance, clad in overalls, and he carried with him a big glass jar full of golden liquid that he announced to be honeysuckle tea. "Been brewin' it for two weeks," he said. "Lettin' it mellow, ya see." He had mason jars all ready for us. "Have a sip!"

I have to say it was very good. Everybody but the Jaybird had a second glass of it. Maybe he knew how potent the stuff was. Within twelve hours, I would be sitting on the pot feeling as if my insides were flooding out, and at home Dad and Mom would be just as bad off. Grandmomma Sarah, who was surely used to such concoctions by now, would sleep like a log through the whole disgusting episode, except in the dead of night she was liable to make a high, banshee keening noise in her sleep that was guaranteed to lift the hair right off your scalp.

Anyway, the time came when Dad and Mom had to be getting back to Zephyr. I felt my face sag, and I must've looked like a wounded puppy because Mom put her arm around me on the porch and said, "You'll be all right. Call me tonight, okay?"

"I will," I vowed, and I watched them as they drove away. The dust settled over the brown cornstalks. Just one week, I thought. One week wouldn't be so bad.

"Hey, Cory!" the Jaybird said from his rocking chair. He was grinning, which was a bad sign. "Got a joke for ya! Three strings walk into a bar. First string says, 'Gimme a drink!' Bartender looks at him, says, 'We don't serve strings in here, so get out!' Second string tries his luck. 'Gimme a drink!' Bartender says, 'Told you we don't serve strings in here, so you hit the trail!' Then the third string's just as thirsty as the devil, so he's got to try, too. 'Gimme a drink!' he says. Bartender looks at him squinty-eyed, says, 'You're a danged-gone *string*, too, ain't ya?' And the string, he puffs out his chest and says, ''Fraid not!''' The Jaybird hooted with laughter, while I just stood there staring at him. "Get it, boy? Get it? ''Fraid not'?" He frowned, the joke over. "Hell!" he growled. "You got a sense of humor as bad as your daddy's!"

One week. Oh, Lord.

There were two subjects the Jaybird could talk about for hours on end: his survival through the Depression, when he held such jobs as coffin polisher, railroad brakeman, and carnival roustabout, and his success as a young man with women, which according to him was enough to turn Valentino green. I would have thought that was a big deal if I'd known who Valentino was. Anytime the Jaybird and I were away from the reach of my grandmother's ear, he might launch into a tale about "Edith the preacher's daughter from Tupelo" or "Nancy the conductor's niece from Nashville" or "that buck-toothed girl used to hang around eatin' candy apples." He rambled on about his "jimbob" and how the girls got all fired up about it. Said there used to be jealous boyfriends and husbands after him by the dozens, but he always escaped whatever trap was closing around him. Once, he said, he'd hung on to the bottom of a railroad trestle above a hundred-foot gorge while two men with shotguns stood right above him, talking about how they were going to skin him alive and nail his hide to a tree. "Thing was," the Jaybird said to me as he chewed lustily on a weed, "I spoiled them girls for every other fella. Yeah, me and my jimbob, we had us a time." Then, inevitably, his eyes would take on a sad cast, and the young man with the flaming jimbob would start slipping away. "I bet you I wouldn't know one of them girls today if I passed her on the street. No sir. They'd be old women, and I wouldn't know a one of them."

Granddaddy Jaybird despised sleep. Maybe it had something to do with his knowing that his days on this earth were numbered. Come five o'clock, rain or shine, he'd rip the covers off me like a whirlwind passing through and his voice would roar in my ear: "Get up, boy! Think you're gonna live *forever*?"

I would invariably mumble, "No, sir," and sit up, and the Jaybird would go on to rouse my grandmother into cooking a breakfast that might have served Sgt. Rock and most of Easy Company.

The days I spent with my grandparents followed no pattern once breakfast was down the hatch. I could just as well be handed a garden hoe and told to get to work as I could be informed that I might enjoy a trip to the pond in the woods behind the house. Granddaddy Jaybird kept a few dozen chickens, three goats—all of whom closely resembled him—and for some strange reason he kept a snapping turtle named Wisdom in a big metal tub full of slimy water in the backyard. When one of those goats stuck his nose into Wisdom's territory, and Wisdom took hold, there was hell to pay. Things were commonly in an uproar at the Jaybird's place: "All snakes and dingleberries" was his phrase to describe a chaotic moment, as when Wisdom bit a thirsty goat and the goat in turn careened into the clean laundry my grandmother was hanging on the line, ending up running around festooned in sheets and dragging them through the garden I'd just been hoeing. The Jaybird was proud of his collection of the skeletons of small animals which he'd painstakingly wired together. You never knew where those skeletons might appear; the Jaybird had a nasty knack for putting them in places you might reach into before looking, like beneath a pillow or in your shoe. Then he'd laugh like a demon when he heard you squall. His sense of humor was, to say it kindly, warped. On Wednesday afternoon he told me he'd found a nest of rattlesnakes near the house last week and killed them all with a shovel. As I was about to drift off to sleep that night, already dreading five o'clock, he opened my door and peered into the dark and said in a quiet, ominous voice, "Cory? Be careful if you get up to pee tonight. Your grandmomma found a fresh-shed snakeskin under your bed this mornin'. Good-sized rattle on it, too. 'Night, now."

He'd closed the door. I was still awake at five.

What I realized, long after the fact, was that Granddaddy Jaybird was honing me like one might sharpen a blade on a grinding edge. I don't think he knew he was doing this, but that's how it came out. Take the snake story. As I lay awake in the dark, my bladder steadily expanding within me, my imagination was at work. I could see that rattler, coiled somewhere in the room, waiting for the squeak of a bare foot pressing on a board. I could see the colors of the forest in its scaly hide, its terrible flat head resting on a ledge of air, its fangs slightly adrip. I could see the muscles ripple slowly along its sides as it tasted my scent. I could see it grin in the dark, same to say, "You're *mine*, bub."

If there could be a school for the imagination, the Jaybird would be its headmaster. The lesson I learned that night, in what you can make yourself describe in your mind as true, I couldn't have bought at the finest college. There was also the subsidiary lesson of gritting your teeth and bearing pain, hour upon hour, and damning yourself for drinking an extra glass of milk at supper.

You see, the Jaybird was teaching me well, though he didn't have a clue.

There were other lessons, all of them valuable. And tests, too. On Friday afternoon Grandmomma Sarah asked him to drive into town to pick up a box of ice cream salt at the grocery store. Normally the Jaybird didn't like to run errands, but today he was agreeable. He asked me to go with him, and Grandmomma Sarah said the sooner we got back the sooner the ice cream would be made.

It was a day right for ice cream. Ninety degrees in the shade, and so hot in the full sun that if a dog went running, its shadow dropped down to rest. We got the ice cream salt, but on the way back, in the Jaybird's bulky old Ford, another test began.

"Jerome Claypool lives just down the road," he said. "He's a good ole fella. Want to drop by and say howdy?"

"We'd better get the ice cream salt to—"

"Yeah, Jerome's a good ole fella," the Jaybird said as he turned the Ford toward his friend's house.

Six miles later, he stopped in front of a ramshackle farmhouse that had a rotting sofa, a cast-off wringer, and a pile of moldering tires and rusted radiators in the front yard. I think we had crossed the line between Zephyr and Dogpatch by way of Tobacco Road somewhere a few miles back. Obviously, though, Jerome Claypool was a popular good ole fella, because there were four other cars parked in front of the place as well. "Come on, Cory," the Jaybird said as he opened his door. "We'll just go in a minute or two."

I could smell the stench of cheap cigars before we got to the porch. The Jaybird knocked on the door: *rap rap rapraprap.* "Who is it?" a cautious voice inquired from within. My grandfather replied, "Blood 'n Guts," which made me stare at him, thinking he'd lost whatever mind he had left. The door opened on noisy hinges, and a long-jawed face with dark, wrinkle-edged eyes peered out. Those eyes found me. "Who's *he?*"

"My grandboy," Jaybird said, and put his hand on my shoulder. "Name's Cory."

"Jesus, Jay!" the long-jawed face said with a scowl. "What're you bringin' a *kid* around here for?"

"No harm done. He won't say nothin'. Will you, Cory?" The hand tightened.

I didn't understand what was going on, but clearly this was not a place Grandmomma Sarah would have enjoyed visiting. I thought of Miss Grace's house out beyond Saxon's Lake, and the girl named Lainie who'd furled her wet pink tongue at me. "No sir," I told him, and the grip relaxed again. His secret—whatever it might be—was safe.

"Bodean won't like this," the man warned.

"Jerome, Bodean can stick his head up his ass for all I care. You gonna let me in or not?"

"You got the green?"

"Burnin' a hole," the Jaybird said, and touched his pocket.

I balked as he started pulling me over the threshold. "Grand-momma's waitin' for the ice cream sa—"

He looked at me, and I saw something of his true nature deep in his eyes, like the glare of a distant blast furnace. On his face there was a desperate hunger, inflamed by whatever was going on in that house. Ice cream salt was forgotten; ice cream itself was part of another world six miles away. "Come on!" he snapped.

I stood my ground. "I don't think we ought to—"

"You don't *think!*" he said, and whatever was pulling him into that house seized his face and made it mean. "You just do what I tell you, hear me?"

He gave me a hard yank and I went with him, my heart scorched. Mr. Claypool closed the door behind us and bolted it. Cigar smoke drifted in a room where no sunlight entered; the windows were all boarded up and a few measly electric lights were burning. We followed Mr. Claypool through a hallway to the rear of the house, and he opened another door. The windowless room we walked into was layered with smoke, too, and at its center was a round table where four men sat under a harsh light playing cards, poker chips in stacks before them and glasses of amber liquid near at hand. "Fuck that noise!" one of the men was saying, making my ears sting. "I ain't gonna be bluffed, no sir!"

"Five dollars to you, then, Mr. Cool," another one said. A red chip hit the pile at the table's center. A cigar tip glowed like a volcano in the maelstrom. "Raise you five," the third man said, the cigar wedged in the side of a scarlike mouth. "Come on, put up or shut—" I saw his small, piggish eyes dart at me, and the man slapped his cards facedown on the table. "*Hey!*" he shouted. "What's that kid doin' in here?"

Instantly I was the focus of attention. "Jaybird, have you gone fuckin' crazy?" one of the other men asked. "Get him out!"

180

"He's all right," my grandfather said. "He's family."

"Not *my* family." The man with the cigar leaned forward, his thick forearms braced on the table. His brown hair was cropped in a crew cut, and on the little finger of his right hand he wore a diamond ring. He took the cigar from his mouth, his eyes narrowed into slits. "You know the rules, Jaybird. Nobody comes in here without gettin' approved."

"He's all right. He's my grandson."

"I don't care if he's the fuckin' prince of England. You broke the rules."

"Now, there's no call to be ugly about it, is th—"

"You're *stupid!*" the man shouted, his mouth twisting as he spoke the word. A fine sheen of sweat glistened on his face, and his white shirt was damp. On the breast pocket, next to a tobacco stain, was a monogram: BB. *"Stupid!"* he repeated. "You want the law to come in and bust us up? Why don't you just give a map to that goddamned sheriff?"

"Cory won't say anythin'. He's a good boy."

"That so?" The small pig eyes returned to me. "You as stupid as your grandpap, boy?"

"No sir," I said.

He laughed. The sound of it reminded me of when Phillip Kenner threw up his oatmeal in school last April. The man's eyes were not happy, but his mouth was tickled. "Well, you're a smart little fella, ain't you?"

"He takes after me, Mr. Blaylock," the Jaybird said, and I realized the man who thought I was so smart was Bodean Blaylock himself, brother of Donny and Wade and son of the notorious Biggun. I recalled my grandfather's brash pronouncement at the door that Bodean could stick his head up his ass; right now, though, it was my grandpop who looked butt-faced.

"Like hell he does," Bodean told him, and when he laughed again he looked around at the other gamblers and they laughed, too, like good little Indians following the chief. Then Bodean stopped laughing. "Hit the road, Jaybird," he said. "We've got some high rollers comin' in here directly. Bunch of flyboys think they can make some money off me."

My grandfather cleared his throat nervously. His eyes were on the poker chips. "Uh . . . I was wonderin' . . . since I'm here and all, mind if I sit in for a few hands?"

"Take that kid and make dust," Bodean told him. "I'm runnin' a poker game, not a baby-sittin' service."

"Oh, Cory can wait outside," the Jaybird said. "He won't mind. Will you, boy?"

"Grandmomma's waitin' for the ice cream salt," I said.

Bodean Blaylock laughed again, and I saw the crimson flare in my grandfather's cheeks. "I don't care about no damned ice cream!" the Jaybird snapped, a fury and a torment in his eyes. "I don't care if she waits till midnight for it, I can do whatever I damn well please!"

"Better run on home, Jaybird," one of the other men taunted. "Go eat yourself some ice cream and stay out of trouble."

You shut up! he hollered. *Here!* He dug into his pocket, brought out a twenty-dollar bill, and slammed it on the table. "Am I in this game, or not?"

I almost choked. Twenty dollars to risk playing poker. That was an awful lot of money. Bodean Blaylock smoked his cigar in silence, and looked back and forth from the money to my granddaddy's face. "Twenty dollars," he said. "That'll hardly get you started."

"I've got more, don't you worry about it."

I realized the Jaybird must've raided the cash jar, or else he had a secret poker-playing fund hidden away from my grandmother. Surely she wouldn't approve of this, and surely the Jaybird had agreed to get the ice cream salt as a ruse to come here. Maybe he'd just planned on dropping by to see who was playing, but I could tell the fever had him and he was going to play come hell or high water. "Am I in, or not?"

"The kid can't stay."

"Cory, go sit in the car," he said. "I'll be there in a few minutes."

"But Grandmomma's waitin' for—"

"Go do like I said and do it right *now!*" the Jaybird yelled at me. Bodean stared at me through a haze of smoke. His expression said: *See what I can do to your granddaddy, little boy?*

I left the house. Before I got to the door, I could hear the sound of a new chair scraping up to the table. Then I walked out into the hot light and I put my hands in my pockets and kicked a pine cone across the road. I waited. Ten minutes went past. Then ten more. A car pulled up, and three young men got out, knocked on the front door, and were admitted by Mr. Claypool. The door closed again. Still my grandfather didn't emerge. I sat in the car for a while, but the heat was so bad my sweat drenched my shirt and I had to peel myself off the seat and get out again. I paced up and down in front of the house, and I paused to watch ants stripping a dead pigeon to the bones. Maybe an hour went past. At some point, though, I realized my grandfather was treating me like a little piece of nothing, and that was how he was treating Grandmomma Sarah, too. Anger started building in me, beginning in the belly like a dull, throbbing heat. I stared at the door, trying to will him to come out. The door remained closed.

The thought came to me, shocking in its decisiveness: *To hell with him.*

I got the box of ice cream salt, and I started walking.

The first two miles were all right. On the third, the heat began getting to me. Sweat was pouring down my face, and my scalp felt as if it were aflame. The road shimmered between its walls of pine forest, and only a couple of cars passed, but they were going in the wrong direction. The pavement started burning my feet through my shoes. I wanted to sit down in some shade and rest, but I did not because resting would be weakness; it would be saying to myself that I shouldn't have tried to walk six miles in hundred-degree heat and blazing sun, that I should have stayed at that house and waited for my grandfather to come out when he was good and ready. No. I had to keep going, and worry about my blisters later.

I started thinking about the story I was going to write about this. In that story, a boy would be crossing a burning desert, a boxful of priceless crystals entrusted to his care. I looked up to watch hawks soaring in the thermals, and when my attention roamed from what I was doing I stepped in a pothole, twisted my ankle, and fell down and the box of ice cream salt burst open beneath me.

I almost cried.

Almost.

My ankle hurt, but I could still stand on it. What hurt me most was the ice cream salt glistening on the pavement. The bottom of the box had broken open. I scooped ice cream salt up in my hands, filled my pockets, and started limping on again.

I was not going to stop. I was not going to sit in the shade and cry, my pockets leaking salt. I was not going to let my grandfather beat me.

I was nearing the end of the third mile when a car's horn honked behind me. I looked around, expecting the Jaybird's Ford. It was, instead, a copper-colored Pontiac. The car slowed, and Dr. Curtis Parrish looked at me through the rolled-down passenger window. "Cory? You need a ride?"

"Yes sir," I said gratefully, and I climbed in. My feet were about burned to the nubs, my ankle swelling up. Dr. Parrish gave it the gas, and we rolled on. "I'm stayin' at my grandfolks'," I said. "About three miles up the road."

"I know where the Jaybird lives." Dr. Parrish picked up his

medical bag, which was sitting between us, and put it onto the back seat. "Awful hot day. Where were you walkin' from?"

"I . . . uh . . ." Here was a crossroads of conscience, thrust upon me. "I . . . had to run an errand for my grandmother," I decided to say.

"Oh." He was quiet for a moment. Then: "What's that spillin' out of your pocket? Sand?"

"Salt," I said.

"Oh," he said, and he nodded as if this made sense to him. "How's your daddy doin' these days? Things ease up at work for him?"

"Sir?"

"You know. His work. When Tom came to see me a few weeks ago, he said his workload was so tough he was havin' trouble sleepin'. I gave him some pills. You know, stress can be a mighty powerful thing. I told your dad he ought to take a vacation."

"Oh." This time I was the one who nodded, as if this made sense. "I think he's doin' better," I said. *I gave him some pills.* Dad hadn't said anything about his work being tough, or that he'd gone to see Dr. Parrish. *I gave him some pills.* I stared straight ahead, at the unfolding road. My father was still trying to escape the realm of troubled spirits. It occurred to me that he was hiding part of himself from Mom and me, just as the Jaybird hid his poker fever from my grandmother.

Dr. Parrish went with me to the front door of my grandparents' house. When Grandmomma Sarah answered his knock, Dr. Parrish said he'd found me walking on the side of the road. "Where's your granddaddy?" she asked me. I must've made a pained face, because after a few seconds of deliberation she answered her own question. "He's gotten himself into some mischief. Uh-huh. That's just what he's done."

"The box of salt busted open," I told her, and I showed a handful of it, my hair wet with sweat.

"We'll get us a new box. We'll save what's in your pockets for the Jaybird." I wasn't to know it for a while, but for the next week every meal the Jaybird sat down to eat would be so loaded with salt his mouth would pucker until it squawked. "Would you come in for a cold glass of lemonade, Dr. Parrish?"

"No, thank you. I've got to get back to the office." His face clouded over; a concern was working its way out of him. "Mrs. Mackenson, did you know Selma Neville?"

"Yes, I know her. Haven't seen her for a month or more, though."

"I just came from her house," Dr. Parrish said. "You know she'd been fightin' cancer for the last year."

"No, I surely didn't!"

"Well, she put up a good fight, but she passed on about two hours ago. She wanted to pass at home instead of a hospital."

"My Lord, I didn't know Selma was sick!"

"She didn't want a fuss. How she got through her last year teachin' I'll never know."

It hit me who they were talking about. Mrs. Neville. My Mrs. Neville. The teacher who'd said I should enter the short-story contest this year. *Good-bye,* she'd said as I'd left her room on the first day of summer. Not *see you next year* or *see you in September,* but a firm and final *good-bye.* She must've known she was dying, as she sat behind that desk in summer's light, and she had known that for her there would be no new class of grinning young monkeys in September.

"Thought you might like to know," Dr. Parrish said. He touched my shoulder with a hand that had two hours ago pulled a sheet over Mrs. Neville's face. "You take care now, Cory." He turned around and walked to his Pontiac, and my grandmother and I watched him drive away.

An hour later, the Jaybird came home. He wore the expression of a man whose last friend had kicked him in the rump and whose last Washington had snickered as it sailed off into another man's pocket. He tried to work up a show of anger at me, for "runnin' off and worryin' me half to death" but before he could get steamed up on that route Grandmomma Sarah derailed him by asking, very quietly, where the ice cream salt was. The Jaybird wound up sitting by himself on the porch in the fading light, moths whirling around him, his face long and haggard and his spirits as low as his flagging jimbob. I felt kind of sorry for him, actually, but the Jaybird was not the kind of man you felt sorry for. One word of regret from me would've made him sneer and swagger. The Jaybird never apologized; he was never wrong. That was why he had no true companions, and that was why he sat alone on that porch in the company of dumb gleaming wings that swirled around him like his ancient memories of pretty farmers' daughters.

One last incident marked my week with my grandparents. I had not slept well on Friday night. I dreamed of walking into my classroom, which was empty of everyone but Mrs. Neville, sitting behind her desk straightening papers. Golden light slanted across the floor, bars of it striping the blackboard. The flesh of Mrs.

Neville's face had shriveled. Her eyes looked bright and large, like the eyes of a baby. She held her back rigid, and she watched me as I stood on the threshold between the hallway and classroom. "Cory?" she said. "Cory Mackenson?"

"Yes ma'am," I answered.

"Come closer," she said.

I did. I walked to her desk, and I saw that the red apple there on its edge had dried up.

"Summer's almost over," Mrs. Neville told me. I nodded. "You're older than you were before, aren't you?"

"I had a birthday," I said.

"That's nice." Her breath, though not unpleasant, smelled like flowers on the verge of decay. "I have seen many boys come and go," she said. "I've seen some grow up and set roots, and some grow up and move away. The years of a boy's life pass so fast, Cory." She smiled faintly. "Boys want to hurry up and be men, and then comes a day they wish they could be boys again. But I'll tell you a secret, Cory. Want to hear it?"

I nodded.

"No one," Mrs. Neville whispered, "ever grows up."

I frowned. What kind of secret was that? My dad and mom were grown-up, weren't they? So were Mr. Dollar, Chief Marchette, Dr. Parrish, Reverend Lovoy, the Lady, and everybody else over eighteen.

"They may look grown-up," she continued, "but it's a disguise. It's just the clay of time. Men and women are still children deep in their hearts. They still would like to jump and play, but that heavy clay won't let them. They'd like to shake off every chain the world's put on them, take off their watches and neckties and Sunday shoes and return naked to the swimming hole, if just for one day. They'd like to feel free, and know that there's a momma and daddy at home who'll take care of things and love them no matter what. Even behind the face of the meanest man in the world is a scared little boy trying to wedge himself into a corner where he can't be hurt." She put aside the papers and folded her hands on the desk. "I have seen plenty of boys grow into men, Cory, and I want to say one word to you. *Remember*."

"Remember? Remember what?"

"Everything," she said. "And anything. Don't you go through a day without remembering something of it, and tucking that memory away like a treasure. Because it is. And memories are sweet doors, Cory. They're teachers and friends and disciplinarians. When you look at something, don't just look. *See* it. Really, really *see* it. See it

186

so when you write it down, somebody else can see it, too. It's easy to walk through life deaf, dumb, and blind, Cory. Most everybody you know or ever meet will. They'll walk through a parade of wonders, and they'll never hear a peep of it. But you can live a thousand lifetimes if you want to. You can talk to people you'll never set eyes on, in lands you'll never visit." She nodded, watching my face. "And if you're good and you're lucky and you have something worth saying, then you might have the chance to live on long after—" She paused, measuring her words. "Long after," she finished.

"How's all this stuff supposed to happen?" I asked.

"First things first. Enter the short-story contest, like I told you."

"I'm not good enough."

"I'm not saying you are. Yet. Just do the best you can, and enter the contest. Will you do that?"

I shrugged. "I don't know what to write about."

"You will," Mrs. Neville said. "When you make yourself sit and look at a blank piece of paper long enough, you will. And don't think of it as writing. Just think of it as telling your friends a story. Will you at least try?"

"I'll think about it," I said.

"Don't think too hard," she cautioned me. "Sometimes thinking gets in the way of doing."

"Yes ma'am."

"Ah, well." Mrs. Neville pulled in a breath and let it slowly out. She looked around the classroom at the empty desks carved with initials. "I have done my best," she said quietly, "and that is all I can do. Oh, you little children, what years you have ahead." Her gaze returned to me. "Class dismissed," she said.

I woke up. It was not quite light yet. A rooster was crowing to herald the sun. The Jaybird's radio was on in their bedroom, tuned to a country station. The sound of a steel guitar, alone and searching over the dark miles of woods and meadows and roads, has always had the power to break my heart in two.

Mom and Dad came to pick me up that afternoon. I kissed Grandmomma Sarah good-bye, and I shook the Jaybird's hand. He put a little extra pressure into his grip. I squeezed back. We knew each other. Then I went out to the pickup truck with my folks, and I found they'd brought Rebel along, so I climbed into the truckbed and let my legs hang over the edge and Rebel nudged up close to me and blew dog breath in my face but it was fine with me.

Grandmomma Sarah and the Jaybird stood on their front porch and waved good-bye. I went home, where I belonged.

7

My Camping Trip

There is nothing more frightening or exciting than a blank piece of paper. Frightening because you're on your own, leaving dark tracks across that snowy plain, and exciting because no one knows your destination but yourself, and even you can't say exactly where you'll end up. When I sat down at my typewriter to chop out that story for the Zephyr Arts Council Writing Contest, I was so scared it was all I could do to spell my name. Concocting a story for yourself and a story that you know strangers are going to read are two different animals; the first is a comfortable pony, the second a crazy bronco. You just have to hold tight, and go along for the ride.

The sheet of paper stared me in the face for quite a while. At last I decided to write about a boy who runs away from his small town to see the world. I got two pages done before it became clear my heart wasn't in it. I started on a tale about a boy who finds a magic lantern in a junkyard. That, too, went into the wastebasket. A story about a ghost car was going pretty well until it hit the wall of my imagination and burst into flames.

I sat there, staring at another fresh sheet of paper.

The cicadas were whirring in the trees outside. Rebel barked at something in the night. From far away I heard a car's engine growl. I thought of my dream about Mrs. Neville, and what she'd said: *Don't think of it as writing. Think of it as telling your friends a story.*

What if? I asked myself. What if I was to write about something that had really happened?

Like . . . Mr. Sculley and the tooth of Old Moses. No, no. Mr. Sculley wouldn't want people coming around to his place to see it. All right then, what about . . . the Lady and the Moon Man? No, I didn't know enough about them. What about . . .

. . . the dead man in the car at the bottom of Saxon's Lake?

What if I was to write a story about what had happened that

morning? Write about the car going into the water, and Dad jumping in after it? Write about everything I'd felt and seen on that March morning before the sun? And what if . . . what if . . . I wrote about seeing the man in the green-feathered hat, standing there at the edge of the woods?

Now, this I could get fired-up about. I began with my father saying, "Cory? Wake up, son. It's time." Soon I was back in the milk truck with him, on our way through the silent early morning streets of Zephyr. We were talking about what I wanted to grow up to be, and then suddenly the car came out of the woods right in front of us, my dad twisted the milk truck's wheel, and the car went over the edge of the red rock cliff into Saxon's Lake. I remembered my father running toward the lake, and how my heart had clutched up as he'd leaped into the water and started swimming. I remembered watching the car starting to go down, bubbles bursting around its trunk. I remembered looking around at the woods across the road and seeing the figure standing there wearing a long overcoat that flapped in the wind and a hat with a green—

Wait.

No, that's not how it had been. I had stepped on the green feather, and found it on the bottom of my muddy shoe. But where else could a green feather come from but the band of a hat? Still and all, I was writing this as it had really been. I hadn't actually seen the green-feathered hat until the night of the flood. So I stuck to the facts, and wrote about the green feather as I'd found it. I left out the part about Miss Grace, Lainie, and the house of bad girls, figuring Mom wouldn't care to read about it. I read the story over and decided it wasn't as good as I could do, so I rewrote it. It was hard making talking sound like talking. Finally, though, after three times through my Royal, the story was ready. It was two pages long, double-spaced. My masterpiece.

When Dad, clad in his red-striped pajamas and his hair still damp from his shower, came in to say good night, I showed him the two sheets of paper.

"What's this?" He held the title up under my desk lamp. " 'Before the Sun,' " he read, and he looked at me with a question in his eyes.

"It's a story for the writin' contest," I said. "I just wrote it."

"Oh. Can I read it?"

"Yes sir."

He began. I watched him. When he got to the part about the car coming out of the woods, a little muscle tensed in his jaw. He put out a hand to brace himself against the wall, and I knew he was reading about swimming out to the car. I saw his fingers slowly grip and relax, grip and relax. "Cory?" Mom called. "Go lock Rebel in for the night!" I started to go, but Dad said, "Wait just a minute," and then he returned to the last few paragraphs.

"Cory?" Mom called again, the TV on in the front room.

"We're talkin', Rebecca!" Dad told her, and he lowered the pages to his side. He stared at me, his face half in shadow.

"Is it okay?" I asked.

"This isn't what you usually write," he said quietly. "You usually write about ghosts, or cowboys, or spacemen. How come you to write somethin' like this?"

I shrugged. "I don't know. I just thought . . . I'd write somethin' true."

"So this is true? This part about you seein' somebody standin' in the woods?"

"Yes sir."

"Then how come you didn't tell me about it? How come you didn't tell Sheriff Amory?"

"I don't know. Maybe . . . I wasn't sure if I really saw somebody or not."

"But you're sure now? Almost six months after it happened, you're sure now? And you could've told the sheriff this, and you didn't?"

"I . . . guess that's right. I mean . . . I *thought* I saw somebody standin' there. He was wearin' a long overcoat, and he—"

"You're sure it was a man?" Dad asked. "You saw his face?"

"No sir, I didn't see his face."

Dad shook his head. His jaw muscle twitched again, and a pulse throbbed at his temple. "I wish to God," he said, "that we'd never driven along that road. I wish to God I'd never jumped in after that car. I wish to God that dead man at the bottom of the lake would leave me alone." He squeezed his eyes shut, and when he opened them again they were bleary and tortured. "Cory, I don't want you showin' this to anybody else. Hear me?"

"But . . . I was gonna enter it in the con—"

"No! God, no!" He clamped a hand to my shoulder. "Listen to me. All this happened six months ago. It's history now, and there's no need dredgin' it all up again."

"But it happened," I said. "It's real."

"It was a bad dream," my father answered. "A very bad dream. The sheriff never found anybody missin' from town. Nobody missin' from anywhere around here who had a tattoo like that. No wife or family ever turned up huntin' a lost husband and father. Don't you understand, Cory?"

"No sir," I said.

"That man at the bottom of Saxon's Lake never was," Dad said, his voice hurt and husky. "Nobody cared enough about him to even *miss* him. And when he died, beat up so bad he hardly looked like a man anymore, he didn't even get a proper burial. I was the last person on this earth to see him before he sank down forever. Do you know what that's done to me, Cory?"

I shook my head.

My father looked at the story again. He put the two pages back on my desk, next to the Royal typewriter. "I knew there was brutality in this world," he said, but he kept his eyes averted from mine. "Brutality is part of life, but . . . it's always somewhere else. Always in the next town. Remember when I was a fireman, and I went out when that car crashed and burned between here and Union Town?"

"Little Stevie Cauley's car," I said. "Midnight Mona."

"That's right. The tire tracks on the pavement said that another car forced Stevie Cauley off the road. Somebody deliberately wrecked him. The car's gas tank ruptured, and it blew sky high. That was brutality, too, and when I saw what was left of a livin', breathin' young man, I—" He flinched, perhaps recalling the sight of charred bones. "I couldn't understand how one human bein' could do that to another. I couldn't understand that kind of hate. I mean . . . what road do you take to get there? What is it that has to get inside you and twist your soul so much you can take a human life as easily as flickin' a fly?" His gaze found mine. "You know what your granddaddy used to call me when I was your age?"

"No sir."

"Yellowstreak. Because I didn't like to hunt. Because I didn't like to fight. Because I didn't like to do any of the things that you're supposed to like, if you're a boy. He forced me to play football. I wasn't any good at it, but I did it for him. He said, 'Boy, you'll never be any good in this life if you don't have the killer instinct.' That's what he said. 'Hit 'em hard, knock 'em down, show 'em who's tough.' The only thing is . . . I'm not tough. I never was. All I ever wanted was peace. That's all. Just peace." He walked to my window, and he stood there for a moment listening to the cicadas. "I guess," he said, "I've been pretendin' for a long time that I'm stronger than I am. That I could put that dead man in the car behind me and let him go. But I can't, Cory. He calls to me."

"He . . . *calls* to you?" I asked.

"Yes, he does." My father stood with his back to me. At his sides, his hands had curled into fists. "He says he wants me to know who he was. He wants me to know where his family is, and if there's anybody on this earth who mourns for him. He wants me to know who killed him, and why. He wants me to *remember* him, and he says that as long as whoever beat him and strangled him to death walks free, I will have no more peace for the rest of my life." Dad turned toward me. I thought he looked ten years older than when he'd taken the two pages of my story in his hand. "When I was your age, I wanted to believe I lived in a magic town," he said softly, "where nothin' bad could ever happen. I wanted to believe every-one was kind, and good, and just. I wanted to believe hard work was rewarded, and a man stood on his word. I wanted to believe a man was a Christian every day of the week, not just Sunday, and that the law was fair and the politicians wise and if you walked the straight path you found that peace you were searchin' for." He smiled; it was a difficult thing to look at. For an instant I thought I could see the boy in him, trapped in what Mrs. Neville's dream-shape had called the clay of time. "There never was such a place," my father said. "There never will be. But knowin' can't stop you from wishin' it was so, and every time I close my eyes to sleep, that dead man at the bottom of Saxon's Lake tells me I've been a damned fool."

I don't know why I said it, but I did: "Maybe the Lady can help you."

"How? Throw a few bones for me? Burn a candle and incense?"

"No sir. Just talk," I said.

He looked at the floor. He drew a deep breath and slowly freed it. Then he said, "I've gotta get some rest," and he walked to the door.

"Dad?"

He paused.

"Do you want me to tear the story up?"

He didn't answer, and I thought he wasn't going to. His gaze flickered back and forth from me to the two sheets of paper. "No," he said at last. "No, it's a good story. It's true, isn't it?"

"Yes sir."

"It's the best you can do?"

"Yes sir."

He looked around at the pictures of monsters taped on the walls, and his eyes came to me. "You're sure you wouldn't rather write about ghosts, or men from Mars?" he inquired with a hint of a smile.

"Not this time," I told him.

He nodded, chewing on his lower lip. "Go ahead, then. Enter it in the contest," he said, and he left me alone.

On the following morning, I put my story in a manila envelope and rode Rocket to the public library on Merchants Street, near the courthouse. In the library's cool, stately confines, where fans whispered at the ceiling and sunlight streamed through blinds at tall arched windows, I handed my contest entry—marked "Short Story" on the envelope in Crayola burnt umber—to Mrs. Evelyn Prathmore at the front desk. "And what little tale might we have here?" Mrs. Prathmore asked, smiling sweetly.

"It's about a murder," I said. Her smile fractured. "Who's judgin' the contest this year?"

"Myself, Mr. Grover Dean, Mr. Lyle Redmond from the English department at Adams Valley High School, Mayor Swope, our well-known published poet Mrs. Teresa Abercrombie, and Mr. James Connahaute, the copy editor at the *Journal*." She picked up my entry with two fingers, as if it were a smelly fish. "It's about a *murder*, you say?" She peered at me over the pearly rims of her eyeglasses.

"Yes ma'am."

"What's a nice, polite young man like you writin' about *murder* for? Couldn't you write about a happier subject? Like . . . your dog, or your best friend, or—" She frowned, at her wit's end. "Somethin' that would enlighten and entertain?"

"No ma'am," I said. "I had to write about the man at the bottom of Saxon's Lake."

"Oh." Mrs. Prathmore looked at the manila envelope again. "I see. Do your parents know you're enterin' this in the contest, Cory?"

"Yes ma'am. My dad read it last night."

Mrs. Prathmore picked up a ball-point pen and wrote my name on the envelope. "What's your telephone number?" she asked, and when I told her she wrote that underneath my name. "All right, Cory," she said, and she summoned up a cool smile, "I'll see that this gets where it needs to go."

I thanked her, and I turned around and walked toward the front door. Before I got out, I glanced back at Mrs. Prathmore. She was bending the envelope's clasp back to unseal it, and when she saw me looking she stopped. I took this as a good sign, that she was eager to read my entry. I went on out into the sunlight, unchained Rocket from a park bench, and pedaled home.

No doubt about it, summer was on the wane.

The mornings seemed a shade cooler. The nights were hungry, and ate more daylight. The cicadas sounded tired, their whirring wings slowing to a dull buzz. From our front porch you could look almost due east and see a single Judas tree up in the forested hills; its leaves had turned crimson almost overnight, a shock amid all that green. And the worst—the very worst for those of us who loved the freedom of summer's days—was that the television and radio trumpeted back-to-school sales with depressing fervor.

Time was running out. So one evening at supper I broached the subject. Bit the bullet. Took the bull by the horns. Jumped in headfirst.

"Can I go campin' overnight with the guys?" was the question that brought silence to the table.

Mom looked at Dad. Dad looked at Mom. Neither of them looked at me. "You said I could if I went to Granddaddy Jaybird's for a week," I reminded them.

Dad cleared his throat and swirled his fork in his mashed potatoes. "Well," he said, "I don't see why not. Sure. You guys can pitch a tent in the back and make a campfire."

"That's not what I mean. I mean campin' out. Like out in the woods."

"There are woods behind the house," he said. "That's woods enough."

"No sir," I said, and my heart was beating harder because for me this was really being daring. "I mean way out in the woods. Out where you can't see Zephyr or any lights. Like real campin'."

"Oh, my," Mom fretted.

Dad grunted and put his fork down. He folded his fingers together, and the thought lines deepened into grooves between his eyes. All this was, I knew from past experience, the first signs of the word "no" being born. "Way out in the woods," he repeated. "Like how far out?"

"I don't know. I thought we could hike somewhere, spend the night, and then come back in the mornin'. We'd take a compass, and sandwiches, and Kool-Aid, and we'd take knapsacks and stuff."

"And what would happen if one of you boys broke an ankle?" Mom asked. "Or got bitten by a rattlesnake? Or fell down in poison ivy, and Lord knows that's everywhere this summer." I hung on; she was working up to full speed. "What would happen if you got attacked by a bobcat? Lord, a hundred things could happen to you in the woods, and none of them good!"

"We'd be all right, Mom," I said. "We're not little kids anymore."

"You're not grown up enough to go wanderin' around out in the woods by yourselves, either! What if you got out there at night two miles from home and a storm blew up? What if it started lightnin' and thunderin'? What if you or one of the others got sick to your stomach? You know, you can't just find a phone and call home out there. Tell him it's a bad idea, Tom."

He made a face; the dirty jobs always fell to the father.

"Go on," Mom urged. "Tell him he can wait until he's thirteen."

"You said last year I could wait until I was twelve," I reminded her.

"Don't talk smart, now! Tom, tell him."

I awaited the firm, resolute "no." It came as a real surprise, then, when my dad asked, "Where would you get the compass?"

Mom looked at him in horror. I felt a spark of hope leap within me. "From Davy Ray's dad," I said. "He uses it when he goes huntin'."

"Compasses can break!" Mom insisted. "Can't they?" she asked Dad.

My father kept his attention on me, his expression solid and serious. "Goin' out on an overnight hike isn't any game for children. I know plenty of men who've gotten lost in the woods, and they'll tell you right off what it feels like to be without a bed or a bathroom, have to sleep on wet leaves and scratch skeeter bites all night. That sound like fun to you?"

"I'd like to go," I said.

"You talk to the other guys about this?"

"Yes sir. They all said they'd like to go, too, if their folks'll let 'em."

"Tom, he's too young!" Mom said. "Maybe next year!"

"No," my father answered, "he's not too young." My mother wore a stricken look; she started to speak again, but Dad put a finger to her lips. "I made a deal with him," he told her. "In this house, a man stands on his word." His gaze swung back to me again. "Call 'em. If their parents say all right, it's all right with us, too. But we'll talk about how far you can go, and when we expect you back, and if you're not back by the time we agree on, you'll have a tough time sittin' down for a week. Okay?"

"Okay!" I said, and I started to go for the phone but Dad said, "Hold on. Finish your supper first."

After this, events gained momentum. Ben's parents gave their approval. Davy Ray's folks said okay. Johnny, however, could not go with us, though he pleaded for my dad to talk to his. Dad did what he could, but the judgment was already passed. Because of Johnny's dizzy spells, his parents were afraid for him to be out in the woods overnight. Once again the Branlins had robbed him.

And so, on a sunny Friday afternoon, laden with knapsacks, sandwiches, canteens of water, mosquito repellent, snakebite kits, matches, flashlights, and county maps we'd gotten from the courthouse, Davy Ray, Ben, and I struck out from my house into the beckoning forest. All our good-byes had been said, our dogs locked up, our bicycles porched and chained. Davy carried his father's compass, and he wore a camouflage-print hunting cap. We all wore long pants, to guard our shins against thorns and snake fangs, and our winter boots. We were in it for the long haul, and we set our faces against the sun like pioneers entering the forest primeval. Before we reached the woods, though, my mother the constant worrier called from the back porch, "Cory! Have you got enough toilet paper?"

I said I did. Somehow, I couldn't imagine Daniel Boone's mother asking him that question.

We climbed the hill and crossed the clearing from where we had flown on the first day of summer. Beyond it the serious woods began, a green domain that might've given Tarzan pause. I looked back at Zephyr lying below us, and Ben stopped and then so did Davy Ray. Everything seemed so orderly: the streets, the roofs, the mowed lawns, the sidewalks, the flowerbeds. What we were about to enter was a wild entanglement, a dangerous realm that offered neither comfort nor safety; in other words, in that one moment I realized exactly what I'd gotten myself into.

"Well," Davy Ray said at last, "I guess we'd better get movin'."

"Yeah," Ben murmured. "Get movin'."

"Uh-huh," I said.

We stood there, the breeze on our faces and sweat on our necks. Behind us, the forest rustled. I thought of the hydra's heads, swaying and hissing, in *Jason and the Argonauts*.

"I'm goin'," Davy Ray said, and he started off. I turned away from Zephyr and followed him, because he was the guy with the compass. Ben hitched his knapsack's straps in a notch tighter, the tail of his shirt already beginning to wander out of his pants, and he said, "Hold up!" and came on as fast as he could.

The forest, which had been waiting a hundred years for three boys just like us, let us in and then closed its limbs and leaves at our backs. Now we had set foot in the wilderness, and we were on our own.

Pretty soon we were drenched with sweat. Going up and down

wooded ridges in the heavy August heat was no easy task, and Ben
started puffing and asking Davy Ray to slow down. "Snake hole!"
Davy Ray shouted, pointing at an imaginary hole at Ben's feet, and
that got Ben moving lickety-split again. We traveled through a green
kingdom of sun and shadow, and we found honeysuckle boiling in
sweet profusion and black-berries growing wild and of course we
had to stop for a while and take a taste. Then we were on the march
again, following the compass and the sun, masters of our destinies.
Atop a hill we found a huge boulder to sit on, and we discovered
what appeared to be Indian symbols carved into the stone. Alas,
though, we weren't the first to make this find, because nearby was a
Moon Pie wrapper and a broken 7-Up bottle. We went on, deeper
into the forest, determined to find a place where no human foot had
ever marked the dirt. We came to a dried-up streambed and
followed it, the stones crunching under our boots. A dead possum,
swarming with flies, snared our attention for a few minutes. Davy
Ray threatened to pick up the possum's carcass and throw it at Ben,
but I talked him out of such a grisly display and Ben shuddered with
relief. Farther ahead, at a place where the trees thinned and white
rocks jutted from the earth like dinosaur ribs, Davy Ray stopped and
bent down. He came up holding a black arrowhead, almost perfectly formed, which he put in his pocket for Johnny's collection.

The sun was falling. We were sweaty and dusty, and gnats spun
around our heads and darted at our eyeballs. I have never understood the attraction of gnats to eyeballs, but I believe it's the
equivalent of moths to flames; in any case, we spent a lot of time
digging the little dead things out of our watering orbs. But as the sun
settled and the air cooled, the gnats went away. We began to wonder
where we might find a place to spend the night, and it was right
about then that the truth of the matter came clear.

There were no mothers and fathers around to make our suppers.
There were no televisions, no radios, no bathtubs, no beds, and no
lights, which we began to fully realize as the sky darkened to the
east. How far we were from home we didn't know, but for the last
two hours we'd seen no mark of civilization. "We'd better stop
here," I told Davy Ray, and I indicated a clearing, but he said, "Ah,
we can go on a little farther," and I knew his curiosity about what
lay over the next ridge was pulling him onward. Ben and I kept up
with him; as I've said before, he was the guy with the compass.

Our flashlights came out to spear through the gathering gloom.
Something fluttered in front of my face and spun away: a bat on the
prowl. Another something scuttled away through the underbrush at
our approach, and Ben kept asking, "What was that? What was

that?'' but neither of us could answer. At last Davy Ray stopped walking, and he shone his flashlight around and announced, ''We'll set up camp here.'' It was none too soon for Ben and me, because our legs were whipped. We shrugged the knapsacks off our aching shoulders and peed in the pine straw and then we set about finding wood for a fire. In this case we were lucky, because there were plenty of pine branches and pine cones lying about and those burned on half a match. So before long we had a sensible fire going, the firepit rimmed with stones as my dad had told me to do, and by its ruddy light we three frontiersmen ate the sandwiches our mothers had made.

The flames crackled. Ben discovered a pack of marshmallows his mom had put in his knapsack. We found sticks and began the joyful task of toasting. All around our circle was nothing but dark beyond the firelight's edge, and lightning bugs blinked in the trees. A breath of wind stirred the treetops, and way up there we could see the blaze of the Milky Way across the sky.

In this forest sanctuary our voices were quiet, respectful for where we were. We talked about our dismal Little League season, vowing that somehow we'd get Nemo Curliss on our team next year. We talked about the Branlins, and how somebody ought to clean their clocks for screwing up Johnny's summer. We talked about how far we must be from home; five or six miles, Davy Ray believed, while Ben said it must be more like ten or twelve. We wondered aloud what our folks were doing at that very same instant, and we all agreed they were probably worried sick about us but this experience would be good for them. We were growing up now, and it was high time they understood our childhood days were numbered.

In the distance an owl began to hoot. Davy Ray talked with great anticipation about Snowdown, who must even now be somewhere in the same woods sharing these sights and sounds, perhaps hearing the same owl. Ben talked about school getting ready to start soon, but we shushed him. We lay on our backs as the firelight dimmed, and stared up at the sky as we talked about Zephyr and the people who lived there. It was a magic town, we all agreed. And we were touched with magic, too, for having been born there.

Sometime after the flames had died and the embers glowed red, after the owl had gone to sleep and the soft warm breeze brought the fragrance of wild cherries into our campsite, we watched shooting stars streak incandescent blue and gold across the heavens. When the show had ended and we were all lying there thinking, Davy Ray said, ''Hey, Cory. How about tellin' us a story?''

''Nah,'' I said. ''I can't think of anythin'.''

"Just make one up," Davy Ray urged. "Come on. Okay?"

"Yeah, but don't make it *too* scary," Ben said. "I don't wanna have bad dreams."

I thought for a while, and then I began. "Did you guys know they had a prison camp for Nazis around here? Dad told me all about it. Yeah, he said they had all these Nazis in this camp in the woods, and all of 'em were the worst killers you can think of. It was right near the Air Force base, only this is before it was an Air Force base."

"Is this for *real?*" Ben asked warily.

"Naw, dummy!" Davy Ray said. "He's makin' it up!"

"Maybe I am," I told him, "and maybe I'm not."

Davy Ray was silent.

"Anyway," I went on, "there was a fire in this prison camp, and some of the Nazis got out. And some of 'em were all burned up, like their faces were all messed up and stuff, but they got out, right in these woods, and—"

"You saw this on 'Thriller,' didn't you?" Davy Ray asked.

"No," I said. "It's what my dad told me. This happened a long time ago, before any of us were even born. So these Nazis got out into the woods right near here, and their leader—his name was Bruno—was a big guy with a scarred-up, burned face and he found a cave for everybody to live in. But there wasn't enough food for everybody, and so when some of them died the others cut up the bodies with knives and—"

"Oh, *gross!*" Ben said.

"And ate 'em, and Bruno always got the brains. He cracked open their skulls like walnuts, scooped out the brains with both hands, and threw 'em down his gullet."

"I'm gonna puke!" Davy Ray cried out, and made retching noises. Then he laughed and Ben laughed, too.

"After a long time—like two years—Bruno was the only one left, and he was bigger'n ever," I continued. "But his face never healed up from the fire. He had one eye on his forehead and the other eye hung down on his chin." This brought more gusts of laughter. "So after all that time in the cave, and eatin' the other Nazis up, Bruno was crazy. He was hungry, but he only wanted one thing to eat: brains."

"*Yech!*" Ben said.

"Brains was all he wanted," I told my audience of two. "He was seven feet tall and he weighed three hundred pounds, and he had a long knife that could slice the top of your head right off. Well, the police and the army were lookin' for him all this time but they never could find him. They found a forest ranger with the top of his head cut off and his brains gone. They found an old moonshiner dead and his brains gone, too, and they figured Bruno was gettin' closer and closer to Zephyr."

"Then they called in James Bond and Batman!" Davy Ray said.

"No!" I shook my head gravely. "There wasn't anybody to call in. There was just the policemen and the army soldiers, and every night Bruno walked through the forest carryin' his knife and a lantern, and his face was so ugly it could freeze people solid like Medusa and then *slash!* he cut somebody's head open and *splatter!* there were the brains down his throat."

"Oh, sure!" Ben grinned. "I'll bet ol' Bruno's still in these woods right now, eatin' people's brains for supper, huh?"

"Nope," I said, formulating the conclusion of my tale. "The police and the soldiers found him, and they shot him so many times he looked like Swiss cheese. But every so often, if you happen to be out in the woods on a real dark night, you can see Bruno's lantern movin' through the trees." I spoke this in an icy whisper, and neither Davy Ray nor Ben did any more laughing. "Yeah, you can see his lantern movin' as he wanders in search of somebody's brains to eat. He casts that light all around, and if you get close to it, you can see the shine of his knife, but don't look at his face!" I held up a warning finger. "No, don't you look at his face, 'cause it'll drive you crazy and it might just make you want to eat some *brains!*" I yelled the last word and jumped as I yelled it, and Ben hollered with fright but Davy Ray just laughed again.

"Hey, that's not funny!" Ben protested.

"You don't have to worry about ol' Bruno," Davy Ray told him. "You don't have any brains, so that lets you off the—"

Davy Ray stopped speaking, and he just sat there staring into the dark.

"What is it?" I asked him.

"Ahhhh, he's tryin' to scare us!" Ben scoffed. "Well, it ain't workin'!"

Davy Ray's face had gone white. I swear I saw his scalp ripple, and the hair stand up. He said, "Guh . . . guh . . . guh . . ." and he lifted his arm and pointed.

I turned around to look in the direction he indicated. I heard Ben make a choked gasp. My own hair jittered on my head, and my heart kaboomed.

A light was coming toward us, through the trees.

"Guh . . . guh . . . God a'mighty!" Davy Ray croaked.

We all three were struck with the kind of horror that makes you want to dig a hole, jump in, and pull the hole in after you. The light was moving slowly, but coming closer. And as it came closer it broke into two, and all of us got down on our quaking bellies in the pine straw. In another moment I could tell what it was: a car's headlights. The car looked like it was going to roll right over our hiding-place, and then it veered away and we watched its red taillights flare as the driver applied the brakes. The car kept going, following a winding trail that was only fifty yards or so from our campsite, and in a couple of minutes it had disappeared amid the trees.

"Did you guys see that?" Davy Ray whispered.

"'Course we saw it!" Ben whispered back. "We're right here, aren't we?"

"Wonder who was in that car, and why they're way out here?" Davy Ray looked at me. "You want to find out, Cory?"

"Probably moonshiners," I answered. My voice trembled. "I think we'd better leave 'em alone."

Davy Ray picked up his flashlight. His face was still pallid, but his eyes shone with excitement. "I'm gonna find out what's goin' on! You guys can stay here if you want to!" He stood up, flicked on the flashlight, and began to stealthily follow the car. He stopped when he realized we weren't with him. "It's okay," he said. "I won't think you guys are scared or anythin'."

"Good," Ben answered, "'cause I'm stickin' right here."

I stood up. If Davy Ray had enough courage to go, then so did I. Besides, I wanted to know who was driving a car way out here in the woods myself. "Come on!" he said. "But watch where you step!"

"I'm not stayin' here alone!" Ben hoisted himself to his feet. "You two are damn *crazy*, you know that?"

"Yeah." Davy Ray sounded proud about it. "Everybody stay low and no talkin'!"

We crept from tree to tree, following the trail that we hadn't even seen when we'd set up camp at nightfall. Davy Ray kept the flashlight's beam aimed at the ground, so it couldn't be spotted by anyone up ahead. The trail wound back and forth between the trees. The owl was hooting again, and lightning bugs blinked around us. We'd gone a couple of hundred yards more along the trail when Davy Ray suddenly stopped and whispered, "There it is!"

We could see the car ahead of us. It was sitting still, but its lights were on and the engine was rumbling. We crouched down in the pine straw, and I don't know about the others, but my heart was going a mile a minute. The car didn't move. Whoever was sitting behind the wheel didn't get out. "I've gotta pee!" Ben whispered urgently. Davy Ray told him to squeeze it.

After five or six minutes, we saw more lights coming through the woods from the opposite direction. It was another car, this one a black Cadillac, and it stopped, facing the first car. Davy Ray looked at me, his expression saying we'd really stumbled into something this time. I didn't particularly care what was going on; I just wanted to get away from what I figured was a meeting of moonshiners. Then the doors of the first car opened, and two people got out.

"Oh, man!" Davy Ray breathed.

Standing in the crossing of headlights were two men wearing ordinary clothes except until you got to their heads, which were covered by white masks. One of the men was medium-sized, the other was big and fat, with a belly that flopped over the waist of his jeans. The medium-sized man was smoking either a cigarette or cigar, it was hard to tell which, and he angled his masked head and blew smoke from the corner of his mouth. Then the Cadillac's doors opened, and I almost swallowed my heart when Bodean Blaylock slid out from behind the wheel. It was him, all right; I remembered his face from when he'd looked across the poker table at me, same to say he had my granddaddy and wasn't about to let him go. A slim man with slicked-back dark hair and a jutting slab of a chin got out of the passenger side; he was wearing tight black pants and a red shirt with cowboy spangles on the shoulders, and at first I thought it was Donny Blaylock but Donny didn't have a chin like that. This man opened the Cadillac's right rear door, and the whole car trembled as whoever was still inside started to climb out.

It was a mountain on two legs.

His gut was tremendous, straining the front of the red-checked shirt and overalls he wore. When he rose up to his full height, he was maybe six and a half feet tall. He was baldheaded except for a wisp of gray hair circling his acorn-shaped skull, and he had a trimmed gray beard that angled to a point below his chin. He breathed like a bellows, his face a ruddy mass of wrinkled flesh. "You boys goin' to a masquerade party?" he growled in a voice like a cement mixer, and he laughed *hut-hut-hut* like a big old engine starting to fire its plugs. Bodean laughed, and the other man laughed, too. The men wearing the masks shifted uneasily. "You fellas look like sacks of shit," the mountainous bulk said as he shambled forward. I swear his hands were the size of country hams, and his feet in their scuffed-up boots looked like they could stomp down small trees.

The masked man with the bulbous belly said, "We're incog . . . incog . . . We don't wanna be recognized."

"Shit, Dick!" the bearded monster said, and he guffawed again. "Have to be a blind fuckin' fool not to recognize your fat gut and ass!" Talk about the pot calling the kettle black, I thought.

"Awwww, you're not supposed to recognize us, Mr. Blaylock!" the man who'd been called Dick answered with a whine of petulance, and I realized with a double start that this man was Mr. Dick Moultry and the other was Biggun Blaylock, the fearsome head of the Blaylock clan himself.

Ben realized it, too. "Let's get outta here!" he whispered, but Davy Ray hissed, "Shut up!"

"Well," Biggun said, his hands on his massive hips, "I don't give a shit if you wear sackcloth and ashes. You bring the money?"

"Yes sir." Mr. Moultry reached into his pocket and brought out a wad of bills.

"Count it," Biggun ordered.

"Yes sir. Fifty . . . one hundred . . . hundred and fifty . . . two hundred . . ." He kept counting, up to four hundred dollars. "Take the money, Wade," Biggun said, and the man in the spangled shirt walked forward to get it.

"Just a minute," the second masked man said. "Where's the merchandise?" He was talking in a low, gruff voice that sounded false, yet I knew that voice from somewhere.

"Bodean, get what the fella wants," Biggun told him, and Bodean took the Cadillac's keys from the ignition and walked back to the trunk. Biggun's gaze stayed fixed on the man with the false voice. I was glad it wasn't directed at me, because it looked so intense it could puddle iron. "It's fine, quality work," Biggun said. "Just what you boys asked for."

"It oughta be. We're payin' enough for it."

"You want a demonstration?" Biggun grinned, his mouth full of gleaming teeth. "If I were you, friend, I'd get rid of that cheroot."

The masked man took a final pull on it, then he turned and flicked it right where we were hiding. It fell into the pine straw about four feet in front of me, and I saw its chewed plastic tip. I knew who smoked cheroots with a tip like that. It was Mr. Hargison, our mailman.

Bodean had opened the trunk. Now he closed it again, and he approached the two masked men carrying a small wooden box in his arms. He carried it gently, as if it might hold a sleeping baby.

"I want to see it," Mr. Hargison said in a voice I'd never heard Mr. Hargison use.

"Show him what he's buyin'," Biggun told his son, and Bodean carefully released a latch and opened the box's top to reveal what lay within. None of us guys could see inside the box, but Mr. Moultry walked over to peer in and he gave a low whistle behind his mask.

"That suit you?" Biggun asked.

"It'll do just fine," Mr. Hargison said. "They won't know what hit 'em until they're tap-dancin' in hell."

"I threw in an extra." Biggun grinned again, and I thought he looked like Satan himself. "For good luck," he said. "Close it up, Bodean. Wade, take our money."

"Davy Ray!" Ben whispered. "Somethin's crawlin' on me!"

"Shut up, goofus!"

"I mean it! Somethin's on me!"

"You hear anythin'?" Mr. Moultry asked, and that question froze the marrow in my bones.

The men were silent. Mr. Hargison gripped the box with both hands, and Wade Blaylock had the fistful of money. Biggun's head slowly turned from side to side, his blast-furnace eyes searching the woods. *Hoot-hoot*, went the distant owl. Ben made a soft, terrified whining noise. I hugged the earth, my chin buried in pine straw, and near my face Mr. Hargison's cheroot smoldered.

"I don't hear nothin'," Wade Blaylock said, and he took the money to his father. Biggun counted it again, his tongue flicking back and forth across his lower lip, and then he shoved the cash into a pocket. "Okey-dokey," he said to the two masked men. "I reckon that concludes our bidness, gents. Next time you want a special order, you know how to find me." He started trudging back to get into the Cadillac again, and Bodean moved fast to open the door for him.

"Thank you kindly, Mr. Blaylock." Something about Mr. Moultry's voice made me think of a ratty dog trying to lick up to a mean master. "We sure do appreciate the—"

"*SPIIIIIDERS!*"

The world ceased its turning. The owl went dumb. The Milky Way flickered on the verge of extinction.

Ben hollered it again: "*Spiders!*" He started thrashing wildly amid the pine needles. "*They're all over me!*"

I couldn't draw a breath. Just couldn't do it. Davy Ray stared at Ben, his mouth hanging open as Ben writhed and yelled. The five men were frozen where they stood, all of them looking in our direction. My heart thundered. Three seconds passed like a lifetime, and then Biggun Blaylock's shout parted the night: "*Get 'em!*"

"Run!" Davy Ray hollered, scrambling to his feet. "Run for it!"

Wade and Bodean were coming after us, their shadows thrown large by the crossing of headlights. Davy Ray was already running back in the direction we'd come, and I said, "Run, Ben!" as I got up and fled. Ben squawked and struggled up, his hands madly plucking at his clothes. I looked over my shoulder and saw Wade about to reach Ben, but then Ben put on a burst of frantic speed and left Wade snatching at empty air. "Come back here, you little bastards!" Bodean yelled as he chased after Davy Ray and me. "Get 'em, damn it!" Biggun bellowed. "Don't let 'em get away!"

Davy Ray was fast, I'll say that for him. He left me behind pretty quick. The only trouble was, he had the flashlight. I couldn't see where I was going, and I could hear Bodean's breath rasping behind me. I dared to glance back again, but Ben had headed off in another direction with Wade at his heels. Whether Mr. Hargison and Mr. Moultry were coming after us, too, I didn't know. Bodean Blaylock was reaching for me, about to snag my collar. I ducked my head and changed directions on him, and he skidded in the pine straw. I kept going, through the dark wilderness. "Davy Ray!" I shouted, because I no longer could see his light. "Where are you?"

"Over here, Cory!" he called, but I couldn't tell where he was. Behind me, I heard Bodean crashing through the underbrush. I had to keep running, the sweat leaking from my face. "Cory! Davy Ray!" Ben shouted from somewhere off to the right. "Goddammit, bring 'em back here!" Biggun raged. I dreaded finding out what that monstrous mountain and his brood would do to us, because whatever had been going on back there was definitely something he'd wanted to keep a secret. I started to call for Ben, but as I opened my mouth my left foot slid on pine needles and suddenly I was rolling down an embankment like a sack of grain. I rolled into bushes and vines, and when I stopped I was so scared and dizzy I almost upchucked my toasted marshmallows. I lay there on my belly, my chin scraped raw by something I'd collided with, while I waited for a hand to winnow from the darkness and grab the back of my neck. I heard branches cracking; Bodean was nearby. I held my breath, fearing he could hear my heartbeat. To me it sounded like a drum corps all slamming an anvil with sledgehammers, and if Bodean couldn't detect it, he was surely as deaf as a post.

His voice drifted to me, from my left. "Might as well give up, kid. I know where you are."

He sounded convincing. I almost answered him, but I realized he was just as much in the dark as I was. I kept my mouth shut and my head low.

A few seconds later, Bodean shouted from a little farther away:

"We're gonna find you! Oh yeah, don't you worry, we'll find every one of you sneakin' bastards!"

He was moving off. I waited a couple of minutes longer, listening to the Blaylocks calling to each other. Evidently, Davy Ray and Ben had both escaped and Biggun was furious about it. "You're gonna find those kids if it takes you all goddamn night!" he roared at his sons, and they meekly answered "Yes sir." I figured I'd better get out while the getting was good, so I got up and crept away like a whipped pup.

I sure didn't know where I was going. I knew only that I needed to put as much distance between my skin and the Blaylocks as possible. I thought about doubling back and trying to find the other guys, but I was scared the Blaylocks would nab me. I just kept walking into the dark. If bobcats and rattlers were anywhere around, they couldn't possibly be worse than the two-legged beasts behind me. Maybe I walked for half an hour before I found a boulder to crouch on, and under the stars I realized my predicament: my knapsack, with all it contained, was back at the campsite, wherever that might be from here. I had no food, no water, no flashlight, no matches, and Davy Ray had the compass.

I had a crushing thought: Mom had been right. I should've waited until I was thirteen.

8

Chile Willow

I have known long nights before. Like when I had strep throat and couldn't sleep and every minute seemed a torment. Or when Rebel had been sick with worms, and I stayed awake worrying as he coughed and whined. The night I spent huddled on that boulder, though, was an eternity of regret, fear, and discomfort all jammed into six hours. I knew one thing for sure: this was my last camping trip. I jumped at every imagined sound. I peered into the dark, seeing hulking shapes where there were only skinny pines. I would've tossed every issue of *National Geographic* on a bonfire for two peanut-butter sandwiches and a bottle of Green Spot. Sometime near dawn, the mosquitoes found me. They were so big I might've grabbed their legs and hitched a ride to Zephyr by air. I was miserable, from my red-blotched bites to my growling belly.

I had plenty of time, between slapping at skeeters and listening for the sounds of footsteps creeping up on me, to wonder what was in the box that Mr. Moultry and Mr. Hargison had paid four hundred dollars for. Man, that was a fortune of money! If the Blaylocks were involved, it had to be something wicked. What were Mr. Moultry and Mr. Hargison planning to do with the contents of that box? Something Mr. Hargison had said came back to me: *They won't know what hit 'em until they're tap-dancin' in hell.*

Whatever this was about, it was a bad enough business to be conducted late at night in the middle of the woods, and I had no doubt the Blaylocks would cut our throats—and maybe Mr. Moultry and Mr. Hargison would, too—to keep it a secret.

At last the sun began to rise, painting the sky pink and purple. I figured I'd better get moving again, in case the Blaylocks were somewhere close. Yesterday we'd been following the sun, and that had been afternoon, so I chose to head due east. I started off on aching legs, my heart hungry for home.

I figured I might be able to get to a high point and see Zephyr, or Saxon's Lake, or at least a road or a railroad track. On the hilltops, however, I could see only more woods. I did get a break, though, about two hours after dawn: a jet plane screamed overhead, and I saw its landing gears slide down. I changed course a few degrees, heading for what I hoped was the Air Force base. The woods, though, seemed to be thickening up rather than thinning. The sun was heating up, the ground rough underfoot, and soon I was wet with sweat. The gnats returned, with all their brothers, sisters, uncles, and cousins, and they swarmed around my head like a dark halo.

Soon I heard more jets shrieking, though I couldn't see them through the trees, and then I heard the dull *whump! whump! whump!* of explosions. I stopped, realizing I was near the bomb testing grounds. From the next ridge I could see dark plumes of smoke and dust rising into the sky to what I reasoned was the northeast. Which meant I was a long, arduous way from my front door.

My belly and the sun at its zenith told me it was high noon. I was supposed to have been home by now. My mother would start going crazy soon, and my dad would start warming up his whipping hand. What would hurt most would be admitting I wasn't as grown-up today as I thought I'd been yesterday.

I continued on, skirting the area where the bombs were dropped. The last thing I needed was to be greeted by a few hundred pounds of high explosive. I pushed through tangles of thorns that bit my skin and tore my clothes, and I gritted my teeth and took what was coming to me. Little panics kept flaring up inside me, my mind seeing rattlesnakes in every shadow. If ever I wished I could really fly, now was the time.

And then, all of a sudden, I emerged from the pine woods into a green, leafy glade. Sunlight glittered off the rippling water of a small pond, and in that water a girl was swimming. She must've not been there long because only the ends of her long, golden hair were wet. She was as brown as a berry, the water glistening on her arms and shoulders as she stroked back and forth. I was about to call to her, and then she flipped over on her back and I saw she was naked.

Instantly my heart jumped and I stepped behind a tree, more afraid to startle her than anything else. Her legs kicked blissfully, the small buds of her breasts visible above the surface. She wore nothing to cover the area between her long, sleek thighs either, and I was ashamed to be looking but my eyes were spellbound. She turned and slid underwater. When she came up again, halfway across the pond, she swept her thick wet tresses back from her forehead and flipped over once more, gazing up at the blue sky as she floated.

Now, this was an interesting situation, I reasoned. Here I stood, hungry and thirsty, covered with mosquito bites and thorn welts, knowing my mother and father were calling up the sheriff and the fire chief by now, and twenty feet in front of me was a shimmering green pond with a naked blond girl floating in it. I hadn't gotten a good look at her face yet, but I could tell she was older than me, maybe fifteen or sixteen. She was long and lean, and she swam not with the splashy giddiness of a child but with an elegant, easy grace. I saw her clothes lying at the base of a tree on the other side of the pond, and a trail led off into the woods. The girl dove under, her legs kicking, then she resurfaced and slowly swam toward her clothes. She stopped, her feet finding the slippery bottom. Then she started wading in toward shore, and the moment of truth was thrust upon me.

"Wait!" I called out.

She spun around. Her face turned red and her hands flew up to cover her breasts, and then she ducked down in the water up to her throat. "Who's there? Who said that?"

"I did." I came out, sheepishly, from my hiding-place. "Sorry."

"Who are *you*? How long have you been standin' there?"

"Just a couple of minutes," I said. I followed it with a white lie. "I didn't see anythin'."

The girl was staring at me with open-mouthed indignation, her wet hair crimped around her shoulders. Her face was illuminated by a spill of sunlight through the trees, and I looked beyond her anger at a vision of beauty. Which surprised me, because the power of her beauty hit me so hard and suddenly. There are many things a boy considers beautiful: the shine of a bike's paint, the luster of a dog's pelt, the singing of a yo-yo as it loops the loop, the yellow harvest moon, the green grass of a meadow, and free hours at hand. The face of a girl, no matter how well-constructed, is usually not in that realm of appreciation. At that moment, though, I forgot about my hungry belly and my mosquito bites and my thorn stings. A girl with the most beautiful face I'd ever seen was staring at me, her eyes pale cornflower blue, and I had the feeling of waking up from a prolonged, lazy sleep into a new world I had never realized existed.

"I'm lost," I managed to say.

"Where'd you come from? Were you spyin' on me?"

"No. I . . . came from that way." I motioned in the direction behind me.

"You're tellin' a story!" she snapped. "Ain't nobody lives up in them hills!"

"Yeah," I said. "I know."

She remained hunkered down in the water, her arms around herself. I could tell that the anger was gradually leaving her, because the expression in her eyes was softening. "Lost," she repeated. "Where do you live?"

"Zephyr."

"Oh, now I know you're tellin' a story! Zephyr's all the way on the other side of the valley!"

"I was campin' out last night," I told her. "Me and my friends. Somethin' happened, and I got lost."

"What happened?"

I shrugged. "Some men got after us."

"Are you tellin' me the honest truth?"

"I am, I swear it."

"All the way from *Zephyr*? You must be worn out!"

"Kinda," I said.

"Turn around," she told me. "Don't you dare look till I say for you to. All right?"

"All right," I agreed, and I turned my back to her. I heard her

209

getting out of the water, and in my mind I saw her naked from head to toe. Clothes rustled. In a minute or two she said, "You can turn around now." When I looked at her again, she was dressed in a pink T-shirt, blue jeans, and sneakers. "What's your name?" she asked, pushing her hair back from her forehead.

"Cory Mackenson."

"I'm Chile Willow," she said. "Come on with me, Cory."

Oh, she spoke my name so fine.

I followed her along the trail through the woods. She was taller than me. She didn't walk like a little girl. She was sixteen, I figured. Walking behind her, I inhaled her scent like the aroma of dew on newly cut grass. I tried to step where she stepped. If I'd had a tail, I would've wagged it. "I don't live too far," Chile Willow said, and I answered, "That's good."

On a dirt road stood a tarpaper shack with a chicken coop next to it and a rust-eaten car hulk sitting on cinderblocks in the weedy yard. The place was even worse than the run-down house where Granddaddy Jaybird had lost his shirt playing poker. I had already taken notice that Chile's jeans were patched and ragged, and there were dime-sized holes in her T-shirt. The house she lived in made the poorest dwelling in Bruton look like a palace. She opened the screen door on squalling hinges and said into the gloom, "Momma? I found somebody!"

I entered the house after her. The front room smelled of harsh cigarette smoke and turnip greens. A woman was sitting in a rocking chair, knitting as she rocked. She stared at me with the same cornflower blue eyes as her beautiful daughter, from a face seamed with wrinkles and burned dry by hard work in the sun. "Throw him back," she said, and her needles never stopped.

"He's lost," Chile told her. "*Was* lost, I mean. Says he came from Zephyr."

"Zephyr," the woman said. Her eyes returned to me. She wore a dark blue shift with yellow needlework across the front, and she had on rubber flipflops. "You're a long way from home, boy." Her voice was low and husky, as if the sun had dried up her lungs, too. On a scarred little table near at hand was an ashtray full of cigarette butts, and half a cigarette still burning.

"Yes, ma'am. I sure would like to call my folks. Can I use your phone?"

"Ain't got no phone," she said. "This ain't Zephyr."

"Oh. Well . . . can somebody take me home?"

Chile's mother plucked the cigarette from the ashtray, took a long pull on it, and set it back down. When she spoke again, the smoke dribbled from her mouth. "Bill's took the truck off. Be back directly, I reckon."

I wanted to ask how long "directly" might be, but that would be impolite. "Can I have a glass of water?" I asked Chile.

"Sure thing. You ought to take off that shirt, too, it's wringin' wet. Go on, take it off." While Chile went back to the dismal little kitchen, I unbuttoned my shirt and peeled it away from my skin. "Done got yourself in some thorns, boy," Chile's mother said, her mouth leaking smoke again. "Chile, bring the iodine in here and doctor this boy." Chile answered, "Yes'm," and I folded my sweat-drenched shirt up and stood waiting for pleasure and pain.

Chile had to pump the water out of the kitchen faucet. Coming out, the water spat and gurgled. When it got to me, it was warm and tinged with brown and contained in a jelly glass with a picture of Fred Flintstone on it. I took a taste and smelled something foul. Then Chile Willow's face was near mine, and the sweetness of her breath was like new roses. She had a swab of cotton and a bottle of iodine. "This might hurt a little bit," she said.

"He can take it," her mother answered for me.

Chile went to work. I winced and drew in my breath as the stinging started and then deepened. As the pain progressed, I watched Chile's face. Her hair was drying, falling in golden waves over her shoulders. Chile got down on her knees before me, the red cotton swab leaving streaks of red across my flesh. My heart was beating harder. Her pale blue eyes met mine, and she smiled. "You're doin' just fine," she said. I smiled back, though I was hurting so bad I wanted to cry.

"How old are you, boy?" Chile's mother inquired.

"Twelve." Another white lie rolled out: "I'll be thirteen soon." I kept looking at Chile's eyes. "How old are *you*?" I asked her.

"Me? I'm an old lady. I'm sixteen."

"You go to the high school?"

"Went one year," she said. "That was enough for me."

"You don't go to *school*?" I was amazed at this fact. "Wow!"

"She goes to school," the mother said, her needles at work. "School of hard knocks, same as I did."

"Aw, Mom," Chile said; from her cupid's-bow mouth, two words could sound like music.

I forgot about the stinging. Pain was nothing to a man like me. As Chile's mother said, I could take it. I looked around the gloomy room, with its stained and battered sticks of furniture, and when I looked at Chile's face again, it was like seeing the sun after a long, stormy night. Though the iodine was cruel, her touch was gentle. I imagined she must like me, to be so gentle. I had seen her naked. In all my life I had seen no female naked but my mother. I had been in the presence of Chile Willow only a short time, but what is time when a heart speaks? My heart was speaking to Chile Willow in that moment, as she bathed my cuts and gave me a smile. My heart was saying *If you were my girlfriend I would give you a hundred lightning bugs in a green glass jar, so you could always see your way. I would give you a meadow full of wildflowers, where no two blooms would ever be alike. I would give you my bicycle, with its golden eye to protect you. I would write a story for you, and make you a princess who lived in a white marble castle. If you would only like me, I would give you magic. If you would only like me.*

If you would only—

"You're a brave little boy," Chile said.

From the rear of the house, a baby began crying.

"Oh, Lord," Chile's mother said, and she put aside her needles. "Bubba's woke up." She stood up and walked in the direction of the crying, her flipflops smacking the splintery floor.

"I'll feed him in a minute," Chile said.

"Naw, I'll do it. Bill's gonna be back soon, and if I was you, I'd put that ring back on. You know how crazy he gets."

"Uh-huh, do I ever." This was said under Chile's breath. Something in her eyes had darkened. She swabbed the last thorn scrape and capped the iodine bottle. "There you go. All done."

Chile's mother returned, holding an infant that wasn't a year old. I stood in the middle of the room, my skin screaming as Chile got off her knees and went back into the kitchen. When she came back, she was wearing a thin gold band on the third finger of her left hand. She took the baby from her mother and began to rock it and croon softly.

"He's a feisty thing," the older woman said. "Gonna be a handful, that's for sure." She went to a window and pulled aside a flimsy curtain. "Here comes Bill now. Gonna get your ride home, fella."

I heard the pickup truck clattering as it pulled up almost to the porch. A door opened and slammed. Then through the screen door came Bill, who was tall and slim and had a crew cut and was all of eighteen years old. He wore dirty jeans and a blue shirt with a grease stain on the front, and he had heavy-lidded brown eyes and was chewing on a match. "Who's *he?*" he asked, first thing.

"Boy needs a ride to Zephyr," Chile's mother told him. "Got hisself lost in the woods."

"I ain't gone take him to Zephyr!" Bill protested with a scowl. "It's hotter'n hell in that truck!"

"Where'd you go?" Chile asked, her arms full of baby.

"Fixed that engine for old man Walsh. And if you think that was fun, you got another think comin'." He glanced at her as he strode past toward the kitchen. I saw him look right through her, as if she wasn't even there, and Chile's eyes had deadened.

"You get any money?" the mother called after him.

"Yeah, I got some money! You think I'm stupid, I wouldn't get no money for a job like that?"

"Bubba needs some fresh milk!" Chile said.

I heard the faucet pumping slimy water. "Shit," Bill muttered.

"You gonna take this boy home to Zephyr, or not?" Chile's mother asked.

"Not," he answered.

"Here." Chile offered the baby to her mother. "I'll drive him, then."

"The hell you say!" Bill came back into the room, holding brown water in another Flintstones jelly glass. "You can't drive nowhere, you ain't got no license!"

"I keep tellin' you I ought to—"

"You don't need to do no drivin'," Bill said, and he looked right through her again. "Your place is in this house. Tell her, Mrs. Purcell."

"I ain't barkin' up nobody's tree," Chile's mother said, but she didn't take the infant. She sat down in her rocking chair, put the cigarette in her mouth, and gripped the knitting needles.

Bill drank down the brown water and made a face. "All right, then. Hell with it. I'll take him to that gas station over near the base. He can use the pay phone."

"That okay with you, Cory?" Chile asked me.

"I . . ." My head was still spinning, and the sight of that gold ring hurt my eyes. "I guess so."

"Well, you better take what I'm offerin' or I'll just kick your butt out the door," Bill warned.

"I don't have any money for the phone," I said.

"Boy, you're in damn sorry shape, ain't you?" Bill took the glass back to the kitchen. "You ain't gettin' none of my work money, that's for sure!"

Chile reached down into the pocket of her jeans. "I've got some

213

money," she said, and her hand came out clutching a small red plastic purse in the shape of a heart. It was cracked and much-used, the kind of thing a little girl might buy at Woolworth's for ninety-nine cents. She popped it open. I saw a few coins inside it. "I just need a dime," I told her. She gave me a dime, one with Mercury's head on it, and I shoved it into my own pocket. She smiled at me, which was worth a fortune. "You'll get home all right."

"I know I will." I looked at the infant's face, and I saw he had her beautiful eyes of cornflower blue.

"Come on, if you're comin'," Bill said on his way past me to the door. He didn't spare a glance at his wife or baby. He went on out, the screen door slammed, and I heard the truck's engine snort.

I could not tear myself away from Chile Willow. In later years I would hear about the "chemistry" between two people, and what that meant; I would be told by my father about the "birds and the bees" but of course by then I would know all about it from my schoolmates. All I knew at that moment was a longing: to be older, taller, stronger, and handsome. To be able to kiss the lips of her lovely face, and crank back time so she didn't have Bill's baby in her arms. What I wanted to say to her, in that moment, was: *You should've waited for me.*

"Go on home where you belong, boy," Mrs. Purcell said. She was watching me intently, her needles paused, and I wondered if she knew what was in my head.

I would never set foot in this house again. I would never again see Chile Willow. I knew this, and I drank her in while I could.

Outside, Bill leaned on the horn. Bubba started crying again.

"Thank you," I told Chile, and I took my wet shirt and walked out into the sunlight. The truck was painted bilious green, its sides dented up, its body sagging to the left. A pair of red velvet dice dangled from the rearview mirror. I climbed into the passenger seat, a spring jabbing my butt. On the floorboard was a toolbox and coils of wires, and though the windows were rolled down, the interior smelled like sweat and a sickly sweet odor I later came to connect with miserable poverty. I looked at the house's doorway and saw Chile emerge into the light, cradling her baby. "Stop and get him some milk, Bill!" she called. I could see her mother standing behind her, in the musty gloom. It occurred to me that their faces were very much alike, though one had already been weathered by time and circumstance, probably a lot of disappointment and bitterness, too. I hoped Chile would be spared such a journey. I hoped she would never lock her smile away, and forget where she'd put the key.

" 'Bye, now!" she said to me.

I waved. Bill pulled the pickup truck away from the house, and dust boiled up off the road between Chile Willow and me.

It was a mile or more until the pavement started. Bill drove in silence, and let me off at a gas station on the edge of the air force base. As I was getting out, he said, "Hey, boy! Better watch where you put your pecker." Then he drove away, and I stood alone on the hot concrete.

Pain was nothing to a man like me.

The gas station's owner showed me where the pay phone was. I started to put the Mercury-head dime into the slot, but I couldn't let go of it. It had come from Chile Willow's purse. I just couldn't. I asked the owner to let me borrow a dime, telling him my dad would pay him back. "I ain't no bank," he huffed, but he took a dime out of the cash register anyway. In another moment it was tinkling down into the pay phone. I dialed the number, and Mom picked up on the second ring.

My folks were there to pick me up in about half an hour. I expected the worst, but I got a rib-busting squeeze from my mother and my dad grinned and cuffed me on the back of my head and I knew I was in high cotton. On the drive home, I learned that Davy Ray and Ben had reached Zephyr together about seven this morning and Sheriff Amory knew the whole story, that two masked men had bought something in a wooden box from Biggun Blaylock and then the Blaylocks had chased us through the forest. "The men with the masks were Mr. Hargison and Mr. Moultry," I said. I felt bad about this, because I recalled that Mr. Hargison had saved our skins from the Branlins. Still and all, the sheriff needed to know.

We passed the Air Force base, its runways and barracks and buildings enclosed by a high mesh fence topped with barbed wire. We drove along the forest road, passing the turnoff to the house of bad girls. Dad slowed almost imperceptibly as we drove past Saxon's Lake, but he didn't look at it. The exact place where I'd seen the figure in the flapping coat was lost in summer growth. As soon as the lake was behind us, Dad picked up speed again.

I was lavished with attention when I got home. I got a big bowl of chocolate ice cream and all the Oreos I could eat. Dad called me "pal" and "partner" with just about every breath. Even Rebel almost licked my face off. I had been delivered from the wilderness, and I was okay.

Of course they wanted to hear about my adventure, and they pressed me to tell them more about the girl who had treated my thorn scrapes. I told them her name, that she was sixteen years old, and that she was as beautiful as Cinderella in that Walt Disney movie. "I do believe our pal's got himself a crush on her," Dad said to Mom, and he grinned. I said, "Awww, I don't have time for any old girl!"

But I fell asleep on the sofa with a dime in my hand.

Before the sun set on Saturday afternoon, Sheriff Amory dropped by. He had been to see Davy Ray and Ben; now it was my turn to be questioned. We sat on the front porch, Rebel sprawled beside my chair and occasionally lifting his head to lick my hand, while in the distance thunder grumbled amid the darkening clouds. He listened to my story about the wooden box, and when I came to the part about the masked men being Mr. Dick Moultry and Mr. Gerald Hargison, he said, "Why do you think it was them, Cory, if you couldn't see their faces?"

"'Cause Biggun Blaylock called the fat one Dick and I saw the cheroot Mr. Hargison threw away and that's what he smokes, the kind with the white plastic tip."

"I see." He nodded, his long-jawed face betraying no emotion. "You know, there are probably a lot of fellas around here who smoke cheroots like that. And just 'cause Biggun Blaylock called a man by his first name doesn't mean it was Dick Moultry."

"It was them," I said. "Both of them."

"Davy Ray and Ben told me they didn't know who the masked men were."

"Maybe they don't, sir, but I do."

"All right, then, I'll make sure I find out where Dick and Gerald were 'round about eleven last night. I asked Davy Ray and Ben if they could take me to where this thing happened, but they said they couldn't find it again. Could you?"

"No sir. It was near a trail, though."

"Uh-huh. Trouble is, there are an awful lot of old loggin' roads and trails cut through those hills. You didn't happen to see what was inside that box, did you?"

"No sir. Whatever it was, Mr. Hargison said it was gonna make some people tap-dance in hell."

Sheriff Amory's brow furrowed. His black eyes held a spark of renewed interest. "Now, why do you think he'd say somethin' like that?"

"I don't know. But Biggun Blaylock would. He said he threw an extra one into the box."

"An extra what?"

"I don't know that, either." I watched lightning flicker on the horizon from sky to earth. "Are you gonna find Biggun Blaylock and ask him?"

"Biggun Blaylock," the sheriff said, "is an invisible man. I hear about him, and I know the things he and his sons do, but I never see him. I think he's got a hideout somewhere in the woods, probably pretty close to where you boys were." He watched the lightning, too, and he wound the fingers of his big hands together and worked his knuckles. "If I could ever catch one of his sons at some mischief, maybe I could smoke Biggun out. But to tell you the truth, Cory, the sheriff's office in Zephyr is pretty much a one-man operation. I don't get a whole lot of money from the county. Heck," he said, and he smiled thinly, "I only got this job 'cause nobody else would have it. My wife's on me all the time to give it up, says I oughta go back into the house-paintin' business." He shrugged. "Well," he said, dismissing those thoughts, "a whole lot of people around here are scared of the Blaylocks. Especially of Biggun. I doubt I could deputize more than five or six men to help me comb the woods for him. And by the time we found him—if we ever did—he'd have known we were comin' long before we got there. See my problem, Cory?"

"Yes sir. The Blaylocks are bigger than the law."

"Not bigger than the law," he corrected me. "Just a whole lot meaner."

A storm was coming. The wind was in the trees. Rebel got up and sniffed the air.

Sheriff Amory stood up. "I'll be goin' now," he said. "Thanks for helpin' me." In the fading light he looked old and burdened, his shoulders slightly stooped. He called good-bye to Mom and Dad through the screen door, and Dad came out to see him off. "You take care of yourself, Cory," he told me, then he and Dad walked together to his car. I stayed on the porch, stroking Rebel, as Sheriff Amory and Dad talked a few minutes more. When the sheriff had driven off and Dad returned to the porch, it was he who appeared burdened. "Come on in, partner," he said, and held the door open for me. "It's gonna get bad out."

The wind roared that night. The rain pounded down, and the lightning was scrawled like the track of a mysterious finger over my hometown.

That was the night I first dreamed about the four black girls, all dressed up and with their shoes shined, who stood beneath a leafless tree calling my name again and again and again.

9

Summer Winds Up

August was dying. So was summer. Schooldays, golden rule days; those lay ahead, on the gilded rim of autumn.

These things happened in the last days of summer: I learned that Sheriff Amory had indeed visited Mr. Hargison and Mr. Moultry. Their wives had told the sheriff that both men were home all night that particular night, that they hadn't even set one foot outside their front doors. The sheriff couldn't do anything else; after all, I hadn't seen the faces of the two men who'd accepted that wooden box from Biggun Blaylock.

The September issue of *Famous Monsters* came to my mailbox. On the envelope that bore my name there was a long green smear of snot.

Mom answered the telephone one morning, and said, "Cory! It's for you!"

I came to the phone. On the other end was Mrs. Evelyn Prathmore, who informed me that I had won third place in the short-story division of the Zephyr Art Council's Writing Contest. I was to be given a plaque with my name on it, she told me. Would I be prepared to read my story during a program at the library the second Saturday of September?

I was stunned. I stammered a yes. Instantly upon putting the telephone down, I was struck first with a surge of joy that almost lifted me out of my Hush Puppies and then a crush of terror that about slammed me to the floor. Read my story? *Aloud?* To a roomful of people I hardly knew?

Mom calmed me down. That was part of her job, and she was good at it. She told me I had plenty of time to practice, and she said I had made her so proud, she wanted to bust. She called Dad at the dairy, and he told me he'd bring me home two cold bottles of chocolate milk. When I called Johnny, Davy Ray, and Ben to tell them the news, they thought it was great, too, and they congratulated me, but all of them quickly pricked the boil of my nascent terror by reacting dolefully to the fact that I had to read my story aloud. What if your zipper breaks and it won't stay up? Davy Ray asked. What if you start shakin' so hard you can't even hold the paper? Ben asked. What if you open your mouth to talk and your voice goes and you can't even say a single word? Johnny asked.

Friends. They really know how to knock you off your pedestal, don't they?

Three days before school started, on a clear afternoon with fleecy clouds in the sky and a cool breeze blowing, we all rode our bikes to the ball field, our gloves laced to the handlebars. We took our positions around the diamond, which was cleated up and going to weed. On the scoreboard was the proof that our Little League team was not alone in agony; the men's team, the Quails, had suffered a five-to-zip loss from the Air Force base team, the High Flyers. We stood with pools of shadow around our ankles and threw a ball back and forth to each other as we talked with some sadness about the passing of summer. We were in our secret hearts excited about the beginning of school. There comes a time when freedom becomes . . . well, too free. We were ready to be regulated, so we could fly again next summer.

We threw fastballs and curves, fly balls and dust-kickers. Ben had the best wormburner you ever saw, and Johnny could make it fishtail an instant before it smacked into your glove. Too bad we were strikeout kings, each and every one. Well, there was always next season.

We'd been there maybe forty minutes or so, working up a sweat, when Davy Ray said, "Hey, look who's comin'!" We all looked. Walking through the weeds toward us was Nemo Curliss, his hands plunged deep into the pockets of his jeans. He was still a beanpole, his skin still buttermilk white. His mother ruled that roost, for sure.

"Hi!" I said to him. "Hey, Nemo!" Davy Ray called. "Come on and throw us a few!"

"Oh, great!" Johnny said, recalling his blistered hand. "Uh . . . why don't you throw some to Ben instead?"

Nemo shook his head, his face downcast. He continued walking across the field, passing Johnny and Ben, and he approached me at home plate. When he stopped and lifted his face, I saw he'd been crying. His eyes behind the thick glasses were red and swollen, the tear tracks glistening on his cheeks.

"What's wrong?" I asked. "Somebody been beatin' up on you?"

"No," he said. "I . . . I . . ."

Davy Ray came up, holding the baseball. "What is it? Nemo, you been cryin'?"

"I . . ." He squeezed out a small sob. He was trying to get control of himself, but it was more than he could manage. "I've gotta go," he said.

"Gotta go?" I frowned. "Go where, Nemo?"

"Away. Jutht . . ." He made a gesture with a skinny arm. "Jutht away."

Ben and Johnny arrived at home plate. We stood in a circle around Nemo as he sobbed and wiped his runny nose. Ben couldn't bear the sight, and he walked off a few paces and kicked a stone around. "I . . . went to your houth, to tell you, and your mom told me you were here," Nemo explained. "I wanted to let you know."

"Well, where do you have to go? Are you gonna go visit somebody?" I asked.

"No." Fresh tears ran down his face. It was a terrible sight to behold. "We've gotta move, Cory."

"*Move?* To where?"

"I don't know. Thomeblathe a long way from here."

"Gosh," Johnny said. "You hardly lived in Zephyr a whole summer!"

"We were hopin' you could play on our team next year!" Davy told him.

"Yeah," I said. "And we thought you were gonna go to our school."

"No." Nemo kept shaking his head, his puffy eyes full of torment. "No. No. I can't. We've gotta move. Gotta move tomorrow."

"*Tomorrow?* How come so fast?"

"Mom thez. Gotta move. Tho Dad can thell thome shirts."

The shirts. Ah yes, the shirts. Nobody wore tailored white shirts in Zephyr. I doubted that anybody wore tailored white shirts in any of the towns Mr. Curliss took his wife and son and his fabric swatches to. I doubted if anybody ever would.

"I can't . . ." Nemo stared at me, and the pain of his gaze made my heart hurt. "I can't . . . ever make no friendth," he said. "'Cauthe . . . we've alwath gotta move."

"I'm sorry, Nemo," I said. "Really I am. I wish you didn't have to move." On an impulse, I took the baseball out of my glove and held it out to him. "Here you go. You keep this, so you can remember your buddies here in Zephyr. Okay?"

Nemo hesitated. Then he reached out and wrapped the skinny fingers of his miracle pitching hand around the ball, and he accepted it. Here Johnny showed his true class; the baseball belonged to him, but he never said a word.

Nemo turned the baseball over and over between both hands, and I saw the red-stitched seam reflected in his glasses. He stared at that baseball as if into the depths of a magic crystal. "I want to thtay here," he said softly. His nose was running, and he sniffled. "I want to thtay here, and go to thcool and have friendth." He looked at me. "I jutht want to be like everybody elth. I want to thtay here so *bad*."

"Maybe you can come back sometime," Johnny offered, but it was a measly crumb. "Maybe you can—"

"No," Nemo interrupted. "I'll never come back. Never. Never even for a thingle day." He turned his head, facing the house they would soon be leaving. A tear crawled down his face and hung quivering from his chin. "Mom thez Dadth gotta thell thirts tho we can have money. At night thometimeth thee hollerth at him and callth him lathee, and thee thez thee never thouda married him. And he thez, 'It'll be the nextht town. The nextht town, that'll be the lucky break.'" Nemo's face swung back to mine. It had changed in that instant. He was still crying, but there was rage in his eyes so powerful that I had to step back a pace to escape its heat. "Ith never gonna be the nextht town," he said. "We're gonna move and move and move, and my mom'th gonna alwath holler and my dad'th gonna alwath thay it'll be the nextht town. But it'll be a lie."

Nemo was silent, but the rage spoke. His fingers squeezed around the baseball, his knuckles whitening, his eyes fixed on nothing.

"We're gonna miss you, Nemo," I said.

"Yeah," Johnny said. "You're okay."

"You'll get up to the mound someday, Nemo," Davy Ray told him. "When you get there, you strike 'em all out. Hear?"

"Yeth," he answered, but there wasn't much conviction in his voice. "I with I didn't have to . . ." He faded off; there was no point in it, because he was a little boy and he had to go.

Nemo began walking home across the field, the baseball gripped in his hand. "So long!" I called to him, but he didn't respond. I imagined what life must be like for him: forbidden to play the game he was so naturally gifted at, shuttered away in a series of houses in a parade of towns, staying in one place only long enough to get picked on and beaten up but never long enough for guys to get to know who and what he was behind the pale skin, the lisp, and the thick glasses. I could never have stood such suffering.

Nemo screamed.

It came out of him with such force that the sound made us jump. The scream changed, became a wail that rose up and up, painful in its longing. And then Nemo spun around, his head and shoulders first and then his hips, and I saw his eyes were wide and enraged and his teeth were clenched. His throwing arm whipped around in a blur, his backbone popped like a whip, and he hurled that baseball almost straight up into the sky.

I saw it go up. I saw it keep going. I saw it become a dark dot. Then the sun took it.

Nemo was on his knees, the scream and the throw having drained all the strength out of him. He blinked, his glasses crooked on his face.

"Catch it!" Davy Ray said, squinting up. "Here it comes down!"

"Where?" Johnny asked, lifting his glove.

"Where is it?" I asked, stepping away from the others to try to find it in the glare.

Ben was looking up, too. His glove hung at his side. "That bugger," he said softly, "is *gone.*"

We waited, searching the sky.

We waited, our gloves ready.

We waited.

I glanced at Nemo. He had gotten up, and was walking home. His stride was neither fast nor slow, just resigned. He knew what was waiting for him in the next town, and in the town after that. "Nemo!" I shouted after him. He just kept walking, and he did not look back.

We waited for the ball to come down.

After a while, we sat down in the red dirt. Our eyes scanned the sky as the fleecy clouds moved and the sun began to sink toward the west.

No one spoke. No one knew what to say.

In later days, Ben would speculate that the wind blew the ball into the river. Johnny would believe a flock of birds had hit it, and knocked it off course. Davy Ray would say something must've been wrong with the ball, that it had come to pieces way up there and we hadn't seen the skin and the innards plummet back to earth.

And me?

I just believed.

Twilight came upon us. At last I climbed on Rocket, the other guys got on their bikes, and we left the ball field and our summer dreams. Our faces now were turned toward autumn. I was going to have to tell somebody soon about the four black girls I saw in my sleep, the ones all dressed up and calling my name under a tree with no leaves. I was going to have to read my story about the man at the bottom of Saxon's Lake in front of a roomful of people. I was going to have to figure out what was in that wooden box Biggun Blaylock had sold in the dead of night for four hundred dollars.

I was going to have to help my father find peace.

We pedaled on, four buddies with the wind at our backs and all roads leading to the future.

THREE
Burning Autumn

Green-Feathered Hat — The Magic
Box — Dinner with Vernon — The Wrath
of Five Thunders — Case #3432 — Dead
Man Driving — High Noon in Zephyr —
From the Lost World

1

Green-Feathered Hat

"**C**ory?"

I pretended I didn't hear the ominous whisper.

"Cory?"

No. I wasn't going to look. At the front of the schoolroom, Mrs. Judith Harper—otherwise known as "Hairpie," "Harpy," and "Old Leather-lungs"—was demonstrating on the blackboard the division of fractions. Arithmetic was for me a walk into the Twilight Zone; this dividing fractions stuff was a mystifying fall into the Outer Limits.

"Cory?" she whispered again, behind me. "I've got a big ole green booger on my finger."

Oh my Lord, I thought. Not again!

"If you don't turn around and smile at me, I'm gone wipe it on the back of your neck."

It was the fourth day of class. I knew on the first day that it was going to be a long year, because some idiot had decreed the Demon a "gifted child" and had double-promoted her, and like the fickle finger of fate, Mrs. Harper had devised a seating chart—boy, girl, boy, girl, boy, girl—that put the Demon in the desk at my back.

And the worst part, the very worst, was that—as Davy Ray told me and laughed wickedly—she had a crush on me as big as the cheesy green moon.

"*Cory?*" Her voice demanded my attention.

I had to turn around. Last time I'd resisted, she'd smeared saliva on the back of my neck in the shape of a heart.

Brenda Sutley was grinning, her red hair oily and ratty and her wandering eyes shining with mischief. She held up her index finger, which had a dirt-grimed nail but no booger on it.

"Got'cha," she whispered.

"*Cory Jay Mackenson!*" Leatherlungs roared. "*Turn around this instant!*"

I did, almost giving myself whiplash. I heard the traitors around me giggling, knowing that the Harpy would not be satisfied with this display of respect. "Oh, I guess you know all about the division of fractions by now, don't you?" she inquired, her hands on hips as wide as a Patton tank. "Well, why don't you come up here and do some division for us, to show us how it's done?" She held the accursed yellow chalk out to me.

If I am ever on death row, the walk to the electric chair will be no more terrifying than that walk from my desk to the chalk in Mrs. Harper's hand and then, ultimately, to the blackboard. "All right," she said as I stood there shoulder-slumped and hang-doggy. "Write down these fractions." She rattled some off, and when I copied them my chalk broke and Nelson Bittner laughed and in two seconds I had a fellow sufferer up there with me.

Everybody knew by now: we weren't going to be able to defeat Mrs. Harper with a frontal attack. We weren't going to be able to storm her ramparts and yell victory over her scattered math books. It would have to be a slow, insidious war of snipers and booby traps, a painstaking probe to learn her weakness. All us kids had found out by now that all teachers had a sore spot; some went crazy over gum chewing, others insane over behind-the-back giggles, still others nuts over the repeated squeaking and scuffing of shoes on the linoleum. Machine-gun coughs, donkeylike snorts, a fusillade of throat clearing, spitballs stuck to the blackboard: all these were arsenals in the battle against Hitlerian teachers. Who knows? Maybe we could get the Demon to bring to class a dead, stinking animal in a shoebox, or get her to sneeze and blow ribbons of snot out of those talented nostrils of hers to make Mrs. Harper's hair uncurl.

"Wrong! Wrong! Wrong!" Leatherlungs bellowed at me as I finished my queasy attempt at fraction division. "Go sit down and pay attention, you blockhead!"

Between Leatherlungs and the Demon, I was really in for it.

After the three o'clock bell had rung and Davy Ray, Johnny, Ben, and I had jawed about the events of the day, I pedaled home on Rocket under a dark, glowering sky. I found Mom at home, cleaning the oven. "Cory!" she said when I walked into the kitchen intent on raiding the cookie jar. "Lady from the mayor's office called for you about ten minutes ago. Mayor Swope wants to see you."

"Mayor Swope?" I paused with my hand reaching for a Lorna Doone. "What for?"

"Didn't say what for, but she said it was important." Mom glanced out the window. "A storm's blowin' up. Your father'll drive you over to the courthouse, if you can wait an hour."

My curiosity was piqued. What would Mayor Swope want with *me?* I looked out the window as Mom continued her oven cleaning, and judged the gathering clouds. "I think I can get there before it starts rainin'," I said.

Mom pulled her head out of the oven, looked at the sky again, and frowned. "I don't know. It might start pourin' on you."

I shrugged. "I'll be all right."

She hesitated, her fretful nature gnawing at her. Ever since my camping trip, though, I could tell she'd been making a mighty effort to stop worrying so much about me. Even though I'd gotten lost, I'd proven I could survive in the face of hardship. Finally, she said, "Go on, then."

I took two Lorna Doones and headed for the porch.

"If it starts comin' down hard, you stay at the courthouse!" she called. "Hear?"

"I hear!" I told her, and I got on Rocket and pedaled as I crunched the Lorna Doones between my teeth. Not too far from the house, Rocket suddenly shuddered and I felt the handlebars jerk to the left. Ahead of me, the Branlins were pedaling side by side on their black bikes, but they were going in the same direction as me and didn't see me. Rocket wanted to turn to the left at the next intersection, and I followed Rocket's sage advice to take a detour.

Thunder was rumbling and it was starting to sprinkle a little as I reached the dark-stoned, gothic-styled courthouse at the end of Merchants Street. The drops were chilly; summer's warm rain was a thing of the past. I left Rocket chained to a fire hydrant and went into the courthouse, which smelled like a moldy basement. A sign on the wall said Mayor Swope's office was on the second floor, and I climbed the wide staircase, the high windows around me letting in murky, storm-blue light. At the top of the staircase, three carved gargoyles sat atop the black walnut banister, their scaly legs curled up and their claws folded across their chests. One wall was decorated with an old tattered Confederate flag and there were dusty display cases holding butternut uniforms riddled with moth holes. Above my head was a darkened glass cupola, reachable only by ladder, and through the cupola I heard thunder resonate as through a bell jar.

I walked along the long corridor, which had a floor of black and white linoleum squares. On either side were offices: License Bureau, County Tax Department, Probate Judge, Traffic Court, and the like. None of their lights were on. I saw a man with dark hair and a blue-paisley bow tie coming out of a pebbled-glass door marked Sanita-

229

tion and Maintenance. He locked the door from a ring of jingling keys and looked at me. "Can I help you, young fella?" he asked.

"I'm supposed to see Mayor Swope," I said.

"His office is at the end of the corridor." He checked his pocket watch. "Might be gone home by now, though. Most everybody leaves around three-thirty."

"Thank you," I told him, and I went on. I heard his keys jingling as he walked toward the stairs, and he whistled a tune I didn't know.

I passed the council's chambers and the recorder's office—both dark—and at the corridor's end I faced a big oak door with brass letters on it that said OFFICE OF THE MAYOR. I wasn't sure if I was supposed to knock or not, and there was no buzzer. I grappled with the question of etiquette here for a few seconds, as the thunder growled outside. Then I balled up my fist and knocked.

In a few seconds the door opened. A woman with horn-rimmed glasses and an iron-gray mountain of hair peered out. Her face was like a chunk of granite, all hard ridges and cliffs. Her eyebrows lifted in a question.

"I'm . . . here to see Mayor Swope," I said.

"Oh. You're Cory Mackenson."

"Yes ma'am."

"Come in." She opened the door wider, and I slipped in past her. As I did, I got a jolt of either violet-scented perfume or hair spray up my nostrils. I had entered a red-carpeted room which held a desk, a row of chairs, and a magazine rack. A map of Zephyr, brown at the edges, adorned one wall. On the desk there was an in tray and an out tray, a neat stack of papers, framed photographs of a baby being held between a smiling young woman and man, and a nameplate that said MRS. INEZ AXFORD and, underneath that in smaller letters, MAYOR'S SECRETARY.

"Just have a seat for a minute, please." Mrs. Axford walked across the room to another door. She rapped softly on it, and I heard Mayor Swope say in his mushmouth accent, "Yes?" from the other side. Mrs. Axford opened it. "The boy's here," she said.

"Thank you, Inez." I heard a chair creak. "I believe that finishes us up for the day. You can go on home if you like."

"Want me to send him in?"

"Two minutes and I'll be with him."

"Yes sir. Oh . . . did you sign that application for the new traffic lights?"

"Need to study that a little more, Inez. Get to it first thing in the mornin'."

"Yes sir. I'll be goin' on, then." She retreated from the mayor's domain and closed the door and said to me, "He'll be with you in two minutes." As I waited, Mrs. Axford locked her desk, got her sturdy brown purse, and straightened the photographs on her desk. She wedged her purse up under her arm, took a long look around the office to make sure everything was in its proper place, and then she walked out the door into the hallway without saying boot, shoot, or scoot to me.

I waited. Thunder boomed overhead and rolled through the courthouse. I heard the rain start—slowly at first, then building up to a hammering.

The door to the mayor's office opened, and Mayor Swope emerged. The sleeves of his blue shirt were rolled up, his initials in white on the breast pocket, his suspenders striped with red. "Cory!" he said, smiling. "Come in and let's have us a talk!"

I didn't know what to make of this. I knew who Mayor Swope was and all, but I'd never spoken to him. And here he was, smiling and motioning me into his office! The guys would believe this about as much as they believed I'd stuck a broomstick down Old Moses's throat!

"Come in, come in!" the mayor urged.

I walked into his office. Everything was fashioned of dark, glistening wood. The air smelled of sweet pipe tobacco. There was a desk in the office that seemed as big as the deck of an aircraft carrier. Shelves were full of thick, leatherbound books. They looked to me as if they had never been touched, because none had bookmarks in them. Two burly black leather chairs faced the desk over an expanse of Persian carpet. Windows afforded a view of Merchants Street, but right now the rain was streaming down them.

Mayor Swope, his gray hair combed back from a widow's peak and his eyes dark blue and friendly, closed the door. He said, "Have a seat, Cory." I hesitated. "Doesn't matter which one." I took the one on his left. The leather pooted when I sat down in it. Mayor Swope settled himself in his own chair, which had scrolled armrests. On his flattop of a desk was a telephone, a leather-covered jar full of pens, a can of Field and Stream tobacco, and a pipe rack cradling four pipes. One of the pipes was white, and had a man's bearded face carved into it.

"Gettin' some rain out there, aren't we?" he asked, his fingers lacing together. He smiled again, and this close I saw his teeth were discolored.

"Yes sir."

"Well, the farmers need it. Just so we don't have another flood, huh?"

"Yes sir."

Mayor Swope cleared his throat. His fingers tapped. "Are your folks waitin' for you?" he asked.

"No sir. I came on my bike."

"Oh. Gosh, you're gonna have a wet ride home."

"I don't mind."

"Wouldn't be good," he said, "if you had an accident on the way. You know, with that rain comin' down so hard, a car could hit you, you could go down in a ditch and . . ." His smile had slipped. Now it crept back. "Well, it wouldn't be good."

"No sir."

"I suppose you're wonderin' why I wanted to see you?"

I nodded.

"You know I was on the panel that judged the writin' contest? I enjoyed your story. Yessir, it deserved a prize." He picked up a briar pipe and popped open the can of tobacco. "It surely did. You're the youngest person ever to win a plaque in the contest." I watched his fingers as he began to fill the pipe's bowl with bits of tobacco. "I checked the records. You're the youngest by far. That ought to make you and your folks very proud."

"I guess so."

"Oh, you don't have to be so modest, Cory! I sure couldn't write like that when I was your age! Nosir! I was good at math, but English wasn't my subject." He produced a pack of matches from his pocket, struck one, and touched it to the tobacco in his pipe. Blue smoke bloomed around his mouth. His eyes were on me. "You've got a keen imagination," he said. "That part in your story about seein' somebody standin' in the woods across the road. I liked that part. How'd you happen to come up with that?"

"It really—" *Happened,* I was going to say. But before I could, somebody knocked at the door. Mrs. Axford looked in. "Mayor Swope?" she said. "Lord, it's pourin' cats and dogs! I couldn't even get to my car, and I just had my hair fixed yesterday! Do you have an umbrella I might borrow?"

"I believe so, Inez. Look in that closet over there."

She opened a closet and rummaged around in it. "Should be one in the corner," Mayor Swope told her. "Smells awfully musty in here!" Mrs. Axford said. "I believe somethin's mildewed!"

"Yeah, gotta clean it out one of these days," he said.

Mrs. Axford came out of the closet clutching an umbrella. But her nose was wrinkled, and in her other hand she was clutching two articles of clothing that were white with mildew. "Look at these!" she said. "I believe mushrooms are growin' in here!"

My heart seized up.

Mrs. Axford was holding a mildew-blotched overcoat and a hat that appeared to have been run through a washer and wringer.

And in the band of that battered hat was a silver disc and a crumpled green feather.

"Whew! Just smell it!" Mrs. Axford made a face that might've stopped a clock. "What're you keepin' this stuff for?"

"That's my favorite hat. Was, at least. It got ruined the night of the flood, but I thought I could get it fixed. And I've had that raincoat for fifteen years."

"No wonder you won't let me clean out your closet! What else is in here?"

"Never you mind! Run on, now! Leroy's waitin' at home for you!"

"You want me to throw these in the garbage on my way out?"

"No, Lord no!" Mayor Swope said. "Just put 'em back in there and close the door!"

"I swear," Mrs. Axford said as she returned the items to the closet, "you men are worse about hangin' on to old clothes than little babies with their blankets." She closed the door with a firm *thunk*. "There. I can still smell that mildew, though."

"It's all right, Inez. You go on home, and be careful on the road."

"I will." She gave me a quick glance, and then she walked out of the office with the umbrella.

I don't think I had drawn a breath during that entire exchange. Now I pulled one in, and I shivered as the air burned my lungs.

"Now, Cory," Mayor Swope said, "where were we? Oh yes: the man across the road. How'd you come up with that?"

"I . . . I . . ." The green-feathered hat was in a closet ten feet from me. Mayor Swope was the man who'd worn it that night when the floodwaters had raged in the streets of Bruton. "I . . . never said it was a man," I answered. "I just said . . . it was somebody standin' there."

"Well, that was a nice touch. I'll bet that was an excitin' mornin' for you, wasn't it?" He reached into another pocket, and when his hand came into view there was a small silver blade in it.

It was the knife I'd seen in his hand, that night when I was afraid he was going to sneak up behind my dad and stab him in the back for what he'd seen at Saxon's Lake.

"I wish I could write," Mayor Swope said. He turned the blade around. On its other end was a blunt little piece of metal, which he used to tamp the burning tobacco down in his pipe. "I've always liked mysteries."

"Me too," I managed to rasp.

He stood up, rain pelting the windows behind him. Lightning zigzagged over Zephyr, and the lights suddenly flickered. Thunder crashed. "Oh my," Mayor Swope said. "That was a little too close, wasn't it?"

"Yes sir." My hands were about to break the armrests of my chair.

"I want you," he said, "to wait right here for a minute. There's somethin' I want to show you, and I think it'll explain things." He crossed the room, the pipe clenched between his teeth and a scrawl of smoke behind him, and he went out into the area where Mrs. Axford's desk was. He left the door ajar, and I could hear him opening the drawer of a filing cabinet.

My gaze went to the closet.

The green feather was in there. So close. What if I was to pluck it from its hat and compare it to the green feather I'd found on the sole of my shoe? If the feathers matched, what then?

I had to move fast if I was going to move at all.

The filing cabinet's drawer closed. Another opened. "Just a minute!" Mayor Swope called to me. "It's not where it's supposed to be!"

I had to go. Right now.

I got up on rubbery legs and opened the closet. The reek of mildewed cloth hit me in the face like a damp slap. But the coat and the hat were there on the floor, nudged up into a corner. I heard the drawer slide shut. I grasped the feather and tugged at it. It wouldn't come loose.

Mayor Swope was coming back into the office. My heart was a cold stone in my throat. Thunder boomed and the rain slammed against the windows, and I grasped that green feather and jerked it and this time it tore loose from the hatband. It was mine.

"Cory? What're you doin' in—"

Lightning flared, so close you could hear the sizzle. The lights went out, and the next crack of thunder shook the windows.

I stood in the dark, the green feather in my hand and Mayor Swope in the doorway.

"Don't move, Cory," he said. "Say somethin'."

I didn't. I edged toward the wall and pressed my back against it.

"Cory? Come on, now. Let's don't play games." I heard him shut the door. A floorboard creaked, ever so quietly. He was moving. "Let's sit down and talk, Cory. There's somethin' very important you need to understand."

Outside, the clouds had gone almost black, and the room was a dungeon. I thought I could see his tall, thin shape gliding slowly toward me across the Persian carpet. I was going to have to get through him to the door.

"No need for this," Mayor Swope said, his voice trying to sound calm and reassuring. It had the same hollow ring as Mr. Hargison's false voice. "Cory?" I heard him release a long, resigned sigh. "You *know*, don't you?"

Darned right I knew.

"Where are you, son? Talk to me."

I didn't dare.

"How'd you find out?" he asked. "Just tell me that."

Lightning flickered and hissed. By its split-second glare I could see Mayor Swope, white as a zombie, standing at the center of the room with pipe smoke drifting around him like a wraith. Now my heart was really hammering; a spark of lightning had jumped off something metal clenched in his right hand.

"I'm sorry you found out, Cory," Mayor Swope said. "I didn't want you to get hurt."

I couldn't help it; in my panic, I blurted it out: "I wanna go home!"

"I can't let you do that," he said, and his shape began moving toward me through the electric-charged dark. "You understand, don't you?"

I understood. My legs responded first; they propelled me across the Persian carpet toward the way out, and my lungs snagged a breath and my hand gripped the green feather. I don't know how near I passed to him, but I got to the door unhindered and tried to twist the doorknob but my palm was slick with cold sweat. He must've heard the rattle, because he said, "Stop!" and I could sense him coming after me. Then the doorknob turned and the door opened and I shot through it as if from the barrel of a cannon. I collided with Mrs. Axford's desk, and I heard the photographs clatter as they fell.

"Cory!" he said, louder. "No!"

I caromed off the side of the desk, a human pinball in motion. I went into the row of chairs, striking my right knee on a hard edge. My lips let out a cry of pain, and as I tried to find the door into the hallway it seemed that the chairs had come to malevolent life and were blocking my way. A cold chill skittered up my spine as Mayor Swope's hand fell on my shoulder like a spider.

"No!" he said, and his fingers started to close.

I pulled loose. A chair was beside me, and I shoved it at Mayor

Swope like a shield. He stumbled into it, and I heard him say "Oof!" as his legs got tangled up and he fell to the floor. Then I turned away from him, frantically searching for the door. At any second I expected a hand to seal itself around my ankle, and that hand to draw me to him like the tentacle of the glass-bowled monster of *Invaders from Mars.* Tears of terror were starting to burn my eyes. I blinked them away, and suddenly my hand found the cold knob of the door that led out. I twisted it, pushed through, and ran along the storm-darkened corridor, my footsteps ringing on the linoleum and thunder echoing through the halls of justice.

"Cory! Come back here!" he hollered as if he really thought I might. He was coming after me, and he was running, too. I had the mental picture of myself beaten to a pulp, my hand cuffed to Rocket, and Rocket tumbling down, down, down into the awful netherworld of Saxon's Lake.

I tripped over my own flying feet, fell, and skidded on my belly across the linoleum. My chin banged into the bottom of a wall, but I scrambled up and kept going, Mayor Swope's footsteps right behind me. *"Cory!"* he shouted, fury in his voice. It was surely the voice of a crazed killer. *"Stop where you are!"*

Like hell, I thought.

And then I saw dank gray light streaming through the cupola over the staircase and I started running down the stairs without even holding on to the railing, which was enough right there to cause my mother to go white-haired. Mayor Swope was puffing behind me, and his voice was losing its steam: "No, Cory! No!" I reached the bottom of the staircase, and I ran across the entrance lobby and out the front door into the chilly rain. The worst of the storm had already swept over Zephyr, and now squatted above the hills like a massive grayish-blue toad-frog. I got Rocket unlocked, but I left the chain hanging. I pedaled away from the courthouse just as Mayor Swope came through the door hollering at me to stop.

The last thing he hollered—and I thought this was strange, coming from a crazed killer—was "For God's sake, be careful!"

Rocket flew over the rain-pocked puddles, its golden eye picking out a path. The clouds were parting, shards of yellow sunlight breaking through. Dad had always told me that when it rained while the sun showed, the devil was beating his wife. Rocket dodged the splashing cars on Merchants Street and I hung on for the ride.

At home, Rocket skidded to a stop at the front porch steps and I ran inside, my hair plastered down with rain and my hand gripping the soggy green feather.

"Cory!" Mom called as the screen door slammed. "Cory Mackenson, come here!"

"Just a minute!" I ran into my room, and I searched the seven mystic drawers until I found the White Owl cigar box. I opened it, and there was the green feather I'd found on the bottom of my shoe.

"Come here this instant!" Mom shouted.

"Wait!" I placed the first green feather down on my desk, and the green feather I'd plucked from the mayor's hatband beside it.

"Cory! Come in here! I'm on the phone with Mayor Swope!"

Oh-oh.

My feeling of triumph cracked, collapsed, cascaded around my wet sneakers.

The first feather, the one that had come from the woods, was a deep emerald green. The one from the mayor's hatband was about three shades lighter. Not only that, but the hatband feather was at least twice as large as the Saxon's Lake feather.

They didn't match one iota.

"Cory! Come talk to the mayor before I get a switch after you!"

When I dared to walk into the kitchen, I saw that my mother's face was as red as a strangled beet. She said into the telephone, "No sir, I promise you Cory doesn't have a mental condition. No sir, he doesn't have panic attacks, either. Here he is right now, I'll put him on." She held the receiver out to me, and fixed me with a baleful glare. "Have you lost your *mind*? Take this phone and talk to the mayor!"

I took it. It was all I could do to utter one pitiable word: "Hello?"

"Cory!" Mayor Swope said. "I had to call to make sure you'd gotten home all right! I was scared to death you were gonna fall down those stairs in the dark and break your neck! When you ran out, I thought you were . . . like . . . havin' a fit or somethin'."

"No sir," I answered meekly. "I wasn't havin' a fit."

"Well, when the lights went out I figured you might be afraid of the dark. I didn't want you to hurt yourself, so I was tryin' to get you settled down. And I figured your mom and dad wouldn't want me to let you try gettin' home in that storm, either! If you'd gotten sideswiped by a car . . . well, thank the Lord it didn't happen."

"I . . . thought . . ." My throat choked up. I could feel my mother's burning eyes. "I thought . . . you were tryin' to . . . kill me," I said.

The mayor was silent for a few seconds, and I could imagine what he must be thinking. I was a pure number-one nut case. "*Kill* you? Whatever for?"

"Cory!" Mom said. "Are you crazy?"

"I'm sorry," I told the mayor. "My . . . imagination got away from me, I guess. But you said I knew somethin' about you, and you wondered how I'd found out, and—"

"No, not somethin' about *me*," Mayor Swope said. "Somethin' about your award."

"My *award*?"

"Your plaque. For winnin' third place in the short story contest. That's why I asked you to come see me. I was afraid somebody else on the awards panel had told you before I could."

"Told me what?"

"Well, I wanted to show it to you. I was bringin' your plaque in to show you when the lights went out and you went wild. See, the fella who engraves the plaques misspelled your name. He spelled Cory with an 'e.' I wanted you to see it before the ceremony so you wouldn't get your feelin's hurt. The fella's promised to do your plaque again, but he's got to do some softball awards first and he can't get to it for two weeks. Understand?"

Oh, what a bitter pill. What a bitter, bitter pill.

"Yes sir," I answered. I felt dazed, and my right knee was really starting to throb. "I do."

"Are you on . . . any medication?" the mayor asked me.

"No sir."

He grunted quietly. That grunt said, *You sure ought to be.*

"I'm sorry I acted a fool," I said. "I don't know what got into me." If he figured I was crazy now, I thought, just wait until he saw what I'd done to his hat. I decided to let him find that out for himself.

"Well," and the mayor gave a little laugh that told me he was finding some humor in this mess, "it's been a real interestin' afternoon, Cory."

"Yes sir. Uh . . . Mayor Swope?"

"Yes?"

"Uh . . . the plaque's okay as it is. Even with my name spelled wrong. You don't have to get it fixed." I figured this was penance of a sort; every time I looked at that plaque, I'd remember the day I shoved a chair at the mayor and knocked him down.

"Nonsense. We'll get it changed for you."

"I'd just as soon have it the way it is now," I told him, and I guess I sounded firm about it because Mayor Swope said, "All right, Cory, if that's what you really want."

He said he had to go get into a bathtub full of Epsom salts, and then he said he'd see me at the awards ceremony. When he hung up, I had to face my mother and explain to her why I'd thought Mayor

Swope was going to kill me. Dad came in during this explanation, and though by all rights I should have been punished for my foolishness, my folks simply sent me to my room for an hour, which was where I was going to go anyhow.

In my room, I looked at the two mismatched green feathers. One bright, one sober. One small, one large. I picked up the Saxon's Lake feather and held it in the palm of my hand, and I found my magnifying glass and examined the feather's rills and ridges. Maybe Sherlock Holmes could've deduced something from it, but I was as confounded as Dr. Watson.

Mayor Swope had been the man in the green-feathered hat. His "knife" had been his pipe-cleaning tool. This feather in my hand had nothing to do with Mayor Swope's hat. Did it have anything to do with the figure I thought I'd seen standing at the edge of the woods, or the dead man at the bottom of the lake? One thing I knew for sure: there were no emerald-green birds in the woods around Zephyr. So where had that feather come from?

I put the mayor's feather aside, intending to return it to him though I knew deep down in my heart I never would, and I slid the Saxon's Lake feather back into the White Owl box which was deposited once more into one of the seven mystic drawers.

That night I dreamed again about the four black girls, all dressed up as if for church. I guessed the youngest was maybe ten or eleven, the other three around fourteen. Only this time they stood talking to each other under a green, leafy tree. Two of them were holding Bibles. I couldn't hear what was being said. One of them laughed, and then the others laughed and the sound was like water rippling. Then there was a bright flash so intense I had to close my eyes, and I was standing at the center of thunder and a hot wind yanked at my clothes and hair. When I opened my eyes again, the four black girls were gone and the tree was stripped bare.

I woke up. There was sweat on my face, as if I had actually been kissed by that scorching breath. I heard Rebel barking in the dark from the backyard. I looked at the luminous dial of my alarm clock, seeing that it was almost two-thirty. Rebel barked on and on, like a machine, and his voice was igniting other dogs, so I figured since I was awake I'd go out and calm him down. I started out of my room, and I saw at once that a light was on in the den.

I could hear a scratching noise. I followed it to the den's threshold, and there I saw my father, wearing his pajamas, sitting at his desk where he wrote out the checks for the bills. He gripped a pen in his hand, and under a pool of light he was writing or drawing something on a sheet of paper. His eyes looked feverish and sunken, and I saw that moisture glistened on his forehead just as it did on mine.

Rebel's barking broke. He started to howl.

Dad muttered, "Damn it," and stood up, being careful not to scrape his chair on the floor. I shrank back into a shadow; I'm not sure why I did this, but Dad looked like he didn't want to be disturbed. He walked to the back door, and I heard him go out to hush Rebel.

Rebel's howling ceased. Dad would be back in a minute or two.

I couldn't help it. I had to know what was so important for him to be up at two-thirty doing.

I walked into the den, and I looked at the sheet of paper.

On it, my father—who was by no means an artist—had drawn a half-dozen crude skulls with wings growing from their temples. There was a column of question marks, and the words *Saxon's Lake* repeated five times. *The Lady* was written there, followed by another series of question marks. *Down in the dark* was there, the pen's point almost tearing through the paper. It was followed in capital letters by two desperate questions: WHO? WHY?

And then a progression that made me feel sick to my stomach:

I am.

I am afraid.

I am about to have a breakd

The back door opened.

I retreated to my shadow, and watched as Dad entered the den. He sat down again, and he stared at what he'd drawn and written.

I had never seen his face before. Not the face he wore now, at this quiet hour before the sun. It was the face of a frightened little boy, tortured beyond his understanding.

He opened a drawer and took out a coffee cup with Green Meadows Dairy stenciled on the side. He brought out a pack of matches. Then he folded the sheet of paper up, and began to tear it into small pieces. The fragments of it went into the coffee cup. When the paper was all torn up, Dad struck a match and dropped it into the cup, too.

There was a little smoke. He opened a window, and then there was none.

I slipped back to my room and lay down to think.

While I was dreaming of the four black girls in their Sunday dresses, what was my father being visited by? A mud-covered figure rising from the lake's murky depths, borne up by a fleet of moss-backed snapping turtles? A beaten and misshapen face, whispering

240

Come with me, come with me, down in the dark? A handcuff on the wrist of a tattooed arm? Or the knowledge that it could be any man and every man who ends his life alone, forgotten, drifting down into oblivion?

I didn't know, and I was afraid to guess. But I knew this for sure: whoever had murdered that unknown man was killing my father, too.

At last sleep overtook me, and gentled me away from these tribulations. I rested, while around me my monsters kept their watch.

2

The Magic Box

The Saturday night of the Zephyr Arts Council awards ceremony arrived. We all put on our Sunday clothes, jammed into the pickup truck, and headed for the library. My fright level, which had been hovering around eight on a scale of ten, now moved past nine. During the week, my so-called buddies had been telling me what might happen when I got up to read my story. If their predictions came true, I would break out in hives, pee in my pants, and lose my dinner from both ends in one simultaneous rush of shame and agony. Davy Ray had told me that to be safe I ought to put a cork in my butt. Ben had said I'd better be careful walking up to the podium in front of all those people, because that's when likely I'd have my accident. Johnny said he'd known a boy who got up to read something in front of people and he forgot how to read right then and there, had started babbling in what sounded like Greek or Zulu.

Well, I'd decided against the cork. But when I saw the lights on in the library and all the cars parked out front, I started regretting my decision. Mom put her arm around my shoulder. "You're gonna do just fine," she said.

"Yep," Dad said. He was wearing his father's face again, but he had dark hollows under his eyes and I'd heard Mom telling him he might need to start taking some Geritol. She knew something was wrong, of course, but she didn't know how deep the troubled current ran. "Just fine," he told me.

The library's meeting room was full of chairs, and at the front there was a table and the dreaded podium. Worse yet, there was a *microphone* at that podium! About forty people occupied the chairs, and Mayor Swope, Mrs. Prathmore, Mr. Grover Dean, and some of the other contest judges were moving around hobnobbing. I wanted to shrivel up and squeeze into a corner when Mayor Swope saw us and started walking over, but Dad placed his hand on my shoulder and I stood my ground.

"Hi there, Cory!" Mayor Swope smiled, but his eyes were wary. I figured he thought I might go crazy at any second. "You ready to read your story tonight?"

No sir, I wanted to say. "Yes sir," was what came out.

"Well, I think we're gonna have a good turnout." His attention went to my folks. "I suspect you two are awfully proud of your boy."

"We sure are," Mom said. "There's never been a writer in the family."

"He's surely got the imagination for it." Mayor Swope smiled again; it was a very tight smile. "By the way, Cory: I got my hat out of my closet to get it reshaped. You don't happen to know what became of the—"

"Luther!" a voice interrupted. "Just the man I need to see!"

Mr. Dollar, all dressed up in a dark blue suit and smelling of Aqua Velva, pushed up beside the mayor. I was never so relieved to see anyone in my life. "Yes, Perry?" Mayor Swope asked, turning away from me.

"Luther, you've gotta do somethin' about that dang-goned *monkey!*" Mr. Dollar insisted. "That thing got on my roof last night and neither me nor Ellen could sleep a wink for all the racket it was makin'! The thing even did its business all over my car! I swear, there's gotta be a way to catch it!"

Ah, Lucifer. The monkey was still loose in the trees of Zephyr, and woe to the occupant of the house on whose roof Lucifer chose to squat. Because of the resulting furor and threatened lawsuits for property damage, Reverend Blessett had slinked out of town in mid-August and left no forwarding address.

"If you come up with a good idea, you let me know," Mayor Swope answered with a hint of irritation. "Short of askin' the Air Force boys to drop a bomb on the town, just about everythin's been tried."

"Maybe Doc Lezander can catch it, or we can pay somebody from a zoo to come in here and . . ." Mr. Dollar was still talking as Mayor Swope moved away, and Mr. Dollar followed him, prattling about the monkey. My folks and I took our seats, and I fidgeted as more people entered the room. Dr. Parrish came in with his wife, and lo and behold the Demon sashayed in with her fireplug mother and candlestick dad. I tried to shrink down in my chair, but she saw me and waved gleefully. Luckily there were no vacant chairs around us, or I'd have walked up to the podium with a booger on the back of my neck. Then my senses got another shock as Johnny Wilson and his parents came in. It wasn't two minutes later that Ben and his mother and dad entered, with Davy Ray and his folks close behind them. I was going to have to brave their leering mugs, but in truth I was glad to see them. As Ben had once told me, they were good old buddies.

It must be said that the people of Zephyr were supportive of their own. Either that, or there wasn't much good on television on Saturday nights. A closet was opened and more folding chairs brought out. The crowd hushed for a few seconds as Vernon Thaxter, wearing only the last shade of his summer tan, strode into the room with a big smile on his face. But people were used to Vernon by now, and they'd learned where to look and where not to. "That feller's still nekkid, Momma!" the Demon pointed out, but except for a few muffled chuckles and flushed faces, nobody made a scene. Vernon pulled a chair into a corner at the back of the room and sat there, contented as a cow. Bull, I mean.

By the time Mayor Swope and Mrs. Prathmore took a box full of plaques up to the table at the front, there were around seventy lovers of fine literature present. Mr. Grover Dean, a slender man of middle age who wore a neatly combed brown wig and round glasses with silver frames, went to the front, carrying a satchel, and he sat down at the table with the mayor and Mrs. Prathmore. He unzipped the satchel and slid out a stack of papers that I presumed were the winning entries in the three categories of short story, essay, and poetry.

Mayor Swope got up and tapped the microphone at the podium. He was greeted with a squeal of feedback and a noise like an elephant breaking wind, which brought a chorus of guffaws and made Mayor Swope motion for the man who operated the sound system. Everybody quietened at last, the microphone was adjusted, and the mayor cleared his throat and was about to speak when a ripple of whispers crossed the audience. I looked back toward the door, and my pounding heart leaped like a catfish. The Lady had just walked in.

She was dressed in violet, with a pillbox hat and gloves. There was a veil of fine netting over her face. She looked frail, her bluish-black arms and legs as thin as sticks. Supporting her with an ever-so-discreet hand to her elbow was Charles Damaronde, he of the massive shoulders and werewolf's eyebrows. Walking three steps behind the Lady was the Moon Man, carrying his cane and wearing a shiny black suit and a red necktie. He was hatless, his dark-and-light-divided face and forehead there for all to see.

I think you could've heard a pin drop. Or, more precisely, a booger fall from the Demon's nose. "Oh my," Mom whispered. Dad shifted nervously in his chair, and I believe he might've gotten up and walked out if he hadn't had to stay for me.

The Lady scanned the audience from behind her veil. All the chairs were taken. I got a quick glimpse of her green eyes—just a glint—but it was enough to make me think I smelled steamy earth and swamp flowers. Then, suddenly, Vernon Thaxter stood up and with a bow offered his chair to her. She said, "Thank you, sir," in her quavery voice and sat down, and Vernon remained standing at the back of the room while Charles Damaronde and the Moon Man stood on either side of the elegant Lady. A few people—not many, only five or six—got up not to offer their chairs but to stalk out. They weren't scared of her like Dad was; it was their indignation that black people had entered a room full of whites without asking permission. We all knew that, and the Lady did, too. It was the time we lived in.

"I guess we can get started," Mayor Swope began. He kept looking around at the crowd, then toward the Lady and the Moon Man, back to the crowd again. "I want to welcome you all to the awards ceremony of the 1964 Zephyr Arts Council Writing Contest. First off, I'd like to thank every one of the participants, without whom there could be no contest."

Well, it went on like that for a while. I might have drowsed off if I hadn't been so full of ants. Mayor Swope introduced all the judges and the Arts Council members, and then he introduced Mr. Quentin Farraday, from the Adams Valley *Journal*, who was there to take pictures and interview the winners. Finally, Mayor Swope sat down and Mrs. Prathmore took his place at the podium to call up the third-place winner in the essay division. An elderly woman named Delores Hightower shuffled up, took her essay from Mr. Dean, and read to the audience for fifteen minutes about the joys of an herb garden, then she was given her plaque and she sat down again. The first-place essay, by a beefy, gap-toothed man named George Eagers, concerned the time he had a flat tire near Tuscaloosa and the one and only Bear Bryant had stopped to ask him if he needed some help, thus proving the Bear's divinity.

The poetry division was next. Imagine my surprise when the Demon's mother stood up to read the second-place poem. This was part of it: "Rain, rain, go away,"/ said the sun, on a summer day./ "I have lots of shinin' to do yet,/ and those dark clouds make me get/ To cryin'." She read it with such emotion, I feared she was going to get to crying and rain on the whole room. The Demon and her father applauded so loud at the end of it, you'd have thought it was the Second Coming.

The first-place poem, by a little wrinkled old lady named Helen Trotter, was in essence a love letter, the first rhyme of which was: "He's always there to show he cares,/ whatever's right, that's what he dares," and the last rhyme: "Oh, how I love to see the smiling face/ Of our great state governor, George C. Wal*lace*."

"Groan," Dad whispered. The Lady, Charles Damaronde, and the Moon Man were gracious enough to make no public comment.

"And now," Mrs. Prathmore announced, "we move into the short-story division."

I needed that cork. I needed it bad.

"This year we have the youngest winner ever on record since we began this contest in 1955. We had a little difficulty deciding if his entry was a short story or essay, since it's based on an actual event, but in the end we decided he showed enough flair and descriptive imagination to consider it a short story. Now, welcome if you will, our third-place winner, reading his story entitled 'Before the Sun': Cory Mackenson." Mrs. Prathmore led the applause. Dad said, "Go get 'em," to me, and somehow I stood up.

As I walked to the podium in a trance of terror, I heard Davy Ray giggling and then a soft *pop* as his dad cuffed him on the back of the neck. Mr. Dean gave me my story, and Mrs. Prathmore bent the microphone down so it could gather my voice. I looked out at that sea of faces; they all seemed to blur together, into a collective mass of eyes, noses, and mouths. I had a sudden fright: was my zipper up? Did I dare to look and see? I caught sight of the *Journal* photographer, his bulky camera poised. My heart was beating like the wings of a caged bird. Queasiness roiled in my belly, but I knew that if I threw up, I could never again face the light of day. Somebody coughed and somebody else cleared his throat. All eyes were on me, and in my hands the paper was shaking.

"Go ahead, Cory," Mrs. Prathmore urged.

I looked at the title, and I started to read it, but what felt like a spiny egg seemed to be lodged in my throat where the words were formed. Darkness lapped around the edges of my vision; was I about to pass out in front of all these people? Wouldn't that make a dandy front-page picture for the *Journal?* My eyes rolled back in my head, my body tumbling for the floor, my underpants white in the maw of my open zipper?

"Just take your time," Mrs. Prathmore said, and in her voice I heard her nerves starting to shred.

My eyes, which felt as if they were about to burst from my head, danced over the audience. I saw Davy Ray, Ben, and Johnny. None of them were grinning anymore; this was a bad sign. I saw Mr. George Eagers look at his wristwatch; another bad sign. I heard some malicious monster whisper, "He's *scared,* poor little boy!"

I saw the Lady rise to her feet at the back of the room. Behind her veil her gaze was cool and placid, like still green waters. She lifted her chin, and that movement spoke a single word: *Courage.*

I pulled in a breath. My lungs rattled like a freight train crossing a rickety bridge. I was here; this was my moment. I had to go on, for better or worse.

I said, " 'Before the—' " My voice, thunderous through the microphone, shocked me silent again. Mrs. Prathmore placed her hand against my back, as if to steady me. " '—Sun,' " I went on. "By C-C-Cory Mackenson."

I started reading. I knew the words; I knew the story. My voice seemed to belong to someone else, but the story was part of me. As I continued on, from sentence to sentence, I was aware that the coughing and throat clearing had ceased. No one was whispering. I read the story as if traveling a trail through a familiar woods; I knew the way to go, and this was a comfort. I dared to glance up again at the audience, and when I did I felt it.

This was to be my first experience with it, and like any first experience, the feeling stays with you forever. What this was exactly I can't say, but it drove into my soul and made a home there. Everyone was watching me; everyone was *listening* to me. The words coming out of my mouth—the words I'd conceived and given birth to—were making time null and void; they were bringing together a roomful of people into a journey of common sights, sounds, and thoughts; they were leaving me and traveling into the minds and memories of people who had never been at Saxon's Lake that chill, early morning in March. I could tell when I looked at them that those people were following me. And the greatest thing— the very greatest thing—is that they *wanted* to go where I led them.

All this, of course, I reasoned out much later. What struck me at the moment, beside getting to the end, was how quiet and still everybody had become. I had found the key to a time machine. I had discovered a current of power I'd never dreamed I possessed. I had found a magic box, and it was called a typewriter.

That voice coming out of me seemed to get stronger. It seemed to speak with expression and clarity rather than being a mumbled drone, which is how it had begun. I was amazed and elated. I actually—wonder of wonders—was enjoying reading aloud.

I reached the final sentence, and ran out of story.

For now.

My mother started applauding first. Then my dad, and the others in the room. I saw the Lady's violet-gloved hands clapping. The applause felt good; but it wasn't nearly as good as that feeling of leading people on a journey and them trusting you to know the way. Tomorrow I might want to be a milkman like Dad, or a jet pilot or a detective, but at that instant I wanted to be a writer more than anything on earth.

I accepted my plaque from Mayor Swope. When I sat down, people around me clapped me on the back, and I could tell by the way my mom and dad smiled that they were proud of me. I didn't mind that my name was misspelled on the plaque. I knew who I was.

The second-place winner, by Mr. Terrence Hosmer, was about a farmer trying to outsmart a flock of ravens after his corn crop. The first-place winner, by Mrs. Ada Yearby, concerned the midnight kneeling down of the animals at the birth of Jesus Christ. Then Mayor Swope thanked everyone for coming and said that we could all go home. On the way out, Davy Ray, Johnny, and Ben swarmed around me, and I believe I got more attention than even Mrs. Yearby. The Demon's mother waddled up to congratulate me, and she looked at my mother with her broad, mustached face and said, "You know, Brenda's birthday party is next Saturday and Brenda sure would like your boy to be there. You know, I wrote that poem for Brenda, 'cause she's a real sensitive child. Would your boy come to Brenda's birthday party? He don't have to bring no present or nothin'."

Mom looked at me for a cue. I saw the Demon, standing with her father across the room. The Demon waved at me and sniggered. Davy Ray elbowed me in the ribs; he didn't know how close he was to getting killed. I said, "Gee, Mrs. Sutley, I think I might have some chores to do at home on Saturday. Don't I, Mom?"

Mom, God love her, was quick. "Yes, you sure do! You've got to cut the grass and help your father paint the porch."

"Huh?" Dad said.

"It's got to be done," Mom told him. "Saturday's the only day we can all work on it together."

"And maybe I can get some guys to help," I offered, which made my buddies find wings on their feet.

"Well, if you wanna come to Brenda's party, she sure would like it. She's havin' her relatives over and all." Mrs. Sutley gave me a defeated smile. She knew. Then she returned to the Demon and said something to her and the Demon gave me that exact same smile. I felt like a heel on a dung-stained boot. But I couldn't encourage the Demon, I just couldn't! It was inhuman to ask me to. And oh brother, I could just imagine what the Demon's relatives must be like! That group would make the Munsters appear lovely.

We were almost out the door when a quiet voice spoke: "Tom? Tom Mackenson?"

My dad stopped and turned around.

He was in the presence of the Lady.

She was smaller than I remembered. She barely stood to my father's shoulders. But there was a strength in her that ten men couldn't have matched; you could see the force of life in her as you can see it in a weathered tree that has bent before the winds of countless storms. She had approached us without Mr. Damaronde or the Moon Man, who stood waiting at a distance.

"Hello again," Mom said. The Lady nodded at her. My dad wore the expression of a man trapped in a dark closet with a tarantula. His eyes were skittering around, searching for a way out, but he was too much of a gentleman to be rude to her.

"Tom Mackenson," she repeated. "You and your wife sure have raised a talented boy."

"I . . . we . . . we've done our best, thank you."

"And such a good *speaker*," the Lady went on. She smiled at me. "You've done well," she said.

"Thank you, ma'am."

"How's that bicycle doin'?"

"Fine. I named it 'Rocket.'"

"That's a nice name."

"Yes ma'am. And . . . ." Tell her, I decided. "And it's got an eyeball in the headlight."

Her brows lifted, ever so slightly. "Is that a fact?"

"*Cory!*" Dad scolded. "Don't make up such things!"

"Seems to me," the Lady said, "a boy's bicycle needs to see where it's goin'. Needs to see whether there's a clear road or trouble ahead. Seems to me a boy's bicycle needs some horse in it, and some deer, and maybe even a touch of *rep*tile. For cleverness, don't you know?"

"Yes ma'am," I agreed. She knew Rocket, all right.

"That was kind of you to give Cory a bike," Dad said to her. "I'm not one to accept charity, but—"

"Oh, it wasn't charity, Mr. Mackenson. It was repayment for a good deed. Mrs. Mackenson, is there anythin' at your house that Mr. Lightfoot needs to fix?"

"No, I think everythin's workin' just fine."

"Well," she said, and she stared at my father. "You never know when things are likely to suffer a breakdown."

"It was good to see you, Mrs. . . . uh . . . Lady." Dad took my mother's elbow. "We'd better be gettin' on home now."

"Mr. Mackenson, we have some matters to discuss," the Lady said as we all started moving away. "I believe you understand when I say they're matters of life and death?"

Dad stopped. I saw a muscle in his jaw work. He didn't want to turn back to her, but she was pulling at him. Maybe he felt her life force—her raw, primal power—heat up a notch, just as I did. He seemed to want to take another step away from her, but he just couldn't do it.

"Do you believe in Jesus Christ, Mr. Mackenson?" the Lady asked.

This question broke through his final barricade. He turned around to face her. "Yes, I do," he said solemnly.

"As do I. Jesus Christ was as perfect as a human bein' can be, yet he got mad and fought and wept and had days of feelin' like he couldn't go on another step. Like when the lepers and the sick folks almost trampled him down, all of 'em beggin' for miracles and doggin' him till he was about miracled out. What I'm sayin', Mr. Mackenson, is that even Jesus Christ needed help sometimes, and he wasn't too proud to ask for it."

"I don't need . . ." He let it go.

"You see," the Lady said, "I believe everybody has visions, now and again. I believe it's part of the human animal. We have these visions—these little snippets of the big quilt—but we can't figure out where they fit, or why. Most times they come in dreams, when you're sleepin'. Sometimes you can dream awake. Just about everybody has 'em, only they can't fathom the meanin'. See?"

"No," Dad said.

"Oh yes, you do." She raised a reedy finger. "Folks get all wrapped up in the sticky tape of this world, makes 'em blind, deaf, and dumb to what's goin' on in the other one."

"The other one? Other what?"

"The other world across the river," she answered. "Where that man at the bottom of Saxon's Lake is callin' to you from."

"I don't want to hear any more of this." But he didn't move.

"Callin' you," she repeated. "I'm hearin' him, too, and he's wreckin' my damn sleep, and I'm an old woman who needs some peace." She took a step closer to my father, and her eyes had him. "That man needs to tell who killed him before he can pass on. Oh, he's tryin', he's tryin' mighty hard, but he can't give us a name or a face. All he can give us are those little snippets of the big quilt. If you were to come see me, and let's us put our thinkin' caps on, maybe we could start sewin' those snippets together. Then you could get a good night's sleep again, so could I, and he could go on where he belongs. Better still: we could catch us a killer, if there's a killer here to be caught."

"I don't . . . believe in . . . that kind of non—"

"Believe it or don't believe it, that's your choice," the Lady interrupted. "But when that dead man comes callin' on you tonight—and he will—you won't have any choice but to hear him. And my advice to you, Mr. Mackenson, is that you ought to start listenin'."

Dad started to say something; his mouth opened, but his tongue couldn't jimmy the words out.

"Excuse me," I said to the Lady. "I wanted to ask you . . . if you've been . . . like . . . havin' any other dreams."

"Oh, most all the time," she said. "Trouble is, at my age, most all my dreams are reruns."

"Well . . . I was wonderin' if . . . you've been havin' any dreams about four girls."

"Four girls?" she asked.

"Yes ma'am. Four girls. You know. Dark, like you. And they're all dressed up, like it's a Sunday."

"No," she said. "I can't say that I have."

"I dream about 'em a lot. Not every night, but a lot. What do you suppose it means?"

"Snippet of a quilt," she said. "Could be somethin' you already know, but you don't know you know."

"Ma'am?"

"Might not be spirits talkin'," she explained. "Might just be your ownself, tryin' to figure somethin' out."

"Oh," I said. This must be why the Lady was picking up Dad's dreams but not mine; mine were not the ghosts of the past, but a shadow of the future.

250

"You'll have to come over to Bruton and see our new museum when it's done," the Lady said to Mom. "We've raised money to start buildin' onto the recreation center. Should be finished in a couple of months. Gonna have a nice exhibition room."

"I've heard about it," Mom said. "Good luck."

"Thank you. Well, I'll let you know when the openin' ceremony's gonna be. Remember what I've told you, Mr. Mackenson." She offered her violet-gloved hand, and my father took it. He might be fearful of the Lady, but he was first and foremost a gentleman. "You know where I live."

The Lady rejoined her husband and Mr. Damaronde, then they walked out into the warm, still night. We went out soon after them, and we saw them drive away in not the rhinestone Pontiac but a plain blue Chevrolet. The last of the attendees were talking on the sidewalk, and they took the time to tell me again how much they'd enjoyed my reading. "Keep up the good work!" Mr. Dollar said, and then I heard him brag to another man, "You know, I cut his hair. Yessir, I've been cuttin' that boy's hair for years!"

We drove home. I kept my plaque on my lap, clenched with both hands. "Mom?" I asked. "What kind of museum's gonna be in Bruton? They gonna have dinosaur bones and stuff?"

"Nope," my father told me. "It's gonna be a civil rights exhibit. I guess they'll have letters and papers and pictures, that kind of thing."

"Slave artifacts is what I hear," Mom said. "Like leg chains and brandin' irons, would be my guess. Lizbeth Sears told me she heard the Lady sold that big Pontiac and donated the money toward the buildin' costs."

"I'll bet whoever burned that cross in her front yard isn't exactly whistlin' 'Dixie' about this," Dad observed. "The Klan'll have somethin' to say, that's for sure."

"I think it's a good thing," Mom said. "I think they need to know where they've been to know where they're goin'."

"Yeah, I know where the Klan wishes they'd go, too." Dad slowed down and turned the pickup truck onto Hilltop Street. I caught a glimpse of the Thaxter mansion through the trees, its windows streaming with light. "She had a hard grip," Dad said, almost to himself. "The Lady, I mean." We knew who he was talking about. "Had a hard grip. And it was like she was lookin' right into me, and I couldn't stop her from seein' things that—" He seemed to realize we were still there, and he abruptly canceled that line of thought.

"I'll go with you," Mom offered, "if you want to go see her. I'll stay right by your side the whole time. She wants to help you. I wish you'd let her."

He was silent. We were nearing the house. "I'll think about it," he said, which was his way of saying he didn't want to hear any more talk about the Lady.

Dad might know where the Lady lived, and he might need her help to exorcise the spirit that called to him from the bottom of Saxon's Lake, but he wasn't ready yet. Whether he was ever going to be ready or not, I didn't know. It was up to him to take the first step, and nobody could make him do it. I had to concern myself with other problems for now: the dream of the four black girls, the Demon's crush on me, how I was going to survive Leatherlungs, and what I was going to write about next.

And the green feather. Always the green feather, its unanswered questions taunting me from one of the seven mystic drawers.

That night, Dad hung the plaque on a wall in my room for me, right over the magic box. It looked nice, up there between the pictures of a large fellow with bolts in his neck and a dark-caped individual with prominent teeth.

I had been charged with power and tasted life tonight. I had taken my own first step, however awkward, to wherever I was going. This feeling of sheer exhilaration might fade, might wane under the weight of days and diminish in the river of time; but on this night, this wonderful never-to-be-again night, it was alive.

3

Dinner with Vernon

To say the Demon pestered me in the following days about coming to her birthday party is like saying a cat has a fondness for the company of mice. Between the Demon's insistent whispering and Leatherlungs' window-shaking bellows, I was a bundle of nerves by Wednesday, and I still couldn't divide fractions.

On Wednesday night, just after supper, I was drying the dishes for

Mom when I heard Dad say from the chair where he was reading the paper, "Car's stoppin' out front. We expectin' anybody?"

"Not that I know of," Mom answered.

The chair creaked as he stood up. He was going out to the porch. Before he went out the door, he gave a low whistle of appreciation. "Hey, you oughta come take a look at this!" he said, and then he went outside. We couldn't resist this invitation, of course. And there parked in front of our house was a long, sleek car with a paint job that gleamed like black satin. It had wire wheels and a shiny chrome grille and a windshield that seemed a mile wide. It was the longest and most beautiful car I'd ever seen, and it made our pickup truck look like a crusty old scab. The driver's door opened and a man in a dark suit got out. He came around the car and stepped onto our lawn, and he said, "Good evening" in an accent that didn't sound like he was from around here. He came on up the walk, into the porch light's circle, and we all saw he had white hair and a white mustache and his shoes were as shiny and black as the car's skin.

"Can I help you?" Dad asked.

"Mr. Thomas Mackenson?"

"Tom. That's me."

"Very good, sir." He stopped at the foot of the steps. "Mrs. Mackenson." He nodded at my mother, then he looked at me. "Master Cory?"

"Uh . . . I'm Cory, yes sir," I said.

"Ah. Excellent." He smiled, and he reached into the inside pocket of his coat and his hand came out holding an envelope. "If you please?" He offered the envelope to me.

I looked at Dad. He motioned for me to take it. I did, and the white-haired man waited with his hands clasped behind his back as I opened it. The envelope was sealed with a circle of red wax that had the letter T embossed in it. I slid from the envelope a small white card on which there were several lines of typed words.

"What's it say?" Mom leaned over my shoulder.

I read it aloud. "'Mr. Vernon Thaxter requests the pleasure of your company at dinner, on Saturday, September 19, 1964, at seven o'clock P.M. Dress optional.'"

"Casual wear recommended," the white-haired man clarified.

"Oh my," Mom said; her worry-bead words. Her brows came together.

"Uh . . . can I ask just who you are?" Dad inquired, taking the white card from me and scanning it.

"My name is Cyril Pritchard, Mr. Mackenson. I am in the employ of the Thaxter household. My wife and I have looked after Mr. Moorwood and young master Vernon for almost eight years."

"Oh. Are you . . . like . . . the butler or somethin'?"

"My wife and I serve as we're required, sir."

Dad grunted and frowned, his own mental worry-beads at work. "How come this was sent from Vernon and not from his father?"

"Because, sir, it's Vernon who wishes to have dinner with your son."

"And why is that? I don't recall Vernon ever meetin' my boy."

"Young master Vernon attended the Arts Council awards ceremony. He was very impressed with your son's command of the language. You know, he had aspirations of being a writer himself at one time."

"He wrote a book, didn't he?" Mom asked.

"Indeed he did. *The Moon My Mistress* was its title. Published in 1958 by Sonneilton Press in New York City."

"I took it out from the library," Mom admitted. "I have to say I wouldn't have bought it, not with that bloody meat cleaver on the front. You know, I always thought that was odd, because the book was more about life in that little town than the butcher who . . . well, you know."

"Yes, I do know," Mr. Pritchard said.

What I didn't know until later was that the butcher in Vernon's book had cut out a different intestine from a number of ladies every time the moon was full. Everybody in the fictional town raved over the butcher's steak-and-kidney pies, spicy Cajun sausages, and lady-finger meat-spread sandwiches.

"It wasn't bad, though, for a first novel," Mom said. "Why didn't he write another one?"

"The book unfortunately didn't sell, for whatever reason. Young master Vernon was . . . shall we say . . . disenchanted." His gaze returned to me. "What shall I tell young master Vernon in regards to the dinner invitation?"

"Hold your horses." Dad spoke up. "I hate to state the obvious, but Vernon's not . . . well, he's not in any mental shape to entertain guests up at that house, is he?"

Here Mr. Pritchard's stare went icy. "Young master Vernon is perfectly capable of entertaining a dinner guest, Mr. Mackenson. In response to your implied concern, your son would be safe with him."

"I didn't mean any offense. It's just that when somebody walks around naked all the time, you've got to believe he's not rowin' with both oars. I can't figure why Moorwood lets him go around like that."

"Young master Vernon has his own life. Mr. Thaxter has decided to let him do as he pleases."

"That's clear to see," Dad said. "You know, I haven't seen hide nor hair of Moorwood in . . . oh, I guess over three years. He was always a hermit, but doesn't he ever come up for air anymore?"

"Mr. Thaxter's business is taken care of. His rents are collected and his properties maintained. That was always his principal pleasure in life, and so it remains. Now: what may I tell young master Vernon, please?"

Vernon Thaxter had had a book published. A mystery, by the sound of it. A real book, by a real New York City publisher. I might never get the chance to talk to a real writer again, I thought. I didn't care if he was crazy, or walked around in his birthday suit. He had knowledge of a world far beyond Zephyr, and though this knowledge may have scorched him, I was interested in finding out his own experiences with the magic box. "I'd like to go," I said.

"That's a yes, I presume?" Mr. Pritchard asked my parents.

"I don't know, Tom," my mother said. "One of us ought to go, too. Just in case."

"I understand your hesitation, Mrs. Mackenson. I can only tell you that my wife and I know young master Vernon to be a gentle, intelligent, and sensitive man. He doesn't have any friends, not really. His father is and has always been very distant to him." Again, the ice crept back into Mr. Pritchard's eyes. "Mr. Thaxter is a single-minded man. He never wanted young master Vernon to be a writer. In fact, up until quite recently he refused to allow the library to stock copies of *The Moon My Mistress*."

"What changed his mind?" Mom asked.

"Time and circumstances," Mr. Pritchard replied. "It became clear to Mr. Thaxter that young master Vernon did not have the aptitude for the business world. As I've said, young master Vernon is a sensitive man." The ice left him; he blinked, and even offered a shade of a smile. "Pardon me. I didn't mean to ramble on about concerns with which I'm sure you don't wish to be bothered. But young master Vernon is eager for an answer. May I tell him yes?"

"If one of us can go, too," Dad told him. "I've always wanted to see the inside of that house." He looked at Mom. "Is that all right with you?"

She thought about it for a minute. I watched for signs of a decision: the chewing of her lower lip usually brought forth a no, whereas a sigh and slight twitch of the right corner of her mouth was a yes being born. The sigh came out, then the twitch. "Yes," she said.

"Very good." Mr. Pritchard's smile was genuine. He seemed relieved that a positive decision had been reached. "I've been instructed to tell you that I'll pick you up here on Saturday evening at six-thirty. Is that suitable, sir?"

The question was directed to me. I said it would be fine.

"Until then." He gave us all a stiff-backed bow and walked to the black-satin-skinned car. The noise the engine made starting up was like hushed music. Then Mr. Pritchard drove away, and turned at the next intersection onto the upward curve of Temple Street.

"I hope everything'll be all right," Mom said as soon as we were back in the house. "I have to say, Vernon's book gave me the willies."

Dad sat down in his chair again and picked up the sports page where he'd left off. All the headlines were about Alabama and Auburn football games, the religions of autumn. "Always wanted to see where ol' Moorwood lives. I guess this is as good an opportunity as I'll get. Anyhow, Cory'll have a chance to talk to Vernon about writin'."

"Lord, I hope you don't ever write anythin' as gruesome as that book was," Mom said to me. "It's strange, too, because all that gruesome stuff just seemed sewn in where it didn't have to be. It would've been a good book about a small town if all that murder hadn't been in there."

"Murders happen," Dad said. "As we all know."

"Yes, but shouldn't a book about *life* be good enough? And that bloody meat cleaver on the cover . . . well, I wouldn't have read it to begin with if Vernon's name hadn't been on it."

"All life isn't hearts and flowers." Dad put down his paper. "I wish it was, God knows I do. But life is just as much pain and mess as it is joy and order. Probably a lot more mess than order, too. I guess when you make yourself realize that, you"—he smiled faintly, with his sad eyes, and looked at me—"start growin' up." He began reading an article about the Auburn football team, then he put it aside again as another thought struck him. "I'll tell you what's strange, Rebecca. Have *you* seen Moorwood Thaxter in the last two or three years? Have you seen him just *once?* At the bank, or the barbershop, or anywhere around town?"

"No, I haven't. I probably wouldn't even know what he looks like, anyway."

"Slim old fella. Always wears a black suit and a black bow tie. I remember seein' Moorwood when I was a kid. He always looked dried up and old. After his wife died, he stopped comin' out of his house very often. But it seems like we would've seen him now and again, don't you think?''

"I've never seen Mr. Pritchard before. I guess they're all hermits."

"Except Vernon," I said. "Until the weather turns cold, I mean."

"Right as rain," Dad said. "But I think I might ask around tomorrow. Find out if anybody I know has seen Moorwood lately."

"Why?" Mom frowned. "What does it matter? You'll probably see him on Saturday night."

"Unless he's dead," came his answer. "Now, wouldn't that be somethin'? If Moorwood's been dead for two years or more, and everybody in Zephyr still jumps at the sound of his name because his dyin's been kept a secret?"

"And why would it be kept a secret? What would be the point?"

Dad shrugged, but I could tell he was thinking in overdrive. "Inheritance taxes, maybe. Greedy relatives. Legal mess. Could be a lot of things." A smile stole across his mouth, and his eyes sparkled. "Vernon would have to know it. Now, wouldn't that just be a hoot if a naked insane man owned most of this town and everybody did what he said to do because we thought it was Moorwood talkin'? Like the night the whole town turned out to keep Bruton from bein' washed away? I always thought that was peculiar. Moorwood was more interested in keepin' his money in a tight fist than givin' it away to Good Samaritans, even if they had to be threatened to be good."

"Maybe he had a change of heart," Mom suggested.

"Yeah. I suspect bein' dead can do that."

"You'll have your chance to find out on Saturday night," Mom said.

And so we would. Between now and then, however, I had to face the Demon and hear about how much fun her birthday party was going to be and how everybody else in the class would be there. Just as my father was asking around about sightings of Moorwood Thaxter, I asked my classmates at recess if they were going to the Demon's birthday party.

No one was. Most made comments that led me to believe they'd rather eat one of her dog dookey sandwiches than go to any party where they'd be at her booger-flicking, Munster-family mercy. I said I'd lie down in red-hot coals and kiss that baldheaded Russian guy who beat his shoe on the table rather than go to the Demon's party and have to smell her stinking relatives.

But I didn't say this where she could hear me, of course. In fact, I was starting to feel more than a little sorry for her, because I couldn't find one single kid who was going to that party.

I don't know why I did it. Maybe because I thought of what it would feel like, to invite a classful of kids to your birthday party, offer to feed them ice cream and cake and they wouldn't even have to bring a present, and have every one of them say no. That is a hurtful word, and I figured the Demon would hear a lot of it in time to come. But I couldn't go to the party; that would be begging for trouble. On Thursday after school, I rode Rocket to the Woolworth's on Merchants Street, and I bought her a fifteen-cent birthday card with a puppy wearing a birthday hat on the front. Inside, under the doggerel poem, I wrote Happy Birthday from Your Classmates. Then I slid it into its pink envelope, and on Friday I got into the room before anybody else and put the envelope on the Demon's desk. I thanked God nobody saw me, either; I never would've lived it down.

The bell rang, and Leatherlungs took command. The Demon sat down behind me. I heard her open the envelope. Leatherlungs started hollering at a guy named Reggie Duffy because he was chewing grape bubble gum. This was part of the overall plan; we'd learned she despised the smell of grape bubble gum, and so almost every day somebody became a purple-mouthed martyr.

Behind me, I heard a faint *sniff*.

That was all. But it was a heart-aching sound, to think that fifteen cents could buy a happy tear.

At recess, on the dusty playground behind the school, the Demon fluttered from kid to kid showing them the card. Everybody had the good sense to pretend they already knew about it. Ladd Devine, a lanky kid with a red crew cut who was already showing signs of being a football star in his quick feet, loping passes, and general fondness for mayhem, began telling all the girls he'd bought the card when he heard they thought it was sweet. I didn't say anything. The Demon was already staring at Ladd with love in her eyes and a finger up her nose.

On Saturday evening, at the appointed time, Mr. Pritchard arrived at our house in the long black car. "Watch your manners!" Mom cautioned me, though it was meant for Dad, too. We weren't dressed up in suits; "casual wear" meant comfortable short-sleeved shirts and clean blue jeans. Dad and I climbed into the back of the car and the impression I had was of finding yourself in a cavern with walls of mink and leather. Mr. Pritchard sat divided from us by a pane of clear plastic. He drove us away from the house and took the turn up onto the heights of Temple Street, and we could hardly hear the engine or even feel a bump.

On Temple Street, amid huge spreading oaks and poplars, were the homes of the elite citizens of Zephyr. Mayor Swope's red brick house was there, on a circular driveway. Dad pointed out the white stone mansion of the man who was president of the bank. A little farther along the winding street stood the house of Mr. Sumpter Womack, who owned the Spinnin' Wheel, and directly across the way in a house with white columns lived Dr. Parrish. Then Temple Street ended at a gate of scrolled ironwork. Beyond the gate, a cobblestoned drive curved between rows of evergreens that stood as straight as soldiers at attention. The windows of the Thaxter mansion were ablaze with light, its slanted roofs topped with chimneys and bulbous onion-shaped turrets. Mr. Pritchard stopped to get out to open the gate, then he stopped again on the other side to close it. The car's tires made pillows out of the cobblestones. We followed the curve between the fragrant pines, and Mr. Pritchard pulled us to a halt under a large canvas awning striped with blue and gold. Beneath the awning, a stone-tiled entryway led to the massive front door. Before Dad could unlatch the car's door, Mr. Pritchard was there to do it for him. Then Mr. Pritchard, moving with the grace and silence of quicksilver, opened the mansion's front door for us, and we walked in.

Dad stopped. "Golly," was all he could say.

I shared his sense of awe. To describe the interior of the Thaxter mansion in the detail it deserves is impossible, but I was struck by the vastness of it, the high ceilings with exposed beams and chandeliers hanging down. Everything seemed to be shining and gleaming and glinting, and our feet were cushioned by gardens of Oriental weave. The air smelled of cedar and saddle soap. On the walls pictures in gilded frames basked in pools of light. A huge tapestry showing a medieval scene adorned one entire wall, and a wide staircase swept up to the second floor like the sweet curve of Chile Willow's shoulder. I saw textures of burled wood, burnished leather, crushed velvet, and colored glass, and even the chandelier bulbs were sparkling clean, not a cobweb between them.

A woman about the same age as Mr. Pritchard appeared from a hallway. She wore a white uniform and had her snowy hair in a bun clasped with silver pins. She had a round, pretty face and clear blue eyes, and she said hello to us in the same accent as her husband. Dad had told me it was British. "Young master Vernon's with his trains," she told us. "He'd like you to join him there."

"Thank you, Gwendolyn," Mr. Pritchard said. "If you'll follow me, gentlemen?" He began walking into a corridor flanked with more rooms, and we were quick to keep up. It was obvious to us that you could put several houses the size of ours in this mansion and still have room left over for a barn. Mr. Pritchard stopped and opened a pair of tall doors and we heard the tinny wail of a train whistle.

And there was Vernon, naked as the day he escaped the womb. He was leaning over, examining something he held close to his face, and we had quite a view of his rear end.

Mr. Pritchard cleared his throat. Vernon turned around, a locomotive in his hand, and he smiled so wide I thought his face would split. "Oh, there you are!" he said. "Come on in!" We did. The room had no furniture but a huge table on which toy trains were chugging across a green landscape of miniature hills, forest, and a tiny town. Vernon was attending to the locomotive's wheels with a shaving brush. "Dust on the tracks," he explained. "If it builds up, a whole train can crash."

I watched the train layout with pure amazement. Seven trains were in motion at the same time. Little switches were being thrown automatically, little signal lights blinking, little cars stopped at little railroad crossings. Sprinkled throughout the green forest were red-leafed Judas trees. The tiny town had matchbox houses and buildings painted to resemble brick and stone. At the terminus of the main street there was a gothic structure with a cupola: the courthouse where I'd fled from Mayor Swope. Roads snaked between the mounded hills. A bridge crossed a river of green-painted glass, and out beyond the town there was a large oblong black-painted mirror. Saxon's Lake, I realized. Vernon had even painted the shoreline red to represent the rocks there. I saw the baseball field, the swimming pool, the houses and streets of Bruton. Even a single rainbow-splashed house, at the end of what must be Jessamyn Street. I found Route Ten, which ran along the forest that opened up a space for Saxon's Lake. I was looking for a particular house. Yes, there it was, the size of my thumbnail: Miss Grace's house of bad girls. In the wooded hills to the west, between Zephyr and the off-map Union Town, there was a round scorch mark where some of the little trees had burned away. "Somethin' caught fire," I said.

"That's where the meteor fell," Vernon replied without even glancing at it. He blew on the locomotive's wheels, a naked Amazing Colossal Man. I found Hilltop Street, and our own house at the edge of the woods. Then I followed the stately curve of

Temple Street, and right there stood the cardboard mansion my father and I were standing in.

"You're in here, Cory. Both of you are." Vernon motioned toward a shoebox beside his right hand, near a scatter of railroad cars, disconnected tracks, and wiring. On the shoebox's lid was written PEOPLE in black crayon. I lifted the lid and looked down at what must've been hundreds of tiny toy people, their flesh and hair meticulously painted. None of them wore any clothes.

One of the moving trains let out a high, birdlike whistle. Another was pulled by a steam engine, which puffed out circles of smoke the size of Cheerios. Dad walked around the gigantic, intricate layout, his mouth agape. "It's all here, isn't it?" he asked. "Poulter Hill's even got tombstones on it! Mr. Thaxter, how'd you do all this?"

He looked up from his work. "I'm not Mr. Thaxter," he said. "I'm Vernon."

"Oh. All right. Vernon, then. How'd you do all this?"

"Not overnight, that's for sure," Vernon answered, and he smiled again. From a distance his face was boyish; up close, though, you could see the crinkly lines around his eyes and two deeper lines bracketing his mouth. "I did it because I love Zephyr. Always have. Always will." He glanced at Mr. Pritchard, who'd been waiting by the door. "Thanks, Cyril. You can go now. Oh . . . wait. Does Mr. Mackenson understand?"

"Understand what?" Dad asked.

"Uh . . . young master Vernon wants to have dinner alone with your son. He wants you to eat in the kitchen."

"I don't get it. Why?"

Vernon kept staring at Mr. Pritchard. The older man said, "Because he invited your son to dinner. You came along, as I understand, as a chaperon. If you still have any . . . uh . . . reservations, let me tell you that the dining room is next to the kitchen. We'll be there eating our dinner while your son and young master Vernon are in the dining room. It's what he wants, Mr. Mackenson." This last sentence was spoken with an air of resignation.

Dad looked at me, and I shrugged. I could tell he didn't like this arrangement, and he was close to pulling up stakes.

"You're here," Vernon said. He put the locomotive down on a track, and it clickety-clicked out from under his hand. "Might as well stay."

"Might as well," I echoed to Dad.

"You'll enjoy the food. Gwendolyn's a fine cook," Mr. Pritchard added.

Dad folded his arms across his chest and watched the trains. "Okay," he said quietly. "I guess."

"Good!" Now Vernon truly beamed. "That's all, Cyril."

"Yes sir." Mr. Pritchard left, and the doors closed behind him.

"You're a milkman, aren't you?" Vernon asked.

"Yes, I am. I work for Green Meadows."

"My daddy owns Green Meadows." Vernon walked past me and around the table to check a connection of wires. "It's that way." He pointed off the table with one of his skinny arms in the direction of the dairy. "You know there's a new grocery store opening in Union Town next month? They're almost finished with that new shopping center there. Going to be what they call a supermarket. Going to have a whole big section of milk in—can you believe this?—plastic jugs."

"Plastic jugs?" Dad grunted. "I'll be."

"Everything's going plastic," Vernon said. He reached down and straightened a house. "That's what the future's going to be. Plastic, through and through."

"I . . . haven't seen your father for a good long while, Vernon. I talked to Mr. Dollar yesterday. Talked to Dr. Parrish and Mayor Swope today, too. Even went by the bank to talk to a few people. Nobody's seen your father for two or more years. Fella at the bank says Mr. Pritchard picks up the important papers and they come back signed by Moorwood."

"Yes, that's right. Cory, how do you like this bird's-eye view of Zephyr? Kind of makes you feel like you could fly right over the roofs, doesn't it?"

"Yes sir." I'd been thinking the exact same thing just a minute or so before.

"Oh, don't 'sir' me. Call me Vernon."

"Cory's been taught to respect his elders," Dad said.

Vernon looked at him with an expression of surprise and dismay. "Elders? But we're the same age."

Dad didn't speak for a few seconds. Then he said, "Oh" in a careful voice.

"Cory, come here and run the trains! Okay?" He was standing next to a control box with dials and levers on it. "Express freight's coming through! Toot toot!"

I walked to the control box, which looked as complicated as dividing fractions. "What do I do?"

"Anything," Vernon said. "That's the fun of it."

Hesitantly, I started twisting dials and pushing levers. Some of the trains got faster, others slower. The steam engine was really puffing now. The signal lights blinked and the whistles blew.

"Is Moorwood still here, Vernon?" my father asked.

"Resting. He's upstairs, resting." Vernon's attention was fixed on the trains.

"Can I see him?"

"Nobody sees him when he's resting," Vernon explained.

"When is he *not* restin', then?"

"I don't know. He's always too tired to tell me."

"Vernon, would you look at me?" Vernon turned his head toward my dad, but his eyes kept cutting back to the trains. "Is Moorwood still alive?"

"Alive, alive-o," Vernon said. "Clams and mussels, alive, alive-o." He frowned, as if the question had finally registered. "Of *course* he's alive! Who do you think runs all this business stuff?"

"Maybe Mr. Pritchard does?"

"My daddy is upstairs resting," Vernon repeated with firm emphasis on the *resting*. "Are you a milkman or a member of the Inquisition?"

"Just a milkman," Dad said. "A curious milkman."

"And curiouser and curiouser you get. Pick up the speed, Cory! Number Six is running late!"

I kept twisting the dials. The trains were zipping around the bends and racing between the hills.

"I liked your story about the lake," Vernon said. "That's why I painted the lake black. It's got a dark secret deep inside, doesn't it?"

"Yes, si—Vernon," I corrected myself. I'd have to get used to being able to call a grown-up by his first name.

"I read about it in the *Journal*." Vernon reached out toward a hillside to straighten a crooked tree, and his shadow fell over the earth. Then, the task done, he stepped back and gazed down upon the town. "The killer had to know how deep Saxon's Lake is. So he has to be a local. Maybe he lives in one of those houses, right there in Zephyr. But, if I'm to understand the dead man was never identified and nobody's turned up missing since March, then he must not have been a local. So: what's the connection between a man who lives here and a man who lived somewhere far away?"

"The sheriff would like to know that, too."

"Sheriff Amory's a good man," Vernon said. "Just not a good sheriff. He'd be the first to admit it. He doesn't have the hound-dog instinct; he lets the birds fly when he's got his paws on them." Vernon scratched a place just below his navel, his head cocked to one side. Then he walked to a brass wallplate and flicked two switches. The room's lights went off; tiny lights in some of the toy houses came on. The trains followed their headlights around the tracks. "So early in the morning," he mused. "But if I was going to kill somebody, I'd have killed them early enough to dump them in the lake and be sure nobody was coming along Route Ten. Why'd the killer wait until almost dawn to do it?"

"I wish I knew," Dad said.

I kept playing with the levers, the dials illuminated before me.

"It must be somebody who doesn't get home delivery from Green Meadows," Vernon decided. "He didn't think about the milkmen's schedules, did he? You know what I believe?" Dad didn't answer. "I believe the killer's a night owl. I think dumping the body into the lake was the last thing he did before he went home and went to bed. I believe if you find a night owl who doesn't drink milk, you've got your killer."

"Doesn't drink milk? How do you figure that?"

"Milk helps you sleep," Vernon said. "The killer doesn't like to sleep, and if he works in the daytime, he'll drink his coffee black."

The only response Dad gave was a muffled grunt, whether in agreement or in sympathy I didn't know.

Mr. Pritchard returned to the darkened room to announce that dinner was being served. Then Vernon turned off the trains and said, "Come on with me, Cory," and I followed him as Dad went with the butler. We walked into a room with suits of armor standing in it, and there was a long table with two places set, one across from the other. Vernon told me to choose a seat, so I sat where I could see the knights. In a few minutes Gwendolyn entered, carrying a silver tray, and so began one of the strangest dinners of my life.

We had strawberry soup with vanilla wafers crumbled up in it. We had ravioli and chocolate cake on the same plate. We had lemon-lime Fizzies to drink, and Vernon put a whole Fizzie tablet in his mouth and I laughed when the green bubbles boiled out. We had hamburger patties and buttered popcorn, and dessert was a bowl of devil's food cake batter you ate with a spoon. As I ate these things, I did so with guilty pleasure; a kid's feast like this was the kind of thing that would've made my mother swoon. There wasn't a vegetable in sight, no carrots, no spinach, no Brussels sprouts. I did get a whiff of what I thought to be beef stew from the kitchen, so I figured Dad was having a grown-up's meal. He probably had no idea what I was assaulting my stomach with. Vernon was a happy eater; he laughed and laughed and both of us wound up licking our batter bowls in a sugar-sopped delirium.

Vernon wanted to know all about me. What I liked to do, who my friends were, what books I liked to read, what movies I enjoyed. He'd seen *Invaders from Mars,* too; it was a linchpin between us. He said he used to have a great big trunk full of superhero comic books, but his daddy had made him throw them away. He said he used to have shelves of Hardy Boys mysteries, until his daddy had gotten mad at him one day and burned them in the fireplace. He said he used to have all the Doc Savage magazines and the Tarzan and John Carter of Mars books and the Shadow and Weird Tales and boxes of *Argosy* and *Boy's Life* magazines, but his daddy had said Vernon had gotten too old for those things and all of them, every one, had gone into the fire or the trash and burned to ashes or been covered in earth. He said he would give a million dollars if he could have them again and he said that if I had any of them I should hold on to them forever because they were magic.

And once you burn the magic things or cast them out in the garbage, Vernon said, you become a beggar for magic again.

" 'I shall wear the bottoms of my trousers rolled,' " Vernon said.

"What?" I asked him. I'd never even seen Vernon wearing shorts before.

"I wrote a book once," he told me.

"I know. Mom's read it."

"Would you like to be a writer someday?"

"I guess," I said. "I mean . . . if I could be."

"Your story was good. I used to write stories. My daddy said it was fine for me to have a hobby like that, but never to forget that someday all this would be my responsibility."

"All what?" I asked.

"I don't know. He never would tell me."

"Oh." Somehow this made sense. "How come you didn't write another book?"

Vernon started to say something; his mouth opened, then closed again. He sat for a long moment staring at his hands, his fingers smeared with cake batter. His eyes had taken on a shiny glint. "I only had the one in me," he said at last. "I looked and I looked for another one. But it's not there. It wasn't there yesterday, it's not there today . . . and I don't think it'll be there tomorrow, either."

"How come?" I asked. "Can't you think of a story?"

"I'll tell you a story," he said.

I waited.

Vernon drew a long breath and let it go. His eyes were unfocused, as if he were struggling to stay awake but sleep was pulling him under. "There was a boy," he began, "who wrote a book about a

265

town. A little town, about the size of Zephyr. Yes, very much like Zephyr. This boy wrote a book, and it took him four years to get everything exactly right. And while this boy was writing his book, his daddy . . ." He trailed off.

I waited.

"His . . . daddy . . ." Vernon frowned, trying to find his thoughts again. "Yes," he said. "His daddy told him he was nothing but a fool. His daddy said it night and day. You fool, you crazy fool. Spending your time writing a book, when you ought to know business. That's what I raised you for. Business. I didn't raise you to spend your time disappointing me and throwing your chances away, I raised you for business and your mother is looking at you from her grave because you disappointed her, too. Yes, you broke her heart when you failed college and that's why she took the pills that reason and that reason alone. Because you failed and all that money was wasted I should've just thrown it out the window let the niggers and the white trash have it." Vernon blinked; something about his face looked shattered. " 'Negroes,' the boy said. We must be civilized. Do you see, Cory?"

"I . . . don't . . ."

"Chapter two," Vernon said. "Four years. The boy stood it for four years. And he wrote this book about the town, and the people in it who made it what it was. And maybe there wasn't a real plot to it, maybe there wasn't anything that grabbed you by the throat and tried to shake you until your bones rattled, but the book was about *life*. It was the flow and the voices, the little day-to-day things that make up the memory of living. It meandered like the river, and you never knew where you were going until you got there, but the journey was sweet and deep and left you wishing for more. It was alive in a way that the boy's life was not." He sat staring at nothing for a moment. I watched his chocolate-smeared fingers gripping at the table's edge. "He found a publisher," Vernon went on. "A real New York City publisher. You know, that's where the heart of things is. That's where they make the books by the hundreds of thousands, and each one is a child different and special and some walk tall and some are crippled, but they all go out into the world from there. And the boy got a call from New York City and they said they wanted to publish his book but would he consider some changes to make it even better than it was and the boy was so happy and proud he said yes he wanted it to be the very best it could be." Vernon's glassy eyes moved, finding pictures in the air.

"So," Vernon said in a quiet voice, "the boy packed his bags while his daddy told him he was a stupid fool that he'd come back to this house crawling and then we'd see who was right, wouldn't we? And the boy was a very naughty boy that day, he told his daddy he'd see him in the bad place first. He went from Zephyr to Birmingham on a bus and Birmingham to New York City on a train, and he walked into an office in a tall building to find out what was going to happen to his child."

Vernon lapsed into silence again. He picked up his batter bowl, trying to find something else to lick. "What happened?" I prodded.

"They told him." He smiled; it was a gaunt smile. "They said this is a business, like any other. We have charts and graphs, and we have numbers on the wall. We know that this year people want murder mysteries, and your town would make a wonderful setting for one. Murder mysteries, they said. Thrill people. We're having to compete with television now, they said. It's not like it used to be, when people had time to read. People want murder mysteries, and we have charts and graphs to prove it. They said if the boy would fit a murder mystery into the book—and it wouldn't be too difficult, they said, it wouldn't be too hard at all to do—then they would publish it with the boy's name right there on the cover. But they said they didn't like the title *Moon Town*. No, that wouldn't do. Can you write hard-boiled? they asked. They said they needed a hard-boiled writer this year."

"Did he do it?" I asked.

"Oh, yes." Vernon nodded. "Oh, he did it. Whatever they wanted. Because it was so close, so close he could taste it. And he knew his daddy was watching over his shoulder. He did it." Vernon's smile was like a fresh wound in scar tissue. "But they were wrong. It was very, very hard to do. The boy got a room in a hotel, and he worked on it. That hotel . . . it was all he could afford. And as he worked on that rented typewriter in that mean little rented room, some of that hotel and some of that city got into him and made its way through his fingers into that book. Then one day he didn't know where he was anymore. He was lost, and there were no signs telling him which way to go. He heard people crying and saw people hurt, and something inside him closed up like a fist and all he wanted to do was get to that last page and get out of it. He heard his daddy laughing, late at night. Heard him say you fool, you little fool you should've stood your ground. Because his daddy was in him, and his daddy had come with him all that way from Zephyr to New York City."

Vernon's eyes squeezed shut for a few agonized seconds. Then they opened again, and I saw they were rimmed with red. "That boy. That stupid little foolish boy took their money, and he ran. Back to Zephyr, back to the clean hills, back where he could think. And then that book came out, with the boy's name on it, and he saw that cover and knew he had taken his child and he had dressed that beautiful child up like a prostitute and now only people who craved ugliness wanted her. They wanted to wallow in her, and use her up and throw her away because she was only one of a hundred thousand and she was crippled. And that boy . . . that boy had done it to her. That evil, greedy boy."

His voice cracked with a noise that startled me.

Vernon pressed his hand to his mouth. When he lowered his hand, a silver thread of saliva hung from his lower lip. "That boy," he whispered. "Found out very soon . . . that the book was a failure. Very soon. He called them. Anything, he said. I'll do anything to save it. And they said we have the charts and tables, and numbers on the wall. They said people were tired of murder mysteries. They said people wanted something different. Said they'd like to see his next book, though. He had promise, they said. Just come up with something different. You're a young man, they said. You have lots of books in you." He wiped his mouth with the back of his hand: a slow, labored movement. "His daddy was waiting. His daddy grinned and grinned and kept on grinning. His daddy's face got as big as the sun and the boy was burned every time he looked at it. His daddy said you're not fit to wear my shoes. And I paid for those shoes. Yes I did. I paid for that shirt and those pants. You're not fit to wear what good money buys you. All you know is failure and failure and that's all you'll ever know for the rest of your life, and he said if I died in my sleep tonight it would be because you killed me with your failures. And that boy stood at the foot of the stairs, and he was crying and he said go on and die, then. I wish to God you would die, you . . . miserable . . . sonofabitch."

On that last terrible, hiss-breathed word I saw the tears jump in his eyes as if he'd been speared. He made a soft moaning sound, his face in torment like a Spanish painting I'd once seen of a naked saint in *National Geographic*. A tear streaked down to his jaw, followed by a second that got caught in a smear of chocolate batter in the corner of his mouth.

"Oh . . ." he whispered. "Oh . . . oh . . . no."

"Young master Vernon?" The voice was as soft as his, but spoken with firmness. Mr. Pritchard had come into the room. Vernon didn't even look at him. I started to stand up, but Mr. Pritchard said,

268

"Master Cory? Please stay where you are for right now." I stayed. Mr. Pritchard crossed the room and stood behind Vernon, and he reached out and put a gentle hand on Vernon's thin shoulder. "Dinner's over, young master Vernon," he said.

The naked man didn't move or respond. His eyes were dull and dead, nothing alive about him but the slow crawl of tears.

"It's time for bed, sir," Mr. Pritchard said.

Vernon spoke in a hollow, faraway voice: "Will I wake up?"

"I believe you will, sir." The hand patted his shoulder; it was a fatherly touch. "You should say good night to your dinner guest."

Vernon looked at me. It was as if he'd never seen me before, as if I were a stranger in his house. But then his eyes came to life again and he sniffled and smiled in his boyish way. "Dust on the tracks," he said. "If it builds up, a train can crash." A frown passed over his features, but it was just a small storm and quickly gone. "Cory." The smile returned. "Thank you for having dinner with me tonight."

"Yes si—"

He held up a finger. "Vernon."

"Vernon," I repeated.

He stood up, and I did, too. Mr. Pritchard said to me, "Your father's waiting for you at the front door. You turn right and walk along the hallway, you'll come to it. I'll be outside to drive you home in a few minutes, if you'll just wait by the car." Mr. Pritchard grasped one of Vernon's elbows, and he guided Vernon to the door. Vernon walked like a very old man.

"I enjoyed my dinner!" I told him.

Vernon stopped and stared at me. His smile flickered off and on, like the sputtering of a broken neon sign. "I hope you keep writing, Cory. I hope everything good happens to you."

"Thank you, Vernon."

He nodded, satisfied that we had made a connection. He paused once more at the entrance to the dining room. "You know, Cory, sometimes I have the strangest dream. In it, I'm walking the streets in broad daylight and I don't have on any clothes." He laughed. "Not a stitch! Imagine that!"

I can't remember smiling.

Vernon let Mr. Pritchard lead him out. I looked around at the carnage of plates, and I felt sick.

The front door was easy to find. Dad was there; from the way he smiled, I could tell he had no inkling of what I'd witnessed. "You have a good talk?" I guess I mumbled something that satisfied him. "He treat you okay?" I just nodded. Dad was jovial and happy now that his belly was full of beef stew and Vernon hadn't hurt me. "Nice house, isn't it?" he asked as we walked to the long black car. "A house like this . . . there's no tellin' how much it cost."

I didn't know either. But I did know that it was more than any one human being ought to pay.

We waited to go home, and in a little while Mr. Pritchard walked out of the house to deliver us at our own front door.

4

The Wrath of Five Thunders

On Monday morning I found the Demon had spurned me. She had eyes now only for Ladd Devine, and her fickle fingers left the back of my neck alone. It was the birthday card that had done it, and Ladd's unknowing declaration that he had sent it. Ladd was going to be a really good football player when he got to high school; between then and now, he would be getting plenty of practice running and dodging.

There was one last incident in the tale of the Demon's birthday. I asked her at recess, as she watched Ladd passing a football to Barney Gallaway, how her party had been. She looked at me as if I were one shade short of invisible. "Oh, we had fun," she said, her stare going back to the young football star. "My relatives came and ate ice cream and cake."

"Did you get any presents?"

"Uh-huh." She began to chew on a dirty fingernail, her hair stringy and oily and hanging in her face. "My momma and daddy gave me a nurse kit, my aunt Gretna gave me a pair of gloves she knitted, and my cousin Chile gave me a dried flower wreath to hang over my door for good luck."

"That's good," I said. "That's real—"

I had been about to move away. Now I stopped in my tracks.

"Chile?" I said. "What's her last name?"

"Purcell. Used to be, I mean. She got married to a fella and the

270

stork brought 'em a little bitty baby." The Demon sighed. "Oh, ain't Ladd just the handsomest thing?"

God has a sense of humor that gets my goat sometimes.

September dwindled away, and one morning it was October. The hills were streaked with red and gold, as if some magician had painted the trees almost overnight. It was still hot in the afternoons, but the mornings began to whisper about sweaters. This was Indian summer, when you saw those purple-and-red-grained ears of corn in baskets in the grocery store and an occasional dead leaf chuckled along the sidewalk.

We had Show-and-Tell Day at our grade in school, which meant that everybody got to bring something important and tell why it was. I brought an issue of *Famous Monsters* to class, the sight of which would probably set Leatherlungs off like a Roman candle but would make me a hero of the oppressed. Davy Ray brought his "I Get Around" record, and the picture of an electric guitar he hoped to learn to play when his parents could afford lessons. Ben brought a Confederate dollar. Johnny brought his collection of arrowheads, all kept in separate drawers in a metal fishing-tackle box and protected by individual cotton balls.

They were a wonder to behold. Small and large, rough and smooth, light and dark: they beckoned the imagination on a journey into the time when the forest was unbroken, the only light was cast from tribal fires, and Zephyr existed only in a medicine man's fever. Johnny had been gathering the arrowheads ever since I'd known him, in the second grade. While the rest of us were running and playing without a moment's interest in that dusty crevice known as history, Johnny was searching the wooded trails and creekbeds for a sharp little sign of his heritage. He had collected over a hundred, lovingly cleaned them—but no shellac, that would be an insult to the hand that carved the flint—and tucked them away in the tackle box. I imagined he took them out at night, in his room, and over them he dreamed of what life was like in Adams Valley two hundred years ago. I wondered if he imagined there were four Indian buddies who had four dogs and four swift ponies, and that they lived in tepees in the same village and talked about life and school and stuff. I never asked him, but I think he probably did.

Before school began that morning of show-and-tell which I had been dreading for several days because of what the Demon would offer up for appraisal—the guys and I met where we usually did, near the monkey bars on the dusty playground, our bikes chained to the fence along with dozens of others. We sat in the sun because the morning was cool and the sky was clear. "Open it," Ben said to Johnny. "Come on, let's see."

It didn't take much urging for Johnny to flip up the latch. He may have kept them protected like rare jewels, but he wasn't stingy about sharing their magic. "Found this one last Saturday," he said as he opened a wad of cotton and brought a pale gray arrowhead to the light. "You can tell whoever did this was in a hurry. See how the cuts are so rough and uneven? He wasn't takin' his time about it. He just wanted to make an arrowhead so he could go shoot somethin' to eat."

"Yeah, and from the size of it I'll bet all he got was a gopher," Davy Ray commented.

"Maybe he was a sorry shot," Ben said. "Maybe he knew he'd probably lose it."

"Could be," Johnny agreed. "Maybe he was a boy, and this was his first one."

"If I'd had to depend on makin' arrowheads to eat," I said, "I would've dried up and blown away mighty fast."

"You sure have got a lot of them." Ben's fingers might have been itching to explore in the tackle box, but he was respectful of Johnny's property. "Have you got a favorite one?"

"Yeah, I do. This is it." Johnny picked up a wad of cotton, opened it, and showed us which one.

It was black, smooth, and almost perfectly formed.

I recognized it.

It was the arrowhead Davy Ray had found in the deep woods on our camping trip.

"That's a beauty," Ben agreed. "Looks like it's been oiled, doesn't it?"

"I just cleaned it, that's all. It does shine, though." He rubbed the arrowhead between his brown fingers, and he placed it in Ben's pudgy hand. "Feel it," Johnny said. "You can hardly feel any cuts on it."

Ben passed it to Davy Ray, who passed it to me. The arrowhead had one small chip in it, but it seemed to melt into your hand. Rubbing it in your palm, it was hard to tell where arrowhead stopped and flesh began. "I wonder who made this one," I said.

"Yeah, I'd like to know, too. Whoever did it wasn't in any hurry. Whoever did it wanted to have a good arrowhead, one that would fly true, even if he lost it. Arrowheads were more than just the tips of arrows to Indians; they were like money, and they showed how much care you put into things. They showed how good of a hunter you were, whether you needed a lot of cheap old arrowheads to do the job, or if you had the time to make a few you could count on. I sure would like to know who made it."

This seemed important to Johnny. "I'll bet it was a chief," I offered.

"A *chief*? Really?" Ben's eyes got wide.

"He's fixin' to make up a story," Davy Ray told him. "Can't believe a thing he says from here on out."

"Sure it was a chief!" I said adamantly. "Yes, he was a chief and he was the youngest chief the tribe ever had! He was twenty years old and his father was a chief before him!"

"Oh, brother!" Davy Ray pulled his knees up to his chest, a knowing smile on his face. "Cory, if there's ever a biggest-liar-in-town contest, you'll win first prize for sure!"

Johnny smiled, too, but his eyes were keen with interest. "Go on, Cory. Let's hear about him. What was his name?"

"I don't know. It was . . . Runnin' Deer, I—"

"That's no good!" Ben said. "That's a girl Indian's name! Make his name . . . oh . . . a warrior's name. Like Heap Big Thundercloud!"

"Big Heap Do-Do!" Davy Ray cackled. "That's you, Ben!"

"His name was Chief Thunder," Johnny said, looking directly at me and ignoring the squabbling duo. "No. Chief *Five* Thunders. Because he was tall and dark and—"

"Cross-eyed," Davy Ray said.

"Had a clubfoot," Johnny finished, and Davy Ray shut up his giggling.

I paused, the arrowhead gleaming on my palm.

"Go ahead, Cory," Johnny urged in a quiet voice. "Tell us a story about him."

"Chief Five Thunders." I was thinking, weaving the story together, as my fingers squeezed and relaxed around the warm flint. "He was a Cherokee."

"Creek," Johnny corrected me.

"Creek, like I said. He was a Creek Indian, and his father was a chief but his father got killed when he was out huntin'. He went out huntin' for deer, and they found him where he'd fallen off a rock. He was dyin', but he told his son he'd seen Snowdown. Yes, he had. He'd seen Snowdown up close, close enough to see that white skin and those antlers that were as big as trees. He said as long as Snowdown lived in the woods, the world would keep goin'. But if anybody ever killed Snowdown, the world would end. Then he died, and Five Thunders was the new chief."

"I thought a chief had to fight to get to be chief," Davy Ray said.

"Well, sure he did!" I answered. "Everybody knows that. He had to fight a whole bunch of braves who thought they ought to be chief. But he liked peace better than he liked fightin'. It wasn't that he couldn't fight when he had to, it was just that he knew when to fight and when not to fight. But he had a temper, too. That's why they didn't call him just 'One Thunder' or 'Two Thunders.' He didn't get mad very much, but when he did—look out! It was like five thunders boomin' out all at the same time."

"The bell's about to ring," Johnny said. "What happened to him?"

"He . . . uh . . . he was the chief for a long, long time. Until he got to be sixty years old. Then he passed bein' chief to his son, Wise Fox." I glanced toward the entrance; kids were starting to go into the school. "But Five Thunders was the chief they remembered best, because he kept peace between his tribe and the other tribes, and when he died they took his best arrowheads and scattered them around the woods for people to find a hundred years later. Then they carved his name in a rock and they buried his body in the secret Indian burial ground."

"Oh, yeah?" Davy Ray grinned. "Where's that?"

"I don't know," I said. "It's a secret."

They groaned. The bell rang, summoning the kids in. I returned the arrowhead of Five Thunders to Johnny, who wrapped it in cotton and returned it to the tackle box. We stood up and started walking across the playground, puffs of dust rising behind our heels. "Maybe there really was somebody like Chief Five Thunders," Johnny said as we neared the door.

"Sure there was!" Ben spoke up. "Cory said so, didn't he?"

Davy Ray made a noise like the breaking of wind, but I knew he didn't mean it. He had a part to play in our group—the part of scoffer and agitator—and this he played very well. I knew what Davy Ray was inside; after all, it was he who had brought Five Thunders to life.

I heard Ladd Devine hollering, "Get away from me with those squirrel heads!" Some girl screamed and somebody shouted, "Oh, gross!" The Demon was in her element.

As I had predicted, the sight of cinematic monsters in her classroom enraged Leatherlungs. She threw a tantrum that made one of Five Thunders' outbreaks seem more like Half-a-Pipsqueak. Leatherlungs demanded to know if my parents knew what kind of garbage I was stuffing my mind with. Then she went into a tirade about how all decency and thoughtfulness in this world was going to ruin, just going to ruin, and why wasn't I interested in good reading instead of this monster trash? I just sat there and took it on the chin, like I was supposed to. Then the Demon opened up the shoebox she'd brought and stuck it in Leatherlungs' face and the sight of those four squirrel heads crawling with ants and their eyes poked out with a toothpick made Leatherlungs beat a hasty retreat to the teachers' lounge.

At last the three o'clock bell rang, and school was behind us for another day. We left Leatherlungs reduced to a raspy whisper. Out on the playground under the hot afternoon sun, clouds of dust stormed through the air as kids ran for freedom. As usual, Davy Ray was ragging Ben about something or other. Johnny put his tackle box on the ground as he unlocked his bike chain, and I knelt down to work the combination lock that secured Rocket.

It happened very fast. Such things always do.

They came out of the dust. I felt them before I saw them. The skin at the back of my neck drew tight.

"Four little pussies, all in a row," came the first taunt.

My head whipped around, because I knew that voice. Davy Ray and Ben ceased their wrangling. Johnny looked up, his eyes darkening with dread.

"There they are," Gotha Branlin said, with Gordo at his side. They wore their grins like open razors, their black bikes crouched behind them. "Ain't they sweet, Gordo?"

"Yeah, ain't they?"

"What's this?" With one quick movement, Gotha tore from my hand the magazine I'd brought for show-and-tell. It ripped along the staples, and on the cover Christopher Lee's Count Dracula hissed with impotent rage. "Look at this shit!" Gotha told his brother, and Gordo laughed at a picture of the sleek female robot from *Metropolis.* "I can see her fuckin' titties!" Gordo said. "Gimme it!" He grabbed the page, Gotha grabbed for it, and between their hands the picture dissolved as if consumed by acid. Gotha got most of it, though—the part showing a glimpse of metallic breasts—and it went down crumpled and dirty in his jeans pocket. Gordo squalled, "You shithole, give it here!" and he wrenched at the rest of the magazine while Gotha pulled at it, too. In another second the rest of the staples surrendered and pages of dark and glittering dreams, heroes and villains and fantastic visions, fluttered through the dust like bats in daylight. "You *ruined* it!" Gotha shrieked, and he shoved his brother so hard Gordo slammed to the ground on his back and a geyser of saliva shot from his mouth. Gordo sat up, his face swollen with rage and his eyes unspeakable, but Gotha cocked a fist back and stood over him like Godzilla over Ghidrah. "Come on and try it!" Gotha said. "Just come on!"

Gordo stayed where he was. His elbow was crushing a picture of King Kong fighting a wet-fleshed giant serpent. Even monsters had their collisions and death battles. Gordo's face was hard and bitter. Any other kid who'd taken so hard a blow would've sobbed at least once. I imagine a tear in the Branlin household was as rare as a dragon's tooth, and all those unshed tears and simmering rages had twisted Gotha and Gordo into what they were: two animals who could not escape their cages, no matter how hard they fought or how far away they roamed on those vulture bikes.

I might have felt sorry for them if they'd given you room to. But then Gotha said, "What's in here?" and he scooped the tackle box off the ground before Johnny could think to grab for it. Johnny made a choking sound as Gotha flipped the latch up and lifted the lid. The big rude hand went in and started plucking the wads of cotton open. "Hey, man!" he said to Gordo. "Look what squawboy's got! Arrowheads!"

"Why don't you leave us alone?" Davy Ray asked. "We're not botherin'—"

"*Shut your hole, dickhead!*" Gotha shouted at him, and Gordo got up grinning, their brotherly hate forgotten for the moment. Both of them started going through the collection of arrowheads, their fingers grasping and gripping; I would've hated to see what dinnertime at the Branlin household was like.

"Those are mine," Johnny said.

Words had never stopped the Branlins before, and they didn't now. "They belong to me," Johnny said, sweat glistening on his cheeks.

This time, something in Johnny's voice made Gotha look up. "What'd you say, niggernuts?"

"They're my arrowheads. I . . . I want 'em back."

"He wants 'em back!" Gordo crowed.

"You little pussies tried to get us in trouble, didn't you?" Gotha's right hand was full of arrowheads. "Went cryin' to the sheriff and tried to get our dad mad at us, too. Didn't you?"

This tactic did not sway Johnny's attention. "Give 'em to me," he said.

"Hey, Gotha! I think squawboy wants his fuckin' arrowheads!"

"Why don't you guys—" I began, but just that quick Gordo was in my face and he grabbed a handful of my shirtfront and pressed me up against the fence.

"Little pussy." Gordo made smacking noises. "Little pussy queer."

I saw Rocket's golden eye in the headlamp, there for just an instant, taking in the situation, then gone.

"Here're your arrowheads, squawboy," Gotha said, and he threw the ones he held across the dusty playground. Johnny trembled, as if he'd been hit by a crosscurrent of winds. He watched Gotha's hand winnow into the box, come up again, and throw arrowheads away as if they were worthless chips of stone.

"Pussy, pussy, pussy!" Gordo chanted, and he laid his wiry forearm across my neck. His nose was running, and he smelled like engine oil and burnt barbecue.

"Quit it," I gasped. His breath was no perfume from France, either.

"Woo-woo, woo-woo!" Gotha started giving Indian whoops as he tossed Johnny's collection away. "Woo-woo, woo-woo!"

"Cut it out!" Davy Ray shouted.

And then Gotha's fingers came up gripping an arrowhead that was smooth and black and almost perfectly formed. Even Gotha could tell that this one was special, because he paused in his pride of meanness and looked closely at it.

"Don't," Johnny said with a note of pleading.

Whatever Gotha might be seeing in the black arrowhead of Chief Five Thunders, it was a passing vision. He reared his arm back, his fingers opened, and the arrowhead took flight. It spun up and up and fell into the grass and weeds near the trash dumpster, and I heard Johnny grunt as if he'd been punched.

"What do you think about *that*, squaw—" Gotha began; he didn't finish it, because in the next second Johnny had made one limp and a leap between them and Johnny's fist came up in a blur and smacked dead solid into Gotha Branlin's chin.

Gotha staggered, blinked, and a wave of pain passed over his face. Then his tongue flicked out, and there was blood on it. He threw aside the tackle box and said, "You're *dead*, niggernuts!"

"Get him, Gotha!" Gordo shouted.

Johnny shouldn't be fighting. I knew this, and I knew he did, too. The Branlin fists had put him in the hospital once. He still suffered an occasional dizzy spell, and he wasn't nearly equal to Gotha Branlin's size. "Run, Johnny!" I shouted.

Johnny was through running.

Gotha came at him swinging. A fist caught Johnny's shoulder and knocked him back, and Johnny dodged a fist to his face and slammed his own punch into Gotha's ribs.

"Fight! Fight!" somebody among the few kids who were left on the field started hollering.

I shoved Gordo back with all my strength. Gordo put out a hand to steady himself, and his fingers gripped Rocket's handlebars. *"Shit!"* he screamed suddenly, and he wrung his hand and stared at his fingers. Blood was showing on the pad of flesh between his thumb and index digit. *"Bastard bit me!"* I imagine he had been cut by a screw, or an edge of metal, though I would later search Rocket and find no protruding screw or metal edge. Gordo twisted around and kicked Rocket, and that's when Five Thunders spoke to me.

He said, as he'd said to Johnny: *Enough.*

I was no puncher. If Gordo wanted to kick, that was fine with me. I stepped forward, my blood bubbling, and I gave him a kick in the shin that made him holler and dance a one-legged jig. Johnny and Gotha were grappling on the ground, the dust swirling around them. Fists rose and fell, and Davy Ray and Ben were ready to jump in if it looked as if Gotha was going to get on top of Johnny and start pummeling him. Johnny, though, was holding his own. He scrambled and twisted and fought, his sweating face paled with dust. Gotha's hand gripped Johnny's hair, but Johnny shook loose. A fist hit Johnny's chin, but Johnny showed no pain. Then Johnny was flailing away at Gotha like a boy with nothing to lose but his dignity, and when those blows connected, they made Gotha grunt with pain and try to curl up like a writhing worm. "Fight! Fight!" the merry call went up, and a knot of onlookers closed around Johnny and Gotha as they battled on the ground.

But Gordo was coming after me with a stick in his right hand.

I didn't care to get my brains knocked out, or have Rocket beaten into submission. I jumped on Rocket, knocked the kickstand up, and wheeled away, trying to put some distance between us. I thought Gordo would turn away from me and then I could try to dart in and knock that stick out of his hand. I was wrong. Gordo got on his black bike and started speeding after me, leaving Gotha to fight his own hateful little war.

I had no time to shout for Ben and Davy Ray. I doubted if they could hear me anyway, over the hollering of the blood-mad crowd. I turned Rocket away from Gordo and pedaled frantically across the playground, going out through the gate in the fence and onto the sidewalk. When I looked back, Gordo was gaining, his head slung forward over the handlebars and his legs pumping. I started to swerve Rocket toward the playground again, to get support from my buddies.

But Rocket wouldn't let me.

Rocket stiffened up. The handlebars wouldn't turn. I had no choice but to keep going along the warped sidewalk, and here a strange thing happened.

The pedals started turning faster, so fast I could hardly keep my feet on them. In fact, my sneakers slid off the grips more than once; the pedals, though, kept going. Rocket's chain rattled through the gears and built up to a high, powerful singing sound.

Rocket raced on, with me doing nothing more than clinging to its back as if on a wild horse. Our speed increased, the wind whipping through my hair. I looked over my shoulder; like doom and the end of time, Gordo was still at my heels.

He wanted my skin, and he wasn't going to stop until he had it.

Back at the playground, Gotha struggled to his feet. Before he could aim a punch, Johnny tackled him at the kneecaps and they went down again as the onlookers shouted their delight. Davy Ray and Ben started looking for me, and they saw Rocket gone and Gordo and one of the black bikes missing.

"Uh-oh!" Ben said.

Gordo's bike was fast. It might've beaten any other bike in Zephyr, but Rocket wasn't like any other bike. Rocket was going like a hellhound, and I dreaded what might happen if that chain jumped its sprocket. We passed a man out raking leaves from his driveway. We passed two women talking in a front yard. I wanted to stop, but whenever I tried to put on the brake there was a high, angry hissing and Rocket would have none of it. I tried to turn right at the next intersection, to try to get home. Rocket wanted to go left, and I yelped as the bike's handlebars took the corner and the rear wheel skidded on the edge of disaster. But Rocket held tight to the pavement, and we were off again with the wind in my teeth. "What're you doin'?" I shouted. "Where're you *goin'*?" There was only one answer to these questions: Rocket had gone insane.

Another backward glance showed me that Gordo was still right on my tail, though he was puffing and his face was mottled with crimson. "Better stop!" he hollered. "I'm gonna get you anyway!"

Not if Rocket could help it. But every time I tried to urge Rocket toward my house, Rocket refused to be guided. The bike had its own destination, and I had no choice but to be swept along with it.

Through the swirling dust, the battlers at the school yard fought to their feet. Gotha, not used to having anybody fight back, was showing his weakness; he was throwing wild punches, and he was so tired he was stumbling like a drunkard. Johnny danced in and out, making Gotha strike air again and again. When Gotha roared with rage and rushed in, the smaller boy dodged aside and Gotha tripped over his own feet and fell headlong, scraping his bruised chin raw over the pebbly ground. He got up again, his arms heavy. Again he attacked, and once more Johnny eluded him, using his clubfoot as Pan might twist and turn on a hoof. "Stand still!" Gotha gasped. "Stand still, you niggerblood!" His chest was heaving, his face as red as a beef chunk.

"All right," Johnny said, his nose bleeding and a gash across his cheekbone. "Come on, then."

Gotha charged him. Johnny feinted to the left. Davy Ray would say later that it was like watching Cassius Clay in action. When Gotha shifted to meet the feint, Johnny put everything he had into a haymaker that caught Gotha's jaw and snapped his head around. Ben said that was when he'd seen Gotha's eyes roll up and go white. But Johnny had one more thunder in him; he stepped forward and hit Gotha in the mouth so hard everybody heard two of Johnny's knuckles pop like gunshots.

Gotha made no noise. Not even a whimper.

He just fell like a big dumb tree.

He lay there, drooling blood. A front tooth slid from his lips, and then Gotha started shaking and he began to cry in hard, angry silence.

Nobody offered to help him. Somebody laughed. Somebody else sneered, "Gonna go cryin' home to his momma!"

Ben clapped Johnny on the back. Davy Ray grabbed his shoulder and said, "You showed him who's tough, didn't you?"

Johnny pulled loose. He wiped his nose with the back of his hand, which Dr. Parrish would be splinting soon for the two broken knuckles. Johnny's parents would give him hell. They would finally understand why he'd spent so much time in his room alone, over the long hot summer, reading a book that had cost three dollars and fifty cents from a mail-order publisher and had the title *Fundamentals of the Fight* by Sugar Ray Robinson.

"I'm not so tough," Johnny replied, and he leaned down beside Gotha and said, "You want some help?"

I, however, did not have the benefit of Sugar Ray's experience. I only had Rocket beneath me and Gordo a relentless pursuer, and when Rocket suddenly turned with a whip of the handlebars and started onto a trail into the woods, I feared I was fast approaching the last roundup.

Rocket refused the brake, refused my frantic tugging on the handgrips. If my bike had gone crazy, I had to get off. I tensed to jump for the underbrush.

But then Rocket burst out through the trees and there was a big ditch right in front of us full of weeds and garbage and with a burst of speed that made the hair stand up on my scalp Rocket took flight.

I think I screamed. I know I wet my pants, and that I hung on so tightly my hands ached for days afterward.

Rocket leaped the ditch and came down on the other side with an impact that cracked my teeth together and made my spine feel like a bowstring that had just been snapped. The jump was too much for even Rocket; the frame thrummed, the tires skidded on a mass of leaves and pine needles, and we went down all tangled up together. I saw Gordo tear along the path toward me, and his face contorted with terror when he saw the ditch yawning for him. He hit the brake, but he was going too fast to stop in time. His black bike slid on its side, and carried Gordo with it as it toppled over into the weeds and trash.

The ditch wasn't all that deep. It wasn't full of thorns, or sharp rocks. Gordo really had a soft landing amid thick green three-leafed vines and a hodgepodge of things: pillows with the stuffing spilling out, garbage can lids, empty tin cans, a few aluminum pie pans, socks and torn-up shirts, rags, and the like. Gordo thrashed around in the green vines for a minute, getting himself loose from the black bike. He was none the worse for wear. He said, "You wait right there, you little shithole. You just wait right—"

He screamed suddenly.

Because something was in the ditch with him.

He had landed right on top of it, as it had been eating the last of a coconut cream pie stolen from the sill of an open kitchen window less than ten minutes before.

And now Lucifer, who did not care to share his den of trash-can treasures, was very, very angry.

The monkey squirted up out of the vines and jumped Gordo, its teeth bared and its rear end spraying forth a nasty business.

Gordo fought for his life. The vicious monkey took plugs of flesh from his arms, his cheek, his ear, and almost gnawed off a finger before Gordo, screaming to high heaven and stinking like hell, was able to scramble out of the ditch and take off running. Lucifer raced after him, chattering, spitting, and shitting, and the last I saw of them Lucifer had leaped onto Gordo's head and had handfuls of peroxided blond hair, riding Gordo like an emperor on an elephant.

I pulled Rocket up and got on. Rocket was docile now, all the willful fight drained away. Before I pedaled off to find a path around the ditch, I thought of how Gordo would be feeling in a few days, his face and arms swollen with bites, when he'd realized all those green three-leafed vines down in Lucifer's domain were poison ivy pregnant with silent evil. He would be a walking fester. If he *could* walk, that is.

"You've got a mean streak," I said to Rocket.

The defeated black bike lay down at the bottom of the ditch. Whoever went in after it had better be stocked up on calamine lotion.

I rode back to school. The fight was over, but three guys were searching the playground. One of them had a tackle box under his arm.

We found most of the arrowheads. Not all. A dozen or so had been swallowed up by the earth. An offering, as it were. Among the lost was the smooth black arrowhead of Chief Five Thunders.

Johnny didn't seem to mind that much. He said he'd look again for it. He said if he didn't find it, somebody else might, in ten years, or twenty years, or who knew how long. It hadn't been his to own anyway, he said. He'd just been keeping it for a while, until the chief needed it on the Happy Hunting Grounds.

I had always wondered what Reverend Lovoy meant when he talked about "grace." I understood it now. It was being able to give up something that it broke your heart to lose, and be happy about it.

By that definition, Johnny's grace was awesome.

I didn't know it yet, but I stood on the verge of my own test of grace.

5

Case #3432

After that day on the playground, the Branlins didn't bother us anymore. Gotha returned to school with a false front tooth and a dose of humility, and when Gordo was released from the hospital he skulked away whenever I was near. The capper came when Gotha actually approached Johnny and asked to be shown—in slow motion, of course—the haymaker punch that he hadn't even seen coming. That's not to say Gotha and Gordo became saints overnight. But Gotha's beating and Gordo's itchy agony had been good for them. They'd been given a drink from the cup of respect, and it was a start.

As October moved along, the hillsides lit up with gold and orange. The smell of burning autumn hazed the air. Alabama and Auburn were both winning, Leatherlungs had eased off her tirades, the Demon was in love with somebody other than me, and everything would have been right with the world.

Except.

I often found myself thinking about Dad, scribbling questions he could not answer, in the small hours of the morning. He was getting downright skinny now, his appetite gone. When he forced a smile, his teeth looked too big and his eyes shone with a false glint. Mom started biting her fingernails, and she was really nagging Dad now but he refused to go to either Dr. Parrish or the Lady. They had a couple of arguments that made Dad stalk out of the house, get in the pickup, and drive away. Afterward, Mom cried in their room. I heard her on the phone more than once, begging Grandmomma Sarah to talk some sense into him. ". . . Eatin' him up inside," I heard Mom say, and then I went out to play with Rebel because it hurt me to hear how much pain my mother was suffering. Dad, as I well knew, was already locked in his own cell of torment.

And the dream. Always the dream: two nights straight, skip a night, there it is again, skip three nights, then seven nights in a row.

Cory? Cory Mackenson? they whispered, standing in their white dresses beneath the scorched and leafless tree. Their voices were as soft as the sound of doves in flight, but there was an urgency about them that struck a spark of fear in me. And as the dream went on, little details began to be revealed as if through misted glass: behind the four black girls was a wall of dark stones, and in that wall the splintered window frame held only a few ragged teeth of glass. *Cory Mackenson?* There was a distant ticking noise. *Cory?* It was getting louder, and the unknown fear welled up in me. *Cor—*

On this seventh night, the lights came on. I looked at my parents, my eyes and brain still drugged with sleep. "What was that noise?" Dad asked. Mom said, "Look at this, Tom." On the wall opposite my bed there was a big scraped mark. Glass and gears lay on the floor; the clock face read two-nineteen. "I know time flies," Mom said to me, "but alarm clocks cost money."

They chalked it up to the Mexican enchilada casserole Mom had made for dinner.

For some time now, an event had been taking shape that was one of those destinies of place and circumstance. I was unaware of it. So were my folks. So, too, was the man in Birmingham who got into his truck at the soft-drink bottling company every morning and drove out to make his deliveries to a prearranged list of gas stations and grocery stores. Would it have made a difference, if that man had decided to spend an extra two minutes in the shower that morning? If he'd eaten bacon instead of sausage with his eggs for breakfast? If I had tossed the stick for Rebel to retrieve just one more time before I'd gone off to school, might that have changed the fabric of what was to be?

Being a male, Rebel was wont to roam when the mood was right. Dr. Lezander had told my folks it would be best if Rebel and his equipment were removed from each other, to cure the wandering itch, but Dad winced every time he thought of it and I wasn't too keen on it, either. So it just didn't get done. Mom didn't like to keep Rebel in his pen all day long, considering the facts that he stayed on the porch most of the day anyhow and our street never got much traffic.

The stage was set. The die was cast.

On the thirteenth of October, when I walked into the front door after school, I found Dad home from work early and waiting for me. "Son," he began. That word instantly told me something terrible had happened.

He took me in the pickup truck to Dr. Lezander's house, which stood on three acres of cleared land between Merchants and Shantuck streets. A white picket fence enclosed the property, and two horses grazed in the sunshine on the rolling grass. A kennel and dog exercise area stood off to one side, a barn on the other. Dr. Lezander's two-storied house was white and square, precise and clean as arithmetic. The driveway curved us around to the rear of the house, where a sign said PLEASE LEASH YOUR PETS. We left the pickup truck parked at the back door, and Dad pulled a chain that made a bell ring. In another minute the door opened, and Mrs. Lezander filled up the entrance.

As I've said before, she had an equine face and a lumpish body that might've scared a grizzly. She was always somber and unsmiling, as if she walked under a thundercloud. But I had been crying and my eyes were swollen, and perhaps this caused the transformation that I now witnessed.

"Oh, you poor dear child," Mrs. Lezander said, and such an expression of care came over her face that I was half stunned by it. "I'm so, so sorry about your dog." *Dok,* she pronounced it. "Please come in!" she told Dad, and she escorted us through a little reception area with portraits of children hugging dogs and cats on the pine-paneled walls. A door opened on stairs leading to Dr.

Lezander's basement office. Each step was a torture for me, because I knew what was down there.

My dog was dying.

The truck bringing soft drinks from Birmingham had hit him as he'd run across Merchants Street around one o'clock. Rebel had been with a pack of dogs, Mr. Dollar had told Mom when he'd called the house. It was Mr. Dollar who had heard the shriek of tires and Rebel's crushed yelp as he'd been coming out of the Bright Star Cafe after lunch. Rebel had been lying there on Merchants Street, the rest of the dogpack barking for him to get up, and Mr. Dollar had gotten Chief Marchette to help him lift Rebel onto the back of Wynn Gillie's pickup truck and bring him to Dr. Lezander. Mom was all torn up about it, too, because she'd meant to put Rebel in his pen that afternoon but had gotten wrapped up in "Search for Tomorrow." Never in his entire life had Rebel roamed as far away as Merchants Street. It was clear to me that he'd been running with a bad bunch, and this was the price.

Downstairs the air smelled of animals; not unpleasant, but musky. There was a warren of rooms lit up with fluorescent lights, a shine of scrubbed white tiles and stainless steel. Dr. Lezander was there, wearing a doctor's white coat, his bald head aglow under the lights. His voice was hushed and his face grim as he said hello to Dad. Then he looked at me, and he placed a hand on my shoulder. "Cory?" he said. "Do you want to see Rebel?"

"Yes sir."

"I'll take you to him."

"He's not . . . he's not dead, is he?"

"No, he's not dead." The hand massaged a tight muscle at the base of my neck. "But he's dying. I want you to understand that." Dr. Lezander's eyes seized mine and would not let me look away. "I've made Rebel as comfortable as possible, but . . . he's been hurt very badly."

"You can fix him!" I said. "You're a doctor!"

"That's right, but even if I operated on him I couldn't repair the damage, Cory. It's just too much."

"You can't . . . just . . . let him *die!*"

"Go see him, son," Dad urged. "Better go on." *While you can,* he was saying.

Dad waited while Dr. Lezander took me into one of the rooms. Upstairs I could hear a whistling noise: a teakettle. Mrs. Lezander was above us, boiling water for tea in the kitchen. The room we walked into had a sickly smell. There was a shelf full of bottles and a countertop with doctor's instruments arranged on a blue cloth. And at the center of the room was a stainless steel table with a form atop it, covered by a dog-sized cotton blanket. My legs almost gave way; blotches of brown blood had soaked through the cotton.

I must've trembled. Dr. Lezander said, "You don't have to, if you don't—"

"I will," I said.

Dr. Lezander gently lifted part of the blanket. "Easy, easy," he said, as if speaking to an injured child. The form shivered, and I heard a whine that all but tore my heart out. My eyes flooded with hot tears. I remembered that whine, from when Dad had brought Rebel home as a puppy in a cardboard box and Rebel had been afraid of the dark. I walked four steps to the side of the table, and I looked at what Dr. Lezander was showing me.

A truck tire had changed the shape of Rebel's head. The white hair and flesh on one side of the skull had been ripped back, exposing the bone and the teeth in a fixed grin. The pink tongue lolled in a wash of blood. One eye had turned a dead gray color. The other was wet with terror. Bubbles of blood broke around Rebel's nostrils, and he breathed with a painful hitching noise. A forepaw was crushed to pulp, the broken edges of bones showing in the twisted leg.

I think I moaned. I don't know. The single eye found me, and Rebel started struggling to stand up but Dr. Lezander grasped the body with his strong hands and the movement ceased.

I saw a needle clamped to Rebel's side, a tube from a bottle of clear liquid feeding into his body. Rebel whimpered, and instinctively I offered my hand to that ruined muzzle. "Careful!" Dr. Lezander warned. I didn't think about the fact that an animal in agony might snap at anything that moves, even the hand of a boy who loves it. Rebel's bloody tongue came out and swiped weakly at my fingers, and I stood there staring numbly at the streak of scarlet that marked me.

"He's suffering terribly," Dr. Lezander said. "You can see that, can't you?"

"Yes sir," I answered, as if in a horrible dream.

"His ribs are broken, and one of them has punctured his lung. I thought his heart might have given out before now. I expect it will soon." Dr. Lezander covered Rebel back over. All I could do was stare at the shivering body. "Is he cold?" I asked. "He must be cold."

"No, I don't think so." *Zo*, he pronounced it. He grasped my shoulder again, and guided me to the door. "Let's go talk to your father, shall we?"

Dad was still waiting where we'd left him. "You okay, partner?"

he asked me, and I said I was though I was feeling very, very sick. The smell of blood was in my nostrils, thick as sin.

"Rebel's a strong dog," Dr. Lezander said. "He's survived what should have killed most dogs outright." He picked up a folder from his desk and slid a sheet of paper out. It was a preprinted form, and at the top of it was Case #3432. "I don't know how much longer Rebel will live, but I think it's academic at this point."

"There's no possibility, you mean?" Dad asked.

"No possibility," the doctor said. He glanced quickly at me. "I'm sorry."

"He's my *dog*," I said, and fresh tears streamed down. My nose felt clogged with concrete. "He can get better." Even as I said that, I knew all the imagination in the world could not make it so.

"Tom, if you'll sign this form, I can administer a drug to Rebel that will . . . um . . ." He darted another glance at me.

"Help him rest," Dad offered.

"That's right. Exactly right. If you'll sign here. Oh, you need a pen, I think." He opened a drawer, fished around, and brought one up.

Dad took it. I knew what this was about. I didn't need to be lulled and coddled as if I were six years old. I knew they were talking about giving Rebel a shot to kill him. Maybe it was the right thing to do, maybe it was humane, but Rebel was my dog and I had fed him when he was hungry and washed him when he was dirty and I knew his smell and the feel of his tongue on my face. I knew him. There would never be another dog like Rebel. A huge knot had jammed in my throat. Dad was bending over the form, about to touch pen to paper. I looked for something to stare at, and I found a black and white photograph in a silver frame on the doctor's desk. It showed a light-haired, smiling young woman waving, a windmill behind her. It took me a few seconds to register the young apple-cheeked face as being that of Veronica Lezander.

"Hold on." Dad lifted the pen. "Rebel belongs to you, Cory. What do you have to say about this?"

I was silent. Such a decision had never been offered to me before. It was heavy.

"I love animals as much as anyone," Dr. Lezander said. "I know what a dog can mean to a boy. What I'm suggesting be done, Cory, is not a bad thing. It's a natural thing. Rebel is in terrible pain, and will not recover. Everything is born and dies. That is life. Yes?"

"He might not die," I murmured.

"Say he doesn't die for another hour. Or two, or three. Say he lives all night. Say he manages somehow to live twenty-four more

287

hours. He can't walk. He can hardly breathe. His heart is beating itself out, he's in deep shock." Dr. Lezander frowned, watching my blank slate of a face. "Be a good friend to Rebel, Cory. Don't let him suffer like this any longer."

"I think I need to sign this, Cory," Dad said. "Don't you?"

"Can I . . . go be with him for a minute? Just alone?"

"Yes, of course. I wouldn't touch him, though. He might snap. All right?"

"Yes sir." Like a sleepwalker, I returned to the scene of a bad dream. On the stainless steel table, Rebel was still shivering. He whined and whimpered, searching for his master to make the pain go away.

I began to cry. It was a powerful crying, and would not be held back. I dropped down to my knees on that cold hard floor, and I bowed my head and clasped my hands together.

I prayed, with my eyes squeezed tightly shut and the tears burning trails down my face. I don't recall exactly what I said in that prayer, but I knew what I was praying for. I was praying for a hand to come down from heaven or paradise or Beulah land and shut the gates on DEATH. Hold those gates firm against DEATH, though DEATH might bluster and scream and claw to get in at my dog. A hand, a mighty hand, to turn that monster away and heal Rebel, to cast DEATH out like a bag of old bleached bones and run him off like a beggar in the rain. Yes, DEATH was hungry and I could hear him licking his lips there in that room, but the mighty hand could seal shut his mouth, could slap out his teeth, could reduce DEATH to a little drooling thing with smacking gums.

That's what I prayed for. I prayed with my heart and my soul and my mind. I prayed through every pore of my flesh, I prayed as if every hair on my head was a radio antenna and the power was crackling through them, the megamegamillion watts crying out over space and eternity into the distant ear of the all-knowing, all-powerful Someone. Anyone.

Just answer me.

Please.

I don't know how long I stayed there on the floor, bowed up, sobbing and praying. Maybe it was ten minutes, maybe longer. I knew that when I stood up, I had to go out there where Dad and Dr. Lezander waited, and tell them yes or—

I heard a grunt, followed by an awful sound of air being sucked into ruined, blood-clogged lungs.

I looked up. I saw Rebel straining to stand on the table. The hair rippled at the back of my neck, my flesh exploding into chill bumps.

Rebel got up on two paws, his head thrashing. He whined, a long terrible whine that pierced me like a dagger. He turned, as if to snap at his tail, and the light glinted in his single eye and the death-grin of his teeth.

"Help!" I shouted. "Dad! Dr. Lezander! Come quick!"

Rebel's back arched with such violence I thought surely his tortured spine would snap. I heard a rattle like seeds in a dry gourd. And then Rebel convulsed and fell onto his side on the table, and he did not move again.

Dr. Lezander rushed in, with my father close behind. "Stand back," the doctor told me, and he put his hand to Rebel's chest. Then he got a stethoscope and listened. He lifted the lid of the good eye; it, too, had rolled back to the white.

"Hold on, partner," Dad said with both hands on my shoulders. "Just hold on."

Dr. Lezander said, "Well," and he sighed. "We won't be needing the form after all."

"No!" I cried out. "No! Dad, no!"

"Let's go home, Cory."

"I *prayed*, Dad! I prayed he wouldn't die! And he's not gonna die! He *can't!*"

"Cory?" Dr. Lezander's voice was quiet and firm, and I looked up at him through a hot blur of tears. "Rebel is—"

Something sneezed.

We all jumped at the sound, as loud as a blast in the tiled room. It was followed by a gasp and rush of air.

Rebel sat up, blood and foam stringing from his nostrils. His good eye darted around, and he shook his grisly head back and forth as if shaking off a long, hard sleep.

Dad said, "I thought he was—"

"He *was* dead!" Dr. Lezander wore an expression of utter shock, white circles ringing his eyes. "*Mein* . . . my God! That dog was dead!"

"He's alive," I said. I sniffled and grinned. "See? I told you!"

"Impossible!" Dr. Lezander had almost shouted it. "His heart wasn't beating! His heart had stopped beating, and he was dead!"

Rebel tried to stand, but he didn't have the strength. He burped. I went to him and touched the warm curve of his back. Rebel started hiccuping, and he laid his head down and began to lick the cool steel. "He won't die," I said confidently. My crying was done. "I prayed Death away from him."

"I don't . . . I can't . . ." Dr. Lezander said, and that's all he could say.

Case #3432 went unsigned.

Rebel slept and woke up, slept and woke up. Dr. Lezander kept checking his heartbeat and temperature and writing everything down in a notebook. Mrs. Lezander came down and asked Dad and me if we would like some tea and apple cake, and we went upstairs with her. I was secure in the knowledge that Rebel would not die while I was gone. Mrs. Lezander poured Dad a cup of tea, while I got a glass of Tang to go with my cake. As Dad called Mom to tell her it looked like Rebel was going to pull through and we'd be home after a while, I wandered into the den next to the kitchen. In that room, four bird cages hung from ceiling hooks and a hamster ran furiously on a treadmill in his own cage. Two of the bird cages were empty, but the other two held a canary and a parakeet. The canary began to sing in a soft, sweet voice, and Mrs. Lezander walked in with a bag of birdseed.

"Would you like to feed our patients?" she asked me, and I said yes. "Just a little bit now," she instructed. "They haven't been feeling well, but they'll be better soon."

"Who do they belong to?"

"The parakeet belongs to Mr. Grover Dean. The canary there—isn't she a pretty lady—belongs to Mrs. Judith Harper."

"Mrs. *Harper*? The teacher?"

"Yes, that's right." Mrs. Lezander leaned forward and made tiny smacking noises to the canary. That noise was strange, coming from such a horsey mouth. The bird picked delicately at the seed I'd poured into its feedtray. "Her name is Tinkerbell. Hello there, Tinkerbell, you angel you!"

Leatherlungs had a canary named Tinkerbell. I couldn't imagine it.

"Birds are my favorite," Mrs. Lezander said. "So trusting, so full of God and goodness. Look over here, at my aviary."

Mrs. Lezander showed me her set of twelve hand-painted ceramic birds, which rested atop a piano. "They came with us all the way from Holland," she told me. "I've had them since I was a little girl."

"They're nice."

"Oh, much better than nice! When I look at them, I have such pleasant memories: Amsterdam, the canals, the tulips bursting forth in spring by the thousands." She picked up a ceramic robin and stroked the crimson breast with her forefinger. "They were broken in my suitcase when we had to pack up quickly and get out. Broken all to pieces. But I put them all together again, each and every one. You can hardly see the cracks." She showed me, but she'd done a good job of repairing them. "I miss Holland," she said. "So much."

"Are you ever goin' back?"

"Someday, maybe. Frans and I talk about it. We've even gotten the travel brochures. Still . . . what happened to us . . . the Nazis and all that terrible . . ." She frowned and returned the robin to its place between an oriole and a hummingbird. "Well, some broken things are not so easily mended," she said.

I heard a dog barking. It was Rebel's bark, hoarse but strong. The sound was coming up from the basement through an air vent. Then I heard Dr. Lezander call, "Tom! Cory! Will both of you come down here, please?"

We found Dr. Lezander taking Rebel's temperature again, by the bottom route. Rebel was still listless and sleepy, but he showed no signs of dying. Dr. Lezander had applied a white ointment to Rebel's wounded muzzle and had him connected now to two needles and bottles of dripping clear liquid. "I wanted you to see this animal's temperature," he said. "I've taken it four times in the last hour." He picked up his notebook and wrote down the thermometer's reading. "This is unheard of! Absolutely unheard of!"

"What is it?" Dad asked.

"Rebel's body temperature has been dropping. It seems to have stabilized now, but half an hour ago I thought he was going to be dead." Dr. Lezander showed Dad the readings. "See for yourself."

"My God." Dad's voice was stunned. "It's that *low?*"

"Yes. Tom, no animal can live with a body temperature of sixty-six degrees. It's just . . . absolutely impossible!"

I touched Rebel. My dog was no longer warm. His white hair felt hard and coarse. His head turned, and the single eye found me. His tail began to wag, with obvious effort. And then the tongue slid from between the teeth in that awful, flesh-ripped grin and licked my palm. His tongue was as cold as a tombstone.

But he was alive.

Rebel stayed at Dr. Lezander's house. Over the following days, Dr. Lezander stitched his torn muzzle, filled him full of antibiotics, and was planning on amputating the crushed leg but then it began to wither. The white hair fell away, exposing dead gray flesh. Intrigued by this new development, Dr. Lezander postponed the amputation and instead wrapped the withering leg to monitor its progress. On the fourth day in Dr. Lezander's care, Rebel had a coughing fit and vomited up a mass of dead tissue the size of a man's fist. Dr. Lezander put it in alcohol in a bottle and showed it to Dad and me. It was Rebel's punctured lung.

But he was alive.

I began riding Rocket over to Dr. Lezander's every day after school to check on my dog. Each afternoon, the doctor wore a freshly puzzled expression and had something new to show me: pieces of vomited-up bones that could only be broken ribs, teeth that had fallen out, the blinded eye that had popped from its socket like a white pebble. For a while Rebel picked at strained meat and slurped a few tonguefuls of water, and the newspapers at the bottom of his cage were clotted and soaked with blood. Then Rebel stopped eating and drinking, wouldn't touch food or water no matter how much I urged him. He curled up in a corner, and stared with his one eye at something behind my shoulder, but I couldn't figure out what had his attention. He would sit like that for an hour or more, as if he'd gone to sleep with his eye open, or he was lost in a dream. I couldn't get him to respond even when I snapped my fingers in front of his muzzle. Then he would come out of it, all of a sudden, and he would lick my hand with his tombstone tongue and whine a little bit. Then he might sleep, shivering, or he might slide off into the haze again.

But he was alive.

"Listen to his heart, Cory," Dr. Lezander told me one afternoon. I did, using the stethoscope. I heard a slow, labored *thud*. Rebel's breathing was like the sound of a creaking door in an old deserted house. He was neither warm nor cold; he just was. Then Dr. Lezander took a toy mouse and wound it up, and he set it loose to twist and turn right in front of Rebel, while I listened to his heartbeat through the stethoscope. Rebel's tail wagged sluggishly. The sound of his heart never changed an iota from its slow, slow beating. It was like the working of an engine set to run at a steady speed, day and night, with no increase or decrease in power no matter what the engine's job required. It was the sound of a machine beating in the darkness without purpose or joy or under-standing. I loved Rebel, but I hated the hollow sound of that heartbeat.

Dr. Lezander and I sat on his front porch in the warm October afternoon light. I drank a glass of Tang and ate a slice of Mrs. Lezander's apple cake. Dr. Lezander wore a dark blue cardigan sweater with gold buttons; the mornings had taken a chilly turn. He sat in a rocking chair, facing the golden hills, and he said, "This is beyond me. Never in my life have I seen anything like this. Never. I should write it up and send it to a journal, but I don't think anyone would believe me." He folded his hands together, a tawny spill of sunlight on his face. "Rebel is dead, Cory."

I just stared at him, an orange mustache on my upper lip.

"Dead," he repeated. "I don't expect you to understand this, when I don't. Rebel doesn't eat. He doesn't drink. He voids nothing. His body is not warm enough to sustain his organs. His heartbeat is . . . a drum, played over and over in the same tattoo without the least variation. His blood when I can squeeze any out—is full of poisons. He is wasting away to nothing, and still he lives. Can you explain that to me, Cory?"

Yes, I thought. *I prayed Death away from him.*

But I didn't say anything.

"Ah, well. Mysteries, mysteries," he said. "We come from darkness, and to darkness we must return." He spoke this almost to himself as he rocked back and forth in his chair with his fingers interwoven. "True of men, and animals, too."

I didn't like this line of thought and conversation. I didn't like thinking about the fact that Rebel was getting skinny and his hair was falling out and he didn't eat or drink but he lived on. I didn't like the empty sound of his heartbeat, like a clock working in a house where no one lived anymore. To get my mind off these thoughts, I said, "My dad told me you killed a Nazi."

"What?" He looked at me, startled.

"You killed a Nazi," I repeated. "In Holland. My dad said you were close enough to see his face."

Dr. Lezander didn't reply for a moment. I remembered Dad telling me not to ask the doctor about this subject, because most men who'd been in the war didn't like to talk about killing. I had feasted on the exploits of Sgt. Rock, Sgt. Saunders, and the Gallant Men, and in my visions of heroes war was a television show adapted from a comic book.

"Yes," he answered. "I was that close to him."

"Gosh!" I said. "You must've been scared! I mean . . . I would've been."

"Oh, I was scared, all right. Very scared. He broke into our house. He had a rifle. I had a pistol. He was a young man. A teenager, actually. One of those blond, blue-eyed teenaged boys who love a parade. I shot him. He fell." Dr. Lezander kept rocking in his chair. "I had never fired a gun before. But the Nazis were in the streets, and they were breaking into our houses, and what could I do?"

"Were you a hero?" I asked.

He smiled thinly; there was some pain in it. "No, not a hero. Just a survivor." I watched his hands grip and relax on the armrests. His fingers were short and blunt, like powerful instruments. "We were all terrified of the Nazis, you know. *Blitzkrieg.* Brownshirt. *Waffen SS. Luftwaffe.* Those words struck us with pure terror. But I met a

German a few years after the war was over. He had been a Nazi. He had been one of the monsters." Dr. Lezander lifted his chin and watched a flock of birds winging south across the horizon. "He was just a man, after all. With bad teeth, body odor, and dandruff. Not a superman, only one man. I told him I'd been in Holland in 1940, when the Nazis had invaded us. He said he wasn't there, but he asked me . . . for forgiveness."

"Did you forgive him?"

"I did. Though I had many friends who were crushed under that boot, I forgave one of the men who wore it. Because he was a soldier, and he was following orders. That is the steel of the German character, Cory. They follow orders, even if it means walking into fire. Oh, I could have struck that man across the face. I could've spat on him and cursed him. I could've found a way to hound him until the day he died, but I am not the beast. The past is the past, and sleeping dogs should be left alone. Yes?"

"Yes sir."

"And speaking of sleeping dogs, we ought to go have a look at Rebel." He stood up, his knees creaking, and I followed him into the house.

The day came when Dr. Lezander said he had done all he could and there was no use to keep Rebel at his house anymore. He gave Rebel back to us, and we took him home in the pickup truck.

I loved my dog, though the gray flesh showed through his thin white hair, his skull was scarred and misshapen, and his withered gray leg was as thin as a warped stick. Mom couldn't be around him. Dad brought up the subject of putting Rebel to sleep, but I wouldn't hear it. Rebel was my dog, and he was alive.

He never ate. Never drank a drop. He stayed in his pen, because he could hardly walk on his withered leg. I could count his ribs, and through his papery skin you could see their broken edges. When I got home from school in the afternoons, he would look at me and his tail would wag a few times. I would pet him—though I have to be honest here and say that the feel of his flesh made my skin crawl—then he would stare off into space and I would be as good as alone until he came back, however long that might be. My buddies said he was sick, that I ought to have him put to sleep. I asked them if they'd like to be put to sleep when they got sick, and that shut them up.

The season of ghosts came upon us.

It was not just that Halloween loomed close at hand, and that the cardboard boxes of silky costumes and plastic masks appeared on the shelves at Woolworth's along with glittery magic wands, rubber pumpkin heads, witches' hats, and spiders jiggling on black webs. It was a feeling in the crisp twilight air; it was a hush across the hills. The ghosts were gathering themselves, building up their strength to wander the fields of October and speak to those who would listen. Because of my interest in monsters, my buddies and even my parents concluded that Halloween was my favorite time of year. They were right, but for the wrong reasons. They thought I relished the skeleton in the closet, the bump in the night, the sheet-wrapped spook in the house on the haunted hill. I did not. What I felt in the hushed October air, as Halloween came nearer, was not the dime-store variety of hobgoblin, but titanic and mysterious forces at work. These forces could not be named; not headless horseman, not howling werewolf or grinning vampire. These forces were as old as the world and as pure in their good or evil as the elements themselves. Instead of seeing gremlins under my bed, I saw the armies of the night sharpening swords and axes for a clash in the swirling mist. I saw in my imagination the tumult on Bald Mountain in all its wild and frantic frenzy, and at the crowing of a rooster to announce the dawn all the thousands of capering demons turning their hideous faces toward the east in sadness and disgust and marching away to their fetid dens in step with the "Anvil Chorus." I saw, as well, the broken-hearted lover pined away to a shade, the lost and sobbing translucent child, the woman in white who wants only kindness from a stranger.

It was thus on one of these still, cool nights approaching All Hallow's Eve that I went out to see Rebel in his pen and found someone standing there with him.

Rebel was sitting on his haunches, his scarred head cocked to one side. He was staring at a figure who stood on the opposite side of the mesh fence. The figure—a little boy, I could tell it was—seemed to be talking to Rebel. I could hear the murmur of his voice. As soon as the back door closed behind me, the little boy jumped, startled, and took off running into the woods like a scalded cat. "Hey!" I shouted. "Wait!"

He didn't stop. He ran over the fallen leaves without making any noise at all. The woods swallowed him up.

The wind blew, and the trees whispered. Rebel circled around and around in his pen, dragging his withered leg. He licked my hand with his chilly tongue, his nose as cold as a lump of ice. I sat with him for a while. He tried to lick my cheek, but I turned my face away because his breath smelled like something dead. Then Rebel went into one of his fixed stares again, his muzzle aimed at the woods. His tail wagged a few times, and he whimpered.

I left him staring at nothing and I went inside because it was getting cold.

Sometime during the night, I woke up in agony because I had refused Rebel my cheek to lick. It was one of those things that grew and grew, until you couldn't stand to live with it inside you. I had rejected my dog, pure and simple. I had prayed Death away from him, and my selfishness had caused him to exist in this state of betwixt and between. I had rejected him, when all he'd wanted to do was lick my cheek. I got up in the dark, put on a sweater, and went to the back door. I was about to turn the back porch light on when I heard Rebel give a single bark that made my hand stop short of the switch.

After years of having a dog, you know him. You know the meaning of his snuffs and grunts and barks. Every twitch of the ears is a question or statement, every wag of the tail is an exclamation. I knew this bark: it spoke of excited happiness, and I hadn't heard it since before Rebel had died and come back to life.

Slowly and carefully, I nudged the back door open. I stood in the dark and listened through the screen. I heard the wind. I heard the last of summer's crickets, a hardy tribe. I heard Rebel bark again, happily.

I heard the voice of a little boy say, "Would you like to be my dog?"

My heart squeezed. Whoever he was, he was trying to be very quiet. "I sure would like for you to be my dog," he said. "You sure are a pretty dog."

I couldn't see Rebel or the little boy from where I stood. I heard the clatter of the fence, and I knew Rebel had jumped up and planted his paws in its mesh just as he used to do when I went out to be with him.

The little boy began to whisper to Rebel. I couldn't make out what was being said.

But I knew now who he was, and why he was here.

I opened the door. I tried to be careful, but a hinge chirped. It was no louder than one of the crickets. As I walked out onto the porch, I saw the little boy running for the forest and the moonlight shone silver on his curly, sandy-colored hair.

He was eight years old. He would be eight years old forever.

"Carl!" I shouted. "Carl Bellwood!"

It was the little boy who had lived down the street, and who had come to play with Rebel because his mother would not let him have a dog of his own. It was the little boy who had burned up in his bed when a bad electrical connection had thrown a spark, and who now slept on Poulter Hill under a stone that read Our Loving Son.

"Carl, don't go!" I shouted.

He glanced back. I caught the white blur of his face, his eyes scared and glittering with trapped moonlight. I don't think he ever got to the edge of the woods. He was just not there anymore.

Rebel began to whine and circle in his pen, the withered leg dragging. He looked toward the forest, and I could not help but see his longing. I stood at the pen's gate. The latch was next to my hand.

He was my dog. *My* dog.

The back porch light came on. Dad, his eyes squinty from sleep, demanded, "What's all this hollerin' about, Cory?"

I had to make up a story about hearing something rummaging around the garbage cans. I couldn't use Lucifer as an excuse, as the second week of October Lucifer had been shotgunned to nasty pieces by Gabriel "Jazzman" Jackson, who'd caught the monkey ravaging his wife's pumpkin patch. I said I thought it might have been a possum.

At breakfast I didn't feel like eating. The ham sandwich in my Clutch Cargo lunchbox remained untouched. At dinner I picked at my hamburger steak. Mom put her hand against my forehead. "You don't have a fever," she said, "but you do look kind of peaked." This was pronounced *peak*-ed, and was Southern for "sick." "How do you feel?"

"All right." I shrugged. "I guess."

"Everythin' okay at school?" Dad inquired.

"Yes sir."

"Those Branlins aren't botherin' you anymore, are they?"

"No sir."

"But somethin' else is?" Mom asked.

I was silent. They could read me like a fifty-foot SEE ROCK CITY sign.

"Want to talk about it, then?"

"I . . ." I looked up at them in the comforting kitchen light. Beyond the windows, the land was dark. A wind sniffed around the eaves, and tonight clouds covered the moon. "I did wrong," I said, and before I could stop them tears came into my eyes. I began to tell my parents how much I regretted praying Death away from Rebel. I had done wrong, because Rebel had been so badly hurt he should've been allowed to die. I wished I hadn't prayed. I wished I could remember Rebel as he had been, bright-eyed and alert, before he had become a dead body living on the sheer power of my

297

selfishness. I wished, I wished; but I had done wrong, and I was ashamed.

Dad's fingers turned his coffee cup around and around. It helped him sort things out, when there were many things to be considered. "I understand," he said, and two words were never more welcome. "You know, no mistake in the world can't be fixed. All it takes is wantin' to fix it. Sometimes it's hard, though. Sometimes it hurts to fix a mistake, but you have to do it no matter what." His eyes rested on me. "You know what ought to be done, don't you?"

I nodded. "Take Rebel back to Dr. Lezander."

"I think so," Dad said.

We were going to do it the next day. Later that night, as my bedtime approached, I took a piece of hamburger steak out for Rebel. It was a real dog's treat. I hoped he might eat it, but he smelled it and then just stared at the woods again as if waiting for someone to come for him.

I was no longer his master.

I sat beside him as the chill wind moved around us. Rebel made little whining noises deep in his throat. He let me pat him, but he was somewhere else. I remembered him as a puppy, full of boundless energy, enthralled by a yellow ball with a little bell in it. I remembered the times we had raced each other, and like a true Southern gentleman he had always let me win. I remembered when we flew, over the hills of summer. Even if that had only been in my imagination, it was truer than true. I cried some. More than some.

I stood up, and I turned toward the woods. I said, "Are you there, Carl?"

He didn't answer, of course. He had always been a shy little boy.

"I'm givin' Rebel to you, Carl," I said. "Okay?"

No answer. But he was there. I knew he was.

"Will you come get him, Carl? I don't want him to be alone very long."

Just silence. Just the silence, listening.

"He likes to have his ears scratched," I said. "Carl?" I called. "You're not burned up anymore, are you? Will Rebel . . . be like he used to be?"

The wind was speaking. Only that and nothing more.

"I'm goin' inside now," I said. "I won't come back out." I looked at Rebel. His attention was fixed on the woods, and his tail wagged the slightest bit. I walked into the house, shut the door, and turned off the back porch light.

Long past midnight, I awakened to the sound of Rebel's happy bark. I knew what I would see if I went to the back door. It was best they get to know each other without me butting in. I turned over, and I went back to sleep.

The next afternoon, at Dr. Lezander's, Dad and the doctor left me alone while I said good-bye to Rebel. He licked me with his cold tongue. I stroked his misshapen head and patted him for a while, and then it was time. Dr. Lezander had the form ready, and Dad held the pen poised for my final word.

"Dad?" I said. "He's my dog, isn't he?"

My father understood. "Yes, he sure is," he answered, and he gave the pen to me.

We left the form that said Case #3432 with Dr. Lezander, my name signed on the dotted line. When we got home again, I walked around in Rebel's pen. It seemed so very small.

I left the gate open when I went out.

6

Dead Man Driving

Toward the end of October, Dad bought a wire basket for me to put on Rocket. At first I thought it was pretty cool, until I realized that now I would be expected to run all sorts of errands for Mom. It was about this time that she put up a hand-lettered sign on the bulletin-board at church, announcing that she was selling pies and other baked goods. A similar sign went up in the barbershop. A few orders began to come in, and soon Mom was elbow-deep in floury mixing bowls, eggshells, and boxes of powdered sugar.

The reason for this, I later learned, was that Dad's hours had been cut back at the dairy. We were hurting for money, though I never would've known it. There was simply less work for Dad to do at Green Meadows. Some of the dairy's oldest customers had canceled their orders. It was because of the new supermarket in Union Town, which had recently opened its doors to the fanfare of the Adams Valley High School marching band. The supermarket, called Big Paul's Pantry, could've swallowed our own little Piggly-Wiggly like a whale swallows a shrimp. It had a section, it seemed, for everything under a fat man's chin. The milk section alone was a whole aisle, and all the milk was in opaque plastic jugs that didn't have to be rinsed out and returned. And because Big Paul stocked so much milk, he could afford to sell it at prices that knocked the stuffing out of Green Meadows Dairy. So it came to pass that Dad's milk route became progressively shorter, if such a thing can be called progress. People liked the newness of going into a clean, air-conditioned supermarket and buying their milk in plastic jugs and then throwing those jugs away without a second thought. Not only that, but Big Paul's Pantry stayed open until eight o'clock at night, which was unheard of.

Putting a basket on Rocket was like saddling Seabiscuit with mailbags. But I did my duty, carrying pies and cakes around to people in the afternoons, and Rocket stiffened up from time to time in protest but never dropped one item.

To show thanks to the Lezanders for being so kind to Rebel, Mom decided to make a pumpkin pie—her best seller—for them free of charge. She put the pie in a box, tied it up with twine, and I slid the box into Rocket's basket and pedaled for Dr. Lezander's house. On the way, I passed Gotha and Gordo Branlin on their black bikes. Gotha acknowledged me with a slight lift of his chin, but Gordo still wearing bandages that covered oozing sores—sped away like blue blazes. I got to Dr. Lezander's house and knocked on the back door, and in a minute Mrs. Lezander answered.

"Mom baked you and the doctor a pie," I said, offering her the box. "It's pumpkin."

"Oh, how very nice." She took it and sniffed around the lid. "Oh dear," she said. "Does this have cream in it?"

"Evaporated milk, I think." I should know. The kitchen was teeming with Pet Milk cans. "My mom made it this mornin'."

"It's very thoughtful of your mother, Cory, but I'm afraid neither of us can eat cream. We're both allergic to anything from a cow." She smiled. "That's how we met, all red and blotched at a clinic in Rotterdam."

"Oh. Gosh. Well, maybe you can give it to somebody else, then. It's a real good pie."

"I'm sure it's a wonderful pie." *Vunderful*, she'd said. "But if I even kept it in the house, Frans would get into it like a little mouse around midnight. He has the sweet tooth, you know. Then in two days he would look like he had the measles and he would itch so much he couldn't wear clothes. So, better not to even let Frans *smell* it, or he'd be walking around like Vernon Thaxter, yes?"

300

I laughed at that image. "Yes, ma'am." I took the pie back. "Maybe Mom can make you somethin' else, then."

"It's not necessary. Just the thought is kind enough."

I paused at the door, wondering if I should mention something that had been on my mind lately.

"Yes?" Mrs. Lezander prodded.

"Can I see the doctor? I'd like to talk to him for a minute."

"He's taking a nap right now. He stayed up all night listening to his radio shows."

"His radio shows?"

"Yes, he's got one of those shortwave radios. Sometimes he stays up until dawn listening to the foreign countries. May I give him a message?"

"Uh . . . I'll just talk to him later." What I wanted to ask was if he needed some help in the afternoons. After watching Dr. Lezander at work, it seemed to me that being a veterinarian was a pretty important job. I could be a veterinarian and a writer at the same time. The world would always need veterinarians, just like it would always need milkmen. "I'll come back some other time," I said, and I returned the pumpkin pie to Rocket's basket and headed for home.

I pedaled leisurely. Rocket acted a little nervous, but I took that to be his dissatisfaction with the basket, like a greyhound with a leash. The sun was warm and the hills were blazing yellow. A week from now the leaves would be brown and tumbling. It was one of those beautiful afternoons when even the blue shadows are lovely, and you know instinctively to slow down and enjoy things because they cannot and will not last.

I grinned, thinking of Dr. Lezander walking around as naked as Vernon Thaxter. That would be a sight, wouldn't it? I'd heard of people being allergic to grass, dogs and cats, ragweed, tobacco and dandelions. Grand Austin was allergic to horses; they made him sneeze until he could hardly stand, which was why he'd stopped going to the Brandywine Carnival when it came through town every November. Grandmomma Sarah said the Jaybird was allergic to work. I supposed people could be allergic to everything under and including the sun. Just think! Neither of the Lezanders could eat ice cream. They couldn't eat banana pudding, or drink a glass of vanilla milk. If I couldn't have any of those things, I'd go just as crazy as—

Vernon came to mind.

Vernon, standing in that room with the trains circling little Zephyr.

You know what I believe?

I remembered the lights off, the windows of the tiny houses glowing.

I believe if you find a night owl who doesn't drink milk, you've got your killer.

I hit the brake. The suddenness of it surprised even Rocket. The bike skidded to a stop.

He stayed up all night listening to his radio shows, Mrs. Lezander had said.

I swallowed hard. I might've had a Pet Milk can wedged in my throat.

Sometimes he stays up until dawn listening to the foreign countries.

"Oh no," I whispered. "Oh no, it can't be Dr. Le—"

A car pulled up beside me, so close it almost skinned my leg, and then it swerved to block my way. It was a dark blue, low-slung Chevy, its right rear side smashed in and rust splotched across it like dead poison ivy leaves. A white rabbit's head on a black square hung from the rearview mirror. The Chevy's engine boomed and popped under the hood, and the whole car trembled with pent-up power. "Hey, boy!" the man behind the wheel said through the rolled-down window. The wheel was covered with blue fur. "You're that little Mackenson shit!"

His voice was slurred, the lids of his red eyes at half mast. Donny Blaylock was three sheets to an ill wind. His face was as craggy as rough-cut rock, a greasy comma hanging down from his dark, slick brilliantined hair. "I 'member you," he said. "Sim's house. Little fucker."

I felt Rocket shiver. The bike suddenly darted forward and banged into the Chevy, like a terrier attacking a Doberman.

"Been seein' things you shouldn't oughta see," Donny went on. "Been causin' us some trouble, ain't you?"

"No sir," I said. Rocket backed up and banged into the Chevy again.

"Oh, yes you have. Biggun's gonna be glad to see you, boy. Gonna have a talk with you 'bout them big eyes and that big ol' mouth of yours. Get in."

If my heart had been pounding any harder, it would've pulled up its root and burst right out of my chest.

"I said, get in. *Now.*" He raised his right hand.

It gripped a pistol, and the pistol was aimed at me.

Once again Rocket attacked the car. Rocket had saved me from Gordo Branlin, but against this dirty rat and his gun, Rocket was powerless.

"Shoot your fuckin' head off in two seconds," Donny vowed.

I was scared half to death, and the other half was terrified. That gun's barrel looked as big as a cannon. It made a convincing argument. In my mind I could hear Mom screaming as I left Rocket and got into the car, but what choice did I have? "Goin' for a ride," Donny said, and he leaned across me—all but suffocating me with the foul odors of stale sweat and moonshine whiskey—and slammed the door shut. He put his foot down on the gas pedal and the Chevy growled and crawled up on the curb before he could get it straightened out again. I looked back at Rocket, which was rapidly shrinking. A little plastic Hawaiian girl did a wobbly hula in the Chevy's rear windshield. "Sit still!" Donny snapped, and I obeyed him because the pistol was right there to jab the obedience into me. Donny's foot pressed harder on the gas. The Chevy's engine was wailing as we tore along Merchants Street and turned toward the gargoyle bridge.

"Where're we goin'?" I dared ask.

"You just wait 'n see."

The speedometer's needle climbed to sixty. We left the gargoyles gasping for breath. The Chevy's engine was making thunder, and we were going seventy miles an hour on the curving road that led past Saxon's Lake. When I gripped the armrest, Donny laughed. On the floorboard an empty bottle rolled back and forth under my feet and the smell of raw rotgut moonshine was harsh enough to make my eyes water.

The woods on either side of the road passed in a yellow blur, the Chevy's rear tires shrieking on the snake-twist road. "I'm fuckin' *alive!*" Donny howled. Maybe so, but he looked near dead. His eyes were sunken, his jaw stubbled with a scraggly beard, his clothes as wrinkled and dirty as if he'd slept for three days in a pigpen. Or maybe just laid in there and drank for three days. "I saw you!" he shouted to me over the wind's blast. "Followed you! Yessir, ol' Donny crept up behind you and bagged him a bird, didn't he?" He threw his shoulders into a curve that made my eyes pop. "That fat sumbitch says I'm stupid! Show his fat ass who the smart Blaylock is!"

If a gun, a fast car, and being drunker than a Shriner made a man smart, then Donny was Copernicus, Da Vinci, and Einstein rolled up into one mass of doughy genius.

We whipped past Saxon's Lake and the red rock cliff. "Whoa! Whoa, Big Dick!" Donny hollered at the car as he stepped on the brake. We slowed down enough for Donny to turn the Chevy to the right and onto a dirt road without flying us into the trees. Then he put on the gas again, and we zoomed the fifty yards between Route Ten and the small white house with a screened-in front porch that stood at the end of that road. I knew the house. The red Mustang was still parked under the green plastic awning, but the old rust-gnawed Cadillac was gone. The rose garden was still there, all thorns and no flowers.

"Whoa!" Donny shouted, and his Big Dick came to a throbbing halt at the door of Miss Grace's house of bad girls.

Lord help me! I thought. What was this all about?

He got out of the car, gun in hand. He showed me its ugly snout. "You better be here when I come back! Better be here, or I'll hunt you down and kill you! Understand?"

I nodded. Donny Blaylock had already killed one man. Mr. Dollar had said so. I had no doubt he would do it again, so my butt stayed glued to the seat. Donny staggered to the door and started beating on it. Somebody hollered from inside. Donny kicked the door open and charged in, shouting, "Where is she? Where's my fuckin' woman?"

I was in deep dookey, that was for sure. Somehow in my fear-seized brain I thought that Dr. Lezander couldn't be the one who'd killed that man at Saxon's Lake; it had to be Donny Blaylock. Mr. Dollar had heard about it from Sim Sears. Donny Blaylock was the killer, not Dr. Lezander!

Donny emerged from the house less than thirty seconds after he'd crashed in. He had hold of a girl by her blond hair, and he was dragging her as she fought and cursed.

That girl was Lainie, who'd furled her tongue at me that very first day.

"Get in that car!" Donny yelled as he dragged her over the ground. She was wearing a pink halter top and purple hot pants, and one of her silver shoes had come off. "Get in there, and do it quick!"

"Lemme go! Lemme go, you sumbitch!"

Out from the doorway shot redhaired, stocky Miss Grace, who wore a white sweater and blue jeans big enough to house a barn dance. She had the look of hellfire on her face and a frying pan in her right hand, and she lifted it to strike Donny over the head.

He shot her. *Bam!* Just that fast.

Miss Grace screamed and grabbed her shoulder as the crimson blossomed against the white like the opening of a rose. She fell to her knees, crying, "You shot me, you asshole! You dumb bastard, you!" Two more girls, both brunette and one as plump as the other was skinny, rushed out to kneel beside Miss Grace, while another blond girl stood in the doorway shouting, "We're callin' the sheriff! Right this minute, we're callin' him!"

"You stupid shit!" Donny yelled as he reached the car. "We *own* the sheriff!" He yanked the door open and threw Lainie in on me, and I scrambled over into the backseat as she clawed and kicked to get out. Donny said, "Stop it!" and he hit her across the face with his free hand so hard, one second I was looking at the back of her head and the next at her face, the tough but pretty features pinched with pain. Blood began crawling from the corner of her mouth. "You want some more, you just keep it up!" Donny warned her, and then he went around and slid under the wheel. The Chevy's engine fired. I started to jump out, but Donny caught my motion in the rearview mirror and the pistol's barrel swatted at my head. If I hadn't ducked in time, I might've earned my wings for real. "Just sit there! The both of you!" Donny shouted, and he whipped the car around in a neck-wrenching circle and headed for Route Ten again.

"You're crazy!" Lainie seethed, one hand pressed to her mouth. "I told you to leave me alone!"

"Do tell!"

"I swear I won't stand for this! Miss Grace'll—"

"What'll she do? I shoulda shot her brains out!"

Lainie made a move for the door handle. But just then we reached Route Ten and Donny laid on the gas. The Chevy's tires screeched as we sped toward Zephyr once more. Lainie's fingers were gripping the handle, but we were already going fifty miles an hour.

"Jump," Donny said, and he grinned. "Go on, I dare ya!"

Her fingers loosened. They let go.

"I'll get the law on you! I swear it!"

"Sure you will." His grin widened. "The law don't have time for trash like you."

"You're drunk and out of your mind!" She glanced back at me. "What're you doin' draggin' a kid around with you for?"

"Family business. You just shut up and look pretty."

"Damn you to hell," she spat at him, but he just laughed.

The Chevy crossed the gargoyle bridge again. We passed Rocket. A crow was perched on the handlebars, trying to pry the pie box open. The indignity of it! Donny tore through Zephyr at sixty miles an hour, blowing dead leaves in our wake. He burst out on the other side and hit Route Sixteen, and we raced across the hills toward Union Town.

"Kidnappin'!" Lainie was still raging. "That's what it is! They can kill you for that!"

"I don't give a shit. I got you. That's what I want."

"I don't want *you!*"

His hand grabbed her chin and squeezed. The Chevy swerved across the road, and I gasped as I saw the woods reaching for us. Then Donny veered us back onto pavement again with a jerk of his arm. We were straddling the centerline. "Don't you say that. Don't you ever say that, or you'll be real sorry."

"I'm just shakin'!" She tried to pull loose, but his wiry fingers tightened.

"I don't wanna hurt you, baby. God knows I don't." His fingers released her, but their marks stayed on her skin.

"I ain't your baby! I told you a long time ago, I don't want nothin' to do with you or them damn brothers of yours!"

"You take our money, don't you? High and mighty for a damned punchboard, ain't you?"

"I'm a *professional*," she said with a measure of pride. "I don't love you, don't you get it? I don't even *like* you! Only one man I ever loved, and he's with Jesus."

"*Jesus*." He mocked her voice. "That bastard's rottin' in hell." His eyes flickered to the rearview mirror. I saw them narrow. "What the *fuck*?" he whispered.

I looked back. A car was behind us, gaining rapidly.

It was a black car. Black as a panther.

"No." Donny shook his head. "Oh, no. I cain't be *that* wasted!"

Lainie looked back, too, her lower lip swollen. "What is it?"

"That car. See it?"

"What car?"

Her deep brown eyes registered nothing. I saw it, though. Clear as light. And Donny did, too. I could tell by the way he was letting the Chevy drift all over the road. The black car was speeding after us. In another moment I could make out the flames painted on the hood. I could see the faint shape of the driver through the slanted windshield. He seemed to be crouched forward, eager to catch us.

"Hell's bells!" Donny's knuckles whitened around the furry wheel. "I'm goin' off my rocker!"

"You just now figurin' that one out? Kidnappin' me is bad enough, but your ass is gonna be in a crack for shootin' Miss Grace! What if you'd killed her?"

"Shut up." Little beads of sweat had broken out on his forehead. His eyes kept ticking back and forth from the rearview mirror to the winding road ahead. The black car was lost for a few seconds behind a curve, and then I saw Midnight Mona slide around it and come out of a shadow, barreling after us. The sun was dull on the black paint and the tinted windshield. The Chevy was on the high side of seventy; Midnight Mona had to be doing near ninety.

"There's where it happened!" Lainie pointed at a place off the roadside, the wind whipping the hair around her strained and lonely face. "That's where my baby got killed!"

She was pointing at a place that might've just looked like weeds and thick underbrush, except two dead and blackened trees stood side by side, their trunks cut by deep and ugly gashes. The limbs of the trees were interlocked, as if embracing each other even in death.

I looked at her blond hair, and I remembered it.

Hers was the head I had seen resting on the shoulder of Little Stevie Cauley, a long time ago in the Spinnin' Wheel's parking lot.

"*Look out!*" Lainie suddenly screamed, and she grabbed for the wheel as a tractor-trailer truck roared over a hill in front of us, its grille filling Big Dick's windshield like a mouthful of silver teeth. Donny had been watching Midnight Mona grow in the rearview mirror, and he shouted with terror and twisted the wheel. The truck's massive tires zoomed past, a deep bass horn bellowing with indignation. I turned around in time to see the truck and Midnight Mona merge together, and then Midnight Mona burst through the truck's rear wheels and kept on coming and the truck went on its way as dumb as Paul Bunyan's ox. Donny hadn't seen this feat of magic; he'd been too busy trying to keep us from crashing. "That was damn close!" Lainie said, and when she looked back I could tell she still saw nothing of the black car.

But I knew. And Donny knew, too. Little Stevie Cauley was coming to save his girlfriend.

"If he wants to fuckin' play, I'll play with him!" Donny yelled, and his foot sank to the floor. The Chevy's engine screamed, the whole car starting to vibrate, everything that wasn't bolted down rattling and groaning. "He never could beat me! Never could!"

"Slow down!" Lainie begged, her eyes filling up with fear. "You'll kill us!"

But Midnight Mona was right on our tail now, hanging there like a black jet plane, matching speed for speed. The driver was a dark shape behind the wheel. The Chevy's tires flayed rubber as Donny gritted his teeth, sweat on his face, and followed the dangerous road. Over the engine and the wind and Lainie's voice crying for Donny to slow down, I couldn't hear a sound from Midnight Mona.

"Come on, you sumbitch!" Donny snarled. "I killed you once! I can kill you again, too!"

"You're *crazy!*" Lainie was clinging to her seat like a cat. "I don't wanna die!"

ROBERT R. McCAMMON

I was thrown from one side of the car to the other as the Chevy took the curves at breakneck speed, Donny fighting the wheel with every ounce of mean strength in his body. My mind was jangled, but not disconnected; I realized, as I was flung around like yesterday's laundry, that Donny Blaylock had killed Little Stevie Cauley. How it had happened I could see in my imagination: two cars—one blue, one black—racing hell-for-sparkplugs on this very road, flames shooting from their tail pipes under last year's October moon. Maybe they were neck and neck, like the chariots in *Ben-Hur*, and then Donny had whipped Big Dick to one side and the right rear panel had slammed into Midnight Mona. Maybe Little Stevie had lost control of the wheel, or maybe a tire had blown. But Midnight Mona had taken flight, as graceful as a black butterfly through the silvery dark, and exploded into fire when she came down. I could hear Donny's fiendish laugh as he'd raced away from the burning ruin of glass and metal.

As a matter of fact, I could hear his fiendish laugh right this minute.

"I'll kill you again! I'll kill you again!" he hollered, his eyes crazed and his brilliantined hair swept back and twisting like Medusa's snakes. It was obvious he was riding on his rims.

He slammed on the brake. Lainie screamed. I screamed. Big Dick screamed, too.

Midnight Mona, which was five feet behind the Chevy's rear fender, hit us.

I saw, as my eyes almost blasted out of my head, the black car's flame-painted snout shove through the back seat. Then, like blurred freeze-frame pictures, Midnight Mona began to fill up the inside of Big Dick. I smelled burning oil and scorched metal, cigarette smoke and English Leather cologne. For the briefest of instants a black-haired young man with eyes as blue as swimming-pool water sat beside me, his hands gripping a steering wheel, his teeth clenching a Chesterfield's stub. The sharp chin of his ruggedly handsome face was set like the prow of the Flying Dutchman. I believe my hair stood on end.

Midnight Mona cleaved through Big Dick. Went right through the front seats, and on its way into the engine block its driver reached out a hand and seemed to touch Lainie's cheek. I saw her blink and jump, her face going as pale as white silk. Donny cringed, yelling in stark-naked fear. He twisted the wheel back and forth because he could see the passing apparition even if Lainie was blind to it. Then Midnight Mona had gone through the front fender, its taillights the shape of red diamonds and its exhaust pipes spouting in Donny's

308

face, and the Chevy started spinning around and around like a Tiltawhirl, the brakes and tires shrieking like drunken banshees at an all-night haunt.

I felt a crunch and heard a thud and I flew into the back of Lainie's seat as if pressed there by an invisible waffle iron. "Jesus!" I heard Donny shout; this time he wasn't mocking anybody. Glass crashed and something *kabong*ed in the car's belly, and with a loud ripping noise of bushes and low tree limbs the Chevy came to a halt with its nose buried in a bank of red dirt.

"*Yi yi yi yi!*" Donny was yelping like a dog with a hurt leg. I tasted blood, and my nose felt as if it had been pushed right through my face. I saw Donny looking wildly about; at his hairline along the sides of his head, the hair had gone gray. "I killed him!" he squalled in a high and giddy voice. "Killed that bastard! Midnight Mona burned up! Saw it burn up!"

Lainie stared at him, her eyes unfocused, an egg-sized knot bulging on her reddened forehead. She whispered thickly, "You . . . killed . . ."

"Killed him! Killed him dead! Went flyin' off the road! *Boom*, he went! *Boom!*" Donny started laughing, and he scrambled out through the driver's-side window without opening the door. His face looked swollen and wet, his eyes cocked and crazy. He began to stagger in a circle, the front of his jeans soggy with urine. "Daddy?" he cried out. "Help me, Daddy!" Then he started gibbering and sobbing and he climbed up the bank of red dirt for the woods beyond.

I heard a *click*.

Lainie had reached down to the floorboard and retrieved the pistol. She had pulled its hammer back, and now she took aim at the struggling, insane wretch who sobbed for his daddy.

Her hand trembled. I saw her finger tighten on the trigger.

"Better not," I said.

Her finger didn't listen.

But her hand did. It moved an inch. The pistol went off, and the bullet threw up a chunk of red dirt. She kept firing, four more times. Four more red dirt chunks, flying in the air.

Donny Blaylock ran for the yellow woods. He got caught up in branches for a moment, and as he thrashed to get loose the branches ripped the shirt right off his back. He hightailed it, but we could hear him laughing and crying until the awful sound faded and was gone.

Lainie lowered her head and pressed her hand to her eyes. Her back began to tremble. She gave a low, moaning sob. My nose was starting to feel like it was on fire.

But through it I could still smell a hint of English Leather.

Lainie looked up, startled. She touched her tear-stained cheek. "Stevie?" she said, her voice alive with hope.

As I've said, it was the season of ghosts. They had gathered themselves, building up their strength to wander the fields—and roads—of October and speak to those who would listen.

Maybe Lainie never saw him. Maybe she wouldn't have believed her own mind if she had, and she would've gone running for a rubber room the same as Donny.

But I believe she heard him, loud and clear. Maybe just in the scent of his skin, or the memory of a touch.

I believe it was enough.

7

High Noon in Zephyr

My nose wasn't broken, though it swelled up like a melon and turned a ghastly purplish-green and my eyes puffed up into black-and-blue slits. To say Mom was horrified about the whole experience is like saying the Gulf of Mexico has some water in it. But I survived, and I was all right after my nose shrank to its regular size.

Sheriff Amory, who'd been called by Miss Grace, found Lainie and me walking back to Zephyr on Route Sixteen. I didn't have much to say to him, because I remembered Donny yelling that the Blaylocks owned him. I told Dad about this when he and Mom came to pick me up at Dr. Parrish's office. Dad didn't say anything, but I could see the thundercloud settling over his head and I knew he wouldn't let it lie.

Miss Grace was okay. She had to be taken to the hospital in Union Town, but the bullet hadn't hit anything that couldn't be fixed. I had the feeling that it would take an awful lot to put Miss Grace down for the count.

This was the story about Lainie and Little Stevie Cauley, as I learned later from Dad, who found it out from the sheriff: Lainie, who'd run away from home when she was seventeen, had met Donny Blaylock while she was a stripper at the Port Said in Birmingham. He had convinced her to come work for his family's "business," promising her all sorts of big money and stuff, saying the Air Force boys really knew how to part with a paycheck. She came, but soon after she arrived at Miss Grace's, she'd met Little Stevie when she'd gone to the Woolworth's in Zephyr to buy her summer wardrobe. Maybe it hadn't been love at first sight, but something close to it. Anyhow, Little Stevie had been encouraging Lainie to leave Miss Grace's and straighten up her act. They'd started talking about getting married. Miss Grace had been in favor of it, because she didn't want any girl working for her who couldn't put her all into the job. But Donny Blaylock fancied himself to be Lainie's boyfriend. He hated Little Stevie anyway because as much as Donny wanted to deny it, Midnight Mona could leave Big Dick dragging. He'd decided the only way to keep Lainie working was to get Stevie out of the picture. The crash and burning of Midnight Mona had been the wreck of Lainie's dreams as well, and from that point on she didn't care about what she did, with who, or where. As Miss Grace had said, Lainie had gotten as rough as a cob.

The last I heard of Lainie, she was going home, older and wiser.

Sadder, too.

But who ever said everybody gets a happy ending?

Some of this information came right from the jackass's mouth. Donny was behind bars in the Zephyr jail, which stood next to the courthouse. He'd been found, dancing with a scarecrow, by a farmer with a very large shotgun. The sight of iron bars in front of his face had squared up some of Donny's raggedy edges, and he had come out of his madness long enough to admit running Little Stevie off the road. It was clear that this time a Blaylock was not going to escape the long arm of the law, even if the hand on that arm was dirty with Blaylock cash.

November had touched the yards of Zephyr with frosty fingers. The hills had gone brown, the leaves falling. They crackled like little fireworks when somebody came up the walk. We heard them on a Tuesday evening, when a fire burned in our hearth, Dad was reading the newspaper, and Mom was poring over her cookbooks for new pie and cake recipes.

Dad answered the door when the knock sounded. Sheriff Junior Talmadge Amory stood under the porch light, his long-jawed face sullen and his hat in his hand. He had the collar of his jacket turned up; it was cold out there.

311

"Can I come in, Tom?" he asked.

"I don't know," Dad said.

"I'd understand if you didn't care to talk to me anymore. I'd take it like a man. But . . . I sure would like to have my say about some things."

Mom stepped up beside my father. "Let him in, Tom. All right?"

Dad opened the door, and the sheriff came in from the night.

"Hi, Cory," he said to me. I was on the floor next to the fireplace, doing my Alabama history homework. A certain area where Rebel used to lounge in the hearth's glow seemed awfully empty. But life went on.

"Hi," I said.

"Cory, go to your room," Dad instructed, but Sheriff Amory said, "Tom, I'd like for him to hear me out, too, seein' as he was the one found out and all."

I stayed where I was. Sheriff Amory sank his slim Ichabod Crane body onto the couch and put his hat on the coffee table. He sat staring at the silver star that adorned it. Dad sat down again, and Mom—ever the hospitable one—asked the sheriff if he'd like some apple pie or spice cake but he shook his head. She sat down, too, her chair and Dad's bracketing the fireplace.

"I won't be sheriff very much longer," Sheriff Amory began. "Mayor Swope's gonna appoint a new man as soon as he can decide on one. I figure I'll be done with it by the middle of the month." He sighed heavily. "I expect we'll be leavin' town before December."

"I'm sorry to hear it," Dad told him. "But I was sorrier to hear what Cory had to tell me. I guess I can't kick you around too much, though. You could've lied when I came to you about it."

"I wanted to. Real bad. But if you can't believe your own son, who in the world *can* you believe?"

Dad scowled. He looked as if he wanted to spit a foul taste from his mouth. "For God's sake, why'd you do it, J.T.? Takin' money from the Blaylocks to shield 'em? Lookin' the other way when they sold their 'shine and suckered people into that crooked gamblin' den? Not to mention Miss Grace's house, and I like and respect Miss Grace but God knows she oughta be in some other line of work. What else did you do for Biggun Blaylock? Polish his boots?"

"Yes," the sheriff said.

"Yes what?"

"I did. Polish his boots." Sheriff Amory gave a wan, tired smile. His eyes were black holes of sadness and regret. His smile slipped off, leaving his mouth twisted with pain. "I always went to Biggun's house to get my money. He had it for me, first day of the month.

Two hundred dollars in a white envelope with my name on it. 'Sheriff Junior.' That's what he calls me." He winced a little at the thought. "When I went in that day, all the boys were there: Donny, Bodean, and Wade. Biggun was oilin' a rifle. Even sittin' in a chair, he can fill up a room. He can look at you and knock you down. I picked up my envelope, and all of a sudden he reaches to the floor and puts his muddy boots on the table, and he says, 'Sheriff Junior, I've got me a mess here to clean up and I don't rightly feel up to doin' it. You think you could clean 'em for me?' And I started to say no, but he takes a fifty-dollar bill out of his shirt pocket and he puts it down inside one of them big boots, and he says, 'Make it worth your while, of course.'"

"Don't tell me this, J.T.," Dad said.

"I want to. I have to." The sheriff peered into the fire, and I could see the flames make light and shadows ripple across his face. "I told Biggun I had to go, that I couldn't be cleanin' anybody's boots. And he grins and says, 'Aw, Sheriff Junior, why didn't you name your price right off?' and he takes another fifty-dollar bill out of his pocket and he slides it down into the other boot." Sheriff Amory looked at the fingers of his traitorous right hand. "My girls needed new clothes," he said. "Needed some Sunday shoes, with bows on 'em. Needed somethin' that wasn't already worn out by somebody else. So I earned myself an extra hundred dollars. But Biggun knew I'd be comin' that day, and he . . . he'd been stompin' around in filth. When his boots were clean, I went outside and threw up, and I heard the boys laughin' in the house." His eyes squeezed shut for a few seconds, and then they opened again. "I took my girls to the finest shoestore in Union Town, and I bought Lucinda a bouquet of flowers. It wasn't just for her; I wanted to smell somethin' sweet."

"Did Lucinda know about this?" Dad asked.

"No. She thought I'd gotten a raise. You know how many times I've asked Mayor Swope and that damn town council for a raise, Tom? You know how many times they've said, 'We'll put it in the budget next year, J.T.'?" He gave a bitter laugh. "Good ol' J.T.! Ol' J.T. can make do, or do without! He can stretch a dime until Roosevelt hollers, and he don't need no raise because what does he do all day? Ol' J.T. drives around in his sheriff's car and he sits behind his desk readin' *True Detective* and he maybe breaks up a fight now and then or chases down a lost dog or keeps two neighbors from squabblin' over a busted fence. Every blue moon there's a robbery, or a shootin', or somethin' like that car goin' down into Saxon's Lake. But it's not like good ol' harmless J.T.'s a *real* sheriff, don't you see? He's just kind of a long, slumpy thing with a star on his hat, and nothin' much ever happens in Zephyr that he should be gettin' a raise, or a half-decent gasoline allowance, or a bonus every once in a while. Or maybe a pat on the back." His eyes glittered with feverish anger. I realized, as my parents did, that we had not known Sheriff Amory's hidden anguish. "Damn," he said. "I didn't mean to come in here and spill all my belly juice like this. I'm sorry."

"If you felt this way so long," Mom said, "why didn't you just quit?"

"Because . . . I liked bein' the sheriff, Rebecca. I liked knowin' who was doin' what to who, and why. I liked havin' people depend on me. It was . . . like bein' a father and big brother and best friend all rolled up into one. Maybe Mayor Swope and the town council don't respect me, but the people of Zephyr do. *Did,* I mean. That's why I kept at it, even though I should've walked away from it a long time ago. Before Biggun Blaylock called me in the middle of the night and said he had a proposition for me. Said his businesses don't hurt anybody. Said they make people feel better. Said he wouldn't be in business to begin with if people didn't come lookin' for what he was sellin'."

"And you believed him. My God, J.T.!" Dad shook his head in disgust.

"There was more. Biggun said if he and his boys weren't in business, the Ryker gang would move in from the next county, and I've heard those fellas are stone-cold killers. Biggun said that by acceptin' his money I might be shakin' hands with the devil, but the devil I knew was better than the devil I didn't know. Yeah, I believed him, Tom. I still believe him."

"So you knew where his hideout was all along. And there you were makin' everybody believe you couldn't find hide nor hair of him."

"That's right. It's near where Cory and the boys saw that box change hands. I honestly don't know what was inside it, but I do know Gerald Hargison and Dick Moultry are Klansmen from way back. But now I'm a sinner and slime of the earth and I'm not fit to walk the streets with decent people." Sheriff Amory directed his hard gaze at my dad. "I don't need to be told I've messed things up, Tom. I know I was wrong. I know I've shamed the office of sheriff. And shamed my family, which is killin' me when people I thought were our good friends look at Lucinda and the girls like they crawled out of a spittoon. Like I say, we'll be leavin' town before long. But I've got one last duty to perform as the elected sheriff of Zephyr."

"What might that be? Openin' the bank vault for Biggun?"

"No," the sheriff said quietly. "Makin' sure Donny goes to prison for murder. Manslaughter, at the very least."

"Oh," Dad said, and I know he must've felt an inch tall. But he grew back quickly enough. "What's Biggun gonna think about that? After he's been payin' you to lay off?"

"Biggun didn't pay me to protect a killer. And that's what Donny is. I just thank God he didn't kill Miss Grace, too. I knew Stevie Cauley. He might've been a tough guy, and he had his share of scrapes with me, but he was decent. His folks are good people, too. So I'm not gonna let Donny slither out of this, Tom. No matter what Biggun threatens me with."

"Has he threatened you?" Mom asked as Dad stood up to shift a fireplace log with the poker.

"Yes. Warned me, is more like it." Sheriff Amory's brows merged, the lines between his eyes deepening. "Day after tomorrow, two marshals from the county seat are comin' on the Trailways bus. It's bus number thirty-three, and it comes in at noon. I'm to have all the transfer papers ready, and they're gonna take custody of Donny."

The Trailways bus came through Zephyr every other day, on its way to Union Town. On rare occasions it stopped, under the little Trailways sign at the Shell gas station on Ridgeton Street, to pick up or disgorge a passenger or two. But most days it sped on, going somewhere else.

"I found a little black book in a pocket under the driver's seat of Donny's car," the sheriff explained. Dad fed another log into the fire, but he was listening. "It's got names and numbers in it that I think have to do with gamblin' on high school football games. Some names are in there that might surprise you. Not Zephyr people, but names you might know from the newspapers if you keep up with politics. I think the Blaylocks might have been payin' a coach or two to throw games."

"My Lord!" Mom breathed.

"Those two marshals are comin' to pick up Donny, and I've gotta make sure he's there to meet 'em." Sheriff Amory ran a finger along the edge of his star. "Biggun says he'll kill me before he lets me put his son on that bus. I figure he means to, Tom."

"He's bluffin'!" Dad said. "Tryin' to scare you into lettin' Donny go!"

"This mornin' there was somethin' dead on our front porch. I think . . . it might've been a cat. But it was all chopped to pieces and the blood was smeared everywhere and on our front door was written *Donny won't go* in cat's blood. You should've seen the girls' faces when they saw that mess." Sheriff Amory lowered his head for a moment, and stared at the floor. "I'm scared. Awful scared. I think Biggun's gonna try to kill me and spring Donny out of jail before that bus comes in."

"I'd be more afraid those damned snakes would go after Lucinda and the girls," Mom said, and I knew she was heated up about it because she hardly ever cursed.

"I sent 'em to Lucinda's mother this mornin', after what happened. She called me around two o'clock, said they'd gotten there fine." He lifted his face and looked at my father with a tortured expression. "I need help, Tom."

Sheriff Amory went on to explain that he needed three or four men to deputize, and that they'd all spend tonight, tomorrow, and tomorrow night at the jail guarding Donny. He said he'd deputized Jack Marchette, who was at the jail pulling guard duty right this minute, but that he was having trouble finding anybody else. He'd asked ten men, he said, and been turned down ten times. It would be dangerous work, he said. The deputies would each get fifty dollars out of his own pocket, and that was all he could afford to pay. But there were pistols and ammunition at the jailhouse, and the jailhouse itself was as firm as a fortress. The tricky part, he said, would be taking Donny from his cell to the bus stop.

"That's the story." Sheriff Amory gripped his bony knees. "Can I deputize you, Tom?"

"*No!*" Mom's voice almost shook the windows. "Are you out of your mind?"

"I'm sorry to have to ask this of Tom, Rebecca. I swear I am. But it's got to be done."

"Ask somebody else, then! Not Tom!"

"Can I get your answer?" the sheriff urged.

Dad stood next to the fireplace, the logs crackling. His eyes went from Sheriff Amory to Mom and back again, with a quick dart toward me. He slid his hands into his pockets, his face downcast. "I . . . don't know what to say."

"You know what's right, don't you?"

"I do. But I know I don't believe in violence. I can't stand the thought of it. Especially . . . not the way I've been feelin' for the last few months. Like I'm walkin' on eggshells with an anvil strapped to my back. I know I couldn't pull a trigger and shoot anybody. I know that for a fact."

"You wouldn't have to carry a gun, then. I wouldn't expect you to. Just be there to show Biggun he can't get away with murder."

"Unless the Blaylocks murder all of you!" Mom fairly leaped from

316

her chair. "No! Tom's been under a lot of stress lately, and he's not in any physical or mental shape to—"

"Rebecca!" Dad snapped. She hushed. "I can speak for myself, thank you," he said.

"Just tell me yes, Tom." Sheriff Amory was pleading now. "That's all I want to hear."

Dad was in pain. I could see its grim mark on his face. He did know what was right, but he was all twisted up and hurting inside, and the chilly hand of the man at the bottom of Saxon's Lake clutched the back of his neck. "No," he said, his voice raspy. "I can't, J.T."

May I be forgiven. I thought one word, and that word was *Yellowstreak*. Immediately I was overcome with shame, and my face was burning as I got up and ran to my room.

"Cory!" Dad called. "Wait a minute!"

"Well, that's just fine!" Sheriff Amory stood up, and he plucked his hat from the coffee table and jammed it on his head. The crown was crushed, the silver star awry. "Just damn fine! Everybody wants the Blaylocks put behind bars and they kick my ass for takin' his dirty money, but when it comes a chance to actually do somethin' about 'em, everybody and their brother, sister, and uncle runs for the hills! Just damned fine!"

Dad said, "I wish I could—"

"Forget it. Stay home. Stay safe. Good night." Sheriff Amory walked out the door into the cold. The leaves crunched under his shoes, the sound fading. Dad stood at the window and watched him drive away.

"Don't worry about him," Mom said. "He'll find enough deputies."

"What if he doesn't? What if everybody *does* run for the hills?"

"Then if this town doesn't care enough about law and order to help their sheriff, Zephyr deserves to dry up and blow away."

Dad turned toward her, his mouth a tight line. "*We're* Zephyr, Rebecca. You and me. Cory. J.T. The ten men he asked who turned him down, they're Zephyr, too. It's people's souls and caring for each other that dries up and blows away before buildin's and houses do."

"You can't help him, Tom. You just can't. If somethin' happened to you . . ." She didn't finish, because that train of thought led to a desolate destination.

"Maybe he did wrong, but he deserves help. I should've said I would."

"No, you shouldn't have. You're not a fighter, Tom. Those Blaylocks would kill you before you could blink."

"Then maybe I shouldn't blink," Dad said, his face stony.

"Just do what J.T. said, Tom. Stay home and stay safe. Okay?"

"Fine example I'm settin' for Cory. Did you see the way he looked at me?"

"He'll get over it," Mom said. She made an effort to summon a smile. "How about a nice piece of spice cake and a cup of coffee?"

"I don't want any spice cake. I don't want any apple pie, or coconut muffins, or blueberry fritters. All I want is some—" He had to stop speaking, but the rush of emotion choked him. *Peace* might have been the next word he was going to say. "I'm gonna go talk to Cory," he told her, and he came to my room and knocked on the door.

I let him in. I had to. He was my dad. He sat down on my bed, while I held a Blackhawk comic book close to my face. Before he'd come in, I'd been remembering something Vernon had said: *Sheriff Amory's a good man, just not a good sheriff. He lets the birds fly when he's got his paws on them.* I guess it could never be said that Sheriff Amory wasn't trying to do well by his family. Dad cleared his throat. "Well, I reckon I'm lower than a snake's pecker, is that right?"

I would've laughed at that any other time. I just stared at my comic book, attempting to climb inside the world of sleek ebony airplanes and square-jawed heroes who used their wits and fists for justice.

Maybe I betrayed myself somehow. Maybe Dad had an instant of reading my mind. He said, "The world's not a comic book, son." Then he touched my shoulder, and he stood up and closed the door on his way out.

I had a bad sleep that night. If it wasn't the four girls calling my name, it was the car going over the red rock cliff into black water, and then Midnight Mona raced through me and Biggun Blaylock's demonic, bearded face said *I threw in an extra for good luck* and Lucifer's shotgun-ripped head screamed from his grave and Mrs. Lezander offered me a glass of Tang and said *Sometimes he stays up until dawn listening to the foreign countries.*

I lay staring into darkness.

I hadn't told Dad or Mom about Dr. Lezander's distaste for milk or his liking to be a night owl. Surely that had nothing to do with the car in Saxon's Lake. What earthly reason would Dr. Lezander have to kill a stranger? And Dr. Lezander was a kind man who loved animals, not a savage beast who had beaten a man half to death and then strangled the other half with a piano wire. It was unthinkable!

Yet I was thinking it.

Vernon had been right about Sheriff Amory. Could he be right about the milk-hating night owl, too?

Vernon was crazy, but like the Beach Boys, he got around. Like the eye of God, he watched the comings and goings of the citizens of Zephyr, saw their grand hopes and mean schemes. He saw life laid bare. And maybe he was aware of more than he even knew.

I decided. I was going to have to start watching Dr. Lezander. And Mrs. Lezander, too. How could he be such a monster under his civilized skin, and her not know it?

The next day, which was cold and drizzly, I pedaled Rocket past Dr. Lezander's after school. Of course he and his wife were both inside. Even the two horses were in the barn. I don't know what I was looking for, I just wanted to look. There had to be more to tie the doctor to Saxon's Lake than Vernon's theories. That night, the silence at the dinner table couldn't have been cleaved with a chain saw. I didn't trust myself to meet Dad's gaze, and Dad and Mom were avoiding looking at each other as well. So it was a merry dinner, all around.

Then, as we were eating the pumpkin pie that we were all getting so heartily sick of, Dad said, "They let Rick Spanner go today."

"Rick? He's been with Green Meadows as long as *you!*"

"That's right," Dad said, and he picked at the crust with his fork. "Talkin' to Neil Yarbrough this mornin'. He hears they're cuttin' back. Have to, because of that damn . . . that supermarket," he corrected himself, though his curse was already flying. "Big Paul's Pantry." He snorted so hard I thought pumpkin pie might come through his nose. "Milk in plastic jugs. What'll they figure out next to mess things up?"

"Leah Spanner just had a baby in August," Mom said. "That's their third one. What's Rick gonna do?"

"I don't know. He left as soon as they told him. Neil says he heard they gave him a month's pay, but that won't go very far with four mouths to feed." He put down his fork. "Maybe we can take 'em a pie or somethin'."

"I'll make a fresh one first thing in the mornin'."

"That'd be good." Dad reached out, and he placed his hand over Mom's. With all that had been going on—said and left unsaid—it was a heartening sight. "I have a feelin' that's just the start of it, Rebecca. Green Meadows can't compete with those supermarket prices. We cut our rates for our regular customers last week, and then Big Paul's Pantry undercut us two days later. I think it's gonna get a whole lot worse before it gets any better." I saw his hand squeeze Mom's, and she squeezed back. They were in it together, for the long haul.

"One other thing." Dad paused. His jaw clenched and relaxed. He was obviously having a hard time spitting this out, whatever it was. "I talked to Jack Marchette this afternoon. He was at the Shell station when I stopped to fill up the truck. He said—" Again, this was a thorny obstruction in his throat. "He said J.T.'s only found one more volunteer deputy other than Jack himself. You know who that is?"

Mom waited.

"The Moon Man." A tight smile flickered across Dad's face. "Can you believe that? Out of all the able-bodied men in this town, only Jack and the Moon Man are gonna stand with J.T. against the Blaylocks. I doubt if the Moon Man can even *hold* a pistol, much less use one if he had to! Well, I suppose everybody else decided to stay home and be safe, don't you?"

Mom pulled her hand away, and she looked somewhere else. Dad stared across the table at me, his eyes so intense I had to shift in my chair because I felt their heat and power. "Some father you've got, huh, partner? You go to school today and tell your friends how I helped uphold the law?"

"No sir," I answered.

"You should have. Should've told Ben, Johnny, and Davy Ray."

"I don't see their fathers linin' up to get themselves killed by the Blaylocks!" Mom said, her voice strained and unsteady. "Where are the people who know how to use guns? Where are the hunters? Where're the big-talkin' men who say they've been in so many fights and they know how to use their fists and guns to solve every problem in this whole wide world?"

"I don't know where they are." Dad scraped his chair back and stood up. "I just know where I am." He started walking toward the front door, and Mom said with a frightened gasp of breath, "Where're you *goin'*?"

Dad stopped. He stood there, between us and the door, and he lifted a hand to his forehead. "Out to the porch. Just out to the porch, Rebecca. I need to sit out there and think."

"It's cold and rainin' outside!"

"I'll live," he told her, and he left the house.

But he came back, in about thirty minutes. He sat before the fireplace and warmed himself. I got to stay up a little later, since it was a Friday night. When it was time for me to go to bed, between ten-thirty and eleven, Dad was still sitting in his chair before the hearth, his hands folded together and supporting his chin. A wind had kicked up outside, and it blew rain like handfuls of grit against the windows.

"Good night, Mom!" I said. She said good night, from her Herculean labors in the kitchen. "Good night, Dad."

"Cory?" he said softly.

"Yes sir?"

"If I had to kill a man, would that make me any different from whoever did that murder at Saxon's Lake?"

I thought about this for a moment. "Yes sir," I decided. "Because you'd only kill to protect yourself."

"How do we know whoever did that murder wasn't protectin' *himself* in some way, too?"

"We don't, I guess. But you wouldn't get any pleasure from it, like he did."

"No," he said. "I sure wouldn't."

I had something else to say. I didn't know if he wanted to hear it or not, but I had to say it. "Dad?"

"Yes, son?"

"I don't think anybody gives you peace, Dad. I think you have to fight for it, whether you want to or not. Like what happened with Johnny and Gotha Branlin. Johnny wasn't lookin' for a fight. It was forced on him. But he won peace for all of us, Dad." My father's expression didn't alter, and I wasn't sure he understood what I was driving at. "Does that make any sense?"

"Perfect sense," he replied. He lifted his chin, and I saw the edge of a smile caught in the corner of his mouth. "Alabama game's on the radio tomorrow. Ought to be a humdinger. You'd better get on to bed."

"Yes sir." I started toward my room.

"Thank you, son," my father said.

I awakened at seven o'clock to the clatter of the pickup truck's cold engine starting. "Tom!" I heard my mother calling from the front porch. "Tom, don't!" I peered out the window into the early sunlight to see Mom in her robe, running to the street. But the pickup truck was already moving away, and Mom cried out, "Don't go!" Dad's hand emerged from the driver's window, and he waved. Dogs barked up and down Hilltop Street, roused from their doghouses by the commotion. I knew where Dad was going. I knew why.

I was scared for him, but during the night he had made a momentous decision. He was going to find peace, rather than waiting for it to find him.

That morning was an exercise in torture. Mom could hardly

speak. She stumbled around in her robe, her eyes glazed with terror. Every fifteen minutes or so she called the sheriff's office to talk to Dad, until finally around nine o'clock he must've told her he couldn't talk anymore because she didn't dial the number again.

At nine-thirty, I got dressed. Pulled on my jeans, a shirt, and a sweater, because though the sun was bright and the sky blue the air was stinging cold. I brushed my teeth and combed my hair. I watched the clock tick toward ten. I thought of the Trailways bus, number thirty-three, on its way over the winding roads. Would it be early, late, or right on time? Today such a thing as seconds might mean life or death for my father, the sheriff, Chief Marchette, and the Moon Man. But I pushed thoughts like that aside, as much as I could. They came back, though, evil as poison ivy. I knew near ten-thirty that I would have to go. I would have to be there, to see my father. I could not wait for the telephone call that would say Donny was on the bus with the two marshals, or my father was lying shot by a Blaylock bullet. I would have to go. I strapped on my Timex, and I was ready.

As eleven o'clock approached, Mom was so nervous she had both the television and the radio on and she was baking three pies at once. The Alabama game was just about to start. I didn't care a damn for it.

I walked into the pumpkin-and-nutmeg-fumed kitchen, and I said, "Can I go to Johnny's, Mom?"

"What?" She looked at me, wild-eyed. "Go where?"

"Johnny's. The guys are gonna meet there to . . ." I glanced at the radio. *Rollllll Tide!* the crowd was cheering. "To listen to the game." It was a necessary lie.

"No. I want you right here with me."

"I told 'em I'd be there."

"I *said* . . ." Her face flamed with anger. She slammed a mixing bowl down onto the counter. Utensils filmed with pumpkin slid to the floor. Tears sprang to her eyes, and she put a hand over her mouth to hold back a cry of anguish.

Cool on the outside, hell-roasted in the guts. That was me. "I'd like to go," I said.

The hand could no longer hold. "Go on, then!" Mom shouted, her nerves at last unraveling to reveal the tormented center. "Go on, I don't care!"

I turned and ran out before the sob that welled up rooted my shoes. As I climbed onto Rocket, I heard a crash from the kitchen. The mixing bowl had met the floor. I started pedaling for Ridgeton Street, the chill biting my ears.

Rocket was fast that day, as if it sensed impending tragedy. Still, the town lay quiet in its Saturday drowse, the cold having chased all but a few hardy kids indoors and most folks tuned to Bear's latest triumph. I leaned forward, my chin slicing the wind. Rocket's tires thrummed over the pavement, and when my shoes lost the pedals the wheels kept turning on their own.

I reached the gas station just past eleven-fifteen. It had two pumps and an air hose. Inside the office part that connected to a two-stall garage, the gas station's owner—Mr. Hiram White, an elderly man with a humped back who shambled around his wrenches and engine belts like Quasimodo amid the bells—sat at his desk, his head cocked toward a radio. At one corner of the cinderblock building a yellow tin sign with TRAILWAYS BUS SYSTEM on it hung from rusted screws. I parked Rocket around back, near the oily trash cans, and I sat on the ground in the sun to wait the coming of high noon.

At ten minutes before twelve, my fingernails gnawed to the bone, I heard the sound of cars approaching. I edged around the corner and took a peek. The sheriff's car pulled in, followed by Dad's pickup truck. The Moon Man, wearing his top hat, was sitting beside Dad. Chief Marchette was in the passenger seat of the sheriff's car, and seated behind Sheriff Amory was the criminal himself. Donny Blaylock wore a gray uniform and a smirk. Nobody got out. They sat there, both engines rumbling.

Mr. White emerged from his office, scuttling sideways like a crab. Sheriff Amory rolled his window down, and they exchanged some words but I couldn't hear what was being said. Then Mr. White returned to his office. A few minutes later, he was leaving wearing a grease-stained jacket and a baseball cap. He got into his DeSoto and drove off, blue smoke in his wake like dots and dashes of Morse code.

The sheriff's window went back up again. I checked my Timex. It was two minutes before twelve.

Two minutes later, the bus had not arrived.

Suddenly a voice behind me said, "Don't move, boy."

A hand seized the nape of my neck before I could turn my head. Wiry fingers squeezed so hard my nerves were frozen. The hand pulled me, and I retreated from the building's corner. Was it Wade or Bodean who had me? Lord, wasn't there some way to warn my dad? The hand kept pulling me until we were back at the trash cans. Then it let me go, and I turned to see my adversary.

Mr. Owen Cathcoate said, "What the damn hell are you doin' here, boy?"

I couldn't speak. Mr. Cathcoate's wrinkled, liver-spotted face was topped by a sweat-stained brown cowboy hat, its shape more of a Gabby Hayes than a Roy Rogers. His scraggly yellow-white hair hung untidily over his shoulders. He wore, over his creased black trousers and a mud-colored cardigan sweater, a beige duster that looked more musty than dusty. Its ragged hem hung almost to the ankles of his plain black boots. But this was not what had stolen my voice. The voice stealer was the tooled-leather gunbelt cinched around his slim waist and the skeleton-grip pistol tucked down into its holster on his left side, turned around so the butt faced out. Mr. Cathcoate's narrow eyes appraised me. "Asked you a question," he said.

"My dad," I managed to say. "He's here. To help the sheriff."

"So he is. That don't explain why *you're* here, though."

"I just wanted to—"

"Get your head blown off? There's gonna be some fireworks, if I know what the Blaylocks are made of. Get on that bike and make a trail."

"The bus is late," I said, trying to stall him.

"Don't stall," he countered. *"Get!"* He shoved me toward Rocket.

I didn't get on. "No sir. I'm stayin' with my dad."

"You want me to whip your tail right this minute?" The veins stood out in his neck. I expect he could deliver a whipping that would make my father's seem like a brush with a powder puff. Mr. Cathcoate advanced on me. I took a single step back, and then I decided I wasn't going any farther.

Mr. Cathcoate stopped, too, less than three feet from me. A hard-edged smile crossed his mouth. "Well," he said. "Got some sand in you, don't you?"

"I'm stayin' here," I told him.

And then we both heard the sound of a vehicle approaching, and we knew the time for debate was ended. Mr. Cathcoate whirled around and stalked to the building's corner, the folds of his duster rustling. He stopped and peered furtively around the edge, and I realized I was no longer seeing Mr. Owen Cathcoate.

I was seeing the Candystick Kid.

I looked around the corner, too, before Mr. Cathcoate waved me back.

My heart jumped at what I saw. Not the Trailways bus, but a black Cadillac. It pulled into the gas station and parked at an angle in front of the sheriff's car. I dodged away from Mr. Cathcoate's restraining hand, and I ran for a pile of used tires near the garage and flopped down on my belly behind them. Now I had a clear view of what was about to happen, and I stayed there despite Mr. Cathcoate motioning me back behind the building's edge.

Bodean Blaylock, wearing an open-collared white shirt and a gray suit that shone with slick iridescence, got out from behind the wheel. His hair was cropped in a severe crew cut, his mean mouth twisted into a thin smile. He reached into the car and his hand came out with a pearl-handled revolver. Then Wade Blaylock, his dark hair slicked back and his chin jutting, got out of the passenger side. He was wearing black pants so tight they looked painted on, the sleeves of his blue-checked cowboy-style shirt rolled up to show his slim, tattooed forearms in spite of the chill. He had a shoulder holster with a gun in it, and he pulled a rifle out of the Cadillac with him and quickly cocked it: *ka–chunk!*

Then the rear door opened, the Cadillac wobbled, and that big brute heaved himself out. Biggun Blaylock was wearing camouflage-print overalls and a dark brown shirt. He looked like one of the November hills come to life, ripped loose from its bedrock to roll across the earth. He wore a toothy grin, his bald head with its tuft of gray hair gleaming with scalp oil. He breathed hard, winded from the exertion of leaving the car. "Do it, boys," he said between wheezes.

Wade leveled the rifle. Bodean cocked his pistol. They aimed at the sheriff's car and started shooting.

I almost left my skin. The bullets hit the two front tires of Sheriff Amory's car and knocked them flat. Then Wade and Bodean took aim at Dad's truck even as Dad threw the gearshift into reverse and tried to skid the truck out of danger. It was fruitless; the two front tires blew, and the truck was left lame and rocking on its shocks.

"Let's talk some business, Sheriff Junior!" Biggun thundered.

Sheriff Amory didn't get out. Donny's grinning face was pressed up against the window glass like a kid looking at fresh cakes in a bakery. I glanced over to see what Mr. Cathcoate was doing. But the Candystick Kid wasn't there anymore.

"Bus ain't comin' for a while!" Biggun said. He leaned into the Cadillac's rear seat and came out holding a double-barreled shotgun in one ham-sized hand and in the other a camouflage shoulder bag. He put the bag on top of the Caddy's roof, unzipped it, and reached in. "Funniest damn thing, Sheriff Junior!" He broke the shotgun open, brought out two shells from the ammo bag, and pushed them in. Then he snapped the weapon shut again. "Damn bus had two flats 'bout six miles down Route Ten! Gonna be hell fixin' them big mothers!" He rested his weight against the Caddy, making it groan and sag. "Always hated changin' tires, myself."

325

A gun spoke: *crack crack!*

The Cadillac's rear tires exploded. Biggun, for all his bulk, jumped two feet in the air. He made a noise that was a combination of hootenanny yodel and opera aria. Wade and Bodean whirled around. Biggun came down with a concrete-cracking concussion.

Smoke drifted around a figure that stood behind the Cadillac, next to Mr. White's parked tow truck. The Candystick Kid was holding his pistol in his right hand.

"What the fuckin' hell of a shit—!" Biggun raged, his face swelling up with blood and the tip of his beard quivering.

Sheriff Amory jumped from his car. "Owen! I told you I didn't want you around here!"

The Candystick Kid ignored him, his cool gaze riveted to Biggun. "Know what this is called, Mr. Blaylock?" He suddenly spun his pistol around and around his trigger finger, the sun glinting off the blued metal, and he delivered the gun to its butt-first position in the left-sided holster with a *shric*king noise of supple leather. "This is called," he said, "a standoff."

"Standoff, my ass!" Biggun shouted. *"Nail him, boys!"*

Wade and Bodean opened fire as Sheriff Amory yelled, "No!" and brought up the rifle he'd been holding at his side.

The Candystick Kid might have been an old, wrinkled man, but whatever was in him that had made him the Kid now showed its mettle. He dived behind the tow truck as bullets crashed through the windshield and pocked the hood. Sheriff Amory squeezed off two shots, and the Cadillac's windshield blew out. Wade yelped and went for the ground, but Bodean turned around with fury contorting his face and his pistol popped. Sheriff Amory's hat flew off his head like a pigeon. The next shot from the sheriff's rifle put a part in the side of Bodean's crew cut, and Bodean must've felt the heat of its passage because he hollered *"Yow!"* and dropped to a snake's view.

Mr. Marchette climbed out of the sheriff's car, holding a pistol. Dad scrambled out of the pickup truck and threw himself to the pavement, and a thrill of mingled pride and fear went through me as I saw he was gripping a gun, too. The Moon Man stayed in the truck and ducked his head, only his top hat showing.

Boom! the double-barreled shotgun said. The tow truck shook, pieces of glass and metal flying off it. Biggun was on his knees beside the Cadillac, and it came to me that he shouldn't destroy that tow truck because he was going to need it to stand up again.

"Daddy!" Donny shouted from the sheriff's car. "Get me outta this, Daddy!"

"Ain't nobody takin' what belongs to me!" Biggun yelled back.

He fired off a shell at the sheriff's car, and the grille exploded. Steaming radiator water spewed like a geyser. From the back seat, where he must've been restrained by cuffs or a rope, Donny hollered, "Don't kill me 'fore you save me, Daddy!"

I saw where Donny got his smarts from.

Biggun reached up and grabbed the ammo bag's strap, and he hauled it down with him to reload. Another bullet smacked into the Cadillac, and a taillight crashed. The Candystick Kid was still at work.

"Ain't no use!" Biggun said, snapping the shotgun shut again. "We're gonna go through you like shit through a goose! Hear me, Sheriff Junior?"

Dad got up. I almost shouted for him to stay down, but he ran alongside the sheriff's car and crouched next to Sheriff Amory. I could see how pale his face was. But he was there, and that's what counted.

There was a lull as everybody got their second gulp of courage. Bodean and Wade began firing at the sheriff's car again, and Donny hunkered down in the back seat. "Stop that shootin', ya damn fools!" Biggun commanded. "You wanna blow your brother's head off?"

Maybe it was my imagination, but neither Wade nor Bodean stopped firing as fast as they should have.

"Get around behind 'em, Wade!" Bodean yelled.

"*You* get around behind 'em, dumb ass!"

Bodean, proving the cunning of a poker player did not translate into common sense, stood up and sprinted for the building's corner. He got about three strides when a single gunshot rang out and he grabbed at his right foot and fell sprawling to the pavement. "I'm shot, Daddy! Daddy, I'm shot!" he whined, his pistol lying out of reach.

"Didn't think you were fuckin' *tickled!*" Biggun roared back. "Lord God, you got the brains of a BB in a boxcar!"

"Gimme somethin' else to shoot at!" the Candystick Kid urged, well-hidden in the shadow of the tow truck. "I got a gun full of lonely bullets!"

"Give it up, Biggun!" Sheriff Amory said. "You're washed up around here!"

"If I am, I'll make you choke on the soap, you bastards!"

"Ain't no use anybody else gettin' hurt! Throw out your guns and let's call it quits!"

"Sheeeeyit!" Biggun snarled. "You think I got anywhere in this life by callin' it quits? You think I come up from hog turds and cotton fields to let a little tin star take my boy away from me and ruin *everythin'*? You shoulda used that money I been payin' you to buy a head doctor with!"

"Biggun, it's over! You're surrounded!" That was my father's voice. To my dying day I shall never forget the steel in it. He was a Blackhawk, after all.

"Surround *this!*" Wade jumped up and started firing with his rifle in my father's direction. Biggun hollered for him to get down, but Wade was balanced on the lunatic edge just like Donny. Bullets struck sparks off the concrete, and one of them thunked into a tire in my nest of concealment. My heart seized up, it was so close. Then the Candystick Kid's gun cracked again, just once, and a chunk of Wade's left ear spun off his head and red blood spattered the Cadillac's hood.

You would've thought the bullet had chopped off something more central, because Wade screamed like a woman. He clutched at his ragged ear, fell to the ground, and started wheeling around and around like the Three Stooges' Curly having a caterwauling fit.

"Oh, my soul!" Biggun moaned.

It was obvious that, like the Branlins, the Blaylocks could dish it out but they sure couldn't take it.

"Damn, I missed!" the Candystick Kid said. "I was aimin' for his head instead of his ass!"

"*I'll kill ya!*" Biggun's voice returned to the thunder zone. "*I'll kill every one of ya and dance on your graves!*"

It was a frightening sound. But with Bodean and Wade writhing on the pavement and Donny yelping like a sad little puppy, there wasn't much lightning left in the storm.

And then the pickup's passenger-side door opened and the Moon Man stepped out. He was wearing a black suit and a red bow tie, as well as his top hat. Around his neck were six or seven strings and attached to the strings were small things that looked like tea bags. A chicken foot was pinned to one lapel, and he wore three watches on each wrist. He didn't duck or dodge. Instead, he began walking past the sheriff's car, past Fire Chief Marchette and my dad and Sheriff Amory. "Hey!" Chief Marchette shouted. "Get your head down!"

But the Moon Man kept going with a deliberate stride, his head held high. He was going right to where Biggun Blaylock crouched by the Cadillac holding a loaded double-barreled shotgun.

"Cease this violence!" the Moon Man intoned in a soft, almost childlike voice. I had never heard him speak before. "Cease this violence, for the sake of all that's good!" His long legs stepped over Wade without hesitation.

"Keep away from me, you nutty nigger!" Biggun warned. But the Moon Man would not be halted. Dad shouted, "Come back!" and started to get up, but Sheriff Amory's hand closed on his forearm.

"I'll blow you to voodoo blazes!" Biggun said, indicating that he indeed knew the reputations of the Moon Man and the Lady. Biggun's eyes had taken on the wet glint of fear. "Stay away from me! Stay away, I said!"

The Moon Man stopped in front of Biggun. The Moon Man smiled, his eyes crinkling up, and he held out his long, slim arms. "Let us search for light," he said.

Biggun aimed the shotgun at the Moon Man at point-blank range. He sneered, "Well, light one for me!" and his thick finger wrenched both triggers at once.

I flinched, my eardrums already cracking from the blast.

But there was no blast.

"Stand up and walk like a man," the Moon Man said, still smiling. "It's not too late."

Biggun gagged and gasped at the same time. He wrenched the triggers again. Still, no blast. Biggun snapped the shotgun open, and what was jammed into the chambers came spilling out over his hands.

They were little green garden snakes. Dozens of them, all tangled together. Perfectly harmless, but they did some damage to Biggun Blaylock, and that's no lie.

"Gaaaaakkkk!" he choked. He knocked the snakes out of the chambers, reached into his ammo bag, and his hand came out full of rippling green bodies. Biggun made a noise like Lou Costello coming face-to-face with Lon Chaney Junior's werewolf—"Wo wo wo wo wo!"—and suddenly that monstrous bulk was up on its feet and showed that he might not walk like a man but he sure could run like a rabbit. Of course, in such cases the reality of physics must eventually intrude and Biggun's weight crashed him to the concrete before he got very far. He struggled and thrashed like a turtle turned on its shell.

Tires shrieked. A pickup truck loaded with men roared into the gas station. I recognized among them Mr. Wilson and Mr. Callan. Most of the men held baseball bats, axes, or guns. Close behind them came a car, followed by another car. Then a second pickup truck skidded to a stop. The men of Zephyr—and many of the Bruton men, too—leaped out ready to bust some heads. "I'll be," Sheriff Amory said, and he stood up.

They were sorely disappointed, to say the least, that it was all over. I later learned the noise of the shootout had thawed their guts and brought them out to defend their sheriff and their town. They had all thought, I suppose, that someone else would shoulder the responsibility, that they could stay home and be safe. A lot of wives had done a lot of crying. But they had come. Not all of the Zephyr and Bruton men, by far, but more than enough to take care of business. I imagine that seeing the crowd of wild men with butcher knives, Louisville Sluggers, hatchets, pistols, and meat cleavers, the Blaylocks thanked their lucky stars they weren't going to jail in snuffboxes.

In all the confusion, I came out from hiding. Mr. Owen Cathcoate was standing over Wade, lecturing him about the straight and narrow path. Wade was listening with only half an ear. My dad was with the Moon Man, over by the Blaylocks' Caddy. I walked to him, and he looked at me and wanted to ask what I was doing there, but he didn't because the answer to that would lead to a whipping. So he didn't ask, he just nodded.

Dad and I stood together, staring down at Biggun's shotgun and the ammo bag. Green garden snakes wriggled around each other like a big mass of seaweed, overflowing from the bag.

The Moon Man just grinned. "My wife," he said. "She one craaaaazy old lady."

8

From the Lost World

The Blaylocks, it may be safe to say, went directly to jail. They did not have a Get Out of Jail Free card, they did not collect two hundred dollars, and their mean monopoly was smashed. I understood that they were as tight-lipped as clams at first, but then the family ties began unraveling as the state investigators drilled them. Wade learned that Donny had stolen a large chunk of his moonshine profits, Bodean found that Wade was skimming the gambling den's money, and Donny suspected that Wade had put some arsenic in his bottle of moonshine and that's why he thought he'd seen a ghost. As the Blaylock brothers began spilling their guts, Biggun decided to take the high road. He fell on his knees at the arraignment and professed, sobbing to shame Shakespeare, that he was Born Again and had been duped into following the paths of Satan by his own misguided sons. They must take after their mothers, he said. He vowed to devote his life to being a minister, if, by the grace of the Lord above, the judge would offer him the cup of mercy.

He was told he would have a very long time in which to practice his preaching, and a nice secure place to catch up on his Bible reading.

When they dragged him out of court, kicking and screaming, he damned everybody in sight, even the stenographer. They said he threw so many curses that if those bad words had been bricks, they'd have made a three-bedroom house with a two-car garage. The brothers went before judges as well, to similar results. I didn't have any sympathy for them. If I knew the Blaylocks, they'd soon be running the prison store and making a killing off every cigarette and square of toilet paper.

One thing, though, the Blaylocks refused to divulge: what was in the wooden box they'd sold to Gerald Hargison and Dick Moultry. It couldn't be proven that any box even existed. But I knew better.

The Amorys left town. Mr. Marchette gave up being fire chief and stepped into the role of sheriff. I understand Sheriff Marchette told Mr. Owen Cathcoate anytime he wanted to wear a deputy's badge it would be fine with him. But Mr. Cathcoate informed the sheriff that the Candystick Kid had gone to roam the frontiers of the Wild West, where he belonged, and from here on out he was just plain old Owen.

Mom was in a zombie state for a while, as visions of what might have been careened through her mind, but she came out of it. I believe that deep in her heart she might have wanted Dad to stay safe at home but she respected him more for making up his own mind about what was right. When my lie became obvious, Dad debated not letting me go to the Brandywine Carnival when it came to town but he wound up making me wash and dry the dinner dishes for a week straight. I didn't argue. I had to pay the piper somehow.

Then the posters began appearing around town. BRANDYWINE CARNIVAL IS ON ITS WAY! Johnny was looking forward to seeing the Indian ponies and trick riders. Ben was excited about the midway, and the rides lit up with pulsing multicolored bulbs. I looked forward to the haunted house, which you rode through on rickety railcars while unseen things brushed your face and howled at you in the dark. Davy Ray's excitement concerned the freak show. I never saw anybody who got so worked up about freaks as he did. They gave me the creeps and I could hardly look at them, but Davy Ray was a true connoisseur of freakdom. If it had three arms, a pinhead, crocodile-scaled skin, or sweated blood, he went into giddy fits of delight.

So it happened that on Thursday night the park area near the baseball field where we'd had our Fourth of July barbecue was empty when the last Zephyr light went off. On Friday morning, kids on their way to school witnessed the transformation a few hours could bring. The Brandywine Carnival appeared like an island in a sea of sawdust. Trucks were chugging around, men were hoisting up tents, the frameworks of rides were being pieced together like dinosaur bones, and the booths were going up where food would be sold and Kewpie dolls not worth a quarter would be won for two dollars' worth of horseshoes.

Before school, my buddies and I took a spin around the park on our bikes. Other kids were doing the same thing, circling like moths in expectation of a light bulb. "There's the haunted house!" I said, pointing toward the bat wings of a gothic mansion being hinged together. Ben said, "Gonna be a Ferris wheel this year, looks like!" Johnny's gaze was on a trailer with horses and Indians painted on its side. Davy Ray hollered, "Looka there! Hoo *boy!*" We saw what he was so excited about: a big, garishly painted canvas with a wrinkled face at its center and in the center of the wrinkled face a single horrible eyeball. FREAKS OF NATURE! the words on the canvas said. IT COULD'VE BEEN YOU!

In truth, it was not a large carnival. It was short of medium-sized, too. Its tents were patched, its trailers rust-streaked, its trucks and workers equally tired. It was the end of the carnival season for them, and our area was almost its last stop. But we never thought that we were getting the leftover crop of caramel apples, that the Indian ponies and trick riders went through their routines with an eye on the clock, that the rides clattered in need of oiling and the barkers were surly not to add flavor but because they were damned bushed. We just saw a carnival out there, aglow and beckoning. That's what we saw.

"Looks like a good one this year!" Ben said as we started to turn back for school.

"Yeah, it sure—"

And then a horn blasted behind me and Rocket zoomed out of the way as a Mack truck passed us. It turned onto the sawdust, its heavy tires crunching down. The truck was a hodgepodge of different-colored parts, and it was hauling a wide trailer with no windows. We could hear the suspension groan. On the trailer's sides, an amateurish hand had painted crude green jungle fronds and foliage. Across the jungle scene was scrawled, in thick red letters that had been allowed to drip like rivulets of blood: FROM THE LOST WORLD.

It rumbled away, toward the maze of other trucks and trailers. But in its wake I caught a smell. Not just exhaust, though of that there was plenty. Something else. Something . . . lizardy.

"Whew!" Davy Ray wrinkled his nose. "Ben let one!"

"I did not!"

"Silent but deadly!" Davy Ray whooped.

"You did it yourself, then! Not me!"

"I smell it," Johnny said calmly. Davy Ray and Ben shut up. We had learned to listen when Johnny spoke. "Came from that trailer," he said.

We watched the Mack truck and trailer turn between two tents and go out of sight. I looked at the ground, and saw the tires had smushed right through the sawdust and left brown grooves in the earth. "Wonder what's in it?" Davy Ray asked on the scent of a freak. I told him I didn't know, but whatever it was, it was mighty heavy.

On the ride to school, we formulated our plans. Parents permitting, we would meet at my house at six-thirty and go to the carnival together like the Four Musketeers. Does that suit everybody? I asked.

"Can't," Ben answered, pedaling beside me. He spoke the word like a grim bell tolling.

"Why not? We always go at six-thirty! That's when all the rides are goin'!"

"Can't," Ben repeated.

"Hey, you got a parrot stuck in your throat?" Davy Ray asked. "What's wrong with you?"

Ben sighed, blowing a wisp of steam in the morning's sunny chill. He had on a woolen cap, his round cheeks flushed with crimson. "Just . . . can't. Not until seven o'clock."

"We *always* go at six-thirty!" Davy Ray insisted. "It's . . . it's . . ." He looked at me for help.

"Tradition," I said.

"Yeah! That's what it is!"

"I think there's somethin' Ben doesn't want to tell us," Johnny said, swerving his bike up on the other side of Davy Ray. "Spit it out, Ben."

"It's just . . . I can't . . ." He frowned, and with another plume of steam decided to give up the game. "At six o'clock I've got a *piana* lesson."

"What?" Davy Ray had fairly yelled it. Rocket wobbled. Johnny looked as if he'd taken a Cassius Clay roundhouse punch to the noggin.

"A *piana* lesson," Ben repeated. The way he said that word, I could see legions of simpering pansies behind legions of upright pianos while their adoring mothers smiled and patted their beanies. "Miss Blue Glass has started teachin' piana. Mom's signed me up, and my first lesson's at six o'clock."

We were horrified. "Why, Ben?" I asked. "Why'd she do it?"

"She wants me to learn Christmas songs. Can you believe it? Christmas songs!"

"Man!" Davy Ray shook his head in commiseration. "Too bad Miss Blue Glass can't teach you guitar!" *Git-tar*, he pronounced it. "Now, that'd be cool! But piana . . . yech!"

"Don't I know it," Ben muttered.

"Well, there's a way around this," Johnny said as we neared the school. "Why don't we just meet Ben at the Glasses' house? We can ride on to the carnival at seven instead of six-thirty."

"Yeah!" Ben perked up. "That way it won't be so awful!"

It was settled, then, pending parental okay. But every year we all got together and went to the carnival on Friday night from six-thirty until ten, and our parents had always said yes. It was really the only night kids our age could go. Saturday morning and afternoon was when the black people went, and Saturday night belonged to the older kids. Then by ten o'clock on Sunday morning the park area was clear again except for a few scatters of sawdust, crushed Dixie cups, and ticket stubs the cleanup crew had left like a dog marking its territory.

The day passed in a slow crawl of anticipation. Leatherlungs called me a blockhead twice and made Georgie Sanders stand with his nose pressed against a circle on the blackboard for smarting off. Ladd Devine went to the office for drawing a lewd picture on the inside cover of his notebook, and the Demon swore she'd fix Leatherlungs' wagon. I sure would've hated to be in Leatherlungs' clunky brown shoes.

From my house, as the blue twilight gathered and the sickle moon appeared, I could see the lights of the Brandywine Carnival. The Ferris wheel was turning, outlined in red. The midway sparkled with white bulbs. The sound of calliope music, laughter, and joyous screams drifted to me over the roofs of Zephyr. I had five dollars in my pocket, a gift from my father. I was wrapped up in my fleece-lined denim jacket against the cold. I was ready to roar.

The Glass sisters lived about a half mile away, on Shantuck Street. By the time I got there on Rocket, near quarter before seven, Davy Ray's bike was parked next to Ben's in front of the house, which looked like a gingerbread cottage Hansel and Gretel might've envied. I left Rocket and went up on the porch. I could hear piano notes being banged behind the door. Then the high, fluty voice of Miss Blue Glass: "Softly, Ben. *Softly!*"

I pressed the doorbell. Chimes rang, and Miss Blue Glass said, "Will you please answer that, Davy Ray?"

He opened the door as the banging continued. I could tell by his sick expression that listening to Ben try to hammer out the same five notes over and over again wasn't good for your health. "Is that Winifred Osborne?" Miss Blue Glass called over the racket.

"No ma'am, it's Cory Mackenson," Davy Ray told her. "He's waitin' for Ben, too."

"Bring him in, then. Too cold to wait outside."

I crossed the threshold into a living room that was a boy's nightmare. All the furniture looked like spindly antiques that wouldn't bear the weight of a starved mosquito. Little tables held porcelain figures of dancing clowns, children holding puppies, and the like. A gray carpet on the floor appeared to indelibly remember footprints. A glass curio cabinet as tall as my dad held a forest of colored crystal goblets, coffee mugs with the faces of all the presidents on them, twenty-odd ceramic dolls clothed in lace costumes, and maybe another twenty rhinestone-decorated eggs each with its own brass four-footed stand. What a crash that thing would make if it went over, I thought. A green-and-blue-streaked marble pedestal held an open Bible as big as my gargantuan dictionary, the type in it large enough to be read from across the room. Everything looked too frail to touch and too precious to enjoy, and I wondered how anybody could live in such a state of frozen pretty. Of course, there was the gleaming brown upright piano, with Ben trapped at its keys and Miss Blue Glass standing beside the bench holding a conductor's baton.

"Hello, Cory. Please have a seat," she said. She was wearing all blue, as usual, except for a wide white belt around her bony waist. Her whitish-blond hair was piled up like a foamy fountain, her black glasses so thick they made her eyes bug.

"Where?" I asked her.

"Right there. On the sofa."

The sofa, covered in velvety cloth that showed shepherds playing their harps to prancing sheep, had legs that looked about as sturdy as rain-soaked twigs. Davy Ray and I eased down into the sofa's cushiony grip. The sofa creaked ever so slightly, but my heart jumped in my throat.

"Now! Thinkin' cap on! Fingers flow like the waves! One, two, three, one, two, three." Miss Blue Glass started motioning up and down with her baton as the pudgy fingers of Ben's right hand tried to play the same five notes with some resemblance to rhythm. Soon enough, though, he was pounding those notes as if trying to crush fire ants. "Flow like the waves!" Miss Blue Glass said. "Softly, softly! One, two, three, one, two, three!"

Ben's playing was less wavy and more sludgy. "I can't do it!" he wailed, and he pulled his hand away from those frightful keys. "My fingers are gettin' all crossed up!"

"Sonia, give that boy a rest!" Miss Green Glass called from the rear of the house. "You're gonna wear his fingers to the bone!" Her voice was more trombone than flute.

"You just mind your own beeswax now, Katharina!" Miss Blue Glass retorted. "Ben's got to learn the proper technique!"

"Well, it's his first lesson, for pity's sake!" Miss Green Glass walked out of a hallway into the living room. She put her hands on her skinny hips and glowered at her sister from behind her own black-framed glasses. She was wearing all green, the shades varying from pale to forest. She made you feel a little seasick just looking at her. Her blondish-white hair was piled higher than Sonia's, and had a vague pyramidal shape about it. "Not everybody's a musical genius like you, you know!"

"Yes I do know, thank you very much!" Swirls of red had crept into Miss Blue Glass's ivory cheeks. "I'll thank you not to interrupt Ben's lesson!"

"His time's about over, anyway. Who's your next victim?"

"Winifred Osborne is my next *student*," Miss Blue Glass said pointedly. "And if it wasn't for your magazine subscriptions, I wouldn't have to go back to teachin' piano to begin with!"

"Don't you blame my magazine subscriptions! It's your own self at fault! I swear, if you buy another set of dinner plates, I'm gonna go straight out of my head! What're you buyin' all those dinner plates for when we don't ever have anybody to dinner?"

"Because they're pretty, that's why! I like pretty things! And I could ask you why you went out and bought a collection of First Lady thimbles when you can't even sew a stitch!"

"Because they're gonna grow in value, that's why! You wouldn't know an investment if it crawled up on one of those dumb dinner plates and begged you to eat it with a biscuit!"

I feared the Glass sisters were going to come to blows. The timbres of their voices sounded like a duel of slightly off-key musical instruments. Caught between them, Ben appeared about to leap from his skin. Then something went *crooaaakk* from the rear of the house. It was the kind of noise I would've imagined the tentacled Martian in the bowl could make. Miss Blue Glass jabbed the baton at her sister and snapped, "See there? You've upset him! Are you satisfied now?"

The door chimes rang. "It's probably the neighbors fussin' about your hollerin'!" Miss Green Glass predicted. "They can hear you all the way to Union Town!"

Johnny stood there when Miss Blue Glass opened the door. He was bundled up in a dark brown jacket over a black turtleneck. "I'm here to wait for Ben," he said.

"Lord have mercy! Is the whole world waitin' for Ben?" She made a face as if she'd bitten into a lemon, but she said, "He's still got five minutes! Come on in, then!" Johnny entered the house, and he saw our edgy faces and realized he had stepped into something that was not a pile of roses.

Crooaaakk! Crooaaakk! the thing in the back room squawked.

"Would you see to him if you aren't too busy?" Miss Blue Glass told her sister. "Since you've stirred him up, at least see to him!"

"I swear I'd move out of here if I could find a cardboard box worth livin' in!" Miss Green Glass groused, but she stalked into the hallway again and the ruckus was over at least for the moment.

"Lord, I'm worn out!" Miss Blue Glass picked up an old church bulletin and fanned herself with it. "Ben, get up and I'll show you what you can be playin' if you'll do your exercises like I've told you."

"Yes ma'am!" He jumped up.

Miss Blue Glass settled herself on the piano bench. Her hands with their long elegant fingers poised over the keyboard. She closed her eyes, getting in the mood I guess. "I used to teach this song to all my students when I was teachin' piano full-time," she said. "Ever heard of 'Beautiful Dreamer'?"

"No ma'am," Ben said. Davy Ray elbowed me in the ribs and rolled his eyes.

"This is it," Miss Blue Glass explained, and she began to play.

It wasn't the Beach Boys, but it was nice. The music swarmed out of that piano and filled up the room, and Miss Blue Glass swayed slightly from side to side on the bench as her fingers rippled across the keyboard. I have to say, it did sound pretty.

Then a terrible screech intruded. The hairs on the back of my neck stood up and strained at their roots. The noise felt like jagged glass hammered into your earhole.

"Skulls and bones! Hannah Furd! Skulls and bones! Cricket in Rinsin!"

Miss Blue Glass stopped playing. "Katharina! Feed him a cracker!"

"He's goin' crazy in here! He's beatin' at his cage!"

"Skulls and bones! Draggin me packin! Skulls and bones!"

I didn't know if those words were what the thing was screaming, but that's what it sounded like to me. Ben, Davy Ray, Johnny, and I looked at each other as if we'd walked into a nuthouse. *"Hannah Furd! Crooaaakk! Cricket in Rinsin!"*

"A cracker!" Miss Blue Glass yelled. "Do you know what a *cracker* is?"

"I'll crack your head in a minute!"

The screaming and screeching went on. Over this tumult, the door chimes rang again.

"It's that song, I'm tellin' you!" Miss Green Glass hollered. "He goes insane every time you play it!"

"Crooaaakk! Draggin me packin! Hannah Furd! Hannah Furd!"

I got up and opened the front door in prelude to running out. A middle-aged man and a little girl eight or nine years old stood on the porch. I recognized the man. Mr. Eugene Osborne was the cook at the Bright Star Cafe. "We're here for Winifred's piano less—" he began, before the caterwauling started up again. *"Skulls and bones! Crooaaakk! Cricket in Rinsin!"*

"What in the *world* is that racket?" Mr. Osborne asked, his hand on the little girl's shoulder. Her blue eyes were wide and puzzled. On Mr. Osborne's knuckles, I saw, were faded tattooed letters. A *U.S.* on the thumb, and on the following fingers *A, R, M,* and *Y.*

"That's my parrot, Mr. Osborne." Miss Blue Glass came up and shoved me aside. She was mighty strong to be so thin. "He's havin' a little trouble lately."

Miss Green Glass emerged from the hallway, carrying a bird cage that contained the source of all that noise. It was a fairly large parrot, and it was fluttering at the bars and shaking like a tornado-spun leaf. *"Skulls and bones!"* it shrieked, showing a black tongue. *"Draggin me packin!"*

"You give him a cracker!" Miss Green Glass put the bird cage down on the piano bench, none too gently. "I'm not gettin' my fingers snapped off!"

"I fed *yours* all the time, and I sure risked my fingers!"

"I'm not feedin' that thing!"

"Hannah Furd! Draggin me packin! Skulls and bones!" The parrot was a bright turquoise blue, not a speck of any other color on him except for the yellow of his beak. He attacked the bars, blue feathers flying.

"Well, then get him to the bedroom!" Miss Blue Glass said. "Put the night cloth over him and settle him down!"

"I'm a slave! I'm just a slave in my own home!" Miss Green Glass wailed, but she picked up the bird cage by its handle again and left the living room.

"Skulls and bones!" the parrot shrieked in parting. *"Cricket in Rinsin!"*

A door closed, and the noise was thankfully muffled.

"He has a little bitty problem," Miss Blue Glass said to Mr. Osborne with a nervous smile. "He doesn't seem to like one of my favorite songs. Please come in, come in! Ben, that finishes your lesson for this evenin'! Remember, now! Thinkin' cap on! Fingers flow like the waves!"

"Yes, ma'am." Then he said under his breath to me, "Let's get outta here!"

I started out, following Davy Ray. The parrot had quieted, perhaps calmed by its night cloth. And then I heard Mr. Osborne say, "First time I ever heard a parrot curse in German."

"I'm sorry, Mr. Osborne?" Miss Blue Glass lifted her penciled-on eyebrows.

I stopped at the door, and turned to listen. Johnny bumped into me.

"Curse in German," Mr. Osborne repeated. "Who taught him those words?"

"Well, I . . . have no idea what you're talkin' about, I'm sure!"

"I was a cook for the Big Red One in Europe. Got the chance to talk to a lot of prisoners, and believe me I know some foul words in German when I hear 'em. I just heard an earful."

"My . . . parrot said those things?" Her smile flickered off and on. "You're mistaken, of course!"

"Let's go!" Johnny told me. "The carnival's waitin'!"

"Wasn't just cursin', either," Mr. Osborne went on. "There were other German words in there, but they were all garbled up."

"My parrot is *American*," Miss Blue Glass informed him with an upward tilt of her chin. "I have no earthly idea what you're talkin' about!"

"Well, okay, then." He shrugged. "Don't matter none to me."

"Boys! Will you close that door and stop lettin' all the heat out?"

"Come on, Cory!" Davy Ray called, already astride his bike. "We're late enough as it is!"

A door opened in the back. Miss Green Glass said from the hallway, "He's quiet now, thank the Lord! Just don't play that song again, whatever you do!"

"I've told you it's not that song, Katharina! I used to play it for him all the time and he loved it!"

"Well, he hates it now! Just don't play it!"

Their squawking was beginning to remind me of two squabbling old parrots, one blue and one green. "Close that door, if you please!" Miss Blue Glass yelled at me, and Johnny gave me a shove onto the porch to uproot my feet. He closed the door behind us, but we could still hear the Glass sisters clamoring like buzz saws. I pitied that poor little Osborne girl.

"Those two are loony!" Ben said as he got on his bike. "Man, that was even worse than *school!*"

"You must've done somethin' to make your mom awful mad at you," was Davy Ray's opinion. "Time's wastin'!" He gave a whoop and took off in the direction of the carnival, his bike's pedals flying.

I lagged behind the others, though they kept yelling for me to catch up. German curse words, I was thinking. How come Miss Sonia Glass's parrot knew German curse words? As far as I knew, neither of the sisters spoke anything but Southern English. I hadn't realized Mr. Osborne was in the Big Red One. That, I knew from my reading, was a very famous infantry division. Mr. Osborne had really been there, on the same war-torn earth as Sgt. Rock! Wow, I thought. Neato!

But how come the parrot knew German curse words?

Then the happy sounds of the carnival drifted to me along with the aromas of buttered popcorn and carameled apples. I left the German-cursing parrot behind, and sped up to catch my buddies.

We paid our dollars at the admission gate and threw ourselves into the carnival like famished beggars at a feast. The strings of light bulbs gleamed over our heads like trapped stars. A lot of kids our age were there, along with their parents, and some older people and high school kids, too. Around us the rides grunted, clattered, and rattled. We bought our tickets and got on the Ferris wheel, and I made the mistake of sitting with Davy Ray. When we got to the very top and the wheel paused to allow riders on the bottommost gondola, he grinned and started rocking us back and forth and yelling that the bolts were about to come loose. "Stop it! Stop it!" I pleaded, my body freezing solid to offset his elasticity. At that height, I could see all across the carnival. My gaze fell on a garish sign with crude green jungle fronds and the red, dripping words FROM THE LOST WORLD.

I paid Davy Ray back in the haunted house. When the warty-nosed witch jumped out of the darkness at our clanking railcar, I grabbed the back of his neck and wailed to shame the scratchy recorded gibberings of ghost and goblin. "Quit it!" he said after he'd come down onto his seat again. Outside, he told me the haunted house was the dumbest thing he'd ever seen in his life and it wasn't even a bit scary. But he sure was walking funny, and he hustled himself off to the row of portable toilets.

We stuffed our faces with cotton candy, buttered popcorn, and glazed miniature doughnuts. We ate candied apples covered with peanuts. We packed away corn dogs and drank enough root beer to make our bellies slosh. Then Ben wanted to ride the Scrambler, with results that were not pretty. We got him into one of the portable toilets, and luckily his aim was good and his clothes were spared a Technicolor splatter.

Ben passed on entering the tent that displayed the big, wrinkled one-eyed face. Davy Ray almost chewed his way through the canvas in his hurry to get in there, but Johnny and I went with him against our better judgment.

In the gloomy confines, a dour-looking man with a nose as large as a dill pickle held court before a half dozen other freak aficiona-dos. He went on for a while about the sins of the flesh and the eye of the Lord. Then he drew back a small curtain and switched on a spotlight and there in a big glass bottle was a shriveled, pink and naked baby with two arms, two legs, and a Cyclops eye in the center of its domed forehead. I winced and Johnny shifted uncomfortably when the man picked up the formaldehyde-filled bottle, the Cyclops baby drifting in its dream. He started showing it to everybody up close. "This is the sin of the flesh, and here's the eye of God as punishment for that sin," he said. I had the feeling he might get along famously with Reverend Blessett. When the man paused in front of me, I saw that the eye was golden, like Rocket's. The baby's face was so wrinkled it might have been that of a tiny old man, about to open his toothless mouth and call for a sip of white lightning to ease his aches. "Notice, son, how the finger of God has wiped clean the means of sin," the man said, his baggy-drawered eyes glinting with a spark of evangelical fever. I saw what he meant: the baby had neither male nor female equipment. There was nothing but wrinkled pink skin down there. The man turned the bottle to show me the baby's back. The baby drifted against the glass, and I heard its shoulder make a soft wet noise of collision.

I saw the Cyclops baby's shoulder blades. They were thick, bony protrusions. Like the stumps of wings, I thought.

And I knew. I really did.

The Cyclops baby was somebody's angel, fallen to earth.

"Woe to the sinner," the man said as he moved on to Johnny and Davy Ray. "Woe to the sinner, under the eye of God."

"Ah, that was a *gyp!*" Davy Ray ranted when we were outside on the midway again. "I thought it was gonna be alive! I thought it could talk to you!"

"Didn't it?" I asked him, and he looked at me like I was halfway around the bend.

We went to a show where motorcycle drivers raced around and around a caged-in cylinder, the engines screaming right in front of our faces and the tires gripping disaster's edge. Then we went to the Indian pony show, under a large tent where palefaces who wouldn't know Geronimo from Sitting Bull jumped around in loincloths and feathers and tried to spur some spirit into horses one hay bale away from the glue factory. The finale came when a wagon with cowboys on it circled the tent with the pseudo-Indians in pursuit, and the cowboys shot off their blanks and the white redmen hollered and ran for their lives. Alabama history was never so boring, but at the end of the show Johnny gave a wan smile and said that one of the ponies, a little tawny thing with a swayed back, looked as if it really could gallop if it had half a field.

By this time Davy Ray was freak-hungry again, so we accompanied him to see a rail-skinny red-haired woman who could make electric bulbs light up by holding them in her mouth. Next was the Al Capone Death Car, the display of which showed bleeding bodies sprawled on a city sidewalk while leering gangsters raked the air with tommy-gun bullets. The actual car, which had a dummy behind the wheel and four dummies standing there gawking at it, was a piece of junk Mr. Sculley would've scorned. We hung in with Davy Ray, as he worked up to speed. The Gator Boy, the Human Caterpillar, and the Giraffe-Necked Woman lured him from behind their canvas folds.

And then we rounded a corner, and we caught that smell.

Just a hint of it, drifting down at the bottom below the reeks of hamburger grease and doughnut fat.

Lizardy, I thought.

"Ben's messed his pants!" Davy Ray said. He should talk.

"Did not!" Ben ought to know by now not to invoke this vicious cycle.

"There it is," Johnny said, and right in front of me was the huge red LOST with THE and WORLD on either side of it.

The trailer had steps that went up into a large, square boxcarlike opening. A dingy brown curtain was pulled across it. At the ticket booth, a man with greasy strands of dark hair combed flat across his bald skull was sitting on a stool, chewing on a toothpick and reading a Jughead comic book. His small, pale blue marbles of eyes flickered up and saw us, and he reached drowsily for a microphone. His voice rasped through a nearby speaker: "Come one, come all! See the beast from the lost world! Come one, come . . ." He lost interest in his spiel and returned to the cartoon balloons.

"Stinks around here," Davy Ray said. "Let's go!"

"Wait a minute," I told him. "Just a minute."

"Why?"

LOST filled up my vision. "I might want to see what this is."

"Don't waste your money on this!" Ben warned. "It'll be a big snake or somethin'!"

"Well, it can't be any dumber than the Death Car!"

They had to agree with that.

"Hey, there's a two-headed bull over yonder!" Davy Ray pointed to the painted canvas. "That's for me!" He started walking off, and Ben took two steps with him but stopped when he realized Johnny and I weren't following. Davy Ray glanced back, scowled, and stopped, too. "It'll be a *gyp!*" he said.

"Maybe," I answered. "But maybe it'll be—"

Something neat, I was about to say.

But there came the sound of a massive body shifting its weight. The trailer groaned. *Boom!* went the noise of bulk hitting wood. The entire trailer shivered, and the man behind the ticket booth reached down at his side and picked up something. Then he started banging on the trailer with a baseball bat studded with nails. I could see where countless nail points had scarred the huge red T of LOST.

Whatever was inside settled down. The trailer ceased its motions. The man put the baseball bat away, his face an expressionless blank.

"Whoa," Ben said quietly. "Mighty big critter in there."

My curiosity was raging. The swampy smell seemed to be keeping customers away, but I had to know. I approached the ticket seller.

"One?" He didn't even look up.

"What is it?" I asked.

"It's from the lost world," he answered. Still he stared at the comic book. His face was gaunt, his cheeks and forehead pitted with acne scars.

343

"Yes sir, but what *is* it?"

This time he did look up. I almost had to step back, because simmering in his eyes was a fierce anger that reminded me of Branlin fury. "If I told you that," he said, sucking noisily on his toothpick, "then it wouldn't be no surprise, would it?"

"Is it . . . like . . . a freak or somethin'?"

"You go in." He smiled coldly, showing little nubs of chewed-down teeth. "Then you tell me what you saw."

"Cory! Come on!" Davy Ray was standing behind me. "This is a gyp, I said!"

"Oh it is, is it?" The man slapped his comic book down. "What do you know, kid? You don't know nothin' but this little blister of a town, do you?"

"I know a gyp when I see it!" He caught himself. "Sir."

"Do you? Boy, you don't know your head from your ass! Get on out of here and quit botherin' me!"

"I sure will!" Davy Ray nodded. "You bet I will! Come on, Cory!" He stalked off, but I stayed. Davy Ray saw I wasn't coming, and he made a noise like a fart and went over to a concession stand near the two-headed bull.

"One," I told the man as I dug a quarter out of my jeans pocket.

"Fifty cents," he said.

"Everythin' else is a quarter!" Ben had come up beside me, with Johnny on my other side.

"This is fifty cents," the man repeated. "Thing's gotta eat. Thing's *always* gotta eat."

I slid the money in front of him. He put the two quarters into a tin can that sounded all but empty, then he tore a ticket and gave me half. "Go up through that curtain and wait for me. There's another curtain on the other side. Don't go through that one till I come up. Hear?" I said I did, and I climbed the steps. The lizardy, swampy odor was terrible, and under that was the sickly-sweet smell of rotting fruit. Before I reached that curtain, I was debating the wisdom of my curiosity. But I pushed through it, and I stood in near darkness. "I'll go, too," I heard Johnny say behind me. Then I waited. I reached out and felt a rough burlap curtain between me and whatever else was in the trailer.

Something rumbled, like a distant freight train.

"Move on in some," the ticket man said, speaking to me as he came up the steps, herding Johnny and Ben. When he pushed the first curtain open, I saw he was holding the nail-studded baseball bat. I gave the other guys room to stand between the curtains. Ben pinched his nostrils shut and said, "That smells *sick!*"

"Likes ripe fruit," the man explained. "Sometimes it goes over."

"What is this thing?" Johnny asked. "And what's the lost world?"

"The lost world is lost! Just like it says. What's lost is no more and can never be again. That get through your skull?"

None of us liked his attitude. Johnny probably could've punched his lights out. But Johnny said, "Yes sir."

"Hey, I'm comin' up!" It was Davy Ray. "Where's everybody?"

The man moved onto the stairs to block his way. "Fifty cents or forget it."

Of course this caused an outburst. I peered through the curtain to watch Davy Ray wrangle with the man. Davy Ray was chewing on a Zero candy bar, the white kind with chocolate nougat in the center. "If you don't shut up," the man warned, "I'm gonna charge you seventy-five cents! Pay up or take a walk!"

Two quarters changed possession. Davy Ray squeezed in with us, and then the man entered muttering sourly. He said to me, "You, boy! Go on through!"

I pushed aside the rough burlap. As I entered, the smell almost knocked me out. The guys filed in behind me, then Mr. Attitude. Four oil lamps, hanging from ceiling hooks, afforded the only light and it was murky at best. In front of me was what appeared to be a big hogpen, enclosed by iron bars the thickness of pythons. Something lay in that pen that was so huge it made my legs go wobbly. I heard Ben gasp behind me. Johnny gave a low whistle. In the pen were piles of rotting, moldy fruit rinds. The fetid decay lay in a soup of greenish-brown mud and, to be delicate here, the mud was adorned with dozens of brown chunks as long as my father's arm and twice as thick. A dark cloud of flies whirled above the pen like a miniature tornado. The smell of all this at close range was bad enough to knock the stripes off a skunk. Little wonder Mr. Attitude's tin can was empty.

"Step up there and take a look!" he said. "Go on, you paid for it!"

"I'm gonna puke!" Ben wailed, and he had to turn and run out.

"I ain't givin' no refunds!" Mr. Attitude hollered after him.

Maybe it was the man's brawling voice. Maybe it was the way we all smelled to that thing in the pen. But suddenly it started heaving itself up from its mud bed, and the huge bulk just kept getting bigger as more of it shucked free from the liquidy mess. The thing gave a single snort that rumbled like a hundred bassoons. Then it lumbered over toward the far side of the trailer, its wet gray flesh glistening with mud and filth, a universe of flies crawling on its hide. With a shriek of shocks and stressed timbers, the entire trailer suddenly began tilting to that side, and all three of us yowled and hollered with the conviction of fear we'd never felt in the haunted house.

"Hold still, you shithead!" Mr. Attitude stood up on a wooden platform. "I said hold still 'fore you throw us over!" He lifted that baseball bat and brought it savagely down.

The sound of that bat smacking flesh made my stomach lurch. I almost lost my carnival feast, but I clenched my teeth together. Mr. Attitude kept hitting the beast: a second time, a third, and a fourth. The creature made no noise, but with the fourth blow it staggered away from the trailer's wall toward the center of the pen again and the trailer righted itself.

"And stay there, ya dumb shit!" Mr. Attitude yelled.

"Are you tryin' to *kill* it, mister?" Davy Ray asked.

"That sonofabitch don't feel no pain! He's got skin like fuckin' armor plate! Hey, don't you be tellin' me my business or I'll throw you outta here on your ass!"

I didn't know if the creature could feel pain or not. All I knew was that I was looking at a big slab of wrinkled gray flesh with dots of blood welling up out of it.

The thing was half the height of an elephant and about as big as our pickup truck. As the thick muscles of its haunches quivered, flies rose lazily into the air. In the murky lamplight, as the creature stood motionless in its mudhole with its stumpy legs mired in rotten fruit rinds and its own excrement, I could see the stubs of three horns rising up from a neckplate of bone covered with leathery gray flesh.

I almost fell down, but I feared what might be on that floor.

"This here's an old thing," Mr. Attitude said. "You know how some turtles can live for two hundred, three hundred years? Well, this thing's so old he makes them turtles look like teenagers. Older'n Methuselah's pecker," he said, and laughed as if this was funny.

"Where'd you find him?" I heard my voice ask, my mind too stunned to connect.

"Bought him for seven hundred dollars, cash on the barrel. Fella had him on the circuit in Louisiana, down in Cajun land. Before that, guy out in Texas was showin' him. Before the Texan, fella in Montana trucked him around. I guess that was in the twenties. Yeah, he's been around some."

Davy Ray said, in a quiet and uneasy voice, "He's bleedin'." He held half of the Zero candy bar down at his side, his appetite vanished.

"Yeah, so what? Gotta smack him some to make him pay attention. Hell, he's got a brain 'bout the size of a walnut, anyhow."

"Where'd he come from?" I asked. "I mean . . . who found him first?"

"It was a long time ago. I don't remember what that Cajun fucker told me. Somethin' about . . . some professor found him. Either in the Amazon jungle or the Belgian Congo, I forget which. Up on some plateau nobody can get to or find again. His name was . . . Professor Chandler . . . no . . ." He frowned. "Callander . . . no, that ain't it." He snapped his fingers. "Professor Challenger! He's the one found it and brung it back! Know what it is? It's a tri . . . a tri—"

"—ceratops," I finished for him. I knew my dinosaurs, and that's no lie.

"Yeah, a tricereytopalis," Mr. Attitude said. "That's just what it is."

"Somebody cut his horns off," Johnny said. He, too, had recognized it, and he walked past me and clamped his hands to the iron bars. "Who cut his horns off, mister?"

"Me, myself, and I. Had to. You shoulda seen them fuckers. Like spears they were. He kept bustin' through the trailer's walls with 'em. Tore right through sheet metal. My chain saw broke all to pieces 'fore I was even half through, had to use a fuckin' ax. He just laid there. That's what he does, just lays there and eats and shits." Mr. Attitude kicked at a white-molded watermelon rind that had somehow been shoved out of the mudhole. "Know how much it costs to keep that old fucker in *fruit* this time of year? Man, that was the dumbest seven hundred dollars I *ever* spent!"

Davy Ray stepped up to the bars beside Johnny. "How come he only eats fruit?"

"Oh, he can eat most anythin'. Once carnival season's over, I feed him garbage and tree bark." Mr. Attitude grinned. "Fruit makes him smell better, y'see."

The triceratops's small black eyes slowly blinked. His massive head moved from one side to the other, searching for a thought. The pen was hardly large enough for him to turn around in. Then he exhaled a long breath and eased down into the mud again, and he stared at nothing with tendrils of blood creeping down his flank.

"Awful tight in there, ain't it?" Davy Ray asked. "I mean . . . don't you ever let him out?"

"Hell, no! How would I get him back in again, genius?" He leaned over the iron bars, which came to his waist when he was standing on the wooden platform. "Hey, shithead!" he yelled. "Why don't you *do* somethin' to earn your fuckin' keep? Why don't you learn to balance a ball on your snout, or jump through a hoop? Thought I could fuckin' *train* you to do some tricks! How come you don't do nothin' but sit there lookin' stupid?" Mr. Attitude's face contorted, and its anger was ugly. "Hey, I'm talkin' to you!" He smacked the beast's back with the baseball bat once and then again, the nails drawing blood. The triceratops's watery eyes closed in what might have been mute suffering. Mr. Attitude lifted the bat for a third blow, his nubby teeth clenched.

"Don't do that, mister," Davy Ray said.

And something in his voice meant it.

The bat paused in its descent. "What'd you say, boy?"

"I said . . . don't do that. Please," he added. "It's not right."

"Might not be right," Mr. Attitude agreed, "but it *is* fun." And he whacked the triceratops across the back a third time with all his strength.

I saw Davy Ray's hand clench as he mashed the remaining half of the Zero candy bar.

"I've had enough," Johnny said. He turned away from the pen and walked past me and out of the trailer.

"Let's go, Davy Ray," I told him.

"It's not right," Davy Ray repeated. Mr. Attitude had stopped beating the beast, and the nails were slicked with red. "Somethin' like this shouldn't be caged up in a mudhole."

"You had your fifty cents' worth," the man said. He sounded drained, sweat glistening on his forehead. I guess it was hard work, whacking those nails in and pulling them out. The act of violence seemed to have sapped some of his anger. "Go on home, country boys," he said.

Davy Ray didn't budge. His eyes reminded me of smoldering coals. "Mister, don't you know what you've *got?*"

"Yep. One big fuckin' headache. You wanna buy him? Hell, I'll cut you a deal! Get your daddy to bring me five hundred dollars, I'll sure as shit unload him in your front yard and he can sleep in your fuckin' bed with you."

Davy Ray was not suckered by this spiel. "It's not right," he said, "to hate somethin' just for bein' alive."

"What do *you* know?" Mr. Attitude sneered. "You don't know shit about *nothin'*, kid! You live twenty more years and see what I seen of this stinkin' world and then you come tell me what to do and what not to do!"

Then Davy Ray did a strange thing. He threw the mashed-up Zero candy bar into the mud right under the triceratops's beaky snout. It made a little *plop* as it went into the liquid. The triceratops just sat there, its eyes heavy-lidded.

"Hey! Don't you be throwin' nothin' in that pen, boy! Both of you just *git!*"

I was on my way out.

I heard a great gobbling sound and looked around to see the triceratops opening its mouth and scooping up the Zero and the surrounding mud like a living bulldozer. The beast chewed a few times and then he tilted his head back to let all the muck slide down his throat.

"Go on!" Mr. Attitude told us. "I'm shuttin' down for the—"

The trailer trembled. The triceratops was standing up, dripping like an ancient swamp oak. I swear his rust-colored tongue, which was as big as a dinner plate, emerged to lick his gray, mud-caked mouth. His head with its three hacked-off horn stumps tilted toward Davy Ray, and he began lumbering forward.

It was like watching a tank build up to speed. And then he lowered his head to collide with the iron bars, and the thick plate of bone made a noise like the popping together of two giants' football helmets. The triceratops stepped back three paces and with a snorting grunt he crashed his head against the iron bars again.

"Hey! Hey!" Mr. Attitude was yelling.

The triceratops shoved forward, his feet or paws or whatever they were sliding in the mud. His strength was awesome; muscles rippled beneath the elephantine flesh, and flies fled the quake. The iron bars groaned and began to bend outward, bolts making a squealing noise as they came loose.

"Hey, quit it! *Quit!*" Mr. Attitude started beating the triceratops again, and droplets of blood flew from the nails. The beast paid no attention, but kept bending the bars in his effort, I realized, to get to Davy Ray. "You sonofabitch! You stupid old fucker!" the man hollered as the baseball bat rose and fell. He looked at us, his eyes wild. "Get out! You've drivin' him crazy!"

I grabbed Davy Ray's arm and pulled at him. He came with me, and we heard more bolts breaking loose behind us. The trailer started rocking like a demonic cradle; the triceratops, it seemed to me, was throwing a fit. We got down the steps, and saw Johnny standing upwind while Ben—a perfect picture of misery—was sitting on an upturned soft-drink case with his face buried in his hands.

"He was tryin' to get out," Davy Ray said as we watched the trailer shake, rattle, and roll. "Did you see that?"

349

"Yeah, I did. He went crazy."

"Bet he never had a candy bar before," he said. "Not in his whole life. He likes Zeros as much as I do, huh? Boy, I've got a whole boxful at home he'd like to get into, I'll bet!"

I wasn't sure the taste of a candy bar had done it, but I said, "I think you're right."

The trailer's rocking subsided. In a few minutes Mr. Attitude came out. His clothes and face were splattered with gobbets of mud and dookey. Both Davy Ray and I started shaking trying to hold in our belly laughs. Mr. Attitude drew the curtain, pulled a door shut, and locked it with a chain and padlock. Then he looked at us and exploded. *"Get outta here, I said! Go on, before I—"* He came at us, waving the nail-studded baseball bat, and we let our laughter go and ran.

The carnival was closing for the night, the midway's crowd dwindling, the rides shutting down and the freak-show barkers hanging up their superlatives. The lights began to go off, one by one.

We walked to where we'd left our bikes. The air had gotten frosty. Winter was on the march.

Ben, his load somewhat lightened, had returned to the land of the living and was chattering happily. Johnny didn't say much, but he did mention how neat the motorcycle riders were. I said I could build a haunted house that would scare the pickles out of people, if I had a mind to. Davy Ray, however, said nothing.

Until we got to our bikes. Then Davy Ray said, "I wouldn't like to live that way."

"What way?" Ben asked.

"In that pen. You know. Like the thing from the lost world."

Ben shrugged. "Ahhhhh, he's probably used to it by now."

"Bein' used to somethin'," Davy Ray answered, "is not the same as likin' it. Numb nuts."

"Hey, don't get mad at *me!*"

"I ain't mad at anybody." Davy Ray sat on his bike, his hands clenching the grips. "It's just . . . I sure would hate to live that way. Could hardly move. Sure couldn't see the sun. And every day would be just like the day before, even if you lived a million days. I can't stand the thought of that. Can you, Cory?"

"It would be pretty awful," I agreed.

"That man'll kill it real soon, the way he's beatin' it. Then he can go dump it on a garbage pile and be done with it." Davy Ray looked up at the sickle moon, his breath white. "Thing wasn't *real*, anyhow. That man was a low-down liar. It was a deformed rhinoceros, that's all it was. So, see? It *was* a gyp, like I told you." And he started pedaling away before I could argue with him.

That was our visit to the Brandywine Carnival.

Early Saturday morning, sometime around three, the civil defense siren atop the courthouse began yowling. Dad got dressed so fast he put his underwear on backward, and he took the pickup to go find out what was happening. I thought the Russians were bombing us, myself. When Dad returned near four o'clock, he told us what he'd learned.

One of the carnival's attractions had escaped. Broken right out of its trailer and left it in kindling. The man who owned it had been sleeping in another trailer. I later heard Dad tell Mom it was a trailer occupied by a red-haired woman who did strange things with light bulbs. Anyway, this thing had gotten loose and rampaged down the midway like a Patton tank, tearing through tents like they were heaps of autumn leaves. This thing had evidently run right down Merchants Street and smashed into several stores, then had turned a number of parked cars into Mr. Sculley's fodder. Had to have done ten thousand dollars' worth of damage, Dad said Mayor Swope had told him. And they hadn't caught the thing yet. It had gotten into the woods and headed for the hills while everybody was still jumping into their boots. Except Mr. Wynn Gillie had seen it when it had crashed its head through the bedroom wall of his house, and Mr. Gillie and his wife were now being treated for shock at the hospital in Union Town.

The beast from the lost world was free, and the carnival left without him.

I let it wait until Sunday evening. Then I called the Callan house from Johnny's, and we used the telephone in the back room while his folks were watching TV. Davy Ray's little brother Andy answered. I asked to speak to Mr. Callan.

"What can I do for you, Cory?" he asked.

"I was callin' for my dad," I told him. "We're gonna be takin' Rebel's pen down this week, and we were wonderin' if you might have . . . oh, a chain cutter we could use?"

"Well, you'll probably need wire cutters for that job. There's a difference."

"There's some chain needs to be cut, too," I said.

"Okay, then. No problem. I'll have Davy Ray bring it over tomorrow afternoon, if that'll suit you. You know, I bought that chain cutter a few years ago but I never use it. Down in the basement in a box somewhere."

"Davy Ray'll probably know where it is," I said.

351

Mr. Attitude had slinked away, most likely because a seven-hundred-dollar loss was cheaper than a ten-thousand-dollar vacation in jail. Many mighty hunters went out on the trail of the beast from the lost world, but they returned with dookey on their boots and their egos busted.

I have a picture in my mind.

I see the park after the carnival has packed up and gone. It is clear again, except for a few scatters of sawdust, crushed Dixie cups, and ticket stubs the cleanup crew has left like a dog marking its territory.

But this year the wind blows Zero wrappers before it, and they make a sound like giggling as they pass.

FOUR
Winter's Cold
Truth

———

**A Solitary Traveler—Faith—Snippets
of the Quilt—Mr. Moultry's Castle—
Sixteen Drops of Blood—The Stranger
Among Us**

1

A Solitary Traveler

"**Y**our father's lost his job," Mom said.

I had just walked in from school, with Thanksgiving four days behind us. This news hit me like a blow to the belly. Mom's face was grim, her eyes already seeing days of hardship ahead. She knew the red-ink realities of her baking business; Big Paul's Pantry had an immense section of pies and cakes as well as milk in disposable plastic jugs.

"They told him when he went in," she continued. "They gave him two weeks' pay and a bonus, and they said they couldn't afford him anymore."

"Where is he?" I dropped my books on the nearest flat surface.

"Gone somewhere, about an hour ago. He sat around most of the day, couldn't eat a bite of lunch or hardly talk. Tried to sleep some, but he couldn't. I believe he's about wrecked, Cory."

"Do you know where he's gone?"

"No. He just said he was goin' somewhere to think."

"Okay. I'm gonna try to find him."

"Where're you goin'?"

"Saxon's Lake, first," I told her, and I walked out to Rocket.

She followed me to the porch. "Cory, you be care—" She stopped herself. It was time to admit that I was on my way to being a man. "I hope you find him," she offered.

I rode away, under a low gray sky threatening sleet.

It was a good haul out there from my house. The wind was blowing against me. As I pedaled on Route Ten, my head thrust forward over the handlebars, I looked cautiously from side to side at the wind-stripped woods. The beast from the lost world was still at large. That in itself wasn't a fearful thing, since I doubted the triceratops wanted to have much to do with the entrapping mudhole of civilization. What made me cautious was the fact that two days before Thanksgiving Marty Barklee, who brought the newspapers in from Birmingham before the sun, had been driving along this very road when a massive bulk had come out of the woods and slammed into his car so hard that its tires left the pavement. I'd seen Mr. Barklee's car. The passenger side was crushed in as if kicked by a giant steel boot, the window smashed all to pieces. Mr. Barklee had said the monster had literally hit and run. I believed the triceratops had staked out his claim in these dense and swampy woods around Saxon's Lake, and any vehicles on Route Ten were in jeopardy because the triceratops thought they were rival dinosaurs. Whether he would think Rocket was worth a snort and charge, I didn't know. I just knew to keep pedaling and looking. Evidently, Mr. Attitude had not realized that instead of a big gray lump that sat snoozing in the mud, he owned a Patton tank that could outrun a car. Freedom will sure speed your legs, that's for sure. And for all its age and size, the triceratops was at heart a boy.

Other than having Davy Ray show up at my front door with a chain cutter, I never let on what I suspected. Johnny didn't either, and we never told Ben because sometimes Ben had a runaway mouth. Davy Ray didn't speak a word about it other than to remark he hoped they just let the creature live out its days in peace. I was never exactly sure, but it seemed like the kind of thing Davy Ray might have done. How was he to know the triceratops was going to do ten thousand dollars' worth of damage? Well, glass could be replaced and metal hammered out. Mr. Wynn Gillie and his wife moved to Florida like they'd been wanting to do for five or six years. Before Mr. Gillie left, Mr. Dollar told him the swamps of Florida were full of dinosaurs, that they came to your back door begging for table scraps. Mr. Gillie turned paste-white and started shaking until "Jazzman" Jackson told him Mr. Dollar was only pulling his leg.

As I turned the curve that would take me past Saxon's Lake, I saw Dad's pickup truck parked over near the red rock cliff. I coasted, trying to figure out what I was going to say. Suddenly I had run out of words. This was not going to be like feeding the magic box; this was real life, and it was going to be very, very hard.

I didn't see him anywhere around the truck as I eased Rocket onto the kickstand. And then I did see him: a small figure, sitting on a granite boulder halfway around the lake. He was staring out across the black, wind-rippled water. As I watched him, I saw him lift a bottle to his lips and drink deeply. Then he lowered the bottle, and sat there staring.

I began walking to him through a morass of reeds and sticker-bushes. The red mud squished under my shoes, and I saw my father's footprints in it. He had come this way many times before, because he'd trampled down a narrow trail through the worst of the undergrowth. In doing this he had unconsciously continued his work as a father, by making the path just a little easier for the son.

When I got nearer, he saw me coming. He didn't wave. He lowered his head, and I knew he, too, had run out of words.

I stood ten feet away from him on the boulder, which at one time had been part of the lip of Saxon's Quarry. He sat with his head bowed and his eyes closed, and beside him was a plastic jug half-full of grape juice. I realized he had gone shopping at Big Paul's Pantry.

The wind shrilled around me and made the trees' bare branches clatter. "You all right?" I asked.

"No," he said.

"Mom told me."

"Figured."

I dug my hands into the pockets of my fleece-lined denim jacket, and I gazed out over the dark, dark water. Dad didn't say anything for a long time, and neither did I. Then he cleared his throat. "Want some grape juice?"

"No sir."

"Got plenty left."

"No sir, I'm not thirsty."

He lifted his face to me. In the hard, cold light he looked terribly old. I thought I could see his skull beneath the thin flesh, and this sight frightened me. It was like looking at someone you loved very much, slowly dying. His emotions had already been balanced on the raw edge. I remembered his desperately scribbled questions in the middle of the night, and his unspoken fears that he was about to suffer a breakdown. I saw all too clearly that my father—not a mythic hero, not a superman, but just a good man—was a solitary traveler in the wilderness of anguish.

"I did everythin' they asked me to," he said. "Worked a double route. Picked up the slack when it needed pickin' up. Got there early and stayed late doin' stock work. I did whatever they wanted." He looked up, trying to find the sun, but the clouds were plates of iron. "They said, 'Tom, you have to understand how it is.' They said, 'We've got to cut to the bone to keep Green Meadows afloat.' And you know what else they said, Cory?"

"No sir."

"They said home milk delivery is as dead as the dinosaurs. They said there's no room for it in all those shelves of plastic jugs. They

357

said the future is gonna be easy come and easy go, and that's what people want." He laced his fingers together, a muscle in his gaunt jaw working. "That's not what *I* want."

"We'll be all right," I said.

"Oh, yeah." He nodded. "Yes, we will be. I'll find somethin' else. I went by the hardware store before I came here and wrote up an application. Mr. Vandercamp Junior might need a truck driver. Heck, I'd work behind a cash register. But I really did think that in three more years I'd be an assistant foreman on the loadin' dock. I really did. Dumb, huh?"

"You didn't know."

"I *never* know," he said. "That's my trouble."

The water rippled as the wind swept across it, kicking up little wavelets. In the woods beyond, unseen crows cawed. "It's cold, Dad," I said. "We ought to go home."

"I can't wait for your granddad to find out about this." He was talking about the Jaybird. "Won't he have a fine old laugh?"

"Mom and me won't be laughin'," I said. "Neither will anybody else."

He picked up the grape juice jug and took another long swig. "Went by Big Paul's Pantry, too. I walked in there and saw all that milk. A white sea of it." He looked at me again. His lips were blue. "I want things to stay the way they are. I don't want a gum-chewin' girl who doesn't know my name to take my money and not even smile when I ask her how she's doin'. I don't want supermarkets open until eight o'clock at night and full of lights that hurt your eyes. Families ought to be home together at eight o'clock at night, not out at the supermarket buyin' stuff that the big banners hangin' from the ceilin' say you ought to buy. I mean . . . if it goes so far, even in the little ways, we can't ever go back. And someday somebody'll say, 'Oh, it's so fine we can go to the supermarket after dark and we can pick and choose from shelves of stuff we've never even heard of before, but whatever happened to those milkmen, or those fellas used to sell watermelons out of the back of their trucks, or that woman who sold fresh vegetables right out of her garden and smiled like the sun when you said good mornin'?' Somebody'll say, 'Oh, they sell all those things at the supermarket now, and you don't have to go hither and yon to buy what you need, it's all under one roof. And why don't they do that to everythin'? Just put a whole town's stores under one roof so the rain won't fall on you and you won't get cold. Wouldn't that be a jim-dandy idea?'" My father worked his knuckles for a moment. "And then you'll have stores and roads and houses, but you won't have towns anymore. Not the way they are now. And you'll walk into one of those stores under one roof and you'll ask for somethin' and the gum-chewin' girl'll say no, we don't have that. We don't have that, and we can't get it for you because they don't make that anymore. That's not what people want, you see. People only want what the big banners hangin' from the ceilin' tell them to want. We only have those things, and they're made by machines a thousand a minute. But they're perfect, she'll say. Not an imperfection in the lot. And when you use it up or get tired of it or when the banners change, you can just throw it away because it's made to be thrown away. Now! she'll say, How many of these perfect things do you need today, and please hurry because there's a line behind you."

He was silent. I heard his knuckles crack.

"It's just one supermarket," I said.

"The first one," he replied.

He narrowed his eyes, and for maybe a minute he stared out at the lake as the wind scrawled patterns across its surface.

"I hear you," he said softly.

I knew who he was talking to. "Dad? Can we go home?"

"You go on. I'm gonna sit here and listen to my friend."

I heard the wind and the crows, but I knew my father heard another voice. "What's he sayin', Dad?"

"He's sayin' the same thing he always says. He's sayin' he's not gonna let me alone until I come with him, down in the dark."

Tears came to my eyes. I blinked them away. "You're not gonna go, are you?"

"No, son," he said. "Not today."

I almost told him about Dr. Lezander. My mouth opened, but my brain posed a question: What would I tell my father? That Dr. Lezander didn't like milk and was a night owl, and Vernon Thaxter believed those were the qualities of a killer? What came out of my mouth was: "The Lady knows things, Dad. She can help us if we ask her."

"The Lady," he repeated. His voice sounded thick. "She pulled a good one on Biggun Blaylock, didn't she?"

"Yes sir, she did. She could help us if we go see her."

"Maybe so. Maybe not." He frowned, as if the thought of asking the Lady's help caused him deep pain. It was surely no worse than the pain already lodged and festering. "I'll tell you what," he said as the frown went away. "I'll ask my friend what he thinks."

I was scared for him. Very, very scared. "Please come home soon," I told him.

"I will." He nodded. "Soon."

I left him there, sitting on the boulder under the low gray clouds. When I made my way to Rocket, I looked back and saw him standing on the boulder's edge. His attention was fixed on the water below him, as if he were searching for the trace of a car in those terrible depths. I started to call to him, to warn him away from the edge, but then he walked back to where he'd been and sat down again.

Not today, he'd said. I had to believe him.

I pedaled home the way I'd come, and I had way too much on my mind to even give a thought to the beast from the lost world.

The following days were gray and cold, the hills around Zephyr brown as the grass on Poulter Hill. We entered December, the jolly month. Dad was around some days when I got home from school, and some days he was not. Mom, who suddenly appeared strained and tired beyond her years, said he was out looking for work. I hoped he wasn't back on that boulder, contemplating the future in a mirror of black glass.

The mothers of my friends were supportive. They started bringing over covered dishes, baskets of biscuits, homemade canned goods, and such. Mr. Callan promised to bring us some venison from his first kill of the season. Mom insisted on baking everyone cakes in return. Dad ate the food, but I could tell it was killing him to take such obvious charity. Evidently the hardware store didn't need a truck driver, nor did it need another man behind the cash register. Often at night I heard Dad up and about, rambling around the house. It started being that he slept much of the day, until eleven or so, and remained awake until after four in the morning. It was a night owl's hours.

One Saturday afternoon Mom asked me to ride to the Woolworth's on Merchants Street and pick her up a box of cake pans. I started out, Rocket easy beneath me. I went to the store, bought the cake pans, and started back.

I stopped in front of the Bright Star Cafe.

Mr. Eugene Osborne worked in there. Mr. Eugene Osborne had been in the Big Red One infantry division. And Mr. Eugene Osborne knew German curse words when he heard them.

This had been nagging at me, like a small little demon's voice at the back of my head, since the night we'd gone to the Brandywine Carnival. How could a parrot know German curse words if its owner spoke no German? And something else I remembered Mr. Osborne saying: *Wasn't just cursin', either. There were other German words in there, but they were all garbled up.*

How could such a thing be?

I left Rocket outside and walked into the Bright Star.

It wasn't much of a place, just a few tables and booths and a counter where people could sit on stools and jaw with the two waitresses, old Mrs. Madeline Huckabee and younger Carrie French. I have to say that Miss French got most of the attention, because she was blond and pretty and Mrs. Huckabee resembled two miles of bad road. But Mrs. Huckabee had been a waitress at the Bright Star long before I was born, and she ruled the cafe with an iron glance. The Bright Star was by no means very active this time of day, but a few people were inside drinking coffee, most of them elderly retired men. Mr. Cathcoate was among them, sitting in a booth reading a newspaper. The television above the counter was on. And sitting at the counter grinning at Miss French was none other than whale-sized Mr. Dick Moultry.

He saw me, and his grin vanished like a ghost at dawn.

"Hi, there!" Miss French said, offering me a sunny smile as I approached the counter. If it weren't for her buck teeth, she might have been as lovely as Chile Willow. "What can I do for you?"

"Is Mr. Osborne here?"

"Sure is."

"Can I talk to him, please?"

"Hold on a minute." She went to the window between the counter and the kitchen. I noticed Mr. Moultry's huge belly pressing against the counter's edge as he leaned forward to get a look at her legs. "Eugene? Somebody wants to talk to you!"

"Who?" I heard him ask.

"Who?" she asked me. Miss French didn't move in my circles, and I didn't come into the Bright Star enough to warrant recognition.

"Cory Mackenson."

"Oh, are you Tom's boy?" she inquired, and I nodded. "Tom's boy!" she told Mr. Osborne.

My dad, like the Beach Boys, got around. I felt Mr. Moultry watching me. He took a loud slurp of coffee, trying to get my attention, but I didn't favor him with it.

Mr. Osborne walked through a swinging door. He was wearing an apron and a white cap, and he wiped his hands on a cloth. "Afternoon," he said. "What can I do for you?"

Mr. Moultry was leaning forward, all ears and belly. I said, "Can we sit down? Over there, maybe?" I motioned toward a back booth.

"Guess so. Lead the way."

When we'd gotten situated, with my back to Mr. Moultry, I said,

"I was at Miss Glass's house when you brought Winifred in for her piano lesson."

"I remember that."

"You remember the parrot? You said it was cursin' in German."

"If I know German, it was. And I do."

"Do you remember what else the parrot was sayin'?"

Mr. Osborne leaned back in the booth. He cocked his head to one side, his hand with its U.S. ARMY tattoo on the fingers toying with a fork from the place setting. "What's all this about, if you don't mind me askin'?"

"Nothin' special." I shrugged. "It just got my curiosity up, that's all."

"Your curiosity, huh?" He smiled faintly. "You came in here to ask me what a parrot said?"

"Yes sir."

"That was almost three weeks ago. How come you didn't want to know before now?"

"I guess I had other things on my mind." I *had* wanted to know, of course, but with the escape of the beast from the lost world and Dad's losing his job, I hadn't given it the highest priority.

"I don't rightly remember what it said, except for the spicy words I couldn't repeat to you without Tom's permission."

"I didn't know my dad came in here."

"Sometimes he does. He came in to fill out an application."

"Oh. Gosh," I said. "I didn't know my dad could *cook.*"

"Dishwasher," Mr. Osborne said, watching me carefully. I think I flinched a little. "Actually, Mrs. Huckabee does all the hirin'. Runs this place like boot camp, she does."

I nodded, trying not to meet his steady gaze.

"That parrot," he said, and his smile widened. "That blue parrot. Cursed a blue streak. Not surprisin', though, is it? Since he belonged to Miss Blue Glass, I mean."

"I guess not." I hadn't known any adults called her Miss Blue Glass.

"What's this about, Cory? Really."

"I want to be a writer," I answered, though I don't know why. "Stuff like this is interestin' to me."

"A *writer?* Like writin' stories and all?"

"Yes sir."

"Seems like that would be a hard row to hoe." He put his elbows on the table. "Is this . . . like . . . research for a story or somethin'?"

"Yes sir." I saw a ray of light. "Yes sir, it sure is!"

362

"You're not writin' a story about Miss Blue Glass, are you?"

"I'm writin' . . . a story about a parrot," I said. "That speaks German."

"Are you, now? Well, how about that! When I was your age, I wanted to be a detective or a soldier. I got my wish on one count." He looked at his tattooed fingers. "I think I might've been better off bein' a detective," he said with a quiet sigh that spoke volumes about what real-life soldiering was as opposed to playing out scenes from *Combat* in the woods.

"Can you remember what else that parrot said, Mr. Osborne?"

He grunted, but his smile was still friendly. "If you've got to have determination to be a writer, you're well on your way. Is knowin' all this so important to you?"

"Yes sir. It's real important."

Mr. Osborne paused, thinking it over. Then he said, "It was all jumbled up, really. Didn't make a whole lot of sense."

"I'd just like to know."

"Let's see, then. Got to crank my mind back some. I'll tell you a secret." He leaned forward a little. "When you work with Mrs. Huckabee, you hear a lot of blue language." I looked around for her, but she was either in the kitchen or the rest room. "I remember the parrot sayin' somethin' about—" He closed his eyes, bringing it back. "Who knows?"

"Can't you remember?" I prodded.

"No, that's it." His eyes opened. "'Who knows?' That's what the parrot was sayin' when it wasn't spoutin' off the curses."

"Who knows what?" I asked.

"Search me. Just 'Who knows?' is all I could get out of it. That, and what I thought sounded like a name."

"A *name*? What was it?"

"Hannaford, I think it was. At least it sounded like it was close to that."

Hannah Furd, I thought.

"I could be wrong, though. I only heard the name once. But I'm not wrong about the cursin', believe you me!"

"Do you remember somethin' Miss Green . . . uh . . . Miss Katharina Glass said about the parrot goin' crazy when that song was played?" I tried to think of the name of it. "'Beautiful Dream'?"

"'Dreamer,'" he corrected me. "Oh, yeah. That's the song Miss Blue Glass taught *me*."

"Taught *you*?"

"That's right. I always wanted to play a musical instrument. I took lessons from Miss Blue Glass . . . oh, I guess it was four years ago when she was teachin' full-time. She had a lot of older students, and she taught us all that song. Now that you mention it, I don't recall that parrot screamin' around back then like he did that night. Funny, huh?"

"Strange." It was my turn to correct him.

"Yeah. Well, I'd best get back to work." He'd seen Mrs. Huckabee emerge from the rest room, and she was dragon enough to scare a soldier. "Does that help you any?"

"I think so," I said. "I'm not sure yet."

Mr. Osborne stood up. "Hey, how about puttin' me in that story?"

"What story?"

He looked at me oddly again. "The story you're writin' about the blue parrot."

"Oh, that story! Yes sir, I sure will!"

"Say somethin' nice about me," he requested, and he started toward the kitchen door again. Some man in a brown uniform was on television, raising a ruckus.

"Hey, Eugene!" Mr. Moultry hollered. "Get a load of this jackass!"

"Mr. Osborne?" I asked, and he gave me his attention before he looked at the television set. "Do you think Miss Blue Glass would mind playin' that song again, with the parrot in the room? And maybe you could listen to it and see what it was sayin'?"

"I think that'd be kinda difficult," he said.

"Sir?"

"Miss Blue Glass took that parrot to Dr. Lezander a couple of weeks ago. It had a brain fever or somethin' birds get. That's what the doc told her. Anyhow, the parrot kicked the bucket. What is it, Dick?"

"Lookit this guy!" Mr. Moultry said, motioning to the man snarling on the television screen. "Name's Lincoln Rockwell! Sonofagun's the head of the American Nazi Party, if you can believe that garbage!"

"American Nazis?" I saw the back of Mr. Osborne's neck redden. "You mean I helped beat their butts over in Europe, and now they're right here in the U.S. of A.?"

"Says they're gonna take over the country!" Mr. Moultry told him. "Listen to him go on, it'll split your ribs!"

"If I could get hold of him, I'd split his ugly *head!*"

I was on my way out, my mind heavy with thoughts. Then I heard

Mr. Moultry—whom ex-Sheriff Amory had said was a member of the Ku Klux Klan—laugh and say, "Well, that's one thing he's got right! I say ship all the niggers back to Africa! I sure as blazes wouldn't want one in my *house*, like a certain somebody invites that Lightfoot nigger right into their front door!"

I had caught this remark, and I knew who it was aimed at. I stopped and looked at him. Mr. Moultry was grinning and talking to Mr. Osborne, the man on the television screen going on about "racial purity," but Mr. Moultry was watching me from the corner of his eye. "Yeah, my house is my castle! I sure as blazes wouldn't stink my castle up by askin' a nigger to come in and make hisself at home! Would you, Eugene?"

"Lincoln Rockwell, huh?" Mr. Osborne said. "That's a hell of a name for a Nazi."

"Seems like some people would know better than to be friends with niggers, don't it, Eugene?" Mr. Moultry plowed on, baiting me.

At last what was being said got through to Mr. Osborne. He regarded Dick Moultry as one might look at rancid cheese. "A man named Ernie Graverson saved my life in Europe, Dick. He was blacker'n the ace of spades."

"Oh . . . listen . . . I didn't mean no . . ." Mr. Moultry's grin was pathetic. "Well," he said as he struggled for his dignity, "there's always one or two gonna have the brains of a white man instead of a gorilla."

"I think," Mr. Osborne said, clamping that U.S. ARMY hand on Mr. Moultry's shoulder and putting some muscle into his grip, "you'd better shut your mouth, Dick."

Mr. Moultry didn't make another peep.

I left the Bright Star, and the brown-uniformed man who was being interviewed on television. I pedaled Rocket home, the cake pans in Rocket's basket. But all the way I was puzzling over the blue parrot—the recently deceased blue parrot, that is—who spoke German.

When I got home, Dad was sleeping in his chair. The Alabama game on the radio had ended before I went to the Woolworth's, and now the radio was tuned to a country music station. I delivered the cake pans to Mom and then watched my father sleep. He was curled up, his arms gripped across his chest. Trying to hold himself together, I thought. He made a soft husking noise, his mouth on the verge of a snore. Something passed through his mind that made him flinch. His eyes came open, red-rimmed, and he seemed to stare right at me for a couple of seconds before his eyes closed again.

I didn't like the way his face looked in sleep. It looked sad and starved, though our food was plentiful. It looked defeated. There was honor in being a dishwasher, of course. I'm not saying there's not, because every labor has its share of honor and necessity. But I couldn't help thinking that he must be on despair's front porch, to have to walk into the Bright Star Cafe and apply to be a dishwasher when assistant foreman of the dairy's loading dock had been so very close. His face suddenly twisted in the grip of a daymare, his mouth letting loose a quiet groan. Even in sleep, he couldn't escape for long.

I walked into my room, shut the door, and I opened one of the seven mystic drawers. I brought out the White Owl cigar box, lifted its lid, and looked at the feather under my desk lamp.

Yes, I decided, my heartbeat quickening. Yes.

It could be a parrot's feather.

But it was emerald green. Miss Blue Glass's German-cursing parrot had been turquoise, not a speck of any other color on it except for the yellow of its beak.

Too bad Miss Green Glass hadn't been the one with the parrot, I thought. That way it would've been emerald green for—

—sure, I thought. And suddenly I felt as if I'd just leaped off a red rock cliff.

Something Miss Blue Glass had said when Miss Green Glass refused to feed the parrot a cracker for fear of losing her fingers.

Three words.

I.

Fed.

Yours.

Your what? Parrot?

Had both Glass sisters, who lived their lives in a strange agreement of mimicry and competition, each owned a parrot? Had there been a second parrot—this one emerald green and missing a feather—somewhere else in that house, as silent as the first was raucous?

A phone call would tell me.

I gripped the feather in my palm. My heart was pounding as I left my room, headed for the telephone. I didn't know the number, of course; I'd have to look it up in the slim directory.

Before I could get to the Glass number, the phone rang.

I said, "I'll get it!" and picked it up.

I would remember for the rest of my life the voice that spoke.

"Cory, this is Mrs. Callan. Let me speak to your mother, please."

The voice was tight and scared. Instantly I knew something was terribly wrong. "Mom!" I shouted. "Mom, it's Mrs. Callan!"

"Don't wake your father!" Mom scolded when she came to the phone, but a grunt and rustle told me it was too late. "Hello, Diane. How are—" She stopped. I saw her smile break. *"What?"* she whispered. "Oh . . . my Jesus . . ."

"What is it? What is it?" I asked. Dad came in, bleary-eyed.

"Yes, we will," Mom was saying. "Of course. Yes. As soon as we can. Oh, Diane, I'm so sorry!" When she returned the receiver to its cradle, her eyes were full of tears and her face bleached with shock. She looked at Dad, and then at me. "Davy Ray's been shot," she said. My hand opened, and the green feather drifted away.

Within five minutes we were in the pickup truck, headed to the hospital in Union Town. I sat between my folks, my mind fogged with what Mom had told me. Davy Ray and his father had gone hunting today. Davy Ray had been excited about being with his dad, out in the winter-touched woods on the trail of deer. They had been coming down a hill, Mrs. Callan had said. Just an ordinary hill. But Davy Ray had stepped into a gopher hole hidden under dead leaves and fallen forward, and as he'd fallen his rifle had gotten caught up beneath him, aimed at his lungs and heart. The rifle had gone off on the impact of body and earth. Mr. Callan, not a man in the best physical shape, had picked up his son in his arms and run a mile through the woods with him back to their truck.

Davy Ray had gone into emergency surgery, Mom said. The damage was very bad.

The hospital was a building of red stone and glass. I thought it looked small to be such an important place. We went in through the emergency entrance, where a nurse with silver hair told us where to go. In a waiting room with stark white walls, we found Davy Ray's parents. Mr. Callan was wearing camouflage-print hunting clothes with blood all over the front, a sight that knocked the breath out of me. He had daubed olive green greasepaint on his cheeks and across the bridge of his nose. It was smeared, and looked like the most horrible bruise. I guess he was in too much shock to even wash his face; what was soap and water compared to flesh and blood? He still had forest dirt crusted under his fingernails. He was frozen in the instant of disaster. Mrs. Callan and Mom hugged each other, and Mrs. Callan began to cry. Dad stood with Mr. Callan at a window. Davy Ray's little brother Andy wasn't there, probably dropped off at a relative's or neighbor's house. He was much too young to understand what a knife was doing inside Davy Ray.

I sat down and tried to find something to read. My eyes couldn't focus on the magazine pages. "So fast," I heard Mr. Callan say. "It happened so fast." Mom sat with Mrs. Callan and they held hands. A bell bonged somewhere in the hospital's halls, and a voice over a loudspeaker called for Dr. Scofield. A man in a blue sweater looked into the waiting room, and everybody gave him their rapt attention but he said, "Any of you folks the Russells?" He went away, searching for some other suffering family.

The minister from the Union Town Presbyterian Church, where the Callans belonged, entered and asked us all to link hands and pray. I held one of Mr. Callan's hands; it was damp with nervous moisture. I knew the power of prayer, but I was through being selfish. I wanted Davy Ray to be all right, of course, and that's what I prayed for with all my heart, but I would never dream of wishing Rebel's death-in-life on a force of nature like Davy Ray.

Johnny Wilson and his mother and father showed up. Johnny's father, a stoic like his son, spoke quietly to Mr. Callan but showed no emotion. Mrs. Wilson and my mom sat on either side of Mrs. Callan, who couldn't do much but stare at the floor and say, "He's a good boy, he's such a good boy," over and over again, as if preparing herself to argue with God for Davy Ray's life.

Johnny and I didn't know what to say to each other. This was the worst thing either of us had ever been through. Ben and his parents came in a few minutes after the Wilsons, and then some of Davy Ray's relatives. The Presbyterian minister took Mr. and Mrs. Callan away with him, for more intimate prayer, I presumed, and Ben, Johnny, and I stood out in the hallway talking about what had happened. "He's gonna be okay," Ben said. "My dad says this is a real good hospital."

"My dad says Davy Ray was lucky it didn't kill him right off," Johnny said. "He says he knew a boy who shot himself in the stomach, and he didn't last but a couple of hours."

I checked my Timex. Davy Ray had been in the operating room for four hours. "He'll make it," I told the others. "He's strong. He'll make it."

Another hour crept slowly past. Night had fallen, and with it a cold mist. Mr. Callan had washed the greasepaint from his face, scrubbed the dirt from beneath his fingernails, and accepted the loan of a green hospital shirt. "That's my last huntin' trip," he said to my father. "I swear to Jesus it is. When Davy Ray gets out of this, we're strippin' the gun rack clear to the wood." He put his hand to his face and choked back a sob. Dad put his arm around Mr. Callan's shoulder. "Know what he said to me today, Tom? Wasn't ten minutes before it happened. He said, 'If we see it, we won't shoot at it, will we? We're just out huntin' deer, aren't we? We won't shoot it if we see it.' You know what he was talkin' about?''

Dad shook his head.

"The thing that ran away from the carnival. Now, what do you think got that in his mind?"

"I don't know," Dad said.

It hurt me to hear these things.

A doctor with short-cropped gray hair and wire-rimmed glasses came in. Instantly the Callans were on their feet. "May I speak with both of you outside, please?" he asked. Mom gripped Dad's hand. I knew, as well, that this was not good news.

When they returned, Mr. Callan told everyone Davy Ray was out of the operating room. Davy Ray's condition was guarded, and the night would tell the tale. He thanked everyone for coming and showing their support, and he said we all ought to go home and get some sleep.

Ben and his parents stayed until ten, and then they left. The Wilsons went home a half-hour later. Gradually, the relatives thinned out. The Presbyterian minister said he would stay as long as they wanted him there. Mrs. Callan grasped my mother's hand, and asked her not to go just yet. So we waited in that room with the stark white walls as the mist turned to rain, the rain stopped, fog drifted across the windows, and mist returned.

Past midnight, Mr. Callan went to get a cup of coffee from a machine down the hall. He returned a few minutes later with the gray-haired doctor. "Diane!" he said excitedly. "Diane, he's come to!"

They rushed out, their hands linked.

Ten minutes passed. Then, after what seemed an eternity, Mr. Callan walked back into the waiting room. I have seen cigarette burns with more life than his eyes possessed. "Cory?" he said softly. "Davy Ray wants to see you."

I was afraid.

"Go on, Cory," my father urged. "It's all right."

I stood up, and I followed Mr. Callan.

The doctor was standing outside Davy Ray's room, talking to their minister. They made a grim picture. Mr. Callan opened the door, and I walked in. Mrs. Callan was in there, sitting in a chair beside a bed enveloped by a filmy oxygen tent. Plastic tubing snaked up from the figure that lay under a pale blue sheet and connected with bags full of blood and clear liquid. A machine showed a green dot, blipping slowly on a round black screen. Mrs. Callan saw me and leaned over toward the head under that tent. "Davy Ray? He's here."

I heard the sound of labored breathing, and I smelled Clorox and Pine Sol. Rain began to tap against the window. Mrs. Callan said, "Cory, sit here," and she stood up. I went to her. Mrs. Callan picked up one of Davy Ray's hands; it was as white as Italian marble. "I'll be right here, Davy Ray." She summoned up a smile with a mighty effort, and then she lowered his hand to the bed once more and moved away.

I stood next to the bed, looking through the oxygen tent at my friend's face.

He was very pale, with dark purplish hollows under his eyes. Somebody had combed his hair, though. The comb had been wet. He was all covered up, so I saw no indication of the wound that had brought him here. Tubes came out of his nostrils, and his lips were gray. His face looked waxen, and his eyes were staring right at me.

"It's me," I said. "Cory."

He swallowed thickly. Maybe the green blip had picked up a little, or maybe it was my imagination.

"You took a fall," I said, and instantly thought that was the stupidest thing ever uttered.

He didn't answer. He couldn't speak, I thought. "Ben and Johnny were here," I offered.

Davy Ray breathed. The breath became a word: *"Ben."* One side of his mouth hitched up. "Numb nuts."

"Yeah," I said, and I tried to smile. I wasn't as strong as Mrs. Callan. "Do you remember much about what happened?"

He nodded. His eyes were feverishly bright. "Tell you," he said, his voice crushed. "Have to tell you."

"All right," I said, and I sat down.

He smiled. "Saw him."

"You did?" I leaned forward conspiratorially. I caught a whiff of something that smelled bloody, but I didn't show it. "You saw the thing from the lost world?"

"No. Better." His smile went away as he swallowed painfully, then came back. "Saw Snowdown," he said.

"Snowdown," I whispered. The great white stag with antlers like oak trees. Yes, I decided. If anyone deserved to see Snowdown, it would be Davy Ray.

"Saw him. That's why I fell down. Wasn't watchin'. Oh, Cory," he said. "He's so pretty."

"I'll bet he is," I said.

"He's *bigger* than they say! And he's a whole lot *whiter*, too!"

"I'll bet," I said, "he's the most beautiful stag there ever was."

"Right there," Davy Ray whispered. "He was right there in front of me. And when I started to tell my dad, Snowdown leaped. He just leaped, and he was gone. Then I fell down, 'cause I wasn't watchin'. But it wasn't Snowdown's fault I fell, Cory. Wasn't anybody's fault. Just happened."

"You're gonna be fine," I said. I watched a bloody bubble of saliva grow at the corner of his mouth.

"I sure am glad I saw Snowdown," Davy Ray said. "I wouldn't have missed it. For nothin'."

He was silent, but for the soft wet rattling of his breath. The machine *blip . . . blip . . . blipped.* "I guess I'd better go," I said, and I started to stand up.

His marble-white hand grasped my own.

"Tell me a story," he whispered.

I paused. Davy Ray watched me, his eyes needful. I settled back down again. He kept hold of my hand, and I didn't try to pull loose. He felt cold.

"All right," I said. I would have to put this together as I went, like the tale of Chief Five Thunders. "There was a boy."

"Yeah," Davy Ray agreed, "gotta be a boy."

"This boy could just think of it, and he could go to other planets. This boy could get the red sand of Mars on his sneakers, or he could skate on Pluto. He could ride his bike on Saturn's rings, and he could fight dinosaurs on Venus."

"Could he go to the sun, Cory?"

"Oh, sure he could. He could go to the sun every day, if he wanted to. That's where he went when he needed a good suntan. He just put on his sunglasses and went there, then he came back brown as a berry."

"Must've gotten awful hot, though," Davy Ray said.

"He took a fan with him," I said. "And this boy was friends with all the kings and queens of the planets, and he visited all their castles. He visited the red sand castle of King Ludwig of Mars, and the cloud castle of King Nicholas of Jupiter. He helped stop King Zanthas of Saturn and King Damon of Neptune from fightin', when they got into a war over who owned a comet. He went to the fire castle of King Burl of Mercury, and on Venus he helped King Swane build a castle in the tall blue trees. On Uranus King Farron asked him to stay all year, and be an admiral in the ice fleet navy. Oh, all

371

the royalty knew about this boy. They knew there'd never be another boy just exactly like him, even if all the stars and planets burned out and were struck to light again a million times. Because he was the only one on the whole earth who could walk on the planets, and he was the only one whose name was written in their invitation books."

"Hey, Cory?"

"Yes?"

His voice was getting drowsy. "I'd kinda like to see a cloud castle, wouldn't you?"

"I sure would," I said.

"Gosh." He wasn't looking at me anymore. He was looking somewhere else, like a solitary traveler about to wish himself to a fabled land. "I never was afraid of flyin', was I?"

"Not a bit."

"I'm awful tired, Cory." He frowned, the red saliva beginning to thread down his chin. "I don't like bein' so tired."

"You oughta rest, then," I said. "I'll come see you tomorrow."

His frown vanished. A smile sneaked across his mouth. "Not if I go to the sun tonight. Then I'll have me a suntan and you'll be stuck here shiverin'."

"Cory?" It was Mrs. Callan. "Cory, the doctor needs to get in here with him."

"Yes ma'am." I stood up. Davy Ray's cold hand clung to mine for a few seconds, and then it fell away. "I'll see you," I said through the oxygen tent. "Okay?"

"Good-bye, Cory," Davy Ray said.

"Good—" I stopped myself. I was thinking of Mrs. Neville, on the first day of summer. "I'll see you," I told him, and I walked past his mother to the door. A sob welled up in my throat before I got out, but I clenched it down. As Chile Willow's mother had said, I could take it.

There was nothing more we could do. We drove home, along misty Route Sixteen, where Midnight Mona arrowed in search of love. We didn't say much; at a time like this, words were empty vessels. At home, the green feather lay on the floor where it had drifted; it went back to its cigar box.

On Sunday morning I awakened with a start. Tears were in my eyes, the sunlight lying in stripes across the floor. My father was standing in the doorway, wearing the same clothes he'd had on all day yesterday.

"Cory?" he said.

Traveling, traveling: to see Kings Ludwig, Nicholas, Zanthas, Damon, Farron, Burl, and Swane. Traveling, traveling: to castles of red sand, hewn of blue trees, formed of fire, shaped of sculpted clouds. Traveling, traveling, with planets and stars beyond and invitation books open to a single name. The solitary traveler has left this world. He will not pass this way again.

2

Faith

I thought I had known Death.

I had walked with it, ever since I could remember sitting in front of the television set, or hunkered down with a box of buttered popcorn before the Lyric's silver screen. How many hundreds of cowboys and Indians had I witnessed fall, arrow-pierced or gut-shot, into the swirling wagon train dust? How many dozens of detectives and policemen, laid low by the criminal bullet and coughing out their minutes? How many armies, mangled by shells and burp guns, and how many monster victims screaming as they're chewed?

I thought I had known Death, in Rebel's flat, blank stare. In the last good-bye of Mrs. Neville. In the rush and gurgle of air as a car with a man at the wheel sank into cold depths.

I was wrong.

Because Death cannot be known. It cannot be befriended. If Death were a boy, he would be a lonely figure, standing at the playground's edge while the air rippled with other children's laughter. If Death were a boy, he would walk alone. He would speak in a whisper and his eyes would be haunted by knowledge no human can bear.

This was what tore at me in the quiet hours: *We come from darkness, and to darkness we must return.*

I remembered Dr. Lezander saying that as I'd sat on his porch with him facing the golden hills. I didn't want to believe it. I didn't want to think that Davy Ray was in a place where he could see no light, not even the candle that burned for him at the Presbyterian church. I didn't want to think of Davy Ray confined, closed away from the sun, unable to somehow breathe and laugh even if doing so was only shadow play. In the days that followed the death of Davy Ray, I realized what fiction I had been a witness to. The cowboys and Indians, the detectives and policemen, the armies and the monster victims, would all rise again, at the dimming of the stage lights. They would go home, to wait for a casting call. But Davy Ray was dead forever, and I could not stand the thought of him in darkness.

It got to where I couldn't sleep. My room was too dark. It got to where I wasn't sure what I'd seen, the night a blurred figure spoke to Rebel. Because if Davy Ray was in darkness, so, too, was Carl Bellwood. Rebel was. And all the sleepers on Poulter Hill and all the generations whose bones lay beneath the twisted roots of Zephyr's trees: they, too, had returned to darkness.

I remembered Davy Ray's funeral. How thick the red earth was, on the edges of the grave. How thick, how heavy. There was no door down there when the minister was finished and the people gone and the dirt shoveled in by Bruton men. There was only dark, and its weight made something crack inside me.

I didn't know where heaven was anymore. I wasn't sure if God had any sense, or plan or reason, or if maybe He, too, was in the dark. I wasn't sure of anything anymore: not life, not afterlife, not God, not goodness. And I anguished over these things as the Christmas decorations went up on Merchants Street.

Christmas was still two weeks away, but Zephyr struggled for a festive air. The death of Davy Ray had drowned everybody's joy. It was talked about at Mr. Dollar's, at the Bright Star Cafe, at the courthouse, and everywhere in between. He was so young, they said. Such a tragic accident, they said. But that's life, they said; whether we like it or not, that's life.

Hearing these things didn't help me. Of course my folks tried to talk to me about it, saying that Davy Ray's suffering was over and that he'd gone to a better place.

But I just couldn't believe them. What place would ever be better than Zephyr?

"Heaven," Mom told me as we sat together before the crackling fire. "Davy Ray's gone to heaven, and you have to believe that."

"Because why?" I asked her, and she looked as if I'd just slapped her face.

I waited for an answer. I hoped for one, but it came in a word that left me unsatisfied, and that word was "faith."

They took me to see Reverend Lovoy. We sat in his office at church, and he gave me a lemon candy from a bowl on his desk. "Cory," he said, "you believe in Jesus, don't you?"

"Yes sir."

"And you believe that Jesus was sent from God to die for the sins of man?"

"Yes sir."

"Then you also believe Jesus was crucified, dead and buried, and on the third day He arose from the grave?"

"Yes sir." Here I frowned. "But Jesus was Jesus. Davy Ray was just a regular boy."

"I know that, Cory, but Jesus came to earth to show us that there's more to this existence than we understand. He showed us that if we believe in Him, and follow His will and way, we, too, have a place with God in heaven. You see?"

I thought about this for a minute as Reverend Lovoy sat back in his chair and watched me. "Is heaven better than Zephyr?" I asked him.

"A million times better," he said.

"Do they have comic books there?"

"Well . . ." He smiled. "We don't really know what heaven will be. We just know it'll be wonderful."

"Because why?" I asked.

"Because," he answered, "we must have faith." He offered the bowl to me. "Would you like another candy?"

I couldn't picture heaven. How could a place be any good at all if it didn't have the things there you enjoyed doing? If there were no comic books, no monster movies, no bikes, and no country roads to ride them on? No swimming pools, no ice cream, no summer, or barbecue on the Fourth of July? No thunderstorms, and front porches on which to sit and watch them coming? Heaven sounded to me like a library that only held books about one certain subject, yet you had to spend eternity and eternity and eternity reading them. What was heaven without typewriter paper and a magic box?

Heaven would be hell, that's what.

These days were not all bleak. The Christmas lights, red and green, glowed on Merchants Street. Lamps shaped like the head of Santa Claus burned on the street corners, and silver tinsel hung from the stoplights. Dad got a new job. He began working three days a week as a stock clerk at Big Paul's Pantry.

One day Leatherlungs called me a blockhead six times. She told me to come up to the blackboard and show the class what I knew about prime numbers.

I told her I wasn't coming.

"Cory Mackenson, you get up here right now!" she roared.

"No, ma'am," I said. Behind me the Demon laughed gleefully, sensing a new assault in the war on Mrs. Harper.

"Get. Up. Here. This. *Minute!"* Leatherlungs' face bloomed red.

I shook my head. "No."

She was on me. She moved a lot faster than I ever would've thought. She grabbed two handfuls of my sweater and wrenched me up out of my desk so hard my knee hit and sent a shiver of pain through my leg, and by the time that pain got to my head it was sheer white-hot anger.

With Davy Ray and darkness and a meaningless word called faith lodged in my mind like thorns, I swung at her.

I hit her right in the face. I couldn't have aimed any better. Her glasses flew off, and she gave a croaking cry of surprise. The anger fled from me just that fast, but Leatherlungs hollered, *"Don't you hit me, don't you dare!"* and she grabbed my hair and started jerking my head. The rest of my classmates sat in stunned amazement; this was too much, even for them. I had stepped into a mythic realm, though I didn't know it yet. Leatherlungs slung me, I crashed into Sally Meachum's desk and about knocked her over, and then Leatherlungs was hauling me out the door on the way to the principal's office, raging every step.

Inevitably, the phone call brought both Mom and Dad. They were, to say the least, appalled at my behavior. I was suspended from school for three days, and the principal—a small, birdlike man named, fittingly, Mr. Cardinale—said that before I could return to class, I would have to write an apology to Mrs. Harper and have both my parents sign it.

I looked at him, with my parents right there in his office, and I told him I could be suspended for three months for all I cared. I told him I wasn't writing her any apology, that I was tired of being called a blockhead, and I was sick of math and sick of everybody.

Dad came up off his chair. "Cory!" he said. "What's wrong with you?"

"Never in the history of this school has a student struck a teacher!" Mr. Cardinale piped up. "Never! This boy needs a whippin' to remember, is what I think."

"I'm sorry to have to say it," Dad told him, "but I agree with you."

I tried to explain to them on the way home, but they wouldn't hear it. Dad said there was no excuse for what I'd done, and Mom said she'd never been so ashamed. So I just stopped trying, and I sat sullenly in the pickup with Rocket riding in the truckbed. The whipping was delivered by my father's hand. It was swift, but it was painful. I did not know that the day before, Dad had been ragged by his boss at Big Paul's Pantry about messing up the count on boxes of Christmas candy. I did not know that Dad's boss was eight years younger than he, that he drove a red Thunderbird, and that he called my father Tommy.

I bore the whipping in silence, but in my room I pressed my face into the pillow.

Mom came in. She said she couldn't understand the way I was acting. She said she knew I was still torn up about Davy Ray, but that Davy Ray was in heaven and life was for the living. She said I would have to write the apology whether I wanted to or not, and the sooner I did it the better. I lifted my face from the pillow, and I told her Dad could whip me every day from now until kingdom come, but I wasn't writing any apology.

"Then I believe you'd better stay in here and think about it, young man," she said. "I believe you'll think better on an empty stomach, too."

I didn't answer. There was no need. Mom left, and I heard my folks talking about me, what was wrong with me and why I was being so disrespectful. I heard the clatter of dinner plates and I smelled chicken frying. I just turned over and went to sleep.

A dream of the four black girls, the flash of light, and a soundless blast awakened me. I had knocked my alarm clock off the bedside table again, but this time my parents didn't come in. The clock was still working; it was almost two in the morning. I got up and looked out the window. A crescent moon appeared sharp enough to hang a hat on. Beyond the window's cold glass the night was still and the stars blazing. I wasn't going to write any apology; maybe this was the Jaybird showing up in me, but I was damned if I'd give the satisfaction to Leatherlungs.

I needed to talk to somebody who understood me. Somebody like Davy Ray.

My fleece-lined jacket hung in the closet near the front door. I didn't want to go out that way, because Dad might be awake. I put on a pair of corduroy jeans, two sweaters, and a pair of gloves. Then I eased the window up. It squeaked once, a hair-raising sound, but I waited for a minute and heard no footsteps. Then I finished the job and slid out the window into the bitter air.

I closed the window behind me, but for a thin slice I could get my fingers hooked into. I got on Rocket, and rode away under the sharp-fanged moon.

The stoplights blinked yellow as I pedaled through the silent streets. My breath billowed out like a white octopus before me. I saw a few lights in houses: bathroom bulbs left on to ease the sleepy stumbling. My nose and ears got cold mighty fast; it was a night not fit for dog or Vernon Thaxter. On my way to Poulter Hill, I took a left turn and pedaled about a quarter mile more than I had to, because I wanted to see something. I coasted slowly past the house that sat on three acres and had a horse barn.

A light burned in an upstairs room. It looked too bright to be a bathroom bulb. Dr. Lezander was up, listening to the foreign countries.

A curious thought occurred to me. Maybe Dr. Lezander was a night owl because he feared the darkness. Maybe he sat up there in that room under the light, listening to voices from around the world, to reassure himself that he was not alone, even as the clock ticked through the lonely hours.

I turned Rocket away from Dr. Lezander's house. I had not pursued the mystery of the green feather any more since Davy Ray had died. A phone call to Miss Blue Glass was too much effort in this time of death and doubt. It was all I could do to fend off my own gathering darkness, much less think of what lay in the mud at the lightless bottom of Saxon's Lake. I didn't want to think that Dr. Lezander had anything to do with that. If he had, then what in this world was real and true anymore?

I reached Poulter Hill. The wrought-iron gates were locked, but since the stone wall around the cemetery was only two feet high, getting in was no feat of magic. I left Rocket to wait there, and I walked up the hill among the moon-splashed tombstones. As Poulter Hill stood on the invisible line between worlds, so, too, did it stand between Zephyr and Bruton. The white dead people lay on one side, the black dead people on the other. It made sense that people who could not eat in the same cafe, swim in the same public pool, or shop in the same stores would not be happy being dead and buried within sight of each other. Which made me want to ask Reverend Lovoy sometime if the Lady and the Moon Man would be going to the same heaven as Davy Ray. If black people occupied the same heaven as white people, what was the point of eating in different cafes here on earth? If black people and white people walked in heaven together, did that mean we were smarter or more stupid than God because on earth we shunned each other? Of course, if we all returned to darkness, there was no God and no heaven, anyway. How Little Stevie Cauley had managed to drive Midnight Mona through a crack of that darkness was another mystery, because I had seen him clear as I now saw the city of stones rising up around me.

There were so many of them. So many. I remember hearing this somewhere: when an old man dies, a library burns down. I recalled Davy Ray's obituary in the Adams Valley *Journal*. They said he had died in a hunting accident. They said who his mother and father were, that he had a younger brother named Andy and that he was a member of the Union Town Presbyterian Church. They said his funeral would be at ten-thirty in the morning. What they had left out stunned me. They hadn't said one word about the way the corners of his eyes crinkled up when he laughed, or how he would set his mouth to one side in preparation for a verbal jab at Ben. There had been no mention of the shine in his eyes when he saw a forest trail he hadn't explored before, or how he chewed his bottom lip when he was about to pitch a fastball. They had written down the cut-and-dried of it, but they had not mentioned the real Davy Ray. I wondered about this as I walked amid the graves. How many stories were here, buried and forgotten? How many old burned libraries, how many young ones that had been building their volumes year by year? And all those stories, lost. I wished there was a place you could go, and sit in a room like a movie theater and look through a catalogue of a zillion names and then you could press a button and a face would appear on the screen to tell you about the life that had been. It would be a living memorial to the generations who had gone on before, and you could hear their voices though those voices had been stilled for a hundred years. It seemed to me, as I walked in the presence of all those stilled voices that would never be heard again, that we were a wasteful breed. We had thrown away the past, and our future was impoverished for it.

I came to Davy Ray's grave. The headstone hadn't arrived yet, but a flat stone marker was set into the bare earth. He was neither at the bottom of the hill nor at the top; he occupied the middle ground. I sat down beside the marker, taking care not to trample on the slight mound that rain would settle and spring would sprout. I looked out into the darkness, under the cold, sharp moon. In the sunlight, I knew, there was a panoramic view of Zephyr and the hills from here. You could see the gargoyle bridge, and the Tecumseh River. You could see the railroad track as it wound its way through those hills, and the trestle as it crossed the river on its passage through Zephyr to the larger towns. It was a nice view, if you had eyes to see it. I somehow doubted that Davy Ray cared much whether he had a view of the hills and river or if his grave overlooked a swamp bowl. Such things might be important to the grievers, but not so much to the leavers.

"Gosh," I said, and my breath drifted out. "I sure am mixed up."

Had I expected Davy Ray to answer? No, I had not. Thus I was not disappointed at the silence.

"I don't know if you're in darkness or heaven," I said. "I don't know what would be so great about heaven if you can't get in a little trouble there. It sounds like church to me. Church is fine for an hour on Sunday, but I wouldn't want to live there. And I wouldn't want darkness, either. Just nothin' and nothin' and more nothin'. Every-thin' you ever thought or did or believed just gone, like a ripple in a pond that nobody sees." I pulled my knees up to my chest, and locked my arms around them. "No voice to speak, no eyes to see, no ears, nothin' at all. Then what are we born for, Davy Ray?"

This question, as well, elicited a burst of silence.

"And I can't figure this faith thing out," I went on. "Mom says I ought to have it. Reverend Lovoy says I've *got* to have it. But what if there's nothin' to have faith in, Davy Ray? What if faith is just like talkin' on a telephone when there's nobody on the other end, but you don't know nobody's there until you ask 'em a question and they don't answer? Wouldn't it make you go kind of crazy, to think you spent all that time jawin' to thin air?"

I was doing some jawing to empty air myself, I realized. But I was comforted, knowing Davy Ray was lying beside me. I shifted over to a place where the brown grass was unmarked by shovels and I reclined on my back. I stared up at the awesome stars. "Look at that," I said. "Just look at that sky. Looks like the Demon blew her nose on black velvet, huh?" I smiled, thinking Davy Ray would've gotten a kick out of that. "Not really," I said. "Can you see that sky from where you are?"

Silence and more silence.

I folded my arms across my chest. It didn't seem so cold, with my back against the earth. My head was next to Davy Ray's. "I got whipped today," I confided. "Dad really blistered me. Maybe I deserved it. But Leatherlungs deserves to get whipped, too, doesn't she? How come nobody listens to kids, even when they've got somethin' to say?" I sighed, and my breath rose toward Capricorn. "I can't write that apology, Davy Ray. I just can't, and nobody's gonna make me. Maybe I was wrong, but I was only half wrong, and they want me to say I was whole wrong. I can't write it. What am I gonna do?"

I heard it then.

Not Davy Ray's voice, chiding me.

But a train's whistle, off in the distance.

The freight was coming through.

I sat up. Off in the hills I could see the headlight like a moving star as the train wound toward Zephyr. I watched it coming.

The freight would slow down as it approached the Tecumseh trestle. It always did. It would slow down even more as it crossed the trestle, its heavy wheels making the old structure moan and clatter.

As it came off the trestle, it would be slow enough to catch if someone had a mind to.

The moment wouldn't last very long. The freight would pick up speed, and by the time it had reached the far side of Zephyr it would be running fast again.

"I can't write any apology, Davy Ray," I said quietly. "Not tomorrow, not the day after that. Not ever. I guess I can't ever go back to school, huh?"

Davy Ray offered neither opinion nor advice. I was on my own.

"What if I was to go away for a while? Not long. Maybe two or three days. What if I was to show 'em I'd rather run away than write an apology? Then maybe they'd listen to me, don't you think?" I watched the moving star come nearer. The whistle blew again, maybe warning a deer off the track. I heard it say *Corrrrryyyyyyyyy*.

I stood up. I could make it to the trestle if I ran to Rocket. But I had to go right this minute. Fifteen more seconds and I would face one more day of anger and disappointment from my parents. One more day of being a boy closed up in a room with an unwritten apology staring me in the face. The freight that was about to pass through always returned again. I reached into my pocket, and found two quarters left over from some purchase of popcorn or candy bar at the Lyric last winter when things were good.

"I'm goin', Davy Ray!" I said. "I'm goin'!"

I started running through the graveyard. As I reached Rocket and swung up onto the saddle, I feared I was already too late. I pedaled like mad for the trestle, the breath blooming around my face. I heard the moan and clatter as I pulled alongside the gravel-edged tracks; the freight was crossing, and I could yet meet it.

And then there it was, the headlight blazing. The huge engine came off the trestle and passed me, going a little faster than I could walk. Then the boxcars began going past: Southern Railroad cars, *bump ka thud, bump ka thud, bump ka thud* on the ties. Already the train was starting to pick up speed. I got off Rocket and put the kickstand down. I ran my fingers along the handlebar. For a second I saw the headlamp's golden eye, luminous with the moon. "I'll be back!" I promised.

All the boxcars were closed up, it seemed. But then here came one toward the end of the freight that had a door partway open. I thought of railroad bulls bashing heads and throwing freeloaders face-first into steam-scalded space, but I shook the thought away. I ran alongside the boxcar with the open door. A ladder was close at hand. I reached up, hooked four gloved fingers around a metal rung, got my thumb wedged there, too, and then I grabbed hold with the other hand and lifted my feet off the gravel.

I swung myself toward the boxcar's open door. I was amazed that I had such dexterity. I guess when you hear a few tons of steel wheels grinding underneath you, you can become an acrobat real quick. I went through that opening into the boxcar, my fingers released the iron rungs, and I hit a wooden floor sparsely covered with hay. The sound of my entrance was not gentle; it echoed in the boxcar, which was sealed shut on the other side. I sat up, hay all over the front of my outermost sweater.

The boxcar rumbled and shook. It was clearly not made for passengers.

But someone was indeed along for the ride.

"Hey, Princey!" a voice said. "A little bird just flew in!"

I jumped up. That voice had sounded like a combination of rocks in a cement mixer and a bullfrog's lament. It had come from the dark before me.

"Yes, I see him," another man answered. This voice was as smooth as black silk and had the lilt of a foreign accent. "I think he almost broke his wings, Franklin."

I was in the company of boxcar-riding tramps who would slit my throat for the quarters in my pocket. I turned to jump through the doorway, but Zephyr was speeding past.

"I wouldn't, young man," the foreign-accented voice cautioned. "It would not be pretty."

I paused on the edge, my heart pounding.

"We ain't gonna bite ya!" the froggish cement-mixer voice said. "Are we, Princey?"

"Speak for yourself, please."

"Ah, he's just kiddin'! Princey's always kiddin', ain't ya?"

"Yes," the black silk voice said with a sigh, "I'm always kidding."

A match flared beside my face. I jumped again, and turned to see who stood there.

A nightmare visage peered at me, so close I could smell his musty breath.

The man would've made a railroad tie look like Charles Atlas. He was emaciated, his black eyes submerged in shadow pools and the cheekbones thrust against the flesh of his face. And what flesh! I had seen summer-baked creekbeds that held more moisture. Every inch of his face was cracked and wrinkled, and the cracks drew his mouth back from his yellow teeth and continued up like a weird cap over the hairless dome of his scalp. His long, skinny fingers, exposed by the matchlight, were likewise shriveled, as was the hand on which they were fixed. His throat was a dried mass of cracks. He wore a dusty white costume of some kind, but where shirt and pants met I couldn't tell. He looked like a stick in a bag of dirty rags.

I was frozen with terror, waiting for the blade to slice my neck.

The wrinkled man's other hand rose like an adder's head. I tensed.

He was holding a package with a few Fig Newtons in it.

"Well, well!" the foreign man said with obvious surprise. "Ahmet likes you! Take a Fig Newton, he doesn't speak."

"I . . . don't think I . . ."

The match went out. I could smell Ahmet next to me, an odor so dry it threatened to crisp the hairs in my nostrils. He breathed like the rustle of dead leaves.

A second match was struck. Ahmet had a black streak across his pointed chin. He still held the Fig Newtons, and now he nodded at me. When he did so, I thought I heard his flesh creak.

He was grinning like warmed-over Death. Baked and crusted Death, to be more exact. I slid a trembling hand into the package and accepted a Fig Newton. This seemed to appease Ahmet. He shambled over toward the boxcar's other side, and he knelt down and touched the match to three candle stubs stuck with wax to the bottom of an upturned bucket.

The light grew. And as it grew, it showed me things I wished I didn't have to look at.

"There," the foreign man said from where he sat with his shoulder against a pile of burlap sacks. "Now we see eye-to-eye."

I wished we'd been back to back with five miles between us.

If this man had ever seen the sun, the Lady was my grandmother. His skin was so pallid, he made the moon appear as dark as Don

Ho. He was a young man, younger at least than my father, and he had fine blond hair combed back from a high forehead. A touch of silver glinted at his temples. He was wearing a dark suit, a white shirt, and a necktie. Only I could tell right off that his suit had seen better days from the patches around the shoulders, the cuffs of his shirt were frayed, and brown blotches marred his tie. Still, there was an elegance about this man; even sitting down, he commanded your attention with a stare that had a trace of well-bred haughtiness in it. His wingtips were scuffed. At first I thought he was wearing white socks, but then I realized those were his ankles. His eyes bothered me, though; in the candlelight, the pupils gleamed scarlet.

But this man, and Ahmet the dried-up one, looked like Troy Donahue and Yul Brynner compared to the third monstrosity in that boxcar.

He was standing up in a corner. His head, which was strangely shovel-shaped, almost brushed the ceiling. The man must have been over seven feet tall. His shoulders looked as wide as some of the wings on the planes at Robbins Air Force Base. His body appeared bulky and lumpy and altogether not right. He was wearing a loose brown jacket and gray trousers with patches on the knees. The trousers looked as if they had gotten drenched and shrunken while he was still in them. The size of the man's shoes astounded me; to call them clodhoppers is like calling an atomic bomb a pregnant grenade. They were more like earthmovers.

"Hi dere," he said as his shoes slammed on the timbers and he came toward me. "I'm Franklin."

He was grinning. I wished he hadn't been. His grin made Mr. Sardonicus look unhappy. What was worse than his grin was a scar that sliced across his Neanderthal forehead and had been stitched together, it seemed, by a cross-eyed medical student with a severe case of hiccups. His huge face looked flattened, his shiny black hair all but painted on his skull. In the candlelight, he appeared as if something he'd recently eaten hadn't agreed with him. The misfortunate oaf was a sickly, grayish hue. And lo and behold! There from each side of the man's bull-thick neck protruded a small rusted screw.

"You want some wadda?" he asked, and he held up a dented canteen. In his hand, it seemed the size of a clamshell.

"Uh . . . no sir. No thank you. Sir."

"Wadda washes down da Fig Newton," he said. "Udderwise get stuck in da troat."

"I'm okay. Really." I cleared my throat. "See?"

"Hokay. Dass fine, den." He returned to his corner, where he stood like a grotesque statue.

"Franklin's a happy sort," Princey explained. "Ahmet's the quiet one."

"What are *you*?" I asked.

"I'm the ambitious type," he said. "What type are you?"

"Scared." I heard the rush of wind behind me. The freight train was speeding now, leaving Zephyr sleeping in peace.

"Sit down if you like," Princey offered. "It's not too clean in here, but neither is it a dungeon."

I looked longingly out the door. We must've been going . . .

". . . sixty miles an hour," Princey said. "Sixty-four, it feels to me. I'm a good judge of the wind."

I sat down, keeping my distance from all three of them.

"So." He slid his hands into the pockets of his coat. "Favor us with your destination, Cory."

"I guess I . . . wait a minute. Did I tell you my name?"

"You must have, I'm sure."

"I don't remember."

Franklin laughed. It sounded like a backed-up drain being Roto-Rootered. "Haw! Haw! Haw! Dere he goes again! Princey's got da best sense'a yuma!"

"I don't think I told you my name," I said.

"Well, don't be stubborn," Princey answered. "Everybody has a name. What's yours?"

"Co—" I stopped. Were these three insane, or was I? "Cory Mackenson. I'm from Zephyr."

"Going to . . . ?" he prompted.

"Where does the train go?" I asked.

"From here?" He smiled slightly. "To everywhere."

I glanced over at Ahmet. He was squatting on his haunches, watching me intently over the flickering candles. He wore sandals on his shriveled feet, his toenails two inches long. "Kinda cold to be wearin' sandals, isn't it?"

"Ahmet doesn't mind," Princey said. "That's his footwear of choice. He's Egyptian."

"*Egyptian*? How'd he get all the way here?"

"It was a long, dusty trail," he assured me.

"Who *are* you people? You look kinda—"

"Familiar if you're a devotee of the sweet science. Boxing, that is," Princey said, shoveling words in my mouth. "Ever heard of Franklin Fitzgerald? Otherwise known as Big Philly Frank?"

"No sir."

"Then why did you say you had?"

"I . . . *did* I?"

"Meet Franklin Fitzgerald." He motioned to the monster in the corner.

"Hello," I said.

"Pleased ta meet ya," Franklin replied.

"I'm Princey Von Kulic. That's Ahmet Too-Hard-to-Pronounce."

"Hee hee hee," Franklin giggled behind a massive hand with scarred knuckles.

"You're not American, are you?" I asked Princey.

"Citizen of the world, at your service."

"Where're you from, then?"

"I am from a nation that is neither here nor there. It is an unnation, if you will." He smiled again. "Unnation. I like that. My country has been ransacked by foreign invaders so many times, we give green stamps for raping and pillaging. It's easier to make a buck here, what can I say?"

"So you're a boxer, too?"

"Me?" He grimaced as if he had a bad taste in his mouth. "Oh, no! I'm the brains behind Franklin's brawn. I'm his manager. Ahmet's his trainer. We all get along famously, except when we're trying to kill each other."

"Haw haw!" Franklin rumbled.

"We are currently between opponents," Princey said with a slight shrug. "Bound from the last place we were to the next place we will be. And such, I fear, is our existence."

I had decided that no matter how fearsome this trio appeared, they really meant me no harm. "Does Mr. Fitzgerald do a lot of fightin'?" I asked.

"Franklin will take on anyone, anywhere, at any time. Unfortunately, though his size is quite formidable, his speed is quite deplorable."

"Princey means I'm slow," Franklin said.

"Yes. And what else, Franklin?"

The huge man's overhanging brow threatened to collapse as he pondered this question. "I don't have da killer instink," he said at last.

"But we're working on that, aren't we, Silent Sam?" Princey asked the Egyptian. Ahmet showed his hooked yellow teeth and nodded vigorously. I thought he'd better be careful, in case his head flew off.

I began staring at Franklin's neck. "Mr. Princey, why does he have those screws in there?"

"Franklin is a man of many parts," Princey said, and Franklin giggled again. "Most of them of the rusted variety. His meetings with other individuals in the squared circle have not always been pleasant. In short, he's had so many broken bones that the doctor's had to wire some of him together. The screws are connected to a metal rod that strengthens his spine. It's painful, I'm sure, but necessary."

"Aw," Franklin said, "it ain't so bad."

"He has the heart of a lion," Princey explained. "Unfortunately, he also has the mind of a mouse."

"Hee hee hee! Dat Princey's a laff riot!"

"I'm thirsty," Princey said, and he stood up. He was tall, too, maybe six four, and slender though not nearly the beanpole Ahmet was.

"Here ya go." Franklin offered him the canteen.

"No, I don't want that!" Princey's pale hand brushed it aside. "I want . . . I don't know what I want." He looked at me. "Has that ever happened to you? Have you ever wanted something but you can't figure out what it is for the life of you?"

"Yes sir," I said. "Like sometimes when I think I want a Co'Cola but I really want root beer."

"Exactly. My throat's as dusty as Ahmet's pillow!" He walked past me and peered out at the passing forest. There were no lights out there, under the firmament. "So!" he said. "You know us now. What about you? I presume you're running away from home?"

"No sir. I mean . . . I'm just gettin' away for a little while, I guess."

"Trouble with your parents? With school?"

"Both of those," I said.

He nodded, leaning against the boxcar's opening. "The universal tribulations of a boy. I, too, had such troubles. I, too, set out to get away for a little while. Do you really think this will help your problems?"

"I don't know. It was all I could think of."

"The world," Princey said, "is not like Zephyr, Cory. The world has no affection for a boy. It can be a wonderful place, but it can also be savage and vile. We should know."

"Why is that?" I asked.

"Because we have traveled all over. We've seen this world, and we know the people who live in it. Sometimes it scares me to death, thinking about what's out there: cruelty, callousness, utter disregard and disrespect for fellow human beings. And it's not getting better, Cory; it's getting worse." He gazed up at the moon, which kept our pace. " 'O world,' " he said. " 'But that thy strange mutations make us hate thee, life would not yield to age.' "

"Ain't dat preddy?" Franklin asked.

"It's Shakespeare," Princey replied. "Talking about the universal tribulations of men." He turned from the moon and stared at me, his pupils scarlet. "Would you like some advice from an older soul, Cory?"

I didn't really want it, but I said, "Yes sir" to be polite.

He wore a bemused expression, as if he knew my thoughts. "I'll give it to you anyway. Don't be in a hurry to grow up. Hold on to being a boy as long as you can, because once you lose that magic, you're always begging to find it again."

That sounded vaguely familiar to me, but I couldn't remember where I'd heard it before.

"Do you want to see something of the world, Cory?" he asked me.

I nodded, transfixed by his bloodred pupils.

"You're in luck, then. I see a city's lights."

I stood up and looked out. And there in the distance, over the dragon's spine of twisted hills, the stars were washed out by earthly phosphorescence.

Princey explained to me that we would come to a part of that city where the freight slowed as it entered the yards. It was then that we could abandon our boxcar without breaking our legs. Gradually the city grew around us, from wooden houses to brick houses to buildings of stone. Even at this late hour, the city was alive. Neon signs blinked and buzzed. Cars sped along the streets, and figures trudged the sidewalks. Then the freight train clattered over the crisscrossed railyard tracks where other trains lay sleeping and began to slow. When it was going the speed of a walking man, Franklin's huge shoes touched the ground. Then Ahmet went out, dust whuffing from his body as he hit. "Go on, if you want to go," Princey told me, standing at my back. I scrambled out and landed all right, and then Princey made his exit. We had arrived in the city, and I was a long way from home.

We walked across the railyard, the sounds of whistles and chugging engines drifting around us. The air smelled burnt, though it was a cold fire. Princey said we'd better find some shelter for the night. We kept going, deeper along the gray streets that stood beneath the tall gray buildings, though several times we had to stop and wait for Franklin, who indeed was a slow mover.

We came to a place where alleys cut the walls, and neon reflected off standing pools of water on the cracked concrete. As we were passing an alley, I heard a grunting noise followed by the smacking of flesh. I stopped to look. One man was holding another with his arms behind him, while a third methodically beat the second man in the face with his fist. The second man was bleeding from the nose and mouth, his eyes dazed and wet with fear. The man who was doing the beating did this as if it were a common labor, like the hacking down of a wayward tree. "Where's the money, you motherfucker?" the first man said in a voice of quiet evil. "You're gonna give us the money." The beating continued, the third man's knuckles red with blood. The victim made a groaning, whimpering noise, and as the fist kept rising and falling, his bruised face began to change shape.

A pale hand gripped my shoulder. "Let's move along, shall we?"

Up ahead, a police car had pulled to the curb. Two policemen stood on either side of a man with long hair and dressed in dirty clothes. They were stocky and their guns gleamed in their black leather holsters. One of the policemen leaned forward and shouted in the long-haired man's face. Then the other policeman grabbed a handful of that hair, spun him around, and slammed his head against the windshield's glass. The glass didn't break, but the man's knees sagged. He didn't try to fight back as he was shoved into the police car. As they drove past us, I caught a glimpse of the man's face peering out, tendrils of blood creeping from his forehead.

Music throbbed and thumped from a doorway. It sounded like all rhyme and no reason. A man sat against a wall, a puddle of urine between his legs. He grinned at the air, his eyes demented. Two young men came along, and one of them held a tin gasoline can. "Get up, get up!" the other one said, kicking at the man on the ground. The demented one kept grinning. "Get up! Get up!" he parroted. In the next second, gasoline sloshed over him. The other young man pulled a pack of matches from his pocket.

Princey guided me around a corner. Franklin, slogging behind Ahmet, sighed like a bellows, his face daubed with shadow.

A siren wailed, but it was going somewhere else. I felt sick to my stomach, my skull pressured. Princey kept his hand on my shoulder, and it was comforting.

Four women were standing on a corner, under the stuttering neon. They were all younger than my mother but older than Chile Willow. They wore dresses that might have been applied with paint, and they appeared to be waiting for somebody important to come along. As we passed them, I smelled their sweet perfume. I looked into the face of one of them, and I saw a blond-haired angel. But something about that face was lifeless, like the face of a painted doll. "Motherfucker better do me right," she said to a dark-haired girl. "Better fuckin' score me, goddammit."

A red car pulled up. The blond-haired angel switched on a smile to the driver. The other girls crowded around, their eyes bright with false hope.

I didn't like what I saw, and Princey guided me on.

In a doorway, a man in a denim jacket was standing over a woman sprawled in a doorway. He was zipping up his pants. The woman's face was a pulped mass of black bruises. "There you go," the man said. "Showed you, didn't I? Showed you who's boss." He reached down and grabbed her hair. "Say it, bitch." He shook her head. "Say who's boss!"

Her swollen eyes were pleading. Her mouth opened, showing broken teeth. "You are," she said, and she began to cry. "You're the boss."

"Keep going, Cory," Princey told me. "Don't stop, don't stop."

I staggered on. Everywhere I looked, there was only mean concrete. I saw not a hill nor a trace of green. I lifted my face, but the stars were blanked out and the night a gray wash. We turned a corner and I heard a clatter. A small white dog was searching desperately through garbage cans, its ribs showing. Suddenly a hulking man was there, and he said, "Now I've got you" as the dog stood staring at him with a banana peel in its mouth. The man lifted a baseball bat and slammed it down across the dog's back. The dog howled with pain and thrashed, its spine broken, the banana peel lost. The man stood over it, and he lifted the baseball bat and brought it down and then the dog had no more muzzle or eyes, just a smashed red ruin. The white legs kept kicking, as if trying to run.

"Little piece a shit," the man said, and he stomped the skinny ribs with his boot.

Tears burned my eyes. I stumbled, but Princey's hand held me up. "Move on," he said. "Hurry." I did, past the carnage. I was about to throw up, and I fell against a wall of rough stones. Behind me, Franklin rumbled, "Da kid's too far from home, Princey. It ain't right."

"You think I *like* this?" Princey snapped. "Numb nuts."

I came to the edge of the wall, and I stopped. I seemed to be looking into a small room. I could hear voices raised in argument, but only a boy sat in the room. He was about my age, I thought, but something in his face looked older by far. The boy was staring at the floor, his eyes glassy as the arguing voices got louder and louder. And then he picked up a sponge and a tube of glue, the kind my buddies and I put plastic models together with. He squeezed glue into the sponge, and then he pressed the sponge over his nose and closed his eyes as he inhaled. After a minute he fell backward, his body starting to convulse. His mouth was open, and his teeth began to clamp down again and again on his tongue.

I shivered, sobbed, and looked away. Princey's hand touched the back of my head, and drew my face into his side.

"You see, Cory?" he whispered, and his voice was tight with strangled rage. "This world eats up boys. You're not ready yet to shove a broomstick down its throat."

"I want to . . . I want to . . ."

"Go home," Princey said. "Home to Zephyr."

We were back at the railyard, amid the whistles and chugs. Princey said they'd go back some of the way with me, to make sure I caught the right train. Here came a Southern Railroad freight train, with one of its boxcars partway open. "This is the one!" Princey said, and he jumped up into the opening. Franklin went next, moving fast on those big old shoes when he had to. Then Ahmet, his cracked flesh puffing dust with every step.

The train was picking up speed. I started running alongside the boxcar, trying to find a grip, but there was no ladder. "Hey!" I shouted. "Don't leave me!"

It began pulling away. I had to run hard to keep up. The boxcar's opening was dark. I couldn't see Princey, Franklin, or Ahmet in there. "Don't leave me!" I shouted frantically as my legs began to weaken.

"Jump, Cory!" Princey urged from the darkness. "Jump!"

The tons of steel wheels were grinding beside me. "I'm scared!" I said, losing ground.

"Jump!" Princey said. "We'll catch you!"

I couldn't see them in there. I couldn't see anything but dark. But the city was at my back, part of the world that ate up boys.

I would have to have faith.

I lunged forward, and I leaped upward toward the dark doorway.

I was falling. Falling through cold night and stars.

My eyes opened with a jolt.

I could hear the freight train's whistle, moving somewhere beyond Zephyr on its way to that other world.

I sat up, next to Davy Ray's grave.

My sleep had lasted only ten minutes or so. But I had gone a long way, and come back shaken and sick inside but safe. I knew the world beyond Zephyr wasn't all bad. After all, I read *National Geographic*. I knew about the beauty of the cities, the art museums, and the monuments to courage and humanity. But just like the moon, part of the world lay hidden. As the man who had been murdered on Zephyr earth lay hidden from the moonlight. The world, like Zephyr, was not all good and not all bad. Princey—or whatever Princey had been—was right; I had some growing up to do before I faced that monster. Right now, though, I was a boy who wanted to sleep in his own bed, and wake up with his mother and father in the house. The apology to Leatherlungs still stuck in my craw. I'd hack through that jungle when I got there.

I stood up, under the blazing stars. I looked at the grave, sadly fresh. "Good-bye, Davy Ray," I said, and I rode Rocket home.

The next day, Mom commented on how tired I looked. She asked if I'd had a bad dream. I said it was nothing I couldn't handle. Then she made me some pancakes.

The apology remained unwritten. While I was in my room that evening, my monsters watching me from the walls, I heard the telephone ring four different times. Dad and Mom came in to talk to me. "Why didn't you tell us?" Dad asked. "We didn't know that teacher was raggin' the kids so hard." He was, as I've said before, familiar with being ragged.

One of the callers had been Sally Meachum's mother. Another had been the Demon's mustachioed mater. Ladd Devine's dad had called, and Joe Peterson's mother. They had told my parents what their kids had told them, and suddenly it appeared that though I was certainly wrong for flying off the handle and whacking Leatherlungs' glasses off, Leatherlungs herself was responsible for some of this.

"It's not right for a teacher to call anybody's child a blockhead. Everybody deserves respect, no matter how old or young they are," Dad told me. "Tomorrow I believe I'll have a little talk with Mr. Cardinale and straighten this thing out." He gave me a puzzled look. "But why in the world didn't you tell us to begin with, Cory?"

I shrugged. "I guess I didn't think you'd take my side of it."

"Well," Dad said, "it seems to me we didn't have enough faith in you, did we, partner?"

He ruffled my hair.

It sure was nice, being back.

3

Snippets of the Quilt

Dad did go to Mr. Cardinale. The principal, who had already heard rumors from the other teachers that Leatherlungs was a burnt-out case two bricks shy of a load, decided that the time I'd spent away from school was enough. No apology was necessary.

I returned to find I was a conquering hero. In years to come, no astronaut home from the moon would feel as welcome as I did. Leatherlungs was cowed but surly, Mr. Cardinale's shrill admonitions ringing in her brain like Noel bells. But I had done my share of wrong, too, and I realized I ought to admit it. So, on that day I returned, which was also the last day of school before Christmas vacation, I raised my hand right after roll call and Leatherlungs snapped, "What is it?"

I stood up. All eyes were on me, expecting another heroic gesture in this grand campaign against injustice, inequality, and the banning of grape bubble gum. "Mrs. Harper?" I said. I hesitated, my grandeur in the balance.

"Spit it out!" she said. "I can't read your mind, you blockhead!"

Whatever Mr. Cardinale had told her, it obviously wasn't enough to persuade her to hang up her guns. But I went ahead anyway, because it was right. "I shouldn't have hit you," I said. "I'm sorry."

Oh, fallen heroes! Idols with feet of miserable clay! Mighty warriors, laid low by flea bites between the cracks in their suits of armor! I knew how they felt, in the groans and stunned gasps that rose around me like bitter flowers. I had stepped from my pedestal and pooted as I hit a mudhole.

"You're *sorry*?" Leatherlungs might have been the most stunned of the lot. She took off her glasses and put them back on. "You're *apologizing* to me?"

"Yes ma'am."

"Well, I . . . I . . . ." Words had fled from her. She was treading the

393

unknown waters of forgiveness, trying to find the bottom of it. "I don't . . . know what to . . ."

Grace beckoned her. Grace, with all its magic and wonder. The grace of a moment, and I saw her face start to soften.

". . . say, but . . ." She swallowed. Maybe there was a lump in her throat.

". . . but . . . *It's high time you showed some common sense, you blockhead!*" she roared.

It had been a lump of nails, obviously. She was spitting them out. *"Sit down and get that math book open!"*

Her face had not softened, I thought as I sighed and sat down. It had just been luffing like a sail before its second wind.

In the hollering madhouse that was called lunch period, I noticed the Demon sneaking out of the lunchroom as Leatherlungs was blasting some poor boy about spending his lunch money on baseball cards. She returned about five minutes later, sliding into her chair near the door before Leatherlungs knew she was gone. I saw the Demon and the other girls at her table giggle and grin. A plot was afoot.

When we were herded back to our room, Leatherlungs sat down at her desk like a lioness curling around a meatbone. "Get those Alabama history books open!" she said. "Chapter Ten! Reconstruction! Hurry it up!" She reached for her own history book, and I heard her grunt.

Leatherlungs couldn't lift the book up off the desktop. As everybody watched, she wrenched at the book with both hands, her elbows planted against the desk's edge, but it wouldn't budge. Somebody chortled. "Is it funny?" she demanded, the fury leaping into her eyes. "Who thinks that it's fun—" And then she squawked, because her elbows wouldn't leave the desk's edge. Sensing calamity, she tried to stand up. Her ample behind would not part with the seat, and when she stood, the chair came with her. "What's going on here!" she shouted as the entire class began to yell with laughter, myself included. Leatherlungs tried to shuffle to the door, but her face contorted as she realized those clunky brown shoes were as good as nailed to the linoleum. There she was, crouched over with her butt stuck to the chair's seat, her shoes mired in invisible iron, and her elbows stuck fast to the desk. She looked as if she were bowing to us, though the expression of rage on her face hardly approved of the courtesy.

"Help me!" Leatherlungs bawled, close to maddened tears. "Somebody help me!" Her cries for assistance were directed at the door, but the way everybody was hollering and laughing I doubted if even her foghorn voice could be heard beyond the frosted glass. She ripped the cloth of one arm of her blouse away as she got an elbow free, and then she made the mistake of placing that free hand against the desktop for added leverage. The hand was free no longer. "Help me!" she shouted. "Somebody get me out of this!"

The upshot of all this was that Mr. Dennis, the black custodian, had to be summoned by Mr. Cardinale to free Leatherlungs. Mr. Dennis was forced to use a hacksaw on the tough fibers of the substance that bound Leatherlungs so firmly to desk, chair, and floor. Mr. Dennis's hand unfortunately slipped during the hacksawing, and a patch of Leatherlungs' rear end was thereafter in need of reconstruction.

I heard Mr. Dennis tell Mr. Cardinale, as the ambulance attendants wheeled Leatherlungs away wheezing and gibbering along the holly-decked hall, that it was the most godawesome glue he'd ever seen. The stuff, he said, changed color depending on what it was smeared on. It was odorless but for the faint smell of yeast. He said Leatherlungs—Mrs. Harper, he called her—was mighty lucky she still had her hand connected to her wrist, the stuff was so powerful. Mr. Cardinale was enraged, in his flighty way. But no jar or tube of glue was found in the room, and Mr. Cardinale was stumped as to how any child could've been cunning and devious enough to perform such trickery.

He did not know the Demon. I never found out for sure, but I assumed she must've had the glue bottle hanging from a string outside the window and had reeled it in while the rest of us were eating lunch. Then, when she was through smearing all the necessary surfaces, the glue bottle had gone out the window again to be collected after school. I'd never heard of such a strong glue before. I learned later that the Demon had concocted it herself, using ingredients that included Tecumseh riverbottom mud, Poulter Hill dirt, and her mother's recipe for angel food cake. If that were so, I would've hated to taste Mrs. Sutley's devil's food. She called it Super Stuff, which made perfect sense.

I knew there had to be a reason the Demon had skipped a grade. I'd had no idea her real talent lay in the realm of chemistry.

Dad and I ventured out into the woods on a chilly afternoon. We found a small pine that would do. We took it home with us, and that night Mom popped corn and we strung the tree with popcorn, gold and silver tinsel, and the scuffed decorations that nestled in a box in the closet except for one week of the year.

Ben was learning his Christmas songs. I asked him whether Miss Green Glass had a parrot, but he didn't know. He'd never seen one, he said. But they might have a green parrot in the back somewhere. Dad and I went in together and bought Mom a new cake cookbook and a baking pan, and Mom and I went in together and bought Dad some socks and underwear. Dad made a solitary purchase of a small bottle of perfume from Woolworth's for Mom while she bought him a plaid muffler. I liked knowing what was inside those brightly wrapped packages under the tree. Two packages were also there, though, that had my name on them and I had no idea what they contained. One was small and one was larger: two mysteries, waiting to be revealed.

I was snakebit about picking up the phone and calling the Glass sisters. The last time I'd intended to, tragedy had struck. The green feather was never far from my hand, though. One morning I woke up, after a dream of the four black girls calling my name, and I rubbed my eyes in the winter sunlight and I picked up the feather from where I'd left it on the bedside table and I knew I had to. Not call them, but go see for myself.

Bundled up, I rode Rocket under the Zephyr tinsel to the gingerbread house on Shantuck Street. I knocked at the door, the feather in my pocket.

Miss Blue Glass opened the door. It was still early, just past nine. Miss Blue Glass wore an azure robe and quilted cyan slippers. Her whitish-blond hair was piled high as usual, which must've been her first labor of the morning. I was reminded of pictures I'd seen of the Matterhorn. She regarded me through her thick black-framed glasses, dark hollows beneath her eyes. "Cory Mackenson," she said. Her voice was listless. "What can I do for you?"

"May I come in for a minute?"

"I am alone," she said.

"Uh . . . I won't take but a minute."

"I am alone," she repeated, and tears welled up behind her glasses. She turned away from the door, leaving it open. I walked into the house, which was the same museum of chintzy art it had been the night I was here for Ben's lesson. Still . . . something was missing.

"I am alone." Miss Blue Glass crumpled down onto the spindly-legged sofa, lowered her head, and began to sob.

I closed the door to keep out the cold. "Where's Miss Gre—the other Miss Glass?"

"No longer *Miss* Glass," she said with the trace of a hurt sneer.

"Isn't she here?"

"No. She's in . . . heaven knows where she is by now." She took off her glasses to blot the tears with a blue lace hanky. I saw that without those glasses and with her hair let down an altitude or two, she might not look nearly so . . . I guess *frightful*'s the word.

"What's wrong?" I asked.

"What's wrong," she said, "is that my heart has been ripped out and *stomped!* Just utterly *stomped!*" Fresh tears streaked down her face. "Oh, I can hardly even think about it!"

"Did somebody do somethin' bad?"

"I have been *betrayed!*" she said. "By my own flesh and blood!" She picked up a piece of pale green paper from beside her and held it out to me. "Read this for yourself!"

I took it. The words, a graceful script, were written in dark green ink.

Dearest Sonia, it began. *When two hearts call to each other, what else can one do but answer? I can no longer deny my feelings. My emotions burn. I long to be joined in the raptures of true passion. Music is fine, dearest sister, but the notes must fade. Love is a song that lives on. I must give myself to that finer, deeper symphony. That is why I must go with him, Sonia. I have no choice but to give myself to him, body and soul. By the time you read this, we shall be . . .*

"Married?" I must've shouted it, because Miss Blue Glass jumped.

"Married," she said grimly.

. . . married, and we hope in time you will understand that we do not conduct our own chorale in this life, but are conducted by the hand of the Master Maestro. Love and Fond Farewell, Your Sister, Katharina.

"Isn't that the damnedest thing?" Miss Blue Glass asked me. Her lower lip began to tremble.

"Who did your sister run off with?"

Miss Blue Glass spoke the name, though speaking it seemed to crush her all the more.

"You mean . . . your sister married . . . *Mr. Cathcoate?*"

"Owen," Miss Blue Glass sobbed, "oh, my sweet Owen ran off with my own sister!"

I couldn't believe what I was hearing. Not only had Mr. Cathcoate gone off and married Miss Green Glass, but he'd been catting with Miss Blue Glass, too! I'd known he had parts of the Wild West in him, but I hadn't imagined his south parts were just as wild. I said, "Isn't Mr. Cathcoate kind of *old* for you ladies?" I put the letter back on the sofa beside her.

"Mr. Cathcoate has the heart of a boy," she said, and her eyes got dreamy. "Oh Lord, I'll miss that man!"

"I have to ask you about somethin'," I told her before her faucets turned on again. "Does your sister have a parrot?"

Now it was her turn to look at me as if my senses had flown. "A *parrot?*"

"Yes ma'am. You had a blue parrot. Does your sister have a green one?"

"No," Miss Blue Glass said. "I'm tellin' you how my heart has been broken, and you want to talk about parrots?"

"I'm sorry. I just had to ask." I sighed and looked around the room. Some of the knickknacks in the curio cabinet were gone. I didn't think Miss Green Glass was ever coming back, and I supposed that Miss Blue Glass knew it. A bird, it seemed, had left its cage. I slid my right hand into my pocket and put my fingers around the feather. "I didn't mean to bother you," I said, and I walked to the door.

"Even my parrot has left me," Miss Blue Glass moaned. "And my parrot was so sweet and gentle . . ."

"Yes ma'am. I was sorry to hear about—"

". . . not like that filthy, greedy parrot of Katharina's!" she plowed on. "Well, I should've known her true nature, shouldn't I? I should've known she had her cap set for Owen, all along!"

"Wait," I said. "I thought you just told me your sister didn't have a parrot."

"That's not what I said. I said Katharina *doesn't* have a parrot. When it died, the devil ate a drumstick!"

I walked back to her, and as I did I brought my hand out of my pocket and opened the fingers. My heart was going ninety miles a minute. "Was that the color of your sister's parrot, Miss Glass?"

She gave it one sniffy glance. "That's it. Lord knows I'd recognize one of his feathers, he was always flyin' against his cage and flingin' 'em out. He was about bald when he died." She caught herself. "Just a minute. What are *you* doin' with one of his feathers?"

"I found it. Somewhere."

"That bird died back in . . . oh, when was it?"

I knew. "March," I said.

"Yes, it *was* March. The buds were startin' to show, and we were choosin' our Easter music. But . . ." She frowned, her stomped heart forgotten for the moment. "How did you know, Cory?"

"A little bird told me," I said. "What did the parrot die of, Miss Glass?"

"A brain fever. Same as my parrot. Dr. Lezander says it's common among tropical birds and when it happens there's not much can be done."

"Dr. Lezander." The name left my lips like frozen breath.

"He loved my parrot. He said my parrot was the gentlest bird he'd ever seen." Her lips curled into a snarl. "But he *hated* that green one of Katharina's! I think he could've killed it the same as me, if I could've gotten away with it!"

"He almost got away with it," I said quietly.

"Got away with what?" she asked.

I let her question slide. "What happened to the green parrot after it died? Did Dr. Lezander come get it?"

"No. It was sick, wouldn't touch a grain of seed, and Katharina took it to Dr. Lezander's office. It died the next night."

"Brain fever," I said.

"That's right, brain fever. Why are you askin' all these strange questions, Cory? And I still don't understand why you have that feather."

"I . . . can't tell you yet. I wish I could, but I can't."

She leaned forward, smelling a secret. "What is it, Cory? I swear I won't breathe it to a soul!"

"I can't say. Honest." I returned the feather to my pocket, and Miss Blue Glass's face slowly dropped again. "I'd better be goin'. I hated to bother you, but it was important." I glanced at the piano as I went to the door, and a thought struck me like the arrowhead of Chief Five Thunders lodging right between my eyes. I remembered the Lady saying she'd dreamed of hearing piano music, and seeing hands holding piano wire and a "crackerknocker." I recalled the piano in the room where all the ceramic birds were, at Dr. Lezander's house. "Did you ever teach Dr. Lezander to play the piano?" I asked.

"Dr. Lezander? No, but his wife took lessons."

His wife. Big, horse-faced Veronica. "Was this real recently?"

"No, it was four or five years ago, when I was teachin' full-time. *Before* Katharina had me knockin' at the poorhouse door," she said icily. "Mrs. Lezander won several gold stars, as I recall."

"Gold stars?"

"I give gold stars for excellence. Mrs. Lezander could've been a professional pianist in my opinion. She has the hands for it. And she loved my song." Her face brightened.

"What song?"

Miss Blue Glass got up and situated herself at the piano. She began to play the song she'd been playing that night her parrot had started squawking in German. "'Beautiful Dreamer,'" she said, and she closed her eyes as the melody filled the room. "It's all I have left now, isn't it? My beautiful, beautiful dreams."

I listened to the music. What had made the blue parrot go so crazy that night?

I remembered the voice of Miss Green Glass: *It's that song, I'm tellin' you! He goes insane every time you play it!*

And Miss Blue Glass, answering: *I used to play it for him all the time and he loved it!*

A small glimmer began to cut through the darkness. It was like a single shard of sunlight, as seen from the bottom of murky water. I couldn't make out anything by it yet, but I knew it was there.

"Miss Glass?" I said. A little louder, because she'd increased the volume and was starting to hammer the keys as if she were playing with Ben's fingers: "*Miss Glass?*"

She stopped on a bitter note. Tears had streamed down all the way to her chin. "What is it?"

"That song right there. Did it make your parrot act strange?"

"No! That was a vile lie of Katharina's, because she hated my favorite song herself!" But the way she said it, I knew it wasn't true.

"You've just started givin' piano lessons again, haven't you? Have you played that song very much since . . . oh . . . the green parrot died?"

She thought about it. "I don't know. I guess . . . I played it at church rehearsal some, to warm up. But because I wasn't givin' lessons, I didn't play the piano much at home. Not that I didn't want to, but Katharina"—she couldn't help but sneer the name—"said my playin' hurt her sensitive ears, that vicious man-stealer!"

The light was still there. Something was taking shape, but it was still a long way off.

"It was Katharina this and Katharina that!" Miss Blue Glass suddenly slammed her hands down on the keyboard with such force the entire piano shook. "I was always bendin' over backward to appease almighty Katharina! And I loathe and despise *green!*" She stood up, a skinny, seething thing. "I'm gonna take everythin' green in this house and burn it, and if that means parts of the house, the very walls, well, I'll burn those, too! If I never see green again, I'll smile in my grave!"

She was working up to a frenzy of destruction. That was a sight I didn't care to witness. I had my hand on the doorknob. "Thank you, Miss Glass."

"Yes, I'm still *Miss* Glass!" she shouted, but she was crying again. "The one and only *Miss* Glass! And I'm proud of it, do you hear me? I'm proud of it!" She plucked the pale green farewell letter from the sofa and, her teeth clenched, she began to rip it to shreds. I got out while the getting was good. As the door closed behind me, I heard the curio cabinet go over. I'd been right; it did make a terrible crash.

As I pedaled home, I was trying to put everything together in my head. *Snippets of the quilt,* the Lady had said. The pieces were there, but how did they fit?

The murder of a man no one knew.

The green feather of a dead parrot, there at the scene of the crime.

A song that caused a second parrot to curse blue blazes in German.

Dr. Lezander, the night owl who hated milk.

Who knows?

Hannaford?

If the green parrot had died at Dr. Lezander's office, how had one of its feathers gotten to the lake?

What was the link between the two parrots, the dead man, and Dr. Lezander?

When I got home, I went straight to the telephone. I called the Glass house again, my fears of tragedy pushed down out of sheer necessity. At first I thought Miss Blue Glass wasn't going to answer, because the phone rang eight times. Then, on the ninth ring: "Yes?"

"Miss Glass, it's me again. Cory Mackenson. I've got one more question for you."

"I don't want to talk about Benedictine Arnold anymore."

"Who? Oh, not your sister. Your parrot. Besides this last time, when it died at Dr. Lezander's, was it ever sick before?"

"Yes. They were both sick on the same day. Katharina and I took them both to Dr. Lezander's office. But that next night her damn bird died." She made a noise of exasperation. "Cory, what is this all *about?*"

The light was a little brighter. "Thanks again, Miss Glass," I said, and I hung up. Mom asked me from the kitchen why I was calling Miss Glass, and I said I was going to write a story about a music teacher. "That's nice," Mom said. I had discovered that being a writer gave you a lot of license to fiddle with the truth, but I'd better not get into the habit of it.

In my room, I put on my thinking cap. It took a while, but I did some sewing with those snippets of the quilt.

And I came to this conclusion: both parrots had been at Dr. Lezander's the night in March the unknown man had been murdered. The green parrot had died that night, and the blue one had come away cursing in German when "Beautiful Dreamer" was played on the piano. Mrs. Lezander played the piano. Mrs. Lezander knew "Beautiful Dreamer."

Was it possible, then, that when Miss Blue Glass had played that song, her parrot remembered something that was said—or cursed and shouted in the German language—while Mrs. Lezander had been playing it? And why would Mrs. Lezander be playing a piano while somebody was shouting and curs—

Yes, I thought. Yes.

I saw the light.

Mrs. Lezander had been playing the piano—that song, "Beautiful Dreamer"—to cover up the shouts and cursing. Only both parrots had been in that room, in the bird cages there. But it seemed unlikely that anybody would be hollering and cursing right over her shoulder, didn't it?

I remembered Dr. Lezander's voice, rising up through the air vent from his basement office. Calling Dad and me to come down. He had known we would hear him clearly through the vent, which was why he hadn't come upstairs. Had he feared, on that night in March, that the noise of shouting might be heard outside the house, and that was why Mrs. Lezander had been playing the first song that came to mind as the two parrots listened and remembered?

Had Dr. Lezander beaten that unknown man with a cracker-knocker in the basement, and strangled him as the parrots listened? Maybe it had taken almost all night, the noises of violence making both parrots thrash against their cages? Then when the deed was done Dr. Lezander and his big horsey wife had carted the naked body out to that unknown man's car, parked in the barn? And either one of them had driven to Saxon's Lake, while the other had followed in their own car? But they hadn't realized that a green feather had whirled out of a bird cage and wound up in the folds of a coat or the depths of a pocket? And since both the Lezanders were allergic to milk, they weren't on the dairy's delivery list and they didn't know what time Dad would be on Route Ten?

Who knows?

Hannaford?

Maybe it had been like that. Maybe.

Or maybe not.

It sure would've made a good Hardy Boys mystery. But all I had was a feather from a dead parrot and a halfway-sewn quilt that seemed a little ragged at the seams. The German cursing, for instance. Dr. Lezander was Dutch, not German. And who was the unknown man? What possible link could a man with the tattoo of a winged skull on his shoulder have with Zephyr's veterinarian? Ragged, ragged seams.

Still . . . there was the green feather, "Beautiful Dreamer," and Who Knows?

Knows *what?* That, it seemed to me, was the key to this dark engine.

I told my parents none of this. When I was ready, I would; I wasn't, so I didn't. But I was convinced now more than ever that a stranger lived among us.

4

Mr. Moultry's Castle

Two days before Christmas, the telephone rang and Mom answered it. Dad was stock-clerking at Big Paul's Pantry. Mom said, "Hello?" and found herself talking to Mr. Charles Damaronde. Mr. Damaronde was calling to invite our family to a reception for the Lady at the Bruton Recreation Center, where the civil rights museum had been completed and was set to open on December 26. The reception was on the afternoon of Christmas Eve, and it was going to be a casual occasion. Mom asked me if I wanted to go, and I said yes. She didn't have to ask Dad, knowing he wouldn't go, and anyway he had to work on Christmas Eve because big boxes of canned eggnog and pressed turkey slices were backing up on the loading dock.

Dad didn't try to stop us from going. He didn't say a word when Mom told him. He just nodded, his eyes somewhere distant. The big boulder at Saxon's Lake, I guessed. So on Christmas Eve morning Mom drove Dad to work in the pickup truck, and when time to get ready for the reception rolled around, Mom suggested that I wear a white shirt and a tie even though Mr. Damaronde had said to come casual. She put on a nice dress, and we set off for Bruton.

One of the interesting things about living in south Alabama is that, though there might be a cold snap in October and maybe even a snow flurry or two in November, Christmas is usually warm. Not summertime warm, of course, but a return to Indian summer. This year was no exception. The sweater I had on was aptly named; I was sweating in it by the time we got to the recreation center, a red brick building next to the basketball court on Buckhart Street. A sign with a red arrow pointed to the Bruton Hall of Civil Rights, which was a white-painted wooden structure a little larger than a house trailer, added on to the recreation center. A red ribbon encircled the entire white building. Although the museum's grand opening wasn't for two more days, there were a lot of cars and quite a bit of activity. People—most of them black, but a few white—were going into the recreation center, and we followed them. Inside, in a big room decorated with pine-cone Christmas wreaths and a huge Christmas tree with red and green bows on the branches, people were lining up to sign a guest book, of which Mrs. Velvadine was in charge. Then the line continued to a punch bowl full of lime-colored liquid, and on to other tables that held a holiday bounty: various chips and dips, little sandwiches, sausage balls, two golden turkeys awaiting the knife, and two weighty hams. The last three tables were true groaning boards; atop them was a staggering selection of cakes, puddings, and pies. Dad's eyes would've shot out of his head if he could've but seen all this feast. The mood was happy and festive, people laughing and talking while a couple of fiddlers sawed their strings on a small stage. And it might have been a casual occasion, but people were dressed to the elevens. The Sunday suits and dresses abounded, the white gloves and flowered hats thrived. I think a peacock might've felt nude in all this rainbow splendor. People were proud of Bruton and proud of themselves, and that was clear to all.

Nila Castile came up and hugged my mother. She pressed paper plates into our hands and guided us through the crowd. The turkeys were about to be carved, she said, and if we didn't hurry, all that fine meat would be sucked right off the bones. She pointed out old Mr. Thornberry, who was wearing a baggy brown suit and buck-dancing to the fiddlers' tune. Beside him, Gavin grinned and matched him step for step. Mr. Lightfoot, elegant as Cary Grant in a black suit with velvet lapels, held a paper plate piled high with ham layered on cake layered on pie layered on sandwiches, and he moved through the throng with slow-motion grace. Then our plates were loaded down with food, our punch cups brimmed with lime fizz. Charles Damaronde and his wife appeared, and thanked Mom for coming. She said she wouldn't have missed it for the world. Children scampered around and grandparents chased futilely after them. Mr. Dennis sidled up to me and asked me in mock serious-ness if I didn't know who had spread that glue down for poor Mrs. Harper to get stuck in like a fly in molasses. I said I had an idea, but I couldn't say for sure. He asked me if my idea went around picking her nose to beat the band, and I said it might.

Somebody began playing an accordion. Somebody else whipped out a harmonica, and the fiddlers had competition. An elderly

woman in a dress the color of fresh orchids started buck-dancing
with Mr. Thornberry, and I imagined that at that moment he was
very glad he had chosen life. A man with an iron-gray beard
grasped my shoulder and leaned his head down beside mine.
"Broomstick in his craw, heh heh heh," he said, and gave my
shoulder a good hard squeeze before he moved on.

Mrs. Velvadine and another rotund woman, both of them wearing
flowered dresses bright enough to shame nature, took the stage and
shooed the musicmakers off. Mrs. Velvadine spoke through a
microphone, telling everybody how glad the Lady was that they'd
come to share this moment with her. The museum they'd worked so
hard to build was almost ready, Mrs. Velvadine said. Come the day
after Christmas, it would open its doors and tell the story of not only
the people of Bruton but the struggles that had brought them to
where they were. There are struggles ahead! Mrs. Velvadine said.
Don't you think there aren't! But though we have a long way to go,
she said, we have come a long way, too, and that's what the
museum was meant to show.

As Mrs. Velvadine spoke, Mr. Damaronde came up beside Mom
and me. "She wants to see you," he said quietly to my mother. We
knew who he meant, and we went with him.

He led us out of the reception area and through a hallway. One
room we passed was set up for table tennis, and had a dartboard
and a pinball machine. Another room held four shuffleboard courts
side by side, and a third contained gymnasium equipment and a
punching bag. Then came to a white door, the smell of paint still
fresh. He held it open for us as we passed through.

We were in the civil rights museum. The floor was made of
varnished timbers, and the lighting was low. Glass display cases
held slave and Civil War clothes on black mannequins, as well as
primitive pottery, needlework, and lace. A section of bookshelves
held maybe a hundred or more thin, leatherbound volumes. They
looked like notebooks or diaries. On the walls were large blown-up
black and white photographs. I recognized Martin Luther King in
one, and in another Governor Wallace blocking the schoolhouse
door.

And at the center of this room stood the Lady, dressed in white
silk, her thin arms adorned with elbow-length white gloves. She
wore a white, wide-brimmed hat, and beneath it her beautiful
emerald eyes shone with light.

"This," she said, "is my dream."

"It's lovely," Mom told her.

"It's *necessary*," the Lady corrected her. "Who on this earth can know where they're going, unless they have a map of where they've been? Your husband didn't come?"

"He's workin'."

"No longer at the dairy, I understand."

Mom nodded. I had the impression the Lady knew exactly where Dad was.

"Hello, Cory," she said. "You've had some adventures lately, haven't you?"

"Yes ma'am."

"You wantin' to be a writer, you ought to be interested in those books." She motioned toward the shelves. "Know what those are?" I said I didn't. "They're diaries," she said. "Voices of people who used to live all around here. Not just black people, either. Anytime somebody wants to find out what life was like a hundred years ago, there are the voices waitin' to be heard." She walked to one of the glass display cases and ran her gloved fingers across the top, checking for dust. She found none, and she grunted with satisfaction. "Everybody needs to know where they've been, it seems to me. Not just blackskins, but whiteskins, too. Seems to me if a person loses the past, he can't find the future either. Which is what this place is all about."

"You want the people of Bruton to *remember* their ancestors were slaves?" Mom asked.

"Yes, I do. I want 'em to remember it not to feel pity for themselves, or to feel put-upon and deservin' of what they don't have, but to say to themselves, 'Look where I have come from, and look what I have become.'" The Lady turned to face us. "Ain't no way out but up," she said. "Readin'. Writin'. *Thinkin'*. Those are the rungs on the ladder that lead up and out. Not whinin' and takin' and bein' a mind-chained slave. That's the used-to-be world. It ought to be a new world now." She moved around the room, and stopped at a picture of a fiery cross. "I want my people," she said quietly, "to cherish where they've come from. Not sweep it under a rug. Not to dwell on it either, because that's nothin' but givin' up the future. But to say, 'My great-granddaddy pulled a plow by the strength of his back. He worked from sunup to sundown, heat and cold. Worked for no wages but a master's food and a roof over his head. Worked *hard*, and was sometimes whipped hard. Sweated blood and kept goin', when he wanted to drop. Took the brand and answered Yes, massa, when his heart was breakin' and his pride was belly-down. Did all this when he knew his wife and children might go up on the auction block and be torn away from him in the blink of an eye. Sang in the fields, and wept at night. He did all this and more, and by God . . . by God, because he suffered this I can at least finish school.'" She lifted her chin in defiance of the flames. "That's what I want 'em to think, and to say. This is my dream."

I left my mother's side, and walked to one of the blown-up photographs. It showed a snarling police dog, its teeth full of shirt as a black man tried to fight away and a policeman lifted a billy club. The next photograph showed a slim black girl clutching school-books and walking through a crowd as rage-swollen white faces shouted derision at her. The third showed . . .

I stopped.

My heart had jumped.

The third picture showed a burned-out church, the stained-glass windows shattered and firemen picking through the ruins. A few black people were standing around, their expressions dull with shock. The trees in front of the church had no leaves on them.

I had seen this picture before, somewhere.

Mom and the Lady were talking, standing over by the slave-spun pottery. I stared at the picture, and I remembered. I had seen this in the copy of *Life* magazine Mom was about to throw out.

I turned my head to the left about six inches.

And there they were.

The four black girls of my recurring dream.

Under individual pictures, their names were etched on brass plaques. *Denise McNair. Carole Robinson. Cynthia Wesley. Addie Mae Collins.*

They were smiling, unaware of what the future held.

"Ma'am?" I said. "Ma'am?"

"What is it, Cory?" Mom asked.

I looked at the Lady. "Who are these girls, ma'am?" My voice trembled.

She came over beside me, and she told me about the dynamite time bomb that had killed those girls in the 16th Street Baptist Church in Birmingham on September 15, 1963.

"Oh . . . *no*," I whispered.

I heard the voice of Gerald Hargison, muffled behind a mask as he held a wooden box in his arms: *They won't know what hit 'em until they're tap-dancin' in hell.*

And Biggun Blaylock, saying: *I threw in an extra. For good luck.*

I swallowed hard. The eyes of the four dead girls were watching me.

I said, "I think I know."

Mom and I left the recreation center about an hour later. Dad was joining us to go to the candlelight service at church tonight. After all, it was Christmas Eve.

"Hello, Pumpkin! Merry Christmas to you, Sunflower! Come right in, Wild Bill!"

I heard Dr. Lezander before I saw him. He was standing there in the church doorway, wearing a red vest with his gray suit and a red-and-green-striped bow tie. He had a Santa Claus pin on his lapel, and when he smiled, light sparkled off his silver front tooth.

My heart started beating very hard, and moisture sprang to my palms. "Merry Christmas, Calico!" he said to my mother for no apparent reason. He grasped my father's hand and shook it. "How are you, Midas?" And then his gaze fell on me, and he put his hand on my shoulder. "And a very happy holiday to you, too, Six-Guns!"

"Thank you, Birdman," I said.

I saw it then.

His mouth was very, very smart. It kept smiling. But his eyes flinched, almost imperceptibly. Something hard and stony came into them, banishing the Christmas light. And then it was gone again, and the whole thing had been perhaps two seconds. "What are you trying to do, Cory?" His hand wouldn't let me go. "Take my job?"

"No sir," I answered, my cleverness squeezed away by Dr. Lezander's increasing pressure. He held my gaze for a second longer, and in that second I knew fear. Then his fingers relaxed and left my shoulder and he was looking at the family who entered behind me. "Come on in, Muffin! Merry Yuletide, Daniel Boone!"

"Tom! Come on and hurry it up, boy!"

We knew who that was, of course. Granddaddy Jaybird, Grandmomma Sarah, Grand Austin, and Nana Alice were there in a pew waiting for us. Grand Austin, as usual, looked thoroughly miserable. The Jaybird was on his feet, waving and hollering and making the same kind of ass out of himself here at Christmas as he had at Easter, proving that he was a fool for all seasons. But when he looked at me he said, "Hello, young man" and I saw in his eyes that I was growing up.

During the candlelight service, while Miss Blue Glass played "Silent Night" on the piano and the organ across from her indeed remained silent, I watched the Lezanders, who were sitting five pews ahead of us. I saw Dr. Lezander turn his bald head and look around, pretending to be quickly scanning the congregation. I knew better. Our eyes met, just briefly. He wore an icy smile. Then he leaned toward his wife and whispered in her ear, but she remained perfectly motionless.

I imagined he might have been answering the question: *Who Knows?* What he whispered to horse-faced Veronica, there between the "darkness flies" and the "all is light," might well have been: *Cory Mackenson knows.*

Who are you? I thought as I watched him during Reverend Lovoy's Christmas prayer. Who are you really, behind that mask you wear?

We lit our candles, and the church was bathed in flickering light. Then Reverend Lovoy wished us a happy and healthy holiday season, said for us to keep the spirit of Christmas first and foremost in our hearts, and the service came to a close. Dad, Mom, and I went home; tomorrow belonged to the grandparents, but Christmas Eve was ours.

Our dinner this year wasn't as grand as in the past, but I did like eggnog and we had plenty of that, courtesy of Big Paul's Pantry. Then came the gift-opening time. As Mom found carols on a radio station, I unwrapped my presents beneath the Yule pine tree.

From Dad I received a paperback book. It was titled *The Golden Apples of the Sun,* by a writer named Ray Bradbury. "You know, they sell books at Big Paul's, too," Dad told me. "Got a whole rack of 'em. This fella who works in the produce department says that Bradbury is a good writer. Says he's got that book himself and there're some fine stories in it."

I paged to the first story. "The Fog Horn," it was called. Skimming it, I saw it was about a sea monster rising to a foghorn's lament. This story had a boy's touch. "Thanks, Dad!" I said. "This is neat!"

As Dad and Mom opened their own presents, I unwrapped my second package. A photograph in a silver frame slid out. I held it up to the hearth's light.

It was a picture of a face I knew well. This was the face of one of my best friends, though he didn't know it. Across the bottom of the photograph was written: *To Cory Mackenson, With Best Wishes. Vincent Price.* I was thrilled beyond words. He actually knew my name!

"I knew you liked his movies," Mom said. "I just wrote the movie studio and asked 'em for a picture, and they sent one right off."

Ah, Christmas Eve! Was there ever a finer night?

When the presents had been opened and the wrappings swept away, the fire fed another log, and a third cup of eggnog warm in our bellies, Mom told Dad what had happened at the Hall of Civil

Rights. He watched the fire crack and sparkle, but he was listening. When Mom was finished, Dad said, "I'll be. I never thought such a thing could happen here." He frowned, and I knew what he was thinking. He'd never thought a lot of things that had happened in Zephyr could ever happen here, starting with the incident at Saxon's Lake. Maybe it was the age that was beginning to take shape around us. The news talked more frequently about a place called Vietnam. Civil strifes broke out in the cities like skirmishes in an undeclared war. A vague sense of foreboding was spreading across the land, as we neared the plastic, disposable, commercial age. The world was changing; Zephyr was changing, too, and there was no going back to the world that used to be.

But: tonight was Christmas Eve and tomorrow was Christmas, and for now we had peace on earth.

It lasted about ten minutes.

We heard the shrieking of a jet plane over Zephyr. This in itself wasn't unusual, since we often heard jets at night either taking off from or landing at Robbins. But we knew the sound of those planes as we knew the freight train's whistle, and this plane . . .

"Sounds awfully low, doesn't it?" Mom asked.

Dad said it sounded to him like it was skimming the rooftops. He got up to go to the porch, and suddenly we heard a noise like somebody whacking a barrel with a fifty-pound mallet. The sound echoed over Zephyr, and in another moment dogs started barking from Temple Street to Bruton and the roving bands of carolers were forced to give up the holy ghost. We stood out on the porch, listening to the commotion. I thought at first that the jet had crashed, but then I heard it again. It circled Zephyr a couple of times, its wingtip lights blinking, and then it veered toward Robbins Air Force Base and sped away.

The dogs kept barking and howling. People were coming out of their houses to see what was going on. "Somethin's up," Dad said. "I think I'll give Jack a call."

Sheriff Marchette had stepped ably into the job J. T. Amory had vacated. Of course, with the Blaylocks behind bars, Zephyr's crime wave was over. The most serious task that lay before Sheriff Marchette was finding the beast from the lost world, which had attacked the Trailways bus one day and gave it such a hard knock with its sawed-off horns that the driver and all eight of the passengers were admitted to the Union Town hospital with whiplash.

Dad reached Mrs. Marchette, but the sheriff had already grabbed his hat and run out, summoned away from Christmas Eve dinner by a phone call. Mrs. Marchette told Dad what her husband had told her, and with a stunned expression Dad relayed the news.

"A bomb," he said. "A bomb fell."

"What?" Mom was already fearing Russian invasion. *"Where?"*

"On Dick Moultry's house," Dad said. "Mrs. Moultry told Jack it went right through the roof, the livin' room floor, and into the basement."

"My Lord! Didn't the whole house blow up?"

"No. The bomb's just sittin' in there." Dad returned the receiver to its cradle. "Just sittin' in there with Dick."

"With *Dick?"*

"That's right. Mrs. Moultry gave Dick a new workshop bench for Christmas. He was in the basement puttin' it together. Now he's trapped down there with a live bomb."

It wasn't very long before the civil defense siren began wailing. Dad got a phone call from Mayor Swope, asking him if he would meet with a group of volunteers at the courthouse and help spread the word from door to door that both Zephyr and Bruton had to be immediately evacuated.

"On Christmas *Eve?"* Dad said. "Evacuate the whole *town?"*

"That's right, Tom." Mayor Swope sounded at his rope's end. "Do you know a bomb fell out of a jet plane right into—"

"Dick Moultry's house, yeah I've heard. It fell out of a jet plane?"

"Right again. And we've gotta get these people out of here in case that damn thing blows."

"Well, why don't you call the air base? Surely they'll come get it."

"I just got off the phone with 'em. Their public relations spokesman, I mean. I told him one of his jets lost a bomb over our town, and you know what he said? He said I must've been in the Christmas rum cake! He said no such thing happened, that none of their pilots were so careless as to accidentally hit a safety lever and drop a bomb on civilians. He said even *if* such a thing happened, their bomb deactivation team was not on duty on Christmas Eve, and *if* such a thing happened, he'd hope the civilians in that town upon which a bomb did *not* drop ought to have sense enough to evacuate because the bomb that did *not* fall from a jet plane could blow most of that town into toothpicks! Now, how about *that?"*

"He's got to know you're tellin' the truth, Luther. He'll send somebody to keep the bomb from explodin'."

"Maybe so, but *when?* Tomorrow afternoon? Do you want to go to sleep tonight with that thing tickin'? I can't risk it, Tom. We've got to get everybody out!"

Dad asked Mayor Swope to come pick him up. Then he hung up

the phone and told Mom she and I ought to take the truck and get to Grand Austin and Nana Alice's for the night. He'd come join us when the work was done. Mom started to beg him to come with us; she wanted to, as much as rain wants to follow clouds. But she saw that he had decided what was right, and she would have to learn to deal with it. She said, "Go get your pajamas, Cory. Get your toothbrush and a pair of fresh socks and underwear. We're goin' to Grand Austin's."

"Dad, is Zephyr gonna blow up?" I asked.

"No. We're movin' everybody out just for safety's sake. The Air Force boys'll send somebody to get that thing real soon, I'm sure of it."

"You'll be careful?" Mom asked him.

"You know it. Merry Christmas." He smiled.

She couldn't help but return it. "You crazy thing, you!" she said, and she kissed him.

Mom and I got some clothes packed. The civil defense siren wailed for almost fifteen minutes, a sound so spine-chilling it even silenced the dogs. Already people were getting the message, and they were driving away to spend the night with relatives, friends in other towns, or at the Union Pines Motel in Union Town. Mayor Swope came by to pick up Dad. Then Mom and I were ready to go. Before we walked out the door, the phone rang and it was Ben wanting to tell me they were going to Birmingham to spend the night with his aunt and uncle. "Ain't it somethin'?" he said excitedly. "Know what I heard? Mr. Moultry's got two busted legs and a broke back and the bomb's lyin' right on top of him! This is really neat, huh?"

I had to agree it was. We'd never experienced a Christmas Eve quite like it.

"Gotta go! Talk to you later! Oh, yeah . . . Merry Christmas!"

"Merry Christmas, Ben!"

He hung up. Mom collared me, and we were on our way to Grand Austin and Nana Alice's house. I'd never seen so many cars on Route Ten before. Heaven help us all if the beast from the lost world decided to attack right about now; there'd be a bomb behind us, cars and trucks tumped over like tenpins, and people flying through the air without wings.

We left Zephyr behind, all lit up for Christmas.

The rest of this story I found out later, since I wasn't there.

Curiosity got the best of Dad. He had to see the bomb. So, as Zephyr and Bruton gradually emptied out, he left the group of volunteers he was riding with and walked a half-dozen blocks to where Mr. Moultry lived. Mr. Moultry's house was a small wooden structure painted pale blue with white shutters. Light was streaming upward through the splintered roof. The sheriff's car was parked out front, its bubble light spinning around. Dad climbed up onto the porch, which had been knocked crooked by the impact. The front door was ajar, the walls riddled with cracks. The bomb's velocity had shoved the house off its foundations. Dad went inside, and he couldn't miss the huge hole in the sagging floor because it had swallowed half the room. A few Christmas tree decorations were scattered about, and a little silver star lay balanced on the hole's ragged edge. The tree itself was missing.

He peered down. Boards and beams were tangled up like a plateful of macaroni. Plaster dust was the Parmesan cheese. There was the meatball of the bomb: its iron-gray tail fins protruded from the debris, its nose plowed right into the basement's dirt floor.

"Get me outta here! Ohhhhh, my legs! Get me to the hospital! Ohhhhh, I'm dyin'!"

"You're not dyin', Dick. Just don't try to move."

Mr. Moultry was lying amid wreckage with a carpenter's work-bench on top of him, and atop that a beam as big around as a sturdy oak. It had split, and Dad figured it had been a support for the living room's floor. Lying across the beam that crisscrossed Mr. Moultry was the Christmas tree, its balls and bulbs shattered. The bomb wasn't on top of Mr. Moultry, but it had dug itself in about four feet from his head. Sheriff Marchette knelt nearby, deliberating the mess.

"Jack? It's Tom Mackenson!"

"Tom?" Sheriff Marchette looked up, his face streaked with plaster dust. "You ought to get outta here, man!"

"I wanted to come see it. Not as big as I thought it would be."

"It's plenty big enough," the sheriff said. "If this thing blows, it'll take the house and leave a crater where the whole block used to be."

"Ohhhhh!" Mr. Moultry groaned. His shirt had been torn open by the falling timbers, and his massive gut wobbled this way and that. "I said I'm dyin', damn it!"

"He hurt bad?" Dad asked.

"Can't get in there close enough to tell. Says he thinks his legs are broken. Maybe a busted rib or two, the way he's wheezin'."

"He always breathes like that," Dad said.

"Well, the ambulance ought to be here soon." Sheriff Marchette checked his wristwatch. "I called 'em directly I got here. I don't know what's keepin' 'em."

"What'd you tell 'em? That a fella got hit by a fallin' bomb?"

"Yes," the sheriff said.

"In that case, I think Dick's in for a long wait."

"Get me outta here!" Mr. Moultry tried to push some of the dusty tangle of lumber off him, but he winced and couldn't do it. He turned his head and looked at the bomb, sweat glistening on his suety cheeks. "Get *that* outta here! Jesus Christ, help me!"

"Where's Mrs. Moultry?" Dad asked.

"Huh!" Mr. Moultry's plaster-white face sneered. "She took off runnin' and left me here, that's what she did! Wouldn't even lift a finger to help me!"

"That's not quite right. She *did* call me, didn't she?" the sheriff pointed out.

"Well, what the hell are *you* good for? Ohhhhhh, my legs! They're broke plumb in two, I'm tellin' ya!"

"Can I come down?" Dad asked.

"Rather you didn't. Rather you got on out of here like any sane man should. But come on if you want to. Be careful, though. The stairs collapsed, so I set up a stepladder."

Dad eased himself down the ladder. He stood appraising the pile of timbers, beams, and Christmas tree on top of Mr. Moultry. "We can probably move that big one," he said. "I'll grab one end if you grab the other."

They cleared the tree aside and did the job, moving the oak-sized beam though their backs promised a rendezvous with deep-heating rub. Mr. Moultry, however, was still in a heap of trouble. "We can dig him out, take him to your car, and get him to the hospital," Dad suggested. "That ambulance isn't comin'."

The sheriff knelt down beside Mr. Moultry. "Hey, Dick. You weighed yourself lately?"

"Weighed myself? Hell, no! Why should I?"

"What did you weigh the last time you had a physical?"

"One hundred and sixty pounds."

"When?" Sheriff Marchette asked. "In the third grade? How much do you weigh right *now*, Dick?"

Mr. Moultry scowled and muttered. Then he said, "A little bit over two hundred."

"Try again."

"Aw, shit! I weigh two hundred and ninety pounds! Does that satisfy you, you sadist you?"

"Maybe got two broken legs. Broken ribs. Possible internal injuries. And he weighs two hundred and ninety pounds. Think we can get him up that ladder, Tom?"

"No way," my father said.

"My thoughts right on the button. He's stuck in here until somebody can bring a hoist."

"What do you mean?" Mr. Moultry squawked. "I gotta stay here?" He looked fearfully at the bomb again. "Well, for God's sake get that damn thing away from me, then!"

"I'd do that for you, Dick," the sheriff said. "I really would, but I'd have to touch it. And what if the thing's primed to go off and all it needs is a finger's touch? You think I want to be responsible for blowin' you up? Not to mention myself and Tom? No, sir!"

"Mayor Swope told me he talked to somebody at Robbins," Dad said to the sheriff. "Said the fella didn't believe—"

"Yeah, Luther came by here before he and his family hit the trail. He told me all about what that sumbitch said. Maybe the pilot was too scared to let anybody know how bad he messed up. Probably staggered out of a Christmas party and climbed right into the cockpit. All I know for sure is, nobody's comin' from Robbins to get this thing anytime soon."

"What am I supposed to do?" Mr. Moultry asked. "Just lie here and suffer?"

"I can go upstairs and fetch you a pilla, if you like," Sheriff Marchette offered.

"Dick? Dick, you okay?" The voice, tentative and afraid, was coming from upstairs.

"Oh, I'm just dandy!" Mr. Moultry hollered. "I'm just tickled pink"—pank, he pronounced it—"to be layin' down here with two busted legs and a bomb next to my melon! God a'mighty! I don't know who you are up there, but you're a bigger idiot than the fool who dropped that damn bomb in the first . . . oh. It's you."

"Hi there, Dick," Mr. Gerald Hargison said sheepishly. "How're you doin'?"

"I could just dance!" Mr. Moultry's face was getting splotched with crimson. "Shit!"

Mr. Hargison stood at the edge of the hole and peered down. "That's the bomb right there, is it?"

"No, it's a big goose turd!" Mr. Moultry raged. " 'Course it's the bomb!"

While Mr. Moultry thrashed to get free again and only succeeded in raising a storm of plaster dust and causing himself considerable pain, Dad looked around the basement. Over in one corner was a desk, and above it a wall plaque that read A MAN'S HOME IS HIS CASTLE. Next to it was a poster of a bug-eyed black minstrel tap-dancing, and underneath it the hand-lettered sign THE WHITE MAN'S BURDEN. Dad wandered over to the desk, the top of which was six inches deep in untidy papers. He slid open the upper drawer and was hit in the face by the enormous mammary glands of a woman on a *Juggs* magazine cover. Underneath the magazine was a hodgepodge of Gem clips, pencils, rubber bands, and the like. An overexposed Kodak picture came to hand. It showed Dick Moultry wearing a white robe and cradling in one arm a rifle while the other embraced a peaked white cap and hood. Mr. Moultry was smiling broadly, proud of his accomplishments.

"Hey, get outta there!" Mr. Moultry swiveled his head around. "It ain't enough I'm layin' here dyin', you've gotta ransack my house, too?"

Dad closed the drawer on the picture and walked back to Sheriff Marchette. Above them, Mr. Hargison nervously scuffed his soles on the warped floor. "Listen, Dick, I just wanted to come by and see about you. Make sure you weren't . . . you know, dead and all."

"No, I'm not dead *yet*. Much as my wife wishes that bomb had clunked me right on the brainpan."

"We're headin' out of town," Mr. Hargison explained. "Uh . . . we probably won't be back until day after Christmas. Probably get back near ten o'clock in the mornin'. Hear me, Dick? Ten o'clock in the mornin'."

"Yeah, I hear you! I don't care what time you get back!"

"Well, we'll get back near ten o'clock. In the mornin', day after Christmas. Thought you might want to know, so you could set your watch."

"Set my *watch*? Are you—" He stopped. "Oh. Yeah. Okay, I'll do that." He grinned, his face sweating as he looked up at the sheriff. "Gerald and me are supposed to help a friend clean out his garage day after Christmas. That's why he's tellin' me what time he'll be back."

"Is that so?" the sheriff asked. "What friend might that be, Dick?"

"Oh . . . fella lives in Union Town. You wouldn't know him."

"I know a lot of people in Union Town. What's your friend's name?"

"Joe," Mr. Hargison said, at the exact second Mr. Moultry said, "Sam."

"Joe Sam," Mr. Moultry explained, still sweatily grinning. "Joe Sam Jones."

"I don't think you're gonna be helping any Joe Sam Jones clean out his garage the day after Christmas, Dick. I think you'll be in a nice secure hospital room, don't you?"

"Hey, Dick, I'm headin' off!" Mr. Hargison announced. "Don't you worry, you're gonna be just fine." And with that last word the toe of his left shoe nudged the silver Christmas tree star that lay balanced on the hole's ragged edge. Dad watched the little star fall as if in graceful slow motion, like a magnified snowflake drifting down.

It hit one of the bomb's iron-gray tail fins, and exploded in a shower of painted glass.

In the seconds of silence that followed, all four of the men heard it.

The bomb made a hissing sound, like a serpent that had been awakened in its nest. The hissing faded, and from the bomb's guts there came a slow, ominous ticking: not like the ticking of an alarm clock, but rather the ticking of a hot engine building up to a boil.

"Oh . . . shit," Sheriff Marchette whispered.

"Jesus save me!" Mr. Moultry gasped. His face, which had been flushed crimson a few moments before, now became as white as a wax dummy.

"The thing's switched on," Dad said, his voice choked.

Mr. Hargison's speech was by far the most eloquent. He spoke with his legs, which propelled him across the warped floor, out onto the crooked porch and to his car at the curb as if he'd been boomed from a cannon. The car sped away like the Road Runner: one second there, the next not.

"Oh God, oh God!" Tears had sprung to Mr. Moultry's eyes. "Don't let me die!"

"Tom? I believe it's time." Sheriff Marchette was speaking softly, as if the weight of words passing through the air might be enough to cause concussion. "To vamoose, don't you?"

"You can't leave me! You can't! You're the *sheriff!*"

"I can't do anythin' more for you, Dick. I swear I wish I could, but I can't. Seems to me you need magic or a miracle right about now, and I think the well's run dry."

"Don't leave me! Get me out of this, Jack! I'll pay you whatever you want!"

"I'm sorry. Climb on up, Tom."

Dad didn't have to be told a second time. He scaled that ladder like Lucifer up a tree. At the top, he said, "I'll steady the ladder for you, Jack! Come on!"

The bomb ticked. And ticked. And ticked.

"I can't help you, Dick," Sheriff Marchette said, and he climbed the ladder.

"No! Listen! I'll do anythin'! Get me out, okay? I won't mind if it hurts! Okay?"

Dad and Sheriff Marchette were on their way to the door.

"Please!" Mr. Moultry shouted. His voice cracked, and a sob came out. He fought against his trap, but the pain made him cry harder. *"You can't leave me to die! It's not human!"*

He was still shouting and sobbing as Dad and the sheriff left the house. Both their faces were drawn and tight. "Great job this turned out to be," Sheriff Marchette said. "Jesus." They reached the sheriff's car. "You need a ride somewhere, Tom?"

"Yeah." He frowned. "No." And he leaned against the car. "I don't know."

"Now, don't look like that! There's not a thing can be done for him, and you know it!"

"Maybe somebody ought to wait around, in case the bomb squad shows up."

"Fine." The sheriff glanced up and down the deserted street. "Are you volunteerin'?"

"No."

"Me, neither! And they're not gonna show up anytime soon, Tom. I think that bomb's gonna explode and we'll lose this whole block, and I don't know about you, but I'm gettin' out while I've still got my skin." He walked around to the driver's door.

"Jack, wait a minute," Dad said.

"Ain't got a minute. Come on, if you're comin'."

Dad got into the car with him, and Sheriff Marchette started the engine. "Where to?"

"Listen to me, Jack. You said it yourself: Dick needs magic or a miracle, right? So who's the one person around here who might be able to give it to him?"

"Reverend Blessett's left town."

"No, not him! *Her.*"

Sheriff Marchette paused with his hand on the gearshift.

"Anybody who can turn a bag of shotgun shells into a bag of garden snakes might be able to take care of a bomb, don't you think?"

"No, I don't! I don't think the Lady had a thing to do with that. I think Biggun Blaylock was so blasted out of his mind on his own rotgut whiskey that he thought he was fillin' that ammo bag full of cartridges when all the time he was shovelin' the snakes in!"

"Oh, come on! You saw those snakes the same as I did! There were *hundreds* of 'em! How long would it have taken Biggun to find 'em all?"

"I don't believe in that voodoo stuff," Sheriff Marchette said. "Not one bit."

Dad said the first thing that came to mind, and saying it left a shocked taste in his mouth: "We can't be afraid to ask her for help, Jack. She's all we've got."

"Damn," the sheriff muttered. "Damn and double-damn." He looked at the Moultry house, light rising from its broken roof. "She might be gone by now."

"She might be. She might not be. Can't we at least drive over there and find out?"

Many houses in Bruton were dark, their owners having obeyed the siren and fled the impending blast. Her rainbow-hued dwelling, however, was all lit up. Tiny sparkling lights blinked in the windows.

"I'll wait right here," Sheriff Marchette said. Dad nodded and got out. He took a deep breath of Christmas Eve air and made his legs move. They carried him to the front door. He took the door's knocker, a little silver hand, and did something he never dreamed he would've done in a million years: he announced to the Lady that he had come to call.

He waited, hoping she would answer.

He waited, watching the doorknob.

He waited.

Fifteen minutes after my father took the silver hand, there was a noise on the street where Dick Moultry lived. It was a rumble and a clatter, a clanking and a clinking, and it caused the dogs to bark in its wake. The rust-splotched, suspension-sagging pickup truck stopped at the curb in front of the Moultry house, and a long, skinny black man got out of the driver's door. On that door was stenciled, not very neatly: LIGHTFOOT'S FIX-IT.

He moved so slowly it seemed that movement might be a painful process. He wore freshly washed overalls and a gray cap that allowed his gray hair to boil out from beneath it. In supreme slow motion, he walked to the truck's bed and strapped on his tool belt, which held several different kinds of hammers, screwdrivers, and arcane-looking wrenches. In a slow extension of time he picked up his toolbox, an old metal fascination filled with drawers that held every kind of nut and bolt under the workman's sun. Then, as if moving under the burden of the ages, Mr. Marcus Lightfoot walked to Dick Moultry's crooked entrance. He knocked at the door, even though it stood wide open: One . . . two . . .

Eternities passed. Civilizations thrived and crumbled. Stars were born in brawny violence and died doddering in the cold vault of the cosmos.

. . . three.

"Thank God!" Mr. Moultry shouted, his voice worn to a frazzle.

"I knew you wouldn't let me die, Jack! Oh, God have mer—" He stopped shouting in mid-praise, because he was looking up through the hole in the living room's floor, and instead of help from heaven he saw the black face of what he considered a devil of the earth.

"Lawdy, lawdy," Mr. Lightfoot said. His eyes had found the bomb, his ear the ticking of its detonation mechanism. "You sure in a big pile'a mess."

"Have you come to watch me get blown up, you black savage?" Mr. Moultry snarled.

"Nossuh. Come ta keep you from gettin' blowed."

"You? Help *me?* Hah!" He pulled in a breath and roared through his ravaged throat: *"Jack! Somebody help me! Anybody white!"*

"Mr. Moultry, suh?" Mr. Lightfoot waited for the other man's lungs to give out. "That there bumb might not care for such a' noise."

Mr. Moultry, his face the color of ketchup and the sweat standing up in beads, began fighting his condition. He thrashed and clawed at the pile of debris; he grasped at his own shirt in a fit of rage and ripped the rest of it away; he gripped at the very air but found no handholds there. And then the pain crashed over him like one wrestler bodyslamming another and Mr. Moultry was left gasping and breathless but still with two broken legs and a bomb ticking next to his head.

"I believe," Mr. Lightfoot said, and he yawned at the lateness of the hour, "I'd best come on down."

It might have been New Year's Eve before Mr. Lightfoot reached the bottom of the stepladder, the tools in his belt jingling together. He grasped his toolbox and started toward Mr. Moultry, but the poster of the bug-eyed minstrel on the wall caught his attention. He stared at it as the seconds and the bomb ticked.

"Heh-heh," Mr. Lightfoot said, and shook his head. "Heh heh."

"What're you laughin' at, you crazy jigaboo?"

"Thass a white man," he said. "All painted up and lookin' the fool."

At last Mr. Lightfoot pulled himself away from the picture of Al Jolson and went to the bomb. He cleared away some nail-studded timbers and roof shingles and sat down on the red dirt, a process that was like watching a snail cross a football field. He drew the toolbox close to his side, like a trusted companion. Then he took a pair of wire-rimmed spectacles from the breast pocket of his shirt, blew on the lenses, and wiped them on his sleeve, all at excruciating slowness.

"What have I done to deserve this?" Mr. Moultry croaked.

Mr. Lightfoot got his spectacles on. "Now," he said. "I can." He leaned closer to the bomb, and as he frowned the small lines deepened between his eyes. "See   what's what."

He took a hammer with a miniature head from his belt. He licked his thumb and—slowly, slowly—marked the hammer's head with his spit. Then he tapped the bomb's side so lightly it hardly made a noise.

"Don't hit it! Oh Jeeeeesus! You'll blow us both to hell!"

"Ain't," Mr. Lightfoot replied as he made small tappings up and down the bomb's side, "plannin' on it." He pressed his ear against the bomb's iron skin. "Uh-huh," he said. "I   hears you   talkin'." As Mr. Moultry agonized in terrified silence, Mr. Lightfoot's fingers were at work, moving across the bomb as one might stroke a small dog. "Uh-huh." His fingers stopped on a thin seam. "Thass   the way   ta   your heart,   ain't it?" He located four screws just below the tail fins, and he lifted the proper screwdriver from its place on his belt like a glacier melting.

"You came here to kill me, didn't you?" Mr. Moultry groaned. He received a punch of insight. "*She* sent you, didn't she? She sent you to kill me!"

"Got," Mr. Lightfoot said as he made the first turn of the first screw, "half   that   right."

Eons later, the final screw fell into Mr. Lightfoot's palm. Mr. Lightfoot had started humming "Frosty, the Snowman," in his somnolent way. Sometime between the removal of the second and third screws, the sound of the detonation mechanism had changed from a tick to a rasp. Mr. Moultry, lying in a stew of sweat, his eyes glassy and his head thrashing back and forth with dementia, had lost five pounds.

Mr. Lightfoot took from his toolbox a small blue jar. He opened it and with the tip of his index finger withdrew some greasy gunk the color of eel's skin. He spat into it, and smeared the gunk onto the seam that circled the bomb. Then he took hold of the tail fins and tried to give them a counterclockwise turn. They resisted. He tried it in the clockwise direction, but that, too, was fruitless.

"Listen here!" Mr. Lightfoot's voice was stern, his brow furrowed with disapproval. "Don't you   gimme no   sass!" With the miniature hammer he clunked the screw holes, and Mr. Moultry lost another few ounces as his pants suddenly got wet. Then Mr. Lightfoot gripped the tail fins with both hands and pulled.

Slowly, with a thin high *skrreeeeek* of resistance, the bomb's tail section began to slide out. It was hard work, and Mr. Lightfoot had to pause to stretch his cramping fingers. Then he went back to it, with the determination of a sloth gripping a tree branch. At last the tail section came free, and exposed were electronic circuits, a jungle of different-colored wires, and shiny black plastic cylinders that resembled the backs of roaches.

"Hoooowheeee!" Mr. Lightfoot breathed, enchanted. "Ain't it pretty?"

"Killin' me . . ." Mr. Moultry moaned. "Killin' me dead . . ."

The rasping was louder. Mr. Lightfoot used a metal probe to touch a small red box from which the noise emanated. Then he used his finger, and he whistled as he drew the finger back. "Oh-oh," he said. "Gettin' kinda   warm."

Mr. Moultry began to blubber, his nose running and the tears trickling from his swollen eyes.

Mr. Lightfoot's fingers were at work again, tracing the wires to their points of origin. The smell of heat rose into the air, which shimmered over the red box. Mr. Lightfoot scratched his chin. "Y'know," he   said,   "I   believe   we   gots us   a   problem   here."

Mr. Moultry trembled on the edge of coma.

"See, I"—Mr. Lightfoot tapped his chin, his eyes narrowed with concentration—"fix   things. I don't break 'em." He drew in a long breath and slowly released it. "Gone have ta   do   a little   breakin', seems ta   me." He   nodded. "Yessuh. Sure   do hate   ta break somethin'   so pretty." He chose another, larger hammer. "Gone   have   ta   do it." He cracked the hammer down on the red box. Its plastic skin split from one end to the other. Mr. Moultry's teeth gripped his tongue. Mr. Lightfoot removed the two plastic sections and regarded the smaller workings and wires within. "Jus'   mysteries   in mysteries," he said. He put his hand down into the toolbox and it came out holding a little wire cutter that still had its ninety-nine-cent price sticker on it. "Now,   listen good," he told the bomb, "don't   you   burp   in my face, hear?"

"Ohhhhh God, oh Jeeeesus above, oh I'm comin' to heaven, I'm comin'," Mr. Moultry gasped.

"You get there," Mr. Lightfoot said with a faint smile, "you   tell St. Peter   he's   got a   fix-it-man   on the way." He reached the cutter toward two wires—one black, the other white—that crisscrossed at the heart of the machine.

"Wait," Mr. Moultry whispered. "Wait . . ."

Mr. Lightfoot paused.

"Gotta get it off my soul," Mr. Moultry said, his eyes as bugged as the minstrel's. "Gotta get light, so I can fly to heaven. Listen to me . . ."

"Listenin'," Mr. Lightfoot told him as the bomb spoke on.

"Gerald and me . . . we . . . it was Gerald did the most of it, really . . . I didn't wanna have nothin' to do with it . . . but . . . it's set to go off at . . . ten in the mornin' . . . day after Christmas. Hear me? Ten in the mornin'. It's a box . . . full of dynamite . . . and an alarm clock timer. We paid Biggun Blaylock, and he . . . he got it for us." Mr. Moultry swallowed, perhaps feeling hell's fire under his buns. "It's set to blow up that civil rights museum. We . . . it was all Gerald's idea, really . . . decided to do it when we first heard the Lady was plannin' on buildin' it. Listen to me, Lightfoot!"

"Listenin'," he said slowly and calmly.

"Gerald planted it, somewhere around that museum. Could be in the recreation center. I don't know where it is, I swear to God . . . but it's over there right now, and it's gonna go off at ten in the mornin', day after Christmas."

"That right?" Mr. Lightfoot asked.

"Yes! It's the truth, and God take me to heaven 'cause I've freed my soul!"

"Uh-huh." Mr. Lightfoot reached out. He gripped the black wire with the cutter and *snip*, the black wire was parted. The bomb, however, would not be silenced so easily.

"Do you hear me, Lightfoot? That box of dynamite is over there right this minute!"

Mr. Lightfoot eased the cutter's blades around the white wire. A muscle clenched in his jaw, and sweat sparkled on his cheeks like diamond dust. He said, "No,   it ain't."

"Ain't what?"

"Over   there.   Not   no   more.   Done   found it.   Gone cut   this   wire   now." His hand trembled. "Might   blow   if   I've   cut   the   wrong wire   first."

"God have mercy," Mr. Moultry whined. "Oh Jesus I swear I'll be a good boy every day of my life if you just let me live!"

"I'm   cuttin'," Mr. Lightfoot said.

Mr. Moultry squeezed his eyes shut. The cutter went *snip*.

KA-BOOOMMMMM!

In that tremendous roar of destruction and fire, Mr. Moultry screamed.

When his screaming wound down, he heard not the harps of the angels nor the devils singing "For He's a Jolly Good Fellow." He heard: "Heh heh heh   heh."

Mr. Moultry's eyes flew open.

Mr. Lightfoot was grinning. He blew a little flicker of blue flame from the snipped end of the white wire. The bomb was tamed and mute. Mr. Lightfoot spoke in a voice made hoarse by the tremendous yell he'd just yelled into Mr. Moultry's ear. "Beggin' your pardon, suh," he said. "Jus' couldn't pass it up."

Mr. Moultry seemed to deflate, as if he'd been punctured. With a slow hissing sound, he fainted dead away.

5

Sixteen Drops of Blood

I'm back.

The time bomb box full of dynamite—with an extra stick thrown in from the gracious hand of Biggun Blaylock—had indeed been found, not long after I had informed the Lady who my dream visitors were. I must've remembered that picture and kept it in the back of my head, and then after the cross-burning and my witnessing Mr. Hargison and Mr. Moultry buy the box from Biggun Blaylock, I must've known subconsciously what the box was. That's why I'd taken to knocking my alarm clock off my bedside table. The only hitch in this theory is that I'd never seen pictures of the girls who'd died at the 16th Street Baptist Church until at the museum. I don't think. Maybe they were in the *Life* magazine. Mom had thrown it out, though, so I can't say for sure.

The Lady put it together as soon as I'd told her. She organized everyone at the reception to start looking for a wooden box either in the recreation center, the civil rights museum, or in the vicinity outside. Nobody could find it, and we tore that place up searching. Then the Lady recalled that Mr. Hargison was a postman. Right outside the center, on the corner of Buckhart Street, was a mailbox. Charles Damaronde held Gavin by his heels as he slid into the mailbox, and we heard his muffled voice say, "Here it is!" He couldn't bring it up, though, because it was too heavy. Sheriff Marchette was called, and he came with Zephyr's postmaster, Mr.

Conrad Oatman, who brought the mailbox key. In that box was enough dynamite to blow up the recreation center, the civil rights museum, and two or three houses across the street. Evidently, four hundred dollars was enough to buy a mighty big bang.

Mr. Hargison, knowing what times the mail was picked up and that the mailbox would not be opened again until sometime on the afternoon of December 26th, had set the alarm clock timer for ten on the dot. Sheriff Marchette said the bomb had been constructed by a professional, because you could adjust the timer to either twelve, twenty-four, or forty-eight hours. He told the Lady that he didn't want Mr. Hargison or Mr. Moultry to know the bomb had been found yet, not until the innards were dusted for fingerprints. Mom and I had told Dad when we'd gotten home from the recreation center, and I have to say that both he and Sheriff Marchette did a good job of not spilling the beans when they were at Dick Moultry's house and Mr. Hargison walked in. Mr. Moultry's confession turned out to be the icing on the cake, since the time bomb yielded five prints that perfectly matched Mr. Hargison's. So those two were taken off pretty soon to visit the Federal Bureau of Investigation office in Birmingham, and needless to say their names were ticked off the roster of the residents of my hometown.

The civil rights museum had its grand opening. I had no more dreams of the four black girls. But if I ever wanted to see them again, I knew where to go.

The falling of the bomb from a jet plane and the finding of a Ku Klux Klan bomb in a mailbox outside the civil rights museum kept Zephyr buzzing in the days following Christmas. Ben, Johnny, and I debated whether Mr. Lightfoot had ever been really afraid of the bomb or not. Ben said he had been, while Johnny and I took the position that Mr. Lightfoot was like Nemo Curliss; instead of baseball, though, Mr. Lightfoot's natural affinity was to anything mechanical, even a bomb, so when he stared those wires down he knew exactly what he was doing every second. Ben, incidentally, had had an interesting experience in Birmingham. He and his mom and dad had stayed with Ben's uncle Miles, who worked at a downtown bank. Miles had given Ben a tour of the vault, and all Ben could talk about was the smell of money, how green it was and how pretty. He said Miles had actually let him hold a pack of fifty one-hundred-dollar bills, and Ben's fingers were still tingling. Ben announced that he didn't know what he was going to do in this life, but as far as possible it was going to involve lots and lots of money. Johnny and I just laughed at him. We missed Davy Ray, because we knew what his comment would've been.

Johnny had asked for and received two Christmas presents. One was a policeman's kit, complete with honorary badge, fingerprint powder, handcuffs, burglar dust that got on the shoes of burglars and only showed up under ultraviolet light, and a policeman's handbook. The other was a wooden display case with little shelves in it, to show his arrowhead collection. He filled it up except for one shelf, which was reserved for a certain smooth black arrowhead if Chief Five Thunders ever decided to give it up again.

A question remained about Mr. Lightfoot and the bomb. Mom voiced it two nights after Christmas, as a cold rain fell on Zephyr.

"Tom?" she said. We were all sitting in the front room, with the fireplace blazing. You couldn't have pried *The Golden Apples of the Sun* out of my hands with a crowbar. "What made Mr. Lightfoot go to Dick Moultry's house, anyway? I wouldn't have thought that was somethin' he might've volunteered to do."

Dad didn't answer.

Just as parents have sixth senses about their children, so, too, do children about their parents. I lowered my book. Dad continued to read the newspaper.

"Tom? Do you know what made Mr. Lightfoot do it?"

He cleared his throat. "Kind of," he said quietly.

"Well, what was it?"

"I guess . . . I had somethin' to do with it."

"*You* did? How?"

He lowered the paper, realizing there was no way out but the truth. "I . . . asked the Lady for help."

Mom sat in stunned silence. Rain struck the windows and the fireplace log popped, and still she didn't budge.

"I figured she was the only chance Dick had. After what she did with Biggun Blaylock's ammo bag . . . I thought she could help him. And I was right, it appears. She called Marcus Lightfoot while I was there at her house."

"Her *house*? I can't believe this! You went to the Lady's house?"

"Not just to it. Inside it. I sat down in her chair. I drank a cup of her coffee." He shrugged. "I suppose I was expectin' shrunken heads on the walls and black widow spiders in every corner. I didn't know she was *religious.*"

"To the Lady's house," Mom said. "I just can't believe it! And after all this time when you were so afraid of her!"

"I wasn't afraid of her," Dad corrected Mom. "I was just . . . a little skittish, that's all."

"And she said she'd help Dick Moultry? Even when she knew he'd had a hand in settin' that time bomb?"

"Well . . . it wasn't quite that simple," my father admitted.

"Oh?" Mom waited. When Dad offered no more information, Mom said, "I'd like to hear it."

"She made me promise to come back. She said she could look at me and tell I was bein' eaten up alive. She said it showed in your face and in Cory's, too. She said we were all livin' under the strain of that dead man at the bottom of Saxon's Lake." Dad put the newspaper down and watched the fire. "And you know what? She's right. I promised to go back to see her tomorrow evenin' at seven o'clock. I was gonna tell you, eventually. Or maybe I wasn't, I don't know."

"Pride, pride," Mom scolded him. "You mean to tell me you did for Dick Moultry what you wouldn't do for *me?*"

"No. It's just that I wasn't ready. Dick needed help. I found it for him. And now I'm ready to find it for myself and both of you, too."

Mom got up from her chair. She stood behind my father, and she put her hands on his shoulders and leaned her chin against his head. I watched their shadows merge. He reached up and put his arm around her neck. They stayed that way for a moment, heart-close, as the fire cracked and sizzled.

It was time to go see the Lady.

When we arrived at her house at ten minutes before seven o'clock, Mr. Damaronde answered the door. Dad had no qualms about crossing the threshold; his fear of the Lady was gone. The Moon Man came out, clad in his robe and slippers, and offered us some pretzels. Mrs. Damaronde put on a pot of coffee—the New Orleans kind with chicory, she said—and we waited in the front room until the Lady was ready to see us.

I was keeping my suspicions about Dr. Lezander to myself. I still couldn't let my heart believe that Dr. Lezander, who had always been so kind and gentle to Rebel, might be a murderer. I had the connection of the two parrots, but there was nothing to connect Dr. Lezander with the dead man except a green feather, and that was just my theory. So he didn't like milk and he was a night owl; did that make him a killer? Before I told my parents, I would need something more solid to go on.

We didn't have to wait very long. Mr. Damaronde asked us to come back with him, and he led us not to the Lady's bedroom but to another room across the hallway. In it, the Lady was sitting in a high-backed chair behind a folding card table. She wore not a voodoo robe or a wizard's cap, but just a plain dark gray dress with a lapel pin in the shape of a dancing harlequin. On the floor of what was obviously her consultation room was a rug of woven reeds, and

427

a crooked tree grew from a big clay pot in the corner. The walls were painted beige and unadorned. Mr. Damaronde closed the door and the Lady said, "Sit down, Tom."

Dad obeyed. I could tell he was nervous, because I could hear his throat click when he swallowed. He flinched a little when the Lady reached down beside her chair and brought up a doctor's bag. She placed it on the table and unzipped it.

"Is this gonna hurt?" Dad asked.

"It might. Depends."

"On what?"

"How deep we have to cut to get at the truth," she answered. She reached into the bag and brought out something wrapped up in blue cloth. Then a silver filigreed box came out, followed by a deck of cards. She brought out a sheet of typing paper. In the overhead light I saw the Nifty watermark; it was the same brand of paper I used. Last out of the bag was a pill bottle containing three polished river pebbles: one ebony, one reddish-brown, one white with gray bands. She said, "Open your right hand," and when Dad did she unscrewed the pill bottle's cap and shook the river pebbles into his palm. "Work those in your hand awhile," she directed.

Dad gave a nervous smile as he did as she asked. "Did these come from Old Moses's stomach or somethin'?"

"No. They're just old pebbles I found. Keep workin' 'em, they'll calm you down."

"Oh," Dad said, rolling the worry-pebbles around and around in his palm.

Mom and I stood to one side, to give the Lady plenty of room to do what she was going to do. Whatever that might be. I don't know what I expected. Maybe one of those torchlit ceremonies with people dancing around in circles and hollering. But it wasn't like that at all. The Lady began to shuffle the cards, and the way she did it I suspected she might have given lessons to Maverick. "Tell me about your dreams, Tom," she said as the cards made a rhythmic *whirr*ing noise between her supple fingers.

Dad glanced uneasily at us. "Do you want them to go?" the Lady asked, but he shook his head. "I dream," he began, "about watchin' the car go into Saxon's Lake. Then I'm in the water with it, and I'm lookin' through the window at the dead man. His face . . . all smashed up. The handcuff on his wrist. The piano wire around his throat. And as the car's goin' down and the water starts floodin' in he—" Dad had to pause a minute. The pebbles clicked together in his palm. "He looks at me and he grins. That awful, smashed face grins. And when he speaks it's like . . . mud gurglin'."

"What does he say?"

"He says . . . 'Come with me, down in the dark.'" Dad's face was a study in pain, and it hurt me to look at it. "That's what he says. 'Come with me, down in the dark.' And he reaches for me, with his hand that isn't shackled. He reaches for me, and I pull back because I'm terrified he's gonna touch me. Then it ends."

"You have other recurrin' dreams?"

"A few. Not as strong as that one, though. Sometimes I think I hear piano music. Sometimes I think I hear somebody hollerin', but it sounds like gibberish. Occasionally I see a pair of hands holdin' that wire, and what looks like a thick wooden baton wrapped up with black tape. There are faces in there that are all blurred up, as if I'm lookin' at 'em through blood or my eyes can hardly hold a focus. But I don't have those nearly as much as the one about the man in the car."

"Did Rebecca tell you that I'm pickin' up some of those snippets, too?" She continued to shuffle the cards. It was a hypnotic, soothing sound. "I hear bits of piano music, the hollerin', and I see the wire and the crackerknocker. I've seen the tattoo, but not the rest of him." She smiled faintly. "You and me are plugged into the same socket, Tom, but you're gettin' more juice than I am. Can you beat that?"

"I thought you were supposed to be the mystic," Dad said.

"I am. Supposed to be. But everybody's got the dream-eyes, Tom. Everybody sees snippets of some quilt or another. You're real close to this one. Closer than I am. That's why."

Dad worked the river pebbles. The Lady shuffled her cards and waited.

"At first," he said, "I was havin' those dreams right when I went to bed. Then later on . . . they started comin' on me when I wasn't even asleep. Durin' the day. I just have a flash of that car, and that man's face, and I hear him callin'. He says the same thing, over and over: 'Come with me, down in the dark.' I hear that mud-gurglin' voice, and I've . . . I've come close to goin' to pieces over it, because I can't shake it. I can't get any rest. It's like I'm up all night, too scared to let myself sleep for fear of . . ." He trailed off.

"Yes?" the Lady prodded.

"For fear of . . . listenin' to that dead man, and doin' what he wants me to do."

"And what might that be, Tom?"

"I think he wants me to kill myself," Dad said.

The card shuffling ceased. Mom's hand found mine and clenched it hard.

"I think he . . . wants me to come to that lake and drown myself in it. I think he wants me to come with him, down in the dark."

The Lady watched him intently, her emerald eyes gathering light. "Why would he want you to do that, Tom?"

"I don't know. Maybe he wants company." He tried for a smile, but his mouth wouldn't work.

"I want you to think very, very carefully. Are those the exact words?"

"Yeah. 'Come with me, down in the dark.' He says it kinda gurgly, because I guess his jaw's busted or there's blood or water or mud in his mouth, but . . . yeah, that's it."

"Nothin' else? Does he call you by name?"

"No. That's all."

"You know, that's funny, don't you think?" the Lady asked.

Dad grunted. "I wish I knew what was so funny about it!"

"This: If the dead man has a chance to speak to you—to give you a message—then why does he waste it on askin' you to commit suicide? Why doesn't he tell you who killed him?"

Dad blinked. Now the clickings of the pebbles stopped. "I . . . never thought about that."

"Think about it, then. The dead man has a voice, however torn up it is. Why doesn't he tell you the name of his killer?"

"I can't say. Seems he would if he could."

"He could." The Lady nodded. "If he was speakin' to *you*, that is."

"I'm not followin' you."

"Maybe," she said, "there are three plugs in that socket."

Realization crawled over Dad's face. Over mine and Mom's, too.

"The dead man isn't speakin' to you, Tom," the Lady said. "He's speakin' to his killer."

"You . . . mean I'm . . ."

"Pickin' up the killer's dreams, like I'm pickin' up yours. Oh, mercy! You've got some *strong* dream-eyes, Tom!"

"He doesn't . . . want me to . . . *kill* myself because I couldn't get him out?"

"No," the Lady said. "Of that I'm sure."

Dad pressed his free hand to his mouth. Tears blurred his eyes, and I heard Mom sob beside me at the sight. He leaned his head forward. A single tear dropped to the table.

"Cuttin' deep," the Lady said, and she put a hand on his forearm. "It's a good hurt, though, isn't it? Like cuttin' away a cancer."

"Yes." His voice cracked. "Yes."

"You want to go outside and walk around a bit, you go right ahead."

Dad's shoulders trembled. But the burden was leaving him, ton by ton. He drew a deep, gasping breath, like the breath of someone whose head has just broken the surface of dark water. "I'm all right," he said, but he didn't lift his face up just yet. "Give me a minute."

"All the minutes you need, take 'em."

At last he looked up. He was still the man he'd been a moment before; his face was still lined, his chin a little saggy. But in his eyes he was a boy again, and he was free.

"You interested in tryin' to find out who that killer might be?" the Lady asked.

Dad nodded.

"I've got my own host of friends across the river. You get to be my age, you've got more of 'em on that side than this. They see things, and sometimes they tell me. But they like to play games with me. They like to throw me a riddle or two. So they never come right out and answer any question directly; it's always a sly answer, but it's always the truth. You want to involve them in this matter?" It sounded like a question she was used to asking.

"I guess I do."

"Either do or not, no damn guessin' about it."

After the least bit of hesitation, my father said, "I do."

The Lady opened the silver filigreed box and shook six small bones out on the table. "Put down the pebbles," she said. "Pick up those in your right hand."

Dad looked distastefully at what lay before him. "Do I have to?"

The Lady paused. Then she sighed and said, "Naw. It's a mood-setter, is all." She used the edge of her hand to sweep the bones back into the silver box. She closed it and set it aside. Then she reached into the doctor's bag again. This time her hand came out with a small bottle of clear liquid and a plastic bag full of cotton swabs. She set these between them and opened the bottle. "You'll have to put the pebbles down, though. Hold out your index finger."

"Why?"

"Because I said so."

He did it. The Lady opened the bottle and upturned it over one of the cotton swabs. Then she dabbed the tip of Dad's index finger. "Alcohol," she explained. "Get it from Dr. Parrish." She spread the Nifty typing paper down on the table. Then she unwrapped the object in the blue cloth. It was a stick with two needles driven through one end. "Keep your finger still," she told him as she picked up the needled stick.

"What're you gonna do? You're not gonna jab me with those, are—"

The needles came down fast and rather roughly into the tip of Dad's finger. "Ouch!" he said. I, too, had winced, my index finger stinging with phantom pain. Instantly blood began to well up from the needle holes. "Keep your blood off that paper," the Lady told him. Working quickly, she dabbed alcohol on the index finger of her own right hand and with her left she whacked the needles down. Here blood was drawn, too. She said, "Ask your question. Not aloud, but in your mind. Ask it clearly. Ask it like you expect an answer. Go ahead."

"All right," Dad said after a few seconds. "What now?"

"What was the date that car went into Saxon's Lake?"

"March sixteenth."

"Squeeze eight drops of blood on the center of the paper. Don't be stingy. Eight drops. Not one more and not one less."

Dad squeezed his finger, and the blood began dripping. The Lady added eight drops of her own red blood to the white paper. Dad said, "Good thing it didn't happen on the thirty-first."

"Take the paper in your left hand and crumple it up with the blood inside it," the Lady instructed him, ignoring his witticism. Dad did as she said. "Hold it and repeat the question aloud."

"Who killed that man at the bottom of Saxon's Lake?"

"Hold it tight," the Lady told him, and she pressed another cotton swab to her bleeding finger.

"Are your friends here right this minute?" Dad asked, his left fist around the crumpled-up paper.

"We'll soon find out, won't we?" She held out her left palm. "Give it to me." When it was lodged there, she said sternly to the air, "Don't ya'll show me up to be a fool, now. This is an important question, and it deserves an answer. Not no riddle, neither. An answer we can figure out. Ya'll gone help us, or not?" She waited perhaps fifteen more seconds. Then she placed the crumpled paper in the middle of the table. "Open it," she said.

Dad took it. As he began to uncrumple it, my heart was slamming. If *Dr. Lezander* was scrawled there in blood, I was going to split my skin.

When the paper was open, Mom and I peered over his shoulder. There was a great big blotch of blood in the middle of the paper and other blotches all around it. I couldn't see a name in that mess to save my life. Then the Lady took a pencil from her bag and studied the paper for a moment, after which she began to play connect-the-blotches.

"I don't see a thing," Dad said.

"Have faith," she told him. I watched the pencil's tip at work, moving between the blood. I watched a long, curvy line swing out and in.

And suddenly I realized I was looking at a 3.

The pencil's tip kept moving. Curving again. Out and in, out and in.

A second 3. And then the pencil's tip ran out of blood blotches to connect.

"That's it," the Lady said. She frowned. "Two threes."

"That's sure not a name, is it?" Dad asked.

"They've riddled me again, is what they've done. I swear, I wish they'd make somethin' *easy* every once in a while!" She thunked the pencil down in disgust. "Well, that's all there's gonna be."

"That's *it*?" Dad sucked at his wounded finger. "You're sure you did this right?"

Words cannot describe the look she gave him. "Two threes," she said. "That's the answer. Three three. Maybe thirty-three. If we can figure out what that means, we'll have the killer's name."

"I can't think of anybody who has three letters in their first and last name. Or maybe it's an address?"

"I don't know. All I know is what I'm lookin' at: three three." She slid the paper toward him; it was his to keep for his pain and trouble. "That's all I can do for you. Sorry there's nothin' more."

"I am, too," Dad said, and he took the paper and stood up.

Then the Lady removed her professional face and became sociable. She said she smelled the fresh coffee, and that there was chocolate roulage made by Mrs. Pearl from the Bake Shoppe. Dad, who had been eating like a bird before we came to the Lady's, ate two whopping pieces of roulage and washed them down with two cups of hot black chicory coffee. He and the Moon Man talked about that day the Blaylocks had been routed at the Trailways bus stop, and Dad laughed at the memory of Biggun running from a bag full of garden snakes.

My father was well and truly returned. Maybe even better than he was before.

"Thank you," Dad said to the Lady as we stood at the door ready to leave. Mom took her hand and kissed her ebony cheek. The Lady regarded me with her shining emerald eyes. "You still gone be a writer?" she asked me.

"I don't know," I said.

"Seems to me a writer gets to hold a lot of keys," she said. "Gets to visit a lot of worlds and live in a lot of skins. Seems to me a writer has a chance to live forever, if he's good and if he's lucky. Would you like that, Cory? Would you like to live forever?"

I thought about it. Forever, like heaven, was an awfully long time. "No ma'am," I decided. "I think I might get tired."

"Well," she said, and she placed a hand on my shoulder, "it seems to me a writer's voice is a forever thing. Even if a boy and a man are not." She leaned her face closer to mine. I could feel the heat of her life, like the sun glowing from her bones. "You're gonna be kissed by a lot of girls," she said. "Gonna kiss a lot of girls, too. But remember this." She kissed me, very lightly, on the forehead. "Remember when you do all that kissin' of girls and women in all the summers left ahead of you that you were first kissed"—her ancient, beautiful face smiled—"by a lady."

When we got home, Dad sat down with the telephone book and scanned the names, looking for the address "thirty-three." There were two residents and a business: Phillip Caldwell at 33 Ridgeton Street, J. E. Grayson at 33 Deerman Street, and the Crafts Barn at 33 Merchants Street. Dad said Mr. Grayson went to our church, and that he was nearing ninety. He believed Phillip Caldwell was a salesman at the Western Auto in Union Town. The Crafts Barn, Mom knew, was run by a blue-haired woman named Edna Hathaway. She seriously doubted if Mrs. Hathaway, who went around supported by a walker, had had anything to do with the incident at Saxon's Lake. Dad decided Mr. Caldwell's house was worth a visit, and he planned to go early in the morning before Mr. Caldwell left for work.

A mystery could always get me out of bed. I was up bright-eyed by the time the clock showed seven, and Dad said I could go with him but I wasn't to say a word while he was talking to Mr. Caldwell.

On the drive over, Dad said he hoped I understood he might have to tell Mr. Caldwell a white lie. I feigned shock and dismay at this, but my own count of white lies had been on the heavy side lately so I couldn't really be disappointed in him. Anyway, it was for the right cause.

Mr. Caldwell's red brick house, four blocks past the gas station, was small and unremarkable. We left the pickup truck at the curb and I followed Dad to the front door. He pressed the buzzer and we waited. The door was opened by a middle-aged woman with jowly cheeks and sleepy eyes. She was still wearing her quilted pink robe. "Is Mr. Caldwell at home, please?" Dad asked.

"Phillip!" she called into the house. "Philllleeeeup!" She had a voice like a buzz saw at high pitch.

In another moment a gray-haired man wearing a bow tie, brown slacks, and a rust-colored sweater came to the door. "Yes?"

"Hi, I'm Tom Mackenson." Dad offered his hand. Mr. Caldwell shook it. "Aren't you the fella who works at the Western Auto in Union Town? Rick Spanner's brother-in-law?"

"That's right. Do you know Rick?"

"Used to work with him at Green Meadows. How's he doin'?"

"Better, now that he found a job. Had to move to Birmingham, though. I pity him, I wouldn't care for the big city myself."

"Me neither. Well, the reason I dropped by so early and all is . . . I lost my job at the dairy, too." Dad smiled tightly. "I'm workin' at Big Paul's Pantry now."

"Been there. Big ol' place."

"Yes, it is. A little too big for me. I was just wonderin' . . . uh . . . if . . . uh . . ." Even a white lie stuck in his craw. "If there were any jobs to be had at the Western Auto."

"No, not that I know of. We hired a new fella last month." He frowned. "How come you just didn't go by there and ask?"

Dad shrugged. "Thought I might save myself the gas, I suppose."

"You ought to go by and fill out an application. You never know what'll come up. The manager's name is Mr. Addison."

"Thank you, I might do that."

Mr. Caldwell nodded. Dad didn't retreat from the door. "Anythin' else I can do for you?"

Dad's eyes were searching the man's face. Mr. Caldwell lifted his eyebrows, waiting. "No," Dad said, and I heard in his voice that his answer had not been found. "I don't think so. Thanks anyway."

"All right. You come on by and fill out an application, Mr. Addison'll keep it on file."

"Okay, I'll remember that."

Back in the truck, Dad started the engine and said, "I believe that was a strikeout, don't you?"

"Yes sir." I had been trying to figure out what the numbers 3 and 3 might have to do with Dr. Lezander, but I, too, was coming up empty.

So was the truck. "Uh-oh!" Dad glanced at the gas gauge. "I'd better stop in and filllleeeeup! Don't you think?" He smiled, and I returned it.

At the station, Mr. Hiram White shambled out of his cathedral of engine belts and radiators and started pumping the gas in. "Pretty day," Mr. White commented, looking up at the blue sky. It had gotten cold again, though; January was champing at its bit like an eager horse.

"Yes, it is," Dad agreed, leaning against the truck.

"Ain't gone be no gunplay today, is there?"

"I don't think so."

Mr. White grinned. "I swear, that was more excitin' than television!"

"I'm just thankful nobody got killed."

"Good thing the bus didn't come in while all that shootin' was goin' on, there would've been some dead bodies to sweep up."

"Right as rain."

"You heard about the bus gettin' hit by that monster out on Route Ten, didn't you?"

"Sure did." Dad checked his watch.

" 'Bout knocked it off its wheels. You know Cornelius McGraw, been drivin' ol' thirty-three for eight years?"

"I don't know him personally."

"Well, he told me that monster was as big as a bulldozer. Said it ran like a deer, too. Said he tried to swerve, but it hit 'em broadside and he said the whole bus 'bout shook itself to pieces. Had to retire the bus is what they had to do."

"Is that right?"

"Sure is." Mr. White finished the job and pulled the nozzle from the truck's gas port. He wiped the end with a cloth so no drop of gas would mar the pickup's paint. "New bus has the route, but Corny's still drivin' it. Still number thirty-three, too, so things don't change so much, do they?"

"I don't know about that," Dad said, and paid him.

"Ya'll take care, now!" Mr. White told us as we drove away.

We were halfway home when Dad said, "I guess I'd better check the phone book again. Maybe I missed somethin'." He glanced at me, then back to the unwinding street. "I was wrong about the Lady, Cory. She's not evil, is she?"

"No sir."

"I'm glad I went. I feel lighter now, knowin' that man isn't callin' for me. I feel sorry for whoever he *is* callin', though. Poor devil must have a hell of a time sleepin', if he sleeps at all."

He's a night owl, I thought. It was time. "Dad?" I said. "I think I know who—"

"*God have mercy!*" Dad suddenly shouted, and he hit the brake so hard the pickup slewed around and went up onto somebody's lawn. The engine shuddered and died. "Did you hear what Mr. White said?" Dad's voice quavered with excitement. "Thirty-three! Ol' thirty-three, he said!"

"Sir?"

"The Trailways bus, Cory! It's number thirty-three! I was standin' right there listenin' to him, and I hardly heard it! You think that could be what those numbers mean?"

I was honored that he was asking my opinion, but I had to say, "I don't know."

"Well, the killer couldn't be Cornelius McGraw. He doesn't even live around here. But what would the bus have to do with whoever killed that man in Saxon's Lake?" He started puzzling it over, his hands clenched hard around the steering wheel. Then a woman holding a broom came out on her porch and started hollering at us to move the truck before she called the sheriff, so we had to go.

We returned to the gas station. Mr. White emerged again. "Sure went through that tank in a hurry, didn't ya?" he asked. Dad wasn't interested in filling up anything but his curiosity, though. When was number thirty-three due back in again? he asked Mr. White, and Mr. White said the next day around noon.

Dad said he'd be there.

Maybe he was wrong, he told Mom that night at dinner, but he was going to be at that gas station waiting for the bus at noon. It wasn't Cornelius McGraw he would be there to see, but he would be watching to find out who the bus brought to Zephyr or who it took away.

I was there with him as noon approached. Mr. White was driving us crazy talking about how hard it was to find good GoJo to clean the grease off your hands anymore. Then Dad said, "Here it comes, Cory," and he walked from cold shadow into crisp sunlight to meet it.

The Trailways bus, with number 33 on the plate above its windshield, swept on past without even slowing, though Mr. McGraw honked the horn and Mr. White waved.

Dad watched it go. But he turned to Mr. White again, and I saw by the set of his jaw that now my father was a man with a mission. "Bus come back through day after tomorrow, Hiram?"

"Sure does. Twelve noon, same as always."

Dad lifted a finger and tapped it against his lips, his eyes narrowed. I knew what he was thinking. How was he going to meet the bus on the days he had to work at Big Paul's Pantry?

"Hiram," he said at last, "you need any help around here?"

"Well . . . I don't know if I—"

"I'll take a dollar an hour," Dad said. "I'll pump the gas, I'll clean

437

the garage, I'll do whatever you ask me to do. You want me to work overtime, that's fine. A dollar an hour. How about it?"

Mr. White grunted and stared at the cluttered garage. "I reckon I do need some stuff inventoried. Brake shoes, gaskets, radiator hoses, and such. And I could use another strong back." This from Quasimodo of the Belts. He stuck out his hand. "Got a job, if you want it. Startin' six in the mornin', if that's all right?"

"I'll be here," Dad said, grasping Mr. White's hand.

My father was nothing if not resourceful.

The bus passed through once more without even a hiss of brakes. But it was due again, twelve noon, same as always, and my dad would be there.

New Year's Eve came, and we watched on television the festivities in Times Square. At the stroke of midnight, someone shot off fireworks over Zephyr, the church bells rang, and horns honked. It had become 1965. On New Year's Day we ate black-eyed peas to bring us silver, and collard greens to bring us gold, and we watched football games until our south ends were sore. Dad sat in his chair with a notepad on his lap, and though he hollered for his teams he was scribbling 33 . . . 33 . . . 33 into an interlocking mosaic of numbers with his ball-point pen. Mom chided him to put down that pen and relax, and he did for a little while but soon his fingers found it again. I could tell by the way she looked at him that she was getting worried about him once more; ol' number thirty-three was becoming as much an obsession as the bad dream had ever been. He was still having that dream, of course, but he knew the dead man was not calling him and that made a big difference. I suppose, though, that in my father's case it took one obsession to break another.

Ben, Johnny, and I and the rest of the childish generation returned to school. In my class, I discovered we had a new teacher. Her name was Miss Fontaine, and she was as young and pretty as spring. Beyond the windows, though, winter was starting to rage.

Every other day, near noon, my father would step outside the gas station's office into chilly wind or blowing sleet or cold pale sun. He would watch the Trailways bus—ol' number thirty-three with Cornelius McGraw at the wheelas it approached, his heart beginning to pound.

But it didn't stop. Not once. It always kept going, bound for somewhere else.

Then Dad would return to the office, where he was likely to be playing dominoes with Mr. White, and he would sit down in a creaky chair and wait for the next move.

6

The Stranger Among Us

January advanced, cold as the tomb.

At eleven o'clock on the morning of Saturday, the sixteenth, I said good-bye to Mom and left home on Rocket to meet Ben and Johnny at the Lyric. The sky was plated with clouds, the threat of freezing rain in the air. I was bundled up like an Eskimo, but I'd soon be shedding my coat and gloves. The movie for today was called *Hell Is for Heroes*, the poster of which showed the sweating faces of American soldiers crouched down behind machine gun and bazooka, awaiting the enemy attack. To accompany this carnage, there would be a program of Daffy Duck cartoons and the next chapter of *Fighting Men of Mars*. The last chapter had ended with the Fighting Men about to be crushed by a falling boulder at the bottom of a Martian mine shaft. I'd already plotted out their escape; they would scramble into a previously hidden tunnel at the very last second, thus escaping a flattening fate.

On my way to the theater, I myself took a fateful turn.

I pedaled to Dr. Lezander's house.

I hadn't seen him at church since Christmas Eve. Since I'd called him "Birdman," and looked him in his eyes of stone. I was beginning to wonder if he and Mrs. Lezander hadn't flown the coop. Several times I'd started to tell Dad my suspicions, but he had thirty-three on his mind and I had nothing but a green feather and two dead parrots. I stopped Rocket at the bottom of the driveway and sat there watching the house. It was dark. Empty? I wondered. Had the doctor and his wife cleared out in the dead of night, alerted by whatever it was I might know? I kept watch; there was no sign of light or life. The heroes and the fighting men could wait. I had to find out, and I began to pedal Rocket up the driveway to the house. I went around back. The PLEASE LEASH YOUR PETS sign was still up. I eased Rocket down on the kickstand and peered into the nearest window.

439

Dark upon dark. At first I saw only shapes of furniture, but as my eyes grew used to the gloom I was able to make out the twelve ceramic birds perched atop the piano. It was the den where the bird cages were. Dr. Lezander's office was below, closer to hell. I couldn't help but see Mrs. Lezander sitting at that piano, playing "Beautiful Dreamer" over and over again as the green and the blue parrots flapped wildly in their cages and shouted curses came up through the air vent. But why were the curses in German?

Lights hit me. My heart hammered; I felt like a prisoner in a jailbreak movie, caught by the roaming circle. I twisted around, and there were a car's headlights as the car pulled up to the back porch. It was a late-model steel-gray Buick with a chrome radiator that resembled a grinning mouthful of silver teeth; the doctor's work was well paid. I made a move toward Rocket, but it was too late to get the kickstand up before I heard a voice say "Who is that?" Mrs. Lezander got out, her bulk made bearish in a brown overcoat. She must've recognized my bike, because my collar was turned up. "Cory?"

I was caught. Easy, I thought. Just take it easy. "Yes ma'am," I answered. "It's me."

"This is providential," she said. "Will you help me, please?" She went around to the passenger side and opened the door. "I've got some groceries."

Rocket might have whispered to me in that second. Rocket might have said in a silken, urgent voice *Get away, Cory. Get away while you still can. I'll take you, if you'll just hang on.*

"Help me, please?" Mrs. Lezander hefted the first of a half-dozen burdened paper bags. On all of them, printed in red letters, was Big Paul's Pantry.

"I'm goin' to the movies," I said.

"It'll just take a minute."

What could be done to me in broad daylight? I took the bag. Mrs. Lezander, a second bag under one arm, slid her key into the back door's lock. A gust of wind blew around us, and I saw the folds of her overcoat move and I knew she had been the figure I saw standing at the edge of the woods.

"Go on," she said, "the door's open."

With Mrs. Lezander hulking at my back and a boulder of fear in my throat, I walked across the threshold as if into a mine shaft.

"Ten points," Mr. White said as he plunked down another domino.

"And ten," Dad said, his own domino going down at the end of the L-shaped pattern.

"I swear I didn't think you had that one!" Mr. White shook his head. "Tricky fella, ain't you?"

"I try my best."

There was a tapping sound. Mr. White peered out the window. The clouds had darkened, the gas station's light splashed across the concrete. Little flecks of sleet were striking the glass. Dad took the opportunity for a glance at the clock on the wall, which showed twelve minutes before noon. "All right, where was I?" Mr. White rubbed his chin and pondered his dominoes like a hunchbacked sphinx. "Here we go!" he said, and reached for one. "Just mark down fifteen points in my fa—"

Something hissed.

Dad turned his head to the left.

The Trailways bus was pulling in.

"—vor," Mr. White finished. "How do, how do! Look who's early this fine day!"

Dad was already on his feet. He walked past the cash register and the shelves of oil and gasoline additives toward the door. "Must've caught a tailwind!" Mr. White said. "Probably caught sight of that monster out on Route Ten, and Corny gave it the lead foot!"

Dad walked out into the cold. The bus pulled to a halt beneath the yellow TRAILWAYS BUS sign. The doors folded outward with a breath of hydraulics. "Watch your step, gents!" Dad heard the driver say.

Two men were getting off. Sleet hit Dad in the face and the wind whirled around him, but he stood his ground. One of the men looked to be in his sixties, the other half those years. The older man, who wore a tweed overcoat and a brown hat, carried a suitcase. The younger, dressed in blue jeans and a beige jacket, carried a duffel bag. "Enjoy your stay, Mr. Steiner!" Corny McGraw said, and the older man lifted a gloved hand and waggled the fingers. Hiram White, who'd come out of the office behind Dad, said, "Howdy" to the two men, and then he looked up the steps at Mr. McGraw. "Hey, Corny! You want some hot coffee?"

"No, I'm gettin' on down the road, Hiram. My sister Jenny had her baby this mornin', and as soon as I finish my route I can go see her. Third young'un, but first boy. Bring you a cigar next time 'round."

"I'll get a match ready. You be careful, Uncle Corny!"

"Ta-ta, ya'll," he said. The doors closed, the bus pulled away, and the two strangers stood facing my father.

The older one, Mr. Steiner, had a wrinkled face but a chin like a slab of granite. He was wearing glasses, flecks of sleet on the lenses. "Sir? Pardon me," he said with a foreign accent. "Is there a hotel?"

"Boardin'house will do," the younger one said; he had thinning blond hair and a flat midwestern brogue.

"No hotel in town," Dad said. "No boardin'house, either. We don't get a lot of visitors here."

"Oh my." Mr. Steiner frowned. "Where's the nearest hotel, then?"

"There's a motel in Union Town. The Union Pines. It's—" He stopped, his arm rising to point the way. "You fellas need a ride?"

"That would be very nice, thank you. Mr. . . . ?"

"Tom Mackenson." He shook the gloved hand. The man's grip jammed his knuckles.

"Jacob Steiner," the older man said. "This is my friend, Lee Hannaford."

"Pleased to meet the both of you," Dad said.

The sixth bag was the heaviest. It was full of dog-food cans. "That goes downstairs," Mrs. Lezander said as she put other canned goods into the cupboard. "Just set it on the counter, I'll take it myself."

"Yes ma'am."

The lights were on in the kitchen. Mrs. Lezander had shed her overcoat, and beneath it she wore a somber gray dress. She took a jar of Folger's instant coffee out of the fourth sack and opened it with a slight wrist-twist. "May I ask," she said, her broad back to me, "why you were looking in the window?"

"I . . . uh . . ." Think fast! I told myself. "I thought I'd drop by because . . . uh . . ."

Mrs. Lezander turned around and watched me, her eyes flat and impassive.

"Because . . . I wanted to ask Dr. Lezander if he . . . like . . . needed some help in the afternoons. I thought maybe I could clean up downstairs, or sweep, or—" I shrugged. "Whatever."

A hand grasped my shoulder from behind.

I almost cried out. I came very close to it. As it was, I felt my face freeze as the blood left it.

Dr. Lezander said, "An ambitious young man. Isn't that right, Veronica?"

"Yes, Frans." She turned away from me and continued putting the groceries up.

He released me. I looked at him. He obviously had just awakened; his eyes were sleep-swollen, the hairs had come out in a grizzle around his neatly trimmed chin beard, and he was wearing a red silk robe over pajamas. He yawned and stifled it with the same hand that had just been on my shoulder. "Coffee, please, dearest," he said. "The blacker the better."

She began to spoon coffee into a cup that had the picture of a collie on it. Then, that task done, she turned on the hot water faucet.

"I heard East Berlin this morning around four," he told her. "A wonderful orchestra was playing Wagner."

Mrs. Lezander filled the collie cup full of steaming water and stirred it. She handed the ebony coffee to her husband, who first inhaled its aroma. "Ahhhhhh, yes!" he said. "This should do the trick!" He took a little slurpy sip. "Good and strong!" he said, satisfied.

"I'd better be goin' now." I edged toward the back door. "Ben Sears and Johnny Wilson are waitin' for me at the Lyric."

"I thought you wanted to ask me about an afternoon job."

"Well . . . I'd better go."

"Oh, nonsense." He reached out again, and his hand found my shoulder. He had iron in his fingers. "I'd be pleased and happy to have you come by and help in the afternoons, Cory. As a matter of truth, I've been looking for a young apprentice."

"Really?" I didn't know what else to say.

"Really." He smiled with his mouth. His eyes were careful. "You're a smart young man, aren't you?"

"Sir?"

"A smart young man. Oh, don't be so modest! You pursue things, don't you? You grip a fact and shake it like a . . . like a terrier." His mouth smiled again, and the silver tooth sparkled. He took a longer sip of coffee.

"I don't know what you mean." I heard my voice tremble, the slightest bit.

"I admire that quality in you, Cory. The terrier determination to get to the root of things. That's a fine quality for a boy to have."

"His bicycle's outside, Frans," Mrs. Lezander said as she put away packs of Rice-A-Roni, the San Francisco treat.

"Bring it in, will you?"

"I've gotta go," I said, and now the fear had started choking me.

"Non"—he answered, smiling—"sense. If we have a freezing rain—and it certainly looks grim out there today you don't want that fine bicycle of yours to be covered with ice, do you?"

"I . . . really have to—"

"I'll bring it in," Mrs. Lezander said, and she went outside. I watched, Dr. Lezander's hand on my shoulder, as the woman pushed Rocket across the threshold and into the den.

"Very good," Dr. Lezander said. He drank some more coffee. "Better safe than sorry, yes?"

Mrs. Lezander returned, sucking her left thumb. She brought it from her mouth to show blood on it. "Look at this, Frans. I cut myself on his bicycle." She said it with an almost clinical detachment. The thumb returned to her mouth. There was blood on her lower lip.

"While you're here, Cory, it seems to me you should see what your job would entail. Don't you agree?"

"Ben and Johnny . . . they're gonna miss me," I said.

"Yes, they will, I'm sure. But they'll go in and sit down and watch the film, won't they? They'll probably think" he shrugged—"that something happened. Like things do to boys." His fingers began to knead my shoulder. "What film is it?"

"Hell Is for Heroes. It's an army picture."

"Oh, an *army* picture. I expect it's the conquering American heroes destroying the wretched German dogs, isn't it?"

"Frans," Mrs. Lezander said quietly.

A look passed between them, as hard and sharp as a dagger.

Dr. Lezander's attention returned to me. "Let's go downstairs, Cory. All right?"

"My mom's gonna be worried," I tried, but I knew it was no good.

"But she believes you're at the *film,* doesn't she?" His eyebrows lifted. "Now, let's go downstairs and see what I'm prepared to pay you twenty dollars a week to do."

My breath was stolen. "Twenty *dollars?*"

"Yes. Twenty dollars a week for an able and understanding apprentice seems like a bargain to me. Shall we go?" His hand guided me toward the steps that led down. It was a powerful hand, and it would not be denied. I had to go. Dr. Lezander flicked a switch that turned on the light over the stairs and flooded light below me. As I descended, I heard the rustle of his red silk robe and the shuffle of his slippers on the stairs. I heard him slurp his coffee. It was a greedy sound, and I was afraid.

My father had not taken Jacob Steiner and Lee Hannaford directly to the Union Pines Motel. On the way, jammed in the pickup truck with the wipers knocking away sleet, he'd asked them if they wanted some lunch. Both men had said yes, and that was how they'd wound up walking into the Bright Star Cafe.

"How about a booth in the back?" Dad asked Carrie French, and she guided them to one and left them with luncheon menu cards.

Mr. Steiner took off his gloves and overcoat. He was wearing a tweed suit and a pale gray vest. He hung his overcoat and his hat on a rack. His hair was as white and thick as a bristle brush. As Mr. Steiner slid into the booth and Dad sat down, too, the younger man peeled off his jacket. He was wearing a blue-checked shirt with the sleeves rolled up past his muscular biceps. And on the right bicep . . . there it was.

Dad said, "Oh my God."

"What is it?" Mr. Hannaford asked. "I'm not supposed to take my jacket off in here?"

"No, it's all right." A sheen of sweat had broken out on my father's forehead. Mr. Hannaford sat down beside Mr. Steiner. "I mean . . . that tattoo . . ."

"You got a problem with it, friend?" The younger man's slate-colored eyes had narrowed into dangerous slits.

"Lee?" Mr. Steiner cautioned. "No, no." It was like telling a bad dog to sit.

"No problem," Dad said. "It's just that . . ." He was having trouble breathing, and the room wanted to spin. "I've seen your tattoo before."

The two men were silent. Mr. Steiner spoke first. "May I ask where, Mr. Mackenson?"

"Before I tell you, I want to know where you've come from and why you're here." Dad pulled his gaze away from the faint outline of a skull with wings swept back from its temples.

"I wouldn't," Mr. Hannaford warned Mr. Steiner. "We don't know this guy."

"True. We don't know anyone here, do we?" Mr. Steiner glanced around, and Dad saw his hawklike eyes take in the scene. A dozen or so people were having lunch and shooting the breeze. Carrie French was fending off the good-natured flirting of a couple of farmers. The television was tuned to a basketball game. "How can we trust you, Mr. Mackenson?"

"What's not to trust?" Something about this man—the way he carried himself, the way his eyes were darting this way and that, sizing things up—made Dad ask the next question. "Are you a policeman?"

"By profession, no. But in a sense, yes."

"What profession are you in, then?"

"I am . . . in the field of historical research," Mr. Steiner answered.

Carrie French came over on her long, pretty legs, her order pad ready. "Help you today?"

"Got any griddle cakes?" Mr. Hannaford plucked a pack of Luckies out of his breast pocket.

"Beg pardon?"

"Griddle cakes! Do you have 'em here or not?"

"I think," Mr. Steiner said patiently as the younger man lit a cigarette, "that they're called pancakes in this part of the country."

"We're not servin' breakfast now." Carrie offered an uncertain smile. "Sorry."

"Just gimme a burger, then." He spouted smoke through his pinched nostrils. "Jesus!"

"Is the chicken noodle soup fresh?" Mr. Steiner asked, examining the menu card.

"Canned, but it's still good."

"I will not eat canned chicken noodle soup, my dear." He gazed at her sternly over the rims of his glasses. "I, too, will have a hamburger. *Very* well done, if you please." *Pliss,* he pronounced it.

Dad ordered the beef stew and a cup of coffee. Carrie paused. "Ya'll aren't from around here, are you?" she asked the two strangers.

"I'm from Indiana," Mr. Hannaford said. "He's from—"

"Warsaw, Poland, originally. And I can speak for myself, thank you."

"Both of you sure are a long way from home," Dad said when Carrie had gone.

"I live in Chicago now," Mr. Steiner explained.

"Still a long way from Zephyr." Dad's eyes kept ticking back to the tattoo. It looked as if the younger man had tried to bleach it out of his skin. "Does that tattoo mean somethin'?"

Lee Hannaford let smoke dribble from the corner of his mouth. "It means," he said, "that I don't like people askin' me my business."

Dad nodded. The first smolderings of anger were reddening his cheeks. "Is that so?"

"Yeah, it's so."

"Gentlemen, please," Mr. Steiner said.

"What would you say to this, hotshot?" Dad propped his elbows on the table and leaned his face closer to the younger man's. "What would you say if I told you that ten months ago I saw a tattoo just like yours on the arm of a dead man?"

Mr. Hannaford didn't respond. His face was emotionless, his eyes cold. He drew cigarette smoke in and blew it out. "Did he have blond hair?" he asked. "Kinda the same color as mine?"

"Yes."

"About the same build, too?"

"I think so, yes."

"Uh-huh." Mr. Hannaford leaned his chiseled face toward my father's. When he spoke, the words left smoke trails. "I'd say you saw my brother."

". . . and these cages must be kept scrupulously clean," Dr. Lezander was saying as he pointed them out. They were empty right now. "As well as the floor. If you come in three times a week, I expect the floor to be scrubbed three times a week. You'll be expected to water and feed all the animals in the kennel, as well as exercise them." I followed along behind him as he showed me from room to room in the basement. Every once in a while I would glance up and see an air vent overhead. "I order my hay in bales. You'd be expected to help unload the truck, cut the baling wire, and spread out hay for the horse stalls. I can attest that cutting baling wire is not an easy endeavor. It's tough enough to string a piano with. Plus your job will include whatever errands I need you to run." He turned to face me. "Twenty dollars a week for three afternoons, say from four until six. Does that sound fair?"

"Gosh." I couldn't believe this. Dr. Lezander was offering me a fortune.

"If you come in on Saturdays, I'll pay you an extra five dollars for . . . say, two until four." He smiled, again with just his mouth. He drank his coffee and set the collie cup down atop an empty wire-mesh cage. "Cory?" he said softly. "I do have two requests before I give you this job."

I waited to hear them.

"One: that your parents don't know how much I'm paying you. I think they should believe I'm paying you perhaps ten dollars a week. The reason I say this is that . . . well, I know your father's working at the gas station now. I saw him the last time I pulled in. I know your mother's struggling in her baking business. Wouldn't it be better for you if they didn't know how much money you were coming home with?"

"You think I ought to keep such a thing from them?" I asked, bewildered.

"It would be your decision, of course. But I believe both your mother and father might be . . . anxious to share your good fortune, if they were to know. And there are so *many* things a boy could buy with twenty-five dollars a week. The only problem is, you'd have to be discreet about those purchases. You couldn't spend it all in one place. I might even have to drive you to Union Town or Birmingham to spend some of that money. But couldn't you think of a few things you might like to have that your parents can't buy you?"

I thought. And then I answered: "No sir, I can't."

He laughed, as if this tickled him. "You will, though. With all that money in your pocket, you will."

I didn't answer. I didn't like what Dr. Lezander thought I would keep from my mother and father.

"Secondly." He folded his arms across his chest, and I saw his tongue probe the inside of his cheek. "There is the matter of Miss Sonia Glass."

"Sir?" My heart, which had settled down some, now speeded up again.

"Miss Sonia Glass," he repeated. "She brought her parrot to me. It died of a brain fever. Right here." He touched the wire-mesh cage. "Poor, poor creature. Now, it happens that Veronica and Miss Glass are in the same Sunday school class. Miss Glass, it seems, was terribly upset and puzzled by questions you asked her, Cory. She said you were very curious about a particular song, and why her parrot had . . . reacted strangely to that song." He smiled thinly. "Miss Glass told Veronica she thought you knew a secret, and might either Veronica or I know what it was? And there was some odd little thing as well, about you being in the possession of a green feather from Miss Katharina Glass's dead parrot. Miss Sonia said she couldn't believe her eyes when she saw it." He began working the knuckles of his right hand as he stared at the floor. "Are these things true, Cory?"

I swallowed hard. If I said they weren't, he'd know I was lying anyway. "Yes sir."

He closed his eyes. A pained expression stole over his face, there and then gone. "And where did you find that green feather, Cory?"

"I . . . found it . . ." Here was the moment of truth. I sensed something in that room coiled up like a snake and ready to strike. Though the overhead light was bright and harsh, the tile-floored room seemed to seethe with shadows. Dr. Lezander, I suddenly realized, had positioned himself between me and the stairs. He waited, his eyes closed. If I made a run for it, Mrs. Lezander would snare me even if I got past the doctor. Again, the choice was stolen from me. "I found it at Saxon's Lake," I said, braving the fates. "At the edge of the woods. Before the sun, when that car went down with a dead man handcuffed to the wheel."

With his eyes closed, Dr. Lezander smiled. It was a terrible sight. The flesh on his face looked tight and damp, his bald head shining under the light. Then he began to laugh: a slow leak of a laugh, bubbling from his silver-toothed mouth. His eyes opened, and they speared me. For a few seconds he had two faces: the lower one wore a silver-glinting smile; the upper one was pure fury. "Well, well," he said, and he shook his head as if he'd just heard the most amazing joke. "What are we going to do about *this?*"

"Have you ever seen this man before, Mr. Mackenson?"

Mr. Steiner had removed his wallet. He had taken a laminated card from it, and now he slid the card before my father as they sat at the back booth in the Bright Star Cafe.

It was a grainy black and white photograph. It showed a man wearing a white knee-length coat, waving and smiling to someone off the frame. He had dark hair that swept back like a skullcap, and he had a square jaw and a cleft in his chin. Behind him was the hood of a gleaming car that looked like an antique, like from the thirties or forties. Dad studied the face for a moment; he paid close attention to the eyes and the white scar of a smile. For all his studying, however, it remained the face of a stranger.

"No," he said as he slid the picture back across the wood. "Never."

"He'll probably look different now." Mr. Steiner studied the picture, too, as if looking into the face of an old enemy. "He might have had some plastic surgery. The easiest way to change appearance is to grow a beard and shave your head. That way even your own mother wouldn't recognize you." *Mudder*, he'd said.

"I don't know that face. Sorry. Who is he?"

"His name is Gunther Down in the Dark."

"What?" Dad almost chewed on his heart.

"Gunther Down in the Dark," Mr. Steiner repeated. He spelled the last name, and then he pronounced it again: "Dahninaderke."

Dad sat back in the booth, his mouth open. He gripped the table's edge to keep from being spun off the entire world. "My God," he whispered. "My God. 'Come with me . . . Dahninaderke.'"

"Excuse me?" Mr. Steiner asked.

"Who is he?" Dad's voice was thick.

Lee Hannaford answered. "He's the man who killed Jeff, if my brother's body is lyin' at the bottom of that damned lake." Dad had told them the story of that morning last March. Mr. Hannaford looked mean enough to snap the head off a cobra. He hadn't eaten much of his hamburger, but he'd almost swallowed three Luckies. "My brother—my stupid-assed brother—must've been black-mailin' him, by what we can figure out. Jeff left a diary hidden in his apartment, back in Fort Wayne. It was in code, written in German. I found the diary in May, when I quit my job in California and came lookin' for him. It took us until a couple of weeks ago to figure the code out."

"It was based on Wagner's *Ring of the Nibelung,*" Mr. Steiner said. "Very, very intricate."

"Yeah, he always was nuts about that code shit." Mr. Hannaford stabbed out another cigarette butt in his ketchupy plate. "Even as a kid. He was always doin' secret writin' and shit. So we pieced it together from the diary. He was blackmailin' Gunther Dahninaderke, first five hundred dollars a month, then eight hundred, then a thousand. It was down in the book that Dahninaderke lived in Zephyr, Alabama. Under a false name, I mean. Jeff and those scumbags helped him come up with a new identity, after he got in touch with 'em. But Jeff must've decided he wanted a payoff for his trouble. In the diary, he said he was gonna make a big score, get his stuff out of the apartment and move to Florida. He said he was drivin' down to Zephyr from Fort Wayne on the thirteenth of March. And that was the last entry." He shook his head. "My brother was fuckin' *crazy* to get involved in this. Well, I was crazy for gettin' involved in it, too."

"Involved in what?" Dad asked. "I don't understand."

"Do you know the term 'neo-Nazi'?" Mr. Steiner asked.

"I know what a Nazi is, if that's what you're askin'?"

"Neo-Nazi. A new Nazi. Lee and his brother were members of an American Nazi organization that operated in Indiana, Illinois, and Michigan. The symbol of that organization is the tattoo on Lee's arm. Lee and Jeff were initiated at the same time, but Lee left the group after a year and went to California."

"Damn straight." A match flared, and a Lucky burned. "I wanted to get as far away from those bastards as I could. They kill people who decide Hitler didn't shit roses."

"But your brother stayed with 'em?"

"Hell, yes. He even got to be some kind of storm-trooper leader or somethin'. Jesus, can you believe it? We were all-Americans on our high school football team!"

"I still don't know who this Gunther Dahninaderke fella is," Dad said.

Mr. Steiner laced his fingers together atop the table. "This is where I come in. Lee took the diary to be deciphered by the Department of Languages at Indiana University. A friend of mine there teaches German. When he got as far as deciphering Dahninaderke's name from that code, he sent the diary directly to me at Northwestern in Chicago. I took over the project from there in

September. Perhaps I should explain that I am the director of the languages department. I am also a professor of history. And last but not least, I am a hunter of Nazi war criminals."

"Say again?" Dad asked.

"Nazi war criminals," Mr. Steiner repeated. "I have helped track down three of them in the last seven years. Bittrich in Madrid, Savelshagen in Albany, New York, and Geist in Allentown, Pennsylvania. When I saw the name Dahninaderke, I knew I was getting closer to the fourth."

"A war criminal? What did he do?"

"Dr. Gunther Dahninaderke was the directing physician at Esterwegen concentration camp in Holland. He and his wife Kara determined who was fit to work and who was ready to be gassed." Mr. Steiner flashed a quick and chilling smile. "It was they, you see, who decided on a sunny morning that I was still fit to live but my wife was not."

"I'm sorry," Dad said.

"That's all right. I knocked his front tooth out and spent a year at hard labor. But it made me hard, and it kept me alive."

"You . . . knocked his front tooth . . ."

"Right out of his head. Oh, those two were quite a pair." Mr. Steiner's face crinkled with the memory of pain. "We called his wife the Birdlady, because she had a set of twelve birds made from clay mixed with the ash of human bones. And Dr. Dahninaderke, who was originally a veterinarian from Rotterdam, had a very intriguing habit."

Dad couldn't speak. He forced it out with an effort. "What was it?"

"As the prisoners passed him on their way to the gas chamber, he made up names for them." Mr. Steiner's eyes were hooded, lost in visions of a horrible past. "Comical names, they were. I'll always remember what he called my Veronica, my beautiful Veronica with the long golden hair. He called her 'Sunbeam.' He said, 'Crawl right in, Sunbeam! Crawl right in!' And she was so sick she had to crawl through her own . . ." Tears welled up behind his glasses. He took them quickly off with the manner of a man who rigidly controlled his emotions. "Forgive me," he said. "Sometimes I forget myself."

"You okay?" Lee Hannaford asked my father. "You look awful white."

"Let me . . . let me see that picture again."

Mr. Steiner slid it in front of him.

Dad took a long breath. "Oh no," he said. "Oh please, no."

Mr. Steiner had heard it in Dad's voice: "You know him now."

"I do. I know where he lives. It's not far from here. Not very far at all. But . . . he's so *nice*."

"I know Dr. Dahninaderke's true nature," Mr. Steiner said. "And the true nature of his wife. You saw it when you looked at the face of Jeff Hannaford. Dr. Dahninaderke and Kara probably tortured him to find out who else knew where he was, or maybe they got the information about the diary out of him, and they beat him to death when he wouldn't tell them where it was or who else knew about it. When you looked at the face of Jeff Hannaford, you saw the twisted soul of Dr. Gunther Dahninaderke. I pray to God you don't have to look upon such a sight again."

Dad stood up and fumbled for his wallet, but Mr. Steiner put money on the table. "I'll take you to him," Dad said, and he started for the door.

"Such a bright young man," Dr. Lezander said, standing between me and the way out. "There's that terrier determination, isn't it? Finding that green feather and then pursuing it to the end? I admire that, Cory, I truly do."

"Dr. Lezander?" I felt as if my chest were constricted by iron bands. "I sure would like to go home."

He took two steps toward me. I retreated as many.

He stopped, aware of his power over me. "I want that green feather. Do you know why?"

I shook my head.

"Because your having it upsets Miss Sonia. It's a reminder of the past, and she doesn't like that. The past should be put behind us, Cory. The world should go on, and leave the things of the past alone, don't you agree?"

"I don't—"

"But no, just like that green feather, the past has to turn up again and again and again. It has to be plowed up and spread out for everyone to see. The past has to be put on exhibit, and everyone who struggled to keep from drowning in that sludge has to pay the price over and over. It's not fair, Cory, it's not right. Do you see?"

I didn't. Somewhere along the line, his train had derailed.

"We were honorable," Dr. Lezander said, his eyes feverish. "We had *honor*. We had pride. And look at the world now, Cory! Look what it's become! We knew the destination, but they wouldn't let us take the world there. And now you see what you see. Chaos and vulgarity on all sides. Gross interbreedings and couplings that even animals wouldn't abide. You know, I had my chance to be a physician to human beings. I did. Many times. And do you know that I would rather kneel in the mud and attend to a swine than save a human life? Because that's what I think of the human race! That's what I think of the liars who turned their backs on us and sullied our honor! That's what I . . . that's what I . . . what I *think!*" He picked up the collie cup and flung it to the floor, and it hit the tiles near my right foot and shattered to pieces with a noise like a gunshot.

Silence.

In another moment, Mrs. Lezander called from upstairs: "Frans? What broke, Frans?"

His brain, I thought.

"We're talking," Dr. Lezander said to her. "Just talking, only that."

I heard her footsteps, heavy on the floor, as she moved away.

Then a scraping sound above us.

And a few seconds later, the piano being played.

The tune was "Beautiful Dreamer." Mrs. Lezander was actually a very talented pianist. She had the hands for it, I recalled Miss Blue Glass saying. I wondered if she also had the hands that were strong enough to wrap hay-baling wire around a man's throat and strangle him to death. Or had Dr. Lezander done that as Mrs. Lezander had played that same tune in the den above and the parrots had squawked and screamed with the memory of brutal violence?

"Twenty-five dollars a week," Dr. Lezander said. "But you must bring me the green feather, and you must never, *never* talk to Miss Sonia Glass about this again. The past is dead. It should stay buried, where it belongs. Do you agree, Cory?"

I nodded. Anything to get out of there.

"Good boy. When can you bring me the feather? Tomorrow afternoon?"

"Yes sir."

"That's very, very good. When you bring it, I'll destroy it so Miss Sonia Glass won't think of the past anymore, and it won't hurt her. When you bring it, I'll give you your first week's money. Is that agreeable?"

"Yes sir." Anything, anything.

"All right, then." He moved aside from the stairs. "After you, *mein herr.*"

I started up.

The front doorbell rang. "Beautiful Dreamer" abruptly stopped. I heard the scrape again: the piano bench being pushed back. At the top of the stairs, Dr. Lezander put his hand on my shoulder again and held me. "Wait," he whispered.

453

We heard the front door opening.

"Tom!" Mrs. Lezander said. "What may I do for—"

"Dad!" I shouted. *"Help—"* Dr. Lezander's hand clamped over my mouth, and I heard him give a muffled cry of anguish that it had all come to this end.

"Cory! Get outta my way, you—!" Dad started into the house, with Mr. Steiner and Lee Hannaford behind him. He shoved the big woman aside, but in the next instant Mrs. Lezander bellowed, *"Nein!"* and slammed a forearm across the side of his face. He fell backward into Mr. Steiner, blood trickling from a gashed eyebrow. Only Mr. Steiner could understand the things Mrs. Lezander shouted to her husband: "Gunther, run! Take the boy and run!" As she was shouting, Mr. Hannaford grabbed her around her throat from behind and with all his weight and strength he wrestled her to the floor. She got up on one knee and fought back, but suddenly Mr. Steiner was on her, too, trying to pin her flailing arms. A coffee table and lamp crashed over. Mr. Steiner, his hat flown off and his lower lip burst open by one of her fists, yelled, "It's over, Kara! It's over, it's over!"

But it was not over for her husband.

At her warning cry, he had picked me up with one arm and scooped the car keys off the kitchen counter where his wife had left them. As I thrashed to get free, he dragged me out the back door into the falling sleet, the wind whipping his red silk robe. He lost a slipper, but he didn't slow down. He flung me into the Buick, slammed the door almost on my leg, and came close to sitting on my head when he leaped behind the wheel. He jammed the key into the ignition, turned it, and the engine roared to life. As he put the gears into reverse and the Buick's tires laid rubber on the driveway, I sat up in time to see Dad run out the back door into the glare of the headlights.

"Dad!" I reached for the door handle on my side. An elbow crashed into my shoulder and paralyzed me with pain, and when the hand gripped the back of my head and flung me down onto the floorboard like an old sack I lay there dazed and hurting. Dr. Gunther Dahninaderke, the murderer—whom I still knew as Dr. Frans Lezander, the murderer—crunched the gearshift into first and the Buick's engine screamed as the car tore away.

Behind us, my father was already running back through the house to get to the pickup. He jumped over the struggling bodies of Mr. Steiner, Mr. Hannaford, and Kara Dahninaderke. The woman was still fighting, but Mr. Hannaford was using his fists on her horsey face and the results were not on the side of beauty.

Dr. Lezander was racing through the streets of Zephyr, the Buick's tires shrieking at every turn. I started to crawl up from the floorboard, but Dr. Lezander shouted, "Stay there! Don't you move, you little bastard!" and he slapped me in the face and I slid back down again. We must've passed the Lyric; I wondered how much hell a hero could stand. We roared onto the gargoyle bridge, and when the steering wheel slipped out of Dr. Lezander's frantic hands for an instant, the Buick sideswiped the left side of the bridge and sent sparks and pieces of chrome flying into the air, the car's frame moaning with the impact. Then he seized control again and, his teeth gritted, he aimed us onto Route Ten.

I saw light leap from the rearview mirror and stab Dr. Lezander in the eyes. He shouted a curse in German that was louder than the Buick's wail, and I could just imagine what the parrots had had to endure that night. But I knew whose lights those were, ricocheting off the mirror. I knew who was behind us, right on the Buick's tail, pushing that old pickup truck to its point of explosion. I knew.

I reached up and grabbed the bottom of the steering wheel, jerking the car to the right. It went off the road onto loose gravel, the tires slipping. Dr. Lezander gave me another Germanic oath, hollered at the velocity and volume of a howitzer shell to the skull, and pounded my fingers loose with his fist. With that same fist, he knocked me in the forehead so hard I saw purple stars and that was the end of my heroics.

"Leave me alone!" Dr. Lezander screamed to the pickup truck whose headlights filled the rearview mirror. *"Can't you leave me alone?"* He fought the wheel around Route Ten's snaky curves, the force of gravity trying its best to rip the tires off. I pulled myself up on the seat again, my head still ringing, and Dr. Lezander yelled, "You little shit!" and grabbed the back of my coat, but he had to use two hands on the wheel so he released me.

I looked back at my father's pickup, twenty feet of sleet and air between Dad's front bumper and Dr. Lezander's rear bumper. We hurtled out of the series of tight curves, and I held on to the seat as Dr. Lezander accelerated, widening the distance between vehicles. I heard a *pop* and twisted my head in time to see Dr. Lezander reaching into the glove compartment, which he'd knocked open with a blow of his fist. His hand emerged gripping a snub-nosed .38 pistol. He threw that arm back, almost cuffing me in the head with the gun's barrel before I ducked, and he fired twice without aiming. The rear windshield exploded, the glass fragments flying toward Dad's pickup like pieces of jagged ice. I saw the pickup swerve and almost go off the road, its rear end wildly fishtailing, but then Dad got it righted. As Dr. Lezander's gun hand passed over my head again, I reached up and grabbed his wrist, pinning that gun against the seat with all my strength. The Buick began to slew from side to side as he grappled with the wheel and with me at the same time, but I hung on.

The gun went off in front of my face, the bullet passing through the seat and out the door with a metallic *clang*. The sound and heat of it going off so close to me sent a shock and shiver through my bones, and I guess I let go but I don't remember and then Dr. Lezander hit me a glancing blow on the right shoulder with that gun barrel. It was perhaps the worst pain I'd ever felt in my life; it filled me up and overspilled from my mouth in a cry. Without the padding of my coat in the way, my shoulder would've surely been broken. As it was, I grabbed at it and fell back against the passenger-side door, my face contorted with pain and my right arm all but dead. I saw, as if locked in a cyclic dream akin to that in *Invaders from Mars*, that we were about to pass the dark plain of Saxon's Lake. And then Dr. Lezander jammed on the brake with his bare foot, and as the Buick slowed and Dad's pickup gained ground, the doctor threw his arm back again and this time he looked over his shoulder to aim. His face was slickly wet in the wash of the lights, his teeth clenched, his eyes those of the savage, hunted animal. He fired, and the windshield of Dad's truck suddenly had a fist-sized hole in it. I saw his finger tighten on the trigger, and I wanted to fight him with all the want in my body, but that pain in my shoulder had me whipped.

Something huge and dark and fast burst out of the woods on the other side of the road, near where I'd seen Mrs. Lezander standing that morning in March.

It was on us before Dr. Lezander even saw it, and it was headed straight for his door.

At the same instant, the gun went off and the beast from the lost world collided with us.

This, truly, was a noise like the end of the world.

Over gunshot and Lezanderscream and crash of glass and folding metal, the Buick was knocked up onto the two tires on my side and they shrieked like constipated banshees as the entire car was shoved off the pavement. Dr. Lezander, his door buckled in as if kicked by God, came tumbling into me across the seat and my breath burst out, my ribs in danger of snapping. I heard a snort and grunt: the triceratops, protecting his territory, was pushing the rival dinosaur off Route Ten. Dr. Lezander's face was pressed up against mine, his weight crushing me, and I smelled his fear like green onions. Then he screamed again and I think I screamed, too, because suddenly the car was falling.

We hit with a bone-jarring jolt and splash.

Dark water seethed up into the floorboard. We had just been received by Saxon's Lake.

The Buick's steaming hood was rising. As it did, water began to surge over the slope of the trunk and pour through the shattered glass. The window on Dr. Lezander's side was broken as well, but the water hadn't yet reached it. He was lying on top of me, the gun lost. His eyes were glassy, blood oozing from his mouth where he must've bitten his lip or tongue. His left arm, the arm which had taken the brunt of the beast's power, was lying at a weird crooked angle. I saw the wet glistening of white bone protruding from the wrist in the red silk sleeve.

The lake was coming in faster now, air bubbles exploding around the trunk. The rear windshield was a waterfall. I couldn't get Dr. Lezander off me, and now the car was turning slowly against me as the Buick rolled over like a happy hog and my side started to submerge. Dr. Lezander was drooling bloody foam, and I realized his ribs must've taken a wallop, too.

"Cory! Cory!"

I looked up, past Dr. Lezander to the broken window rising above me.

My father was there, his hair plastered flat, his face dripping. Blood was creeping down from his cut eyebrow. He started wrenching out bits of glass from the window frame with his fingers. The Buick shuddered and moaned. Water edged up over the seat and its cold touch shocked me and made Dr. Lezander start thrashing.

"Can you grab my hand?" Dad wedged his body in through the crumpled window and strained to reach me.

I couldn't, not with that weight on me. "Help me, Dad," I croaked.

He fought to winnow in farther. His sides must've been raked and clawed by glass, but his face showed no pain. His lips were tight and grim, his eyes fixed on me like red-rimmed lamps. His hand tried to part the distance between us, but still the distance was too great.

Dr. Lezander's body lurched. He said something, but it must've been a snarl of German. He blinked, his eyes coming into painful focus. Water sloshed over us, a touch of the grave. He looked at his broken wrist, and he made a deep moaning noise.

"Get off him!" Dad shouted. "For God's sake, get off my son!"

Dr. Lezander shuddered and coughed. On the third cough, bright red blood sprayed from his nose and mouth. He grasped at his side, and suddenly there was blood on his hand. The beast from the lost world had staved his ribs right through his innards.

The water was roaring now. The Buick was sinking at the trunk.

"Please!" Dad begged, still straining to reach me. "Please give me my son!"

Dr. Lezander looked around as if trying to figure out exactly where he was. He lifted himself off me a few inches, which made me able to breathe without feeling like I was jammed in a sardine can. Dr. Lezander looked back at the sinking trunk and the water surging dark and foamy where the rear windshield had been and I heard him whisper "*Oh.*"

It was the whisper of surrender.

Dr. Lezander's face turned. He stared at me. Blood dripped from his nose and ran down my cheek. "Cory," he said, and his voice gurgled. His good hand closed on my wrist.

"Up you go," he whispered. "Bronco."

He lifted himself up with an effort that must've racked him, and he guided my hand into my father's.

Dad pulled me out, and I flung my arms around his neck. He held me, his legs treading water and tears streaming down his heroic face.

With a great buckling and moaning noise, the Buick was going down. The water rushed around us, drawing us in. Dad started kicking us away from it, but the pull was too strong. Then, with a hissing noise of heat and liquid at war, the Buick was drawn down into the depths. I felt my father fighting the suction, and then he gasped a breath and I knew he had lost.

We went under.

The car was sinking below us, into a huge gloomy vault where the sun was a stranger. Air bubbles rose from it like silver jellyfish. Dad was kicking frantically, trying to break the pull, but we were going down with Dr. Lezander. In the underwater blur I saw the doctor's white face pressed up against the windshield. Bubbles were streaming from his open mouth.

And suddenly something had drifted up from below and was clinging to the trunk. Something that might have been a big clump of moss or rags somebody had dumped into Saxon's Lake with their garbage. Whatever this thing was, it moved slowly and inexorably into the Buick through the broken rear windshield. The car was turning, turning over like a bizarre ride at the Brandywine Carnival, suspended against darkness. As my lungs burned for breath I saw the blur of Dr. Lezander's white face again, only this time the ragged mossy thing had wrapped itself around him like a putrid

458

robe. Whatever this thing was, it had hold of his jaw. I saw a faint glint of a silver tooth, like a receding star. Then the Buick turned over on its back like a huge turtle and as air bubbles rushed up again I felt them hit us and break us loose from the suction. We were rising toward the realm of light.

Dad lifted me up, so my head broke the surface first.

There wasn't much light up there today, but there was a whole lot of air. Dad and I clung together in the choppy murk, breathing.

At last we swam to where we could pull ourselves out, through mud and reeds to solid earth. Dad sat down on the ground next to the pickup truck, his hands scraped raw with glass cuts, and I huddled on the red rock cliff and looked out over Saxon's Lake.

"Hey, partner!" Dad said. "You okay?"

"Yes sir." My teeth were chattering, but being cold was a passing thing.

"Better get in the truck," he said.

"I will," I answered, but I wasn't ready yet. My shoulder, which would become one swollen lump of bruise in the next couple of days, was mercifully numb.

Dad pulled his knees up to his chest. The sleet was falling, but we were already cold and wet, so what of it? "I've got a story to tell you about Dr. Lezander," he said.

"I want to tell you one, too," I answered. I listened; the wind swept over the lake's surface and made it whisper.

He was down in the dark now. He had come from darkness and to darkness he had returned.

"He called me Bronco," I said.

"Yeah. How about that?"

We couldn't stay here very much longer. The wind was really getting cold. It was the kind of weather that made you catch your death.

Dad looked up at the low gray clouds and the January gloom. He smiled, with the face of a boy unburdened.

"Gosh," he said, "it's a beautiful day."

Hell might have been for heroes, but life was for the living.

These things happened, in the aftermath.

When Mom got up off the floor from her faint, she was all right. She hugged both Dad and me, but she didn't cling on to us. We had come back to her a little worse for wear, but we were back. Dad in particular; his dreams of the man at the bottom of Saxon's Lake were ended, good and truly.

Mr. Steiner and Mr. Hannaford, though dismayed that they had never even gotten a finger on Dr. Gunther Dahninaderke, were at least satisfied with the outcome of rough justice. They had Mrs. Kara Dahninaderke and her birds of human bone in their custody, however, and that was a great consolation. The last I heard of her, she was going to a prison where even the light lay chained.

Ben and Johnny were beside themselves. Ben jumped up and down in a fit and Johnny scowled and stomped when they realized they had been sitting in front of a movie while I'd been battling for my life against a Nazi war criminal. To say this made me a celebrity at school was like saying the moon is the size of a river pebble. Even the teachers wanted to hear my tale. Pretty Miss Fontaine was enthralled by it, and Mr. Cardinale asked to hear it twice. "You ought to be a writer, Cory!" Miss Fontaine said. "You surely do know your words!" Mr. Cardinale said, "You'd make a fine author, in my opinion."

Writer? Author?

Storyteller, that's what I decided to be.

On a cold but sunny Saturday morning toward the end of January, I left Rocket on the front porch and got into the pickup truck with Mom and Dad. He drove us across the gargoyle bridge and along Route Ten—slowly, all the time watching for the beast from the lost world. Though the beast remained loose in the woods, I never saw him again. I believe he was a gift to me from Davy Ray.

We reached Saxon's Lake. The water was smooth. There was no trace of what lay at its bottom, but we all knew.

I stood on the red rock cliff, and I reached into my pocket and pulled out the green feather. Dad had tied twine around it, with a little lead-ball weight on its end. I threw it into the lake, and it went down faster than you can say Dahninaderke. Much faster, I'm sure.

I wanted no souvenirs of tragedy.

Dad stood on one side of me, and Mom on the other. We were a mighty good team.

"I'm ready now," I told them.

And I went home, where my monsters and my magic box were waiting.

FIVE
Zephyr as It Is

———

It has been a long, cold winter, and I am going home.

South from Birmingham on Interstate 65, that busy highway leading to the state capital. A left turn at Exit 205, and then following the road as it narrows and winds past drowsing towns named Coopers, Rockford, Hissop, and Cottage Grove. No sign spells out the name Zephyr anymore, but I know where it is and I am going home.

I am not going alone, on this beautiful Saturday afternoon at the beginning of spring. My wife, Sandy, is beside me, and our own "young'un" in the back, curled up wearing a Birmingham Barons baseball cap on backward and baseball cards scattered over the seat. These days there might be a fortune back there, who knows? The radio—pardon me, the stereo cassette player—is on, with Tears For Fears coming out of the speakers. I think Roland Orzabal is a fantastic singer.

It's 1991. Can you believe it? We're poised on the edge of a new century, for better or worse. I guess we'll all make up our own minds which. The year 1964 seems like ancient history now. The Polaroids taken in that year have turned yellow. No one wears their hair like that anymore, and the clothes have changed. People have changed, too, I think. Not just in the South, but everywhere. For better or worse? You can decide for yourself.

And what we and the world have been through since 1964! Think of it! It's been a faster, more brain-busting ride than ever could be devised by the Brandywine Carnival. We've lived through Vietnam—if we've been fortunate—and the era of Flower Power, Watergate and the fall of Nixon, the Ayatollah, Ronnie and Nancy, the cracking of the Wall and the beginning of the end of Communist Russia. We truly are living in the time of whirlwinds and comets. And like rivers that flow to the sea, time must flow into the future. It boggles the mind to think what might be ahead. But, as the Lady once said, you can't know where you're going until you figure out where you've been. Sometimes I think we have a lot of figuring out to do.

"It's such a lovely day," Sandy says, and she leans back in her seat to watch the countryside glide past. I glance at her and my eyes are blessed. She wears sunlight in her blond hair like a spill of golden flowers. There's some silver in there, too, and I like it though she frets some. Her eyes are pale gray and her gaze is calm and steady. She is a rock when I need strength, and a pillow when I need comfort. We're a good team. Our child has her eyes and her calm, the dark brown of my hair and my curiosity about the world. Our child has my father's sharp-bridged nose and the slim-fingered "artist's hands" of my mother. I think it's a fine combination.

"Hey, Dad!" The baseball cards have been forgotten for the moment.

"Yeah?"

"Are you nervous?"

"No," I say. Better be honest, I think. "Well . . . maybe a little bit."

"What's it gonna be like?"

"I don't know. It's been . . . oh . . . let's see, we left Zephyr in 1966. So it's been . . . you tell me how many years."

A few seconds' pause. "Twenty-five."

"Right as rain," I say. Our child gets an aptitude in math strictly from Sandy's side of the family, believe me.

"How come you never came back here? I mean, if you liked it so much?"

"I started to, more than a few times. I got as far as the turnoff from I-65. But Zephyr's not like it was. I guess I know things can't stay the same, and that's all right but . . . Zephyr was my home, and it hurts to think it's changed so much."

"So how's it changed? It's still a town, isn't it?" I hear the baseball cards being flipped through again, being sorted by team and alphabetized.

"Not like it was," I say. "The air force base near here closed down in 1974, and the paper mill up on the Tecumseh shut down two years later. Union Town grew. It's about four or five times the size it was when I was a boy. But Zephyr . . . just got smaller."

"Um." The attention is drifting now.

I glance at Sandy, and we smile at each other. Her hand finds mine. They were meant to be clasped together, just like this. Before us, the hills rise around Adams Valley. They are covered by trees that blaze with the yellow and purple of new buds. Some green is appearing, too, though April's not here yet. The air outside the car is still cool, but the sun is a glorious promise of summer.

My folks and I indeed did leave Zephyr, in August of 1966. Dad, who had found a job working at Mr. Vandercamp's hardware store, sensed the changing winds and decided to search for greener pastures. He found a job in Birmingham, as the assistant manager on the night shift at the Coca-Cola bottling plant. He was making twice as much money as he'd ever made when he was a milkman. By 1970, he'd moved up to be the night-shift manager, and he thought we were in high cotton. That was the year I started college, at the University of Alabama. Dad saw me graduate, with a degree in journalism, before he died of cancer in 1978. It was, thankfully, a quick passing. Mom grieved terribly, and I thought I was going to lose her, too. But in 1983, on a cruise to Alaska with a group of friends from her church, Mom met a widowed gentleman who owned a horse breeding farm near Bowling Green, Kentucky. Two years later, she became his wife and she lives on that farm still. He's a great guy and is very good to my mother, but he's not my dad. Life goes on, and the roads always lead to unexpected destinations.

ROUTE TEN, reads a sign pocked with rust-edged bullet holes.

My heart is starting to beat harder. My throat is dry. I expect change, but I'm afraid of it.

I've tried my damnedest not to get old. This in itself is a tough job. I don't mean age old, because that's an honorable thing. I mean attitude old. I've seen guys my age suddenly wake up one morning and forget their fathers forbade them to listen to those demonic Rolling Stones. They've forgotten their fathers demanding that they get out of the house if they're going to wear their hair down on their foreheads. They've forgotten what it meant, to be the bossee instead of the bosser. Of course the world is tougher now, no doubt about it. There are harder choices to be made, with more terrible conse- quences. Kids need guidance, for sure. I did, and I'm glad I got guided because it helped me miss making a lot of mistakes. But I think parents aren't teachers anymore. Parents—or a whole lot of us, at least—lead by mouth instead of by example. It seems to me that if a child's hero is their mother or father—or even better, both of them in tandem—then the rough road of learning and experience is going to be smoothed some. And every little bit of smoothing helps, in this rough old world that wants children to be miniature adults, devoid of charm and magic and the beauty of innocence.

Well, my last name's neither Lovoy nor Blessett, so I ought to get off my pulpit now.

ROBERT R. McCAMMON

I've changed somewhat since 1964, of course. I don't have as much hair, and I wear glasses. I've picked up some wrinkles, but I've gained some laugh lines, too. Sandy says she thinks I'm more handsome now than I ever was. This is called love. But as I say, I really have tried to hold off the attitude aging. In this regard, music came to my rescue. I believe music is the language of youth, and the more you can accept as being valid, the younger your attitude gets. I credit the Beach Boys with getting me interested in music to begin with. Now my record collection—excuse me, my CD collection— includes artists like Elvis Costello, U2, Sinéad O'Connor, Concrete Blonde, Simple Minds, and Technotronic. I have to say, however, that sometimes I feel the classics pulling at me, like Led Zeppelin and the Lovin' Spoonful. But with all this choice on my platter, I have a feast.

I drive past a weeded-up road that cuts through the woods, and I know what ruin lies at its end fifty yards away. Miss Grace and her bad girls folded their tents right after the Blaylocks went to prison. The house's roof was blown off during a windstorm in July of 1965. I doubt if there's much left at all now. The kudzu vines around here have always been hungry.

Ben started college at the University of Alabama the same year I did, majoring in business. He even stayed to go to graduate school, and I would never in a million years have thought that Ben would actually enjoy school. He and I got together from time to time at the university, but gradually he was more and more involved with his business fraternity and I didn't see a whole lot of him. He joined Sigma Chi social fraternity and became vice president of the chapter. He lives now in Atlanta, where he's a stockbroker. He and his wife, Jane Anne, have a boy and a girl. The guy is rich, he drives a gold-colored BMW, and he's fatter than ever. He called me three years ago, after he read one of my books, and we see each other every few months. Last summer we drove down to a small town near the state line between Alabama and Florida to visit the chief of police there. His name is John Wilson.

I always knew Johnny had the blood of a chief in his veins. He runs a tight ship in that town, and he accepts no nonsense. But I understand that he's a fair man, and everybody there seems to like him, because he's in his second term. While we were there, Ben and I met Johnny's wife, Rachel. Rachel is a stunning woman who looks like she could easily be a fashion model. She hangs all over that guy. Though they have no children, Johnny and Rachel are perfectly happy. We all went deep-sea fishing off Destin one weekend, and Johnny caught a marlin, I got my line tangled up under the boat, and

Ben got the sunburn of his life. But we sure did do a lot of laughing and catching up.

It is there before I realize it. My stomach tightens.

"Saxon's Lake," I tell them. They both crane their necks to look.

It hasn't changed at all. The same size, the same dark water, the same mud and reeds, the same red rock cliff. It wouldn't take much effort to imagine Dad's milk truck parked there, and him leaping into the water after a sinking car. It likewise wouldn't take much effort to remember a Buick wallowing there, water flooding through the broken rear windshield, and my father straining to reach me with a glass-slashed hand. Not much effort at all.

Dad, I love you, I think as we leave Saxon's Lake behind.

I remember his face, washed by firelight, as he sat there in the house and explained to me about Dr. Gunther Dahninaderke. It took us both—and Mom, too, and just about everybody in town—a long time to accept the fact that he and his wife had done such evil things. Though he wasn't evil through and through, or else why would he have saved my life? I don't think anyone is evil beyond saving. Maybe I'm like Dad that way: naive. But better naive, I think, than calloused to the core.

It dawned on me sometime later about Dr. Dahninaderke and his nightly vigils at the shortwave radio. I firmly believe he was listening to the foreign countries for news on who else in the Nazi regime had been captured and brought to justice. I believe that under his cool exterior he lived in perpetual terror, waiting for that knock on the door. He had delivered agonies, and he had suffered them, too. Would he have killed me once he had that green feather in his fist, as he and Kara had tortured and killed Jeff Hannaford over blackmail money? I honestly don't know. Do you?

Oh, yes! The Demon!

Ben told me this. The Demon, who had demonstrated later in high school that she was indeed a genius, went to college at Vanderbilt and became a chemist for DuPont. She did very well at that, but her strange nature would not let her alone. The last Ben understood, the Demon has become a performance artist in New York City and is locking horns with Jesse Helms over an art piece she does in which she screams and rants about corporate America while sitting in a baby pool full of . . . you can guess what.

All I can say is, Jesse Helms better not get on her bad side. If he does, I pity him. He might find himself glued to his desk one fine day.

I follow the same curves that scared the yell out of me when Donny Blaylock flew around them. And then the hills move aside and the road becomes as cleanly straight as a part made by Mr. Dollar and there is the gargoyle bridge.

Missing its gargoyles. The heads of the Confederate generals have been hacked away. Maybe it was vandalism, maybe it was somebody who would get a thousand dollars apiece for them on the art market as examples of Southern primitivism. I don't know, but they are gone. There is the railroad trestle, which is about the same, and there is the shine of the Tecumseh River. I imagine that Old Moses is happier, now that the paper mill has closed. He doesn't get pollution in his teeth when he bites a mouthful of turtle. Of course, he doesn't get his Good Friday feast anymore, either. That ended, Ben told me, when the Lady passed over her own river in 1967 at the grand old age of one hundred and nine. The Moon Man, Ben said, left town soon afterward, heading for New Orleans, and after that the community of Bruton began to dwindle, getting smaller at even a faster rate than Zephyr. The Tecumseh River may be cleaner now, but I wonder if on some nights Old Moses doesn't lift his scaly head to the surface and spout steam and water from the twin furnaces of his nostrils. I wonder if he doesn't listen to the silence beyond the sounds of water sloshing over rocks and think in his own reptilian language "Why doesn't anybody ever come to play with me anymore?"

Maybe he's still here. Maybe he's gone, following the river to the sea.

We cross the gargoyle-less bridge. And there on the other side is my hometown.

"Here we are," I hear myself say as I slow the car down, but instantly I know I am incorrect. We may be in a particular place in time, but this place is no longer Zephyr.

At least not the Zephyr I knew. The houses are still here, but many of them are tumbling down, the yards forlorn. It's not totally a ghost town, however, because some of the houses—a small, small number, it appears—are still being lived in, and there are a few cars on the streets. But already I feel that a great gathering—a wonderful party and celebration of life—has moved on somewhere else, leaving its physical evidence behind like a garden of dead flowers.

This is going to be a lot tougher than I thought.

Sandy senses it. "You all right?"

"We'll find out," I tell her, and I manage a feeble smile.

"There's hardly anybody here, is there, Dad?"

"Hardly a soul," I answer.

I turn off Merchants Street before I get to the center of town. I can't take that yet. I drive to the ball field where the Branlins made

their savage attack on us that day, and I stop the car on the field's
edge.

"Mind if we sit here for a minute, kids?" I ask.

"No," Sandy says, and she squeezes my hand.

About the Branlins. Johnny supplied me with this information,
being an officer of the law. It seems that the brothers were not of a
single nature after all. Gotha started playing football in high school
and became the man of the hour when he intercepted a Union Town
High School pass right on their goal line and ran it back for a big
TD. The acclaim did wonders for him, proving that all the time he
only craved the attention his mother and father were too stupid or
mean to give him. Gotha, Johnny told me, now lives in Birmingham
and sells insurance, and he coaches a peewee football team on the
side. Johnny told me Gotha needs no peroxide in his hair anymore,
since he has not a strand of it left.

Gordo, on the other hand, continued his descent. I'm sorry to say
that in 1980 Gordo was shot to death by the owner of a 7-Eleven in
Baton Rouge, Louisiana, where he'd fallen in with a bad crowd.
Gordo died trying to steal less than three hundred dollars from the
register and all the Little Debbie cakes he could carry. It seems to me
that once upon a time he did have a chance, but he didn't listen to
the poison ivy.

"I'm gonna get out for a minute and stretch my legs," I say.

"Want us to go with you, Dad?"

"No," I answer. "Not right now."

I get out and walk across the overgrown baseball field. I stand on
the pitcher's mound, caressed by cool breeze and warm sun. The
bleachers where I first saw Nemo Curliss are sagging. I hold my arm
out with my palm toward the sky, and I wait.

What would happen if that ball Nemo Curliss flung to heaven
suddenly came down into my hand after all these years?

I wait.

But it doesn't happen. Nemo, the boy with a perfect arm who was
trapped by all-too-imperfect circumstances, threw that ball beyond
the clouds. It never came down and it never will, and only Ben,
Johnny, and I remember.

I close my palm, and return my arm to my side.

I can see Poulter Hill from here.

It, too, has been allowed to deteriorate. The weeds are pushing up
amid the headstones, and it appears that no new flowers have been
put up there for a long time. That's a shame, I think, because there
lie Zephyr's faithful ones.

I don't want to walk amid those stones. I had never been back,

469

after my train trip. I had said my good-bye to Davy Ray, and he said his to me. Anything else would be a numb-nuts thing to do.

I turn away from Death, and walk back to the living.

"This was my school," I tell my wife and child as I stop the car beside the playground.

We all get out here, and Sandy walks at my side as my shoes stir the playground's dust. Our "young'un" begins to run around in wider and wider circles, like a pony set free after a long period of confinement. "Be careful!" Sandy warns, because she's seen a broken bottle. Worrying, it seems, comes with the job.

I put my arm around Sandy, and her arm goes around my back. The elementary school is empty, some of the windows shattered. There is a crushing silence, where so many young voices whooped and hollered. I see the place near the fence where Johnny and Gotha Branlin squared off. I see the gate where I fled from Gordo on Rocket and led him to Lucifer's judgment. I see—

"Hey, Dad! Look what I found!"

Our "young'un" comes trotting back. "I found it over there! Neat, huh?"

I look into the small, offered palm, and I have to smile.

It is a black arrowhead, smooth and almost perfectly formed. There are hardly any cuts on it at all. It was obviously fashioned by someone who was proud of his labors. A chief, most likely.

"Can I keep it, Dad?" my daughter asks.

Her name is Skye. She turned twelve in January, and she's going through what Sandy calls the "tomboy stage." Skye would rather put on a baseball cap backward and run grinning through the dust than play with dolls and dream about the New Kids on the Block. These things will come later, I'm sure. For right now, Skye is fine.

"I believe you ought to," I tell her, and she eagerly pushes that arrowhead down into the pocket of her jeans like a secret treasure.

You see, it's a girl's life, too.

And now we drive along Merchants Street, into the center of the stilled heart.

Everything is closed. Mr. Dollar's barbershop, the Piggly-Wiggly, the Bright Star Cafe, the hardware store, the Lyric, everything. The windows of the Woolworth's are soaped over. The growth of retail outlets, apartments, and a shopping mall with four theaters in Union Town consumed the spirit of Zephyr, as Big Paul's Pantry finished off the milkman's route. This is a going-forward, but is it progress?

We drive past the courthouse. Silence. Past the public swimming pool and the shell of the Spinnin' Wheel. Silence, silence. We drive past the house of Miss Blue Glass, and the silence where there used to be music is heavy indeed.

Miss Blue Glass. I wish I can say I know what happened to her, but I don't. She would be in her eighties now, if she is still alive. I just don't know. The same is true with so many others, who drifted away from Zephyr in the waning years: Mr. Dollar, Sheriff Marchette, Jazzman Jackson, Mr. and Mrs. Damaronde, Nila Castile and Gavin, Mrs. Velvadine, Mayor Swope. I think they are all alive, in other towns. I think they have kept part of Zephyr with them, and wherever they go they leave Zephyr's seeds in the earth. As I do.

I worked for a newspaper in Birmingham for two years after I finished college. I wrote headlines and edited other people's stories. When I went to my apartment in that big city after work, I sat down at my magic box—not that same one, but a new magic box—and I wrote. And I wrote. The stories went out into the mail and the stories came back. Then, out of desperation, I tried to write a novel. Lo and behold, it found a publisher.

I am a library now. A small one, but I'm growing.

I slow the car as we move past a house set back off the street next to a barn. "He lived right there," I tell Sandy.

"Wow!" Skye says. "It's creepy! It looks like a haunted house!"

"No," I tell her, "I think it's just a house now."

Like Bo knows football, my daughter knows haunted houses. She knows Vincent Price and Peter Cushing, the films of Hammer, the works of Poe, the chronicles of Mars and the town called 'Salem's Lot. But she knows Alice through the looking glass, too, and the Faithful Tin Soldier, the Ugly Duckling, and the journeys of Stuart Little. She knows Oz and the jungles of Tarzan, and though she is too young to fully appreciate anything but the colors, she knows the hands of Van Gogh, Winslow Homer, and Miró. She will listen to Duke Ellington and Count Basie, as well as to the Beach Boys. Just last week she asked me if she could put a picture in a frame on her dresser. She said she thought this particular dude was cool.

His name is Freddy.

"Skye," I said, "I really think havin' that in here is gonna give you night—"

And then I stopped. Oh-oh, I thought. Oh-oh.

Freddy, meet Skye. Talk to her about the power of make-believe, will you?

I turn the car onto Hilltop Street, and we rise toward my house.

I'm doing all right with my writing. It's a hard job, but I enjoy it. Sandy and I aren't the kind of people who need to own half the world to be happy. I have to say, though, that once I did splurge. I bought an old red convertible that called to me from a used car lot when Sandy and I were taking a vacation in New England. I think they used to refer to such cars as roadsters. I've restored it back to how it must've looked when Zephyr was new. Sometimes, when I'm alone out in that car, speeding along with the wind in my hair and the sun on my face, I forget myself and speak to it. I call it by a certain name.

You know what I call it.

That bicycle went with me when we left Zephyr. We had more adventures, and that golden eye saw a lot of trouble coming and kept me from getting into it on more than several occasions. But eventually it creaked under my weight, and my hands didn't seem to fit on the grips anymore. It was consigned to the basement, under a blue tarp. I imagined it went to sleep like a bird. One weekend I returned from college to find that Mom had had a garage sale, which included the contents of the basement. And here's your money a fella paid for your old bike! she'd said as she handed me a twenty-dollar bill. He bought it for his own boy, isn't that grand, Cory? Cory? Isn't that grand?

It's grand, I'd told my mother. And that night I put my head on my dad's shoulder and cried as if I were twelve again instead of twenty.

My heart stutters.

There it is. Right there.

"My house," I tell Sandy and Skye.

It has aged, under sun and rain. It needs paint and care. It needs love, but it is empty now. I stop the car at the curb, and I stare at the porch and see my father suddenly emerge smiling from the front door. He looks strong and fit, like he always does when I remember him.

"Hey, Cory!" he says. "How ya gettin' along?"

Just fine, sir, I answer.

"I knew you would be. I did all right, didn't I?"

Yes sir, you did, I say.

"Sure do have a pretty wife and a good daughter, Cory. And those books of yours! I knew you were gonna do well, all the time I knew it."

Dad? Do you want me to come in and stay awhile?

"Come in *here*?" He leans against the porch column. "Why would you want to do that, Cory?"

Aren't you lonely? I mean . . . it's so quiet here.

"Quiet?" He laughs heartily. "Sometimes I wish it *was* quiet! It's not a bit of quiet here!"

But . . . it's empty. Isn't it?

"It's full to the brim," my father says. He looks up at the sun, over the hills of spring. "You don't have to come here to see them, Cory. Or to see me, either. You really don't. You don't have to leave what is, to visit what was. You've got a good life, Cory. Better than I dreamed. How's your mom doin'?"

She's happy. I mean, she misses you, but . . .

"But life is for the livin'," he tells me in his fatherly voice. "Now go on and get on with it instead of wantin' to come in an old house with a saggy floor."

Yes sir, I say, but I can't leave yet.

He starts to go in, but he pauses, too. "Cory?" he says.

Yes sir?

"I'll always love you. Always. And I'll always love your mother, and I am so very happy for the both of you. Do you understand?"

I nod.

"You'll always be my boy," Dad says, and then he returns to the house and the porch is empty.

"Cory? Cory?"

I turn my face and look at Sandy.

"What do you see?" she asks me.

"A shadow," I say.

I want to go one more place before I turn the car around and drive away. I head us up the winding path of Temple Street, toward the Thaxter mansion at its summit.

Here things have really changed.

Some of the big houses have actually been torn down. Where they were is rolling grass. And here is another surprise: the Thaxter mansion has grown, sprouting additions on either side. The property around it is huge. My God! I realize. Vernon must still live there! I drive through a gate and past a big swimming pool. A treehouse has been constructed in the arms of a massive oak. The mansion itself is immaculate, the grounds beautiful, and smaller buildings have been constructed in its style.

I stop the car in front. "I can't believe this!" I tell Sandy. "I've gotta find out if Vernon's still here!"

I get out and start for the front door, my insides quaking with excitement.

But before I reach it, I hear a bell ring. *Ding . . . ding . . . ding . . . ding.*

I hear what sounds like a tidal wave, gaining speed and force.

And my breath is well and truly swept away.

Because here they come.

Swarming out of the front door, like wasps from the nest in the church's ceiling on Easter Sunday. Here they come, laughing and hollering and jostling each other. Here they come, in a wonderful riot of noise.

The boys. Dozens of them, dozens. Some white, some black. Their numbers surge around me, as if I am an island in the river. Some of them run for the treehouse, others scamper across the rolling green yard. I am at the center of a young universe, and then I see the brass plaque on the wall next to the door.

It says THE ZEPHYR HOME FOR BOYS.

Vernon's mansion has become an orphanage.

And still they stream out around me, furious in their freedom on this glorious Saturday afternoon. A window opens on the second floor, and a wrinkled face peers out. "James Lucius!" her voice squawks. "Edward and Gregory! Get up here for your piano lessons right this very minute!"

She wears blue.

Two older women I don't know come out, chasing after the crowd of boys. Good luck to them, I think. And then a younger man emerges, and he stops before me. "Can I help you?"

"I . . . used to live here. In Zephyr, I mean." I am so stunned I can hardly talk. "When did this become an orphanage?"

"In 1985," the man tells me. "Mr. Vernon Thaxter left it to us."

"Is Mr. Thaxter still alive?"

"He left town. I'm sorry, but I don't know what became of him." This man has a gentle face. He has blond hair, and eyes of cornflower blue. "May I ask your name?"

"I'm—" I stop, because I realize who he must be. "Who are *you*?"

"I'm Bubba Willow." He smiles, and I can see Chile in him. "Reverend Bubba Willow."

"I'm very pleased to meet you." We shake hands. "I met your mother once."

"My mom? Really? What's your name?"

"Cory Mackenson."

The name doesn't register. I was a ship, passing through Chile's night. "How's your mother doin'?"

"Oh, just great. She moved to St. Louis, and she's teachin' sixth grade now."

"I'll bet her students sure feel lucky."

"Parson?" A wizened voice says. "Par son Willa?"

An elderly black man in faded overalls has come out. Around his skinny waist he wears a tool belt holding hammers, screwdrivers, and arcane-looking wrenches. "Parson, I done   fixed   that   slow   leakupastairs. Oughta lookat that ol' freezer now." His eyes find me. "Oh," he says with a soft slow gasp. "I   know   you."

And a smile spreads across his face like day following night.

I hug him, and when he grasps me his tool belt jingle-jangles.

"Cory Mackenson! My Lord! Is that you?"

I peer up at the woman in blue. "Yes ma'am, it is."

"My Lord, my Lord! Excuse me, Reverend! *My Lord, my Lord!"* Then her attention goes where it ought to: toward the new generation of boys. "James Lucius! Don't you get up in that treehouse and break those fingers!"

"Would you and your family like to come in?" Reverend Willow asks.

"Please   do," Mr. Lightfoot says, smiling. "Lots   ta talk   about."

"Got coffee and doughnuts inside," the reverend tempts me. "Mrs. Velvadine runs a grand kitchen."

"Cory, you get on in here!" Then: "James Luuuuucius!"

Sandy and Skye have gotten out of the car. Sandy knows me, and she knows I'd like to stay for just a little while. We will not tarry long here, because my hometown is not our home, but an hour would be time well spent.

As they go in, I pause outside the door before I join them.

I look up, into the bright blue air.

I think I see four figures with wings, and their winged dogs, swooping and playing in the rivers of light.

They will always be there, as long as magic lives.

And magic has a strong, strong heart.

Acknowledgments

No book is ever written without help and influence. *Boy's Life* is no exception. I would like to thank, then, some of the people and things that helped create *Boy's Life*, whether they're aware of such help or not.

My thanks to Forrest J. Ackermann; Roger Corman; Boris Karloff; Vincent Price; Lon Chaney Senior and Junior; Jungle Jim; Sky King and Penny; *Screen Thrills Illustrated;* Ian Fleming and Bond, James Bond; Eudora Welty; Bob Kane; Barbara Steele; Big Daddy Roth; the Boys from Hawthorne though a young man is gone; Clutch Cargo; Space Angels; Super Car; the Captain and Tom Terrrrific; Yancy Derringer; *Famous Monsters of Filmland;* Gordon Scott; Vic Morrow and the *Combat* squad; Jim Warren (sorry, Forry!); Boston Blackie; Zorro; Cisco Kid and Pancho; the Whistler; Kirk Douglas in *Sparta-cus;* the Rolling Stones; *Thriller* and those pigeons from hell; the Hammer Films bunch; Peter Cushing, the ultimate Van Helsing; Christopher Lee; Edgar Rice Burroughs; Red Skelton and the passing parade; *Creepy* and *Eerie;* Ray Harryhausen and the Ymir; Mr. Television, Milton Berle; *It's A Mad, Mad, Mad, Mad* (Did I miss one?) *World;* Edgar Allan Poe; Lester Dent or Kenneth Robeson or whoever cranked out all those great Doc Savages; Three Dog Night (hello, Cory!); Clayton Moore, the one and only Lone Ranger; Richard Matheson; Roy Rogers and Trigger; *X–Men;* Buffalo Bob and Howdy; the Brothers Grimm; Bela Lugosi; Paladin; *The Outer Limits;* Brigitte Bardot (I didn't spend all my time with *Geographics!*); Basil Rathbone; Mister Dillon! Mister Dillon!; Sir Arthur Conan Doyle; *Invaders from Mars;* Gene Autry; Steve Reeves; Aunt Bea; Dr. Richard Kimble; the Who; Hans Christian Andersen; *13 Ghosts* and those weird glasses; Sergeant Preston of the Yukon; Mr. and Mrs. North; the Thin Man; Peter Lorre; Alfred Hitchcock; Here, Lassie!; Errol Flynn, the perfect Robin Hood; a man named Jed; the *Aquanauts;* Steve Roper and Mike Nomad; Clint Walker; Kookie, my hair's

477

falling out!; *Gorgo; Rodan; Reptilicus;* Charles Laughton; Oral Roberts heal thyself; *The Gallant Men;* Victor Mature swinging that jawbone; Walt Disney; Mr. Lucky; Burt Lancaster; *Through the Looking Glass;* Bronco and Sugarfoot; the Mavericks, wild as the wind in Or-e-gon; Joe and Frank; *Fantasia;* that house on haunted hill; Guy Madison and Andy Devine; *The Mysterians; Dementia 13* (Yikes!); Captain America and Bucky; Harper Lee; Steve McQueen (Cooler!) on that motorcycle, jumping the barbed wire; Tom Swift and His; and so many, many more whom I will think of as soon as I believe I've finished writing this.

To two very special influences on this boy's life and writing: Mr. Rod Serling,, for his talent and imagination that continues on far beyond the *Zone;* and to Mr. Ray Bradbury. Your lake will always be deeper and sweeter than mine, your jar hold greater mysteries, your rockets travel truer to the heart. Thank you so very, very much.

Well, I see by the old clock on the wall that it's time to go. Good-bye, kids!

Robert R. McCammon
April 14, 1990–September 23, 1990

GONE

SOUTH

For my family

1

The Good Son

It was hell's season, and the air smelled of burning children.

This smell was what had destroyed Dan Lambert's taste for barbecued pork sandwiches. Before August of 1969, the year he'd turned twenty, his favorite food had been barbecue crispy at the edges and drenched with sloppy red sauce. After the eleventh day of that month, the smell of it was enough to make him sick to death.

He was driving east through Shreveport on 70th Street, into the glare of the morning sun. It glanced off the hood of his gray pickup truck and stabbed his eyes, inflaming the slow ache in his skull. He knew this pain, and its vagaries. Sometimes it came upon him like a brute with a hammer, sometimes like a surgeon with a precise scalpel. During the worst times it hit and ran like a Mack truck and all he could do was chew on his rage and lie there until his body came back to him.

It was a hard thing, dying was.

In this August of 1991, a summer that had been one of the hottest in Louisiana's long history of hellish seasons, Dan was forty-two years old. He looked ten years older, his rawboned, heavily lined face a testament to his ceaseless combat with pain. It was a fight he knew he couldn't win. If he knew for certain he would live three more years, he wasn't sure if he'd be happy about it. Right now it was day-to-day. Some days were all right, some weren't worth a bucket of warm spit. But it wasn't in his nature to give up, no matter how tough things got. His father, the quitter, had not raised a quitter. In this, at least, Dan could find strength. He drove on along the arrow-straight line of 70th Street, past strip malls and car lots and fast-food joints. He drove on into the merciless sun and the smell of murdered innocents.

Lining the commercial carnival of 70th Street was a score of barbecue restaurants, and it was from their kitchen chimneys that this odor of burned flesh rose into the scalded sky. It was just after

483

nine, and already the temperature sign in front of the Friendship Bank of Louisiana read eighty-six degrees. The sky was cloudless, but was more white than blue, as if all the color had been bleached from it. The sun was a burnished ball of pewter, a promise of another day of misery across the Gulf states. Yesterday the temperature had hit a hundred and two, and Dan figured that today it was going to be hot enough to fry pigeons on the wing. Afternoon showers passed through every few days, but it was just enough to steam the streets. The Red River flowed its muddy course through Shreveport to the bayou country and the air shimmered over the larger buildings that stood iron-gray against the horizon.

Dan had to stop for a red light. The pickup's brakes squealed a little, in need of new pads. A job replacing rotten lumber on a patio deck last week had made him enough to pay the month's rent and utilities, and he'd had a few dollars left over for groceries. Still, some things had to slide. He'd missed two payments on the pickup, and he needed to go in and see Mr. Jarrett to work something out. Mr. Jarrett, the loan manager at the First Commercial Bank, understood that Dan had fallen on hard times, and cut him some slack.

The pain was back behind his eyes. It lived there, like a hermit crab. Dan reached beside himself on the seat, picked up the white bottle of Excedrin, and popped it open. He shook two tablets onto his tongue and chewed them. The light turned green and he drove on, toward Death Valley.

Dan wore a rust-colored short-sleeve shirt and blue jeans with patches on the knees. Under a faded blue baseball cap, his thinning brown hair was combed back from his forehead and spilled over his shoulders; haircuts were not high on his list of priorities. He had light brown eyes and a close-cropped beard that was almost all gray. On his left wrist was a Timex and on his feet was a sturdy pair of brown, much-scuffed workboots. On his right forearm was the bluish-green ghost of a snake tattoo, a reminder of a burly kid who'd had one too many cheap and potent zombies with his buddies on a night of leave in Saigon. That kid was long gone, and Dan was left with the tattoo. The Snake Handlers, that's what they'd been. Not afraid to stick their hands in the jungle's holes and pull out whatever horror might be coiled up and waiting in there. They had not known, then, that the entire world was a snake hole, and that the snakes just kept getting bigger and meaner. They had not known, in their raucous rush toward the future, that the snakes were lying in wait not only in the holes but in the mowed green grass of the American Dream. They got your legs first, wound around your ankles, and slowed you down. They slithered into your guts and made you sick and afraid, and then you were easy to kill.

In the years since that Day-Glo memory of a night in Saigon, Dan Lambert had shrunken. At his chest-thumping, Charlie-whomping best he'd stood six-two and carried two hundred and twelve pounds of Parris Island–trained muscle. Back then, he'd felt as if he could swallow bullets and shit iron. He weighed about a hundred and seventy pounds now, and he didn't think he was much over six feet. There was a gauntness in his face that made him think of some of the old Vietnamese people who'd huddled in their hootches with eyes as terrified as those of mongrel dogs expecting a boot. His cheekbones jutted, his chin was as sharp as a can opener under the beard. It was the fact that he rarely ate three meals a day, and of course a lot of his shrinkage was due to the sickness, too.

Gravity and time were the giant killers, he thought as he drove along the sun-washed highway with the back of his sweat-wet shirt stuck to the seat. Gravity shrank you and time pulled you into the grave, and not even the Snake Handlers could beat such fearsome enemies as those.

He drove through pale smoke that had drifted from the chimney of Hungry Bob's Barbecue Shack, the cook getting all that meat good and black for the lunch crowd. A tire hit a pothole, and in the truck's bed his box of tools jangled. They were the hammers, nails, levels, and saws of a carpenter.

At the next intersection he turned right and drove south into an area of warehouses. It was a world of chain-link fences, loading docks, and brick walls. Between the buildings the heat lay trapped and vengeful. Up ahead a half-dozen pickup trucks and a few cars were parked in an empty lot. Dan could see some of the men standing around talking. Another man was sitting in a folding chair reading a newspaper, his CAT hat throwing a slice of shade across his face. Standing near one of the cars was a man who had a sign hanging around his neck, and on that sign was hand-lettered WILL WORK FOR FOOD.

This was Death Valley.

Dan pulled his truck into the lot and cut the engine. He unpeeled his damp shirt from the backrest, slipped the bottle of aspirin into his pocket, and got out. "There's Dan the man!" Steve Lynam called from where he stood talking with Darryl Glennon and Curtis Nowell, and Dan raised a hand in greeting.

"Mornin', Dan," Joe Yates said, laying his newspaper in his lap. "How's it hangin'?"

"It's still there," Dan answered. "I think."

"Got iced tea." A plastic jug and a bag of Dixie cups sat on the ground next to Joe's folding chair. "Come on over."

Dan joined him. He drew iced tea into a cup and eased himself down beside Joe's shadow. "Terry got a ticket," Joe said as he offered Dan some of the newspaper. "Fella came by 'bout ten minutes ago, lookin' for a man to set some Sheetrock. Picked Terry and off they went."

"That's good." Terry Palmeter had a wife and two kids to feed. "Fella say he might be needin' some more help later on?"

"Just the one Sheetrock man." Joe squinted up toward the sun. He was a lean, hard-faced man with a nose that had been broken and flattened by a vicious fist somewhere down the line. He'd been coming here to Death Valley for over a year, about as long as Dan had been. On most days Joe was an amiable gent, but on others he sat brooding and dark-spirited and was not to be approached. Like the other men who came to Death Valley, Joe had never revealed much about himself, though Dan had learned the man had been married and divorced the same as he had. Most of the men were from towns other than Shreveport. They were wanderers, following the promise of work, and for them the roads on the map led not so much from city to city as from hot-tarred roofs to mortared walls to the raw frameworks of new houses with pinewood so fresh the timbers wept yellow tears. "God, it's gonna be a cooker today," Joe said, and he lowered his head and returned to his reading and waiting.

Dan drank the iced tea and felt sweat prickling the back of his neck. He didn't want to stare, but his eyes kept returning to the man who wore the desperate hand-lettered sign. The man had sandy-blond hair, was probably in his late twenties, and wore a checked shirt and stained overalls. His face was still boyish, though it was starting to take on the tautness of true hunger. It reminded Dan of someone he'd known a long time ago. A name came to him: *Farrow*. He let it go, and the memory drifted away like the acrid barbecue smoke.

"Looky here, Dan." Joe thumped an article in the paper. "President's economics honcho says the recession's over and everybody ought to be in fine shape by Christmas. Says new construction's already up thirty percent."

"Do tell," Dan said.

"Got all sorts of graphs in here to show how happy we oughta be." He showed them to Dan, who glanced at the meaningless bars and arrows and then watched the man with the sign again. "Yeah, things are sure gettin' better all over, ain't they?" Joe nodded, answering his own cynical question. "Yessir. Too bad they forgot to tell the workman."

"Joe, who's that fella over there?" Dan asked. "The guy with the sign."

"I don't know." He didn't lift his gaze from the paper. "He was there when I got here. Young fella, looks to be. Hell, every man jack of us would work for food if it came to that, but we don't wear signs advertisin' it, do we?"

"Maybe we're not hungry enough yet."

"Maybe not," Joe agreed, and then he said nothing else.

More men were arriving in their pickups and cars, some with wives who let them out and drove off. Dan recognized others he knew, like Andy Slane and Jim Neilds. They were a community of sorts, scholars in the college of hard knocks. Fourteen months ago Dan had been working on the payroll of the A&A Construction Company. Their motto had been We Build the Best for Less. Even so, the company hadn't been strong enough to survive the bottom falling out of the building business. Dan had lost his job of five years and quickly found that nobody was hiring carpenters full-time. The first thing to go had been his house, in favor of a cheaper apartment. His savings had dwindled amazingly—and frighteningly—fast. Since his divorce in 1984 he'd been paying child support to Susan, so his bank account had never been well padded. But he'd never been a man who needed or expected luxuries, anyway. The nicest thing in his possession was his Chevy pickup—"metallic mist" was the correct name of its color, according to the salesman—which he'd bought three months prior to the crash of A&A Construction. Being behind the two payments bothered him; Mr. Jarrett was a fair man, and Dan was not one to take advantage of fairness. He was going to have to find a way to scrape some cash together.

He didn't like looking at the man who wore the hand-lettered sign, but he couldn't help it. He knew what trying to find a steady job was like. With all the layoffs and businesses going under, the help-wanted ads had dried up to nothing. Skilled laborers like Dan and the others who came to Death Valley were the first to feel the hurt. He didn't like looking at the man with the desperate sign because he feared he might be seeing his own future.

Death Valley was where men who wanted to work came to wait for a "ticket." Getting a ticket meant being picked for a job by anyone who needed labor. The contractors who were still in business knew about Death Valley, and would go there to find help when a regular crewman was sick or they needed extra hands for a day or two. Regular homeowners sometimes drove by as well, to hire somebody to do such jobs as patching a roof or building a fence. The citizens of Death Valley worked cheap.

And the hell of it, Dan had learned by talking to the others, was that places like Death Valley existed in every city. It had become clear to him that thousands of men and women lived clinging to the edge of poverty through no fault of their own but because of the times and the luck of the draw. The recession had been a beast with a cold eye, and it had wrenched families young and old from their homes and shattered their lives with equal dispassion.

"Hey, Dan! How many'd ya kill?"

Two shadows had fallen across him. He looked up and made out Steve Lynam and Curtis Nowell standing beside him with the sun at their backs. "What?" he asked.

"How many'd ya kill?" Curtis had posed the question. He was in his early thirties, had curly dark brown hair, and wore a yellow T-shirt with NUKE THE WHALES stenciled on it. "How many chinks? More than twenty or less than twenty?"

"Chinks?" Dan repeated, not quite grasping the point.

"Yeah." Curtis dug a pack of Winstons and a lighter from his jeans pocket. "Charlies. Gooks. Whatever you dudes called 'em back then. You kill more than twenty of 'em?"

Joe pushed the brim of his cap up. "You fellas don't have anythin' better to do than invade a man's privacy?"

"No," Curtis said as he lit up. "We ain't hurtin' anythin' by askin', are we, Dan? I mean, you're proud to be a vet, ain't you?"

"Yes, I am." Dan sipped his tea again. Most of the Death Valley regulars knew about his tour of duty, not because he particularly cared to crow about it but because Curtis had asked him where he'd gotten the tattoo. Curtis had a big mouth and he was on the dumb side: a bad combination. "I'm proud I served my country," Dan said.

"Yeah, you didn't run to Canada like them draft-dodgin' fuckers did, huh?" Steve asked. He was a few years older than Curtis, had keen blue eyes and a chest as big as a beer keg.

"No," Dan answered, "I did what I was told."

"So how many?" Curtis urged. "More than twenty?"

Dan released a long, weary breath. The sun was beating down on his skull, even through the baseball cap. "Does it really matter?"

"We want to know," Curtis said, the cigarette clenched between his teeth and his mouth leaking smoke. "You kept a body count, didn't you?"

Dan stared straight ahead. He was looking at a chain-link fence.

Beyond it was a wall of brown bricks. Sun and shadow lay worlds apart on that wall. In the air Dan could smell the burning.

"Talked to this vet once in Mobile," Curtis plowed on. "Fella was one-legged. He said he kept a body count. Said he knew how many chinks he'd killed right to the man."

"Jesus Christ!" Joe said. "Why don't you two go on and pester the shit outta somebody else? Can't you see Dan don't want to talk about it?"

"He's got a voice," Steve replied. "He can say if he wants to talk about it or not."

Dan could sense Joe was about to stand up from his chair. When Joe stood up, it was either to go after a ticket or knock the ugly out of somebody. "I didn't keep a body count," Dan said before Joe could leave the folding chair. "I just did my job."

"But you can kinda figure out how many, right?" Curtis wasn't about to give up until he'd gnawed all the meat off this particular bone. "Like more or less than twenty?"

A slow pinwheel of memories had begun to turn in Dan's mind. These memories were never far from him, even on the best of days. In that slow pinwheel were fragments of scenes and events: mortar shells blasting dirt showers in a jungle where the sunlight was cut to a murky gloom; rice paddies shimmering in the noonday heat; helicopters circling overhead while soldiers screamed for help over their radios and sniper bullets ripped the air; the false neon joy of Saigon's streets and bars; dark shapes unseen yet felt, and human excrement lying within the perimeter wire to mark the contempt the Cong had for Uncle Sam's young men; rockets scrawling white and red across the twilight sky; Ann-Margret in thigh-high boots and pink hot pants, dancing the frug at a USO show; the body of a Cong soldier, a boy maybe fifteen years old, who had stepped on a mine and been blown apart and flies forming a black mask on his bloody face; a firefight in a muddy clearing, and a terrified voice yelling *motherfucker motherfucker motherfucker* like a strange mantra; the silver rain, drenching the trees and vines and grass, the hair and skin and eyes and not one drop of it clean; and the village.

Oh, yes. The village.

Dan's mouth was very dry. He took another swallow of tea. The ice was almost gone. He could feel the men waiting for him to speak, and he knew they wouldn't leave him alone until he did. "More than twenty."

"Hot damn, I knew it!" Grinning, Curtis elbowed Steve in the ribs and held out his palm. "Cough it up, friend!"

"Okay, okay." Steve brought out a battered wallet, opened it, and slapped a five-dollar bill into Curtis Nowell's hand. "I'll get it back sooner or later."

"You boys ain't got trouble enough, you gotta gamble your money away?" Joe sneered.

Dan set his cup down. A hot pulse had begun beating at his temples. "You laid a bet," he said as he lifted a wintry gaze to the two men, "on how many corpses I left in 'Nam?"

"Yeah, I bet it'd be more than twenty," Curtis said, "and Steve bet it'd be—"

"I get the drift." Dan stood up. It was a slow, easy movement though it hurt his knees. "You used me and what I did to win you some cash, Curtis?"

"Sure did." It was said proudly. Curtis started to push the fiver into his pocket.

"Let me see the money."

Still grinning, Curtis held the bill out.

Dan didn't smile. His hand whipped forward, took the money, and had it in his grip before Curtis's grin could drop. "Whoa!" Curtis said. "Give it here, man!"

"You used me and what I did? What I *lived* through? I think I deserve half of this, don't you?" Without hesitation, Dan tore the bill in two.

"Hey, man! It's against the fuckin' law to tear up money!"

"Sue me. Here's your half."

Curtis's face had reddened. "I oughta bust your fuckin' head is what I oughta do!"

"Maybe you ought to. Try, at least."

Sensing trouble, a few of the other men had started edging closer. Curtis's grin returned, only this time it was mean. "I could take you with one hand, you skinny old bastard."

"You might be right about that." Dan watched the younger man's eyes, knowing that in them he would see the punch coming before Curtis's arm was cocked for the strike. "Might be. But before you try, I want you to know that I haven't raised my hand in anger to a man since I left 'Nam. I wasn't the best soldier, but I did my job and nobody could ever say I'd gone south." Dan saw a nerve in Curtis's left eyelid begin to tick. Curtis was close to swinging. "If you swing on me," Dan said calmly, "you'll have to kill me to put me down. I won't be used or made a fool of, and I won't have you winnin' a bet on how many bodies I left in my footprints. Do you understand that, Curtis?"

"I think you're full of shit," Curtis said, but his grin had weakened. Blisters of sweat glistened on his cheeks and forehead.

He glanced to the right and left, taking in the half-dozen or so onlookers, then back to Dan. "You think you're somethin' *special* 'cause you're a vet?"

"Nothin' special about me," Dan answered. "I just want you to know that I learned how to kill over there. I got better at it than I wanted to be. I didn't kill all those Cong with a gun or a knife. Some of 'em I had to use my hands. Curtis, I love peace more than any man alive, but I won't take disrespect. So go on and swing if you want to, I'm not goin' anywhere."

"Man, I could break your damn neck with one punch," Curtis said, but the way he said it told Dan he was trying to decide whether to push this thing any further.

Dan waited. The decision was not his to make.

A few seconds ticked past. Dan and Curtis stared at each other.

"Awful hot to be fightin'," Joe said. "Grown men, I swear!"

"Hell, it's only five dollars," Steve added.

Curtis took a deep drag on his cigarette and exhaled smoke through his nostrils. Dan kept watching him, his gaze steady and his face placid though the pain in his skull had racheted up a notch.

"Shit," Curtis said at last. He spat out a shred of tobacco. "Give it here, then." He took the half that Dan offered. "Keep you from tapin' it back together and spendin' it, at least."

"There ya go. Ya'll kiss and make up," Joe suggested.

Curtis laughed, and Dan allowed a smile. The men who'd thronged around began moving away. Dan knew that Curtis wasn't a bad fellow; Curtis just had a bad attitude sometimes and needed a little sense knocked into him. But on this day, with the sun burning down and no breeze stirring the weeds of Death Valley, Dan was very glad push had not come to shove.

"Sorry," Steve told him. "Guess we didn't think it'd bother you. The bet, I mean."

"Now you know. Let's forget it, all right?"

Curtis and Steve moved off. Dan took the Excedrin bottle from his pocket and popped another aspirin. His palms were damp, not from fear of Curtis, but from fear of what he might have done had that particular demon been loosed.

"You okay?" Joe was watching him carefully.

"Yeah. Headache."

"You get a lot of those, don't you?"

"A few."

"You seen a doctor?"

"Yeah." Dan put the bottle away. "Says it's migraine."

"Is that so?"

"Uh-huh." He knows I'm lyin', Dan thought. There was no need to tell any of the men here about his sickness. He crunched the aspirin between his teeth and washed it down with the last of his iced tea.

"Curtis is gonna get his clock cleaned one fine day," Joe said. "Fella don't have no sense."

"He hasn't lived enough, that's his problem."

"Right. Not like us old relics, huh?" Joe looked up at the sky, measuring the journey of the sun. "Did you see some hell over there, Dan?"

Dan settled himself back down beside his friend's chair. He let the question hang for a moment, and then he said, "I did. We all did."

"I just missed gettin' drafted. I supported you fellas all the way, though. I didn't march in the streets or nothin'."

"Might've been better if you had. We were over there way too long."

"We could've won it," Joe said. "Yessir. We could've swept the floor with them bastards if we'd just—"

"That's what I used to think," Dan interrupted quietly. "I used to think if it wasn't for the protesters, we could've turned that damn country into a big asphalt parkin' lot." He drew his knees up to his chest. The aspirin was kicking in now, dulling the pain. "Then I went up to Washington, and I walked along that wall. You know, where the names are. Lots of names up there. Fellas I knew. Young boys, eighteen and nineteen, and what was left of 'em wouldn't fill a bucket. I've thought and thought about it, but I can't figure out what we would've had if we'd won. If we'd killed every Charlie to a man, if we'd marched right into Hanoi and torched it to the ground, if we'd come home the heroes like the Desert Storm boys did . . . what would we have won?"

"Respect, I guess," Joe said.

"No, not even that. It was past time to get out. I knew it when I saw all those names on that black wall. When I saw mothers and fathers tracin' their dead sons' names on paper to take home with 'em because that's all they had left, I knew the protesters were right. We never could've won it. Never."

"Gone south," Joe said.

"What?"

"Gone south. You told Curtis nobody could ever say you'd gone south. What's that mean?"

Dan realized he'd used the term, but hearing it from the mouth of another man had taken him by surprise. "Somethin' we said in

'Nam," he explained. "Somebody screwed up—or cracked up—we said he'd gone south."

"And you never screwed up?"

"Not enough to get myself or anybody else killed. That was all we wanted: to get out alive."

Joe grunted. "Some life you came back to, huh?"

"Yeah," Dan said, "some life."

Joe lapsed into silence, and Dan offered nothing else. Vietnam was not a subject Dan willingly talked about. If anyone wanted to know and they pressed it, he might tell them hesitantly about the Snake Handlers and their exploits, the childlike bar girls of Saigon and the jungle snipers he'd been trained to hunt and kill, but never could he utter a word about two things: the village and the dirty silver rain.

The sun rose higher and the morning grew old. It was a slow day for tickets. Near ten-thirty a man in a white panel truck stopped at Death Valley and the call went up for two men who had experience in house-painting. Jimmy Staggs and Curtis Nowell got a ticket, and after they left in the panel truck everybody else settled down to waiting again.

Dan felt the brutal heat sapping him. He had to go sit in his truck for a while to get out of the sun. A couple of the younger bucks had brought baseball gloves and a ball, and they peeled off their wet shirts and pitched some as Dan and the older men watched. The guy with the hand-lettered sign around his neck was sitting on the curb, looking expectantly in the direction from which the ticket givers would be coming like God's emissaries. Dan wanted to go over and tell him to take that sign off, that he shouldn't beg, but he decided against it. You did what you had to do to get by.

Again the young man reminded Dan of someone else. Farrow was the name. It was the color of the hair and the boyish face, Dan thought. Farrow, the kid from Boston. Well, they'd all been kids back in those days, hadn't they? But thinking about Farrow stirred up old, deep pain, and Dan shunted the haunting images aside.

Dan had been born in Shreveport on the fifth of May in 1950. His father, who had been a sergeant in the Marine Corps but who liked to be called "Major" by his fellow workers at the Pepsi bottling plant, had departed this life in 1973 by route of a revolver bullet to the roof of the mouth. Dan's mother, never in the best of health, had gone to south Florida to live with an older sister. Dan understood she had part interest in a flower shop and was doing all right. His sister, Kathy, older than he by three years, lived in Taos, New Mexico, where she made copper-and-turquoise jewelry. Of the two of them, Kathy had been the rebel against the major's rigid love-it-or-leave-it patriotism. She'd escaped just past her seventeenth birthday, jumping into a van with a band of folksingers—"scum of the earth," the major had called them—and hitting the road to the golden West. Dan, the good son, had finished high school, kept his hair cut short, had become a carpenter's apprentice, and had been driven by his father to the Marine recruiting center to do his duty as a "good American."

And now Dan was waiting, in the city of his birth, for a ticket in the hot stillness of Death Valley.

Around eleven-thirty another panel truck pulled up. Dan was always amazed at how quickly everybody could move when the day was passing and tickets were in short supply. Like hungry animals the men jostled for position around the panel truck. Dan was among them. This time the call was for four laborers to patch and tar a warehouse's roof. Joe Yates got a ticket, but Dan was left behind when the panel truck drove away.

As twelve noon passed, some of the men began leaving. Experience taught that if you hadn't gotten a ticket by noon, you'd struck out. There was always tomorrow. Rain or shine, Death Valley and its citizens would be here. As one o'clock approached, Dan got into his pickup, started the engine, and drove through the charred-meat smoke for home.

He lived in a small apartment complex about six miles from Death Valley, but on the same side of town. Near his apartment stood a combination gas station and grocery store, and Dan stopped to go inside and check the store's bulletin board. On it he'd placed an ad that said "Carpenter Needs Work, Reasonable Rates" with his telephone number duplicated on little tags to be torn off by potential customers. He wanted to make sure all the tags weren't gone; they were not. He spent a few minutes talking to Leon, the store's clerk, and asked again if Mr. Khasab, the Saudi-Arabian man who owned the store, needed any help. As usual, Leon said Mr. Khasab had Dan's application on file.

The apartment building was made of tawny-colored bricks, and on these blistering days the little rooms held heat like closed fists. Dan got out of his truck, his back sopping wet, and opened his mailbox with his key. He was running an ad in the Jobs Wanted section of the classifieds this week, with his phone number and address, and he was hoping for any response. Inside the mailbox were two envelopes. The first, addressed to "Occupant," was from a city councilman running for reelection. The second had his full name on it—Mr. Daniel Lewis Lambert—and its return address was the First Commercial Bank of Shreveport.

"Confidential Information" was typed across the envelope in the lower left corner. Dan didn't like the looks of that. He tore open the envelope, unfolded the crisp white sheet of paper within, and read it.

It was from the bank's loan department. He'd already assumed as much, though this stiff formality was not Mr. Jarrett's style. It took him only a few seconds to read the paragraph under the *Dear Mr. Lambert,* and when he'd finished he felt as if he'd just taken a punch to the heart.

. . . valued loan customer, however . . . action as we see proper at this time . . . due to your past erratic record of payment and current delinquency . . . surrender the keys, registration, and appropriate papers . . . 1990 Chevrolet pickup truck, color metallic mist, engine serial number . . .

"Oh my God," Dan whispered.

. . . immediate repossession . . .

Dan blinked, dazed in the white glare of the scorching sun.

They were taking his truck away from him.

2

Ticking

When he pushed through the revolving door into the First
Commercial Bank at ten minutes before two, Dan was wearing his
best clothes: a short-sleeve white shirt, a tie with pale blue stripes,
and dark gray slacks. He'd removed his baseball cap and combed
his hair, and on his feet were black shoes instead of the workman's
boots. He'd expected the usual cold jolt of full-blast air-
conditioning, but the bank's interior wasn't much cooler than the
street. The air-conditioning had conked out, the tellers sweating in
their booths. Dan walked to the elevator, his fresh shirt already
soaked. In his right hand was the envelope, and in the envelope was
the letter of repossession.

He was terrified.

The loan department was on the second floor. Before he went
through the solemn oak door, Dan stopped at a water fountain to
take another aspirin. His hands had started trembling. The time of
reckoning had arrived.

The signature on the letter was not that of Robert "Bud" Jarrett. A
man named Emory Blanchard had signed it. Beneath Blanchard's
signature was a title: *Manager.* Two months ago Bud Jarrett had been
the loan department's manager. As much as he could, Dan steeled
himself for whatever lay ahead, and he opened the door and walked
through.

In the reception area was a sofa, a grouping of chairs, and a
magazine rack. The secretary, whose name was Mrs. Faye Duvall,
was on the telephone at her desk, a computer's screen glowing blue
before her. She was forty-nine, gray-haired, fit, and tanned, and
Dan had talked to her enough to know she played tennis every
Saturday at Lakeside Park. She had taken off the jacket of her peach-
hued suit and draped it over the back of her chair, and a fan aimed
directly at her whirred atop a filing cabinet.

Dan saw that the closed door behind her no longer had Mr.

Jarrett's name on it. On the door was embossed MR. E. BLANCHARD. "One minute," Mrs. Duvall said to Dan, and returned to her phone conversation. It was something to do with refinancing. Dan waited, standing before her desk. The window's blinds had been closed to seal out the sun, but the heat was stifling even with the fan in motion. At last Mrs. Duvall said good-bye and hung up the phone, and she smiled at Dan but he could see the edginess in it. She knew, of course; she'd typed the letter.

"'Afternoon," she said. "Hot enough for you?"

"I've known worse."

"We need a good rain, is what we need. Rain would take the sufferin' out of that sky."

"Mr. Jarrett," Dan said. "What happened to him?"

She leaned back in her chair and frowned, the corners of her mouth crinkling. "Well, it was sudden, that's for sure. They called him upstairs a week ago Monday, he cleaned out his desk on Tuesday, and he was gone. They brought in this new fella, a real hard charger." She angled her head toward Blanchard's door. "I just couldn't believe it myself. Bud was here eight years; I figured he'd stay till he retired."

"Why'd they let him go?"

"I can't say." The inflection of her voice, however, told Dan she was well aware of the reasons. "What I hear is, Mr. Blanchard was a real fireball at a bank in Baton Rouge. Turned their loan department around in a year." She shrugged. "Bud was the nicest fella you'd ever hope to meet. But maybe he was too nice."

"He sure helped me out a lot." Dan held up the letter. "I got this today."

"Oh. Yes." Her eyes became a little flinty, and she sat up straighter. The time for personal conversation was over. "Did you follow the instructions?"

"I'd like to see Mr. Blanchard," Dan said. "Maybe I can work somethin' out."

"Well, he's not here right now." She glanced at a small clock on her desk. "I don't expect him back for another hour."

"I'll wait."

"Go ahead and sit down, then. We're not exactly crowded at the minute." Dan took a seat, and Mrs. Duvall returned to her task on the computer screen. After a few moments, during which Dan was lost in his thoughts about how he was going to plead his case, Mrs. Duvall cleared her throat and said, "I'm sorry about this. Do you have enough money to make one payment?"

"No." He'd gone through his apartment like a whirlwind in

search of cash, but all he'd been able to come up with was thirty-eight dollars and sixty-two cents.

"Any friends you could borrow it from?"

He shook his head. This was his problem, and he wasn't going to drag anybody else into it.

"Don't you have a steady job yet?"

"No. Not that, either."

Mrs. Duvall was silent, working on the keyboard. Dan put the letter in his pocket, laced his fingers together, and waited. He didn't have to be told that he was up Shit Creek without a paddle and that his boat had just sprung a leak. The heat weighed on him. Mrs. Duvall got up from her chair and angled the fan a little so some of the breeze came Dan's way. She asked if he wanted a cold drink from the machine down the hall, but he said he was fine.

"I tell you, this damn heat in here is somethin' awful!" she said as she backed the cursor up to correct a mistake. "Air-conditionin' busted first thing this mornin', can you believe it?"

"It's bad, all right."

"Listen, Mr. Lambert." She looked at him, and he winced inside because he could see pity in her expression. "I've gotta tell you that Mr. Blanchard doesn't go for hard-luck stories. If you could make up for one payment, that might help a whole lot."

"I can't," Dan said. "No work's been comin' in. But if I lose my truck, there's no way I can get to a job if somebody calls me. That truck . . . it's the only thing I've got left."

"Do you know anythin' about guns?"

"Pardon?"

"Guns," she repeated. "Mr. Blanchard loves to go huntin', and he collects guns. If you know anythin' about guns, you might get him talkin' about 'em before you make your pitch."

Dan smiled faintly. The last gun he'd had anything to do with was an M16. "Thank you," he said. "I'll remember that."

An hour crept past. Dan paged through all the magazines, looking up whenever the door to the hallway opened, but it was only to admit other loan customers who came and went. He was aware of the clock on Mrs. Duvall's desk ticking. His nerves were beginning to fray. At three-fifteen he stood up to go get a drink of water from the fountain, and that was when the door opened and two men entered the office.

"Hello, Mr. Blanchard!" Mrs. Duvall said cheerfully, cueing Dan that the boss had arrived.

"Faye, get me Perry Griffin on the phone, please." Emory

Blanchard carried the jacket of his light blue seersucker suit over his right arm. He wore a white shirt and a yellow tie with little blue dots on it. There were sweat stains at his armpits. He was a heavyset, fleshy man, his face ruddy and gleaming with moisture. Dan figured he was in his mid-thirties, at least ten years younger than Bud Jarrett. Blanchard had close-cropped brown hair that was receding in front, and his square and chunky face coupled with powerful shoulders made Dan think the man might've played college football before the beers had overtaken his belly. He wore silver-wire-rimmed glasses and he was chewing gum. The second man had likewise stripped off the coat of his tan-colored suit, and he had curly blond hair going gray on the sides. "Step on in here, Jerome," Blanchard said as he headed for his office, "and let's do us a li'l bidness."

"Uh . . . Mr. Blanchard?" Mrs. Duvall had the telephone to her ear. She glanced at Dan and then back to Blanchard, who had paused with one hand on the doorknob. "Mr. Lambert's been waitin' to see you."

"Who?"

Dan stepped forward. "Dan Lambert. I need to talk to you, please."

The force of Blanchard's full gaze was a sturdy thing. His eyes were steely blue, and they provided the first chill Dan had felt all day. In three seconds Blanchard had taken Dan in from shoetips to the crown of his head. "I'm sorry?" His eyebrows rose.

"Repossession," Mrs. Duvall explained. "Chevrolet pickup truck."

"Right!" Blanchard snapped his fingers. "Got it now. Your letter went out yesterday, I recall."

"Yes sir, I've got it here with me. That's what I need to talk to you about."

Blanchard frowned, as if his teeth had found a fly in his chewing gum. "I believe the instructions in that letter were clear, weren't they?"

"They were, yeah. But can I just have two minutes of your time?"

"Mr. Griffin's on the line," the secretary announced.

"Two minutes," Dan said. *Don't beg,* he thought. But he couldn't help it; the truck was his freedom, and if it was taken from him, he'd have nothing. "Then I'll be gone, I swear."

"I'm a busy man."

"Yes sir, I know you are. But could you just please hear me out?"

The chilly blue eyes remained impassive, and Dan feared it was all over. But then Blanchard sighed and said resignedly, "All right, sit down and I'll get to you. Faye, pipe ol' Perry into my office, will you?"

"Yes sir."

Dan settled into his chair again as Blanchard and the other man went into the inner office. When the door had firmly closed, Mrs. Duvall said quietly, "He's in a good mood. You might be able to get somewhere with him."

"We'll see." His heart felt like a bagful of twisting worms. He took a long, deep breath. There was pain in his skull, but he could tough it out. After a few minutes had passed, Dan heard Blanchard laugh behind the door; it was a hearty, gut-felt laugh, the kind of laugh a man makes when he's got money in his pockets and a steak in his belly. Dan waited, his hands gripped together and sweat leaking from his pores.

It was half an hour later when the door opened again. Jerome emerged. He looked happy, and Dan figured their business had been successful. He closed the door behind him. "See ya later on, Faye," he told Mrs. Duvall, and she said, "You take care, now." Jerome left, and Dan continued to wait with tension gnawing his nerves.

A buzzer went off on Mrs. Duvall's desk, and Dan almost jumped out of his chair. She pressed a button. "Yes sir?"

"Send Mr. Lambert in," the voice said through the intercom.

"Good luck," Mrs. Duvall told Dan as he approached the door, and he nodded.

Emory Blanchard's office was at a corner of the building, and had two high windows. The blinds were drawn but shards of sunlight arrowed white and fierce between the slats. Blanchard was sitting behind his desk like a lion in his den, imperial and remote. "Shut the door and have a seat," he said. Dan did, sitting in one of two black leather chairs that faced the desk. Blanchard removed his glasses and wiped the round lenses with a handkerchief. He was still chewing gum. The sweat stains at his armpits had grown; moisture glistened on his cheeks and forehead. "Summertime." He spoke the word like a grunt. "Sure not my favorite season."

"It's been a hot one, all right." Dan glanced around the office, noting how this man had altered it from Bud Jarrett's homey simplicity. The carpet was a red-and-gold Oriental, and behind Blanchard on oak shelves that still smelled of the sawmill were thick leather-bound books, meticulously arranged tomes that were for display more than for reading. A stag's head with a four-point rack of antlers was mounted on a wall, and beneath it a brass plaque read

THE BUCK STOPS HERE. Prints of fox hunts were hung on either side of the stopped buck. On the wide, smooth expanse of Blanchard's desk were framed photographs of an attractive but heavily made-up blond woman and two children, a girl of seven or eight and a boy who looked to be ten. The boy had his father's cool blue eyes and his regal bearing; the girl was all bows and white lace.

"My kids," Blanchard said.

"Nice-lookin' family."

Blanchard returned the glasses to his face. He picked up the boy's picture and regarded it with admiration. "Yance made all-American on his team last year. Got an arm like Joe Montana. He sure raised a holler when we left Baton Rouge, but he'll do fine."

"I've got a son," Dan said.

"Yessir." Blanchard put the photograph back in its place next to a small Lucite cube that had a little plastic American flag mounted inside it. Written on the cube in red, white, and blue were the words I Supported Desert Storm. "You wait about nine more years, you'll see Yance Blanchard breakin' some passin' records at LSU, I guarandamntee it." He swiveled his chair around to where a computer screen, a telephone, and the intercom were set up. He switched the computer on, pressed a few keys, and black lines of information appeared. "Okay, there's your file," he said. "You a Cajun, Mr. Lambert?"

"No."

"Just wonderin'. Sometimes you can't tell who's a Cajun and who's not. Alllllrighty, let's see what we've got here. Carpenter, are you? Employed at A&A Construc—oh, you *were* employed at A&A Construction until November of last year."

"The company went bankrupt." He'd told Mr. Jarrett about it, of course, and it had gone into his file.

"Construction bidness hit the rocks, that's for sure. You free-lancin' now, is that it?"

"Yes sir."

"I see Jarrett was lettin' you slide some months. Delinquent two payments. See, that's not a good thing. We can let you get by sometimes if you're one payment behind, but two payments is a whole different story."

"Yes sir, I know that, but I . . . kind of had an understandin' with Mr. Jarrett."

Even as he said it, Dan knew it was the wrong thing to say. Blanchard's big shoulders hunched up almost imperceptibly, and he slowly swiveled his chair around from the computer screen to face Dan. Blanchard wore a tight, strained smile. "See, there's a problem," he said. "There is no Mr. Jarrett at this bank anymore. So any understandin' you might've had with him isn't valid as far as I'm concerned."

Dan's cheeks were stinging. "I didn't mean to be—"

"Your record speaks for itself," the other man interrupted. "Can you make at least one payment today?"

"No sir, I can't. But that's what I wanted to talk to you about. If I could . . . maybe . . . pay you fifteen dollars a week until a job comes along. Then I could start makin' the regular payments again. I've never been so long between jobs before. But I figure things'll pick up again when the weather cools off."

"Uh-huh," Blanchard said. "Mr. Lambert, when you lost your job did you look for any other kind of work?"

"I looked for other jobs, yeah. But I'm a carpenter. That's what I've always done."

"You subscribe to the paper?"

"No." His subscription had been one of the first items to be cut.

"They run classified ads in there every day. Page after page of 'em. All kinds of jobs, just beggin'."

"Not for carpenters. I've looked, plenty of times." He saw Blanchard's gaze fix on his snake tattoo for a few seconds, then veer away with obvious distaste.

"When the goin' gets tough," Blanchard said, "the tough get goin'. Ever hear that sayin'? If more people lived by it, we wouldn't be headin' for a welfare state."

"I've never been on welfare." The pain flared, like an engine being started, deep in Dan's skull. "Not one day in my life."

Blanchard swiveled to face the computer's screen again. He gave a grunt. "Vietnam vet, huh? Well, that's one point in your favor. I wish you fellas had cleaned house like the boys did over in Iraq."

"It was a different kind of war." Dan swallowed thickly. He thought he could taste ashes. "A different time."

"Hell, fightin's fightin'. Jungle or desert, what's the difference?"

The pain was getting bad now. Dan's guts were clenched up. "A lot," he said. "In the desert you can see who's shootin' at you." His gaze ticked to the Lucite cube that held the plastic flag. Something small was stamped on its lower left corner. Three words. He leaned forward to read them. *Made in China.*

"Health problem," Blanchard said.

"What?"

"Health problem. Says so right here. What's your health problem, Mr. Lambert?"

Dan remained silent.

Blanchard turned around. "You sick, or not?"

Dan put one hand up against his forehead. Oh, Jesus, he thought. To have to bare himself before a stranger this way was almost too much for him.

"You aren't on drugs, are you?" Blanchard's voice had taken on a cutting edge. "We could've cleaned house over there if so many of you fellas hadn't been on drugs."

Dan looked into Blanchard's sweating, heat-puffed face. A jolt of true rage twisted him inside, but he jammed it back down again, where it had been drowsing so long. He realized in that moment that Blanchard was the kind of man who enjoyed kicking a body when it was beaten. He leaned toward Blanchard's desk, and slowly he pulled himself out of the black leather chair. "No, sir," he said tersely, "I'm not on drugs. But yeah, I *am* sick. If you really want to know, I'll tell you."

"I'm listenin'."

"I've got leukemia," Dan said. "It's a slow kind, and some days I feel just fine. Other days I can hardly get out of bed. I've got a tumor the size of a walnut right about here." He tapped the left side of his forehead. "The doctor says he can operate, but because of where the tumor lies I might lose the feelin' on my right side. Now, what kind of carpenter would I be if I couldn't use my right hand or leg?"

"I'm sorry to hear that, but—"

"I'm not finished," Dan said, and Blanchard was quiet. "You wanted to know what was wrong with me, you oughta have the manners to hear the whole story." Blanchard chose that moment to glance at the gold Rolex watch on his wrist, and Dan came very close to reaching across the desk and grabbing him by his yellow necktie. "I want to tell you about a soldier." Dan's voice was roughened by the sandpaper of raw emotion. "He was a kid, really. The kind of kid who always did what he was told. He drew duty in a sector of jungle that hid an enemy supply route. And it was always rainin' on that jungle. It was always drippin' wet, and the ground stayed muddy. It was a silver rain. Sometimes it fell right out of a clear blue sky, and afterward the jungle smelled like flowers gone over to rot. The silver rain fell in torrents, and this young soldier got drenched by it day after day. It was slick and oily, like grease off the bottom of a fryin' pan. There was no way to get it off the skin, and the heat and the steam just cooked it in deeper." Dan drew up a tight, terrible smile. "He asked his platoon leader about it. His platoon leader said it was harmless, unless you were a tree or a vine. Said you could bathe in it and you'd be all right, but if you dipped a blade of sawgrass in it, that sawgrass would blotch up brown and crispy as quick as you please. Said it was to clear the jungle so we could find the supply route. And this young soldier . . . you know what he did?"

"No," Blanchard said.

"He went back out in that jungle again. Back out in that dirty rain, whenever they told him to. He could see the jungle dyin'. All of it was shrivelin' away, bein' burned up without fire. He didn't feel right about it because he knew a chemical as strong as that had to be bad for skin and bones. He knew it. But he was a good soldier, and he was proud to fight for his country. Do you see?"

"I think so. Agent Orange?"

"It could kill a jungle in a week," Dan said. "What it could do to a man didn't show up until a long time later. That's what bein' a good soldier did to me, Mr. Blanchard. I came home full of poison, and nobody blew a trumpet or held a parade. I don't like bein' out of work. I don't like feelin' I'm not worth a damn sometimes. But that's what my life is right now."

Blanchard nodded. He wouldn't meet Dan's eyes. "I really, truly, am sorry. I swear I am. I know things are tough out there."

"Yes sir, they are. That's why I have to ask you to give me one more week before you take my truck. Without my truck, I don't have any way to get to a job if one comes open. Can you please help me out?"

Blanchard rested his elbows on his desk and laced his fingers together. He wore a big LSU ring on his right hand. His brows knitted, and he gave a long, heavy sigh. "I feel for you, Mr. Lambert. God knows I do. But I just can't give you an extension."

Dan's heart had started pounding. He knew he was facing disaster of the darkest shade.

"Look at my position." Blanchard's chewing gum was going ninety miles a minute. "My superiors kicked Bud Jarrett out of here because of the bad loans he made. They hired me because I don't make bad loans, and part of my job is to fix the mess Jarrett left behind. One week or one month: I don't think it would really matter very much, do you?"

"I need my truck," Dan rasped.

"You need a social worker, not a loan officer. You could get yourself checked into the VA hospital."

"I've been there. I'm not ready to roll over and die yet."

"I'm sorry, but there's nothin' I can do for you. It's bidness, you see? You can bring the keys and the paperwork tomorrow mornin'. I'll be in the office by ten." He swiveled around and switched the computer's screen off, telling Dan that their conversation was over.

"I won't do it," Dan said. "I can't."

"You will, Mr. Lambert, or you'll find yourself in some serious trouble."

"Jesus Christ, man! Don't you think I'm already in serious trouble? I don't even have enough money to buy decent groceries! How am I gonna get around without my truck?"

"We're finished, I think. I'd like you to leave now."

Maybe it was the pain building in Dan's skull; maybe it was this final, flat command from the man who was squeezing the last of the dignity from his life. Whatever it was, it shoved Dan over the edge.

He knew he should not. Knew it. But suddenly he was reaching out toward the photographs and the Made in China American flag, and as he gritted his teeth the rage flew from him like a dark bird and he swept everything off the top of Blanchard's desk in a swelling crash and clatter.

"Hey! Hey!" Blanchard shouted. "What're you doin'?"

"Serious trouble," Dan said. "You want to see some serious trouble, mister?" He hefted the chair he'd been sitting on and slammed it against the wall. The sign that said The Buck Stops Here fell to the floor, and books jittered on the perfect shelves. Dan picked up the wastebasket, tears of frustration and shame stinging his eyes, and he threw its contents over Blanchard, then flung the wastebasket against the stag's head. A small voice inside Dan screamed at him to stop, that this was childish and stupid and would earn him nothing, but his body was moving on the power of single-minded fury. If this man was going to take his freedom from him, he would tear the office apart.

Blanchard had picked up the telephone. "Security!" he yelled. "Quick!"

Dan grabbed the phone and jerked it away from him, and it too went flying into the shelves. As Dan attacked the fox-hunt pictures, he was aware in a cold, distant place that this was not only about the truck. It was about the cancer in his bones and the growth in his brain, the brutal heart of Death Valley, the jostling for tickets, the dirty silver rain, the major, the village, his failed marriage, the son who had been infected with his father's poison. It was all those things and more, and Dan tore the pictures off the walls, his face contorted, as Blanchard kept shouting for him to stop. *A good soldier,* Dan thought as he began pulling the books off the shelves and flinging them wildly around the office. *A good soldier good soldier I've always been a good—*

Someone grabbed him from behind.

"Get him out!" Blanchard hollered. "He's gone crazy!"

A pair of husky arms had clamped around Dan's chest, pinning his own arms at his sides. Dan thrashed to break free, but the security guard was strong. The grip tightened, forcing the air from Dan's lungs. "Get him outta here!" Blanchard had wedged himself into a corner, his face mottled with red. "Faye, call the police!"

"Yes, sir!" She'd been standing in the open door, and she hurried to the phone on her desk.

Dan kept fighting. He couldn't stand to be confined, the pressure on his chest driving him to further heights of frenzy. "Hold still, damn it!" the guard said, and he began dragging Dan to the door. "Come on, you're goin' with—"

Panic made Dan snap his head backward, and the guard's nose popped as bone met cartilage. The man gave a wounded grunt, and suddenly Dan was free. As Dan turned toward him, he saw the guard—a man as big as a football linebacker, wearing a gray uniform—sitting on his knees on the carpet. His cap had spun away, his black hair cropped in a severe crew cut, his hands cupped over his nose with blood leaking between the sausage-thick fingers. "You busted my nose!" he gasped, his eyes slitted and wet with pain. "You sumbitch, you busted my nose!"

The sight of blood skidded Dan back to reality. He hadn't meant to hurt anyone; he hadn't meant to tear up this man's office. He was in a bad dream, and surely he must soon wake up.

But the bad dream took another, more wicked turn.

"You sumbitch," the guard said again, and he reached with bloody fingers to the pistol in a holster at his waist. He pulled the gun loose, snapping off the safety as it cleared the leather.

Going to shoot me, Dan thought. He saw the man's finger on the trigger. For an instant the smell of ozone came to him—a memory of danger in the silver-dripping jungleand the flesh prickled at the back of his neck.

He lunged for the guard, seized the man's wrist, and twisted the gun aside. The guard reached up with his free hand to claw at Dan's eyes, but Dan hung on. He heard Mrs. Duvall shout, "The police are comin'!" The guard was trying to get to his feet; a punch caught Dan in the rib cage and almost toppled him, but still he held on to the guard's wrist. Another punch was coming, and Dan snapped his left hand forward with the palm out and smashed the man's bleeding nose. As the guard bellowed and fell back, Dan wrenched the pistol loose. He got his hand on the grip and fumbled to snap the safety on again.

He heard a *click* behind him.

He knew that sound.

Death had found him. It had slid from its hole here in this sweltering office, and it was about to sink its fangs.

Dan whirled around. Blanchard had opened a desk drawer and was lifting a pistol to take aim, the hammer cocked back and a finger on the trigger. Blanchard's face was terrified, and Dan knew the man meant to kill him.

It took a second.

One second.

Something as old as survival took hold of Dan. Something ancient and unthinking, and it swept Dan's sense aside in a feverish rush.

He fired without aiming. The pistol's *crack* vibrated through his hand, up his snake-tattooed forearm and into his shoulder.

"Uh," Blanchard said.

Blood spurted from a hole in his throat.

Blanchard staggered back, his yellow necktie turning scarlet. His gun went off, and Dan flinched as he heard the bullet hiss past his head and thunk into the doorjamb. Then Blanchard crashed to the floor amid the family photographs, fox-hunt prints, and leather-bound books.

Mrs. Duvall screamed.

Dan heard someone moan. It was not Blanchard, nor the guard. He looked at the pistol in his hand, then at the splatter of red that lay across Blanchard's desk. "Oh, God," Dan said as the horror of what he'd just done hit him full force. "Oh, my God . . . no . . . ."

The gears of the universe seemed to shift. Everything shut down to a hazy slow-motion. Dan was aware of the guard cowering against a wall. Mrs. Duvall fled into the corridor, still shrieking. Then Dan felt himself moving around the desk toward Blanchard, and though he knew he was moving as fast as he could, it was more like a strange, disembodied drifting. Bright red arterial blood was pulsing from Blanchard's throat in rhythm with his heart. Dan dropped the pistol, got down on his knees, and pressed his hands against the wound. "No!" Dan said, as if to a disobedient child. "No!" Blanchard stared up at him, his chilly blue eyes glazed and his mouth half open. The blood kept spurting, flowing between Dan's fingers. Blanchard shuddered, his legs moving feebly, his heels plowing the carpet. He coughed once. A red glob of chewing gum rolled from his mouth, followed by rivulets of blood that streamed over his lower lip.

"No oh God no please no don't die," Dan began to beg. Something broke inside him, and the tears ran out. He was trying to stop the bleeding, trying to hold the blood back, but it was a tide that would not be turned. "Call an ambulance!" he shouted. The guard didn't move; without his gun the man's courage had crumpled like cheap tin. "Somebody call an ambulance!" Dan pleaded. "Hang on!" he told Blanchard. "Do you hear? Hang on!"

Blanchard had begun making a harsh hitching noise deep in his chest. The sound filled Dan with fresh terror. He knew what it was. He heard it before, in 'Nam: the death watch, ticking.

The police, Mrs. Duvall had said.

The police are comin'.

Blanchard's face was white and waxen, his tie and shirt soaked with gore. The blood was still pulsing, but Blanchard's eyes stared at nothing.

Murder, Dan realized. *Oh Jesus, I've murdered him.*

No ambulance could make it in time. He knew it. The bullet had done too much damage. "I'm sorry, I'm sorry," Dan said, his voice cracking. His eyes blurred up with tears. "I'm sorry, dear God I'm sorry."

The police are comin'.

The image of handcuffs and iron bars came to him. He saw his future, confined behind stone walls topped with barbed wire.

There was nothing more he could do.

Dan stood up, the room slowly spinning around him. He looked at his bloodied hands, and smelled the odor of a slaughterhouse.

He ran, past the guard and out of the office. Standing in the corridor were people who'd emerged from their own offices, but when they saw Dan's bloody shirt and his gray-tinged face they scurried out of his way. He ran past the elevator, heading for the stairwell.

At the bottom of the stairwell were two doors, one leading back into the teller's area and another with a sign that said EMERGENCY EXIT ONLY! ALARM WILL SOUND! As Dan shoved the exit door open, a high-pitched alarm went off in his ear. Searing sunlight hit him; he was facing the parking lot beside the bank. His truck was in a space twenty yards away, past the automatic teller machine and the drive-up windows. There was no sign yet of a police car. He ran to his truck, frantically unlocked the door, and slid behind the wheel. Two men, neither of them a police officer, came out of the emergency exit and stood gawking as Dan started the engine, put the truck into reverse, and backed out of the parking space. His brakes shrieked when he stomped on the pedal to keep from smashing the car parked behind him. Then he twisted the wheel and sped out of the lot, and with another scream of brakes and tires he took a left on the street. A glance in his rearview mirror showed a police car, its bubble lights spinning, pulling up to the curb in front of the building. He had no sooner focused his attention on the street ahead than a second police car flashed past him, trailing a siren's wail, in the direction of the bank.

Dan didn't know how much time he had. His apartment was five miles to the west. Beads of sweat clung to his face, blood smeared all over the steering wheel.

A sob welled up and clutched his throat.

He cried, silently.

He had always tried to live right. To be fair. To obey orders and be a good soldier no matter what slid out of this world full of snake holes.

As he drove to his apartment, fighting the awful urge to sink his foot to the floorboard, he realized what one stupid, senseless second had wrought.

I've gone south, he thought. He wiped his eyes with his snake-clad forearm, the metallic smell of blood sickening him in the hellish August heat. *Gone south, after all this time.*

And he knew, as well, that he'd just taken the first step of a journey from which there could be no return.

3

Mark of Cain

Hurry! Dan told himself as he pulled clothes from a dresser drawer and jammed them into a duffel bag. *Movin' too slow hurry they'll be here soon any minute now . . .*

The sound of a distant siren shocked his heart. He stood still, listening, as his pulse rioted. A precious few seconds passed before he realized the sound was coming through the wall from Mr. Wycoff's apartment. The television set. Mr. Wycoff, a retired steelworker, always watched the *Starsky and Hutch* reruns that came on every day at three-thirty. Dan turned his mind away from the sound and kept packing, pain like an iron spike throbbing in his skull.

He had torn off the bloody shirt, hastily scrubbed his hands in the bathroom's sink, and struggled into a clean white T-shirt. He didn't have time to change his pants or his shoes; his nerves were shredding with each lost second. He pushed a pair of blue jeans into the duffel bag, then picked up his dark blue baseball cap from the dresser's top and put it on. A framed photograph of his son, Chad, taken ten years ago when the boy was seven, caught his attention and it too went into the bag. Dan went to the closet, reached up to the top shelf, and brought down the shoebox that held thirty-eight dollars, all his money in the world. As he was shoving the money into his pocket, the telephone rang.

The answering machine—a Radio Shack special clicked on after three rings. Dan heard his own voice asking the caller to leave a message.

"I'm callin' about your ad in the paper," a man said. "I need my backyard fenced in, and I was wonderin'—"

Dan might have laughed if he didn't feel the rage of the law bearing down on him.

"—if you could do the job and what you'd charge. If you'd call me back sometime today I'd appreciate it. My number's . . ."

510

Too late. Much, much too late.

He zipped the bag shut, picked it up, and got out.

There were no sounds yet of sirens in the air. Dan threw the bag into the back of his truck, next to the toolbox, and he got behind the wheel and tore out of the parking lot. He crossed the railroad tracks, drove six blocks east, and saw the signs for Interstate 49 ahead. He swung the pickup onto the ramp that had a sign saying I-49 SOUTHBOUND. Then he steadily gave the truck more gas, and he merged with the afternoon traffic, leaving the industrial haze of Shreveport at their backs.

Killer, he thought. The image of blood spurting from Blanchard's throat and the man's waxen face was in his brain, unshakable as gospel. It had all happened so fast, he felt still in a strange, dreamlike trance. They would lock him away forever for this crime; he would die behind prison walls.

But first they had to catch him, because he sure as hell wasn't giving himself up.

He switched on his radio and turned the dial, searching Shreveport's stations for the news. There was country music, rock 'n' roll, rap, and advertisements but no bulletin yet about a shooting at the First Commercial Bank. But he knew it wouldn't take long; soon his description and the description of his truck would be all over the airwaves. Not many men bore the tattoo of a snake on their right forearms. He realized that what he'd worn as a badge of pride and courage in 'Nam now was akin to the mark of Cain.

Tears were scorching his eyes again. He blinked them away. The time for weeping was over. He had committed the most stupid, insane act of his life; he had gone south in a way he would never have thought possible. His gaze kept ticking to the rearview mirror, and he expected to see flashing lights coming after him. They weren't there yet, but they were hunting for him by now. The first place they'd go would be the apartment. They would've gotten all the information about him from the bank's computer records. How long would it take for the state troopers to get his license number and be on the lookout for a metallic-mist Chevrolet pickup truck with a killer at the wheel?

A desperate thought hit him: maybe Blanchard hadn't died.

Maybe an ambulance had gotten there in time. Maybe the paramedics had somehow been able to stop the bleeding and get Blanchard to the hospital. Then the charge wouldn't be murder, would it? In a couple of weeks Blanchard could leave the hospital and go home to his wife and children. Dan could plead temporary insanity, because that's surely what it had been. He would spend some time in jail, yes, but there'd be a light at the end of the tunnel. Maybe. May—

A horn blew, jarring him back to reality. He'd been drifting into the next lane, and a cream-colored Buick swept past him with a furious *whoosh.*

He passed the intersection of the Industrial Loop Expressway, and was moving through the outskirts of Shreveport. Subdivisions of blocky tract houses, strip malls, and apartment complexes stood near warehouses and factories with vast parking lots. The land was flat, its summer green bleached to a grayish hue by the merciless sun. Ahead of him, the long, straight highway shimmered and crows circled over small animals that had been mangled by heavy wheels.

It came to Dan that he didn't know where he was going.

He knew the direction, yes, but not the destination. Does it matter? he asked himself. All he knew is, he had to get as far from Shreveport as he could. A glance at the gas gauge showed him the tank was a little over a quarter full. The Chevy got good gas mileage for a pickup truck; that was one of the reasons he'd bought it. But how far could he get with thirty-eight dollars and some change in his pocket?

His heart jumped. A state trooper's car was approaching, heading north on the other side of the median. He watched it come nearer, all the spit drying up in his mouth. Then the car was passing him, doing a steady fifty-five. Had the trooper behind the wheel looked at him? Dan kept watching the rearview mirror, but the trooper car's brake lights didn't flare. But what if the trooper had recognized the pickup truck and radioed to another highway patrol car waiting farther south? On this interstate the troopers could be massing in a roadblock just through the next heat shimmer. He was going to have to get off I-49 and take a lesser-traveled parish road. Another four miles rolled under the tires before he saw the exit of Highway 175, heading south toward the town of Mansfield. Dan slowed his speed and eased onto the ramp, which turned into a two-lane road bordered by thick stands of pines and palmettos. As he'd figured, this route was all but deserted, just a couple of cars visible far ahead and none at his back. Still, he drove the speed limit and watched warily for the highway patrol.

Now he was going to have to decide where to go. The Texas line was about twenty miles to the west. He could be in Mexico in fifteen hours or so. If he continued on this road, he would reach the bayous and swampland on the edge of the Gulf in a little over three hours.

He could get to the Gulf and head either west to Port Arthur or east to New Orleans. And what then? Go into hiding? Find a job? Make up a new identity, shave off his beard, bleach out the tattoo?

He could go to Alexandria, he thought. That city was less than a hundred miles away, just below the heart of Louisiana. He'd lived there for nine years, when he'd been working with Fordham Construction. His ex-wife and son lived there still, in the house on Jackson Avenue.

Right. His mouth settled into a grim line. The police would have that address too, from the bank's records. Dan had faithfully made his child support payments every month. If he went to that house, the police would swarm all over him. And besides, Susan was so afraid of him anyway that she wouldn't let him in the door even if he came as a choirboy instead of a killer. He hadn't seen his ex-wife and seventeen-year-old son in over six years. It had been better that way, because his divorce was still an open wound.

He wondered what the other Snake Handlers would think of a father who had attacked his own little boy in the middle of the night. Did it matter that in those days Dan had been half crazy and suffered nightmarish flashbacks? Did it matter that when he'd put his hands around the boy's throat he'd believed he was trying to choke to death a Viet Cong sniper in the silver-puddled mud?

No, it didn't. He remembered coming out of the flashback to Susan's scream; he remembered the stark terror on Chad's tear-streaked face. Ten seconds more—just ten—and he might have killed his own son. He couldn't blame Susan for wanting to be rid of him, and so he hadn't contested the divorce.

He caught himself; the truck was drifting toward the centerline again as his attention wandered. He saw some dried blood between his fingers that he'd missed with the soap and rag, and the image of Blanchard's bleached face stabbed him.

A glance in the rearview mirror almost stopped his heart entirely. Speeding after him was a vehicle with its lights flashing. Dan hesitated between jamming the accelerator and hitting the brake, but before he could decide to do either, a cherry-red pickup truck with two grinning teenagers in the cab roared past him and the boy on the passenger side stuck a hand out with the middle finger pointed skyward.

Dan started trembling. He couldn't stop it. Sickness roiled in his stomach, a maniacal drumbeat trapped in his skull. He thought for a few seconds that he was going to pass out as dark motes spun before his eyes like flecks of ash. Around the next bend he saw a narrow dirt road going off into the woods on his right. He turned onto it and followed it fifty yards into the sheltering forest, his rear tires throwing up plumes of yellow dust.

Then he stopped the truck, cut the engine, and sat there under the pines with beads of cold sweat on his face.

His stomach lurched. As the fire rose up his throat, Dan scrambled out of the truck and was able to reach the weeds before he threw up. He retched and retched until there was nothing left, and then he sat on his knees, breathing sour steam as birds sang in the trees above him.

He pulled the tail of his T-shirt out and blotted the sweat from his cheeks and forehead. Dust hung in the air, the sunlight lying in shards amid the trees. He tried to clear his mind enough to grapple with the problem of where to go. To Texas and Mexico? To the Gulf and New Orleans? Or should he turn the truck around, return to Shreveport, and give himself up?

That was the sensible thing, wasn't it? Go back to Shreveport and try to explain to the police that he'd thought Blanchard was about to kill him, that he hadn't meant to lose his temper, that he was so very, very sorry.

Stone walls, he thought. Stone walls waiting.

At last he stood up and walked unsteadily back to his truck. He got in, started the engine, and turned on the radio. He began to move the dial through the stations; they were weaker now, diminished by distance. Seven or eight minutes passed, and then Dan came upon a woman's cool, matter-of-fact voice.

". . . shooting at the First Commercial Bank of Shreveport just after three-thirty this afternoon . . ."

Dan turned it up.

". . . according to police, a disturbed Vietnam veteran entered the bank with a gun and shot Emory Blanchard, the bank's loan manager. Blanchard was pronounced dead on arrival at All Saints Hospital. We'll have more details as this story develops. In other news, the city council and the waterworks board found themselves at odds again today when . . ."

Dan stared at nothing, his mouth opening to release a soft, agonized gasp.

Dead on arrival.

It was official now. He was a murderer.

But what was that about entering the bank with a gun? "That's wrong," he said thickly. "It's wrong." The way it sounded, he'd gone to the bank intent on killing somebody. Of course they had to

514

GONE SOUTH

put the "disturbed Vietnam veteran" in there, too. Might as well make him sound like a psycho while they were at it.

But he knew what the bank was doing. What would their customers think if they knew Blanchard had been killed with a security guard's gun? Wasn't it better, then, to say that the crazy Vietnam veteran had come in packing a gun and hunting a victim? He kept searching the stations, and in another couple of minutes he found a snippet: ". . . rushed to All Saints Hospital, where he was pronounced dead on arrival. Police caution that Lambert should be considered armed and dangerous . . ."

"Bullshit!" Dan said. "I didn't go there to kill anybody!"

He saw what would happen if he gave himself up. They wouldn't listen to him. They'd put him in a hole and drop a rock on it for the rest of his life. Maybe he might live only three more years, but he wasn't planning to die in prison and be buried in a pauper's grave.

He engaged the gears. Head to the bayou country, he decided. From there he could go either to New Orleans or Port Arthur. Maybe he could find a freighter captain who needed cheap labor and didn't care to ask questions. He turned the truck around and then he drove back to Highway 175. He took a right, southbound again.

The truck's cab was a sweat box, even with both windows down. The heat was weighing on him, wearing him out. He thought about Susan and Chad. If the news was on the radio, it wouldn't be long before it hit the local TV stations. Susan might already have gotten a call from the police. He didn't particularly care what she thought of him; it was Chad's opinion that mattered. The boy was going to think his father was a cold-blooded killer, and this fact pained Dan's soul.

The question was: what could be done about it?

He heard an engine gunning behind him.

He looked in the rearview mirror.

And there was a state trooper's car right on his tail, its blue bubble lights spinning.

Dan had known true terror before, in the jungles of Vietnam and when he'd seen Blanchard's gun leveling to take aim. This instant, though, froze his blood and stiffened him up like a dime-store dummy.

The siren yowled.

He was caught.

He jerked the wheel to the right, panic sputtering through his nerves.

515

The trooper whipped past him and was gone around the next curve in a matter of seconds.

Before he could think to stop and turn around, Dan was into the curve and saw the trooper pulling off onto the road's shoulder. A cherry-red pickup truck was down in a ditch, and one of the teenage boys was standing on the black scrawl the tires had left when he'd lost control of the wheel. The other boy was sitting in the weeds, his head lowered and his left arm clasped against his chest. As Dan glided past the accident scene, he saw the trooper get out of the car and shake his head as if he knew the boys were lucky they weren't scattered like bloody rags amid the pines.

When the trooper's car was well behind, Dan picked up his speed again. Dark motes were still drifting in and out of his vision, the sun's glare still fierce even as the afternoon shadows lengthened. He'd had not a bite of food since breakfast, and he'd lost the meager contents of his stomach. He considered stopping at a gas station to buy a candy bar and a soft drink, but the thought of pulling off while a state trooper was so close behind him put an end to that idea. He kept going, following the sun-baked road as it twisted like the serpent on his forearm.

Mile after mile passed. The traffic was sparse, both in front and behind, but the strain of watching in either direction began to take its toll. The shooting replayed itself over and over in his mind. He thought of Blanchard's wife—widow, that is—and the two children, and what they must be going through right now. He began to fear what might be lying in wait for him around the curves. His headache returned with a vengeance, as did his tremors. The heat was sapping his last reserves of strength, and soon it became clear to him that he had to stop somewhere to rest. Another few miles passed, the highway leading between pine forest broken by an occasional dusty field, and then Dan saw a gravel road on his right. As he slowed down, prepared to turn into the woods and sleep in his truck, he saw that the road widened into a parking lot. There was a small whitewashed church standing beneath a pair of huge weeping willow trees. A little wooden sign in need of repainting said: VICTORY IN THE BLOOD BAPTIST.

It was as good a place as any. Dan pulled into the gravel lot, which was deserted, and he drove the truck around to the back of the church. When he was hidden from the road, he cut the engine and slid the key out. He pulled his wet shirt away from the backrest and lay down on the seat. He closed his eyes, but Blanchard's death leapt at him to keep him from finding sleep.

He'd been lying down for only a few minutes when someone

516

rapped twice against the side of his truck. Dan bolted upright, blinking dazedly. Standing there beside his open window was a slim black man with a long-jawed face and a tight cap of white hair. Over the man's deep-set ebony eyes, the thick white brows had merged together. "You okay, mister?" he asked.

"Yeah." Dan nodded, still a little disoriented. "Just needed to rest."

"Heard you pull up. Looked out the winda and there you were."

"I didn't know anybody was around."

"Well," the man said, and when he smiled he showed alabaster teeth that looked as long as piano keys, "just me and God sittin' inside talkin'."

Dan started to slide the key back into the ignition. "I'd better head on."

"Now, hold on a minute, I ain't runnin' you off. You don't mind me sayin', you don't appear to be up to snuff. You travelin' far?"

"Yes."

"Seems to me that if a fella wants to rest, he oughta rest. If you'd like to come in, you're welcome."

"I'm . . . not a religious man," Dan said.

"Well, I didn't say I was gonna *preach* to you. 'Course, some would say listenin' to my sermons is a surefire way to catch up on your sleep. Name's Nathan Gwinn." He thrust a hand toward Dan, who took it.

"Dan . . ." His mind skipped tracks for a few seconds. A name came to him. "Farrow," he said.

"Pleased to meet you. Come on in, there's room to stretch out on a pew if you'd like."

Dan looked at the church. It had been years since he'd set foot in one. Some of the things he'd seen, both in Vietnam and afterward, had convinced him that if any supernatural force was the master of this world, it smelled of brimstone and devoured innocent flesh as its sacrament.

"Cooler inside," Gwinn told him. "The fans are workin' this week."

After a moment of deliberation, Dan opened the door and got out. "I'm obliged," he said, and he followed Gwinn—who wore black trousers and a plain light blue short-sleeve shirt—through the church's back door. The interior of the church was Spartan, with an unvarnished wooden floor that had felt the Sunday shoes of several generations. "I was writin' my sermon when I heard you," Gwinn said, and he motioned into a cubicle of an office whose open window overlooked the rear lot. Two chairs, a desk and lamp, a file cabinet, and a couple of peach crates full of religious books had been squeezed into the little room. On the desk was a pad of paper and a cup containing a number of ballpoint pens. "Not havin' much luck, I'm a'feared," he confided. "Sometimes you dig deep and just wind up scrapin' the bottom. But I ain't worried, somethin'll come to me. Always does. You want some water, there's a fountain this way."

Gwinn led him through a corridor lined with other small rooms, the floor creaking underfoot. A ceiling fan stirred the heat. There was a water fountain, and Dan went to work satisfying his thirst. "You a regular camel, ain't you?" Gwinn asked. "Come on in here, you can stretch yourself out." Dan followed him through another doorway, into the chapel. A dozen pews faced the preacher's podium, and the sunlight that entered was cut to an underwater haze by the pale green glass of the stained windows. Overhead, two fans muttered like elderly ladies as they turned, fighting a lost cause. Dan sat down on a pew toward the middle of the church, and he pressed his palms against his eyes to ease the pain throbbing in his skull.

"Nice tattoo," Gwinn said. "You get that around here?"

"No. Someplace else."

"Mind if I ask where you're headin' from and where you're goin'?"

"From Shreveport," Dan said. "I'm goin' to—" He paused. "I'm just goin'."

"Your home in Shreveport, is it?"

"Used to be." Dan took his hands away from his eyes. "I'm not real sure where I belong right now." A thought struck him. "I didn't see your car outside."

"Oh, I walked from my house. I just live 'bout a half-mile up the road. You hungry, Mr. Farrow?"

"I could do with somethin', yeah." Hearing that name was strange, after all this time. He didn't know why he'd chosen it; probably it was from seeing the young man who was begging work at Death Valley.

"You like crullers? I got some in my office; my wife baked 'em just this mornin'."

Dan told him that sounded fine, and Gwinn went to his office and returned with three sugar-frosted crullers in a brown paper bag. It took about four seconds for Dan to consume one of them. "Have another," Gwinn offered as he sat on the pew in front of Dan. "I believe you ain't et in a while."

A second pastry went down the hatch. Gwinn scratched his long jaw and said, "Take the other one, too. My wife sure would be tickled to see a fella enjoyin' her bakin' so much." When the third one was history, Dan licked the sugar from his fingers. Gwinn laughed, the sound like the rasp of a rusty saw blade. "Part camel, part goat," he said. "Don't you go chewin' on that bag, now."

"You can tell your wife she makes good crullers."

Gwinn reached into a trouser pocket, pulled out a silver watch, and checked the time. "'Bout quarter to five. You can tell Lavinia yourself if you want to."

"Pardon?"

"Supper's at six. You want to eat with Lavinia and me, you're welcome." He returned the watch to his pocket. "Won't be no fancy feast, but it'll warm your belly up. I can go call her, tell her to put another plate on the table."

"Thanks, but I've gotta get back on the road after I rest some."

"Oh." Gwinn lifted his shaggy white brows. "Decide where you're goin', have you?"

Dan was silent, his hands clasped together.

"The road'll still be there, Mr. Farrow," Gwinn said quietly. "Don't you think?"

Dan looked into the preacher's eyes. "You don't know me. I could be . . . somebody you wouldn't want in your house."

"True enough. But my Lord Jesus Christ says we should feed the wayfarin' stranger." Gwinn's voice had taken on some of the singsong inflections of his calling. "'Pears to me that's what you are. So if you want a taste of fried chicken that'll make you hear the heavenly choir, you just say the word and you got it."

Dan didn't have to think very long to make a decision. "All right. I'd be grateful."

"Just be hungry! Lavinia always makes a whoppin' supper on Thursday nights anyhow." Gwinn stood up. "Lemme go on back and call her. Why don't you rest some and I'll fetch you when I'm ready to go."

"Thank you," Dan said. "I really do appreciate this." He lay down on the pew as Gwinn walked back to his office. The pew was no mattress, but just being able to relax for a little while was glorious. He closed his eyes, the sweat cooling on his body, and he searched for a few minutes of sleep that might shield him from the image of Emory Blanchard bleeding to death.

In his office, Reverend Gwinn was on the telephone to his wife. She stoically took the news that a white stranger named Dan Farrow was joining them for supper, even though Thursday was always the night their son and daughter-in-law came to visit from Mansfield.

But everything would work out fine, Lavinia told her husband, because Terrence had called a few minutes before to let her know he and Amelia wouldn't be there until after seven. There'd been a raid on a house where drugs were being sold, she told Nathan, and Terrence had some paperwork to do at the jail.

"That's our boy," Gwinn said. "Gonna get elected sheriff yet."

When he hung up, the reverend turned his attention again to the unwritten sermon. A light came on in his brain. Kindness for the wayfarin' strange. Yessir, that would do quite nicely!

They always amazed him, the mysterious workings of God did. You never knew when an answer to a problem would come right out of the blue; or, in this case, out of a gray Chevy pickup truck.

He picked up a pen, opened a Bible for reference, and began to write an outline of his message for Sunday morning.

4

The Hand of Clint

"**T**wo cards."

"I'll take three."

"Two for me."

"One card."

"Oh, oh! I don't like the sound of that, gents. Well, dealer's gonna take three and see what we got."

The poker game in the back room of Leopold's Pool Hall, on the rough west end of Caddo Street in Shreveport, had started around two o'clock. It was now five forty-nine, according to the Regulator clock hanging on the cracked sea-green wall. Beneath a gray haze of cigarette and stogie smoke, a quintet of men regarded their cards in silence around the felt-topped table. Out where the pool tables were, balls struck together like a pistol shot, and from the aged Wurlitzer jukebox Cleveland Crochet hollered about Sugar Bee to the wail of a Cajun accordion.

The room was a hotbox. Three of the men were in shirtsleeves, the fourth in a damp T-shirt. The fifth man, however, had never removed the rather bulky jacket of his iridescent, violet-blue sharkskin suit. In respect of the heat, though, he'd loosened the knot of his necktie and unbuttoned the starched collar of his white shirt. A glass of melting ice and pale, cloudy liquid was placed near his right hand. Also within reach was a stack of chips worth three hundred and nineteen dollars. His fortunes had risen and fallen and risen again during the progress of the game, and right now he was on a definite winning jag. He was the man who'd requested one card, so sure was he that he owned a hand no one else could touch.

The dealer, a bald-headed black man named Ambrose, finally cleared his throat. "It's up to you, Royce."

"I'm in for five." Royce, a big-bellied man with a flame-colored beard and a voice like a rodent's squeak, tossed a red chip on top of the ante.

521

"I fold." The next man, whose name was Vincent, laid his cards facedown with an emphatic *thump* of disgust.

There was a pause. "Come on, Junior," Ambrose prodded.

"I'm thinkin'." At age twenty-eight, Junior was the youngest of the players. He had a sallow, heavy-jawed face and unruly reddish-brown hair, sweat gleaming on his cheeks and blotching his T-shirt. He stared at his cards, a cigarette clenched between his teeth. His lightless eyes ticked to the player next to him. "I believe I got you this time, Mr. Lucky."

The man in the sharkskin suit was engrossed in his own cards. His eyes were pallid blue, his face so pale the purple-tinged veins were visible at his temples. He looked to be in his mid-thirties, his body as lean as a drawn blade. His black hair was perfectly combed, the part straight to the point of obsessiveness. At the center of his hairline a streak of white showed like a touch of lightning.

"Put up or fold 'em," Ambrose said.

"See the five and raise you ten." The chips clattered down.

"Fifteen dollars," the man in the sharkskin suit said, his voice so soft it neared a whisper, "and fifteen more." He tossed the chips in with a flick of his right wrist.

"Oh, lawwwwdy!" Ambrose studied his cards with heightened interest. "Talk to me, chillen, talk to me!" He picked up his cigar stub from an ashtray and puffed on it as if trying to divine the future in smoke signals.

Nick, the pool hall's bartender, came in while Ambrose was deliberating and asked if anybody needed their drinks freshened. Junior said he wanted another Budweiser, and Vincent said he'd have a refill of iced tea. The man in the sharkskin suit downed his cloudy drink in two long swallows and said, "I'll have another of the same."

"Uh . . . you sure you don't want some sugar in that?" Nick asked.

"No sugar. Just straight lemon juice."

Nick returned to the front room. Ambrose puffed out a last question mark and put his cards facedown. "Nope. My wife's gone have my ass as it is."

Royce stayed in and raised another five spot. Junior chewed his lower lip. "Damn it, I've *gotta* stay in!" he decided. "Hell, I'll raise five to you!"

"And fifteen more," came the reply.

"Sheeeeyit!" Ambrose grinned. "We gots us a showdown here!"

"I'm out." Royce's cards went on the table.

Junior leaned back in his chair, his cards close to his chest and fresh sweat sparkling on his face. He glowered long and hard at the man beside him, whom he'd come to detest in the last two hours. "You're fuckin' bluffin'," he said. "I caught you last time you tried to bluff me, didn't I?"

"Fifteen dollars to you, Junior," Ambrose said. "What'cha gone do?"

"Don't rush me, man!" Junior had two red chips in front of him. He'd come into the game with over a hundred dollars. "You're tryin' to fox me, ain't you, Mr. Lucky?"

The man's head turned. The pale blue eyes fixed upon Junior, and the whispery voice said, "The name is Flint."

"I don't give a shit! You're tryin' to rob me, I figure I can call you whatever I please!"

"Hey, Junior!" Royce cautioned. "Watch that tongue, now!"

"Well, who the hell knows this guy, anyhow? He comes in here, gets in our game, and takes us all for a ride! How do we know he ain't a pro?"

"I paid for my seat," Flint said. "You didn't holler when you took my money."

"Maybe I'm hollerin' *now!*" Junior sneered. "Does anybody know him?" he asked the others. Nick came in with the drinks on a tray. "Hey, Nick! You ever see this here dude before?"

"Can't say I have."

"So how come he just wandered in off the street lookin' to play poker? How come he's sittin' there with all our damn money?"

Flint snapped the cards shut in his left hand, drank some of the fresh lemon juice, and rubbed the cold glass across his forehead. "Meet the raise," he said, "or go home and cry to your mommy."

Junior exhaled sworls of smoke. Crimson had risen in his cheeks. "Maybe you and me oughta go dance in the alley, what do you think about that?"

"Come on, Junior!" Ambrose said. "Play or fold!"

"Nick, loan me five dollars."

"No way!" Nick retreated toward the door. "This ain't no bank in here, man!"

"Somebody loan me five dollars," Junior said to the others. This demand was met with a silence that might have made stones weep. "Five dollars! What's wrong with you guys?"

"We don't loan money in this room," Ambrose reminded him. "Never have and never will. You know the house rules."

"I'd loan it to you if you were in a tight!"

"No you wouldn't. And I wouldn't ask. The rule is: you play with your own money."

"Well, it's sure nice to know who your friends are!" Junior wrenched the cheap wristwatch off his arm and slid it in front of Flint. "Here, damn it! That's gotta be worth fifteen or twenty bucks!"

Flint picked up the watch and examined it. Then he returned it to the table and leaned back, his cards fanned out again and resting against his chest. "Merchandise isn't money, but since you're so eager to walk out of here a loser, I'll grant you the favor."

"*Favor.*" Junior almost spat the word. "Yeah, right! Come on, let's see what you've got!"

"Lay yours down first," Flint said.

"Glad to!" *Slap* went the cards on the table. "Three queens! I always was lucky with the women!" Junior grinned, one hand already reaching out to rake in the chips and his watch.

But before his hand got there, it was blocked by three aces.

"I was always smart at poker," Flint said. "And smart beats lucky any day."

Junior's grin evaporated. He stared at the trio of aces, his mouth crimping around the cigarette.

Flint scooped up the chips and put the wristwatch into his inside coat pocket. While Nick didn't loan money, he did sell poker chips. It was time, Flint knew, to cash in and be on his way. "That does it for me." He pocketed the rest of his winnings and stood up. "Thank you for the game, gentlemen."

"*Cheater.*"

"Junior!" Ambrose snapped. "Hush up!"

"*Cheater!*" Junior scraped his chair back and rose to his feet. His sweating face was gorged with blood. "You cheated me, by God!"

"Did I?" Flint's eyes were heavy-lidded. "How?"

"I don't know how! I just know you won a few too many hands today! Oh, yeah, maybe you lost some, but you never lost enough to put you too far behind, did you? Nosir! You lost just to keep us playin', so you could set me up for this shit!"

"Sit down, Junior," Vincent told him. "Some people gotta win, some gotta lose. That's why they call it gamblin'."

"Hell, can't you see it? He's a pro is what he is! He came in here off the street, got in our game, and made fools outta every damn one of us!"

"I see," Ambrose said wearily, "that it's almost six o'clock. Honey'll skin my butt if I don't get home."

"Gone skin your butt anyhow for losin' that paycheck," Royce said with a high giggle.

"Humility keeps me an honest man, my friends." Ambrose stood up and stretched. "Junior, that look on your face could scare eight lives out of a cat. Forget it now, hear? You can't win every day, or it wouldn't be no fun when you did."

Junior watched Flint, who was buttoning his jacket. Beneath Flint's arms were dark half-moons of sweat. "I say that bastard *cheated!* There's somethin' not right about him!"

Flint suddenly turned, took two strides forward, and his face and Junior's were only inches apart. "I'll ask you once more. Tell me how I cheated, sonny boy."

"You know you did! Maybe you're just slicker'n owl shit, but I know you cheated somehow!"

"Prove it," Flint said, and only Junior saw the faint smile that rippled across his thin-lipped mouth.

"You dirty sonofa—" Junior hauled back his arm to deliver a punch, but Ambrose and Royce both grabbed him and pulled him away. "Lemme go!" Junior hollered as he thrashed with impotent rage. "I'll tear him apart, I swear to God!"

"Mister," Ambrose said, "it might be best if you don't come 'round here again."

"I wasn't plannin' on it." Flint finished off his lemon juice, his face impassive. Then he turned his back on the other men and walked out to the bar to cash in his chips. His stride was as slow and deliberate as smoke drifting. While Nick was counting the money, Junior was escorted to the street by Ambrose, Vincent, and Royce. "You'll get yours, Mr. Lucky!" was Junior's parting shot before the door closed.

"He flies off the handle sometimes, but he's okay." Nick laid the crisp green winnings in Flint's pale palm. "Better not walk around with that kinda cash in this neighborhood."

"Thank you." He gave Nick a twenty. "For the advice." He started walking toward the door, his hand finding the car keys in his pocket, and over the zydeco music on the jukebox he heard the telephone ring.

"Okay, hold on a minute. Hey, your name Murtaugh?" Nick called.

Flint stopped at the door, dying sunlight flaring through the fly-specked windows. "Yes."

"It's for you."

"Murtaugh," Flint said into the phone.

"You seen the TV in the last half hour?" It was a husky, ear-hurting voice: Smoates, calling from the shop.

525

"No. I've been busy."

"Well, wrap up your bidness and get on over here. Ten minutes."
Click, and Smoates was gone.

Even as six o'clock moved past and the blue shadows lengthened, the heat was suffocating. Flint could smell the lemon juice in his perspiration as he strode along the sidewalk. When Smoates said ten minutes, he meant eight. It had to be another job, of course. Flint had just brought a skin back for Smoates this morning and collected his commission—forty percent—on four thousand dollars. Smoates, who was the kind of man who had an ear on every corner and in every back room, had told him about the Thursday afternoon poker game at Leopold's, and with some time to kill before going back to his motel Flint had eased himself into what had turned out to be child's play. If he had any passion, it was for the snap of cards being shuffled, the clack of spinning roulette wheels, the soft thump of dice tumbling across sweet green felt; it was for the smells of smoky rooms where stacks of chips rose and fell, where cold sweat collected under the collar and an ace made the heartbeat quicken. Today's winnings had been small change, but a game was a game and Flint's thirst for risk had been temporarily quenched.

He reached his ride: a black 1978 Cadillac Eldorado that had seen three or four used car lots. The car had a broken right front headlight, the rear bumper was secured with burlap twine, the passenger door was crumpled in, and the southern sun had cracked and jigsawed the old black paint. The interior smelled of mildew and the chassis moaned over potholes like a funeral bell. Flint's appetite for gambling didn't always leave him a winner; the horses, greyhounds, and the casinos of Vegas took his money with a frequency that would have terrified an ordinary man. Flint Murtaugh, however, could by no stretch of the imagination be called ordinary.

He slipped his key into the door's lock. As it clicked open, he heard another noise—a metallic *snap*—very close behind him, and he realized quite suddenly that he would have to pay for his inattention.

"Easy, Mr. Lucky."

Flint felt the switchblade's tip press at his right kidney. He let the breath hiss from between his teeth. "You're makin' a real big mistake."

"Do tell. Let's walk. Turn in that alley up there."

Flint obeyed. There weren't many people on the sidewalk, and

Junior kept close. "Keep walkin'," Junior said as Flint turned into the alley. Ahead, in the shadows between buildings, was a chain-link fence and beyond it a parking garage. "Stop," Junior said. "Turn around and look at me."

Flint did, his back to the fence. Junior stood between him and the street, the knife low at his side. It was a mean-looking switchblade, and Junior held it as if he had used it before. "I believe your luck's run out." Junior's eyes were still ashine with anger. "Gimme my money."

Flint smiled coldly. He unbuttoned his sharkskin jacket, and in so doing he tapped a finger twice on his belt buckle, which bore his initials in scrolled letters. He lifted his hands. "It's inside my coat. Come get it, sonny boy."

"I'll cut you, damn it! I'll give you some shit like you never had before, man!"

"Will you? Sonny boy, I'm gonna give you three pieces of wisdom. One." He raised a finger of his left hand. "Never play poker with a stranger. Two." Two fingers of his right hand went up. "Never raise against a man who asks for a single card. And three . . ."

Something moved at Flint's chest, underneath the white linen shirt.

Flint's necktie was pushed aside. Through the opening of an undone button emerged a dwarf-sized hand and a slim, hairless white arm. The hand gripped a small double-barreled derringer aimed at Junior's midsection.

"When you've got the drop on a man," Flint continued, "never, never let him face you."

Junior's mouth hung open. *"Jesus,"* he whispered. "You've . . . got . . . three . . ."

"Clint. Steady." Flint's voice was sharp; the derringer had wobbled a few inches to the right. "Drop the knife, sonny boy." But Junior was too stunned to respond. "Clint. Down. Down. Down." The arm obeyed, and now the derringer was pointed in the vicinity of Junior's knees. "You'll be a cripple in three seconds," Flint promised.

The knife clattered to the gritty pavement.

Flint frowned, sliding his two hands into his pants pockets. The third hand held the derringer steady. "I should've figured on this," Flint said, mostly to himself. "Clint. Holster."

The wiry arm retreated into his shirt. Flint felt the gun slide into the small holster under his right shoulder. The arm twitched once, a muscle spasm, and then lay pressed against Flint's chest with the fingers wedged beneath his belt buckle. "Good Clint," Flint said, and he walked quickly toward Junior, who still stood shocked and gaping. Flint withdrew his right hand, which now wore the set of brass knuckles that had been in his pocket. The blow that followed was fast and decisive, hitting Junior on the chin and snapping his head back. Junior gave a garbled cry and staggered into some garbage cans, and then Flint swung again—a graceful, almost balletic motion—and the brass knuckles crunched into the cheek-bone on the left side of Junior's face.

Gasping, Junior fell to his knees. He stayed there, his head swaying from side to side and the anger washed from his eyes by the tears of pain.

"You know," Flint observed, "what you said about givin' me some shit is really funny. It really, truly is." Flint touched the knuckles of Junior's right hand with the toe of his polished black wingtip. The cheap wristwatch fell to the pavement beside Junior's fingers. "See, nobody on this earth can give me any more shit than I've already had to endure. Do you understand?"

"Ahhhhplleesh," Junior managed.

"I've been where you are," Flint said. "It made me meaner. But it made me smarter, too. Whatever doesn't kill you makes you smarter. Do you believe that?"

"Immmmaeuff," Junior said.

"Take your watch," Flint told him. "Go on. Pick it up."

Slowly, Junior's hand closed around the watch.

"There you go." The cold smile had never left Flint's face. "Now I'm gonna help your education along."

He summoned up his rage.

It was an easy thing to find. It had grinning faces in it, and harsh, jeering laughter. It had the memory of a bad night at the blackjack table, and of a loan shark's silky threats. It had Smoates' voice in it, commanding *Ten minutes.* It had a lifetime of torment and bitterness in it, and when it emerged from Flint it was explosive. The hand of Clint felt that rage and clenched into a knotty fist. Flint inhaled, lifted his foot, exhaled in a *whoosh*, and stomped Junior's fingers beneath his shoe.

The watch broke. So did two of the fingers and the thumb. Junior gave a wail that shattered into croaking, and he lay writhing on his side with his hand clasped to his chest and bits of watch crystal sticking into his palm.

Flint stepped back, sweat on his face and the blood pounding in his cheeks. It took him a few seconds to find his voice, and it came out thick and raw. "You can tell the police about this if you want to." Flint returned the brass knuckles to his pocket. "Tell 'em a freak with three arms did it, and listen to 'em laugh."

Junior continued to writhe, his attention elsewhere.

"Fare thee well," Flint said. He stepped over Junior, walked out of the alley, and got into his car. In another moment he had fired up the rough and rumbling engine and pulled away from the curb en route to the Twilight Zone Pawn Shoppe on Stoner Avenue.

As he drove, Flint felt sick to his stomach. The rage was gone, and in its place was shame. Breaking the boy's fingers had been cruel and petty; he'd lost control of himself, had let his baser nature rule him. Control was important to Flint. Without control, men fell to the level of animals. He pushed a cassette tape into the deck and listened to the cool, clean sound of Chopin's piano preludes, some of his favorite music. It made him think of his dream. In the dream, he stood on a rolling, beautiful emerald-green lawn, looking toward a white stone mansion with four chimneys and a huge stained-glass window in front.

He believed it was his home, but he didn't know where it was.

"I'm not an animal." His voice was still coarse with emotion. "I'm not."

A dwarf-sized left hand suddenly rose up before his face, swatting at his cheek with the ace of spades.

"Stop that, you bastard," Flint said, and he pushed Clint's arm back down where it belonged.

The Twilight Zone Pawn Shoppe stood between Uncle Joe's Loans and the Little Saigon Take-out Restaurant. Flint drove around back and parked next to Eddie Smoates's late-model Mercedes-Benz. The door at the rear of the pawn shop had a sign identifying it as DIXIE BAIL BONDS AND COLLECTIONS. Clint was moving around under Flint's shirt, getting hungry, so Flint reached into the backseat for a box of Ritz crackers before he got out of the car. He pressed a button on the brick wall beside the door, and a few seconds later Smoates's voice growled through an intercom mounted there: "You're late."

"I came as soon as I—"

A buzzer cut him off, announcing that the door had been electronically unlocked. Flint pushed through it into the air-conditioning. The door locked again at his back; Smoates kept a lot of valuables around, and he was a careful man. There was a small reception area with a few plastic chairs, but the office had closed for regular business an hour ago. Flint knew where he was going; this place was as familiar to him as his brother's arm. He walked past the reception desk and knocked on a door behind it.

"In!" Smoates said, and Flint entered.

As usual, Eddie Smoates sat at the center of a rat's nest of piled-up papers and file folders. The office smelled of garlic, onions, and grease: the prime ingredients of the Little Saigon take-out dinner that lay in Styrofoam plates and cups atop Smoates's untidy desk. The man was stuffing the rubber-lipped mouth in his moon-round face with stringy chicken. Smoates had the quick, dark eyes of a ferret, his broad scalp shaved bald and a gray goatee adorning his chin. He had massive forearms and shoulders that swelled his lime-green Polo shirt, though his belly was becoming voluminous as well. Twenty years ago Smoates had been a professional wrestler, wearing a mask and going by the name X the Unknown. He said, "Siddahn" as he sucked pieces of garlic chicken off the bones, and Flint sat in one of the two chairs that faced the desk. Behind Smoates was a metal door that led into the pawn shop, which he also owned. On a rack of shelves pushed precariously against a wall were a half-dozen TV sets, ten VCRs, and a dozen or so stereo amps. The TV sets were on, all tuned to different channels, though their volumes were too low to be audible.

Smoates, a noisy eater, kept feasting. Grease glistened on his chin and in his goatee. Flint was repulsed by Smoates's lack of manners. He stared fixedly at his employer's prized collection of what Smoates called his "pretties." Held in a glass curio cabinet were such items as a mummified cat with two heads, a severed human hand with seven fingers floating in a jar of murky preservative, the skull of a baby with an extra eyehole in the center of its forehead, and—nature's cruelest trick, it seemed to Flint—an embalmed monkey with a third arm protruding from its neck. On a shelf above the "pretties" were eight photo albums that contained the pictures Smoates had collected of what seemed to be his driving passion next to making money and eating. Smoates was a connoisseur of freaks. As other men enjoyed vintage wine, fine paintings, or sculpture, Smoates craved grotesque oddities of flesh and bone. Flint, who lived in an apartment in the town of Monroe a hundred miles east of Shreveport, had never visited his employer's home in the six years he'd been on the Dixie payroll, but he understood from one of his fellows that Smoates kept a basement full of freak memorabilia gleaned from five decades of carnival sideshows. Whatever it was that made a man long to gaze upon the most bizarre and hideous of malformed creations, it ran dark and twisted right to the roots of Smoates's soul.

Such fascination disgusted Flint, who considered himself a well-bred gentleman. But then, Flint himself might still be an object of disgusting fascination had Smoates not visited the sideshow tent that advertised, among other attractions, Flint and Clint, the Two in One. Smoates had paid Flint to go with him to a photography studio and pose shirtless for a series of pictures, which had presumably wound up with the others in the photo albums. Flint had no desire to page through the albums; he'd seen enough freaks in the flesh to last him a lifetime.

"You win or lose?" Smoates asked, not looking up from his garlic chicken.

"I won."

"How much?"

"Around three hundred and fifty."

"That's good. I like when you win, Flint. When you're happy, I'm happy. You *are* happy, right?"

"I am," Flint said gravely.

"I like for my boys to be happy." Smoates paused, searching his plate of bones for a shred of meat. "Don't like 'em to be late, though. Ten minutes ain't fifteen. You need a new watch?"

"No." Clint's arm suddenly slid from the front of Flint's shirt and began scratching and tickling at his chin. Flint took a Ritz cracker from the box and put it into the fingers. Immediately the arm withdrew, and from beneath Flint's shirt came the sound of crunching.

Smoates pushed his plate aside, his fingers gleaming with grease. His eyes had taken on a feverish glint. "Open your shirt," he commanded. "I like to watch him eat."

As much as he detested to, Flint obeyed. Smoates was the man with the wallet, and he didn't tolerate disobedience from his "boys." Flint's fingers undid the buttons, letting Smoates have a clear view of the slim white dwarfish arm that was connected at the elbow to an area just beneath Flint's solar plexus. "Feed him," Smoates said. Flint took another cracker from the box. He felt the soft bones of his brother move within him, a slow shifting that pressed against his own organs. Clint could smell the cracker and his hand searched the air for it, but Flint guided it toward the fist-sized growth that protruded from his right side. Smoates was leaning forward, watching. The growth was as pale as the arm, was hairless and eyeless but had a set of flared nostrils, ears like tiny seashells, and a pair of thin lips. As the cracker came nearer, the lips parted with a soft, wet noise to show the small, sharp teeth and tongue that might have belonged to a kitten. The mouth accepted the cracker, the teeth crunched down, and Flint pulled his fingers back to avoid being nicked. Sometimes Clint was overeager in his feeding.

"Amazin'." Smoates wore a dreamy smile. "I swear, I don't know how your wires got crossed, but they sure did, didn't they?"

Flint rebuttoned his shirt, except for the single button at the center he usually left open. His face was impassive. "What did you want to see me about?"

"Take a look at this." Smoates picked up a remote control from his desk, pressed down with a big, greasy thumb, and one of the VCRs clicked into Play mode. Static sizzled on one of the TV screens for a few seconds, then the attractive face of a dark-haired news-woman appeared. She was speaking into a microphone, while behind her was a police car and a knot of people standing around a building's revolving door. Smoates used a second remote control to boost the volume.

". . . this afternoon in what police are saying was the act of a desperate and disturbed man," the newswoman said. "Emory Blanchard, who was the loan manager of the First Commercial Bank, was pronounced dead on arrival at All Saints Hospital. This was the scene just a few moments ago when Clifton Lyles, the bank's president, made a public statement."

The picture changed. A grim-faced man with white hair was standing in front of the building, reporters holding a forest of microphones around him. "I want to say we don't intend to sit still for this outrage," Lyles said. "I'm announcin' right now a reward in the amount of fifteen thousand dollars for Lambert's capture." He held up a hand to ward off the shouts. "No, I'm not takin' questions. There'll be a full statement for the press later. I just hope and pray that man is caught before he kills anybody else. Thank you very much."

The newswoman came on again. "That was Clifton Lyles, presi-dent of the First Commercial Bank. As you can see behind me, there's still a lot of activity here as the police continue to—"

The videotaped image stopped. Smoates turned the volume down. "Crazy fucker went in there and shot Blanchard. Fella lost his marbles when he found out his pickup truck was bein' repossessed. You up to goin' after this skin?"

Flint had been feeding Clint during the videotape. Now he chewed on a cracker himself, leaving his brother's fingers searching through the opening of the undone button. "I always am," he answered.

"Figured so. I got a call in." Smoates had a connection in the police department who, for a fee, fed him all the information he required. "Have to move fast on this one. Tell you the truth, I don't think there's much chance of gettin' him. Every badge in the state'll be gunnin' for him. But there's nothin' else on the docket, so you might as well give it a try." He struck a kitchen match and lit a black cheroot, which he gripped between his teeth. He leaned back in his chair and spewed smoke toward the ceiling. "Give you a chance to take the new man out on a trainin' run."

"The new man? What new man?"

"The new man I'm thinkin' of hirin' on. Name's Eisley. Came in to see me this afternoon. He's got potential, but he's green. I need to see what he's made of."

"We work alone," Flint said quietly.

"Eisley's stayin' at the Ol' Plantation Motel out by the airport." Smoates fished for his notepad on the cluttered desktop. "Room Number Twenty-three," he said when he'd found it.

"We work alone," Flint repeated, a little more forcefully.

"Uh-huh. That may be, but I want you to take Eisley along this time."

Flint shifted uneasily in his chair. A small terror had begun building within him. "I don't . . . I don't allow anyone else into my car."

"Are you *jivin'* me?" Smoates scowled across the desk, and his scowl was not pretty. "I've seen that bucket of bolts. Nothin' special about it."

"I know, but . . . I'm particular about who I ride with."

"Well, Eisley ain't a nigger, if that's what bothers you."

"No, that's not it. I just . . . Clint and me . . . we'd rather work alone."

"Yeah, you already said that. But you're elected. Billy Lee's in Arkansas on a job, Dwayne's still laid up with the flu, and I ain't heard from Tiny Boy in two weeks. Figure he must've gone back to the sideshow, so we need some fresh blood 'round here. Eisley might work out just fine."

Flint choked. He lived alone—if a man whose brother was trapped inside his body in a wicked twist of genetics could ever be truly alone—and preferred it that way. Having to deal with another person at close quarters might drive him right up the wall. "What's wrong with him?"

"Who?"

"Eisley," Flint said, speaking slowly and carefully. "Somethin' must be wrong with him, or you wouldn't want to hire him on."

Smoates drew on his cheroot and tapped ashes to the floor. "I like his personality," he said at last. "Reminds me of a fella I used to think real highly of."

"But he's a freak, right? You don't hire anybody but freaks."

"Now, that ain't exactly correct. I hire—" He paused, mulling it over. "Special talents," he decided. "People who impress me, for one reason or 'nother. Take Billy Lee, for instance. He don't have to say a word, all he has to do is stand there and show his stuff, and he gets the job done. Am I right?"

Flint didn't answer. Billy Lee Klaggens was a six-foot-six-inch-tall black man who had paid his dues on the freak-show circuit under the name of Popeye. Klaggens, a fearsome visage, could stand there and stare at you and the only thing moving about him would be his eyeballs as blood pressure slowly squeezed them almost out of his skull. Faced with such a sight, the skins Klaggens hunted became as hypnotized as rabbits watching a cobra flare its hood—and then Klaggens sprayed a burst of Mace in their eyes, snapped on the handcuffs, and that was all she wrote. Klaggens had worked for Smoates for over ten years, and he had taught Flint the ropes.

"Eisley's got a special talent, if that's what you're gettin' at." A little thread of smoke leaked from the gap between his front teeth. "He's a born communicator. I think he could make the fuckin' sphinx talk. He knows how to work people. Used to be in show business."

"Didn't we all," Flint said.

"Yeah, but Eisley's got the gift of gab. You and him, you'll make a good team."

"I'll take him out on a trainin' run, but I'm *not* teamin' up with him. Or with *anybody*."

"Okay, okay." Smoates grinned, but on his face it looked more like a sneer. "Flint, you gotta loosen up, boy! You gotta get over this antisocial problem, you'll be a lot happi—" The telephone half buried beneath file folders rang, and Smoates snatched up the receiver. "Dixie Bail Bonds and Collections . . . well, you took your sweet fuckin' time, didn't you? Let's have the story." He tossed Flint the notepad and a ballpoint pen. "Daniel Lewis Lambert . . . Vietnam veteran . . . unemployed carpenter . . ." He snorted smoke through his nostrils. "Shit, man, gimme somethin' I can *use!*" He listened, the cheroot at a jaunty angle in his mouth. "Cops think he's left town. Armed and dangerous. Ex-wife and son in Alexandria. What's the address?" He relayed it to Flint, who wrote it down.

"No other relatives in state? Sumbitches are gonna be waitin' for him to show up in Alexandria then, right? Hell, they gone get him 'fore I even send my boy out. But gimme the license number and a description of his truck anyhow; we might get lucky." Flint wrote that down as well. "What's Lambert look like?" was the next question, and Lambert's description went on the notepad's page. "Anythin' else? Okay, then. Yeah, yeah, you'll get your money this week. You hear that they've picked Lambert up, you gimme a call pronto. I'll be home. Yeah, same to you." He hung up. "Cops figure he might be on his way to Alexandria. They'll have the house staked out, for sure."

"Doesn't sound to me like I've got a snowball's chance in Hell of grabbin' him." Flint tore off the page and folded it. "Too many cops in the picture."

"It's worth a shot. Fifteen thousand smacks ain't hay. If you're lucky, you might catch him 'fore he gets to the house."

"I'd agree with you if I didn't have to haul freight."

Smoates drew on his cheroot and released a ragged smoke ring that floated toward the ceiling. "Flint," he said, "you been with me—what?—six years, goin' on seven? You're one of the best trackers I ever had. You're smart, you can think ahead. But you got this attitude problem, boy. You forget who pulled you out of that sideshow and who pays your bills."

"No, I don't," Flint answered crisply. "You won't let me."

Smoates was silent for a few seconds, during which he stared without blinking at Flint through a haze of smoke. "You tired of this job?" he asked. "If you are, you can quit anytime you please. Go on and find yourself some other line of work. I ain't stoppin' you."

Flint's mouth was dry. He held Smoates's haughty stare as long as he could, and then he looked away.

"You work for me, you follow my orders," Smoates continued. "You do what I say, you draw a paycheck. That make sense to you?"

"Yeah," Flint managed to say.

"Maybe you can grab Lambert, maybe you can't. I think Eisley's got potential, and I want to see what he's made of. Only way to do that is to send him out on a run with somebody, and I say that somebody is *you*. So go get him and hit the road. You're wastin' my time and money."

Flint took the box of crackers and stood up. He pushed his brother's arm down under his shirt and held it there. Now that he'd been fed, Clint would be asleep in a few minutes; unless he was called upon, all he basically did was eat and sleep. Flint's eyes found the three-armed monkey in the curio cabinet, and the same surge of anger that had made him break Junior's fingers swelled up in him and almost spilled out.

"I'll give Eisley a call and tell him you're on the way," Smoates said. "Check in with me from the motel."

I'm not an animal, Flint thought. Blood pulsed in his face. He felt Clint's bones twitch within him like the movement of someone trapped in a very bad dream.

"Standin' there ain't gonna get you nowhere," Smoates told him.

Flint turned away from the three-armed monkey and the bald-headed man behind the desk. When the door had closed at Flint's back, Smoates released a harsh little hiccup of a laugh. His belly shook. He crushed his cheroot out in the plate of grease and bones, and it perished with a bubbly hiss. His laughter gurgled and swelled.

Flint Murtaugh was on his way to meet the Pelvis.

5
A Ways to Go

Three hours after shooting a man to death, Dan Lambert found himself sitting on a screened porch, a ceiling fan creaking overhead, with a glass of honeysuckle tea in his hand and a black woman offering him a refill from a purple pitcher.

"No ma'am, thank you," he said.

"Lemme get on back to the kitchen, then." Lavinia Gwinn put the pitcher down on the wicker table between Dan and Reverend Gwinn. "Terrence and Amelia oughta be here 'bout another half hour."

"I hope you don't mind me stayin'. I didn't know your son was comin' over when your husband invited me."

"Oh, don't you worry, we gots plenty. Always cook up a feast on Thursday nights." She left the porch, and Dan sipped his tea and listened to the cicadas droning in the green woods around the reverend's white clapboard house. The sun was sinking lower, the shadows growing between the trees. Reverend Gwinn occupied a wicker rocking chair, his fingers laced around his tea glass and his face set with the expression of a man who is calm and comfortable with life.

"You have a nice house," Dan said.

"We like it. Had a place in the city once, but it was like livin' in an alarm clock. Lavinia and me don't need much to get by on."

"I used to have a house. In Alexandria. My ex-wife and son still live there."

"Is that where you're headed, then?"

Dan took a moment to think about his answer. It seemed to him now that all along he'd known the house on Jackson Avenue was his destination. The police would be waiting for him there, of course. But he had to see Chad, had to tell his son that it had been an accident, a terrible collision of time and circumstance, and that he wasn't the cold-blooded killer the newspapers were going to make him out to be. "Yes," he said. "I believe I am."

"Good for a man to know where he's goin'. Helps you figure out where you've been."

"That's for damn sure." Dan caught himself. "Uh . . . sorry."

"Oh, I don't think the Lord minds a little rough language now and again, long as you keep His commandments."

Dan said nothing. *Thou shalt not kill,* he was thinking.

"Tell me about your son," Gwinn said. "How old is he?"

"Seventeen. His name's Chad. He's . . . a mighty good boy."

"You see a lot of him?"

"No, I don't. His mother thought it was for the best."

Gwinn grunted thoughtfully. "Boy needs a father, I'd think."

"Maybe so. But I'm not the father Chad needs."

"How's that, Mr. Farrow?"

"I messed up some things," Dan said, but he didn't care to elaborate.

A moment passed during which the smell of frying chicken drifted out onto the porch and made the hunger pangs sharpen in Dan's belly. Then Reverend Gwinn said, "Mr. Farrow, excuse me for sayin' so, but you look like a man who's seen some trouble."

"Yes sir." Dan nodded. "That's about right."

"You care to unburden it?"

Dan looked into the reverend's face. "I wish I could. I wish I could tell you everythin' I've been through, in Vietnam and after I left that damned place, but that's no excuse for what I did today." He looked away again, shamed by Gwinn's compassion.

"Whatever you did, it can be forgiven."

"Not by me. Not by the law, either." He lifted the cool glass and pressed it against his forehead for a few seconds, his eyes closed. "I wish I could go back and make everythin' right. I wish I could wake up and it'd be mornin' again, and I could have another chance." He opened his eyes. "That's not how life works though, is it?"

"No," Gwinn said. "Not *this* life, at least."

"I'm not much of a religious man. Maybe I saw too many young boys get blasted to pieces you couldn't have recognized as part of anythin' human. Maybe I heard too many cries for God that went unanswered." Dan swigged down the rest of his tea and set the glass aside. "That might sound cynical to you, Reverend, but to me it's a fact."

"Seems to me no one's life is easy," Gwinn said, a frown settling over his features. "Not the richest nor the poorest." He rocked gently back and forth, the runners creaking. "You say you've broken the law, Mr. Farrow?"

"Yes."

"Can you tell me what you've done?"

Dan took a long breath and let it go slowly. The cicadas trilled in the woods, two of them in close harmony. "I killed a man today," he answered, and he noted that Gwinn ceased his rocking. "A man at a bank in Shreveport. I didn't mean to. It just happened in a second. It was . . . like a bad dream, and I wanted to get out of it but I couldn't. Hell, I was never even a very good shot. One bullet was all it took, and he was gone. I knew it, soon as I saw where I'd hit him."

"What had this man done to you?"

Dan had the sudden realization that he was confessing to a stranger, but Gwinn's sincere tone of voice urged him on. "Nothin', really. I mean . . . the bank was repossessin' my pickup. I snapped. Just like that. I started tearin' up his office. Then all of a sudden a guard was there, and when he pulled a gun on me I got it away from him. Blanchard—the man I shot—brought a pistol out of his desk and aimed it at me. I heard the hammer of his gun click. Then I pulled the trigger." Dan's fingers gripped the armrests, his knuckles white. "I tried to stop the bleedin', but there wasn't much I could do. I'd cut an artery in his neck. I heard on the radio that he was dead on arrival at the hospital. I figure the police are gonna catch me sooner or later, but I've got to see my son first. There are some things I need to tell him."

"Lord have mercy," Gwinn said very quietly.

"Oh, I'm not deservin' of mercy," Dan told him. "I'd just like some time, that's all."

"Time," the reverend repeated. He took the silver watch from his pocket, snapped it open, and looked at the numerals.

"If you don't want me sittin' at your table," Dan said, "I can understand."

Gwinn's watch was returned to the pocket. "My son," he said, "will be here any minute now. You didn't ask what kinda work Terrence does."

"Never thought to."

"My son is a deputy sheriff in Mansfield," Gwinn said, and those words caused the flesh to tighten at the back of Dan's neck. "Your description on the radio?"

"Yes."

"Terrence might not have heard about it. Then again, he might've." Gwinn held Dan's gaze with his dark, intense eyes. "Is what you've told me the truth, Mr. Farrow?"

"It is. Except my name's not Farrow. It's Lambert."

"Fair enough. I believe you." Gwinn stood up, leaving the chair rocking. He went into the house, calling for his wife. Dan left his chair as well, his heart beating hard. He heard the reverend say, "Yeah, Mr. Farrow's got a ways to go and he's not gonna be stayin' for dinner after all."

"Oh, that's a shame," Lavinia answered. "The chicken's all done!"

"Mr. Farrow?" There was just a trace of tension in Gwinn's voice. "You care to take some chicken for the road?"

"Yes sir," Dan said from the front door. "I sure would."

The reverend returned carrying a paper bag with some grease stains on the bottom. His wife was following along behind him. "What's your hurry, Mr. Farrow? Our boy oughta be here directly!"

"Mr. Farrow can't stay." Gwinn pushed the paper bag into Dan's hand. "He's gotta get to . . . New Orleans, didn't you say, Mr. Farrow?"

"I believe I might have," Dan said as he accepted the fried chicken.

"Well, I'm awful sorry you're not gonna be joinin' us at the table," Lavinia told him. "You gots family waitin' for you?"

"Yes, he does," Gwinn said. "Come on, Dan, I'll walk you to your truck."

"You take care on that road now," Lavinia continued, but she didn't leave the porch. "Crazy things can happen out there."

"Yes ma'am, I will. Thank you." When he and the reverend had reached the pickup and Lavinia had gone back inside, Dan asked, "Why are you helpin' me like this?"

"You wanted some time, didn't you? I'm givin' you a little bit. You better get on in there."

Dan slid into the driver's seat and started the engine. He realized that some of Blanchard's dried blood still streaked the steering wheel. "You could've waited. Just turned me in when your son got here."

"What? And scare Lavinia half to death? Take a chance on my boy gettin' hurt? Nosir. Anyhow, seems like you've had enough trouble today without me makin' more for you. But you listen to me now: the sensible thing to do is turn yourself in after you see your son. The police ain't savages; they'll give an ear to your story. All runnin's gonna do is make things worse."

"I know that."

"One more thing," Gwinn said, his hand on the window frame. "Maybe you're not a religious man, but I'll tell you somethin' true:

God can take a man along many roads and through many mansions. It's not where you are that's important; it's where you're goin' that counts. Hear what I'm sayin'?"

"I think so."

"Well, you keep it to heart. Go on now, and good luck to you."

"Thanks." *I'll need it*, he thought. He put the Chevy into reverse.

"So long." Gwinn let go of the truck and stepped back. "The Lord be with you."

Dan nodded and reversed the truck along the dirt drive that led from the reverend's house to the cracked concrete of Highway 175. Gwinn stood watching him go as Dan backed onto the road and then put the truck's gears into first. The reverend lifted his hand in a farewell gesture and Dan drove away, heading southbound again but this time rested, his head clear and for the moment free of pain and a paper bag full of fried chicken on the seat beside him. He had driven perhaps a mile from Gwinn's house when a car came around the bend and passed him, going north, and he saw a young black man at the wheel and a black woman on the passenger side. Then he was around the curve himself, and he gave the truck a little more gas. *The Lord be with you*, he thought. But where had the Lord been at three o'clock this afternoon?

Dan reached into the bag and found a drumstick, and he chewed on it as he followed the curvy country road deeper into the Louisiana heartland. As the sun continued to settle in the west and the miles clicked off, Dan focused his thoughts on what lay ahead of him. If he swung east and got on the freeway again, he would reach Alexandria in about an hour. If he stayed on this slower route, it would take double that. The sun would be gone in another thirty minutes or so. The police would surely be staking out the house on Jackson Avenue, and those prowl cars had mighty strong spotlights. He couldn't even risk driving past the house. How long would it take before the police slacked off their surveillance? He might think about giving himself up after he'd talked to Chad, but he wasn't going to let the boy see him wearing handcuffs. So the question was: how was he going to get to Chad without the police jumping all over him first?

South of a small hamlet called Belmont, Dan pulled into a Texaco station, bought five dollars worth of gas, a Buffalo Rock ginger ale to wash down the excellent fried chicken, and a Louisiana roadmap. The gray-haired woman who took his money was too interested in her *Soap Opera Digest* to pay him much attention. In the steamy blue evening Dan switched on the pickup's headlights and followed Highway 175 as it connected with Highway 171 and became a little smoother. At the town of Leesville, where he found himself stopped at a traffic light right in front of the police station, he took a left onto Highway 28 East, which was a straight shot into Alexandria. He had about thirty miles to go.

Fear started clawing at him again. The dull throbbing in his head returned. Full dark had fallen, a sickle moon rising over the trees. Traffic was sparse on the road, but every set of headlights in his rearview mirror stretched Dan's nerves. The nearer he got to Alexandria, the more he doubted this mission could be accomplished. But he had to try; if he didn't at least try, he wouldn't be worth a damn.

He passed a sign that said ALEXANDRIA 18 MI.

The police are gonna be there, he told himself. They'll get me before I can walk up the front steps. Would they have the telephone tapped, too? If I called Susan, would she put Chad on the phone or would she hang up?

He decided he couldn't drive up to the house. There had to be another way. But he couldn't drive around in circles, either.

ALEXANDRIA 10 MI. the next sign said.

He didn't know what to do. He could see the glow of Alexandria's lights on the horizon. Two more miles reeled off the odometer. And then he saw a blinking sign through the trees on his right—HIDEAWAY M TOR CO RT—and he lifted his foot from the accelerator. Dan slowed down as the turnoff to the motor court approached. He had another instant of indecision, but then he turned off Highway 28 and guided the pickup along a dirt road bordered by scraggly pines and palmettos. The headlights revealed green-painted cottages tucked back amid the trees. A red wooden arrow with OFFICE on it pointed in the direction he was going. Dan saw no lights in any of the cottages, and a couple of them looked as if their roofs were an ill wind away from collapse. The grounds were weeded-up and forlorn, a swing set rusted and drooping next to an area of decaying picnic tables. Then the driveway stopped at a house painted the same shade of vomito green as the cottages, a rust-splotched station wagon parked alongside. A yellow buglight burned on the front porch, and other lights showed in the windows. The Hideaway, it appeared, was open for business.

As Dan cut the engine, he saw a figure peer through a window at him, then withdraw. He'd just gotten out when he heard a screen door's hinges skreek.

"Howdy," a man said. "How're you doin'?"

"I'm all right," Dan lied. He was facing a slim, bucktoothed gent who must've stood six-four, his dark hair cut as if a bowl had been placed on his head as a guide for the ragged scissors. "You got a vacancy?"

The man, who wore blue jeans and a black Hawaiian-print shirt with orange flowers on it, gave a snorty laugh. "Nothin' but," he said. "Come on in and we'll fix you up."

Dan followed the man up a set of creaky stairs onto the porch. He was aware of a deep, slow rumbling noise on the sultry air; frogs, he thought it must be. Sounded like hundreds of them, not very far away. Dan went into the house behind the man, who walked to a desk in the dingy little front room and brought out a Nifty notebook and a ballpoint pen. "Allrighty," the man said, offering a grin that could've popped a bottle top. "Now we're ready to do some bidness." He opened the notebook, which Dan saw was a registration log that held only a few scribbled names. "I'm Harmon DeCayne, glad you decided to stop over with us."

"Dan Farrow." They shook hands. DeCayne's palm felt oily.

"How many nights, Mr. Farrow?"

"Just one."

"Where you from?"

"Baton Rouge," he decided to say.

"Well, you're a long way from home tonight, ain't you?" DeCayne wrote down the fake information. He seemed so excited, his hand was trembling. "We got some nice cottages, real nice and comf'table."

"That's good." Dan hoped the cottages were cooler than the house, which might've served as a steam bath. A small fan on a scarred coffee table was chattering, obviously overmatched. "How much?" He reached for his wallet.

"Uh—" DeCayne paused, his narrow brow wrinkling. "Does six dollars suit you?"

"*Seven* dollars. Paid in advance, if you please."

DeCayne jumped. The woman's voice had been a high, nasty whiplash. She had come through a corridor that led to the rear of the house, and she stood watching Dan with small, dark eyes.

"Seven dollars," she repeated. "We don't take no checks or plastic."

"My wife," DeCayne said; his grin had expired. "Hannah."

She had red hair that flowed over her thick-set shoulders in a torrent of kinky curls. Her face was about as appealing as a chunk of limestone, all sharp edges and forbidding angles. She wore a shapeless lavender-colored shift and rubber flipflops, and she stood maybe five feet tall, her body compact and wide-hipped and her legs like white tree trunks. She was holding a meat cleaver, her fingers glistening with blood.

"Seven dollars it is," Dan agreed, and he paid the man. The money went into a metal tin that was instantly locked by one of the keys on a key ring attached to DeCayne's belt. Hannah DeCayne said, "Give him Number Four. It's cleanest."

"Yes, hon." De Cayne plucked the proper key from a wall plaque where six other keys were hanging.

"Get him a fan," she instructed her husband. He opened a closet and brought out a fan similar to the one that fought the steam currents. "A pilla, too."

"Yes, hon." He leaned into the closet again and emerged with a bare pillow. He gave Dan a nervous smile that didn't do much to hide a glint of pain in his eyes. "Nice and comf'table cottage, Number Four is."

"Does it have a phone?" Dan asked.

"Phone's right here," the woman said, and she motioned with the meat cleaver toward a telephone on a table in the corner. "Local calls cost fifty cents."

"Are Alexandria numbers long distance?"

"We ain't in Alexandria. Cost you a dollar a minute."

And she'd time him to the second, too, he figured. He couldn't call Susan with this harpy listening over his shoulder. "Is there a pay phone around anywhere?"

"One at the gas station couple of miles up the road," she said. "If it's workin'."

Dan nodded. He stared at the cleaver in the woman's fist. "Been choppin' some meat?"

"Froglegs," she said.

"Oh." He nodded again, as if this made perfect sense.

"That's what we live on," she continued, and her lower lip curled. "Ain't no money in this damn place. We sell froglegs to a restaurant in town. Come out of the pond back that way." She motioned with the cleaver again, toward the rear of the house. Dan saw jewels of blood on the blade. "What'd you say your name was?"

"Farrow. Dan Farrow."

"Uh-huh. Well, Mr. Farrow, you ever seen a cockeyed fool before?" She didn't wait for an answer. "There's one, standin' right beside you. Ever heard of a cockeyed fool buyin' a damn motel on the edge of a swamp pond? And then puttin' every damn penny into a damn fairyland?"

"Hon?" Harmon's voice was very quiet. "Please."

"Please, my ass," she hissed. "I thought we was gonna be makin' some money by now, but no, I gotta damn fool for a husband and I'm up to my elbows in froglegs!"

"I'll show you to your cottage." Harmon started for the door.

"Watch where you step!" Hannah DeCayne warned Dan. "Damn frogs are breedin' back in that pond. There's hundreds of 'em 'round here. Show our guest the fairyland while you're at it, why don'tcha?" This last statement had been hurled at her husband like a bucketful of battery acid. He ducked his shoulders and got out of the house, and Dan darted another glance at the woman's meat cleaver before he followed.

"Enjoy your stay," she said as he went through the door.

Holding the fan and the pillow, Harmon climbed into the pickup truck and Dan got behind the wheel. Harmon made a slight nasal whistling sound as he breathed, kind of like a steam kettle on a slow boil. "Number Four's up that road," he said with an upward jerk of his chin. "Turn right."

Dan did. "Woman's always on me," Harmon said bitterly. "So I messed up, so what? Ain't the first man in the world to mess up. Won't be the last neither."

"That's true," Dan agreed.

"It's that way." Harmon motioned to a weed-grown pathway meandering off into the woods.

"What is? The cottage?"

"No. The fairyland. There's your cottage up ahead."

The headlights showed a dismal-looking green-daubed dump waiting ahead, but at least the roof appeared sturdy. Also revealed by the headlights was a squattage of frogs, maybe two dozen or more, on the dirt road between Dan's truck and the cottage. Dan hit the brake, but Harmon said, "Hell, run 'em over, I don't give a damn."

Dan tried to ease through them. Some squawked and leapt for safety, but others seemed hypnotized by the lights and met their maker in a flattened condition. Dan parked in front of the cottage and followed DeCayne inside, the noise of the frogs a low, throbbing rumble.

He hadn't expected much, so he wasn't disappointed. The cottage smelled of mildew and Lysol, and the pent-up heat inside stole the breath from his lungs. DeCayne turned on the lights and plugged in the fan, which made a racketing sound as if its blades were about to come loose and fly apart. The bed's mattress had no sheet, and none was offered. Dan checked the bathroom and found two fist-size frogs croaking on the shower tiles. DeCayne scooped them up and tossed them out the back door. Then he presented the key to Dan. "Checkout time's twelve noon. 'Course, we're not expectin' a rush, so you can take your time."

"I'll be leavin' early anyway."

"Okay." He'd already put the pillowcase on the pillow and directed the fan's sullen breeze toward the bed. "You need anythin' else?"

"Not that I can think of." Dan didn't plan to sleep here; he was going to bide his time for a few hours and then call Susan from the gas station's pay phone. He walked outside with DeCayne and got his duffel bag from the truck.

"Hannah's right about watchin' where you step," the man said. "They can make an awful mess. And if you find any more in the cottage, just pitch 'em out back." DeCayne looked toward his own house, which stood fifty yards or so away, the lights just visible through the woods. "Well, I'd better get on back. You married, Mr. Farrow?"

"Used to be."

"I knew you were a free man. Got the look of freedom about you. I swear, sometimes I'd give anythin' to be free."

"All it takes is a judge."

DeCayne grunted. "And let her steal me blind? Oh, she laughs at me and calls me a fool, but someday I'll show her. Yessir. I'll fix up the fairyland the way it oughta be and the tourists'll come from miles around. You know, I bought all that stuff for a song."

"What stuff?"

"In the fairyland. The statues and stuff. It's all in there: Cinderella's castle, Hansel and Gretel, the whale that swallowed Jonah. All they need is patchin' and paint, they'll be like new."

Dan nodded. It was obvious the man had constructed some kind of half-baked tourist attraction along that weeded-up pathway, and obvious too that the tourists had failed to arrive.

"One of these days I'll show her who's a fool and who's smart," DeCayne muttered, mostly to himself. He sighed resignedly. "Well, hope you have a good night's sleep." He began walking back to his house, frogs jumping around his shoes.

Dan carried his duffel bag into the cottage. In the bathroom he found a sliver of soap on the sink, and he removed his baseball cap and damp shirt and washed his face and hands with cool water. He was careful to get rid of the last traces of blood between his fingers and under his nails. Then he took a wet piece of toilet paper outside and cleaned the pickup's steering wheel. When he returned to the cottage, he discovered in the bedside table's drawer a six-month-old

Newsweek magazine with Saddam Hussein's face on the cover. Beneath the magazine was the more useful discovery of a deck of cards. He sat down on the bed, leaning back against the plastic headboard, and he took off his wristwatch and laid it beside him. It was twelve minutes after nine; he'd decided that he'd go make the call at eleven o'clock.

He dealt himself a hand of solitaire, the first of many, and he tried with little success to get Blanchard's dying face out of his mind. In a couple of hours he might either see Chad or be in the back of a police car heading for jail. Was it worth the risk? He thought it was. For now, though, all he could do was wait and play out the cards before him. The wristwatch's second hand was moving, and the future would not be denied.

6

Meet the Pelvis

As Dan had been driving away from Reverend Gwinn's house, a black 1978 Cadillac Eldorado with a broken right headlight and a crumpled passenger door turned into the parking lot of the Old Plantation Motel near Shreveport's regional airport.

In the sultry twilight gloom, the place looked as if Sherman had already passed through. Flint Murtaugh guided his car past a rusted cannon that defiantly faced the north. A tattered Confederate flag drooped on its warped pole. The motel's office was constructed to resemble a miniature plantation manor, but the rest of the place was definitely meant for the slaves. Trash floated on the brown surface of the swimming pool's water, and two men sat sharing a bottle beside an old Lincoln up on cinder blocks. Flint stopped his car before the door marked twenty-three and got out. Beneath Flint's shirt, Clint twitched in an uneasy sleep. Flint heard a man's and woman's voices tangled in argument through an open door, cursing each other purple. Beer cans and garbage littered the parched grass. Flint thought that the South wasn't what it used to be.

He knocked on the door of number twenty-three. A dog began barking from within, a high-pitched *yap yap yap yap*.

"It's all right, Mama," he heard a man say.

That voice. Familiar, wasn't it?

A latch clicked. The door opened a few inches before the chain stopped it.

Flint was looking at a slice of pudgy face and a sapphire-blue eye. An oily comma of dark brown hair hung down over the man's forehead. "Yes sir?" that deep, slightly raspy, oh-so-familiar voice asked as the dog continued to yap in the background.

"I'm Flint Murtaugh. Smoates sent me."

"Oh, yessir! Come on in!" The man took the chain off, opened the door wider, and Flint caught his breath with a startled gasp.

Standing before him, wearing a pair of black pants and a red shirt

548

with a wide, tall collar and silver spangles on the shoulders, was a man who had died fourteen years before.

"Don't mind Mama," Elvis Presley said with a nervous grin. "She's got a bark, but she don't have no bite."

"You're . . ." No, of course it wasn't! "Who the hell are you?"

"Pelvis Eisley's the name." He offered a fleshy hand, the fingers of which were laden with gaudy fake diamond rings. Flint just looked at it, and the other man withdrew it after a few seconds as if fearful he'd caused offense. "Mama, get on back now! Give him some room! Come on in, pardon the mess!"

Flint crossed the threshold as if in a daze. Pelvis Eisley—the big-bellied, fat-jowled twin of Elvis Presley as he'd been the year of his death at Graceland—closed the door, relocked it, and scooped up a grocery sack from the nearest chair. It was filled, Flint saw, with potato chip bags, boxes of doughnuts, and other junk food. "There you go, Mr. Murtaugh, you can set yourself right here."

"This is a joke, isn't it?" Flint asked.

"Sir?"

A spring jabbed his butt, and only then did Flint realize he'd sat down in the chair. "This has got to be a—" Before he could finish, a little barking thing covered with brown-and-white splotches leapt onto his lap, its wet pug nose mashed flat and its eyes bulbous. It began yapping in his face.

"Mama!" Pelvis scolded. "You mind your manners!" He lifted the bulldog off Flint and put her down, but the animal was instantly up on Flint's lap again.

"I reckon she likes you," Pelvis said, smiling an Elvis sneer.

"I . . . hate . . . dogs," Flint replied in his chill whisper. "Get it off me. *Now.*"

"Lordy, Mama!" Pelvis picked the dog up and held her against his jiggling belly while the animal continued to bark and struggle. "Don't ever'body in this world enjoy your shenanigans, you hear? Hold still!" The dog's thrashings made Flint think of a Slinky. Its watery eyes remained fixed on him as he used his handkerchief to brush the dog hairs from the knees of his pants.

"You want somethin' to drink, Mr. Murtaugh? How 'bout some buttermilk?"

"*No.*" The very smell of buttermilk made him deathly ill.

"Got some pickled pig's feet, if you want a bite to—"

"Eisley," Flint interrupted, "how much did that bastard pay you?"

"Sir?"

"Smoates. How much did he pay you to pull this joke on me?"

Pelvis frowned. He and the struggling dog wore the same expression. "I don't believe I know what you mean, sir."

"Okay, it was a good joke! See, I'm laughin'!" Flint stood up, his face grim. He glanced around the cramped little room and saw that Eisley's living habits were the equivalent of buttermilk and pickled pig's feet. On one wall a large poster of Elvis Presley had been thumb-tacked up; it was the dangerous, cat-sneer face of the young Elvis before Las Vegas stole the Memphis from his soul. On a table was a beggar's banquet of cheap plaster Elvis statues and busts; a cardboard replica of Graceland; a framed photograph of Elvis standing with his gloomy, hollow-eyed mother, and a dozen other Elvis knickknacks and geegaws that Flint found utterly repugnant. Another wall held a black velvet portrait of Elvis and Jesus playing guitars on the steps of what was presumably heaven. Flint felt nauseated. "How can you stand to live in all this crap?"

Pelvis looked stunned for a few seconds. Then his grin flooded back. "Oh, now you're joshin' me!" The dog got away from him and slipped to the floor, then leapt up onto the bed amid empty Oreo and Chips Ahoy cookie bags and started yapping again.

"Listen, I've got a job to do, so I'll just say fare thee well and get out." Flint started for the door.

"Mr. Smoates said you and me was gonna be partners," Pelvis said with a hurt whine. "Said you was gonna teach me ever'thin' you knew."

Flint stopped with his hand on the latch.

"Said you and me was gonna track a skin together," Pelvis went on. "Hush, Mama!"

Flint wheeled around, his face bleached to the shade of the white streak in his hair. "You mean . . . you're tellin' me . . . this is *not* a joke?"

"No sir. I mean, yes sir. Mr. Smoates called. Fella come from the office to get me, 'cause that's where the phone is. Mr. Smoates said you was on your way, and we was gonna track a skin together. Uh . . . is that the same as bein' a bounty hunter?" Pelvis took the other man's shocked silence as agreement. "See, that's what I wanna be. I took a detective course by mail from one of them magazines. I was livin' in Vicksburg then. Fella who runs a detective agency in Vicksburg said he didn't have a job for me, but he told me all about Mr. Smoates. Like how Mr. Smoates was always on the lookout for—let's see, how'd he put it?—special talent, I think he said. Anyhow, I come from Vicksburg to see Mr. Smoates and we had us a talk this afternoon. He said for me to hang 'round town a few days, maybe he'd give me a tryout. So I guess this is what this is, huh?"

"You've got to be insane," Flint rasped.

Pelvis kept grinning. "Been called worse, I reckon."

Flint shook his head. The walls seemed to be closing in on him, and on all sides there was an Elvis. The dog was yapping, the noise splitting his skull. The awful stench of buttermilk wafted in the air. Something close to panic grabbed Flint around the throat. He whirled toward the door, wrenched the latch back, and leapt out of the foul, Elvisized room. As he ran along the breezeway toward the office with Clint twitching under his shirt, he heard the nightmare calling behind him: "Mr. Murtaugh, sir? You all right?"

In the office, where a Confederate flag was nailed to the wall next to an oil portrait of Robert E. Lee, Flint all but attacked the pay phone. "Hey, careful there!" the manager warned. He wore blue jeans, a Monster Truck T-shirt, and a Rebel cap. "That's motel property!"

Flint shoved a quarter into the slot and punched Smoates's home number. After four rings Smoates answered: "Yeah?"

"I'm not goin' out with that big shit sack!" Flint sputtered. "No way in Hell!"

"Ha," Smoates said.

"You tryin' to be funny, or what?"

"Take it easy, Flint. What's eatin' you?"

"You know what, damn it! That Eisley! Hell, he thinks he's *Elvis!* I'm a professional! I'm not goin' on the road with somebody who belongs in an asylum!"

"Eisley's sane as you or me. He's one of them Elvis impersonators." Smoates let out a laugh that so inflamed Flint, he almost jerked the phone off the wall. "Looks just like him, don't he?"

"Yeah, he looks like a big shit sack!"

"Hey!" Smoates's voice had taken on a chill. "I was a fan of Elvis's. Drilled my first piece of pussy with 'Jailhouse Rock' playin' on the radio, so watch your mouth!"

"I can't believe you'd even *think* about hirin' him on! He's as green as grass! Did you know he took a detective course by *mail?*"

"Uh-huh. That puts him ahead of where *you* were when I hired you. And as I recall, you were pretty green yourself. Billy Lee raised hell about havin' to take you out your first time."

"Maybe so, but I didn't look like a damn fool!"

"Flint," Smoates said, "I like the way he looks. That's why I want to give him a chance."

"Are you crazy, or am I?"

"I hire people I think can get the job done. I hired you 'cause I figured you were the kind of man who could get on a skin's track and not let loose no matter what. I figured a man with three arms was gonna have to be tough, and he was gonna have somethin' to prove, too. And I was right about that, wasn't I? Well, I've got the same feelin' about Eisley. A man who walks and talks and looks like Elvis Presley's gotta have a lot of guts, and he's already been down a damn hard road. So you ain't the one to be sittin' in judgment of him and what he can or can't do. Hear?"

"I can't stand bein' around him! He makes me so nervous I can't think straight!"

"Is that so? Well, that's just what Billy Lee said about you, as I remember. Now, cut out the bellyachin' and you and Eisley get on your way. Call me when you get to Alexandria."

Flint opened his mouth to protest again, but he realized he would be speaking to a deaf ear because Smoates had already hung up. *"Shit!"* Flint seethed as he slammed the receiver back onto its hook.

"Watch your language there!" the manager said. "I run a refined place!" Flint shot him a glance that might've felled the walls of Fort Sumter, and wisely the manager spoke no more.

At Number Twenty-three Flint had to wait for Eisley to unlock the door again. The heat hung on him like a heavy cloak, anger churning in his constricted belly. He understood the discomfort of pregnancy, only he had carried this particular child every day of his thirty-three years. Inside the room, the little bulldog barked around Flint's shoes but was smart enough not to get in range of a kick. "You okay, Mr. Murtaugh?" Eisley asked, and the dumb innocence of his Elvis-voice was the match that ignited Flint's powder keg.

He grasped Eisley's collar with both hands and slammed his bulk up against the Elvis poster. "Ouch," Pelvis said, showing a scared grin. "That kinda smarted."

"I dislike you," Flint said icily. "I dislike you, your hair, your clothes, your dead fat hillbilly, and your damn ugly dog." He heard the mutt growling and felt it plucking at his trouser leg, but his anger was focused on Eisley. "I believe I've never met anybody I dislike worse. And Clint doesn't care for you worth a shit, either." He let go of Pelvis's collar to unhook a button. "Clint! Out!" His brother's hand and arm slid free like a slim white serpent. The fingers found Pelvis's face and began to explore his features. Pelvis made a noise like a squashed frog. "You know what you are to me?" Flint asked. "Dirt. If you get under my feet, I'll step on you. Got it?"

"Lordy, lordy, lordy." Pelvis stared transfixed at Clint's roving hand.

"You have a car?"

"Sir?"

"A *car!* Do you have one?"

"Yes sir. I mean, I did. Ol' Priscilla broke down on me when I was comin' back from seeing Mr. Smoates. Had to get her towed to the shop." His eyes followed the searching fingers. "Is that . . . like . . . a magic trick or somethin'?"

Flint had hoped that if he had to take this fool with him, Eisley would at least be confined to his own car. Then, without warning, Eisley did the unthinkable thing.

"Mr. Murtaugh," he said, "that's the damnedest best trick I ever saw!" And he reached out, took Clint's hand in his own, and shook it. "Howdy there, pardner!"

Flint almost passed out from shock. He couldn't remember anyone ever touching Clint. The sensation of a stranger's hand clasped to Clint's was like a buzz saw raked up his spine.

"I swear you could go on television with a trick as good as that!" Eisley continued to pump Clint's arm, oblivious to the danger that coiled before him.

Flint gasped for breath and staggered backward, breaking contact between Eisley and his brother. Clint's arm kept bobbing up and down, the little hand still cupped. "You . . . you . . ." Words could not convey Flint's indignation. Mama had seen this new development and had skittered away from Flint's legs, bouncing up onto the bed where she rapid-fired barks at the bobbing appendage. "You . . . don't touch me!" Flint said. "Don't you ever dare touch me again!" Eisley was still grinning. This man, Flint realized, had the power to drive him stark raving insane. "Get packed," he said, his voice choked. "We're leavin' in five minutes. And that mutt's stayin' here."

"Oh . . . Mr. Murtaugh, sir." At last Eisley's face showed genuine concern. "Mama and me go everywhere together."

"Not in my car." He shoved Clint's arm back down inside his shirt, but Clint came out again and kept searching around as if he wanted to continue the hand shaking. "I'm not carryin' a damn mutt in my car!"

"Well, I can't go, then." Pelvis sat down on the bed, his expression petulant, and at once Mama was in his lap, licking his double chins. "I don't go nowhere without Mama."

"Okay, good! Forget it! I'm leavin'!"

553

Flint had his hand on the doorknob when Pelvis asked, in all innocence, "You want me to call Mr. Smoates and tell him it didn't work out?"

Flint stopped. He squeezed his eyes shut for a few seconds. The rage had leapt up again from where it lived and festered, and it was beating like a dark fist behind the door of his face.

"I'll call him," Pelvis said. "Ain't no use you wastin' the quarter."

Leave the hillbilly jerk, Flint thought. To hell with Smoates, too. I don't need him or his lousy job. I don't need *anybody*.

But his anger began to recede like a bayou tide, and beneath it was the twisted, busted-up truth: he could not go back to the sideshow, and without Smoates, what would he do?

Flint turned toward Pelvis. Mama sat in Pelvis's lap, warily watching Flint. "Do you even know what this job is *about*?" Flint asked. "Do you have any idea?"

"You mean bounty huntin'? Yes sir. It's like on TV, where—"

"*Wrong!*" Flint had come close to shouting it, and Mama stiffened her back and began a low growling. Pelvis stroked her a couple of times and she settled down again. "It's not like on TV. It's dirty and dangerous, and you're out there on your own with nobody to help you if things screw up. You can't ask the cops for help, 'cause to them you're trash. You have to walk—or crawl—through hellholes you couldn't even imagine. Most of the time all you're gonna do is spend hours sittin' in a car, waitin'. You're gonna be tryin' to get information from the kind of slimeballs who'd just as soon be cuttin' your throat to see your blood run."

"Oh, I can take care of myself," Pelvis asserted. "I ain't got a gun, but I know how to use one. That was chapter four in the manual."

"Chapter four in the manual." Flint's voice dripped sarcasm. "Uh-huh. Well, bein' a gunslinger in this business'll either get you killed or behind bars. You can't use firepower on anybody unless it's in self-defense and you've got witnesses, otherwise it's you who's goin' to prison. And let me tell you, a bounty hunter in prison would be like a T-bone steak in a dog pound."

"You mean if the fella's runnin' away from you, you can't shoot him?"

"Right. You nail somebody in the back and he dies, it's your neck in the noose. So you have to use your wits and be a good poker player."

"Sir?"

"You've got to know how to stack the deck in your favor," Flint explained. "I've got my own tricks. At close range I use a can of Mace. Know what that is?"

"Yes sir. It's that spray stuff that burns your skin."

"The kind I use can blind a man for about thirty seconds. By that time you ought to have the cuffs on him and he's on the ground, docile as a little lamb."

"Well, I'll be!" Pelvis said. "Mr. Smoates told me you were gonna be a mighty good teacher."

Flint had to endure another wave of anger; he lowered his head and waited it out. "Eisley," he said, "you know what a loan shark is?"

"Yes sir, I do."

"That's what Smoates is. He owns five or six loan companies in Louisiana and Arkansas and ninety percent of the work he'll expect you to do is collectin' money. And that's not pretty work either, I promise you, 'cause you have to shut your eyes to people's misfortunes and either scare the cash out of them or get rough, if it comes to that. The bounty-huntin' thing is just kind of a sideline. You can make some good money out of it if the reward's high enough, but it's no game. Every time you go out after a skin, you're riskin' your life. I've been shot at, swung on with knives and billy clubs, I've had a Doberman set on me, and one skin even tried to take my head off with a samurai sword. You don't get a lot of second chances in this business, Eisley. And I don't care how many mail-order detective courses you took; if you're not cold-blooded enough, you'll never survive your first skin hunt." Flint watched the other man's eyes to see if his message was getting through, but all he saw was dumb admiration. "You know anythin' about the skin we're supposed to collect?"

"No sir."

"His name's Lambert. He's a Vietnam veteran. Killed a man at a bank this afternoon. He's probably half crazy and armed to the teeth. I wouldn't care to meet him if there wasn't a chance of some big money in it. And if I were you, I'd just go call Smoates and tell him you've thought this thing over and you've decided to pass."

Pelvis nodded. From the glint in Pelvis's eye, Flint could tell that a spark had fired in the man's brain like a bolt of lightning over Lonely Street.

"Is that what you're gonna do, then?"

"Well, I just figured it out," Pelvis said. "That ain't no trick, is it? You really *do* have three arms, don't you?"

The better to strangle you with, Flint thought. "That's right."

"I never saw such a thing before! I swear, I thought it was a trick at first, but then I got to lookin' at it and I could tell it was real! What does your wife have to say about it?"

"I've never been married." Why did I tell him that? Flint asked himself. There was no reason for me to tell him about myself! "Listen to me, Eisley. You don't want to go with me after this skin. Believe me, you don't."

"Yes sir, I do," Pelvis answered firmly. "I want to learn everythin' I can. Mr. Smoates said you was the best bounty hunter there is, and I was to listen to you like you was God hisself. You say jump, I'll ask how high. And don't you worry about Mama, she don't have accidents in the car. When she wants to pee or dookie, she lets out a howl." He shook his head, awestruck. "Three arms. Now I've seen it all. Ain't we, Mama? Ain't we seen it all now?"

Flint drew a long breath and let it out. Time was wasting. "Get up," he said, and those were two of the hardest words he'd ever uttered. "Pack enough for two nights."

"Yes sir, yes sir!" Pelvis fairly jumped up from the bed. He started throwing clothes into a brown suitcase covered with Graceland, Memphis, and Las Vegas stickers. Mama had sensed Pelvis's excitement, and she began running in circles around the room. For the first time, Flint saw that Pelvis was wearing a pair of honest-to-God blue suede shoes that were run down at the heels.

"I can't believe I'm doin' this," he muttered. "I must be out of my mind."

"Don't you worry, I'll do whatever you say," Pelvis promised. Underwear, socks, and gaudy shirts were flying into the suitcase. "I'll be so quiet, you'll hardly know I'm there!"

"I'll bet."

"Whatever you say, that's my command. Uh . . . you mind if I load up some groceries? I get kinda hungry when I travel."

"Just do it in a hurry."

Pelvis stuffed another grocery sack with glazed doughnuts, peanut butter crackers, Oreos, and dog biscuits. He smiled broadly, his idol sneering at Flint over his shoulder. "We're ready!"

"One very, very important rule." Flint stepped toward Pelvis and stared at him face-to-face. "You're not to touch me. Understand? And if that dog touches me, I'm throwin' it out the window. Hear?"

"Yes sir, loud and clear." Pelvis's breath made Flint wince; it smelled of buttermilk.

Flint turned away, pushed Clint's arm under his shirt, and stalked out of the wretched room. Pelvis hefted the suitcase and the groceries, and with a stubby, wagging tail, Mama followed her king.

7

Big Ol' Frog

Dan pushed a quarter into the pay phone's slot outside an Amoco gas station on Highway 28, less than seven miles west of Alexandria. It was twenty minutes after eleven, and the gas station was closed. He pressed the *O* and told the operator his name was Daniel Lewis and he wanted to make a collect call to Susan Lambert at 1219 Jackson Avenue in Alexandria.

He waited while the number clicked through. Pain thrummed in his skull, and when he licked his lips his tongue scraped like sandpaper. One ring. Two. Three. Four.

They're not home, he thought. *They're gone, because Susan knew I'd want to see—*

Five rings. Six.

"Hello?" Her voice was as tight as barbed wire.

"I have a collect call for Susan Lambert from Daniel Lewis," the operator said. "Will you accept the charges?"

Silence.

"Ma'am?" the operator urged.

The silence stretched. Dan heard his heartbeat pounding. Then: "Yes, I'll accept the charges."

"Thank you," Dan said when the operator had hung up.

"The police are here. They're waitin' to see if you'll show."

"I knew they would be. Are they listenin' in?"

"Not from in here. They asked me if I thought you'd call and I said no, we hadn't talked for years. It *has* been years, you know."

"I know." He paused, listening for clicks on the line. He heard none, and he'd have to take the risk that the police had not gone through the process of tapping the wires. "How's Chad?"

"How would you think he is, to find out his father's shot a man dead?"

That one hurt. Dan said, "I don't know what you've heard, but would you like to hear my side of it?"

557

Again she was silent. Susan had always had a way of making silence feel like a chunk of granite pressed down on your skull. At least she hadn't hung up yet. "The bank fired Mr. Jarrett, their loan manager," he began. "They hired a new man, and he was gonna repossess my truck. He said some bad things to me, Susan. I know that's no excuse, but—"

"You're right about that," she interrupted.

"I just went crazy for a minute. I started tearin' his office up. All I could think of was that without my truck I was one more step down the hole. A guard came in and he pulled a gun on me. I got it away from him, and then all of a sudden Blanchard had a pistol too and I knew he was gonna shoot me. I swear I didn't mean to kill him. Everythin' was happenin' so fast, it was like fallin' off a train. No matter what the TV or radio says, I didn't go to that bank lookin' to kill somebody. Do you believe me?"

No answer.

"We've had our troubles," Dan said. His knuckles were aching, he was gripping the receiver so tightly. "I know . . . you got afraid of me, and I can't blame you. I should've gotten help a long time ago, but I was afraid to. I didn't know what was wrong with me, I thought I was losin' my mind. I had a lot to work through. Maybe you won't believe me, but I never lied to you, did I?"

"No," she replied. "You never lied to me."

"I'm not lyin' now. When I saw the gun in Blanchard's hand, I didn't have time to think. It was either him or me. After it was done, I ran because I knew I'd killed him. I swear to God that's how it happened."

"Oh, Jesus," Susan said in a pained voice. "Where are you?"

Here was the question Dan had known she would ask. Did he trust her that the police were not listening? Wouldn't she have had to sign forms or something to permit them to run a tap? They were no longer man and wife and had a troubled history, so why would the police assume she wouldn't tell them if he called? "Are you going to tell them?" he asked.

"They said if I heard from you, I was to let them know."

"Are you?"

"They told me you'd be armed and dangerous. They said you might be out of your mind, and you'd probably want money from me."

"That's a crock of bullshit. I'm not carryin' a gun, and I didn't call you for money."

"Why *did* you call me, Dan?"

"I . . . I'd like to see Chad."

558

"No," she said at once. "Absolutely not."

"I know you don't care much for me. I don't blame you. But please believe me, Susan. I don't want to hurt anybody. I'm not dangerous. I made a mistake. Hell, I've made a *lot* of mistakes."

"You can fix this one," she said. "You can give yourself up and plead self-defense."

"Who's gonna listen to *me*? Hell, that guard's gonna say I had the gun stashed in my clothes. The bank'll stand behind him, 'cause they sure won't admit a sick old vet could get a pistol away from—"

"Sick? What do you mean, sick?"

He hadn't wanted this thing to come up, because he needed no sympathy. "I've got leukemia," he said. "From the Agent Orange, I think. The doctors say I can last maybe two years. Three at the most."

Susan didn't respond, but he could hear her breathing.

"If the police take me, I'll die in prison," he went on. "I can't spend the last two years of my life witherin' away behind bars. I just can't."

"You . . . you damn *fool!*" she suddenly exploded. "My God! Why didn't you let me know?"

"It's not your concern."

"I could've given you some money! We could've worked somethin' out if you were in trouble! Why'd you keep sendin' the money for Chad every month?"

"Because he's my son. Because I owe you. Because I owe *him*."

"You were always too stubborn to ask for help! That was always your problem! Why in the name of God couldn't you"—her voice cracked, a sound of emotion that astonished Dan—"couldn't you break down just a little bit and call me?"

"I'm callin' you now," Dan said. "Is it too late?"

She was silent. Dan waited. Only when he heard her sniffle and clear her throat did he realize she was weeping.

"I'll put Chad on," she said.

"Please," he said before she could leave, "can't I see him? Just for five minutes? Before I called I thought it'd be enough to hear his voice, but I need to see him, Susan. Isn't there some way?"

"No. The police told me they're gonna watch the house all night."

"Are they out front? Could I slip in the back?"

"I don't know where they are or how many. All I've got is a phone number they gave me. I figure it's to a mobile phone, and they're sittin' in a car somewhere on the street."

"The thing is," Dan said, "I'd like to see both of you. After tonight I'm hittin' the road. Maybe I can get out of the country if I'm lucky."

"Your name and picture's all over the news. How long do you think it'll be before somebody recognizes you and the law either tracks you down or *shoots* you down? You do know about the reward, don't you?"

"What reward?"

"The president of that bank's put fifteen thousand dollars on your head."

Dan couldn't hold back an edgy laugh. "Hell, all I was askin' for was a week's extension. Now they're ready to spend fifteen thousand dollars on me? No wonder the economy's so screwed up."

"You think this is funny?" Susan snapped, and again her voice was thick with emotion. "It's not a damn bit funny! Your son's gonna always know his father was a killer! You think that's funny, too?"

"No, I don't. But that's why I want to see him. I want to explain things. I want to see his face, and I want him to see mine."

"There's no way, unless you want to give yourself up first."

"Listen . . . maybe there is," he said, his shoulder pressed against a wall of rough bricks. "If you're willin', I mean. It depends on you."

A few seconds passed in which Susan made no response.

"You want to hear the idea?" he urged.

"I can't make any promises."

"Just hear me out. When I hang up, dial that number and tell 'em I called."

"*What?*"

"Tell 'em they were right. I've got two or three guns and I sound like I'm out of my head. Tell 'em I said I was comin' over to see you as soon as I could get there. Then tell 'em you're afraid to stay in the house and you want to spend the night at a motel."

"That won't work. They'll know I'm lyin'."

"Why will they? They're not watchin' you, they're watchin' the house. They already believe I'm carryin' a load of guns and I'm ravin' mad, so they'll want you to get out. They'll probably clear the whole block."

"They'd follow me, Dan. No, it wouldn't work."

"It's worth a try. They might send a man to follow you to the motel and make sure you get checked in, but likely as not he won't stay around very long. The only thing is, you've got to make 'em believe you're scared to death of me."

"That used to be true," she said.

"You're not still scared of me, are you?"

"No, not anymore."

"All I'm askin' for is five minutes," Dan said. "Then I'm gone."

She paused, and Dan knew he'd said all he could. At last she sighed heavily. "I'll need some time to get a suitcase packed. You want me to call you when we get settled?"

"No, I shouldn't stay where I am and I don't have a phone in my room. Can we meet somewhere?"

"All right. How about Basile Park? At the amphitheater?"

Basile Park was about three miles from the house. "That'll do. What time?"

"An hour or so, I guess. But listen: if a policeman comes with me, or they won't let me take my own car, I won't be there. They might follow me without me knowin'. Are you willin' to chance it?"

"I am."

"All right. I'm crazy for doin' it, but all right. I'll try to make it, but if I'm not there—"

"I'll wait as long as I can," Dan said. "Thank you, Susan. You don't know how much this means to me."

"I'll try," she repeated, and then she hung up.

He returned the receiver to its cradle. His spirit felt lightened. He and Susan had gone to several outdoor concerts at Basile Park, and he knew the amphitheater there. He checked his watch to give himself an hour, then he got back into the pickup truck and drove toward the Hideaway. He thought about the fifteen thousand dollars, and he wished he'd seen that much money in a year's time. They wanted him caught fast, that was for sure.

Before he reached the turnoff to the motor court, it crossed Dan's mind that Susan might be setting him up. The police might have been listening after all, and would be waiting for him at the park. There was no way to know for certain. He and Susan had parted on bitter terms, yes, but there *had* been some good times, hadn't there? A few good memories to hold on to? He remembered some, and he hoped she did. He was Chad's father, and that was a link to Susan that could never be broken. He would have to take the risk that she wasn't planning on turning him in. If she was . . . well, he'd cross that bridge when he came to it.

He drove past the DeCaynes' house on the way to his cottage, and he was unaware that the sound of his engine awakened Hannah from a troubled sleep.

She wasn't sure what had wakened her. Harmon was snoring in the other bed, his mouth a cavern. Hannah got up from under the sweat-damp sheet, her red hair—the texture of a Brillo pad—

confined by a shower cap. She recalled bits and pieces of a nightmare she'd had; the monster in it had been a warty frog with skinny human legs. Wearing only a bra and panties that barely held her jiggling mounds in check, she padded into the kitchen, opened the refrigerator's freezer, and got an ice cube to rub over her face. The kitchen still smelled of blood and frog guts, and in the freezer were dozens of froglegs wrapped in butcher's paper for delivery to the restaurant. While she was at it, Hannah opened the carton of vanilla ice cream that was in the freezer as well, and she got a spoon and took the carton with her to the front room to gorge herself until she was sleepy again. She switched on the radio, which was tuned to the local country music station. Garth Brooks was singing about Texas girls. Hannah walked to a window and pushed aside the curtain.

The lights were on in Number Four. Something about that man she didn't like, she'd decided. Of course, she didn't like too many people to begin with, but that man in Number Four gave her a creepy feeling. He looked sick, for one thing. Skinny and pale, like he might have AIDS or something. She didn't like his tattoo, either. Her first husband had been in the merchant marine, was illustrated from wrists to shoulders, and she couldn't abide anything that reminded her of that shiftless sonofabitch.

Well, he'd be gone soon enough. They'd be seven dollars richer, and every cent helped. Hannah plopped down on the sofa, her spoon strip-mining the ice cream. Reba McEntire serenaded her, and Hannah saw the bottom of the carton. The news came on, the newscaster talking about a fire last night in Pineville. The Alexandria town council was meeting to discuss pollution in the Red River. An Anandale woman had been arrested for abandoning her baby in the bus station's bathroom. A mentally disturbed Vietnam veteran had shot to death an official at a bank in Shreveport, and—

". . . fifteen thousand dollars reward has been offered . . ."

Hannah's spoon paused in its digging.

". . . by the First Commercial Bank for the capture of Daniel Lewis Lambert. Police consider Lambert armed and extremely dangerous. Lambert was last seen driving a gray 1989 Chevrolet pickup truck. He is forty-two years old, six-feet-one with a slim build; he wears a beard and . . ."

Hannah had a mouthful of ice cream. She stared at the radio, her eyes widening.

". . . has the tattoo of a snake on his right forearm. Police advise extreme caution if Lambert is sighted. The number to call is . . ."

She couldn't swallow. Her throat had seized up. As she bolted to her feet, she spat the contents of her mouth onto the floor and a cry spiraled out: *"Harrrrrrmon!* Harmon, get up *this minute!"*

Harmon wasn't fast enough for her. He found himself being grabbed by both ankles and hauled out of bed. "You crazy?" he yelped. "Whatzamatter?"

"He's a killer!" Hannah's hair, which had a life of its own, had burst free from the shower cap. Her eyes were wild, her mouth rimmed with ice cream foam. "I knew somethin' was wrong with him I knew it when I seen him he killed a man in Shreveport got that tattoo on his arm fifteen thousand dollars reward hear me?"

"Huh?" Harmon said.

Hannah grasped him by the collar of his red-checked pajamas. "Fifteen thousand dollars!" she shrieked into his face. "By God, we're gonna get us that money! Now, stand up and put your clothes on!"

As Harmon pulled on his pants and Hannah struggled into her shapeless shift, she managed to drill the story through his thick skull. Harmon's face blanched, his fingers working his shirt buttons into the wrong holes. He started for the telephone. "I'll go call the law right n—"

A viselike hand clamped to his shoulder. "You listen to *me!"* she thundered. "You want to throw that money out the window? You think the cops won't cheat us outta every damn penny, you're dumber than a post! We're gonna catch him and take him in *ourselves!"*

"But . . . Hannah . . . he's a *killer!"*

"He ain't nothin' but a big ol' frog!" she glowered, her hands on her stocky hips. " 'Cept his legs are worth fifteen thousand dollars, and you and me are gonna take him to market! So you just shut up and do what I say! Understand?"

Harmon shut up, his thin shoulders bowed under the redheaded pressure. Hannah left the room, and Harmon heard her rummaging around in the hallway's closet. Harmon got his ring of keys from the bureau and hooked them around a belt loop, his fingers trembling. When he looked up, Hannah was holding the double-barreled shotgun that was their protection against burglars. He said, "That gun's so old, I don't know if it'll even—" She squelched him with a stare that would freeze time. Hannah also held a box of shells; there were five inside, and she loaded the shotgun and then pushed the other three shells into a pocket.

"We gotta get him out in the open," she said. "Get him outside where he can't get to his guns."

"We ought to call the law, Hannah! Jesus, I think I'm 'bout to heave!"

"Do it *later!*" she snarled. "He might be a crazy killer, but I don't know many men who can do much killin' when they've got their legs blowed off! Now, you just do what I say and we'll be rich as Midas!" She snapped the shotgun's breech shut, slid her feet into her rubber flipflops, and stalked toward the front door. "Come on, damn it!" she ordered when she realized Harmon wasn't following, and he came slinking after her as pale as death.

8

Mysterious Ways

In Number Four, Dan checked his watch and saw it was time to go. He'd swallowed two aspirin and laid down for a while, then had put on clean underwear and socks and the pair of blue jeans from his duffel bag. Now he stood before the bathroom's dark-streaked mirror, wetting his comb and slicking his hair back. He put on his baseball cap and studied his face with its deep lines and jutting cheekbones.

Susan wasn't going to recognize him. He was afraid again, the same kind of gnawing fear as when he'd walked into the bank. More than likely, this was the last time he would ever see his son. He hoped he could find the words he needed.

First things first: getting to Basile Park without being stopped by the police. Dan hefted the duffel bag over his shoulder, picked up the cottage's key, and opened the front door into the humid night. The frogs had quieted except for a few low burps. Dan went to hit the wall switch to turn off the ceiling's bulb when he heard a metallic *clink* from the direction of his pickup truck, and he realized with a jolt that someone was standing there at the light's edge, watching him.

Dan whipped his head toward the sound. "Hey, hey!" a man said nervously. It was Harmon DeCayne, sweat sparkling on his cheeks. He lifted his hands to show the palms. "Don't do nothin' rash, now!"

"You scared the hell out of me! What're you doin' here?"

"Nothin'! I mean to say . . . I saw the lights." He kept his hands upraised. "Thought you might need somethin'."

"I'm pullin' out," Dan said, his nerves still jangling. "I was gonna stop at your house and leave the key on the porch."

"Where you headin'? It's awful late to be on the road, don't you think?"

"No, I've got places to go." He advanced on DeCayne, intending

565

to stow his duffel bag in the rear of the truck, and the other man retreated, that clinking noise coming from the key ring that Dan saw was fixed to one of DeCayne's belt loops. Dan abruptly stopped. His radars had gone up. He smelled a snake coiled in its hole. "You all right?"

"Sure I'm all right! Why wouldn't I be all right?"

Dan watched the man's eyes; they were glassy with fear. *He knows*, Dan thought. *Somehow, he knows.* "Here's the key," he said, and he held it out.

"Okay. Sure. That's fi—"

Dan saw DeCayne's eyes dart at something behind him.

The woman, Dan realized. He had the mental image of a meat cleaver coming at him.

He set himself and whirled around, bringing the duffel bag off his shoulder in a swinging blow.

BOOM! went a gun seemingly right in his face. He felt the heat and the shock wave and suddenly the burning rags of the duffel bag were ripped from his hands and the fiery shreds of his clothes were flying out of it like luminous bats. Hannah DeCayne staggered backward holding a shotgun with smoke boiling from the breech. Dan had an instant to register that the duffel bag had absorbed a point-blank blast, and then the woman righted herself and a holler burst from her sweat-shining face. Dan saw the shotgun leveling at his midsection. He jumped away from its dark double eyes a heartbeat before a gout of fire spewed forth and he landed on his belly in the weeds. His ears were ringing, but over that tintinnabulation he heard a wet smack and the *crump* of buckshot hitting metal. He scrambled into the woods that lay alongside the cottage, his mind shocked loose of everything but the need to run like hell.

Behind Dan, Harmon DeCayne was watching his shirt turn red. The impact had lifted him up and slammed him back against the pickup truck, but he was still on his feet. He pressed his hands against his stomach, and the blood ran between his fingers. He stared, blinking rapidly, through the haze of smoke that swirled between him and his wife.

"Now you've done it," he said, and it amazed him that his voice was so calm. He couldn't feel any pain yet; from his stomach to his groin was as cold as January.

Hannah gasped with horror. She hadn't meant to fire the first time; she'd meant to lay the barrels up against the killer's skull, but his bag had hit the gun and her finger had twitched. The second time she'd been aiming to take him down before he could rush her. Harmon kept staring at her as his knees began to buckle. And then the rage overcame Hannah's shock and she bellowed, "I *told* you to get out of the way! Didn't you *hear* what I told you?"

Harmon's knees hit the ground. He swallowed thickly, the taste of blood in his mouth. "Shot me," he rasped. "You . . . damn bitch. Shot me."

"It's not *my* fault! I told you to move! You stupid ass, I told you to move!"

"Ahhhhhh," Harmon groaned as the first real pain tore at his tattered guts. Blood was pooling in the dust below him.

Hannah turned toward the woods, her face made even uglier by its rubber-lipped contortion. "You ain't gettin' away!" she yelled into the dark. She popped the shotgun open and reloaded both barrels. "You think I'm lettin' fifteen thousand dollars get away in my woods, you're crazy! You hear me, Mr. Killer?"

Dan heard her. He was lying on his stomach in the underbrush and stubbly palmettos forty feet from where the woman was standing. He'd seen Harmon fall to his knees, had seen the woman reloading her shotgun. Now he watched as Hannah walked to her husband's side.

She looked down at Harmon's damp, agonized face. "You mess up every damn thing," she said coldly, and then she lifted the shotgun and fired a shell into the pickup's left front tire. The tire exploded with a whoosh of air and the pickup lurched like a poleaxed horse. Dan almost cried out, but he clasped a hand over his mouth to prevent it.

"You ain't goin' nowhere in your truck!" Hannah shouted toward the woods. "You might as well come on out!"

Dan still wore his baseball cap, beads of sweat clinging to his face. All his other clothes were blown to rags, his metallic-mist Chevrolet pickup crippled, his hopes of getting to Basile Park blasted to pieces, too. The red-haired witch held the shotgun at hip level, its barrels aimed in his direction. "Come on out, Mr. Killer!" she yelled. Beside her, Harmon was still on his knees, his hands pressed to the wet mess of his midsection and his head drooping. "All right then!" she said. "I can play hide-and-seek if you want to, and first chance I get I'll blow your damn brains out!" She suddenly began stalking into the woods almost directly toward where Dan was stretched out. Panic skittered through him; there was no way he could fight a loaded shotgun. He bolted up and ran again, deeper into the thicket. His spine crawled in expectation of the blast. "I hear you!" Hannah squalled. He heard the noise of her stocky body smashing through the foliage. "Don't you run, you bastard!"

She was coming like a hell-bound freight train. Low pine

branches whipped into Dan's face as he ran, thorns grabbing at his trousers. Under his feet, frogs grumped and jumped. His right shoe caught a root and he staggered, coming perilously close to falling. The underbrush was dense, and the noise he was making would've brought his Vietnam platoon leader down on his head like a fifty-pound anvil. He had neither the quick legs nor the balance of his youth. All he cared about at the moment was putting distance between himself and a shotgun shell.

And then he smelled oily stagnance and his shoes splashed into water. Mud bogged him down. It was the frog pond.

"You wanna go swimmin'?" Hannah shouted from behind him.

Dan couldn't see how large the pond was, but he knew he didn't dare try to get across it. The woman would shoot him while he was knee-deep in muck. He backed out of the water to firmer earth and set off again through weeds and brush that edged the pond. No longer could he hear the woman following him, and it leapt through his mind that she knew these woods and might be hunkered down somewhere ahead. He pushed through a tangle of vines. Up beyond the canopy of pines and willow trees he caught sight of a few stars, as distant as Basile Park seemed to be. And then he entered a stand of waist-high weeds and he walked right into the arms of the figure that stood in front of him.

In that instant he probably gained a dozen or so new gray hairs. He came close to wetting his pants. But he swung at the figure's head and pain shot through his knuckles when he connected with its jaw. The figure toppled over, and it was then that Dan realized it was a plaster mannequin.

He stood over it, wringing his bruised hand. He could make out two more mannequins nearby as if frozen in hushed conversation, their clothes weatherbeaten rags. Dark shapes lay before him, but he was able to discern what seemed to be a carousel half covered with kudzu. He had stumbled into Harmon DeCayne's fairyland.

He went on, past the rotting façade of a miniature castle. There was a broken-down Conestoga wagon and a couple of rusted car hulks. Bricks were underfoot, and Dan figured this was supposed to have been the main street of an enchanted village. Other manne-quins dressed as cowboys and Indians stood about, the citizens of DeCayne's imagination. Dan moved past a huge tattered fabric shape with rotting wooden ribs that he thought might have been Jonah's whale, and suddenly he was looking at a high mesh fence topped with barbed wire that marked the edge of DeCayne's property.

I can climb the fence, he decided. The barbs'll be tough, but they'll be kinder than that damn shotgun. Once I get over, I can—

Can *what?* he asked himself. Without my truck I'm not gettin' very far.

But there was another set of wheels close by, wasn't there?

The station wagon parked next to the DeCaynes' house.

He remembered the key ring on Harmon's belt loop. Would the station wagon's key be on it? Would the car even run? It had to; how else did they get their froglegs to market? But to get the key ring he would have to double back through the woods and avoid the woman, and that was a tall and dangerous order.

He stood there for a moment, his hands grasping the fence's mesh. Beyond the fence was just more dark woods.

If he had any hope of getting to Basile Park, he would have to go back for the key ring.

Dan let go of the fence. He drew a deep breath and released it. His head was hurting again, but the ringing in his ears had ceased. He turned away from the fence and started back the way he'd come, creeping slowly and carefully, his senses questing for sound or motion.

A one-armed mannequin wearing a crown or tiara of some kind—a deformed fairy princess—stood on his right in the high weeds as he neared Jonah's whale. And suddenly Dan caught a sinuous movement from the corner of his eye, over beside a crumbling structure festooned with kudzu. He was already diving into the weeds as the shotgun boomed, and a split second later the princess's head and neck exploded in a shower of plaster. He lay on his side, breathing hard. "Got you, didn't I?" Hannah shouted. "I know I winged you that time!"

He heard the shotgun snap open and then shut again. The woman was striding toward him, her flipflops making a smacking noise on the bricks. Dan felt what seemed to be a length of pipe next to his shoulder. He reached out and touched cold fingers. It was the princess's missing arm.

He picked it up and rose to his feet. There was Hannah DeCayne, ten feet in front of him, the shotgun aimed just to his left. He flung the plaster arm at her, saw it pinwheel around and slam into her collarbone, and she bellowed with pain and fell on her rump, the shotgun going off into the air. Then Dan tore away through the weeds with the speed of desperation, leaving the woman cursing at his back.

He found the pond again, and ran along its boggy edge. In

another few minutes he pushed out of the underbrush twenty yards away from his lamed pickup truck. Harmon DeCayne was still in the same position, kneeling with his head bowed and his hands clasping his bloody middle.

Dan leaned over the man and grasped the key ring. DeCayne's eyes were closed, his breathing ghastly. Dan pulled the keys loose, and suddenly DeCayne's eyes opened and he lifted his head, blood leaking from the corner of his mouth.

"Hannah?" DeCayne gasped.

"Be still," Dan told him. "Which key starts the station wagon?"

"Don't . . . don't hurt me."

"I'm not gonna hurt you. Which key starts the—"

DeCayne's mouth stretched open. He shrieked in a voice that sliced the night: *"Hannah! He's got the keys!"*

Dan would've slugged him if the man hadn't been gutshot. He stood up as DeCayne continued to sound the alarm. In a couple of minutes the woman would be all over him. Dan ran along the road toward the DeCaynes' house. Harmon's shouting faded, but the damage was done. Reaching the station wagon, Dan opened the door on its groaning hinges and slid behind the wheel. The inside of the car smelled like the frog pond. He tried to jam a key into the ignition, but it refused. The next key balked as well. He saw a blurred movement, and by the house lights made out Hannah DeCayne running toward him on the road, her hair streaming behind her, her sweating face a rictus of rage. She was holding the shotgun like a club, and Dan realized she must be out of shells but she still could knock his brains out of his ears.

The third key would not fit.

"You ain't gettin' away!" she roared. "You ain't gettin' away!"

Dan's fingers were slippery with sweat. He chose not the fourth key, but the fifth.

It slid in.

He turned it and pressed his foot down on the gas pedal.

The station wagon went *ehehehehBOOM* and a gout of black smoke flew from the exhaust. Dan jammed the gearshift into reverse and the car obeyed like a glacier, and then Hannah DeCayne was right there beside him and she jerked his door open and swung at his skull with the shotgun's stock. Dan had seen the blow coming, and he ducked down in the seat as the shotgun slammed against the door frame. Then Hannah was lunging into the car after him even as Dan picked up speed in reverse, and she tried to claw at his eyes with one hand while the other beat at him with the gun. He kicked out at her, caught her right hip, and she staggered back. Then he swerved the car around in a bone-jarring half circle and dust bloomed up between him and the woman. Dan shoved the gearshift into drive, floored the accelerator, and the car rattled forward. One of the side windows suddenly shattered inward from another blow of the shotgun's stock, bits of glass stinging Dan's neck. He looked back, saw Hannah DeCayne running after him as the station wagon picked up speed, and she cursed his mother and tried to grab hold of the open door again. Then he was leaving her behind and he found the headlight switch an instant before he would've smashed into a weeping willow tree. As it was, he jerked the wheel and scraped a dent along the passenger side. He got the door closed, looked in the rearview mirror but could see nothing through the swirling dust. It wouldn't have surprised him, though, if Hannah DeCayne had been hanging on to the exhaust pipe with her teeth.

Then he reached Highway 28 and steered toward Alexandria and Basile Park. The woman had given him a blow on the left shoulder with the shotgun's stock, and though it hurt like hell, it wasn't broken. Better that than a cracked skull. He debated stopping at the Amoco station to call an ambulance, but he figured Hannah would run into the house first thing and do it. The station wagon's tank was a little less than three-quarters full, which was a real blessing. He had his wallet, the clothes on his back, and his baseball cap. He still had his skin on, too. He counted himself lucky.

Hannah had stopped running. There was no use in it, and her lungs were on fire. She watched the station wagon's lights move away. For a long time she stood in the dark, her hands clenching and loosening again on the empty shotgun. She heard his voice—a weak voice now—calling her: "Hannah? Hannah?"

At last she turned her back on the highway and limped— painfully, a bruise blackening on her right hip—to where Harmon was crouched on his knees.

"Hannah," he groaned, "I'm hurt bad."

She'd lost her flipflops. She looked at the bottom of her left foot, which had been cut by a shard of glass. The sight of that wound, with its angry edges, made something start ticking like a bomb in her brain.

"Call somebody," Harmon said. His eyelids were at half mast, his hands clasped together in the gory swamp of his stomach. "You . . . gotta . . ."

"Lost us fifteen thousand dollars." Hannah's voice was hollow and weary. "You mess up every damn thing."

"No . . . I didn't. It was you . . . messed up."

She shook her head. "He read you, Harmon. He knew. I told you

571

to get out of the way, didn't I? And there went fifteen thousand dollars down the road. Oh my God, what I could've done with that mo—" She stopped speaking and stared blankly at the dust, a pulse beating at her temple.

"I'm hurtin'," Harmon said.

"Uh-huh. The thing is, they could prob'ly sew you up at the hospital."

He reached up a bloody hand for her. "Hannah . . . I need help."

"Yes, you do," she answered. "But from now on I think I'm gonna help myself." Her eyes had taken on the glitter of small, hard stones. "Too bad that killer stopped here. Too bad we found out who he was. Too bad he fought the shotgun away from you."

"What?" Harmon whispered.

"I tried to help you, but I couldn't. I ran into the woods and hid, and then I seen what he done to you."

"Have you . . . lost your mind?"

"My mama always told me the Lord moves in mysterious ways," Hannah said. "I never believed her till this very minute."

Harmon watched his wife lift the shotgun over her head like a club.

He made a soft, mewling noise.

The shotgun's stock swung down with all the woman's bitter fury behind it. There was a noise like an overripe melon being crushed. The shotgun rose up again. Sometime during the next half-dozen blows, the stock splintered and broke away. When it was done, Hannah DeCayne was bathed in sweat and gasping, and she had bitten into her lower lip. She looked down at the ruins and wondered what she had ever seen there. She wiped the shotgun's barrel off with the hem of her shift, dropped it on the ground beside the crumpled form, and then she limped into the house to make the call.

9

Time the Thief

The rust-splotched station wagon crept through the streets of Alexandria, past the dark and quiet houses, past the teardrop-shaped streetlamps, past sprinklers hissing on the parched brown lawns.

Dan drove slowly, alert for the police. His shoulder was stiffening, his body felt as if he'd been tumbled a few times inside a cement mixer, but he was alive and free and Basile Park was less than a mile away.

He'd seen no police cars and only a few other vehicles out at this late hour. He turned onto a street that led into the manicured park, following it past an area of picnic tables and tennis courts. A sign pointed the way to the amphitheater, beyond the public parking lot. His heart sank; the lot was empty. But maybe she hadn't been able to shake the police. Maybe a lot of things. Or maybe she'd just decided not to show up.

He decided to wait. He stopped the station wagon, cut the lights and the engine, and sat there in the dark, the song of cicadas reaching him from a nearby stand of pines.

What had happened to his pickup truck still speared him. This whole nightmare was accountable to the truck, and it had taken that red-haired witch two seconds to destroy its usefulness. Damn, but he was going to miss it. A real workingman's truck, he recalled the salesman saying. Easy payments, good warranty, made in America.

Dan wondered what Blanchard's wife and children were feeling like about now, and he let the thoughts of his pickup truck go.

Time ticked past. After thirty minutes Dan decided to give her fifteen more. When the fifteen was gone, he stopped looking at his watch.

She wasn't coming.

Five more minutes. Five more, and then he'd accept it and leave.

573

He leaned back and closed his eyes, listening to the night sounds.

It took only a few heartbeats, only a few breaths, and he was back in the village again.

The name of the village was Cho Yat. It was in the lowlands, where rice paddies steamed under the August sun and the jungle hid sniper nests and snake holes. The platoon had stopped at Cho Yat while Captain Aubrey and the South Vietnamese translator hunkered down in the shade to ask the village elders about Cong activity in the sector. The elders answered reluctantly, and in riddles. It was not their war. As the other Snake Handlers waited, eight or nine children gathered around for a closer look at the foreign giants. A new man—green as grass, just in a few days before—sitting next to Dan opened his knapsack and gave one little boy a chocolate bar. "Hershey," the man said. He was from Boston, and he had a clipped Yankee accent. "Can you say that? Her-shey."

"*Hishee*," the child answered.

"Good enough. Why don't you give some of that to your—" But the little boy was already running away, peeling the tinfoil back and jamming the chocolate into his mouth, with other children yelling in pursuit. The Bostonian—his eyes cornflower blue in a young, unlined face, his hair as yellow as the sun—had looked at Dan and shrugged. "I guess they don't go in for sharing around here."

"Nope," Dan had replied. "If I were you, I'd leave it to the captain to do the tradin'. You'll be wanting that in a few hours."

"I'll survive."

"Uh-huh. Well, if I were you, I'd do what I was told and no more. Don't offer, don't volunteer, and don't be givin' away your food."

"It was just a chocolate bar. So what?"

"You'll find out in a minute."

It was actually less than a minute before the green Bostonian was surrounded by shouting children with their hands thrust out. Some of the other villagers came over to see what they might scrounge from the bountiful knapsacks of the foreign giants. The commotion interrupted Captain Aubrey's questioning of the elders, and he came storming at the Bostonian like a monsoon cloud. It was explained to the soldier that he was not to be giving away his food or any other item in his possession, that the elders didn't want gifts because the Cong had been known to slaughter whole villages when they found canned goods, mirrors, or other trinkets. All this had been said with Captain Aubrey's face about two inches from the Bostonian's, and by the time the captain was finished speaking in his voice that could curl a chopper's rotors, the Bostonian's face had gone chalky under his fresh sunburn.

"It was just a piece of candy," the young man had said when Captain Aubrey returned to his business and the children had been scattered away. "It's no big deal."

Dan had looked at the Bostonian's sweat-damp shirt and seen his name printed there in black stencil over the pocket: *Farrow*. "Out here everythin's a big deal," Dan had told him. "Just lay low, do what you're supposed to, and don't go south, you might live for a week or two."

The platoon had left Cho Yat, moving across the flat, gleaming rice paddies toward the dark wall of jungle that lay beyond. Their patrol had lasted four hours and discovered not so much as the print of a Goodyear-soled sandal.

It was on the way out when the point team had radioed to Captain Aubrey with the message that something was burning in Cho Yat.

Emerging from the jungle with the others, Dan had seen the dark scrawl of smoke in the ugly yellow sky. A harsh, hot wind had washed over him, and in it he'd smelled a sickly-sweet odor like pork barbecue.

He'd known what the odor was. He'd smelled it before, after a flamethrower had done its work on a snake hole. Captain Aubrey had ordered them to double-time it to the village, and Dan had done what he was told because he'd always been a good soldier, the smell of burning flesh swirling around him in the pungent air and his boots slogging through rice-paddy mud.

His eyes opened in the dark.

He peered into the rearview mirror.

Headlights were approaching along the park road.

He stopped breathing. If it was a police car . . . His fingers went to the key in the ignition switch. The headlights came closer. Dan watched them coming, sweat glistening on his face. Then the car stopped about twenty feet away and the lights went out.

His breathing resumed on a ragged note. It was a dark-colored Toyota, not a police car. Dan watched the rearview mirror for a few seconds longer, but he saw no other lights. He sat there waiting. So did the Toyota's driver. Well, he would have to make the first move. He got out and stood beside the station wagon. The driver's door of the Toyota opened, and a woman got out. The courtesy light gave Dan a brief glimpse of the young man who sat in the passenger seat.

"Dan?" If the sound of her voice had been glass, it would have cut his throat.

"It's me," he answered. His palms were wet. His nerves seemed twisted together in the pit of his stomach.

She came toward him. She stopped suddenly, when she could see his face a little better. "You've changed," she said.

"Lost some weight, I guess."

Susan had never been one to shrink from a challenge. She showed him she still had her grit. She continued to walk toward him, toward the man who had suffered midnight rages and deliriums, who had attacked their son in his bed, who had brought some of the hell of that war back with him when the last helicopter left Saigon. Susan stopped again when she was an arm's length away.

"You look good," he told her, and it was the truth. Susan had been on the thin side when they'd divorced, but now she looked fit and healthy. He figured her nerves were a lot steadier without him around. She'd cut her dark brown hair to just above her shoulders, and Dan could tell that there was a lot of gray in it. Her face was still firm-jawed and more attractive than he remembered. More confident, too. There was some pain in her eyes, which were a shade between gray and green. She wore jeans and a short-sleeved pale blue blouse. Susan was still Susan: a minimum of makeup, no flashy jewelry, nothing to announce that she was anything other than a woman who accepted no pretense. "You must be doin' all right," he said.

"I am. We both are."

He looked anxiously toward the park road. Susan said, "I didn't bring the police."

"I believe you."

"I told 'em you called, and that I was afraid to stay at the house. I wouldn't have taken so long, but they had one of their men follow me to the Holiday Inn. He sat out in the parkin' lot for about an hour. Then all of a sudden he raced off, and I thought for sure they'd caught you."

Dan figured the man had gotten a radio call. By now the police must be swarming all over the Hideaway Motor Court.

"I thought you'd be in a pickup truck," Susan said.

"I stopped at a motel outside town and the couple who own the place found out who I was. They tried to get the reward by blastin' me with a shotgun. The woman gut-shot her own husband by accident and then blew out one of the truck's tires. Only way I could get here was by takin' their car."

"Dan—" Susan's voice cracked. "Dan, what're you gonna *do*?"

"I don't know. Keep from gettin' caught, I hope. Maybe find a place where I can rest awhile and think some things through." He offered a grim smile. "This hasn't been one of my best days."

"Why didn't you *tell* me you needed money? Why didn't you tell me you were sick? I would've helped you!"

"We're not man and wife anymore. It's not your problem."

"Oh, that's just great!" Her eyes flashed with anger. "It's not my problem, so you get yourself jammed in a corner and you wind up killin' somebody! You think it's always you against the world, you never would let anybody help you! I could've given you a loan if you'd asked! Didn't you ever think about that?"

"I thought about it," he admitted. "Not very long, though."

"Bullheaded and stubborn! Where'd it get you? Tell me that!"

"Susan?" he said quietly. "It's too late for us to be fightin', don't you think?"

"The stubbornest man in this *world!*" Susan went on, but the anger was leaving her. She put a hand up against her forehead. "Oh Jesus. Oh my God. I don't . . . I can't even believe this is real."

"You ought to see it from where I'm standin'."

"The leukemia. When'd you find out?"

"In January. I figure it had to be the Agent Orange. I knew it was gonna show up in me sooner or later." He started to tell her about the knot in his brain—that, too, he felt had to do with the chemical—but he let it slide. "They ran some tests at the V.A. hospital. Doctors wanted me to stay there, but I'm not gonna lie in a bed and wait to die. At least I could work. When I had a job, I mean."

"I'm sorry," she said. "I swear to God I am."

"Well, it's the hand I got dealt. What happened at that bank was my own damn fault. I went south, Susan. Like we used to say in 'Nam. I screwed up, the second passed and there was no bringin' it back again." He frowned, staring at the pavement between them. "I don't want to spend whatever time I have left in prison. Worse yet, in a prison hospital. So I don't know where I'm goin', but I know I can't go back." He leveled his gaze at her again. "Did you tell Chad my side of it?"

She nodded.

"You took a big chance comin' out here to meet me. I know it's not easy for you, the way I used to be and all. But I couldn't just say a few words to him over the phone and leave it like that. Lettin' me see him is the kindest thing you ever could've done for me."

"He's your son, too," she said. "You've got the right."

"You mind if I sit in the car with him for a few minutes? Just the two of us?"

She motioned toward the Toyota. Dan walked past her, his heart pounding. He opened the driver's side door and looked in at the boy.

Hi, Chad, he meant to say, but he couldn't speak. At seventeen years, Chad was hardly a boy anymore. He was husky and broad-shouldered, as Dan himself used to be. He was so changed from the picture Dan had—the picture left behind at the Hideaway Motor Court—that the sight of him was like a punch to Dan's chest. Chad's face had lost its baby fat and taken on the angles and planes of manhood. His sandy-brown hair was cut short, and the sun had burnished his skin. Dan caught the scent of Aqua Velva; the young man must've shaved before they'd left the motel. Chad wore khaki trousers and a blue-and-red tie-dyed T-shirt, the muscles in his arms defined. Dan figured he did outdoor work, maybe light construction or yardkeeping. He looked fine, and Dan realized this was going to be a lot tougher than he'd thought.

"Do you recognize me?" he asked.

"Kinda," Chad said. He paused, thinking it over. "Kinda not."

Dan eased into the driver's seat, but he left the door ajar to keep the courtesy light on. "It's been a long time."

"Yes sir," Chad said.

"You workin' this summer?"

"Yes sir. Helpin' Mr. McCullough."

"What kind of work?"

"He's got a landscapin' business. Puts in swimmin' pools, too."

"That's good. You helpin' your mom around the house?"

"Yes sir. I keep the grass cut."

Dan nodded. Chad's speech was a little hesitant and there was a dullness in his eyes. Otherwise, there was no outward sign of Chad's mental disability. Their son had been born—as the counselor put it—"learning disabled." Which meant his thinking processes were always going to be labored, and tasks involving intricate detail would be difficult for him. This fact of life had added to the fuel of Dan's anger in those bad years, had made him curse God and strike out at Susan. Now, tempered by time, he thought that the Agent Orange might have afflicted Chad. The poison that had seeped into Dan had dwelled in his sperm for years, like a beast in a basement, and passed from him through Susan into their son. None of what he suspected could be proven in any court of law, but Dan thought it was true as surely as he remembered the oily feel of the dirty silver rain on his skin. Watching Chad try to put his thoughts together was like someone struggling to open a rusted lock. Most times the tumblers fell into place, but Dan remembered that when they didn't, the boy's face became an agony of frustration.

"You've really grown up," Dan said. "I swear, time's a thief."

"Sir?" Chad frowned; the abstract statement had passed him by.

Dan rubbed the bruised knuckles of his right hand. The moment had arrived. "Your mom told you what I did, didn't she?"

"Yes sir. She said the police are after you. That's why they came to the door."

"Right. You'll probably hear a lot of bad things about me. You're gonna hear people say that I'm crazy, that I walked into that bank with a gun, lookin' to kill somebody." Dan was speaking slowly and carefully, and keeping eye contact with his son. "But I wanted to tell you, face-to-face, that it's not true. I did shoot and kill a man, but it was an accident. It happened so fast it was like a bad dream. Now, that doesn't excuse what I did. There's no excuse for such a thing." He paused, not knowing what else to say. "I just wanted you to hear it from me," he added.

Chad looked away from him and worked his hands together. "Did . . . that man you killed . . . did he do somethin' bad to you?"

"I wish I could say he did, but he was just doin' his job."

"You gonna give yourself up?"

"No."

Chad's gaze came back to him. His eyes seemed more focused and intense. "Mom says you can't get away. She says they'll find you sooner or later."

"Well," Dan said, "I'm plannin' on it bein' later."

They sat in silence for a moment, neither one looking at the other. Dan had to say this next thing; he couldn't recall his father—the spit-and-polish major—ever saying it to him, which made saying it doubly difficult and doubly important. "I wasn't such a good father," he began. "I had some things inside me that wouldn't let go. They made me blind and scared. I wasn't strong enough to get help, either. When your mom told me she wanted a divorce, it was the best thing she could've done for all of us." Tears suddenly burned his eyes, and he felt a brick wedged in his throat. "But not one day goes by that I don't think about you, and wonder how you're doin'. I know I should've called, or written you a letter, but . . . I guess I didn't know what to say. Now I do." He cleared his throat with an effort. "I just wanted you to know I love you very, very much, and I hope you don't think too badly of me."

Chad didn't respond. Dan had said everything he needed to. It was time to go. "You gonna take good care of your mom?"

"Yes sir." Chad's voice was thick.

"Okay." He put his hand on his son's shoulder, and it crossed his mind that he would never do this again. "You hang tough, hear?"

Chad said, "I've got a picture."

"A picture? Of what?"

"You." Chad reached into his back pocket and brought out his wallet. He slid from it a creased photograph. "See?"

Dan took it. The photo, which Dan recalled was snapped at a Sears studio, showed the Lambert family in 1978. Dan—burly and beardless, his face sunburned from some outdoors carpentry job but his eyes deepset and haunted—and Susan were sitting against a paper backdrop of summer mountains, the four-year-old Chad smiling between them. Chad's arms were clutched to their shoulders. Susan, who appeared frail and tired, wore a brave smile. Looking at the picture, Dan realized it was the image of a man who hadn't yet learned that the past was a more implacable enemy than any Viet Cong crouched in a snake hole. He had given his nightmares power over him, had refused to seek help because a man—a good soldier—did not admit weakness. And in the end that war he'd survived had taken everything of worth away from him.

It was the picture, he thought, of a man who'd gone south a long, long time ago.

"You have a picture of me?" Chad asked. Dan shook his head, and Chad took a folded piece of paper from the wallet. "You can have this one if you want it."

Dan unfolded the paper. It was a picture of Chad in a football uniform, the number fifty-nine across his chest. The camera had caught him in a posed lunge, his teeth gritted and his arms reaching for an off-frame opponent.

"I cut it out of last year's annual," Chad explained. "That was the day the whole team got their pictures taken. Coach Pierce said to look mean, so that's what I did."

"You did a good job of it. I wouldn't care to line up against you." He gave his son a smile. "I do want this. Thank you." He refolded the picture and put it in his own pocket, and he returned the Sears studio photograph to Chad. And now, as much as he wished it weren't so, he had to leave.

Chad knew it, too. "You ever comin' back?" he asked.

"No," Dan said. He didn't know quite how to end this. Awkwardly, he offered his hand. "So long."

Chad leaned into him and put his arms around his father's shoulders.

Dan's heart swelled. He hugged his son, and he wished for the impossible: a rolling-back of the years. He wished the dirty silver rain had never fallen on him. He wished Chad had never been contaminated, that things could've been patched up with Susan, and that he'd been strong enough to seek help for the nightmares and flashbacks. He guessed he was wishing for a miracle.

Chad said, up close to his ear, "So long, Dad."

Dan let his son go and got out of the car. His eyes were wet. He wiped them with his forearm as he walked to the station wagon, where Susan waited. He'd almost reached her when he heard a dog barking, a high-pitched *yap yap yap*.

Dan stopped in his tracks. The sound had drifted across the park, its direction hard to pinpoint. It was close enough, though, to instantly set Dan's nerves on edge. Where had it come from? Was somebody walking a dog in the park at *this* hour? Wherever it was, the dog had stopped barking. Dan glanced around, saw nothing but the dark shapes of pine trees that stood in clusters surrounding the parking lot.

"You all right?" Susan looked as if she'd aged five years in the last few minutes.

"Yeah." A tear had trickled down his cheek into his beard. "Thanks for bringin' him."

"Did you think I wouldn't?"

"I didn't know. You took a chance, that's for sure."

"Chad needed to see you as much as you needed to see him." Susan reached into her jeans pocket. "I want you to have this." Her hand emerged with some greenbacks. "I raided the cookie jar before we left the house."

"Put it away," Dan said. "I'm not a charity case."

"This isn't the time to be proud or stupid." She grabbed his hand and slapped the money into it. "I don't know how much cash you've got, but you can use another sixty dollars."

He started to protest, but thought better of it. An extra sixty dollars was, in its own way, a small miracle. "I'll call it a loan."

"Call it whatever you please. Where're you goin' from here?"

"I don't know yet. Maybe I'll head to New Orleans and sign on a freighter. I can still do a day's work."

Susan's face had taken on the grave expression Dan remembered that meant she had something important to say but she was working up to it. "Listen," she said after a moment, "you mentioned findin' a place to rest. I've been seein' a fella for the past year. He works for an oil company, and we've talked about . . . maybe gettin' more serious."

"You mean married serious?" He frowned, not exactly sure how he felt about this bolt from the blue. "Well, you picked a fine time to tell me."

"Just hear me out. He's got a cabin in a fishin' camp, down in the bayou country south of Houma. The camp's called Vermilion. Gary's in Houston, he won't be back till next week."

It took a few seconds for what Susan was saying to get through to him. Before Dan could respond, Susan went on. "Gary's taken Chad and me down there a few weekends. He checks on the oil rigs and we do some fishin'. There's no alarm system. Nothin' much there to steal. The nearest neighbor's a mile or so away."

"Bringin' Chad was enough," Dan told her. "You don't have to—"

"I *want* to," she interrupted. "The cabin's two or three miles past the bridge, up a turnoff on the left. It's on the road that's a straight shot out of Vermilion. Painted gray with a screened-in porch. Wouldn't be hard to get past the screen and break a windowpane."

"What would Gary say about that?"

"I'll explain things. There'll be food in the pantry; you wouldn't have to go out."

Dan grasped the door's handle, but he wasn't yet ready to leave. The police would be out there, hunting him in the night, and he was going to have to be very, very careful. "I could use a day or two of rest. Figure out what to do next." He hesitated. "Is this fella . . . Gary . . . is he good to you?"

"He is. He and Chad get along real well, too."

Dan grunted. It was going to take him some time to digest this news. "Chad needs a father," he said in spite of the pain it caused him. "Somebody who takes him fishin'. Stuff like that."

"I'm sorry," Susan said. "I wish I could do more for you."

"You've done enough. More than enough." He pushed the money into his pocket. "This is my problem, and I'll handle it."

"Stubborn as hell." Her voice had softened. "Always were, always will be."

He opened the station wagon's door. "Well, I guess this is good—"

A flashlight clicked on.

Its dazzling beam hit Dan's eyes and blinded him.

"Freeze, Lambert!" a man's voice ordered.

10

Line of Fire

The shock paralyzed Dan. Susan caught her breath with a harsh gasp and spun around to face the intruder.

"Easy, easy," the man behind the flashlight cautioned. He had a whispery, genteel southern accent. "Don't do anythin' foolish, Lambert. I'm armed."

He was standing about twenty feet away. Dan expected to be hit by a second light, and then the policemen would rush in, slam him against the car, and frisk him. He lifted his hands to shield his face from the stabbing white beam. "I'm not packin' a gun."

"That's good." It was a relief to Flint Murtaugh, who had crept up from the edge of the parking lot by keeping the woman's car between himself and the fugitive. He'd been standing there for a couple of minutes in the darkness, listening to their conversation. In his left hand was the flashlight, in his right was a .45 automatic aimed just to Lambert's side. "Put your hands behind your head and lock your fingers."

It's over, Dan thought. He could run, maybe, but he wouldn't get very far. Where were the other policemen, though? Surely there wasn't just the one. He obeyed the command.

Susan was squinting into the light. She'd talked to the policemen in charge of the stakeout on her house and to the one who'd followed her to the Holiday Inn; she hadn't heard this man's voice before. "Don't hurt him," she said. "It was self-defense, he's not a cold-blooded killer."

Flint ignored her. "Lambert, walk toward me. Slowly."

Dan paused. Something was wrong; he could feel it in the silence. Where were the backup policemen? Where were the police cars, the spinning bubble lights and the crackling radios? They should've converged on him by now, if they were even here.

"Come on, move it," Flint said. "Lady, step out of the way."

Lady, Susan thought. The other policemen had addressed her as *Mrs. Lambert*. "Who are you?"

"Flint Murtaugh. Pleased to meet you. Lambert, come on."

"Wait, Dan." Susan stepped in front of him to take the full force of the light. "Show me your badge."

Flint clenched his teeth. His patience was already stretched thin from the hellish drive with Pelvis Eisley and Mama. He was in no mood for complications. Flint had never cared to know the names of all the characters Elvis Presley had played in his wretched movies. Trying to make Eisley cease jabbering about Presley was as futile as trying to make that damn mutt stop gnawing at fleas. Flint was tired and his sharkskin suit was damp with sweat, Clint was agitated by the heat and kept twitching, and it was long past time for a cold shower and a glass of lemon juice.

"I'd like to see your badge," Susan repeated, the man's hesitation fueling her doubt. *Flint Murtaugh*, he'd said. Why hadn't he said *Officer Murtaugh*?

"Listen, I'm not plannin' on a long relationship with you people, so let's cut the chatter." Flint had taken a sidestep so the light hit Lambert's face again. Susan moved to shield her ex-husband once more. "Lady, I told you to step out of the way."

"Do you have a badge, or not?"

Flint's composure was fast unraveling. He wanted Lambert to come to him because he didn't want to have to pass the woman; if she grabbed for the flashlight or the gun, things could get messy. He wished he'd circled around the other side and crept up on Lambert from behind to keep the woman from being between them. It was Eisley's fault, he decided, for screwing up his concentration. Flint had a small spray can of Mace in his inside coat pocket, and he suspected that he might have to use it. "Lady," he replied, "that man standin' there is worth fifteen thousand dollars to me. I've come from Shreveport to find him, and I've had a hard night. You really don't want to get yourself involved in this."

"He's not a policeman," Dan said to Susan. "He's a bounty hunter. You workin' for the bank?"

"Independent contract. Keep your fingers locked, now; let's don't cause anymore trouble."

"You mind if I ask how you found me?"

"Time for that when we're drivin'. Come on, real slow and easy." It had been a lucky break, actually. Flint had driven along Jackson Avenue and had seen the police surveillance teams, one at either end of the block. He'd parked two streets away and sat beside a hedge in someone's yard, watching the house to see what developed. Then the woman had pulled out of her garage, followed by another policeman in an unmarked car, and Flint had decided to tag along at a distance. At the Holiday Inn he'd been on the verge of calling it quits when her watchdog had rushed off, obviously answering a radio summons, but then the woman had emerged again and Flint had smelled an opportunity.

"Don't do it," Susan said before Dan could move. "If he doesn't work for the state of Louisiana, he doesn't have any right to take you in."

"I've got a *gun!*" Flint was about ready to snort steam. "You understand me?"

"I know a gun's not a badge. You're not gonna be shootin' an unarmed man."

"Mom?" Chad called from the car. "You need some help?"

"No! Just stay where you are!" Susan directed her attention at the bounty hunter again. She took two steps toward him.

"Susan!" Dan said. "You'd better keep—"

"*Hush.* Let somebody help you, for God's sake." She advanced another step on Flint. "You're a vulture, aren't you? Swoopin' in on whatever meat you can snatch."

"Lady, you're tryin' to make me forget my manners."

"You ready to shoot a woman, too? You and Dan could share the same cell." She moved forward two more paces, and Flint retreated one. "Dan?" Susan said calmly. "He's not takin' you anywhere. Get in your car and go."

"*No!* No, goddamn it!" Flint shouted. "Lambert, don't you move! I won't kill you, but I'll sure as hell put some hurt on you!"

"He's empty talk, Dan." Susan had decided what needed to be done, and she was getting herself into position to do it. She took one more step toward the bounty hunter. "Go on, get in the car and drive away."

Flint hollered, "No, you don't!" It was time to put Lambert on the ground. Flint jammed the automatic into his waistband and plucked the small red can of Mace from inside his coat. He popped the cap off with his thumb and put his index finger on the nozzle. The concentrated spray had a range of fifteen feet, and Flint realized he was going to have to shove the woman aside to get a clear shot at Lambert. He was so enraged he almost fired a burst into her eyes, but he'd never Maced a woman and he wasn't going to start now. He stalked toward her and was amazed when she stood her ground. "To hell with this!" he snarled, and he jabbed an elbow at her shoulder to drive her out of the line of fire.

But suddenly she was moving.

She was moving very, very fast.

She clamped a wiry hand to his right wrist, stepped into him with her own shoulder, and pivoted, her elbow thunking upward into Flint's chin and rattling his brains. His black wingtips left the pavement. His trapped wrist was turned in on itself, pain shooting up his arm. Somewhere in midair he lost both the flashlight and the Mace. As he went over the woman's hip, one word blazed in Flint's consciousness: *sucker.* Then the ground came up fast and hard and he slammed down on his back with a force that whooshed the breath from his lungs and made stars and comets pinwheel through his skull. Susan stepped back from the fallen man and scooped up the flashlight. "Way to go, Mom!" Chad yelled, leaning out of the Toyota's window.

"Damn" was all Dan could think to say. It had happened so quickly that his hands were still locked behind his head. "How did you—"

"Tae kwon do," Susan said. She wasn't even breathing hard. "I've got a brown belt."

Now Dan understood why Susan hadn't been afraid to meet him. He lowered his hands and walked to her side, where he looked down the flashlight's beam at the bounty hunter's pained and pallid face. A comma of white-streaked hair hung over Flint Murtaugh's sweat-glistening forehead, and he'd curled up on his side and was clutching his right wrist.

Dan saw the automatic and freed it from the man's waistband. "Brown belt or not, that was a damn fool thing to do. You could've gotten yourself killed." He removed the bullet clip, threw it in one direction and the gun in another.

"He had somethin' in his other hand." Susan shone the light around. "I couldn't tell what it was, but I heard him drop it." She steadied the beam on Murtaugh again. "I can't figure out where he came from. I thought I made sure nobody was follow—" She stopped speaking. Then, her voice tight: "Dan. What is *that?*"

He looked. The front of the man's white shirt was twitching, as if his heart were about to beat through his chest. Dan stared at it, transfixed, and then he reached down to touch it.

"Mr. Murtaugh! Mr. Murtaugh, you all right?"

Dan straightened up. Another man was out there in the dark. Both Dan and Susan had the eerie sensation that they recognized the voice's deep, snarly resonance, but neither one of them could place it. A dog began to yap again, and on the pavement Flint gave a muffled half-groan, half-curse.

Susan switched the light off. "You'd better hit it. Gettin' kind of crowded around here."

Dan hurried to the station wagon and Susan followed him, and so neither of them saw the slim, pale third arm push free from Flint Murtaugh's shirt and flail angrily in the air. Dan got behind the wheel, started the engine, and turned on the headlights. Susan reached in and grasped his shoulder. "Good luck," she said over the engine's rumbling.

"Thanks for everythin'."

"I did love you," she told him.

"I know you did." He put his hand over hers and squeezed it. "Take care of Chad."

"I will. And you take care of yourself."

"So long," Dan said, and he put the station wagon in reverse and backed away past the bounty hunter. Flint pulled himself up to his knees, pain stabbing through his lower back and his right wrist surely sprained. Clint's arm was thrashing around, the hand clenched in a fighting fist. Through a dreamlike haze Flint watched the fifteen-thousand-dollar skin twist the station wagon around and drive across the parking lot. Flint tried to summon up a yell, but a hoarse rasp emerged: "Eisley! He's comin' at you!"

In another moment Dan had to stomp on the brake. He feared he must be losing his mind, because right there in front of the pickup stood a big-bellied, pompadour-haired Elvis Presley, a beat-up black Cadillac behind him blocking the road. Elvis—a credible impersonator for sure—was holding on to a squirming little bull-dog. "Where's Mr. Murtaugh?" Elvis shouted in that husky Memphis drawl. "What'cha done to him?"

Dan had seen everything now. He hit the gas pedal again, taking the station wagon up over the curb onto the park's grass. The rear tires fishtailed and threw up clods of earth. Elvis scrambled out of the way, bellowing for Mr. Murtaugh.

Flint had gotten to his feet and was hobbling in the direction of the Cadillac. His left shoe hit something that clattered and rolled away: the can of Mace. "Eisley, stop him!" he hollered as he paused to retrieve the spray can, the bruised muscles of his back stiffening. "Don't let him get—awwwww, *shit!*" He'd seen the station wagon maneuvering around the Caddy, and he watched with helpless fury as it bumped over the curb again onto the road, something underneath the vehicle banging with a noise like a dropped washtub. Then the skin was picking up speed and at the park's entrance turned right with a shriek of flayed rubber onto the street.

"Mr. Murtaugh!" Pelvis cried out with relief as Flint reached him. "Thank the Lord! I thought that killer had done—"

"Shut up and get in the car!" Flint shouted. "Move your fat ass!" Flint flung himself behind the wheel, started the engine, and as he jammed down on the gas pedal Pelvis managed to heave his bulk and Mama into the passenger side. Flint got the Cadillac turned around with a neck-twisting spin in the parking lot, the single headlight's beam grazing past the woman who stood beside her car. He had an instant to see that her son had reached out for her and their hands were clasped. Then Flint, his face a perfect picture of hellacious rage, took the Cadillac roaring out of Basile Park in pursuit.

"I thought sure he'd done killed you!" Pelvis hollered over the hot wind whipping through the car. His frozen pompadour was immobile. Mama had slipped from his grasp and was wildly bounding from backseat to front and back again, her high-pitched barks like hot nails being driven into the base of Flint's skull. Clint's arm was still thrashing, angry as a stomped cobra. Pelvis shouted, "You see that fella try to run me down? If I'd've been a step slower, I'd be lookin' like a big ol' waffle 'bout now! But I foxed him, 'cause when I jigged to one side he jagged to the other and I just kept on jiggin'. You saw it, didn't you? When that fella tried to run me—"

Flint pressed his right fist against Pelvis's lips. Mama seized Flint's sleeve between her teeth, her eyes wide and wet and a guttural growl rumbling in her throat. "I swear to Jesus," Flint seethed, "if you don't shut that mouth I'm puttin' you out right here!"

"It's shut." Pelvis caught Mama and pulled her against him. Reluctantly, she let go of Flint's sleeve. Flint returned both hands to the steering wheel, the speedometer's needle trembling toward sixty. He saw the station wagon's taillights a quarter-mile ahead.

"You want me to shut up," Pelvis said with an air of wounded dignity, "all you have to do is ask me kindly. No need to jump down my throat jus' 'cause I was tellin' you how I stared Death square in the face and—"

"Eisley." Tears of frustration sprang to Flint's eyes, which utterly amazed him; he couldn't remember the last time he'd shed a tear. His nerves were jangling like fire alarms, and he felt a hair away from a rubber room. The speedometer's needle was passing sixty-five, the Cadillac's aged frame starting to shudder. But they were gaining on the station wagon, and in another few seconds they'd be right up on its rear fender.

GONE SOUTH

Dan had the gas pedal pressed to the floor, but he couldn't kick any more power out of the engine. The thing was making an unearthly metallic roar as if on the verge of blowing its cylinders. He saw in his rearview mirror the one-eyed Cadillac speeding up on his tail, and he braced for collision. There was a blinking caution light ahead, marking an intersection. Dan had no time to think about it; he twisted the wheel violently to the left. As the station wagon sluggishly obeyed, its worn tires skidding across the pavement, the Cadillac hit him, a grazing blow from behind, and sparks shot between their crumpled fenders. Then, as Dan fought the wheel to keep from sliding over the curb into somebody's front yard, the Cadillac zoomed past the intersection.

"Hold on!" Flint shouted, his foot jamming the brake pedal. The Eldorado was heavy, and would not slow down without screaming, smoking protest from the tires. Pelvis clung to Mama, who was trying her damnedest to jump into the backseat. Flint reversed to the intersection, the bitter smoke of burned rubber swirling through the windows, and turned left onto a winding street bordered by brick homes with manicured lawns and honest-to-God white picket fences. He sped after Lambert, but there was no sign of the station wagon's taillights. Other streets veered off on either side, and it became clear after a few seconds that Lambert had turned onto one of them.

"I'll find you, you bastard!" Flint said between clenched teeth, and he whipped the car to the right at the next street. It, too, was dark.

"He's done gone," Pelvis said.

"Shut up! Hear me? Just shut your mouth!"

"Statin' a fact," Pelvis said.

Flint took the Cadillac roaring to the next intersection and turned left. His palms were wet on the wheel, sweat clinging to his face. Clint's hand came up and stroked his chin, and Flint cuffed his brother aside. Flint took the next right, the tires squealing. He was in a mazelike residential area, the streets going in all directions. Anger throbbed like drumbeats at his temples, pain lancing his lower back. He tasted panic like cold copper in his mouth. Then he turned right onto another street and his heart kicked.

Three blocks away was a pair of red taillights.

Flint hit the accelerator so hard the Cadillac leapt forward like a scalded dog. He roared up behind Lambert's car, intending to swerve around him and cut him off. But in the next instant Flint's triumph shriveled into terror. The Cadillac's headlight revealed the car was not a rust-eaten old station wagon but a new Chevrolet Caprice. Across its fast-approaching rear end was silver lettering that spelled out ALEXANDRIA POLICE.

Flint stood on the brake pedal. A thousand cries for God, Jesus, and Mother Mary rang like crazy bells in his brain. As the Cadillac's tires left a quarter-inch of black rubber on the pavement, the prowl car's driver punched it and the Caprice shot forward to avoid the crash. The Caddy slewed to one side before it stopped, the engine rattled and died, and the police cruiser's bubble lights started spinning. It backed up, halting a couple of feet from Flint's busted bumper. A spotlight on the driver's side swiveled around and glared into Flint's face like an angry Cyclopean eye.

"Well," Pelvis drawled, "now we've done shit and stepped in it."

Over nearer the intersection with the flashing caution light, Dan started the station wagon's engine and backed out of the driveway he'd pulled into. He eased onto the street, his headlights still off. The black Cadillac had sped past about two minutes before, and Dan had expected it to come flying back at any second. As the saying went, it was time to git while the gittin' was good. He switched on his lights and at the caution signal took a left toward Interstate 49 and the route south. There were no cars ahead of him, nor any in his rearview mirror. But it was going to be a long night, and a long drive yet before he could rest. He breathed a good-bye to Alexandria, and a good riddance to the bounty hunters.

Flint, still stunned by the sudden turn of events, was watching the red and blue lights spin around. "Eisley, you're a jinx," he said hoarsely. "That's what you are. A jinx." Two policemen were getting out of the car. Flint pushed the can of Mace under his seat. Clint's arm resisted him, but he forced it inside his shirt and buttoned his coat. The two officers both had young, rawboned faces, and they didn't appear happy. Before they reached the Cadillac, Flint dug his wallet out and pressed his left arm over his chest to pin Clint down. "Keep your mouth zipped," he told Pelvis. "I'll do all the talkin'."

The policeman who walked up on Flint's side of the car had a fresh crew cut and a jaw that looked as if it could chop wood. He shone a flashlight into Flint's eyes. "You near 'bout broke our necks, you know that? Look what you did to my cap." He held up a crushed and formless thing.

"I'm awful sorry, sir." Flint's voice was a masterpiece of studied remorse. "I'm not from around here, and I'm lost. I guess I panicked, 'cause I couldn't find my way out."

"Uh-huh. You had to be goin' at least sixty. Sign back there says fifteen miles an hour. This is a residential zone."

"I didn't see the sign."

"Well, you seen the *houses*, didn't you? You seen our car in front of you. Seems to me you're either drunk, crazy, or mighty stupid." He shifted the light, and its beam fell upon Pelvis. "Lordy, Walt! Look what we've got here!"

"How you fellas doin'?" Pelvis asked, grinning. In his arms Mama had begun a low, menacing growl.

"I bet this'll be a real interestin' story," the policeman with the light said. "Let's see a driver's license. Your ID, too, Mr. Presley sir."

Flint fumbled to remove the license from his eelskin wallet and hold Clint immobile at the same time. His wrist was still hurting like hell. Eisley produced a battered wallet that had the face of Elvis on it in brightly colored Indian beads. "I never did believe he was dead, did you, Randy?" Walt said with undisguised mirth. He was taller than his partner and not quite as husky. "I always knew it was a wax body in that coffin!"

"Yeah, we might get ourselves on Gerrado Riviera for this," Randy said. "This is better'n seein' green men from Mars, ain't it? Call the tag in." Walt walked around back to write it down and then returned to the cruiser. Randy inspected the licenses under the light. "Flint Murtaugh. From Monroe, huh? What're you doin' here in the middle of the night?"

"Uh . . . well, I'm . . ." Flint's mind went blank. He tried to pull up something, anything. "I'm . . . that is to say . . ."

"Officer, sir?" Pelvis spoke up, and Flint winced. "We're tryin' to find the Holiday Inn. I believe we must've took the wrong turn."

The light settled on Pelvis's face. "The Holiday Inn's over toward the interstate. The sign's lit up; it's hard to miss."

"I reckon we did, though."

Randy spent a moment examining Pelvis's license. Clint gave a twitch under Flint's shirt, and Flint felt sweat dripping from his armpits. "Pelvis Eisley," Randy said. "That can't be your born name."

"No sir, but it's my legal name."

"What's your born name?"

"Uh . . . well, sir, I go by the name that's written down right—"

"Pelvis ain't a name, it's a bone. What name did your mama and daddy give you? Or was you hatched?"

Flint didn't care for the nasty edge in the policeman's voice. "Hey, I don't think there's any call to be—"

"Hush up. I'll come back to you, don't you worry about it. I asked for your born name, sir."

"Cecil," came the quiet reply. "Cecil Eisley."

"Cecil." Randy slurred the name, making it sound like something that had crawled out from under a swamp log. "You dress like that all the time, Cecil?"

"Yes sir," Pelvis answered in all honesty. In his lap Mama continued her low growling.

"Well, you're 'bout the damnedest sight I ever laid eyes on. You mind tellin' me what you're in costume for?"

"Listen, Officer," Flint said. He was terrified Pelvis was going to start blabbering about being a bounty hunter, or about the fact that Lambert was somewhere close by. "I was the one drivin', not him."

"Mr. Murtaugh?" Randy leaned his head nearer, and Flint had the startling thought that he'd seen the policeman's face before, when its thin-lipped mouth was twisted into a cruel grin and the garish midway lights threw shadows into the deep-set eye sockets. "When I want you to speak, I'll ask you a question. Hear me?"

His was the face of a thousand others who had come to the freak show to leer and laugh, to fondle their girlfriends in front of the stage and spit tobacco on Flint's polished shoes. Flint felt a hard nut of disgust in his throat. Clint lurched under his shirt, but luckily Flint had a firm grip and the policeman didn't see. "There's no reason to be rude," Flint said.

Randy laughed, which was probably the worst thing he could've done. It was a humorless, harsh laugh, and it made Flint want to smash it back through the man's teeth. "You want to see rude, you keep on pushin' me. You come flyin' up on my rear end and almost wreck my car, I'm not about to kiss you for it. Now you're real, real close to a night in jail, so you'd best just sit there and keep your mouth shut."

Flint stared sullenly at him, and the policeman glared back. "It's a clean tag," Walt said, returning from the cruiser's radio.

"I'm just about to get the story from Cecil," Randy told him. "Let's hear it."

"Well, sir . . ." Pelvis cleared his throat. Flint waited, his head lowered. "We're on our way to New Orleans. Goin' to a convention there, at the Hyatt Hotel. It's for Elvis interperators like me."

"Now I can retire. I've heard everythin'," Randy said, and Walt laughed.

"Yes sir." Pelvis wore his stupid smile like a badge of honor. "See, the convention kicks off tomorrow."

"If that's so, how come you're lookin' for the Holiday Inn?"

"Well . . . see, we're supposed to meet some other fellas goin' to the convention, too. We're all gonna travel together. I reckon we just missed seein' the sign, and then we got all turned around. You know how it is, bein' in a strange place not knowin' where you are and it so late and everythin'. Couldn't find no phone, and I'm tellin' you we were gettin' mighty scared 'cause these days you gotta be careful where you wind up, all them murders you see on the news every time you turn on the—"

"All right, all right." Randy gasped like a man surfacing for air. He stabbed the light into Flint's eyes again. "You an Elvis 'interpera-tor,' too?"

"No sir, he's my manager," Pelvis said. "We're like two peas in a pod."

Flint felt queasy. Clint's arm jumped and almost got away from him.

"Walt? You got any ideas on what to do with these two? Should we take 'em in?"

"That's the thing to do, seems to me."

"Yeah." The light was still aimed at Flint's face. "Gettin' lost is no excuse for speedin' through a residential area. You could've killed somebody."

"Us, for instance," Walt said.

"Right. You need to spend a night in jail, to get your thinkin' straight."

Great, Flint thought bitterly. When they searched him down before putting him in the cell, they were going to jump out of their jackboots.

" 'Course," Randy went on, "if everybody at the station was to find out we almost got rear-ended by Elvis Presley, we'd be takin' it in the shorts for God only knows how long. So, Mr. Manager Man, you'd best be real glad he's with you, 'cause I don't like your face and if I had my druthers I'd put you smack-dab *under* the jail. Here." The policeman handed him the licenses. For a few seconds Flint was too dumbfounded to take them.

"Mr. Murtaugh, sir?" Pelvis said. "I believe he's lettin' us go."

"With a *major* warnin'," Randy added sternly. "Hold the speed down. Next time you might be goin' to a cemetery instead of a convention."

Flint summoned up his wits and took the licenses. "Thank you," he forced himself to say. "It won't happen again."

"Damn straight it won't. You follow us, we'll take you to the Holiday Inn. But I want Cecil to drive."

"*Sir?*"

593

"I want Cecil where you're sittin'," Randy said. "I don't trust you behind my car. Come on, get out and let him take the wheel."

"But . . . it's . . . *my* car," Flint sputtered.

"He's got a valid driver's license. Anyway, the Holiday Inn's not very far. Come on, do like I'm tellin' you."

"No . . . listen . . . I don't let anybody else drive my—"

Pelvis put a hand on Flint's shoulder, and Flint jumped as if he'd received an electric shock. "Mr. Murtaugh? Don't you worry, I'll be real careful."

"Move it," Randy said. "We've got other places to be."

Pelvis put Mama into the backseat and came around to the driver's side. With an effort that bordered on the superhuman, Flint got out and, holding Clint's arm firmly against his chest, eased into the passenger seat. In another moment they were following the police cruiser out of the maze of residential streets, and Pelvis smiled and said, "I never drove me a Cadillac before. You know, Elvis loved Cadillacs. Gave 'em away every chance he got. He seen some people lookin' at a Cadillac in a showroom one time, he pulled out a big wad of cash and bought it for 'em right there on the spot. Yessir." He nodded vigorously. "I believe I could get to like drivin' a Cadillac."

"Is that so?" Flint had broken out in a cold sweat, and he couldn't help but stare at Eisley's fleshy hands guiding the car. "You'd better enjoy it, then, because ten seconds after those hick cops drive off will be the last time you sit behind my steerin' wheel! Do you have a cement block for a brain? I told you to keep your mouth shut and leave the talkin' to me! Now we've gotta go back to that damn Holiday Inn when we could've been on Lambert's ass! I could've talked our way out of trouble if you hadn't opened your big mouth! Jesus Christ! All that crap about an Elvis convention in New Orleans! We're lucky they didn't call the men with the butterfly nets right then and there!"

"Oh, I went to that convention last year," Pelvis said. "At the Hyatt Hotel, just like I said. 'Bout two hundred Elvises showed up, and we had us a high old time."

"This is a nightmare." Flint pressed his fingers against his forehead to see if he was running a fever. Reality, it seemed, had become entangled with delirium. "I'm at home in my bed, and this is the chili peppers I ate on my pizza."

Pelvis wheezed out a laugh. "Nice to know you still got your sense of humor, seein' as how we lost Lambert and all."

"We haven't lost him. Not yet."

"But . . . he's gone. How're we gonna find him again?"

"You're ridin' with a *professional*, Eisley!" Flint said pointedly. "First thing you learn in this business is to keep your eyes and ears open. I got close enough to hear Lambert and his ex-wife talkin'. She was tellin' him about a cabin in a fishin' camp south of Houma. Vermilion, she said the camp was called. I heard her tell him where it is. She said to break a windowpane, and that there'd be food in the pantry. So that might be where he's headed."

"I swanee!" Pelvis gushed. "Mr. Smoates said you was gonna be a good partner!"

"Get that partners shit out of your head!" Flint snapped. "We're not partners! I'm saddled with you for this one skin hunt, and that's all! You've already screwed up big-time, when I told you to keep that mutt quiet back in the park! That damn barkin' almost shot me out of my shoes! Made me so nervous I let him get the drop on me, and that's how he got away!"

"I was meanin' to ask you about that," Pelvis said. "What happened?"

"That damn woman—" Flint paused. No, he thought; being knocked on your ass by a woman was not a thing Smoates needed to hear about. "She distracted me," he said. "Then Lambert charged in before I could use the Mace. He's a Vietnam vet, he put me down with some kind of judo throw."

"Lucky he didn't take your gun and shoot you," Pelvis said. "Him bein' such a crazy killer, I mean."

"Yeah." Flint nodded. "Lucky."

Which led him to a question: why hadn't Lambert used the gun on him when he was lying helpless on the ground? Maybe because he hadn't wanted to commit another murder in front of his ex-wife and son, Flint decided. Whatever the reason, Flint could indeed count himself fortunate to still be alive.

At the Holiday Inn—the same motel where Flint and Pelvis had sat in the parking lot watching the door to Susan Lambert's room—the two Alexandria policemen gave them a further warning about getting the broken headlight repaired, and as soon as the police cruiser had driven away, Flint took the Cadillac's wheel and banished Pelvis and Mama to the rear seat. In another five minutes Flint was back on Interstate 49, heading south again. He kept his speed below sixty-five. There was no point courting trouble from the highway patrol, and if Lambert was going to the fishing camp cabin, he'd still be there by the time Flint found the place. *If* the troopers didn't stop Lambert first, and *if* Lambert hadn't headed off in another direction. But it was a gamble worth taking, just as Flint had gambled on following Lambert's ex-wife.

The way ahead was dark. Houma was down in swamp and Cajun territory. Flint had never heard of Vermilion before, but he'd find it when they got down there. It wasn't an area Flint would've ventured into without a good reason, though. Those swamp dwellers were a rough breed, and best left alone. At least—thank God—Eisley was quiet and Flint could get his thoughts in order.

Something that sounded like a warped buzz saw started whining in the backseat.

Flint looked into the rearview mirror. Pelvis was stretched out and snoring, with Mama's head cradled on his shoulder. The bulldog added to the noise by growling in her sleep.

A thought came to Flint unbidden: *At least he's got somethin' that gives a damn about him.*

Which was more than he could say for himself.

But then, there was always Clint. Good ol' blind and mute Clint, who had ruined his life as surely as if he had been born a leper.

The way ahead was dark. Flint was determined to find Lambert now; this was a matter of honor. He wasn't afraid of anything on this earth, least of all a crazy killer too stupid to shoot a man who was down and defenseless. This was a game to be played out to the last card, winner take all. He was going to drag that skin back to Smoates and show that bastard what being a professional was all about.

Flint thought of the mansion in his dream, the white stone mansion with four chimneys and a huge stained-glass window in front. His home, he believed. The place where his mother and father lived. The rich, refined people who had seen a mass of twitching flesh growing from their baby's chest and, horrified, had given the baby up to the four winds of adoption. His home. It had to be, because he dreamed of it so often. He would find it yet, and he would find that man and woman and show them he was their son, born of refinement into a cold and dirty world. Maybe it lay to the south. Maybe it lay somewhere at the end of this road, and if he'd gone south long before this he would've found it like a hidden treasure, an answer, a shining lamp.

Maybe.

But right now the way ahead was dark.

11

Traveling by Night

Forty-six miles south of Alexandria, as the sultry nightwind swept in through the station wagon, Dan felt sleep pulling at him.

He was on Highway 167, which paralleled I-49 and twisted through cane-field country. It was all but deserted. Dan had seen no trooper cars since leaving Basile Park, and there'd been no headlights behind him for the last twenty minutes. Houma was still a good seventy miles away, and Vermilion maybe twelve or fifteen miles beyond that. He had to find another roadmap; his last one had been left in his pickup truck. But the fishing camp cabin would be worth the extra miles. He could hide there for a couple of days, get some decent rest, and decide where to go.

His eyelids were heavy, the drone of the tires hypnotic. He'd tried the radio, but it was lifeless. The pain in his skull was building again, and maybe this was the only thing keeping him awake. He needed a cup of coffee, but on this road the few cafes he passed looked to have been closed up since nightfall. After three more miles he came to a crossroads that had a sign pointing east to I-49. He sat there, weighing the risk of trying to find a truckstop on the interstate. It won out over the chance of nodding off at the wheel and running into a ditch.

The interstate was a dangerous place, because the troopers prowled there. At this time of the morning, though nearing three o'clock—the truck drivers in their big, snorting rigs were masters of the four-lane. Dan passed a sign that said Lafayette—"the heart of Acadiana"—was thirty miles ahead. Five miles later he saw green neon that announced CAJUN COUNTRY TRUCK STOP 24 HOURS and he took the next exit. The truck stop was a gray cinder-block building, not much to look at, but he could see a waitress at work through the restaurant's plate-glass window. A tractor-trailer truck was parked at the diesel pumps, its tank being filled by an attendant. In front of the restaurant was a red Camaro with a Texas vanity plate that proclaimed its owner to be AN A1 STUD. Dan drove around back and parked next to two other cars, an old brown Bonneville and a dark blue Mazda, both with Louisiana plates, that probably belonged to the employees. He felt light-headed with weariness as he trudged into the restaurant, which had a long counter and stools and a row of red vinyl booths.

"How you be doin'?" the waitress asked from behind the counter in thick Cajun dialect. "Goan set you'self anywhere." She was a heavyset blond woman, maybe in her mid-forties, and she wore a red-checked apron over a white uniform. She returned to her conversation with a gray-haired gent in overalls who sat at the counter nursing a cup of coffee and a glazed doughnut.

Dan chose a booth beside the window so he had full view of the parking lot. Sitting three booths in front of him were a young man and woman. Her back was to Dan, her wavy shoulder-length hair the color of summer wheat. The young man, who Dan figured was twenty-seven or twenty-eight, wore his dark brown hair pulled back into a ponytail, and he had a sallow, long-jawed face and deepset ebony eyes that fixed Dan with a hard stare over his companion's shoulder. Dan nodded toward him, and the young man blinked sullenly and looked away.

The waitress came with a menu. Her name tag read DONNA LEE. "Just a cup of coffee," Dan told her. "As strong as you can make it."

"Hon, I can make it jump out the cup and two-step," she promised, and she left him to go back through a swinging door to the kitchen.

Dan took off his baseball cap and ran a hand over his forehead to collect the sheen that had gathered there. Fans were turning at the ceiling, their cool breezes welcome on his skin. He leaned against the backrest and closed his eyes. But he couldn't keep them shut because the death of Emory Blanchard was still repeating itself in the haunted house of his mind. He rubbed his stiff shoulder and then reached back to massage his neck. He'd escaped two tight squeezes since midnight, but if a state trooper car pulled up right then, he didn't know if he would have the energy to get up from his seat.

"You know what I think? I think the whole thing's a pile of shit!" It was the young man in the booth, talking to the woman. His voice dripped venom. "I thought you said I was gonna make some money out of this!"

"I said I'd pay you." Her voice was smoky and careful. "Keep it down, all right?"

"No, it ain't all right! I don't know why the hell I said I'd do this! It's a bunch of lies is what it is!"

"It's not lies. Don't worry, you'll get your money."

The young man looked as if he were about to spit something back at her, but his piercing gaze suddenly shifted, locking onto Dan. "Hey! What're you starin' at?"

"I'm just waitin' for a cup of coffee."

"Well look somewhere else while you do it!"

"Fine with me." Dan averted his eyes, but not before he'd noted that the young man wore a black T-shirt imprinted with yellow skulls and the legend HANOI JANES. The woman got him to quiet down a little, but he was still mouthing off about money. He kept cutting his eyes at Dan. Lookin' for trouble, Dan thought. Pissed off about something and ready to pick a fight.

The waitress brought his coffee. Donna Lee had been right; this java had legs. "Keep the pot warm, will you?" Dan suggested as he sipped the high octane. She answered, "Goan do it," and walked behind the cash register to take the gray-haired man's money. "See you next run-through," she told him, and Dan watched him walk out to his tractor-trailer rig at the diesel pumps.

"Made a fool of me is what you did!" the young man started up again. "Come all this way to find a fuckin' fairy tale!"

"Joey, come on. Calm down, all right?"

"You think I'm supposed to be *happy*? Drive all this way, and then you gimme this big load of shit and ask me to calm down?" His voice was getting louder and harsher, and suddenly he reached out across the table and seized his companion's wrist. "You played me for a fuckin' fool, didn't you?"

"Ease up there, friend!" Donna Lee cautioned from behind the counter.

"I ain't talkin' to you!" Joey snapped. "So just shut up!"

"Hey, listen here!" She strode toward their booth on her chunky legs, her cheeks reddening. "You can get your sassy tail gone, I won't cry."

"It's okay," the young woman said, and Dan saw her pug-nosed profile as she glanced to the left at Donna Lee. "We're just talkin'."

"Talks kinda rough, don't he?"

"Gimme the damn check, how 'bout it?" Joey said.

"Pleased to." Donna Lee pulled the checkpad and a pencil from a pocket of her apron and totaled up their order. "Hon, you need any help?"

"No." She'd worked her wrist free and was rubbing where his fingers had been. "Thanks anyhow."

Dan happened to catch Joey's glare again for a split second, and the young man said, "God *damn!*" and stood up from the booth. His cowboy boots clacked on the linoleum, approaching Dan. "Joey, don't!" the young woman called, but then Joey was sliding into the seat across from him.

Dan drank down the rest of his coffee, paying him no attention. Inside, he was steeling himself for the encounter. "I thought I told you to quit starin' at me," Joey said with quiet menace.

Dan lifted his gaze to meet Joey's. The young man's eyes were red-rimmed, his gaunt face strained by whatever inner demons were torturing him. A little tarnished silver skeleton hung from the lobe of his left ear. Dan had met his kind before: a walking hair-trigger, always a hot flash away from explosion. Dan said calmly, "I don't want any trouble."

"Oh, I think you're askin' for a whole truckload of it, old man."

Dan was in no shape to be fighting, but damned if he'd take this kind of disrespect. If he was going down, he was going down swinging. "I'd like to be left alone."

"I'll leave you alone. After I take you out in the parkin' lot and beat the shit outta—" Joey didn't finish his threat, because Dan's right hand shot out, grasped the silver skeleton, and tore it from his earlobe. As Joey shouted with pain, Dan caught a left handful of T-shirt and jerked the young man's chest hard against the table's edge. Dan leaned forward, their faces almost touching. "You need some manners knocked into you, boy. Now, I'd suggest that you stand up and walk out of here, get in your car, and go wherever you're goin'. If you don't want to do that, I'd be glad to separate you from your teeth."

A drop of blood was welling from Joey's ripped earlobe. He sneered and started to fire another taunt into Dan's face, which might have cost the young punk at least a broken nose.

Whack!

Something had just slammed onto the tabletop.

Dan turned his head and looked at a baseball bat that had eight or nine wicked nails stuck through it.

"Pay attention," Donna Lee said. She was speaking to Joey, who had abruptly become an excellent listener. "You goan stand up, pay your check, leave me two dollars tip, and haul ass out my sight. Mister, let him loose."

Dan did. Joey stood up, his nervous gaze on the brainbuster. Donna Lee stepped back and then followed him to the cash register. "Get you 'nother cup in a minute," she told Dan.

"Sorry. He gets like that sometimes."

It was the young woman, standing next to his booth. Dan looked up at her, said, "No harm d—" and then he stopped because of her face.

The left side of it, the side he'd seen in profile, was very pretty. Across the bridge of her pug nose was a scatter of freckles. Her mouth had the lush lips lonely men kissed in their dreams, and her blond hair was thick and beautiful. Her eyes were soft blue, the blue of a cool mountain lake.

But the right side of her face was another story, and not a kind one.

It was covered by a huge purplish-red birthmark that began up in her hair and continued all the way down onto her throat. The mark had ragged edges like the coast on a map of some strange and unexplored territory. Because the left side of her face was so achingly perfect, the right side was that much harder to look at. "Done," Dan finished, his gaze following the maroon inlets and coves. Then he met her eyes, and he recognized in them the same kind of deep, soul-anchored pain he'd seen in his own mirror.

The instant of an inner glimpse passed. She glanced at his empty coffee cup. "You'd better get somethin' to eat, mister," she said in that voice like velvet and smoke. "You don't look so hot."

"Been a rough day." Dan noted that she wore no makeup and her clothes were simple: a violet floral-patterned short-sleeve blouse and a pair of lived-in blue jeans. She carried a small chestnut-colored purse, its strap around her left shoulder. She was a slim girl, not a whole lot of meat on her bones, and she had that wiry, hardscrabble Texas look. Maybe she stood five-two, if that. Dan tried to envision her without the birthmark; lacking it, she might resemble the kind of fresh-faced girl-next-door in magazine ads. With it, though, she was traveling by night in the company of Joey the punk.

"Arden!" His money had been slapped down beside the cash register. "You comin' or not?"

"I am." She started to walk away, but Dan said, "Hey, you think he wants this?" and he offered her the silver skeleton. "Reckon he does," she answered as she took it from his palm. "Fuck it, I'm goin'!" Joey shouted, and he stormed through the front door.

"He's got a mouth on him," Dan told the girl.

"Yeah, he does get a little profane now and again. Sorry for the trouble."

"No apology needed."

She followed Joey, taking long strides with her dusty brown boots, and Donna Lee said to her, "Honey, don't you suffer no shit, hear?" After the girl was gone, Donna Lee brought the coffeepot over to Dan and refilled his cup. "I hate a bastard think he can stomp on a woman," she confided. "Remind me of my ex-husband. Didn't have a pot to pee in the way he laid 'round all day, and he had that mean mouth, too. You travelin' far?"

"A distance," Dan said.

"Where to?"

Dan watched her set the coffeepot down on his table, a sure sign she wanted to stick around and talk. "South," he decided to say.

"Such a shame, huh?"

"What is?"

"That girl. You know. Her face. Never seen a birthmark so bad before. No tellin' what that do to a person."

Dan nodded and tasted his fresh cup.

"Listen," Donna Lee continued, "you don't mind me bein' so personal, you don't look to be feelin' well. You up to drivin'?"

"I'm all right." He felt, however, as if he had the strength of a wrung-out dishrag.

"How 'bout a piece of strawberry pie? On the house?"

He was about to say that sounded fine, when Donna Lee's eyes suddenly flicked up from him and she stared out the window. "Uh-oh. Looky there, he's at it again!"

Dan turned his head and saw Joey the punk and the girl named Arden arguing beside the red Camaro. She must've said something that made his hair-trigger flare, because he lifted his arm as if to strike her a backhanded blow and she retreated a few steps. His face was contorted with anger, and now Dan and Donna Lee could hear his shouting through the glass. "I swear to gumbo," Donna Lee said resignedly, "I knew when I stuck eye on him he was gonna be trouble. Lemme go get my slugger." She went behind the counter, where she'd stashed the nail-studded baseball bat.

Outside, Joey had stopped short of attacking the girl. Dan watched him throw open the Camaro's trunk and toss a battered brown suitcase onto the pavement. Its latches popped, the suitcase spilling clothes in a multicolored spiral. A small pink drawstring bag fell out, and Joey attacked it with relish. He charged it and gave it a vicious kick, and Arden scooped it up and backed away, holding it protectively against her chest, her mouth crimped with bitterness.

"You get on outta here!" Donna Lee yelled from the door, her slugger ready for action. Two attendants from the gas station were coming over to see what the ruckus was about, and they looked like fellows who could chew Joey up at least as well as the slugger could. "Go on, 'fore I call the law!"

"Kiss my ass, you old bitch!" Joey hollered back, but he'd seen the two men coming and he started moving faster. He banged the trunk shut and climbed into the car. "Arden, I'm quits with you! Hear me?"

"Go on, then! Here, take it and go on!" She had some money in her fist, and she flung the bills at him through the Camaro's window. The engine boomed. Joey shouted something else at her, but it was drowned by the engine's noise. Then he threw the Camaro into reverse, spun the car around in a half circle facing the way out, and laid on the horn at the same time as he hit the accelerator. The wide rear tires shrieked and smoked, and when they bit pavement they left black teethmarks. As the Camaro roared forward, the two gas station attendants had to jump for their lives. Dan watched through the window as the studmobile tore off across the parking lot and in three eyeblinks it had dwindled to the size of its red taillights. The car headed for the I-49 northbound ramp, and very soon it was lost from sight.

Dan took a drink of coffee and watched the girl.

She didn't cry, which is what he'd expected. Her expression was grim but resolute as she opened her purse and put the pink drawstring bag into it, and then she began to pick up her scattered items of clothing and return them to the suitcase. Donna Lee had a few words with the gas station boys, the nail-pierced slugger held at her side. Arden kept glancing in the direction the Camaro had gone as she retrieved her belongings. Donna Lee helped her round up the last few items, and then the girl snapped her suitcase shut and stood there with her birthmarked face aimed toward the northern dark. The two attendants returned to their building, Donna Lee came back into the restaurant and put the slugger away behind the counter, but Arden stood alone in the parking lot.

"She okay?" Dan asked.

"Say he'll be back," Donna Lee told him. "Say he got a bad temper and sometime it make him get crazy, but after a few minute he come to his sense."

"Takes all kinds, I guess."

"Yes, it do. I swear I would've brained him if I'd got close enough to swing. Knocked some that meanness out his ears." Donna Lee walked over to Dan's booth and motioned with a lift of her chin. "Look at her out there. Hell, if a man treat me that way, I swanee I wouldn't stand 'round waitin' on him. Would you?"

"No, I sure wouldn't."

Donna Lee gave him a smile of approval. "I'm gonna get you that strawberry pie, on the house. That suit you?"

"Sounds fine."

"You got it, then!"

The pie was mostly sugary meringue, but the strawberries were fresh. Dan was about halfway through it when Arden came back into the restaurant, lugging her suitcase. "Awful warm out there," she said. "Mind if I sit and wait?"

" 'Course you can, hon! Sit down and rest you'self!" Donna Lee had found a stray to mother, it seemed, and she hurriedly poured a glass of iced tea and took it to Arden, who chose a booth near the door. Donna Lee sat down across from her, willing to lend an ear to the girl's plight, and Dan couldn't help but overhear since they were sitting just a couple of booths away. No, Joey wasn't her husband, Arden told Donna Lee. Wasn't even really her boyfriend, though they'd gone out together a few times. They lived in the same apartment complex in Fort Worth, and they'd been on their way to Lafayette. Joey played bass guitar in a band called the Hanoi Janes, and Arden had worked the sound board and lights for them on weekends. Mostly fraternity parties and such. Joey was so high-strung because he had an artistic temperament, Arden said. He threw a fit every once in a while, to let off steam, and this wasn't the first time he'd ditched her on the roadside. But he'd be back. He always came back.

Dan looked out the window. Just dark out there, and nothing else.

"Hon, I wouldn't wait for him, myself," Donna Lee said. "I'd just as soon take the bus back home."

"He'll be here. He'll get about ten miles up the road, then he'll cool off."

"Ain't no kinda man throw a girl out his car to take her chance. I'd go on home and tell that sucker to kiss my Dixie cup. You got business in Lafayette?"

"Yeah, I do."

"Family live there?"

"No," Arden said. "I'm goin' to meet somebody."

"That's where I'd go, then. I wouldn't trust no fella threw me out the car. Next time he might throw you out where there's not a soul to help you."

"Joey'll be back." Arden kept watching through the window. "Any minute now."

"Damned if I'd be waitin' here for him. Hey, friend!"

Dan turned his head.

"You goin' south, aren't you? Gotta go through Lafayette. You want to give this young lady a ride?"

"Sorry," Dan answered. "I'm not carryin' passengers."

"Thanks anyway," Arden said to Donna Lee, "but I wouldn't ride with a stranger."

"Well, I'll tell you somethin' 'bout Donna Lee Boudreax. I've worked here goin' on nine year, I've seen a lot of folk come and go, and I've got to where I can read 'em real good. I knew your friend was trouble first sight, and if I say that fella over there's a gentleman, you can write it in the book. Friend, you wouldn't harm this young lady, would you?"

"No," Dan said, "but if I was her father I sure wouldn't want her ridin' with a stranger in the middle of the night."

"See there?" Donna Lee lifted her penciled-on eyebrows. "He's a gentleman. You want to go to Lafayette, you'd be safe with him."

"I'd better stay here and wait," Arden insisted. "Joey'd really blow up if he came back and found me gone."

"Hell, girl, do he *own* you? I wouldn't give him the satisfaction of findin' me waitin'."

Dan took the last bite of his pie. It was time to get moving again, before this booth got too comfortable. He put his baseball cap back on and stood up. "How much do I owe you?"

"Not a thing, if you'll help this young lady out."

He looked out the window. Still no sign of a Camaro's headlights. "Listen, I'd like to, but I can't. I've got to get on down the road."

"Road goes south," Donna Lee said. "Both of you headin' that way. Ain't no skin off your snout, is it?"

"I think she's old enough to make up her own mind." Dan saw that Arden was still staring out at the dark highway. He felt a pang of sadness for her. If the right side of her face were as pretty as the left, she sure wouldn't have to be waiting for a punk who cursed her and left her to fend for herself. But he had enough problems without taking on another one. He put two dollars down on the table for the coffee, said "Thanks for the pie," and he started for the door.

"Speak up, hon," Donna Lee urged. "Train's pullin' out."

But Arden remained silent. Dan walked out of the restaurant into humidity that steamed the sweat from his pores before he'd even reached the station wagon. He drove over to the self-serve pumps, where he intended to top off the tank. He needed another roadmap as well, and when the gas stopped flowing he went into the office, bought a Louisiana map, and paid what he owed for the fill-up.

He was standing under the lights, searching the map south of

Houma for a place called Vermilion, when he heard the sound of boots coming up behind him. He looked around and there she stood, suitcase in hand, her birthmark dark purple in the fluorescent glow.

"I don't think he's comin' back this time," she said. "You got room?"

"I thought you said you wouldn't ride with a stranger."

"Everybody's a stranger when you're a long way from home. I don't want to wait around here anymore. If you give me a ride, I'll pay you ten dollars."

"Sorry." Dan folded the map and got behind the steering wheel.

"It's a birthmark, not leprosy," Arden said with some grit in her voice. "You won't catch it."

Dan paused with his hand on the ignition. "A southbound trucker ought to be along pretty soon. You can hitch a ride with him."

"If I wait for a trucker, no tellin' what might turn up. You look too damn tired to try anythin', and even if you did, I believe I could outrun you."

He couldn't argue with her logic. Even with all that caffeine in his system, he still felt as weak as a whipped pup, his joints ached like bad teeth, and a glance into the rearview mirror had shown him a pasty-white face with what looked like dark bruises under his eyes. In truth, he was just about used up. The girl was waiting for his answer. Lafayette was about twenty-five miles. Maybe it would be good to have somebody along to keep him awake, and then he could find a place to rest until nightfall.

"Climb in," he said.

Arden hefted her suitcase into the rear seat. "Got a lot of glass back here."

"Yeah. Window was broken, I haven't had a chance to clean it out."

She took the passenger seat. Dan started the engine and followed the ramp to I-49 southbound. The truck stop fell behind, and in a couple of minutes the glow of green neon was gone. Arden looked back only once, then she stared straight ahead as if she'd decided that where she was going was more important than where she'd been.

Dan imagined that her birthmark would bleach white if she knew who she was riding with. Donna Lee would've taken the slugger to him rather than put this girl in his care. Dan kept his speed at fifty-five, the engine laboring. State troopers were lurking somewhere on the interstate; maybe waiting around the next curve, looking for a stolen station wagon with a killer worth fifteen thousand dollars behind the wheel.

He never had put much faith in prayer.

Right now, with the dark pressing all around, his strength tattering away, and his future a question mark, a silent prayer seemed to be the only shield at hand.

12

Jupiter

The first lights of Lafayette were ahead. Dan said, "We're almost there. Where do you need to go?"

Arden had been quiet during the drive, her eyes closed and her head tilted to one side. Now she sat up straight and took her bearings. She opened her purse, unfolded a piece of paper, and strained to read by the highway lights what was written there. "Turn off on Darcy Avenue. Then you'll go two miles east and turn right on Planters Road."

"What are you lookin' for? Somebody's house?"

"The Twin Oaks nursin' home."

Dan glanced quickly at her. "A *nursin'* home? That's why you came all the way from Fort Worth?"

"That's right."

"You have a relative livin' there?"

"No, just somebody I have to see."

Must be somebody mighty important, Dan thought. Well, it wasn't his business. He took the turn onto Darcy Avenue and drove east along a wide thoroughfare lined with fast-food joints, strip malls, and restaurants with names like King Crawdaddy and Whistlin' Willie's Cajun Hut. Everything was closed but an occasional gas station, and only a couple of other cars passed by. Dan turned right on Planters Road, which ran past apartment complexes and various small businesses. "How far is it from here?"

"Not far."

His curiosity about the nursing home was starting to get the best of him. If she hadn't come the distance from Fort Worth on account of a relative, then who was it she needed to see? He had his own problems, for sure, but the situation intrigued him. "Mind if I ask who you're goin' to visit?"

"Somebody I used to know, growin' up."

"This person know you're comin'?"

608

"No."

"You think quarter to four in the mornin' is a good time to visit somebody in a rest home?"

"Jupiter always liked early mornin'. If he's not up yet, I'll wait."

"Jupiter?" Dan asked.

"That's his name. Jupiter Krenshaw." Arden stared at him. "How come you've taken such an interest?"

"No special reason. I guess I just wanted to know."

"All right, I reckon that's only fair. I used to know Jupiter when I was fifteen, sixteen years old. He worked on the farm where I was livin'. Groomed the horses. He used to tell me stories. Things about his growin' up, down in the bayou. Some of 'em made-up stories, some of 'em true. I haven't seen him for ten years, but I remember those stories. I tracked down his nearest relative, and I found out Jupiter was in the nursin' home." She watched Planters Road unreel in the headlights. "There's somethin' I need to talk to him about. Somethin' that's very, very important to me."

"Must be," Dan commented. "I mean, you came a long way to see him."

She was silent for a moment, the warm wind blowing in around them. "You ever hear of somebody called the Bright Girl?"

Dan shook his head. "No, can't say I have. Who is she?"

"I think that might be it," Arden said, lifting her chin to indicate a low-slung brick building on the right. In another moment Dan could see the small, tastefully lit sign that announced it was indeed the Twin Oaks Retirement Home. The place was across from a strip mall, but it didn't look too bad; it had a lot of windows, a long porch with white wicker furniture, and two huge oak trees stood on either side of the entrance. Dan pulled up to the front, where there was a wheelchair ramp and steps carpeted with Astroturf. "Okay," he said. "This is your stop."

She didn't get out. "Can I ask a favor of you?"

"You can ask."

"How much of a hurry are you in?"

"I'm not hurryin', but I'm not dawdlin', either."

"Do you have time to wait for me? It shouldn't take too long, and I sure would appreciate a lift to a motel."

He thought about it, his hands on the wheel. A motel room was what he needed, too; he was just too tired to make it the rest of the way to Vermilion. He'd found the fishing camp on the roadmap: a speck on Highway 57 about fifteen miles south of Houma, near where the pavement ended in the huge bayou swamp of Terrebonne Parish. "I'll wait," he decided.

"Thanks." She leveled her gaze at him. "I'm gonna leave my suitcase. You won't run off soon as I walk in the door, will you?"

"No, I'll stick." And maybe catch some sleep while he waited, he thought.

"Okay." She nodded; he seemed trustworthy, and she counted herself lucky that she'd met him. "I don't even know your name."

"Dan," he said.

"I'm Arden Halliday." She offered her hand, and Dan shook it. "I appreciate you helpin' me like this. Hope I didn't take you too far out of your way."

He shrugged. "I'm headed down south of Houma anyhow." Instantly he regretted telling her that, because if she happened to find out who he was, that information would go straight to the police. He was so tired, he was forgetting a slip of the lip could lead him to prison.

"I won't be long," she promised, and she got out and walked up the steps, entering the building through a door with etched-glass panels.

It occurred to him that the smart thing to do might be to set her suitcase on the porch and hit the accelerator, but he dismissed the idea. Weariness was creeping through his bones, his eyes heavy-lidded. He was going to ask her to get behind the wheel when she was finished inside. He cut the engine and folded his arms across his chest. His eyes closed, and he listened to the soft humming of insects in the steamy night.

"Mister?"

Dan opened his eyes and sat bolt upright. A man was standing beside his window, peering in. Dan had an instant of cold terror because the man wore a cap and uniform with a badge at his breast pocket.

"Mister?" the policeman said again. "You can't park here."

"Sir?" It was all Dan could get out.

"Can't park here, right in front of the door. It's against the fire code."

Dan blinked, his vision blurred. But he could make out that the face was young enough to have acne eruptions, and on the badge was stamped TWIN OAKS SECURITY.

"You can park 'round the side there," the security guard said. "If you don't mind, I mean."

"No. No, I don't mind." He almost laughed; a lanky kid who was probably all of nineteen had just about scared his hair white. "I'll move it." He reached down to restart the engine, and at that moment Arden came out of the building and down the steps.

"Any problem?" she asked when she saw the security guard, and the kid looked at her and started to answer, but then his eyes got fixed on the birthmark and his voice failed him.

"I was about to move the car," Dan explained. "Fire code. You finished already?"

"No. Lady at the front desk says Jupiter usually wakes up around five. I told her he'd want to see me, but she won't get him up any earlier. That's about another hour."

Dan rubbed his eyes. An hour wasn't going to make much difference one way or another, he figured. "Okay. I'll park the car and try to get some sleep."

"Well, there's a waitin' area inside. Got a sofa you might stretch out on, and it's sure a lot cooler in there." Arden suddenly looked into the security guard's face. "You want to tell me what you're starin' at?"

"Uh . . . uh . . ." the kid stammered.

Arden stepped toward him, her chin uplifted in defiance. "It's called a port-wine stain," she said. "I was born wearin' it. Go on and take a good long look, just satisfy the hell out of yourself. You want to touch it?"

"No ma'am," he answered, taking a quick backward step. "I mean . . . no thank you, ma'am."

Arden continued to lock his gaze with her own, but she'd decided he meant no disrespect. Her voice was calmer when she spoke again. "I guess I wouldn't want to touch it, either, if I didn't have to." She returned her attention to Dan, who could see the anger fading from her eyes like the last embers of a wind-whipped fire. "Probably be more comfortable inside."

"Yeah, I guess so." He figured he could've slept in a cement mixer, but the sofa would be kinder to his bones. He fired up the engine, which sounded as rugged as he felt. "I'll pull around to the side and come on in." The security guard moved away and Dan parked the station wagon in a small lot next to the Twin Oaks. It was a tribulation to walk the distance back to the front door. Inside, though, the air-conditioning was a breath from heaven. A thin, middle-aged woman with a hairdo like a double-dip of vanilla ice cream sat behind a reception desk, her lips pursed as she absorbed the contents of a paperback romance. Arden was sitting nearby in a waiting area that held a number of overstuffed chairs, brass reading lamps, and a magazine rack, and there was the full-length sofa as pretty as a vision of the Promised Land.

Dan eased himself down, took off his shoes, and stretched out. Arden had a dog-eared *National Geographic* in her lap, but she looked needful of some sleep, too. The place was quiet, the corridors only dimly lit. From somewhere came the sound of a low, muffled coughing. Dan had the thought that no policeman in Louisiana would think to look for him at a Lafayette nursing home. Then his mind and body relaxed, as much as was possible, and he slept a dreamless sleep.

Voices brought him back to the land of the living.

"Ma'am? I believe Mr. Krenshaw's awake by now. Can I tell him who you are?"

"Just tell him Arden. He'll know."

"Yes ma'am." There was the sound of rubber-soled shoes squeaking on the linoleum.

Dan opened his eyes and looked out the nearest window. Violet light was showing at the horizon. Nearing six o'clock, he figured. His mouth was as dry as a dust bowl. He saw a water fountain a few steps away, and he summoned his strength and sat up, his joints as stiff as rusty hinges. The girl was still sitting in the chair, her face turned toward a corridor that went off past the reception desk. She'd opened her purse, Dan noted, and she had removed the small pink drawstring bag from it. The bag was in her lap, both her hands clutched together around it in an attitude that struck Dan as being either of protection or prayer. As he stood up to walk to the water fountain, he saw her pull the drawstring tight and push it into her purse again. Then she rose to her feet as well, because someone was coming along the corridor.

There were two people, one standing and one sitting. A brown-haired woman in a white uniform was pushing a wheelchair, her shoes squeaking with every step, and in the wheelchair sat a frail-looking black man wearing a red-checked robe and slippers with yellow-and-green argyle socks. Dan took a drink of water and watched Arden walk forward to meet the man she'd come so far to see.

Jupiter was seventy-eight years old now, his face was a cracked riverbed of wrinkles, and his white hair had dwindled to a few remaining tufts. Arden was sure she'd changed just as much, but he would have to be blind not to know her, and the stroke he'd suffered two years before had not robbed him of his eyes. They were ashine, and their excitement jumped into Arden like an electric spark. His nephew had told Arden about the stroke, which had happened just five months after the death of Jupiter's wife, and so Arden had been prepared for the palsy of his head and hands and the severe downturn of the right side of his mouth. Still, it was hard because she remembered how he used to be, and ten years could do a lot of damage. She took the few last steps to meet him, grasped one of his palsied hands as he reached up for her, and with an effort he opened his mouth to speak.

"Miz Arden," he said. His voice was like a gasp, almost painful to hear. "Done growed up."

She gave him the best smile she had. "Hello, Jupiter. How're they treatin' you?"

"Like I'm worn out. Which I *ain't*. Gone be back to work again soon as I get on my feet." He shook his head with wonder, his hand still gripping Arden's. "My, my! You have surely become a young lady! Doreen would be so proud to see you!"

"I heard what happened. I'm sorry."

"I was awful down at first. Awful down. But Doreen's the pride of the angels now, and I'm happy for her. Gone get on my feet again. Louis thinks I'm worn out can't do a thing for m'self." He snorted. "I said you gimme the money they chargin' you, I'll show you how a man can pull hisself up. I ain't through, no ma'am." Jupiter's rheumy eyes slid toward Dan. "Who is that there? I can't—" He caught his breath. "Lord have mercy! Is that . . . is that Mr. Richards?"

"That's the man who brought me—"

"Mr. *Richards!*" The old man let go of Arden and wheeled himself toward Dan before the nurse could stop him. Dan stepped back, but the wheelchair was suddenly right there in front of him and the old man's crooked mouth was split by an ecstatic grin. "You come to see me, too?"

"Uh . . . I think you've got me mixed up with some—"

"Don't you worry, now I *know* I'm gone get up out this thing! My, my, this is a happy day! Mr. Richards, you still got that horse eats oranges skin and all? I was thinkin' 'bout that horse th'other day. Name right on the tip of my tongue, right there it was but I couldn't spit it out. What was that horse's name?"

"Jupiter?" Arden said quietly, coming up behind him. She put a hand on one of his thin shoulders. "That's not Mr. Richards."

"Well, sure it is! Right here he is, flesh and bone! I may be down, but I ain't out! Mr. Richards, what was the name of that horse eats oranges skin and all?"

Dan looked into Arden's face, seeking help. It was obvious the old man had decided he was someone else, and to him the matter was settled. Arden said, "I think the horse's name was Fortune."

"Fortune! That's it!" Jupiter nodded, his eyes fixed on Dan. "You still got that ol' wicked horse?"

"I'm not who you—" But Dan paused before he went any further. There seemed to be no point in it. "Yeah," he said. "I guess I do."

"I'll teach him some manners! God may make the horse, but I'm the one takes off the rough edges, ain't that right, Miz Arden?"

"That's right," she said.

Jupiter grunted, satisfied with the answer. He turned his attention away from Dan and stared out the window. "Sun's comin' up directly. Be dry and hot. Horses need extra water today, can't work 'em too hard."

Arden motioned the nurse aside for a moment and spoke to her, and the nurse nodded agreement and withdrew to give them privacy. Dan started to move away, too, but the old man reached out with steely fingers and caught his wrist. "Louis don't think I'm worth a damn no more," he confided. "You talk to Louis?"

"No, I didn't."

"My nephew. Put me in here. I said Louis, you gimme the money they're chargin' you, I'll show you how a man can pull hisself up."

Arden drew up a chair beside the old man and sat down. Through the window the sky was becoming streaked with pink. "You always did like to watch the sun rise, didn't you?"

"Got to get an early start, you want to make somethin' of you'self. Mr. Richards knows that's gospel. Water them horses good today, yessir."

"You want me to step outside?" Dan asked the girl. But Jupiter didn't let go of him, and Arden shook her head. Dan frowned; he felt as if he'd walked on stage in the middle of a play without knowing the title or what the damn thing was about.

"I am so pleased," Jupiter said, "that you both come to see me. I think a lot 'bout them days. I dream 'bout 'em. I close my eyes and I can see everythin', just like it was. It was a golden time, that's what I believe. A golden time." He drew a long, ragged breath. "Well, I ain't done yet. I may be down, but I ain't out!"

Arden took Jupiter's other hand. "I came to see you," she said, "because I need your help."

He didn't respond for a moment, and Arden thought he hadn't heard. But then Jupiter's head turned and he stared quizzically at her. "My help?"

She nodded. "I'm goin' to find the Bright Girl."

Jupiter's mouth slowly opened, as if he were about to speak, but nothing came out.

"I remember the stories you used to tell me," Arden went on. "I never forgot 'em, all this time. Instead of fadin' away, they kept gettin' more and more real. Especially what you told me about the

Bright Girl. Jupiter, I need to find her. You remember, you told me what she could do for me? You used to say she could touch my face and the mark would come off on her hands. Then she'd wash her hands with water and it'd be gone forever and ever."

The birthmark, Dan realized she was talking about. He stared at Arden, but her whole being seemed to be focused on the old man.

"Where is she?" Arden urged.

"Where she always was," Jupiter answered. "Where she always will be. Road runs out, meets the swamp. Bright Girl's in there."

"I remember you used to tell me about growin' up in LaPierre. Is that where I need to start from?"

"LaPierre," he repeated, and he nodded. "That's right. Start from LaPierre. They know 'bout the Bright Girl there, they'll tell you."

"Beg pardon," Dan said, "but can I ask who ya'll are talkin' about?"

"The Bright Girl's a faith healer," Arden told him. "She lives in the swamp south of where Jupiter grew up."

It came clear to Dan. Arden was searching for a faith healer to take the birthmark off her face, and she'd come to see this old man to help point the way. Dan was tired and cranky, his joints hurt, and his head was throbbing; it frankly pissed him off that he'd taken a detour and risked traveling on the interstate because of such nonsense. "What is she, some kind of voodoo woman lights incense and throws bones around?"

"It's not voodoo," Arden said testily. "She's a holy woman."

"Holy, yes she is. Carries the lamp of God," Jupiter said to no one in particular.

"I had you figured for a sensible person. There's no such thing as a faith healer." A thought struck Dan like an ax between the eyes. "Is that why Joey left you? 'Cause he figured out you were chasin' a fairy tale?"

"Oh, Mr. Richards sir!" Jupiter's hand squeezed Dan's harder. "Bright Girl ain't no fair' tale! She's as real as you and me! Been livin' in that swamp long 'fore my daddy was a li'l boy, and she'll be there long after my bones done blowed away. I seen her when I was eight year old. Here come the Bright Girl down the street!" He smiled at the memory, the warm pink light of the early sun settling into the lines of his face. "Young white girl, pretty as you please. That's why she called bright. But she carries a lamp, too. Carries a lamp from God that burns inside her, and that's how she gets her healin' touch. Yessir, here come the Bright Girl down the street and a crowd of people followin' her. She on the way to Miz Wardell's house, Miz Wardell so sick with cancer she just lyin' in bed, waitin' to die. She see me standin' there and she smile under her big purple hat and I know who she is, 'cause my mama say Bright Girl was comin'. I sing out Bright Girl! Bright Girl! and she touch my hand when I reach for her. I feel that lamp she carryin' in her, that healin' lamp from God." He lifted his eyes to Dan's face. "I never felt such light before, Mr. Richards. Never felt it since. They said the Bright Girl laid her hands on Miz Wardell and up come the black bile, all that cancer flowin' out. Said it took two days and two nights, and when it was done the Bright Girl was so tired she had to be carried back to her boat. But Miz Wardell outlived two husbands and was dancin' when she was ninety. And that ain't all the Bright Girl did for people 'round LaPierre, neither. You ask 'em down there, they'll tell you 'bout all the folks she healed of cancers, tumors, and sicknesses. So nosir, all due respect, but Bright Girl ain't no fair' tale 'cause I seen her with my own livin' eyes."

"I believe you," Arden said. "I always did."

"That's the first step," he answered. "You go to LaPierre. Go south, you'll find her. She'll touch your face and make things right. You won't never see that mark no more."

"I want things made right. More than anythin' in this world, I do."

"Miz Arden," Jupiter said, "I 'member how you used to fret 'bout you'self, and how them others treated you. I 'member them names they called you, them names that made you cry. Then you'd wipe your eyes, stick your chin out again, and keep on goin'. But it seems to me you might still be cryin' on the inside." He looked earnestly up at Dan. "You gone take care of Miz Arden?"

"Listen," Dan said. "I'm not who you think I am."

"I know who you are," Jupiter replied. "You the man God sent Miz Arden."

"Come again?"

"That's right. You the man God provided to take Miz Arden to the Bright Girl. You His hands, you gone have to steer her the right direction."

Dan didn't know what to say, but he'd had enough of this. He pulled loose from the old man's spidery fingers. "I'll be waitin' outside," he growled at Arden, and he turned toward the door.

"Good-bye!" Jupiter called after him. "You heed what I say now, hear?"

Outside, the eastern horizon was the color of burnished copper. Already the air smelled of wet, agonizing heat. Dan stalked to the station wagon, got behind the wheel, and sat there while the sweat began to bloom from his pores. Again he pondered ditching her suitcase and hitting the road, but the heat chased such thoughts away; in his present condition he wouldn't get more than a few miles before he fell asleep at the wheel. He was nodding off when the girl opened the passenger door. "You look pretty bad," she said. "Want me to drive?"

"No," he said. Don't be stupid, he told himself. Weaving all over the road was a sure way to get stopped by a police car. "Wait," he said as she started to climb in. "Yeah, I think you'd better drive."

They started off, Arden retracing the way they'd come. To Dan's aching bones the pitch and sway of the station wagon's creaking frame was pure torture. "Gonna have to pull over," he said when they were back on Darcy Avenue. He made out a small motel coming up on the right; its sign proclaimed it the Rest Well Inn, which sounded mighty good to him. "Turn in there."

She did as he said, and she drove up under a green awning in front of the motel's office. A sign in the window said that all rooms were ten dollars a night, there were phones in all of them, and the cable TV was free. "You want me to check us in?"

Dan narrowed his eyes at her. "What do you mean, check *us* in? We ain't a couple."

"I meant separate rooms. I could do with some sleep, too."

"Oh. Yeah, okay. Fine with me."

She cut the engine and got out. "What's your last name?"

"Huh?"

"Your last name. They'll want it on the register."

"Farrow," he said. "From Shreveport, if they need that, too."

"Back in a couple of minutes."

Dan leaned his head back and waited. Stopping here seemed the only thing to do; he wouldn't have driven the rest of the way to Vermilion in daylight even if he'd felt able. He was fading fast. That crazy old man, he thought. Here come the Bright Girl down the street. Laid her hands on Miz Wardell. All that cancer flowin' out. I never felt such light before, Mr. Rich—

"Here's your key."

Dan got his eyes open and took the key Arden offered. The sun had gotten brighter. Arden drove them a short distance, and then somehow he was fitting the key into a door and walking into a small but clean room with beige-painted cinder-block walls. He locked the door behind him, walked right to the bed, and climbed onto it without removing his cap or shoes. If the police were to suddenly burst into the room, they would've had to pour him into handcuffs.

Pain was throbbing through his body. He had pushed himself too far. But there was still a distance to go, and he couldn't give up. Get seven or eight hours of sleep, he'd feel better. Drive after dark, down into the swampland. They know 'bout the Bright Girl there. Go south, you'll find her. You His hands, you gone have to steer her the right direction.

Crazy old man. I'm a killer, that's what I am.

Dan turned over onto his side and curled his knees up toward his chest.

You His hands.

And with that thought he slipped away into merciful and silent darkness.

13

Satan's Paradise

"**Y**ou know, Elvis almost gave up singin' when he was a young boy. Signed on as a truck driver, and that's what he figured on bein'. Did I tell you I used to be a truck driver?"

"Yes, Eisley," Flint said wearily. "Two hours ago."

"Well, what I was meanin' is that you never know where you're goin' in this life. Elvis thought he was gonna be a truck driver, and look where he went. Same with me. Only I guess I ain't got to where I'm goin' yet."

"Um," Flint said, and he let his eyes slide shut again.

The sun was hot enough to make a shadow sweat. The Eldorado's windows were down but the air was still, not a whisper of a breeze. The car was parked on a side road under the shade of weeping willow trees, otherwise they couldn't have stayed in it as they had for almost twelve hours. Even so, Flint had been forced to take off his coat and unbutton his shirt, and Clint's arm dangled from its root just below the conjunction of Flint's rib cage, the hand clenching every so often as if in lethargic protest of the heat. The reflexes of Clint's hand had kept Mama entertained for a while, but now she lay asleep in the backseat, her pink tongue flopped out and a little puddle of drool forming on the black vinyl.

There was one cracked and potholed highway from Houma to Vermilion, no other road in or out. It had brought Flint and Pelvis along its winding spine south through the bayou country in the predawn darkness, and though they hadn't been able to see much but the occasional glimmer of an early morning fisherman's lamp upon the water, they could smell the swamp itself, a heavy, pungent odor of intermingled sweet blossoms and sickly wet decay. They had crossed a long, concrete bridge and come through the town of Vermilion, which was a shuttered cluster of ramshackle stores and clapboard houses. Three miles past the bridge, on the left, was a dirt road that led through a forest of stunted pines and needle-tipped palmettos to a gray-painted cabin with a screened-in porch. The cabin had been dark, Lambert's car nowhere around. While Pelvis and Mama had peed in the woods, Flint had walked behind the cabin and found a pier that went out over a lake, but because of the darkness he couldn't tell how large or small the lake was. A boathouse stood nearby, its doors secured by a padlock. Lambert might or might not be on his way here, Flint decided, but it was fairly certain he hadn't shown up yet. Which was for the best, because Pelvis let out a loud yelp when a palmetto pricked him in a tender spot and then Mama started rapid-firing those high-pitched yips and yaps that made Flint's skin crawl.

They'd driven back to Vermilion and Flint had used the phone booth in front of a bait-and-tackle shop. He'd called Smoates's answering service and been told by the operator on duty that the light was still green, which meant that so far as Smoates knew, Lambert hadn't been caught. Flint had found a dirt side road about fifty yards south of the turnoff to the cabin that he could back the Cadillac onto and still have a view through the woods. It was here that they'd been sitting since four o'clock, alternately keeping watch, sleeping, or eating the glazed doughnuts, Oreo cookies, Slim Jims, and other deadly snacks from Eisley's grocery sack. They had stopped at a gas station just south of Lafayette to fill up and get something to drink, and there Flint had bought a plastic jug of water while Pelvis had opened his wallet for a six-pack of canned Yoo-Hoos.

"I swear," Pelvis said between sips from the last can, "that's an amazin' thing."

Flint remained silent; he was wise to Eisley's methods of drawing him into pointless talk.

"I swear it is," Pelvis tried again. "That little fella inside you, I mean. You know, I went to a freak show one time and saw a two-headed bull, but you take the cake."

Flint pressed his lips together tightly.

"Yessir." *Slllurrrrp* went the final swallow of the Yoo-Hoo. "People'd pay to see you, they surely would. I know *I* would. I mean, if I couldn't see you for free. Make you some money that way. You ever want to give up bounty-huntin' and go into show business, I'll tell you everythin' you need to—"

"Shut—your—mouth." Flint had whispered it, and instantly he regretted it because Eisley had worn him down yet again.

Pelvis dug down into the bottom of the sack and came up with the last three Oreos. Three bites and they were history. He wiped his lips with the back of his hand. "Really, now. You ever think about show business? All jokin' aside. You could get to be famous."

Flint opened his eyes and stared into Pelvis's sweat-beaded face. "For your information," he said coldly, "I grew up in the carnival life. I had a stomach full of 'show business,' so just drop it, understand?"

"You was with the carnival? You mean a freak show, is that right?"

Flint lifted a hand to his face and pressed index finger and thumb against his temples. "Oh, Jesus, what have I done to deserve this?"

"I'm int'rested. Really I am. I never met nobody was a real live freak before."

"Don't use that word."

"What word?"

"*Freak!*" Flint snapped, and Mama jumped up, growling. "Don't use that word!"

"Why not? Nothin' to be 'shamed of, is it?" Pelvis looked honestly puzzled. "I reckon there's worse words, don't you think?"

"Eisley, you kill me, you know that?" Flint summoned up a tight smile, but his eyes were fierce. "I've never met anybody so . . . so *dense* before in my entire life."

"Dense," Pelvis repeated. He nodded thoughtfully. "How do you mean that, exactly?"

"Thick-skulled! Stupid! How do you think I mean it?" Flint's smile had vanished. "Hell, what's wrong with you? Have you been in solitary confinement for the last five or six years? Can't you just shut your mouth and keep it shut for *two* minutes?"

"Course I can," Pelvis said petulantly. "Anybody can do that if they want to."

"Do it, then! Two minutes of silence!"

Pelvis clamped his mouth shut and stared straight ahead. Mama yawned and settled down to sleep again. "Whose watch we usin' to time this by?" Pelvis asked.

"Mine! I'll time it on my watch! Startin' right now!"

Pelvis grunted and rummaged down in the sack, but there was nothing left but wrappers. He upturned the last Yoo-Hoo can to try to catch a drop or two on his tongue, then he crumpled the can in a fist. "Kinda silly, I think."

"There you go!" Flint rasped. "You couldn't last fifteen seconds!"

"I'm not talkin' to *you!* Can't a man speak what's on his mind? I swear, Mr. Murtaugh, you're tryin' your very best to be hard to get along with!"

"I don't want you to get along with me, Eisley!" Flint said. "I want you to sit there and zipper your mouth! You and that damn mutt have already messed things up once, you're not gonna get a chance to do it again!"

"Don't blame that on Mama and me, now! We didn't have nothin' to do with it!"

Flint gripped the steering wheel with both hands, red splotches on his cheeks. Clint's hand rose up and clutched at the air before it fell back down again. "Just be quiet and leave me alone. Can you do that?"

"Sure I can. Ain't like I'm *dense* or anythin'."

"Good." Flint closed his eyes once more and leaned his head back.

Maybe ten seconds later Pelvis said, "Mr. Murtaugh?"

Flint's eyes were red-rimmed when he turned them on Eisley, his teeth gritting behind his lips.

"Somebody's comin'," Pelvis told him.

Flint looked through the pines along the road. A vehicle—one of only the dozen or so they'd seen on the road all day—was approaching from the direction of Vermilion. In another few seconds Flint saw it wasn't a station wagon but a truck about the size of a moving van. As the truck grew nearer, Flint made out the blue lettering on its side: BRISCOE PROCESSING CO. Under that was BATON ROUGE, LA. The truck rumbled past them and kept going south, took a curve, and was gone from sight.

"I don't think Lambert's comin'," Pelvis said. "Should've been here by now if he was."

"We're waitin' right here. I told you waitin' was a big part of the job, didn't I?"

"Yessir," Pelvis agreed, "but how do you know he ain't been caught already? We could sit here till crows fly back'ards, and if he's done been caught he ain't comin'."

Flint checked his wristwatch. It was eighteen minutes until four. Eisley was right; it was time to make a call to Smoates again. But Flint didn't want to drive into Vermilion to use the phone, because if Lambert was coming, it would be across that bridge and Flint didn't care to be spotted. It would be easier to take Lambert when he thought he was safe in the cabin rather than chasing him north on the highway. Flint looked in the direction the truck had gone. There had to be some trace of civilization farther south. He unfolded his Louisiana road map, one of a half-dozen state maps he always kept in the car, and found the dot of Vermilion. About four or five miles south of that was another speck called Chandalac, and then Highway 57 ended three miles or so later at a place named LaPierre. Beyond that was swampland all the way to the Gulf of Mexico.

The truck had to be going somewhere, and there had to be at least one pay phone down there, too. Flint started the engine and eased the Eldorado out of its hiding place. He ignored Pelvis's question of "Where we headed?" and turned right, the sun's glare sitting like a fireball on the long black hood.

In the brutal afternoon light they could see the type of country they'd driven through in darkness: on both sides of the road the flat, marshy land was alternately cut by winding channels of murky water and then stubbled with thick stands of palmettos and huge ancient oak trees. Around the next curve a brown snake that had to be a yard long was writhing on the hot pavement on Flint's side of the road, and he figured the truck had just crushed it a couple of minutes earlier. His spine crawled as the car passed over it, and when he glanced in the rearview mirror he saw two hulking birds that must've been vultures swoop down on the dying reptile and start tearing it to pieces with their beaks.

Flint didn't believe in omens. Nevertheless, he hoped this wasn't one.

They'd gone maybe a couple of miles when the spiny woods fell away on the right side of the road and the sun glittered off a blue channel of water that meandered out of what appeared to be primeval swamp. Just ahead was a white clapboard building with a tin roof and a sign that said Vermilion Marina & Groceries, and jutting off from shore was a pier where several small boats were tied up. One larger craft—a shrimp boat, Flint thought it was because of the nets and various hoists aboard—had just arrived and its crew was tying ropes down to the pier. And there sat the Briscoe Processing Company truck as well, parked next to the clapboard building with its loading bay facing the pier. Beside the marina, near a sun-bleached sign that advertised live bait, chewing tobacco, and fresh onions, stood a phone booth.

Flint pulled the car to a stop on a surface of crushed oyster shells. He buttoned up his shirt and shrugged into his loose-fitting suit jacket. "Stay here," he instructed Pelvis as he got out. "I'll be right back." He'd taken three strides toward the phone booth when he heard the Eldorado's passenger door creak open and Pelvis was climbing out with Mama tucked under his arm. "Just go on 'bout your business," Pelvis said when Flint fired a glare at him. "I'm goin' in there and get me some vittles. You want anythin'?"

"No." *Vittles,* Flint thought. Wasn't that what Granny fixed on

623

"The Beverly Hillbillies"? "Wait. Yeah, I do," he decided. "Get me a bottle of lemon juice, if they've got it. And don't go in there and flap your lips about Lambert, hear me? Anybody asks, you're here to do some fishin'. Understand?"

"You don't think I've got a lick of sense, do you?"

"Bingo," Flint said, and he turned his back on Pelvis and went into the phone booth. He placed a call through to Smoates's office. "It's Flint," he said when Smoates answered. "What's the situation on Lambert?"

"Hold on a minute."

Flint waited, sweat trickling down his face. It had to be over ninety degrees, even as the sun began to fall toward the west. The heat had stunned Clint, who lay motionless. The air smelled of the steamy, sickly sweet reek of the swamp, and his own bodily aroma wasn't too delicate, either. He wasn't used to being unclean; a gentleman knew the value of cleanliness, of crisp white shirts and freshly laundered underwear. These last twenty-four hours had been a little slice of hell on earth, and this swampland looked like Satan's paradise, too. From where he was standing, Flint could see four men unloading cargo from the shrimp boat. The cargo was greenish-brown and scaly, with long snouts bound shut by copper wire, four stubby legs fastened together with wire as well. Alligators, he realized with a start. The men were unloading alligators, each three or four feet long, from the deck of the boat and then carrying them to the Briscoe Processing Company truck and heaving them into the back. The men's workclothes were wet and muddy, the boat's deck heaped with maybe twenty or more live and squirming alligators. But there was a fifth man—slimmer than the others, with shoulder-length grayish-blond hair and wearing blue jeans and a Harvard T-shirt—who stood apart from the workers and seemed to be supervising. As Flint watched, the man in the Harvard T-shirt glanced at him and the sun flared in the round lenses of his dark glasses. The glance became a lingering stare.

"Flint?" Smoates had come back on the line. "Latest word's that Lambert's still on the loose. Where are you?"

"Down south. Little hellhole called Vermilion. I want you to know I'm standin' here watchin' a bunch of geeks unload honest-to-God live alligators off a boat."

"You ought to ask 'em if they need a hand," Smoates said with a wet chuckle.

Flint chose to let the remark pass. "I came close to nailin' Lambert last night."

"You're shittin' me! He showed up at the ex-wife's house?"

"No, not there. But I found him. I think he's on his way here, too. Probably holed up somewhere and gonna be on the move again after dark." Flint saw the man in the Harvard T-shirt still staring at him; then the dude motioned one of the workers—a shirtless, shaven-headed wall of a black man who must've stood six-four and weighed close to three hundred pounds—over to him and they started talking, their backs toward the phone booth, as the others continued to unload the alligators and throw them into the truck. "Smoates," Flint said, "Eisley's drivin' me crazy. Even God couldn't get him to shut his mouth. I don't know what you saw in him, but he's all wrong for the job."

"So he talks a lot, so what? That could be a plus. He's got the ability to wear people down."

"Yeah, he's good at that, all right. But he's slow upstairs. He can't think on his feet. I'd hate to be in a tight spot and have to depend on him, I'll tell you that."

"Forget about Eisley for a minute. You ain't heard the news, huh?"

"What news?"

"Lambert's a double murderer now. He killed a fella at a motel outside Alexandria 'round midnight. Blasted him with a shotgun, and when the fella didn't die fast enough, Lambert beat him to death. Stole his station wagon. Cable TV's picked up the story, it's on every hour."

"He was in the station wagon when I found him. I would've had him, but his ex-wife helped him get away."

"Well, sounds to me like Lambert's turned into a mad dog. Man who's killed twice won't think nothin' 'bout killin' a third time, so watch your ass."

"He's in the grocery store right now," Flint said.

"Huh? Oh, yeah! Ha! See, Flint? Eisley's givin' you a sense of humor!"

"It's his lack of sense I'm worried about. I've done all right at stayin' alive so far, but that was before you shackled him on me."

"He's gotta learn the ropes somehow," Smoates said. "Just like you did." He paused for a moment, then released a heavy sigh. "Well, I reckon you're right. Lambert's an awful dangerous skin to train Eisley on. Neither one of you are any good to me in a grave, so you can call it quits and come on in if you want to."

Flint was knocked off his wheels. He thought the earth might shake and the heavens crack open. Smoates was offering him a way out of this nightmare.

"You still there, Flint?"

"Uh . . . yeah. Yeah, I'm here." His joy had been a short-lived thing. He was thinking the unthinkable; he needed his share of the reward money for his gambling debts, and if Lambert was coming to the cabin after dark, it would be foolish to give up and go back to Shreveport now. Then again, Lambert might not even be in Louisiana anymore. It was Flint's call to make. He had the can of Mace and his brass knuckles in the car's glove compartment, and Clint's derringer was in its small holster against the skin under his right arm. The derringer's bullets didn't have much stopping power, but no man—not even a mad dog Vietnam vet—was going to do a whole lot of running or fighting with a hole through his kneecap. "If Lambert shows up here," Flint said, "I believe I can take him. I'll hang in until tomorrow mornin'."

"You don't have to prove anythin'. I know what you can do. But somebody as crazy as Lambert could be awful unpredictable."

Flint grunted. "Smoates, if I didn't know you better, I'd think you were concerned about me."

"You've been a damn fine investment. Eisley's gonna turn out to be a good investment, too, once he gets the green worn off him."

"Oh, I see. Well, just so I know where I stand." He wiped sweat from his eyebrows with his sleeve. The long-haired man in the Harvard T-shirt was watching the others work again, and paying Flint no attention. "I'll stay here awhile longer. If Lambert doesn't show by six in the mornin', I'll start back."

"Okay, play it how you want."

"I'll check in again around dark." Flint hung the phone back on its cradle. He was drenched with sweat under his jacket and totally miserable. Still, the game had to be played out. He saw that Eisley hadn't returned to the car, and when he looked through a window into the grocery store he saw Pelvis standing at the cash register eating an ice cream sandwich as he talked to a fat red-haired girl behind the counter. The girl wore an expression of rapture on her pudgy-cheeked face, and Flint guessed it wasn't every day she had a customer like him. Flint spotted a sign that said REST ROOMS and there was an arrow pointing around the side of the building. He followed it and found two doors, one marked GENTS and the other GALS. The GENTS door had a hole where the knob should've been. As he pushed through the door, he was aware of the sounds of distress the trussed-up alligators were making as they were being thrown into the truck, a combination of guttural burps and higher-pitched bleats. He figured the things were going to Baton Rouge to wind up as shoes, belts, and purses. Hell of a way to make a living, that was.

Flint stood in a small bathroom that smelled strongly of Lysol, but there were other more disagreeable odors wafting about as well. One of the two urinals seemed to have moss growing in it, and the other held a dark yellow lake clogged with cigarette butts. He didn't care to take a look into the toilet stall. He chose the mossy urinal, which had a Tropical Nights condoms machine mounted on the wall above it, and he unzipped his pants and went about the task.

As he relieved himself, he thought about what Smoates had said: *Man who's killed twice won't think nothin' 'bout killin' a third time.* So why, Flint wondered, am I still alive? Lambert had just come from his second murder, and he wouldn't have had much to lose by a third, especially the execution of a bounty hunter who'd tracked him from Shreveport. Why hadn't Lambert used the gun when he'd had the chance? Maybe because he hadn't wanted his ex-wife and son to be witnesses?

It was self-defense, Flint remembered the woman saying. *He's not a cold-blooded killer.*

Lambert's turned into a mad dog, was Smoates's opinion.

Which was the truth? *I'll let the judge sort it out,* Flint thought as he stared at the aged photo of a smiling, heavily made-up blond girl on the condom machine. He looked down to shake and zip.

The edge of a straight razor was laid against the crown of Flint's penis, which suddenly and decisively dried up.

"Get the door."

The door bumped shut.

"Easy, man. Be cool, now. Don't pee on my hand. I wouldn't like it if you peed on my hand, I might get all bent outta shape and this razor might twitch." The long-haired man wearing round-lensed sunglasses and the Harvard T-shirt was standing beside Flint; he had a soft, almost feminine voice with just a hint of a refined southern accent, but he was jabbering as if he might be flying on speed. "Wouldn't want that, man, no you wouldn't. Bummer to have all that blood shootin' out your stump. Messy, messy, messy. Virgil, find his wallet."

An ebony hand the size of a roast slid into Flint's jacket and went to the inside pocket, almost grazing Clint.

"Just look straight ahead, man. Hold on to your joy stick, both hands. That's right. Car 54, where are you?"

"No badge," Virgil said in a voice like a cement mixer turning over. "Lou'zana license. Name's Flint Murtaugh. Monroe address."

"Our man Flint!" The razor remained where it was, a threat to three shriveled inches of Flint's flesh. "Do not adjust the horizontal, do not adjust the vertical. We are in control. Talk to me."

"What's this all about?" he managed to say though his throat had seized up.

"Beeeep! Wrong answer! I'm askin' the questions, *kemo sabe!* Who are you and what're you doin' here?"

"I'm here to do some fishin'."

"Oh, yeahhhhh! Fishin' he says, Virgil! What's your nose tell us?"

Flint heard the black man sniffing the air next to his face. "Don't smell like no fisherman," Virgil rumbled. "Got kinda like a cop smell, but . . ." He kept sniffing. "Somethin' real funny 'bout him."

Flint turned his head to the left and looked into the dark lenses. The Harvard man, who stood about the same height as Flint, was in his late forties or early fifties. He was lean and sun-browned, gray grizzle covering the jaw of his deeply lined and weathered face. His hair had once been sand-colored, but most of it was now nearing silver. Part of his right ear looked as if it had been either chewed off or shot off. His T-shirt with the name of that hallowed university was mottled with sweat stains, and his blue jeans appeared to be held together by crusty patches of grime. Flint concluded his brief inspection by noting that the man wore Top-Siders without socks. "I'm not a cop," he said, lifting his gaze again to the opaque lenses. "I came down to fish for the weekend, that's all."

"Wore your best suit to fish in, did you? Come all the way here from Monroe just to hook a big mudcat? If you're a fisherman, I'm Dobie Gillis."

"Ain't no fisherman." Virgil was standing on the other side of Flint, his broad bare chest smeared with 'gator mud. His nose had wide, flared nostrils and he wore purple paisley shorts and Nikes on size thirteen feet. "Fish won't bite, weather this hot. Ain't been no fishermen 'round here all week."

"This is true," the man with the razor said. "So, Flinty, what's your story?"

"Look, I don't know who you fellas are or what this is about, but all I did was come in here to use the bathroom. If you want to rob me, go ahead and take my money, but I wish you'd put the razor away."

"Maybe it's *you* who wants to rob *us.*"

"What?"

"I saw you on the phone, Flinty. You reached out and touched somebody. Who was it? Couldn't have been Victor Medina, could it? You one of his spies, Flinty?"

"I don't know any Victor Medina. I had to call my office."

"What line of work you in?"

"I sell insurance," Flint answered.

"Smellin' a lie," Virgil said, sniffing.

"The nose knows. Virgil's got a mystic snout, Flinty. So let's try it again: what line of work you in?"

Flint couldn't tell these two swamp rats why he was really there; they'd want the reward for themselves. Anger welled up inside him. "I'm an astronaut," he said before he could think better of it. "What business is it of yours?"

"Ohhhhhh, an astronaut, Virgil!" The man grinned, his greenish teeth in dire need of brushing. "We've got us a celebrity here! What do you say about that?"

"Say he wants it done the hard way, Doc."

"This is true." Doc nodded, his grin evaporating. "The hard way it shall be, then."

Virgil looked into the toilet stall. Now it was his turn to grin. "Heh-heh! Somebody done forgot to flush!"

"Oh me oh me oh my!" Doc pulled the razor away from Flint's penis and closed the blade with a quick snap of his wrist, and Flint took the opportunity to zip himself up out of harm's way. "I believe this is a job for an astronaut, don't you?"

"Surely." Virgil took a step forward and gripped the nape of Flint's neck with one huge hand while the other grasped Flint's right wrist and wrenched his arm up behind his back.

"Hey, hey! Wait a minute!" Flint yelled, true fear kicking his heart and pain shooting through his arm. Clint had awakened and was thrashing under his shirt, but Virgil was manhandling Flint like a sack of straw into the toilet stall. Though Flint grabbed the stall's door with his left hand and tried to fight free, Virgil made short work of that attempt by sweeping his legs out from under him and forcing him to his knees on the gritty floor. The hair rose up on the back of Flint's neck when he saw the brown mess in the slimy bowl and what might have been fist-size crabs scuttling around down in the murk.

"Yum-yum!" Doc said. "Candygram for Mongo!"

Virgil pushed Flint's face toward the toilet bowl. The man's strength was awesome, and though Flint did his damnedest at resisting, all he could do was slow the inevitable. He couldn't get to the derringer and neither could he find the breath to command Clint to get it. His only hope was that he would pass out before his face broke the scummy, clotted surface.

"Sir?"

Doc turned his head toward the husky voice behind him. He gasped; Elvis Presley was standing there, framed by the hot white glare through the open doorway. Doc stood gaping and stunned as

Pelvis Eisley reached up with his left hand and plucked off the sunglasses. Doc blinked, his pale green eyes overloaded with light.

" 'Scuse me," Pelvis said, and he lifted his right hand—the hand that held the red can of Mace he'd taken from the Cadillac's glove compartment—and sprayed a burst of fine mist squarely into Doc's face.

The result was immediate. Doc let out a scream that curled Pelvis's ducktail, and he staggered back, raking at his inflamed eyeballs. In the toilet stall, Flint's nose was two inches away from disaster when the scream echoed off the tiles and Virgil's hand left the back of his head. Flint jabbed an elbow backward into the man's chest, but Virgil just grunted and turned away to help Doc.

"Lord have mercy," Pelvis said when he saw the size of the black man who'd just emerged from the toilet stall. Virgil took one look at Doc, who was down on the floor clutching his face with both hands and writhing in agony, then he stared at Pelvis as if seeing an alien from another planet. The shock didn't last but three seconds, after which Virgil charged Pelvis like a mad bull.

Pelvis stood his ground and got off another spray of Mace, but Virgil saw it coming and he jerked his head to one side, throwing up a thick forearm to protect his face. The spray wet his shoulder and burned like the furies of Hell, but Virgil was still moving and he hit his target with a body block that all but knocked Pelvis out of his blue suede shoes. Pelvis slammed against the wall, his jowls and belly quaking, and Virgil chopped at his wrist and knocked the Mace out of his hand. The stomp of a Nike crushed the can flat. Virgil grabbed Pelvis by the throat and lifted him off his feet. Pelvis's eyes bulged as he started choking, his fingers scrabbling to loosen Virgil's massive hands.

Flint had staggered out of the stall. He saw Pelvis's face swelling with blood and he knew he had to do something anything—fast. He yanked his shirt open, pulled the derringer from its holster, and cocked it. "Leave him alone!" Flint shouted, but Virgil paid no attention. There was no time for a second try. Flint stepped forward, pressed the derringer's double barrels against the back of Virgil's left knee, and squeezed the trigger. The little weapon made only a polite firecracker *pop*, but the force of the slug couldn't help but shatter the big man's kneecap. Virgil cried out and released Pelvis, and he went down on the floor, gripping at the ruins of his knee.

"Gone pass out!" Pelvis gasped. "Lordy, I can't stand up!"

"Yes you can!" Flint saw his wallet on the floor where Virgil had dropped it, and he snatched it up and then took Pelvis's weight on his shoulder. "Come on, *move!*" He kicked the door open and pulled

Pelvis out with him into the scorching light. The loading of the alligators was still proceeding, which made Flint think that the other three workmen had believed Doc's scream of pain to be his own. The red-haired grocery girl had probably been too scared to come look; either that, or screams of pain were commonplace around there. But then one of two workers carrying a squirming alligator along the pier saw them and let out a holler: "Hey, Mitch! Doc and Virgil are down!" The third man was on the boat, and he reached under his muddy yellow shirt and pulled out a pistol before he came running across the gangplank.

It was definitely time to vacate the premises.

Pelvis, who could hardly stand up one second, was in the next second a fairly impressive sprinter. The man with the gun got off a shot that knocked a chunk of cinder block from the wall eight inches above Flint's head, and Flint fired the derringer's other bullet without aiming though he knew he was out of range. All the workmen threw themselves flat on the pier, the 'gator landing belly-up. Then Flint was running for the car, too, where Mama was barking frantically in the driver's seat. He almost crushed her as he flung himself behind the wheel, and Pelvis did crush the sack of Twinkies, potato chips, and cookies that occupied his own seat. Flint jammed the key in, started the engine, and roared away from the store in reverse. The man with the gun hadn't come around the corner yet. Flint put the pedal to the metal, the engine still shrieking in reverse.

And then there was the gunman, skidding around the building's edge. He planted his feet in a firing stance and took aim at the retreating car. Flint shouted, "Get down!" and Pelvis ducked his head, both arms clutching Mama. But before the man could pull the trigger, the Eldorado got behind the cover of woods and Flint's heart fell back into his chest from where it had lodged in his throat. He kept racing backward another fifty yards before he found a clear place on the weedy shoulder to turn the car around, then he gave it the gas again.

Pelvis had hesitantly lifted his head. The first faint blue bruises were coming up on his neck. "I come to the bathroom and heard 'em in there!" he croaked over the howl of wind and engine. "Looked through the hole in the door and seen 'em tryin' to rob you! I 'membered what you said 'bout the Mace blindin' a man!"

"They were crazy, that's what they were!" Flint's face glistened with sweat, his eyes darting back and forth from the rearview mirror to the road. The truck wasn't following. He cut his speed to keep from flying off the dangerous curves into the marsh. Clint was still writhing, as if he shared his brother's fury. "Goddamned swamp rats, tried to drown me!" Still the truck wasn't following, and Flint eased up on the gas some more. Pelvis kept looking back, too, his face mottled with crimson splotches. "I don't see 'em yet!"

In another moment Flint realized—or hoped—the truck wasn't coming after them at all. The dirt road where they'd been sitting watching for Lambert would soon be on the left. It was time to take a gamble. What were the odds that the truck was following as opposed to the odds that it was not? Doc probably couldn't see yet, and Virgil was going to need a stretcher. Flint put his foot on the brake as they approached the dirt road.

"What're you doin'? You ain't stoppin', are you?" Pelvis squawked.

"I'm here to get Lambert," Flint said as he backed off the highway into the shade of the weeping willows once more. "I'm not lettin' a bunch of swamp rats run me off." He got far enough down the road so as not to be seen by anyone coming from either direction, then he opened the glove compartment, brought out a box of bullets for the derringer, and reloaded its chambers. He cut the engine, and they sat there, all four of them breathing hard.

A minute passed. "That toy gun might do fine in a pinch," Pelvis said, "but I wouldn't stake my life on it." Flint didn't respond. Five minutes went by, during which Pelvis kept mumbling to himself or Mama. After fifteen minutes they heard a vehicle approaching from the south. "Oh, Lord, here they come!" Pelvis said, scrunching down in his seat.

The truck passed their hiding place at a lawful speed and kept going. They listened to it moving away, and then its sound faded.

"I'll be." Pelvis sat up, wincing as pain lanced his lower back. If he hadn't been carrying such a pad of fat around his midsection, he might be laid out on the bathroom floor right then. "What do you make of that?"

Flint shook his head. A lot of strange things had happened to him in his bounty-hunting career, but this might have been the strangest. What had all that been about? Doc and Virgil hadn't been trying to rob him; they'd wanted to know who he was, why he was there, and who he'd been talking to on the phone. "Damned if I can figure it out." He slid Clint's derringer back into its holster. "You all right?"

"Hurtin' some, but I reckon I'm okay."

Flint kept listening for a siren that would be an ambulance or police car. If the cops showed up, they could wreck everything. But he was starting to have the feeling that the swamp rats didn't care to see the police around, either. Law-abiding citizens didn't usually carry straight razors and threaten the bodily parts of strangers. And what was all that about somebody named Victor Medina, and them thinking he might be there to rob *them?*

Rob them of what? A truckload of live alligators?

It made no sense, but Flint hadn't come this distance to worry about some crazy 'gatormen. He turned his attention back to snaring Lambert. Stupid of Eisley to have lost the Mace; he should've held on to it, no matter what. Without the Mace, the job was going to be that much tougher.

"Mr. Murtaugh, sir?"

Flint looked at Pelvis, and saw that his face had turned milky white.

"Never seen a fella get shot before," Pelvis said, in obvious distress. "Never *been* shot at, neither. Got to thinkin' 'bout it, and . . . believe I'm gone have to heave."

"Well, get out and do it! Don't you mess up my car!"

"Yes sir." Pelvis opened the door, pulled himself out and staggered into the woods, and Mama leapt from the car after him.

Flint grunted with disgust. Man who couldn't take a little violence and blood sure wasn't suited to hunt skins for bounty. His own nerves had stopped jangling several minutes earlier, but he was going to see that toilet bowl in his nightmares.

Clint had settled down to rest again. Flint looked into the crumpled sack of groceries, and he was gratified to find a small green bottle. He uncapped the lemon juice and took a long, thirsty swallow. Ever since he could remember, his system had craved acid. He decided that in a few minutes he should walk up to the cabin and make sure Lambert hadn't arrived while they'd been gone.

Still there was no siren. The police and ambulance weren't coming.

Alligators, he thought. What made alligators worth protecting with a pistol?

Well, it wasn't his business. His business was finding Lambert and taking him back to Shreveport, which he was determined to do. He could hear Eisley retching out all that junk food he'd packed himself with. Flint took another drink from the green bottle, and he thought that this was a hell of a life for a gentleman.

14

The Small Skulls

Dan was one of the first to reach the village. The sky was stained yellow by drifting smoke, the air thick with the reek of burned flesh.

He heard the wailing, like the sound of muted trumpets.

He moved forward through the haze at a slow-motion gait, his M16 clutched before him. Sweat had stiffened the folds of his uniform, his heart thudding in his chest like distant artillery. Someone was screaming up ahead: a woman's scream, hideous in its rising and falling. The ugly smoke swirled around him, its smell stealing his breath. He pushed past a couple of other grunts from his platoon, one of whom turned away and vomited on the dirt.

At the center of the village was a smoldering pile of twisted gray shapes. Dan walked nearer to it, feeling the heat tighten his face. Some of the villagers were on their knees, shrieking. He saw four or five children clinging to their mothers' legs, their faces blank with shock. Small orange flames flickered in the burned pile; nearby was a United States Marine–issue gasoline can, probably stolen from a supply dump, that had been left as a taunt.

Dan knew what had been set afire. He knew even before he saw the small skulls. Before he saw a crisped hand reaching up from the mass of bodies. Before he saw that some of them had not burned to the bone, but were swollen and malformed and pink as seared pork.

Someone clutched his arm. He looked into the wrinkled, tear-streaked face of an old Vietnamese man who was jabbering with what must have been a mixture of rage and terror. The old man thrust his hand at Dan, and in the palm lay a tiny airplane formed out of tinfoil.

He understood, then. It was from the Hershey bar's wrapper. The Cong had circled around behind them, and had found this tinfoil toy as evidence of collusion with the enemy. How many children had been executed was difficult to tell. Flesh had melted and run together in glistening pools, bones had blackened and fused, facial features had been erased. The old Vietnamese staggered away from Dan, still jabbering, and thrust his palm in an accusatory gesture at another marine. Then he went to the next and the next, his voice breaking and giving out but his hand still flying up to show them the reason for this massacre of the innocents.

Dan backed away from the burned corpses, one hand over his mouth and nose and sickness churning in his stomach. Captain Aubrey was trying to take charge, yelling for someone to shovel dirt over the flames, but his face was pallid and his voice was weak. Dan turned his eyes from the sight, and he saw the young Bostonian with cornflower-blue eyes—Farrow—standing near him, staring fixedly at the fire as the Vietnamese elder thrust the tinfoil airplane into his face. Then Dan had to get away from the smoke before it overcame him, had to get away from the smell of it, but it was everywhere, in his khakis and his hair and in his skin. He had to get away from this war and this death, from the mindless killing and the numbing horror, and as he ran into the rice paddies he was sick all over himself but the odor was still in his nostrils and he feared he would smell it for the rest of his life.

He fell down in the wet vegetation and pushed his face into the muck. When he lifted his head, he could still smell the burned meat. Smoke drifted above him, a dark pall against the sun. Something strained to break loose inside him, and he was afraid of it. If this thing collapsed, so, too, might the wall of willpower and bravado he'd been shivering behind every moment, every hour, every day of his tour of duty. He was a good soldier, he did what he was told and he'd never gone south, never. But with brown mud on his face and black despair in his soul he fought the awful urge to get up and run toward the jungle, toward where they must be watching from the lids of their snake holes, and once there he would squeeze the trigger of his M16 until his ammo was gone and then they would emerge silently from the shadows and cut him to pieces.

Never gone south. Never. But he could feel himself trembling on the edge of the abyss, and he gripped handfuls of mud to keep from falling.

The feeling slowly passed. He was all right again. No, not all right, but he would make it. Death and cruel waste were no strangers in this land. He had seen sights enough to make him wish for blindness, but he had to stand up and keep going because he was a man and a marine and he was there to get the job done. He turned over on his back and watched the smoke drifting, a dark scrawl of senseless inhumanity, a sickening cipher. The wailing in the village behind him seemed to be growing more shrill and louder, a chorus of agony, though Dan clasped his hands to his ears *louder louder* though he squeezed his eyes shut and tried to neither think nor feel *louder louder* though he prayed for God to deliver him from this place and there was no answer but the wailing louder and louder and loud—

"*Uh,*" he said.

He sat up, his face contorted.

"Jesus!" somebody said. A female voice. "You 'bout scared the stew outta me!"

Wailing. He could still hear it. He didn't know where he was, his mind was still hazed with the smoke of Vietnam. It came to him in another few seconds that he was no longer hearing the wailing from the village in his memory. A police car! he thought as panic streaked through him. He saw a window and started to get up and hobble toward it, but his joints had tightened and the pain in his skull was excruciating. He sat on the edge of what he realized was a bed, his hands pressed to his temples.

"I've been tryin' to wake you up for five minutes. You were dead to the world. Then all of a sudden you sat up so fast I thought you were goin' right through the wall."

He hardly heard her. He was listening to the siren. Whatever it was—police car, fire truck, or ambulance—it was moving rapidly away. He rubbed his temples and tried to figure out where he was. His brain seemed to be locked up, and he was searching desperately for the key.

"You all right?"

Dan looked up at the girl who stood next to him. The right side of her face was a deep violet-red. A birthmark, terrible in its domination. Arden was her name, he remembered. Arden Holiday. No. Halliday. He remembered the Cajun Country Truck Stop, a young man in a Hanoi Janes T-shirt, and a baseball bat studded with nails thunking down on the table.

"Brought you a barbecue," she said, and she offered him a grease-stained white sack. "Restaurant's right across the road."

The smell of the charred pork made his stomach lurch. He lowered his head, trying to think through the pain.

"Don't you want it? You must be hungry. Slept all day."

"Just get it away from me." His voice was a husky growl. "Please."

"Okay, okay. I thought you'd want somethin' to eat."

She left the room. His memory was coming back to him in bits and pieces, like a puzzle linking together. A pistol shot. The dying face of Emory Blanchard. Reverend Gwinn and his wife's crullers. The DeCaynes and a shotgun blast tearing the tire of his truck apart. Fifteen thousand dollars reward. Susan and Chad at Basile Park, and her telling him about the cabin in Vermilion. The bounty hunter with the flashlight, and Elvis Presley hollering for Mr. Murtaugh.

The girl, now. He'd given her a ride to Lafayette to see a man at a nursing home. Mr. Richards, the man's name was. No, no; it was Jupiter. Old man, talking about somebody called the Bright Girl. Faith healer, down in the swamp. Take that mark right off your face. You His hands, you gone have to steer her the right direction.

A motel in Lafayette. That's where he was. Slept all day, Arden had said. The sun was still high outside, though. He struggled to focus on his wristwatch's dial, and read the time as eight minutes after four. His cap. Where was his cap? He found it lying on the bed beside him. His shirt was stiff with dried sweat, but there wasn't much he could do about that. He sat there gathering the strength to stand up. He'd pushed himself yesterday to the limit of his endurance, and now he was going to have to pay the price. His headache was easing somewhat, but his bones throbbed in raw rhythm with his pulse. At last he stood up and staggered into the bathroom, where he caught a glimpse in the mirror of a white, sunken-eyed Halloween mask with a graying beard that couldn't possibly be his face. There was a shower stall, this one thankfully with no frogs hopping about, and Dan reached in and turned on the cold tap and then put his head under the stream.

"Hey!" Arden had returned. "You decent?"

He just stood there in the downpour, wishing he'd had the sense to lock her out.

"Got somethin' to show you. Just take a minute."

The sooner he could get rid of her, the better. He turned off the water, found a towel to dry his hair, and walked into the front room. Arden was sitting in a chair at a round table next to the bed, a map spread out on the tabletop. She still wore her blue jeans, but she'd changed into a fresh beige short-sleeve blouse. "Wow," she said, staring at him. "You really look beat."

He reached back and massaged the cramped muscles of his shoulders. "I thought I locked that door before I went to sleep. How'd you get in?"

"I stood out there knockin' till my knuckles were raw. You wouldn't answer your phone, either. So I got an extra key from the lady at the front desk. I told her we were travelin' together. Look here."

"We're not travelin' together," Dan said. He saw that what she'd spread out was his own Louisiana roadmap, taken from the station wagon.

"Here's LaPierre. See?" She put her finger on a dot where Highway 57 ended at the swamp. "It's about twenty-five miles south of Houma. Didn't you say you were headed that way?"

"I don't know. Did I?"

"Yes. You said you were goin' somewhere south of Houma. Not a whole lot down there, from the looks of the map. Where're you headed?"

He examined the map a little closer. LaPierre was maybe three miles past a town called Chandalac, which was four or five miles past Vermilion. South of LaPierre the map showed nothing but Terrebonne Parish swamp. "I'm not takin' you any farther. You can catch a bus from here."

"Yeah, I guess I could, but I figured since you were goin' that way you'd help me—"

"*No,*" he interrupted. "It's not possible."

She frowned. "Not possible? Why not? You're goin' down there, aren't you?"

"Listen, you don't know me. I could be . . . somebody you wouldn't want to be travelin' with."

"What's that mean? You a bank robber or somethin'?"

Dan eased himself down on the bed again. "I'll give you a ride to the bus station. That's the best I can do."

Arden sat there chewing her bottom lip and studying the map. Then she watched him for a moment as he wedged a pillow beneath his head and closed his eyes. "Can I ask you a personal question?"

"Depends," he said.

"Somethin' wrong with you? I mean . . . are you sick? You sure don't look healthy, if you don't mind my sayin'."

Dan opened his eyes and peered up at the ceiling tiles. There was no point in trying to hide it. He said, "Yeah, I'm sick."

"I thought so. What is it? AIDS?"

"Leukemia. Brain tumor. Worn out and at the end of my rope. Take your pick."

She didn't say anything for a while. He heard her folding the map up, or trying to, but road maps once unfolded became stubborn beasts. Arden cleared her throat. "The Bright Girl's a healer. You heard Jupiter say that, didn't you?"

"I heard an old man callin' me Mr. Richards and talkin' nonsense."

"It's not nonsense!" she answered. "And you bear a resemblance to Mr. Richards. He had a beard and was about your size. I can see how Jupiter mistook you."

Dan sat up again, his neck painfully tight, and looked at her. "Listen to me. The way I figure this, you're tryin' to track down a faith healer—who I don't think even exists—to get that mark off your face. If you're goin' on the tall tales of some crazy old man, I think you're gonna be real disappointed."

"Jupiter's not crazy, and they're not tall tales. The Bright Girl's down there. Just because you don't believe it doesn't make it not true."

"And just because you *want* to believe it doesn't make it true. I don't know anything about you, or what you've been through, but seems to me you ought to be seein' a skin doctor instead of tryin' to find a faith healer."

"I've seen dermatologists and plastic surgeons." Arden said icily. "They all told me I've got the darkest port-wine stain they ever saw. They can't promise me they can get it all off, or even half of it off without scarrin' me up. I couldn't afford the cost of the operations, anyway. And you're right about not knowin' anything about me. You sure as hell don't know what it's like to wear this thing on your face every day of your life. People lookin' at you like you're a freak, or some kind of monster not fit to be out in public. When somebody's talkin' to you, they'll try to look everywhere but your face, and you can tell they're either repulsed or they're feelin' pity for you. It's a bad-luck sign, is what it is. My own father told me that when I was six years old. Then he left the house for a pack of cigarettes and kept on goin', and my mama picked up a bottle and didn't lay it down again until it killed her. From then on I was in and out of foster homes and I can tell you none of 'em were paradise." She stopped speaking, her mouth tightening into a grim line.

"When I was fifteen," Arden went on after a long pause, "I stole a car. Got caught and put on a ranch for 'troubled youth' outside San Antonio. Mr. Richards ran it. Jupiter worked at the stable, and his wife was a cook. It was a hard place, and if you stepped out of line you earned time in the sweat box. But I got my high school diploma and made it out. If I hadn't I'd probably be dead or in prison by now. I used to help Jupiter with the horses, and he told me stories about the Bright Girl. How she could touch my birthmark and take it away. He told me where he'd grown up, and how everybody down there knew about the Bright Girl." She paused again, her eyes narrowing as she viewed some distant scene inside her head. "Those stories . . . they were so real. So full of light and hope.

That's what I need right now. See, things haven't been goin' so good in my life. Lost my job at the Goodyear plant, they laid off almost a whole shift. Had to sell my car. My credit cards were gettin' me in trouble, so I put the scissors to 'em. I went to apply for a job at a burger joint, and the fella took one look at my face and said the job was already filled and there wasn't anything comin' open anytime soon. Same thing happened with a couple of other jobs I went lookin' for. I'm behind two months on my rent, and the bill collectors are barkin' after me. See . . . what I need is a new start. I need to get rid of my bad luck once and for all. If I can find the Bright Girl and get this thing off my face . . . I could start all over again. That's what I need, and that's why I pulled every cent I've got out of the bank to make this trip. Do you understand?"

"Yeah, I do," Dan said. "I know things are tough, but lookin' for this Bright Girl person's not gonna help you. If there ever *was* such a woman, she's dead by now." He met Arden's blank stare. "Jupiter said the Bright Girl was livin' in the swamp long before his daddy was a little boy. Right? So Jupiter said she came to LaPierre when *he* was a kid. He said she was a young and pretty white girl. *Young,* he said. Tell me how that can be."

"I'll tell you." Arden finished refolding the map before she continued. "It's because the Bright Girl never ages."

"Oh, I see." He nodded. "Not only is she a healer, she's found the fountain of youth."

"I didn't say anything about the fountain of youth!" Anger lightened Arden's eyes but turned the birthmark a shade darker. "I'm tellin' you what Jupiter told me! The Bright Girl doesn't ever get old, she always stays young and pretty!"

"And you believe this?"

"Yes! I do! I—I just do, that's all!"

Dan couldn't help but feel sorry for her. "Arden," he said quietly, "you ever heard of somethin' called *folklore?* Like stories about Johnny Appleseed, or Paul Bunyan, or . . . you know, people who're bigger than life. Maybe a long, long time ago there was a faith healer who lived down in that swamp, and after she died she got bigger than life, too, because people didn't want to let her go. So they made up these stories about her, and they passed 'em down to their children. That way she'd never die, and she'd always be young and pretty. See what I'm sayin'?"

"You don't know!" she snapped. "Next thing you'll be sayin' Jesus was a made-up story, too!"

"Well, it's your business if you want to go sloggin' through a swamp lookin' for a dead faith healer. I'm not gonna stop you."

"Damn right you're not!" Arden stood up, taking the map with her. "If I was as sick as you are, I'd be hopin' I could find the Bright Girl, too, not sittin' there denyin' her!"

"One thing that'll kill you real quick," he said as she neared the door, "is false hope. You get a little older, you'll understand that."

"I hope I never get that old."

"Hey," Dan said before she could leave. "You want a ride to the bus station, I'll be ready to go after dark."

Arden hesitated with her hand on the doorknob. "How come you don't want to go until dark?" She had to ask another question that had bothered her as well. "And how come you're not even carryin' a change of clothes?"

He thought fast. "Cooler after dark. I don't want my radiator boilin' over. And I've got friends where I'm goin', I wasn't plannin' on stoppin'."

"Uh-huh."

He avoided her eyes because he feared she was starting to see through him. "I'm gonna take a shower and get some food. *Not* barbecue. You ought to call the bus station and find out where it is."

"Even if I take a bus to Houma, I still have to get down to LaPierre somehow. Listen," she said, determined to try again, "I'll pay you thirty dollars to take me there. How about it?"

"No."

"How much out of your way can it be?" Desperation had tightened her voice. "I can do some of the drivin' for you. Besides, I've never been down in there before and . . . you know . . . a girl travelin' alone could get into trouble. That's why I paid Joey to drive me."

"Yeah, he sure took good care of you, all right. I hope you get where you're goin', but I'm sorry. I can't take you."

She kept staring at him. Something mighty strange was going on, she thought. There was the broken glass in the back of the station wagon, the fact that he was traveling without even a toothbrush, and was it happenstance that he hadn't awakened until a shrieking siren had gone past the motel? *I could be somebody you wouldn't want to be travelin' with,* he'd said. What did that mean?

She was making him nervous. He stood up and pulled off his T-shirt. She could see the outline of every rib under his pale skin. "You want to watch me get naked and take a shower, that's fine with me," Dan said. He began unbuckling the belt of his jeans.

"Okay, I'm leavin'," she decided when he pushed down his zipper. "My room's right next door, when you get ready." She retreated, and Dan closed the door in her face and turned the latch.

He breathed a sigh of relief. She was starting to wonder about him, that much was clear. He knew he should never have given her a ride; she was a complication he didn't need. But right now there was nothing to be done but take his shower and try to relax, if he could. Get some food, that would make him feel a whole lot better. He started for the bathroom, but before he got there, curiosity snared him and he turned on the TV and clicked through the channels in search of a local newscast. He found CNN, but it was the financial segment. He switched the set off. Then, after a few seconds of internal debate, he turned it back on again. Surely he wouldn't have made the national news, but a local broadcast might come on at five and he'd find out if Lafayette had picked up the story. He felt as grimy as a mudflap at a tractor pull, and he went into the bathroom and cranked the shower taps to full blast.

Arden had gone to the office to return the extra key. The small-boned, grandmotherly woman behind the registration desk looked up over her eyeglasses from working a crossword puzzle in the Lafayette newspaper. "Your friend all right?"

"Yeah, he is. He was just extra tired, didn't hear me knockin'." She laid the key down on the desk. "Could you tell me how to get to the bus station from here?"

"Got a phone book, I'll look up the address." The woman reached a vein-ridged hand into a drawer for the directory. "Where you plannin' on goin'?"

"To Houma, first. Then on down south."

"Ain't much south of Houma but the bayou. You got relatives down there?"

"No, I'm on my own."

"On your *own*? What about your friend?"

"He's . . . goin' somewhere else."

"Lord, I wouldn't go down in that swamp country by myself, that's for gospel!" The woman had her finger on the bus station's address, but first she felt bound to deliver a warning. "All kinda roughnecks and heathens livin' down there, they don't answer to no law but their own. Look right here." She picked up the newspaper's front page and thrust it at Arden. "Headline up top, 'bout the ranger. See it?"

Arden did. It said *Terrebonne Ranger Still Missing,* and beneath that was a smaller line of type that said *Son of Lafayette Councilman Giradoux.* A photograph showed a husky, steely-eyed young man wearing a police uniform and a broad-brimmed hat.

"Missin' since Tuesday," the woman told Arden. "Been the big news here all week. He went down in that swamp one too many times, is what he did. Swallowed him up, you can bet on it."

"I'm sorry about that," Arden said, "but it's not gonna stop me from—" And then she did stop, because her gaze had gone to a story at the bottom of the page and a headline that read *Second Murder Attributed to Shreveport Fugitive.* A photograph was included with this story, too, and the bearded face in it made Arden's heart freeze.

It wasn't the best quality picture, but he was recognizable. It looked like a mug shot, or a poorly lit snapshot for a driver's license. He was bare headed and unsmiling, and he'd lost twenty pounds or more since the camera had caught him. Beneath the picture was his name: Daniel Lewis Lambert.

"They found his boat," the woman said.

"Huh?" Arden looked up, her insides quaking.

"Jack Giradoux's boat. They found it, but there wasn't hide nor hair of him. I know his folks. They eat breakfast every Saturday mornin' at the Shoneys down the road. They thought that boy hung the moon, and they're gonna take it awful hard."

Arden returned to reading the story. "I'd be mighty careful in that swamp country," the woman urged. "It's bad people can make a parish ranger disappear." She busied herself writing the bus station's address down on a piece of notepad paper.

Arden felt close to passing out as she realized what kind of man Dan Farrow—no, Dan *Lambert*—really was. Vietnam veteran, had the tattoo of a snake on his right forearm. Shot and killed the loan manager at a bank in Shreveport. Shot and beat to death a man at a motel outside Alexandria and stole his station wagon. "Oh my God," she whispered.

"Pardon?" The woman lifted her silver eyebrows.

Arden said, "This man. He's—"

. . . the man God sent Miz Arden.

Jupiter had said it. *You the man God provided to take Miz Arden to the Bright Girl. You His hands, you gone have to steer her the right direction.*

No, Dan Lambert was a killer. This newspaper said so. He'd killed two people, so what was to stop him from killing her if he wanted to? But he was sick, anybody could look at him and tell that. If he wanted to kill her, why hadn't he just pulled off the highway before they'd reached Lafayette?

"You say somethin'?" the woman asked.

"I . . . yeah. I mean . . . I'm not sure."

"Not sure? About what?"

Arden stared at the photograph. *The man God sent.* She'd wanted to believe that very badly. That there was some cosmic order of things, some undercurrent in motion that had brought her to this time and place. But if Jupiter had been so wrong, then what did that say about his belief in the Bright Girl?

She felt something crumbling inside her, and she feared that when it fell away she would have nothing left to hold her together.

"You still want the address?"

"What?"

"The bus station. You want me to tell you how to get there? It's not far."

The walls were closing in on her. She had to get out of there, had to find a place to think. "Can I take this?" She held the newspaper's page so the woman couldn't see Dan's picture.

"Sure, I'm through with it. Don't you want the—"

Arden was already going out the door.

"Guess not," the woman said when the door closed. She'd wanted to ask the girl if that mark on her face hurt, but she'd decided that wouldn't be proper. It was a shame; that girl would've been so pretty if she weren't disfigured. But that was life, wasn't it? You had to take the bad with the good, and make the best of it. Still, it was a terrible shame.

She turned her attention again to the crossword puzzle. The next word across was four letters, and its clue was "destiny."

15

The Truth

Dan had stepped out of the shower and was toweling off when he heard someone speak his name.

He looked at the television set. His face—his driver's license picture—was looking back at him from the screen. He thought he'd been prepared for the shock, but he was wrong; in that instant he felt as if he'd simultaneously taken a gut punch and had icy water poured on the back of his neck. The newscaster was talking about the shooting of Emory Blanchard, and the camera showed scenes of policemen at the First Commercial Bank. And then the vision truly became nightmarish, because suddenly a distraught face framed with kinky red curls was talking into a reporter's microphone.

"He went crazy when he found out we knew who he was," Hannah DeCayne was saying. "Harmon and me tried to stop him, but he was out of his mind. Grabbed the shotgun away from Harmon and blasted him right there in front of me, and then he— oh, dear Lord, it was terrible—then he started beatin' my husband in the head with the gun. I never saw anybody so wild in my life, there wasn't a thing I could do!"

The camera showed the dismal Hideaway Motor Court in daylight, then focused on the crippled pickup truck. There was a shot of blood on the sandy ground. "DeCayne was pronounced dead early this morning at an Alexandria hospital," the newscaster said.

Dan's knees gave way. He sat down on the edge of the bed, his mouth agape.

"Police believe Lambert may be on his way to Naples, Florida, where his nearest family member lives . . ."

Christ! Dan thought. They'd brought his mother into this thing now!

". . . but there've been reports that Lambert's been seen both in New Orleans and Baton Rouge. Repeating what we understand from Alexandria police, Lambert may be traveling under the name

645

Farrow, and he should be considered extremely dangerous. Again, the First Commercial Bank of Shreveport has put a fifteen-thousand-dollar reward on Lambert, and the number to call with information is 555-9045." The photograph of Dan came up on the screen again. "Lambert is forty-two years old, has brown hair and brown eyes and stands—"

Dan got up and snapped the TV off. Then he had to sit down once more because his bones felt rubbery and his head was reeling. Anger started boiling up inside him. What kind of damned shit was that woman trying to shovel? No, not *trying;* she was doing a pretty good job of it, fake tears and all. Dan saw what had happened. The bitch had killed her husband, and who was going to call her a liar? He sensed the net starting to close around him. Who would believe he hadn't murdered DeCayne? Pretty soon the newscasts were going to make him out to be a bloodthirsty fiend who killed everybody in his path. With his picture on TV, the reward, the police looking for the station wagon—what chance did he have of getting to Vermilion, much less out of the country?

He clasped his hands to his face. His heart was beating hard, the pulse pounding at his temples. How much farther could he get? Even traveling with the shield of darkness he knew it was only a matter of time now before the law found him. And his time, it seemed, was fast ticking away. Should he try to keep going, or just give it up and call the police? What was the point of running anymore? There was no escaping prison; there was no escaping the disease that was chewing his life away. Gone south, gone south, he thought. Where could you run to when all roads were blocked?

He didn't know how long he sat there, his eyes squeezed shut and his head bowed, his thoughts scrambling like mice in mazes. There was a tentative knock at the door. Dan didn't say anything. The knock came again, a little louder this time.

"Go away!" he said. It had to be her. Or the police. He'd find out soon enough.

A long silence followed. Then her voice: "I . . . want to talk to you for a minute."

"Just go away and leave me alone. Please."

She was silent, and Dan thought she'd gone. But then he heard a rustling at the bottom of the door and something slid under it into the room. It was a newspaper page.

Dan had the feeling that the bad news was about to get worse. He put the towel around his waist, went to the door, and picked up the page. There at the lower right was his picture, the same photo he'd seen on television. *Second Murder Attributed to Shreveport Fugitive,* the headline read. He reached out, unlatched the door, and pulled it open.

Arden took a backward step, half of her face pale with fear, and she lifted a tire iron she'd taken from the back of the station wagon over her head. "Don't touch me," she said. "I'll knock your head in!"

They stared at each other for a few seconds, like two wary and frightened animals. At last Dan said, "Well, you've got my attention. What'd you want to talk about?"

"That's you, isn't it? You killed two people?"

"It's me," he answered. "But I didn't kill two people. Just the man in Shreveport."

"Oh, is that supposed to make me feel better?"

"Right now I don't give a damn what you feel. You're not the one goin' to prison. I guess you've already called the police?"

"Maybe I have," she said. "Maybe I haven't."

"You saw there's fifteen thousand dollars reward on me, didn't you? That ought to be enough to get your birthmark off. See? This must be your lucky day."

"Don't try to rush me," she warned. "I swear I'll hit you."

"I'm not rushin' anybody. Where am I gonna go wearin' a towel? You mind if I get dressed before the police get here?"

"I haven't called 'em. Not yet, I mean."

"Well, do what you have to do. I figure I'm through runnin'." He turned his back on her and went to his clothes, which were lying on a chair near the bathroom door.

Arden didn't enter the room. She watched him as he dropped the towel and put on his underwear and socks. His body was thin and sinewy, the vertebrae visible down his spine. His muscles looked shrunken and wasted. There was nothing physically threatening about him at all. Arden lowered the tire iron, but she didn't cross the threshold. Dan put on his T-shirt and then his jeans. He sat down in the chair to slip his shoes on. "I didn't kill the man in Alexandria," he told her. "For what it's worth, his wife did it and she's blamin' me. Yeah, I did steal their station wagon, only because the damn woman shot my pickup truck's tire out. She blasted him with a shotgun, aimin' at me, but when I left there he was still alive. She beat him to death and she's tellin' the police I did it. That's the truth."

Arden swallowed thickly, the fear still fluttering around in her throat. "The paper said you went crazy in a bank. Shot a man dead. That you're supposed to be armed and dangerous."

"They got the crazy part right. Bank was repossessin' my truck. It was the last thing I had left. I got in a fight with a guard, the loan manager pulled a pistol on me, and . . . it just happened. But I'm not armed, and I never was carryin' a gun. I guess I ought to be flattered that they think I'm so dangerous, but they're wrong." He sat back in the chair and put his hands on the armrests. "I meant it about the reward money. Ought to be you who gets it as much as anybody else. You want to go call the law, I'll be right here."

Her common sense told her to go to her room and use the phone there, but she hesitated. "How come you didn't give yourself up after you shot that man?"

"I panicked. Couldn't think straight. But I was tellin' you the truth about the leukemia. The doctors don't give me a whole lot of time, and I don't care to pass it in prison."

"So how come you're just gonna sit there and let me turn you in?"

"Somebody will, sooner or later. I thought I could get out of the country, but . . . there's no use in tryin' to run when your name and face is plastered all over TV and the newspapers. It's just hurtful to my family."

"Your *family*? You married?"

"Ex-wife. A son. I stopped to see 'em in Alexandria, that's why I was stayin' at that damn motel. I was headin' to a place called Vermilion. Cabin down there I was gonna hide in for a while, until I could decide what to do." He shook his head. "No use in it."

Arden didn't know exactly what she'd expected, but this wasn't it. After she'd digested the newspaper story, she'd gone to the station wagon to search it, looking for a gun. She'd found the tire iron in the back and in the glove compartment a couple of old receipts—for froglegs, of all things—made out to Hannah DeCayne from the Blue Gulf Restaurant. The hell of this thing was that the fifteen thousand dollars would bail her out of her financial troubles and buy her a car, but after the bills were paid off there still wouldn't be enough left for the plastic surgery. The doctors had told her there would have to be two or more operations, and they couldn't promise what the results would be. But here was fifteen thousand dollars sitting in front of her if she wanted it.

"Go on," Dan said. "Call 'em, I don't care."

"I will. In a minute." She frowned. "If you're so sick, why aren't you in a hospital?"

"Ever set foot in a V.A. hospital? I was in one for a while. People waitin' to die, hollerin' and cryin' in their sleep. I wasn't gonna lie there and fade away. Besides, most days I could still work. I'm a carpenter. Was, I mean. Listen, are you gonna call the police, or do you want to write my life story?"

Arden didn't answer. She was thinking of what it had felt like when she was joy-riding in that car she'd stolen—speeding from nowhere to nowhere, trying to outrace reality—and the state troopers' car had roared up behind her with its siren wailing and the bubble light awhirl. She remembered the snap of cuffs on her wrists, and the sharp, dark terror that had pierced her tough fuck-you attitude. She'd had a lot to learn in those days. If it hadn't been for a few people like Mr. Richards and Jupiter and his wife, the lessons would've fallen like seeds on stony ground. Stealing a car was a lot different from committing murder, of course, and maybe Dan Lambert belonged in prison, but Arden wasn't sure she was the one to put him there.

"One thing I'd like to do for myself," Dan said while she was pondering the situation. He stood up, causing Arden's heart to start thumping again, and he went to the telephone on the table beside his bed. He dialed the operator and asked for directory assistance in Alexandria.

"Who're you callin'?" Arden's knuckles were aching, she was gripping the tire iron so hard.

"I'd like the police department," he said to the Alexandria operator when the call clicked through. "The main office at City Hall."

"What're you *doin'*?" Arden asked, incredulous. "Givin' yourself up?"

"Quiet," he told her. He waited until a voice answered. "Alexandria police, Sergeant Gil Parradine speakin'."

"Sergeant, my name is Dan Lambert. I think you people are lookin' for me."

There was no reply, just stunned—or suspicious silence. Then: "Is this a joke?"

"No joke. Just listen. I didn't kill Harmon DeCayne. I saw his wife shoot him with that shotgun, but when I left there, he was still alive. She must've decided to beat him to death and blame it on me. See what I'm sayin'?"

"Uh . . . I'm . . . hold on just a minute, I'll connect you to—"

"*No!*" Dan snapped. "You pass the phone, I'm gone! I'm tellin' you, that woman killed her husband. You check the shotgun for fingerprints, you won't find one of mine on it. Will you do that for me?"

"I—I'll have to let you talk to Captain—"

"I'm through talkin'." Dan hung up.

"I can't believe you just did that! Don't you know they'll trace the call?"

"I just wanted to start 'em thinkin'. Maybe they'll check for prints and ask that damn woman some more questions. Anyway, they don't know it wasn't a local call. There's enough time for you to turn me in."

"Do you *want* to go to prison? Is that it?"

"No, I don't want to go to prison," Dan said. "But I don't have a whole hell of a lot of choice, do I?"

Arden had to do the next thing; she had to test both herself and him. She took a deep breath, crossed the threshold into his room, and closed the door behind her. She stood with her back against it, the tire iron ready if he jumped at her.

He raised his eyebrows. "Takin' a risk bein' in a room alone with me, aren't you?"

"I'm not sure yet. Am I?"

He showed her his palms and eased down on the edge of the bed. "Whatever's on your mind," he told her, "now's the time to tell me about it."

"All right." She took two steps toward him and stopped again, still testing both her own nerves and his intentions. "I don't want to turn you in. That's not gonna help me."

"Fifteen thousand dollars is a lot of money," he said. "You could buy yourself—"

"I want to find the Bright Girl," Arden went on. "That's why I'm here. Findin' the Bright Girl and gettin' this thing off my face is all I'm interested in. Not the money, not why you killed some man in Shreveport." Her intense blue gaze didn't waver. "I've seen her in my dreams, only I never could tell what she looked like. But I think I'm close to her now, closer than I've ever been. I can't give it up. Not even for fifteen thousand dollars."

"It would pay for an operation, wouldn't it?"

"The doctors can't say for sure they can get it off. They say tryin' to remove it could leave a scar just as bad as the birthmark. Then where would I be? Maybe worse off, if that's even possible. No, I'm not doin' it that way, not when I'm so close."

"You're not thinkin' straight," Dan said. "The doctors are your best chance. The Bright Girl . . . well, you know what I think about that story."

"I do. It doesn't matter. I want you to drive me to LaPierre."

He grunted. "Now I *know* you're out of your mind! Look who you're talkin' to. I killed a man yesterday. I've got a stolen car sittin' out in the parkin' lot. You don't know I wouldn't try to kill you if I could, and you're wantin' to travel with me another ninety miles

650

down into the swamp. Wouldn't you say that might be pushin' your luck?''

"If you were gonna hurt me, you would've done it between here and the truck stop. I believe you about what happened at the motel. There's not a gun in the car, and you're not carryin' one. I've got a tire iron, and I still think I could outrun you."

"Maybe, but you can't outrun the police. Ever heard of aidin' and abettin' a fugitive?"

"If the police stop us," Arden said, "I'll say I didn't know who you were. No skin off your teeth to tell 'em the same thing."

Dan looked at her long and hard. He figured she'd had a rough life, and this obsession with the Bright Girl had grown stronger as things had started falling apart. He saw only disappointment ahead for her, but he was in no position to argue. She was right; it was no skin off his teeth. "You sure about this?"

"Yes, I am." The truth was that she hadn't decided he was worth trusting until he'd made the call to Alexandria. Still, she was going to hang on to the tire iron awhile longer.

He stood up and walked toward her. It flashed through her mind to retreat to the door, but she stayed where she was. She knew from experience that once you showed fear to a horse, the animal would never respect you again; she knew it was true with people, too. He reached out for her, and she lifted the tire iron to ward him off.

He stopped. "My cap," he said. "It's on the chair behind you."

"Oh." She stepped aside to let him get it.

Dan put his cap on and checked his wristwatch. Five thirty-four. Outside the window the shadows were lengthening, but it wouldn't be full dark until after seven. "I'll want to travel the back roads," he told her. "A little safer that way, but slower. Less likely to run across a state trooper. I hope. And I'm not gonna jump you, so you can put that thing down." He nodded toward the tool in her hand. When she didn't lower it, he narrowed his eyes and said, "If you don't trust me now, just think how you're gonna feel in a couple of hours when we're out in the dark and there's nobody around for miles."

Arden slowly let her arm fall.

"Okay, good. I'd hate to sneeze and get my brains knocked out. You got any deodorant?"

"Huh?"

"Deodorant," he repeated. "I need some. And toothpaste or mouthwash, if you've got either of those. Aspirin would help, too."

"In my suitcase. I'll bring it over."

"That's all right, I'll go with you," Dan said, and he saw her stiffen up again. "My room, your room, or the car, what does it matter?" he asked. "Better be certain you want to do this before we get started."

She realized she was going to have to turn her back on him sooner or later. She said, "Come on, then," and she went out the door first, her stomach doing slow flip-flops.

In Arden's bathroom Dan applied roll-on deodorant and he'd never thought the day would come when he'd be using Secret—and then he wet a washcloth, put a glob of Crest on it, and scrubbed his teeth. Arden brought him a small first aid kit that contained a bottle of Tylenol, a tube of skin ointment, some adhesive bandages, and a bottle of eyedrops. "You must've been a girl scout," Dan said as she shook two aspirin onto his palm.

"Joey always said I missed my callin', that I should've been a nurse. That's because I took care of the band when they had hangovers or were too strung out to play. Somebody had to be responsible."

Dan swallowed the Tylenol tablets with a glass of water and gave her back the first aid kit. "I'll need to get some food and coffee somewhere. We'd better not stick around here too much longer."

"I'm ready."

It was six o'clock by the time the bill was paid and they were pulling away from the motel. Arden kept the tire iron on the seat near her right hand, and Dan decided not to make an issue of it. Not far from the motel Dan turned into a McDonald's and in the drive-through bought three hamburgers, a large order of fries, and a cup of coffee. They sat in the parking lot while he ate, and Dan unfolded the roadmap and saw that Highway 182 was the route to follow through the towns of New Iberia, Jeanerette, Baldwin, and on to Morgan City, where Highway 90 would take them deeper into the bayou country to Houma.

"Where're you gonna go?" Arden asked when he'd finished the second burger. "After you take me to LaPierre, I mean. You still gonna try to get out of the country?"

"I don't know. Maybe."

"Don't you have any relatives you could go to? Are your parents still alive?"

"Father's dead. My mother's alive, but she's old and I don't want to get her messed up in this. It'll be hard enough on her as it is."

"Does she know about the leukemia?"

"No. It's my problem." He speared her with a glance. "What do you care, anyway? You hardly know me."

She shrugged. "Just interested, I guess. You're the first killer I ever met."

Dan couldn't suppress a grim smile. "Well, I hope I'm the last one you meet." He offered her his french fries. "Take some."

She accepted a few and crunched them down. "You don't really have anywhere to go, do you?"

"I'll find a place."

Arden nodded vacantly and watched the sun sinking. The Bright Girl—a dream without a face—was on her mind, and if she had to travel with a wanted fugitive to reach that dream, then so be it. She wasn't afraid. Well, maybe a little afraid. But her life had never been easy, and no one had ever given her a free ticket. She had nowhere to go now but toward the Bright Girl, toward what she felt was the hope of healing and a new start.

I know who you are, she recalled Jupiter saying to the killer beside her.

You the man God sent Miz Arden.

She hoped that was true. She wanted to believe with all her heart it was.

Because if Jupiter could be so wrong about Dan Lambert, he could be wrong about the Bright Girl, too.

Dan finished his food and they started off again. Four miles south of Lafayette, they passed a state trooper who'd pulled a kid on a motorcycle over to the roadside. The trooper was occupied writing a ticket and they slid by unnoticed, but it was a few minutes before Arden stopped looking nervously back.

The light was fading. Purple shadows streamed across the road, and on either side there were woods broken by ponds of brackish water from which tree stumps protruded like shattered teeth. The road narrowed. Traffic thinned to an occasional car or pickup truck. A sign on stilts said KEEP YOUR HEART IN ACADIANA OR GET YOUR— there was the crude drawing of a mule's hind end here—OUT. Spanish moss festooned the trees like antebellum lace, and the mingled odors of wild honeysuckle and Gulf salt drifted on the humid air. As the first stars emerged from the darkening sky, heat lightning began to ripple across the southern horizon.

Dan switched on the headlights and kept an eye on the rearview mirror. The heat lightning's flashes reminded him of the battle zone, with artillery shells landing in the distance. He had the eerie sensation of traveling on a road that led back into time, back into the wet wilderness of a foreign country where the reptiles thrived and death was a silent shadow. He was afraid of what he might find—or what might find him—there, but it was the only road left for him to go. And like it or not, he had to follow it to its end.

16

Black Against Yellow

It was just after nine o'clock when the station wagon's headlight beams grazed a rust-streaked sign that said VERMILION 5 MI., CHANDELAC 12 MI., LaPIERRE 15 MI. "Almost there," Dan said, relief blooming in him like a sweet flower. Arden didn't answer. She'd opened her purse two miles back and taken from it the pink drawstring bag, which she now held in her lap. Her fingers kneaded the bag's contents, but Arden stared straight ahead along the cone of the lights.

"What's in that thing?" Dan asked.

"Huh?"

"That bag. What's in it?"

"Nothin' special," she said.

"You're sure rubbin' it like it's somethin' special."

"It's . . . just what I carry for good luck."

"Oh, I should've figured." He nodded. "Anybody who believes in faith healers has to have a good-luck charm or two lyin' around."

"If I were you, I wouldn't be laughin'. I'd think you'd want to find the Bright Girl as much as I do."

"There's an idea. After she heals me, she can go back to Shreveport with me and raise Emory Blanchard from the dead. Then I can get right back to where I was, beggin' for work."

"Laugh if you want to. All I'm sayin' is, what would it hurt for you to go with me?"

"It would hurt," he said. "I told you what I think about false hope. If there really was a Bright Girl—which there's not—the only way she could help me is to crank back time and bring the man I killed back to life. Anyway, I said I'd take you to LaPierre, and that's what I'll do, but that's *all*."

"What're you gonna do, dump me out on the street once we get there?"

"No, I'll help you find someplace to spend the night." He hoped.

The last motel they'd passed was ten miles behind them in the small town of Houma. Since the woods had closed in on either side of the road, they'd seen the scattered lights of only a few houses. They had left civilization behind, it seemed, and the bittersweet smell of the swamp thickened the air. If worse came to worst and a motel or boardinghouse couldn't be found anywhere near LaPierre, Dan had decided to offer Arden lodging at the cabin and then he'd take her on into town in the morning. But *only* if nothing else could be found; he didn't like having somebody depending on him, and the sooner she went on her way the better he'd feel about things.

They crossed a long, concrete bridge and suddenly they were passing through the hamlet of Vermilion. It wasn't much, just a few clapboard houses and closed-up stores. The only place that was lit up with activity was a little dump called Cootie's Bar, and Dan noted that the four pickup trucks parked around the place all had shotguns or rifles racked in the rear windows. This did not help Dan's hopes of finding a decent motel room for Arden. He had the feeling that a woman alone in this territory could find herself pinned to a pool table, and a man with a fifteen-thousand-dollar reward on his head would be torn clean apart. He drove on through Vermilion, luckily attracting the attention of only a couple of dogs who stopped scrapping over a bone to get out of the road.

As they drew away from town, Dan watched the odometer. Susan had said the turnoff to Gary's cabin was three miles past the bridge, on the left. It ought to be coming up any minute now. He didn't plan on stopping there yet, but he wanted to make sure he found it. And then, yes, there it was, a dirt road snaking off to the left into the woods. Good. Now at least he knew where he'd be resting his head tonight. He passed the turnoff, and neither he nor Arden saw the black Eldorado hidden close by.

Pelvis was asleep and snoring with Mama sprawled out on his chest when Flint saw headlights approaching. As darkness had fallen, Flint had pulled the car closer up the dirt road to the highway's edge, and he'd kept vigilant watch while Pelvis had drowsed, awakened to prattle about Elvis's pink Cadillac and love of his mother's coconut cakes, and then drowsed again. Flint could have counted on one hand how many cars had passed, and none of them had even slowed at the turnoff to the cabin. This one, though, did slow down, if almost imperceptibly. But it didn't turn, and now here it came on the southbound road. Still, Flint's heartbeat had quickened, and Clint felt the change and responded with a questioning twitch under his brother's sweat-soaked shirt. Flint turned the key in the ignition and switched on the single headlight as the car began to glide past their hiding place.

The beam jabbed out and caught the rust-splotched station wagon. Flint saw a blond-haired woman sitting in the passenger seat; she glanced toward the light, her eyes squinted, and Flint made out that the entire right side of her face seemed to be covered with an ugly violet bruise. He couldn't see the driver's face, but he saw a head wearing a dark blue baseball cap. Then the station wagon had gone out of the light. Flint's breath hissed between his teeth; it was the same car Lambert had driven out of Basile Park.

He started the engine. Pelvis sat up bleary-eyed and rasped, "Whazhappenin?"

"He's here. Just passed us, goin' south." Flint's voice was calm and quiet, his heart pumping hot blood but his nerves icy. "He didn't turn, but that's him all right. Hold the mutt." He put the engine into gear and eased the Eldorado onto the road, turning right to follow Lambert. The station wagon's taillights were just going around a curve. "There's a woman with him," Flint said as they gained speed. "Could be a hostage. Looks like he might've beaten her up."

"A *hostage*?" Pelvis said, horrified. His arms were clamped tightly around Mama. "My Lord, what're we gonna *do*?"

"What we came for." They rounded the curve, and there was the station wagon forty yards ahead. "Hang on," Flint said. His foot pressed down on the accelerator, a cold smile of triumph twisting his mouth. "I'm gonna run the sonofabitch off the road."

The light suddenly hitting them had startled Arden as much as it had Dan. "You think that was a trooper?" she asked, her voice shaky as they started into the curve.

"Could've been. We'll find out in a minute."

"He's pullin' out!" She had her head outside the window. "Comin' after us!"

Dan watched the rearview mirror. No siren yet, no flashing light. He kept his speed steady, the needle hanging at fifty. There was no need to panic yet. Might've been just somebody parked on a side road getting stoned. No need to panic.

"Here he comes!" Arden yelled. "Pickin' up speed!"

Dan saw the car coming around the curve, closing the distance between them. The car had only one headlight.

One headlight.

A knot the size of a lemon seemed to swell in Dan's throat.

The bounty hunters' black Cadillac had one headlight.

But no, it couldn't be! How the hell would Flint Murtaugh and the Elvis clone have known where he was going? No, it wasn't them. Of course it wasn't.

He heard the roar of their engine.

Arden pulled her head in, her eyes wide. "I think he's gonna—"

Ram us, she was about to say. But then the headlight was glaring into the rearview mirror and the Cadillac was right on their bumper and Dan tried to jerk the station wagon to one side but he was a muscle-twitch too late. The Cadillac banged into their rear with threatening authority, then abruptly backed off again. The station wagon's frame was shivering, but Dan had control of the wheel. Another curve was coming up, and he had to watch where he was going. The Cadillac leapt forward again with what sounded like an angry snort, and once more banged their rear bumper and then drew back. "He's tellin' me to pull over!" Dan said above the rush of the wind. He glanced at the speedometer and saw the needle trembling at sixty.

"Who is it? The police?"

"Uh-uh! Couple of bounty hunters are after me! Damned if I know how they found me, but—"

"Comin' fast again!" Arden shouted, gripping onto the seat back.

This time the Cadillac's driver meant business. The knock rattled their bones and almost unhinged Dan's hands from the shuddering wheel. The Cadillac didn't back away, but instead began shoving the station wagon off the road. Dan put his foot on the brake pedal and the tires shrieked in protest, but the Cadillac was too strong. The station wagon was being inexorably pushed to the roadside, and now something clattered and banged under the front axle and the smell of scorched metal came up through the floorboard. The brake pedal lost its tension and slid right to the floor, and Dan realized the brakes had just given up the ghost.

Whoever was driving, Murtaugh or the imitation Elvis, they wanted to play rough. Dan was damned if he'd let those two have him without a fight. He lifted his foot from the dead pedal and jammed it down on the accelerator, at the same time twisting the wheel violently away from the roadside. A gout of oil smoke boomed from the exhaust pipe, and the station wagon jumped forward, putting six feet between its crumpled rear bumper and the Cadillac's teeth. Dan swerved back and forth across the road, trying to cut their speed and also to keep the Cadillac from shoving them again. They passed what looked like a marina on the right and then the woods closed in once more on both sides of the pavement. A SPEED LIMIT 45 MPH sign pocked with bullet holes swept past. The

Cadillac roared up on them, smacking their left rear fender before Dan could jerk the station wagon aside. Now the road began a series of tight twists and turns, and it was all Dan could do to keep them from flying off. He dared to look at the speedometer and saw that it too had gone haywire, the needle flipping wildly back and forth across the dial.

"Slow down!" Arden shouted. "You'll wreck us!"

He pulled up on the emergency brake, but there was no tension in that either. Whatever had fried underneath the car had burned out the brake system, which probably had been hanging together with spit and chicken wire anyway. "No brakes!" he answered, and then he fought the car around the next sharp curve with the Cadillac on his tail, his teeth clenched and his heart pounding. Welcome To Chandelac a sign announced, and they were through a one-block strip of darkened stores in a blast of engine noise and whirlwind of sandy grit. On the other side of Chandelac, the road straightened out and overhead huge oak trees locked branches. The Cadillac suddenly veered into the left lane and came up beside Dan, and Dan looked into the puffy face of an aged Elvis Presley, who was holding on to his bulldog with one arm and waving him to pull over with the other.

Dan shook his head. The Elvis impersonator said something to Murtaugh, probably relaying Dan's answer. Murtaugh then delivered his next response by slamming the Cadillac broadside against the station wagon. Arden had been holding back a scream, but the collision of metal knocked it loose. Dan felt the right-side tires slide off the pavement and into the weeds. He had no choice but to hit the accelerator and try to jump ahead of Murtaugh, but the bounty hunter stayed with him. Dan thought they must be going seventy miles an hour, the woods blurring past and the station wagon's engine moaning with fatigue. The road curved to the right, and suddenly there were headlights coming in the left lane. Murtaugh instantly cut his speed and drifted back behind Dan, who took the curve on smoking tires. They rocketed past an old Ford crawling north, and as soon as they were out of the curve the Cadillac was banging on Dan's back door again.

He darted a glance at Arden, saw her hunched forward with the pink drawstring bag clenched between her hands. "I told you not to travel with me, didn't I?" he yelled, and then he saw in the rearview mirror the Cadillac trying to pull alongside him. He veered to the left, cutting the bounty hunter off. Murtaugh swung the Cadillac to the right, and again Dan cut him off.

* * *

"He's not gonna let you get up there!" Pelvis shouted over the windstorm. His hair was a molded ebony still life. He saw the speedometer and blanched. "Lord God, Mr. Murtaugh! We're goin' seventy—"

"I know how fast!" Flint yelled back. The station wagon's beat-up rear fender was less than ten feet ahead. Lambert had stopped using his brakes. Either the man was crazy, or demonically desperate. Flint pressed his foot down on the accelerator and the Cadillac's battered front fender again slammed into Lambert's car. This time some serious damage was done: white sparks exploded from underneath the station wagon, a piece of metal coming loose and dragging the concrete. As Flint let the Eldorado drift back he saw Lambert's left rear tire start shredding apart. "That got him!" Flint crowed. "He'll have to pull over!"

Within seconds the tire had disintegrated into flying fragments and now the wheel rim was dragging a line of sparks. But Lambert made no move to pull off, and the man's stupid stubbornness infuriated Flint. He twisted the wheel, his knuckles white and Clint's hand seizing at the air, and he veered into the left lane and powered the Eldorado up alongside Lambert to deliver the coup de grâce.

Dan saw Murtaugh coming. The big black car was going to knock them into the next parish. His heart had been gripped by a cold fist when he'd felt the rear tire going, but actually the drag was slowing them down. Still, here came Murtaugh up alongside, and what the Cadillac was going to do to them wouldn't be pretty.

He swung the car to the left and bashed the Cadillac so hard he heard the frames of both cars groan in discordant harmony. Murtaugh returned the favor with a broadside blow, and suddenly Dan's door tore off its rusted hinges and fell away. Both cars whammed together in the center of the road, what remained of the station wagon's left side buckling inward like a stomped beer can.

Dan's speed was falling past sixty, the engine making a harsh *lug-lug-lug*ging. He smelled burned rubber and hot metal, and ahead on the road a half-dozen ravens leapt up from the roadkill on which they were feasting and scattered with enraged cries. He looked at the dashboard and saw the needle on the water temperature gauge vibrating at the far limit of the red line. Murtaugh hit him again, his own car being reduced to rolling wreckage and steam swirling from the Cadillac's hood, and the impact knocked the station wagon across the right lane onto the shoulder.

Dan heard Arden's breath hitch.

They hit a sign, black against yellow, that he had only an instant to read before it was crushed down.

Dangerous Bridge, 10mph.

With a *boom* and a burst of escaping steam from the volcanic radiator the hood flew up in front of the windshield. Dan twisted the wheel to get on the pavement again, but the rear end fishtailed out of control. Three seconds later they hit something else that cracked like a pistol shot, and abruptly Dan felt his butt rise up off the seat and he knew with sickening certainty that the station wagon had left the road. Branches and vines whipped at the top of the car, he heard Arden scream again, and his own mouth was opening to cry out when they came down, the station wagon hitting water like a fatman doing a graceless bellyflop. Dan had the sensation of his body being squeezed and then stretched by the impact, his skull banging the roof and bright comets of red light streaking behind his eyes. He heard what sounded like a wall of water crashing against the hood and windshield, and the engine sizzled and moaned before it began an iron-throated gurgling. Dazed at the quickness of what had happened, his head packed with pain and his consciousness flagging, Dan sat in the darkness still gripping the steering wheel.

His feet were submerged. Water had sloshed up through the floorboard and was flooding over the crumpled sill where the door had been. He thought the car was sinking, and the terror that swept through him cleared away some of the haze. He turned his head— his neck muscles felt sprained—and made out the girl lying sprawled on the seat. He couldn't leave her there, and though he thought he was moving as fast as he could, it seemed like a slow-motion nightmare; he got his arms around Arden and pulled her with him out of the car, stepping into knee-deep water bottomed with mud. The girl was a dead weight. Dan lost his footing and splashed down with her. Her face went under, and he turned over on his back to support her so her head was above water. She didn't struggle or sputter, but she was breathing. The taste of blood was in Dan's mouth. The darkness was closing in again, but he felt a slow current flowing around his body. It came to him that the current, as weak as it might be, must be flowing south to the Gulf, however far away that was. He knew for sure that if he passed out, both of them would drown. The bounty hunters. Where were they? Somewhere close, that was for sure. He couldn't hesitate any longer. Dan began pushing himself and Arden through the muddy water, giving them up to the current's southward drift.

17

Corridors and Walls

"They went off!" Pelvis had yelled. "Smack off the bridge!"

Flint had fought the Eldorado to a stop fifty yards past the wooden bridge. Steam was hissing around the hood, the radiator ready to blow. Mama was barking her head off, Clint was whipping in a frenzy, and Pelvis was yelling in Flint's ear.

"Shut up! Just shut your mouth!" Flint shouted. He put the car in reverse and started backing to the bridge. The structure, except for the broken railing the station wagon had torn through, was festooned with orange reflectors. They were still twenty yards from the bridge when the engine shuddered and died, and Flint had to guide the car off into the weeds on the right side of the road. "Get out!" he told Pelvis, and then he popped open the glove compartment, removed his set of handcuffs and their key, and put them into his suit jacket's inside pocket. He got out, Clint's arm still flailing around outside his shirt, then he shrugged into his jacket and unlocked the trunk.

"He never even slowed down, did he?" Pelvis was jabbering. "Never slowed down, went right off that bridge like he had wings!"

"Take one of these." Flint had pushed aside a pair of jumper cables and a toolbox and brought out two red cylinders that were each about twelve inches long.

Pelvis recoiled. "What is that? Dynamite?"

Flint closed the trunk, set one of the cylinders on the hood, and yanked a string attached to the end of the cylinder in his hand. There was a sputter of sparks as the friction fuse ignited, and then the cylinder grew a bright red glow that pushed back the night in a fifteen-foot radius and made Pelvis squint. "Safety flare," Flint said. "Don't look at the flame. Take the other one and pull the fuse."

Pelvis did, holding Mama in the crook of his arm. His flare cooked up a bright green illumination.

"Let's see what we've got." Flint strode toward the snapped railing, and Pelvis followed behind.

The bridge was only two feet above water. There was the station wagon, mired to the tops of its wheels and glistening with mud. Flint could see the driver's seat. Lambert wasn't in it. Flint reached into his shirt with his left hand, slid the derringer from its holster, and then switched the gun to his right hand and the flare to his left. He lifted the flare higher, searching for movement. The bridge spanned a channel that was maybe ten or twelve feet wide, with thickets of sharp-tipped palmettos and other thorny swamp growth protruding from the water on either side. He saw no dry land out there; neither did he see Lambert or the woman with the bruised face. Leaning over, he shone the flare under the bridge, but Lambert wasn't there either. "Damn it to hell," he said as he eased off the bridge into the morass. He started slogging toward the car, the flare sizzling over his head, and then he stopped and looked back when Pelvis didn't join him. "Are you waitin' for a written invitation?"

"Well . . . no sir, but . . . my shoes. I mean, they're real blue suede. I paid over a hundred dollars for 'em."

"Tough. Get in here and back me up!"

Pelvis hesitated, his face folded in a frown. He looked down at his shoes and sighed, and then he got a good grip on Mama and stepped into the swamp. He flinched as he felt the mud close over his hound dogs.

His derringer ready, Flint shone the flare into the car. Water was still filling up the floorboard. He saw something floating in there: Lambert's baseball cap. In the backseat was a suitcase, and the red glare revealed a purse on the passenger side. He said, "Clint! Take!" and pushed the derringer into his brother's hand. Then he leaned in, retrieved the purse and opened it, finding a wallet and a Texas driver's license made out to Arden Halliday with a Fort Worth address. The picture showed the face of a young woman with wavy blond hair. Her face might have been valuable on the freak-show circuit: the left side was pretty enough, but the right side was covered with a dark deformity that must've been a terrible birthmark. In the wallet were no credit cards, but it held a little over a hundred dollars and some change.

"I swear, that's some trick!" Pelvis said, staring at Clint's hand with the derringer in it. "Can he shoot that thing?"

"If I tell him to." Flint slid the license and the money into his jacket, then he returned the wallet to the purse and the purse to the car.

"He can understand you?"

"I've trained him with code words, same as trainin' a dog. Clint! Release!" Flint took the derringer as Clint's fingers loosened. He scanned the swamp while he moved the light around, making the shadows shift.

"Bet you wish he could talk sometimes."

"He'd say he's as sick of me as I am of him. Get your mind back on your business. Lambert couldn't be far away, and he's got the woman with him."

"You think we ought to—"

"Hush!" Flint snapped. "Just listen!"

Pelvis, as much as he loved to hear the voice of his idol coming from his own throat, forced himself to be quiet. Mama began to growl, but Flint gave Pelvis a hellfire-and-damnation look and Pelvis gently scratched under her chin to silence her. They listened. They could hear the swamp speaking: a drone of insects pulsing like weeping guitars; something calling in the distance with a voice like a bandsaw; little muffled grunts, trills, and chitters drifting in the oppressive heat.

And then, at last, a splash.

Flint whispered, "There he is." He moved past the car and stopped again, the water up to his knees. He offered the flare toward the darkness, shards of crimson light glinting off the channel's ripply surface. He could feel a slight current around his legs. Lambert was tired and probably hurt, and he was taking the path of least resistance.

"Hey, Lambert!" Flint shouted. It could've been his imagination, but the swamp seemed to go quiet. "Listen up!" He paused, his ears straining, but Lambert had stopped moving. "It's over! All you're doin' is diggin' yourself a deeper hole! Hear me?" There was no answer, but Flint hadn't expected one yet. "Don't make us come in there after you!"

Dan was crouched down in the water forty yards ahead of the two bounty hunters' flares. He was supporting Arden's head against his shoulder. She hadn't fully come to, but she must have been waking up because her body had involuntarily spasmed and her right hand, balled into a fist, had jerked up and then splashed down again. Dan didn't recall striking his face on the steering wheel, but his nose felt mashed and blood was trickling from both nostrils. Probably broken, he'd decided; it was all right, he'd survived worse punches. Pain drummed between his temples and his vision was clouded, and he'd almost blacked out a couple of minutes before but he thought he was past it now. He had backed up as far as he could against the right side of the channel, where gnarly vegetation grew out of the muck. Something with thorns was stabbing into his shoulder. He waited, breathing hard as he watched the two figures in their overlapping circles of red and green light.

"Show yourself, Lambert!" the one named Murtaugh called. "You don't want to hurt the woman, now, do you?"

He thought of leaving her, but her head might slip under and she'd drown before they reached her. He thought of surrendering, but it had occurred to him that at his back was a wilderness where a man could disappear. It was in his mind like a fixed star to head south with the current and keep heading south, and sooner or later he would have to reach the Gulf.

Murtaugh said, "Might as well give it up! You're not goin' anywhere!"

The cold arrogance in the man's voice sealed Dan's decision. He was damned if he'd give up to those two money-hungry bastards. He began pushing himself and Arden away from them, the bottom's soft mud sucking at his legs. Arden gave a soft moan, and then water must have gotten in her mouth because her body twitched again and her arms flailed, causing another splash, and then she started coughing and retching.

Murtaugh sloshed two strides forward and threw the flare toward the noise. Dan watched the red light spin up in a high arc, illuminating twisted branches bearded with Spanish moss, and the flare began coming down. There was no hiding from the light; as it bloomed the water red around him, Dan stood up and with the strength of desperation heaved Arden's body over his shoulder in a fireman's carry. He heard the Elvis impersonator yell, "I see him!" Dan was struggling through the mire when the flare hit the surface behind him. It kept burning for four seconds more before the chemical fire winked out. He managed only a few steps before his knees gave way and he fell again, dowsing them both, and Arden came up choking and spitting.

In her mind she'd been sixteen again, when she'd lived on the youth ranch. She'd been riding full-out on one of Jupiter's horses, and suddenly the animal had stepped into a gopher hole and staggered and she'd gone flying over his head, the treacherous earth coming up at her as fast as a slap from God. But water, not Texas dust, was in her eyes and mouth now; she didn't know where she was, though the pain in her head and body told her she'd just been thrown from horseback. A flickering green light floated in the darkness. She heard a man's voice whisper, "Easy, easy! I've got you!" and an arm hooked under her chin. She was being pulled through water. There was no strength in her to resist. She reached up to grasp hold of the arm, and she realized there was something gripped in her right fist and it was vitally important not to let go of it. Then she remembered what it was, and as that came clear, so did the memory of a black-and-yellow sign that said DANGEROUS BRIDGE, 10MPH.

Flint took the flare from Pelvis and holstered his derringer. "He won't get far. Come on." He slogged after their quarry, his shoes weighted with mud.

"Mr. Murtaugh . . . we're not followin' him in *there*, are we?"

Flint turned his face, his eyes deep-socketed and his skin a sepulchural shade. "Yes, Eisley, we are. We're gonna rag his tail all night if we have to. That's the job. You wanted an audition, now, by God, you're gonna get it."

"Yes sir, but . . . it's a *swamp*, Mr. Murtaugh. I mean . . . you saw those 'gators today, and that big whopper of a snake lyin' in the road. What're we gonna do when the light burns out?"

"It'll last half an hour. I give Lambert twenty minutes at most." He'd considered rushing Lambert, but decided it was safer to wear him down. Anyway, nobody was going to do much rushing in this mud. "I don't think he's got a gun, but he must be carryin' some kind of weapon. A knife, maybe. If we crowd him too close, he might get crazy and hurt the girl."

Pelvis's sweat-shiny face was a study of Tupelo torment. "I don't want to get anybody hurt. Maybe we ought to go find the law and let 'em take it from here."

"Eisley," Flint said gravely, "no bounty hunter worth a shit goes cryin' to the police for help. They hate *us*, and we don't need *them*. We let Lambert get away from us, there goes the fifteen thousand dollars *and* the girl's life, too, most likely. Now, come on." He started off again, and again stopped when Pelvis didn't follow. Flint nodded. "Well," he said, "I figured it. I knew you were nothin' but a windbag. You thought it'd be easy, didn't you?"

"I . . . didn't know I was gonna have to wade through a swamp full of 'gators and snakes! I've got Mama to look out for."

Flint's fuse had been sparking; now, like the flare's, it ignited his charge. "God *damn* it!" he shouted, and he sloshed back to stand face-to-jowls with Pelvis. "You got us in this mess! It was you who couldn't keep your mutt quiet back in the park! It was you who lost the Mace! It's been you who's messed up my rhythm—my *life*— ever since Smoates hung you around my neck! You're an insult to me, you understand? I'm a *professional*, I'm not a freak or a clown like you are! I don't give up and quit! Hear me?" His voice ended on a rising, stabbing note.

Pelvis didn't answer. His face was downcast. A drop of sweat fell from his chin into the quagmire that was already leaching the blue dye from his mail-order shoes. In his arms, Mama's bulbous eyes stared fixedly at Flint, a low growl rippling in her throat.

Flint's anger turned incandescent. He reached out, grabbed Mama by the scruff of her neck, and jerked her away from Pelvis. Mama's growling had increased, but her ferocity was a bluff; she began yelping as Flint reared his arm back to throw her as hard and far as he could.

Pelvis seized Flint's wrist. "Please, Mr. Murtaugh!" he begged. "Please don't hurt her!"

Flint was a heartbeat away from flinging Mama farther into the swamp, but he looked into Pelvis's eyes and saw a terror there beyond any he'd ever glimpsed. Something about Eisley's face had shattered. It was like watching an Elvis mask crumble and seeing behind it the face of a frightened, simpleminded child.

"She don't mean no harm." The voice was even different now; some of the Memphis huskiness had fallen away. "She's all I got. Please don't."

Flint hesitated, his arm still flung back. Then, just that quickly, his anger began to dissolve and he realized what a mean, petty thing he'd been on the verge of doing. He thrust the shivering dog at Pelvis and backed away, a muscle working in his jaw. Pelvis enfolded Mama in his arms. "It's all right, it's all right," he said, speaking to the dog. "He won't hurt you, it's all right."

Flint turned away and began following the channel. He felt sick to his stomach, disgusted at himself and at Eisley, too. There was no doubt about it now, the man was making him crack up. Then he heard splashing behind him, and he glanced over his shoulder and saw Eisley following. It would've been better, Flint thought, if Eisley had gone back to the car and waited. It would've been better for Eisley to leave this ugly, miserable work to somebody who was more suited to it.

Clint's hand rose up and the little fingers stroked at the stubble of beard on his brother's usually clean-scraped chin. Flint swatted Clint's hand away, but it came willfully up again to feel the hairs. He pinned the hand down against his chest with his right arm, and Clint fought him. It was a silent and internal war, sinewy muscles straining, and Flint felt Clint's head jerk as if trying to tear itself and the malformed lump of tissue and ligaments it was attached to finally and completely free. Flint staggered forward, his mouth a tight line and his eyes set on the darkness yet to be traveled through. A feeling of panic rose up, like Clint's clammy hand, and seized his throat. He would never find the clean white mansion of his birth. Never. He could pore through magazines of splendid estates and drive through the immaculate streets of wealthy enclaves in town after town, but he would never find his home. Never. He was lost, a gentleman of breeding cast out on the dirty current, fated to slog through the mud with the Pelvis Eisleys of this world breathing buttermilk breath on the back of his neck.

It seemed to Flint now, in the spell of this panic, that he'd always been searching for a way out of one swamp or another: the dismal, humiliating grind of the freak shows, his overwhelming gambling debts, this soul-killing job, and the freak-obsessed lunatic who jerked his strings. His life had been a series of swamps populated with the dregs of the earth. Grinning illiterates had taunted him, hard-eyed prostitutes had shrieked and fled when they'd discovered his secret, children had been reduced to fearful tears and later, probably, he'd crept into their nightmares. For a few dirty dollars he'd used the brass knuckles on some of Smoates's loan customers, and he couldn't say that from time to time it hadn't been a pleasure using that festering rage inside him to pummel promptness into unfortunate flesh. He had kicked men when they were down. He had broken ribs and noses and grinned inside at the sound of begging. What was one more swamp to be slogged through, with all that mud already stuck to his shoes?

He had taken a wrong turn somewhere. He had taken many wrong turns. Wasn't there some way out of this filth, back toward the road that led him to the clean white mansion? Dear God of deformities and wretchedness, wasn't there some escape?

He knew the answer, and it made him afraid.

The cards have been dealt. Play or fold, your choice. It's late in the game, very very late, and it seems you're running out of chips.

Play or fold. Your choice.

Flint stopped. He felt the blood burning his face. His mouth opened and out swelled a shout that was bitter anger and pain, wounded pride and feverish determination all bound up and twisted together. At first it was a mangled, inhuman sound that scared Pelvis into believing a wild animal was about to leap at them, and then words exploded out of it: *"Lambert! I'll follow you till you drop! Understand? Until you drop!"*

The swamp had hushed again. The sound of Flint's voice rolled away across the wilderness like muffled thunder. Pelvis stood a distance behind Flint in the green flarelight, both his arms clutching Mama close. Slowly, the insect hums and buzzes and strange chittering birdcalls weaved together and grew in volume once more, the dispassionate voice of the swamp telling Flint who was master of this domain. When Flint drew a long, ragged breath and continued wading southward with the sluggish current, Pelvis got his legs moving, too.

Flint held the flare high, his eyes darting from side to side. Sweat was trickling down his face, his clothes drenched with it. He heard splashing ahead, but how far, it was hard to say. The channel took a leftward curve, and suddenly Flint realized the water level had risen three inches above his knees. "Gettin' deeper," Pelvis said at about the same time.

"Gettin' deeper for him, too," Flint answered.

The mud gripped their shoes. Pelvis watched the surface for gliding shadows. The air was rank with the odors of wet, rotting vegetation, and breathing it left the sensation of slime accumulating at the back of the throat.

Behind them, the two edges of disturbed darkness the light had passed through first linked tendrils, grew joints, and then silently sealed together again.

Up ahead, barely twenty yards beyond the light's range, Dan was down in the water with Arden. She was fully conscious now, though her vision kept fading in and out, and she could remember everything up until when they'd hit the warning sign; her bell had been rung hard, a bloody inch-long gash just past her hairline where her head had glanced off something on the dashboard, a cut inside her mouth, and a bruised chin, courtesy of a flying knee.

Dan could see the blotch of dark wetness in her hair. He figured she might have a concussion, and she was lucky she hadn't smashed her skull. "I want you to stay right here," he whispered. "They'll take you back with 'em."

"No!" She'd spoken too loudly, and he put his finger on her mouth.

"Comin' for you, Lambert!" Murtaugh called. "Nowhere else to run!"

"No!" Arden whispered. "I'm all right! I can keep goin'!"

"Listen to me!" He had his face right up against hers. "I'm headin' into the swamp, just as deep as I can get! You've gone far enough with me!" He saw the flare-lit figures wading slowly and steadily nearer. In another minute the light would find them.

"I'm goin' with you," Arden said. "I'm too close to turn back."

She was out of her mind, he decided. Her eyes had taken on the shine of religious fervency, like those of the walking wounded who flocked, desperate for a healing miracle, to television evangelists. She had come to the end of her rope and found herself dangling, and now all she could think to do was hold on to him. "Stay here," he told her. "Just stay here, they'll get you out." He stood up and began sloshing southward, the water up to the middle of his thighs.

Arden saw the circle of green light approaching, and the two figures at its center. Her distorted vision made them out to be monsters. She tried to stand up, slipped, and fell again. Dan looked briefly back at her and then continued on. Arden got her feet planted in the mud and pushed herself up, and then she started fighting to reach Dan with the light glinting on the frothy water just behind her.

"He's tirin' out," Flint told Pelvis. "Hear him strugglin'?" The splashing was over on the right, and Flint angled toward it.

Pelvis suddenly jumped and bellowed, "Oh Jesus!"

Flint whipped the flare around. "What the hell is it?"

"Somethin' swam by me!" Pelvis had almost dropped Mama in his jig of terror. "I think it was a snake!"

Flint's gaze searched the water, his own skin starting to crawl. The light showed something dark and about three feet long, sinuously moving with the current. He watched it until it slithered beyond the light. "Just keep goin'," he said, as much to himself as to Pelvis, and he started wading again. The sound of splashing had quieted, but Lambert couldn't go on much longer.

Dan looked back. Arden was still straining to catch up with him, but she'd found her balance and her strides were careful and deliberate. The water was almost at her waist. He started to turn and go on, but like a flash of shock the moment took him spinning back in time.

He remembered a night patrol, and a wide, muddy stream that cut through the jungle. He remembered the crossing, and how almost all but the grunts guarding the rear—of which he was one— had climbed up a slippery bank when the first white flare had exploded over their heads. The enemy had gotten around behind them, or had come up from hidden snake holes. "Move it, move it, move it!" somebody began yelling as the second white flare popped. The rifles started up, Dan was standing in knee-deep muck and tracers were zipping past him out of the jungle. Other grunts were running and falling, trying to scramble up the bank. Within an instant the situation became as all night combat did in that jungle: a confused, surrealistic montage of shadows fleeing from the flare-light, blurred motion, screams as bullets thunked into flesh. He couldn't move; his legs were frozen. Figures were falling, some struggling up, some thrashing in the mud. It seemed pointless to move because the others were getting cut down as they tried to climb up the bank, and if he stood still, if he stood very very still with the tracers passing on either side of him, he might make himself disappear from the face of this hellish earth.

Someone gripped his shirt and yanked him.

"*Go,*" a voice urged; it was not a shout, but it was more powerful than a shout.

Dan looked at the man. He had the gaunt, sunken-eyed face of a hard-core veteran, a man who had seen death and smelled it, who had killed after hours of silent stalking and escaped being killed by inches of miraculous grace. He had a blond beard and eyes of cornflower blue, only the eyes seemed ancient now and lifeless. They had been lifeless since that day months ago at the village.

"Go," Farrow said again. Farrow, who since that day had retreated into himself like a stony sphinx, who suffered in silence, who always volunteered with a nod for the jobs no other grunt would dare take.

And now, in this little cell of time, Dan saw something glisten and surface from Farrow's eyes that he hardly recognized.

It might have been joy.

Farrow pushed him hard toward the bank, and the push got Dan moving. Dan reached the bank and started up it, clawing at vines and over the bodies of dying men. He dared to look over his shoulder, and he saw a sight that would stay with him all his days.

Farrow was walking to the other side, and he was spray-firing his M16 back and forth into the jungle. Dan saw the enemy's tracers start homing in on Farrow. The young man did not pause or cringe. One bullet hit him, then a second. Farrow kept moving and firing. A third bullet knocked him to his knees. He got up. Somebody was shouting at him to come back, for the love of God come back. Farrow staggered on, his M16 tearing down the foliage and scattering black-clad figures. Either the weapon choked or the clip was gone, because it ceased firing. There was a stretch of silence, broken by the cries of the wounded. The Cong had stopped shooting. Dan saw Farrow jerk the clip out and pop another one in. He took two more steps and his M16 blazed again, and then maybe four or five tracers came out of the jungle and hit him at once and he was knocked backward and splashed down into the muddy water that rolled over him like a brown shroud.

All of it had taken only a span of seconds, but it had taken years for Dan to digest what he'd seen. Even so, it still sometimes came up to lodge in his throat.

He watched Arden pulling herself toward him, as resolute in her decision as Farrow had been in his. Or as crazy, Dan thought. There had been no doubt in his mind that Farrow had gone quietly insane after that day at the village, and had been—whether he was aware of it or not—searching for a way to commit suicide. How the death of those children had weighed on Farrow was impossible to say, but it must've been a terrible burden that ultimately led him to choose a slow walk into a dozen Viet Cong rifles. If Farrow hadn't taken that walk, Dan and at least three other men might have been cut to pieces. Dan's life had been spared, and for what reason? For him to be tainted by the Agent Orange and later pull the trigger that killed an innocent man? For him now to be standing in this swamp, watching a girl with a birthmarked face struggling to reach him? Life made no sense to him; it was a maze constructed by the most haphazard of hands and he, Arden, the bounty hunters, all humanity alike, were blindly searching its corridors and banging into walls.

She was almost to him. The green flarelight was chasing her.

"Give it up, Lambert!" Murtaugh shouted. "It's no use!"

Maybe it wasn't. But the girl believed it was, enough to trust a killer. Enough to fight her way into the unknown. Enough to make Dan think that if he had half of her desire, he might find his way through this wilderness to freedom.

He waded to meet her and caught her left hand. She looked at him with an expression of amazement and relief. Then Dan started pulling her with him, racing against the oncoming light.

18

The Most Dangerous Place

Though Flint still couldn't see Lambert or the girl, he knew they must not be more than fifteen or twenty yards beyond the light's edge. He was moving as fast as he could, but the channel was hard going. The water had crept up toward his waist, and it had occurred to him that if it deepened to his chest, Clint would drown. He was dripping sweat in the hot and clammy air. In another moment he heard Pelvis's lungs wheezing like the pipes of an old church organ.

"Mr. Murtaugh!" Pelvis gasped. "I'm gonna have to . . . have to stop for a minute. Get my breath."

"Keep movin'!" Flint told him, and he didn't pause.

The wheezing only worsened. "Please . . . Mr. Murtaugh . . . I gotta stop."

"Do what you want! I'm not stoppin'!"

Pelvis fell behind, his chest heaving. Oily beads of sweat were trickling down his blood-gorged face, his heart furiously pounding. Flint glanced back and then continued on, step after careful step. Pelvis tried to follow, but after a half-dozen more strides he had to stop again. Mama had sensed his distress and was frantically licking his chin. "Mr. Murtaugh!" Pelvis called, but Flint was moving away and taking the light with him. Terror of the dark and of the things that slithered through it made Pelvis slog forward once more, the blood pulsing at his temples. He couldn't get his breath, it was as if the air itself were waterlogged. He wrenched one foot free from the mud and put it down in front of him, and he was pulling the other one up when his throat seemed to close, darkness rippled across his vision, and he fell down into the water.

Flint heard splashing and looked back. He saw the mutt, paddling to keep her head up.

Pelvis was gone.

Flint's heart jumped. "Christ!" he said, and he struggled back toward the swirling water where Pelvis had submerged. The dog

672

was trying to reach him, her eyes wide with panic. Bubbles burst from the surface to Flint's left, followed by a flailing arm, and then Pelvis's butt broached like a flabby whale. Flint got hold of the arm, but it slipped away from him. "Stand up, stand up!" he was shouting. A dark, dripping mass came up from the water, and Flint realized it was Pelvis's hair. He grabbed it and pulled, but suddenly he found himself gripping a pompadour with no head beneath it.

A wig. That's what it was. A cheap, soaked and sopping wig.

And then something white and vulnerable-looking with a few strands of dark hair plastered across it broke the surface, and Flint dropped the wig and got his arm underneath the man's chin. Pelvis was a weight to be reckoned with. He coughed out a mouthful of water and let go a mournful groan that sounded like a freight train at midnight. "Get your feet under you!" Flint told him. "Come on, stand up!"

Still sputtering, the baldheaded Pelvis got his muddy suedes planted. "Mama!" he cried out. "Where is she?"

She wasn't far, yapping against the current. Pelvis staggered to her and scooped her up, and then he almost fell down again and he had to lean his bulk against Flint. "I'll be all right," Pelvis said between coughs. "Just gotta rest. Few minutes. Lord, I thought . . . thought my ticker was givin' out." He lifted a hand to his head, and when his fingers found nothing there but pasty flesh he looked to Flint, his face contorted with abject horror, as if he indeed might be about to suffer heart failure. "My hair! Where's my hair?" He started thrashing around again, searching for it in the froth.

"It's gone, forget it!" Flint registered that Pelvis's naked head was pointed like a bullet at the crown. On the sides and back was a fringe of short, ratty hairs. Flint spotted the wig floating away like a lump of Spanish moss, and he sloshed the few feet to it and plucked it up. "Here," he said, offering it to its master. Pelvis snatched it away from him and, holding Mama in the crook of an arm, began wringing the wig out. Flint might've laughed if he hadn't been thinking of how far Lambert was getting ahead of them. "You okay?"

Pelvis snorted and spat. He was trembling. He wiped his nose on his forearm and then carefully, reverently, replaced the wet wig back on his skull. It sat crooked and some of its wavy peaks had flattened, but Flint saw relief flood into Pelvis like a soothing drug, the man's tormented face relaxing. "Can you go on, or not?" Flint asked.

"Gimme a minute. Heart's beatin' awful hard. See, I get dizzy spells. That's why I had to quit my stage show. Is it on straight?"

"Crooked to the right."

Pelvis made the adjustment. "I passed out onstage last year. Oldie Goldie's Club in Little Rock. They took me to the hospital, thought I was about to croak." He paused to draw a few slow, deep breaths. "Wasn't the first time. Word went 'round, and I couldn't get no more jobs. Gimme a minute, I'll be fine. Can you breathe? I can't hardly breathe this air."

"You weigh too much, that's your trouble. Ought to give up all that junk you eat." Flint was staring down the channel, gauging the distance that Lambert must be putting between them. The going had to be hard on Lambert, too, but he'd probably push himself and the girl until they both gave out. When he looked at Pelvis again, Flint thought that the wig resembled a big, spongy Brillo pad stuck to the man's head. "I'll give you three minutes, then I'm goin' on. You can either stay here or go back to the car."

Pelvis didn't care to lose the protection of Flint's light. "I can make it if you just go a step or two slower."

"I told you it wasn't gonna be easy, didn't I? Don't fall down and drown on me, now, you hear?"

"Yes sir." His misshapen wig was dripping water down his face. "I reckon this washes me up, huh? I mean, with Mr. Smoates and the job and all?"

"I'd say it does. You should've told him about this, it would've saved everybody a hell of a lot of trouble." Flint narrowed his eyes and glanced quickly at the flare. Maybe they had fifteen minutes more light. Maybe. "You're not cut out for this work, Eisley. Just like I'm not cut out to . . . to dress up like Elvis Presley and try to impersonate him."

"Not impersonate," Pelvis corrected him firmly. "I'm an interperator, not an impersonator."

"Whatever. You ought to cut out the junk food and go back to it."

"That's what the doctor told me, too. I've tried, but Lord knows it ain't easy to pass up the peanut butter cookies when you can't sleep at three in the mornin'."

"Yes, it is. You just don't buy the damn things in the first place. Haven't you ever heard of self-discipline?"

"Yes sir. It's somethin' other folks have got."

"Well, it's what you *need*. A whole lot of it, too." He checked his wristwatch, impatient to get after Lambert. But Pelvis's face was still flushed, and maybe he needed another minute. If Pelvis had a heart attack, it'd be hell dragging that bulk of a body out of the swamp. Flint had become acutely aware of the flare sizzling itself toward extinction. He watched Mama licking Pelvis's chin, her stubby tail wagging. A pang of what might have been envy hit him. "How come you carry that mutt around everywhere? It just gets in the way."

"Oh, I wouldn't leave Mama, no sir!" Pelvis paused, stroking Mama's wet back before he went on in a quieter voice. "I had another dog, kinda like Mama. Had Priss for goin' on six years. Left her at the vet one weekend when I went on the road. When I got back . . . the place was gone. Just bricks and ash and burned-up cages. Electrical fire, they said. Started late at night, nobody was there to put it out. They should've had sprinklers or somethin', but they didn't." He was silent for a moment, his hand stroking back and forth. "For a long time after that . . . I had nightmares. I could see Priss burnin' up in a cage, tryin' to get out but there wasn't no way out. And maybe she was thinkin' she'd done somethin' awful bad, that I didn't come to save her. Seems to me that would be a terrible way to die, thinkin' there was nobody who gave a damn about you." He lifted his gaze to Flint's, his eyes sunken in the green glare. "That's why I wouldn't leave Mama. No sir."

Flint turned his attention to his watch again. "You ready to move?"

"I believe I am."

Flint started off, this time at a slower pace. Pelvis drew another deep breath, *whoosh*ed it out, and then began slogging after Flint.

Ahead, Dan still gripped Arden's hand as they followed the channel around a curve. He glanced back; they'd outdistanced the light, and he thought the bounty hunters must've stopped for some reason. His eyes were getting used to the dark now. Up through the treetops he could see pieces of sky full of sparkling stars. The water was still deepening, the bottom's mud releasing bursts of gaseous bubbles beneath their feet. Sweat clung to Dan's face, his breath rasping, and he could hear Arden's lungs straining too in the steamy heat. Something splashed in the water on their left; it sounded heavy, and Dan prayed it was simply a large catfish that had jumped instead of a 'gator's tail steering a set of jaws toward them. He braced for the unknown, but whatever it had been it left them alone for the moment.

Looking back once again, he could see the green light flickering through the undergrowth. They were still coming. Arden looked over her shoulder, too, then concentrated on getting through the water ahead. Her vision had cleared, but where she'd banged her skull against the dashboard was raw with pain. She was wearing out with every step; she felt her strength draining away, and soon she was going to have to stop to catch her breath. She wasn't on the run;

it was Dan the bounty hunters were after, but when they'd take him away they'd take the man she had come to believe was her best hope of finding the Bright Girl. From a deep place within her the voice of reason was speaking, trying to tell her that it was pointless to go any farther into this swamp, that a wanted killer had her by the hand and was leading her away from civilization, that she probably had a concussion and needed a doctor, that her brain was scrambled and she wasn't thinking straight and she was in the most dangerous place she'd ever been in her life. She heard it, but she refused to listen. In her right hand was clutched the small pink drawstring bag containing what had become her talisman over the years, and she fixed her mind on Jupiter's voice saying that this was the man God had provided to take her to the Bright Girl. She had to believe it. She had to, or all hope would come crashing down around her, and she feared that more than death.

"I see a light," Dan suddenly said.

She could see it, too. A faint glow, off to the right. Not electricity. More like the light cast from a candle or oil lamp. They kept going, the water at Dan's waist and above Arden's.

Shapes emerged from the darkness. On either side of the channel were two or three tarpaper shacks built up on wooden platforms over the water. The light was coming from a window covered with what looked like waxed paper. The other shacks were dark, either empty or their inhabitants asleep. Dan had no desire to meet the kind of people who'd choose to live in such primitive arrangements, figuring they'd shoot an intruder on sight. But he made out something else in addition to the shacks: a few of them, including the one that showed a light, had small boats—fishing skiffs—tied up to their pilings.

They needed a boat in the worst way, he decided. He put his finger to his lips to tell Arden to remain silent, and she nodded. Then he guided her past the shack where the light burned and across the channel to the next dwelling. The skiff there was secured by a chain and padlock, but a single paddle with a broken handle was lying down inside it. Dan eased the paddle out and went on to the third shack. The boat that was tied there held about six inches of trash-filled water in its hull. There were no other paddles in sight, but the leaky craft was attached to a piling only by a plastic line. In this case beggars couldn't be choosers. Dan spent a moment untying the line's slimy knot, then he pulled himself as quietly as he could over into the boat though his foot thumped against the side. He waited, holding his breath, but no one came out of the shack. He helped Arden in. She sat on the bench seat at the bow, while Dan sat in the stern and shoved them away from the platform. They glided out toward the channel's center, where the current flowed the strongest, and when they were a safe distance away from the shack, Dan slid the stubby paddle into the water and delivered the first stroke.

"Grave robbers!" a woman's voice shrilled, the sound of it startling Dan and making goose bumps rise on Arden's wet arms. "Go on and steal it, then, you donkey-dick suckers!"

Dan looked behind. A figure stood back at the first shack, where the light burned.

"Go on, then!" the woman said. "Lord's gonna fix your asses, you'll find out! I'll dance on your coffins, you maggot-eaters!" She began spitting curses that Dan hadn't heard since his days in boot camp, and some that would've curled a drill sergeant's ear hairs. Another voice growled, "Shut up, Rona!" It belonged to a man who sounded very drunk. "Shut your hole, I'm sleepin' over here!"

"I wouldn't piss on your face if it was on fire!" Rona hollered across the channel. "I'm gonna cook up a spell on you. Your balls gonna dry up like little bitty black raisins!"

"Awwwww, shut up 'fore I come over there and knock your head out your ass!" A door whacked shut.

Dan's paddling had quickened. The woman continued to curse and rave, her voice rising and falling with lunatic cadence. Then she retreated into her hovel and slammed her own door so hard Dan was surprised the place hadn't collapsed. He saw the light move away from the window, and he could imagine a wizened, muttering crone in there stooped over a smoking stewpot with a goat's head in it. Well, at least they had a boat though they were sitting in nasty water. The phrase *up Shit Creek* came to him, but they did have a paddle. When he glanced back again, he no longer saw the green flare's glow. Maybe the bounty hunters had given up and turned away. If so, good riddance to them. Now all he could do was guide this boat down the center of the bayou and hope it would lead them eventually out to the Gulf. From there he could find somewhere safe to leave the girl and strike out on his own again.

He didn't like being responsible for her, and worrying about that knock she'd suffered, and feeling her hand clutch his so hard his knuckles cracked. He was a lone wolf by nature, that's how things were, so just as soon as he could, he was getting rid of her. Anyway, she was crazy. Her obsession with the Bright Girl made Dan think of something he'd seen on the news once: hundreds of people had converged from across the country to camp out day after day in an Oklahoma cornfield where a farmer's wife swore the Virgin Mary had materialized. He remembered thinking how desperately those people had wanted to believe in the wisdom of a higher power, and how they'd believed that the Virgin Mary would appear again at that same place with a message for mankind. Only she'd never showed up, and the really amazing thing was that none of those hundreds of people had regretted coming there, or felt betrayed or bitter. They'd simply felt that the time wasn't right for the Virgin Mary to appear again, but they were certain that sometime and somewhere she would. Dan couldn't understand that kind of blind faith; it flew in the face of the wanton death and destruction he'd witnessed in 'Nam. He wondered if any of that multitude had ever put a bullet between the eyes of a sixteen-year-old boy and felt a rush of exultation that the boy's AK-47 had jammed. He wondered if any of them had ever smelled the odor of burning flesh, or seen flames chewing on the small skulls. If any of them had walked in his boots, had stood in the dirty silver rain and seen the sights that were seared in his mind, he doubted they would put much faith in waiting for the return of Mary, Jesus, or the Holy Ghost.

Dan paddled a few strokes and then let the boat drift. Arden faced southward, the warm breeze of motion blowing past her. The water made a soft, chuckling sound at the bow, and the bittersweet swamp was alive with the hums and clicks and clacks of insects, the occasional sharp keening of a night bird, the bass thumping of frogs and other fainter noises that were not so identifiable. The only light now came from the stars that shone through spaces in the thick canopy of branches overhead.

Dan started to look back, but he decided not to. He knew where he'd been; it was where he was going that concerned him now. The moment of Emory Blanchard's death was still a bleeding wound in his mind, and maybe for the rest of his days it would torture him, but the swamp's silken darkness gave him comfort. He felt a long way from the law and prison walls. If he could find food, fresh water, and a shelter over his head—even the sagging roof of a tarpaper shack—he thought he could live and die here, under these stars. It was a big swamp, and maybe it would accept a man who wanted to disappear. An ember of hope reawakened and began to burn inside him. Maybe it was an illusion, he thought, but it was something to nurture and cling to, just as Arden clung to her Bright Girl. His first task, though, was getting her out, then he could decide on his own destination.

The boat drifted slowly onward, embraced by the current flowing to the sea.

Pelvis held Mama with one arm and his other hand gripped the back of Flint's soggy suit jacket. The green flarelight had burned out several minutes before, and the night had closed in on them. Pelvis had been asking—begging was the more correct term—Flint to turn back when they'd heard a woman's voice hollering and cursing ahead. As they'd slogged on through the stomach-deep water, Flint's left hand slid under his shirt and supported Clint's head; their eyes had started acclimating to the dark. In another moment they could make out the shapes of the tarpaper shacks, a light moving around inside the nearest one on the right. Flint saw a boat tied up to the platform the shack stood on, and as they got closer he made out that it had a scabrous-looking outboard motor. It occurred to him that Lambert might be hiding in one of the darkened shacks, waiting for them to move past. He guided Pelvis toward the flickering light they could see through a waxed-paper window, and at the platform's edge Flint said, "Stay here" and pulled himself up on the splintery boards. He paused to remove the derringer, then he pushed Clint's arm under his shirt and buttoned up his dripping jacket. He held the derringer behind his back and knocked at the shack's flimsy door.

He heard somebody scuttling around inside, but the knock wasn't answered. "Hey, in there!" he called. "Would you open up?" He reached out, his fist balled, to knock a second time.

A latch slammed back. The door swung open on creaking hinges, and from it thrust the business end of a sawed-off shotgun that pressed hard against Flint's forehead.

"I'll open *you* up, you dog-ass lickin' sonofabitch!" the woman behind the gun snarled, and her finger clicked back the trigger.

Flint didn't move; it swept through his mind that at this range the shotgun would blast his brains into the trees on the other side of the bayou. By the smoky light from within the shack, Flint saw that the woman was at least six feet tall and built as solidly as a truck. She wore a pair of dirty overalls, a gray and sweat-stained T-shirt, and on her head was a battered dark green football helmet. Behind the helmet's protective face bar was a forbidding visage with burning, red-rimmed eyes and skin like saddle leather.

"Easy," Flint managed to say. "Take it easy, all I want to do is ask—"

"I know what you want, you scum-sucker!" she yelled. "You ain't takin' me back to that damn shithole! Ain't gettin' me in a rubber room again and stickin' my head full of pins and needles!"

Crazy as a three-legged grasshopper, he thought. His heart was galloping, and the inside of his mouth would've made the Sahara feel tropical. He stared at the woman's grimy-nailed finger on the trigger in front of his face. "Listen," he croaked. "I didn't come to take you anywhere. I just want to—"

"Satan's got a silver tongue!" she thundered. "Now I'm gonna send you back to hell, where you belong!"

Flint saw her finger twitch on the trigger. His breath froze.

"Ma'am?" There was the sound of muddy shoes squeaking on the timbers. "Can I talk to you a minute, ma'am?"

The woman's insane eyes blinked. "Who is that?" she hissed. "Who said that?"

"I did, ma'am." Pelvis walked into the range of the light, Mama cradled in his arms. "Can I have a word with you, please?"

Flint saw the woman stare past him at Eisley. Her finger was still on the trigger, the barrel pressing a ring into his forehead. He was terrified to move even an inch.

Pelvis offered up the best smile he could find. "Ain't nobody wants to hurt you, ma'am. Honest we don't."

Flint heard the woman draw a long, stunned gasp. Her eyes had widened, her thin-lipped mouth starting to tremble.

"You can put that gun down if you like," Pelvis said. "Might better, 'fore somebody gets hurt."

"Oh," the woman whispered. "Oh my Jesus!" Flint saw tears shine in her eyes. "They . . . they told me . . . you died."

"Huh?" Pelvis frowned.

"They told her you died!" Flint spoke up, understanding what the madwoman meant. "Tell her you didn't die, Elvis!"

"Shut your mouth, you Satan's asshole!" the woman ranted at him. "I'm not talkin' to you!" Her finger twitched on the trigger again.

"I do wish you'd at least uncock that gun, ma'am," Pelvis said. "It'd make an awful mess if it was to go off."

She stared at him, her tongue flicking out to wet her lips. "They told me you died!" Her voice was softer now, and there was something terribly wounded in it. "I was up there in Baton Rouge, when I was livin' with Billy and that bitch wife he had. They said you died, that you took drugs and slid off the toilet and died right there, wasn't a thing nobody could do to save you but I prayed for you I cried and I lit the candles in my room and that bitch said I wanted to burn down the house but Billy, Billy he's been a good brother he said I'm all right I ain't gonna hurt nobody.''

"Oh." Pelvis caught her drift. "Oh . . . ma'am, I ain't really—"

"Yes you are!" Flint yelped. "Help me out here, Elvis!"

"You dirty sonofabitch, you!" the woman hollered into his face. "You call him *Mr. Presley!*"

Flint gritted his teeth, the sweat standing out in bright oily beads on his face. "Mr. Presley, tell this lady how I'm a friend of yours, and how hurtin' me would be the same as hurtin' you. Would you tell her that, please?"

"Well . . . that'd be a lie, wouldn't it? I mean, you made it loud and clear you think I stand about gut-high to an ant."

"That was then. This is now. I think you're the finest man I've ever met. Would you please tell her?"

Pelvis scratched Mama's chin and cocked his head to one side. A few seconds ticked past, during which a bead of sweat trickled down to the end of Flint's nose and hung there. Then Pelvis said, "Yes'm, Mr. Murtaugh's a friend of mine."

The woman removed her shotgun from Flint's forehead. Flint let his breath rattle out and staggered back a couple of steps. "That's different, then," she said, uncocking the gun. "Different, if he's your friend. My name's Rona, you remember me?"

"Uh . . ." Pelvis glanced quickly at Flint, then back to the madwoman. "I . . . believe I . . ."

"I seen you in Biloxi." Her voice trembled with excitement. "That was in—" She paused. "I can't think when that was, my mind gets funny sometimes. I was sittin' in the third row. I wrote you a letter. You remember me?"

"Uh . . ." He saw Flint nod. "Yes'm, I believe so."

"I sent my name in to that magazine, you know that *Tiger Beat* magazine was havin' that contest for a date with you? I sent my name in, and my daddy said I was the biggest fool ever lived but I did anyway and I went to church and prayed I was gonna win. My mama went to live in heaven, that's what I wrote in my letter." She looked down at her dirty overalls. "Oh, I—I must look a fright!"

"No ma'am," Pelvis said quietly. "Rona, I mean. You look fine."

"You sure have got fat," Rona told him. "They cut your balls off in the army, didn't they? Then they made you stop singin' them good songs. They're the ones fucked up the world. Put up them satellites in outer space so they could read people's minds. Them monkey-cock suckers! Well, they ain't gettin' to me no more!" She tapped her helmet. "Best protect yourself while you can!" She let her hand drop, and she looked dazedly back and forth between Flint and Pelvis. "Am I dreamin'?" she asked.

"Rona?" Flint said. "You mind if I call you Rona?" She just stared blankly at him. "We're lookin' for somebody. A man and a woman. Did you see anybody pass by here?"

Rona turned her attention to Pelvis again. "How come they tell such lies about you? That you was takin' drugs and all? How come they said you died?"

"I . . . just got tired, I reckon," Pelvis said. Flint noted that he was standing a little taller, he'd sucked his gut in as much as possible, and he was making his voice sound more like Elvis than ever, with that rockabilly Memphis sneer in it. "I wanted to go hide someplace."

"Uh-huh, me, too." She nodded. "I didn't mean to burn that house down, but the light was so pretty. You know how pretty a light can be when it's dark all the time? Then they put me in that white car, that white car with the straps, and they took me to that place and stuck pins and needles in my head. But they let me go, and I wanted to hide, too. You want some gumbo? I got some gumbo inside. I made it yesterday."

"Rona?" Flint persisted. "A man and a woman. Have you seen them?"

"I seen them grave robbers, stealin' his boat." She motioned across the channel. "John LeDuc lived there, but he died. Stepped in a cottonmouth nest, that's what the ranger said. Them grave robbers over there, stealin' his boat. I hollered at 'em, but they didn't pay no mind."

"Uh-huh. What do you get to if you keep followin' this bayou?"

"Swamp," she said as if he were the biggest fool who ever lived. "Swamp and more swamp. 'Cept for Saint Nasty."

"Saint Nasty? What's that?"

"Where they work on them oil rigs." Rona's gaze was fixed on Pelvis. "I'm dreamin', ain't I? My mama comes and visits me sometimes, I know I'm dreamin' awake. That's what I'm doin' now, ain't that right?"

"How far's Saint Nasty from here?" Flint asked.

"Four, five miles."

"Is there a road out from there?"

"No road. Just the bayou, goes on to the Gulf."

"We need a boat," he said. "How much for yours?"

"What?"

"How much money?" He took the opportunity to slip the

derringer into his pocket and withdraw the wet bills he'd taken from the girl's wallet. "Fifty dollars, will that cover the boat and motor?"

"Ain't no gas in that motor," she told him. "That ranger comes 'round and visits me, he brings me gas. His name's Jack, he's a nice young fella. Only he didn't come this week."

"How about paddles, then? Have you got any?"

"Yeah, I got a paddle." She narrowed her eyes at Flint. "I don't like your looks. I don't care if you are his friend and he's a dream I'm havin'. You got somethin' mean in you."

"Sixty dollars," Flint said. "Here's the cash, right here."

Rona gave a harsh laugh. "You're crazier'n hell. You better watch out, they'll be stickin' pins and needles in your head 'fore long."

"Sooner than you think, lady." He shot a scowl at Pelvis. "Mr. Presley, how about openin' those golden lips and helpin' me out a little bit?"

Pelvis was still thinking about two words the madwoman had uttered: *Cottonmouth nest*. "We sure do need your boat, Rona," he said with genuine conviction. "It'd be doin' us a big favor if you'd sell it to us. You can even keep the motor, we'll just take the boat and paddle."

Rona didn't reply for a moment, but Flint could see her chewing on her lower lip as she thought about the proposal. "Hell," she said at last, "you two ain't real anyhow, are you?" She shrugged. "You can buy the boat, I don't care."

"Good. Here." Flint offered sixty dollars to her, and the woman accepted the cash with an age-spotted hand and then sniffed the wet bills. "We'll need the paddle, too," he told her, and she laughed again as if this were a grand illusion and walked into her shack, the interior of which Flint could see was plastered with newspaper pages and held a cast-iron stove. Flint told Pelvis to help him get the motor unclamped from the boat's stern, and they were laying it on the platform when Rona returned—without her shotgun—bringing a paddle.

"Thank you, ma'am," Pelvis said. "We sure do 'preciate it."

"I got a question for you," Rona said as they were getting into the boat. "Who sent you here? Was it Satan, to make me think I'm losin' my mind, or God, to give me a thrill?"

Pelvis stared into her leathery face. Behind the football helmet's protective bar her deep-socketed eyes glinted with what was surely insanity but might also have been—at least for a passing moment— the memory of a teenaged girl in her finest dress, sitting in the third row of a Biloxi auditorium. He worked one of the gaudy fake diamond rings from a finger and pushed it into her palm. "Darlin'," he said, "you decide."

Sitting in the stern, Flint untied the rope that secured the boat to the platform and then pushed them off with the paddle. Pelvis took the bow seat, Mama warm and drowsy against his chest. Flint began to stroke steadily toward the center of the channel, where he got them turned southward. He felt the current grasp their hull, and in another moment they were moving at about the pace of a fast walk. When Pelvis looked back at the woman standing in front of her decrepit shack, Flint said acidly, "Made yourself another fan there, didn't you, Mr. Presley?"

Pelvis stared straight ahead into the darkness. He pulled in a long breath and slowly released it, and he answered with some grit in his voice. "You can pucker up and kiss my butt."

19

Home Sweet Hellhole

In the starfire dark Dan and Arden drifted past other narrower bayous that branched off from the main channel. They saw no other lights or shacks, and it was clear that their detour off the bridge had left LaPierre miles behind.

When the mosquitoes found them, there was nothing they could do but take the bites. Something bumped hard against the boat before it swam away, and after his heart had descended from his throat, Dan figured it had been an amorous alligator looking for some scaly tush. He got into a pattern of paddling for three or four minutes and then resting, and he and Arden both cupped their hands and bailed out the water that was seeping up through the hull. He said nothing about this to Arden, but he guessed the boat was a rusty nail or two from coming apart.

Most of the pain had cleared from Arden's head. Her vision had stopped tunneling in and out, but her bones still ached and her fingers found a crusty patch of dried blood in her hair and a lump so sore the lightest pressure on it almost made her sick. Her purse and suitcase were gone, her money, her belongings, her identification, everything lost. Except her life, and the drawstring bag in her right hand. But that was okay, she thought. Maybe it was how things were supposed to be. She was shedding her old skin in preparation for the Bright Girl's touch. She was casting off the past, and getting ready for the new Arden Halliday to be born. How she would find the Bright Girl in this wilderness she didn't exactly know, but she had to believe she was close now, very close. When she'd seen the light in the shack's window back there, she'd thought for a moment they might have found the Bright Girl, but she didn't think—or she didn't want to think—that the Bright Girl would choose to live in a tarpaper hovel. Arden hadn't considered what kind of dwelling the Bright Girl might occupy, but now she envisioned something like a green mansion hidden amid the cypress trees, where sunlight streamed through the high branches like liquid gold. Or a house-boat anchored in a clear, still pool somewhere up one of these bayous. But not a dirty tarpaper shack. No, that didn't suit her image of the Bright Girl, and she refused to believe it.

She strained to see through the darkness, thinking—or wishing—that just ahead would be the glow of another lantern and a cluster of squatters' shacks, somebody to help her find her way. She glanced back at Dan as he slid the paddle into the water again. *The man God provided,* Jupiter had said. She'd never have left the motel with Dan if she hadn't been clinging to Jupiter's instincts about him. Jupiter had always been a mystic; he had the sixth sense about horses, he knew their temperaments and their secret names. If he said a docile-looking animal was getting ready to snort and kick, it was wise to move away from the hindquarters. And he knew other things, too; if he smelled rain in the midst of a Texas drought, it was time to get out the buckets. He read the sky and the wind and the pain in Arden's soul; she had come to realize during her years at the youth ranch that Jupiter Krenshaw was connected to the flowing currents of life in a way she couldn't fathom. She had trusted and believed him, and now she had to trust and believe he'd been telling her the truth about the Bright Girl, and that he'd seen something in Dan Lambert that no one else could recognize.

She had to, because there was no turning back.

They drifted on, the skiff being drawn along with the slow but steady current. They passed evidence that others had come this way: a few abandoned and crumbling shacks, a wharf jutting out over the water on rotten pilings, a wrecked and vine-draped shrimp boat whose prow was jammed between the trunks of two huge moss trees. Dan felt weariness overtaking him, and he caught himself dozing off between stretches of paddling. Arden likewise had begun to close her eyes and rest, fighting thirst but not yet ready to drink any of the water they were gliding through.

Dan let himself sleep for only a few minutes at a time, then his internal alarm went off and roused him to keep the boat from drifting into the half-submerged trees on either side. The water was probably eight or ten feet deep, he figured. Their boat was still in the slow process of sinking, but he went to work bailing with his hands and Arden helped him until their craft had lightened up again.

Dan noted that the branches overhead were beginning to unlock and draw apart. In another twenty minutes or so—a little over an hour since they'd set off in the boat—the bayou merged into a wider channel that took a long curve toward the southwest. Heat lightning shimmered in the sky, and an occasional fish jumped from the channel's ebony surface and splashed down again. Dan looked at the water in the boat and decided it wasn't wise to think too much about what might be roaming the depths, making those fish want to grow wings. He paddled a few strokes and then rested again, the muscles of his back starting to cramp.

"You want me to paddle awhile?" Arden asked.

"No, I'm all right." Resting the paddle across his knees, he let the current do the work. He scratched the welts on his forehead where a couple of mosquitoes had been feasting, and he sorely missed his baseball cap. "How about you? You hangin' in?"

"Yeah."

"Good." He listened to the quiet sound of the hull moving through the water. "I sure could use a cold six-pack. I wouldn't kick a pizza out of bed, either."

"I'll take a pitcher of iced tea with some lime in it," she said after a moment of deliberation. "And a bowl of strawberry ice cream."

Dan nodded, looking from side to side at the dense walls of foliage that lined the bayou. Yes, he decided; a man could get lost in here and never be found. "This ought to take us out to the Gulf, sooner or later," he said. "Could be daylight before we get there, though." He made out ten forty-four by the luminous hands of his watch. "Once we clear the swamp, maybe we can find a fishin' camp or somethin' along the coast. Could be we can find a road and flag a car down, get you a ride out of here."

"Get *me* a ride out? What about you?"

"Never mind about me. You took a pretty hard knock on the head, you need to see a doctor."

"I don't need a doctor. You know who I need to find."

"Don't start that again!" he warned. "Hear me? Wherever LaPierre is, we're long past it. I'm gettin' you out of here, then you can do what you please. You ought to get back to Fort Worth and count yourself lucky to be alive."

"And how am I gonna do that? I lost my purse and all my money. Even if I could find a bus station, I couldn't buy a ticket."

"I've got some money," he said. "Enough to buy you a bus ticket, if you can hitch a ride back to Houma."

"Yeah, I've sure got a lot to go back to," she answered tersely. "No job, no money, nothin'. Pretty soon I'll be out on the street. How do you think I'll do at a shelter for the homeless?"

"You'll find a job, get back on your feet."

"Uh-huh. I wish it was that easy. Don't you know what it's like out there?"

"Yeah," he drawled, "I believe I do."

She grunted and allowed herself a faint, bitter smile. "I guess so. Sorry. I must sound like a whinin' fool."

"Times are hard for everybody. Except the rich people who got us into this mess." He listened to the distant call of a night bird off to the left, a lonely sound that tugged at his heart. "I never wanted to be rich," he said. "Seems to me, that's just askin' for more problems. But I always wanted to pull my own weight. Pay my bills and take pride in my work. That's what was important to me. After I got back from 'Nam, I had some tough times, but things were workin' out. Then . . . I don't know." He caught himself from going any further. "Well, you've got your own road to travel; you don't need to walk down mine."

"I think we're both headin' in the same direction."

"No, we're not," he corrected her. "How old are you?"

"Twenty-seven."

"The difference between us is that you've got your whole life ahead of you, and I'm windin' it down. Nobody said livin' was gonna be easy or fair, that's for damn sure. I'm here to tell you it's not. But you don't give up. You're gonna get knocked down and beat up and stomped, but you don't quit. You can't."

"Maybe you can," Arden said quietly. "I'm tired of bein' knocked down, beaten up, and stomped. I keep gettin' up, and somethin' comes along to knock me down again. I'm tired of it. I wish to God there was a way to . . . just find some peace."

"Go back to Fort Worth." He slid the paddle into the water and began pushing them forward again. "Somethin's bound to open up for you. But you sure don't belong in the middle of a swamp, tryin' to find a faith healer."

"Right now I don't know where I belong. I don't think I ever have known." She was silent for a moment, her hands working around the pink drawstring bag. "What was your best time?" she asked. "I mean, the time when you thought everything was right, and you were where you were supposed to be. Do you know?"

He thought about it, and the longer he thought the harder the question became to answer. "I guess . . . maybe when I'd first joined the marines. In boot camp, on Parris Island. I had a job to do—a mission—and I was gettin' ready for it. Things were black and white. I thought my country needed me, and I thought I could make a difference."

"You sound like you were eager to fight."

"Yeah, I was." Dan paddled another stroke and then paused. "I liked bein' over there the first couple of months. At first it seemed like I was doin' somethin' important. I didn't like to kill—no man in his right mind does—but I did it because I was fightin' for my country. I thought. Then, later on, it all changed. I saw so many boys get killed, I couldn't figure out what they were dyin' for. I mean, what were we tryin' to do? The Viet Cong didn't want my country. They weren't gonna invade us. They didn't have anything we needed. What was that all about?" He shook his head. "Here it's been over twenty years, and I still don't know. It was a hell of a lot of wasted lives is what it was. Lives just thrown away."

"It must've been bad," Arden said. "I've seen a couple of movies about Vietnam, and it sure wasn't like Desert Storm, was it?"

"Nope, it sure wasn't." *Movies about Vietnam*, he thought, and he lowered his head to hide his half-smile. He'd been forgetting that Arden was all of four years old when he'd shipped to 'Nam.

"My best time was when I was livin' on the youth ranch," she said. "It was a hard place, and you did your chores and toed the line, but it was all right. The others there were like I was. All of us had been through a half-dozen foster homes, and we'd screwed up and gotten in trouble with the law. It was our last chance to get straight, I guess. I hated it at first. Tried to run away a couple of times, but I didn't get very far. Mr. Richards put me to work cleanin' out the barn. There were five horses, all of 'em old and swaybacked, but they still earned their keep. Jupiter was in charge of the stable, that's where I met him."

"You think a lot of him, don't you?"

"He was always kind to me. Some of those foster homes I was in . . . well, I think solitary confinement in prison would've been better. I had trouble, too, because of . . . you know . . . my mark. Somebody looked at me too long, I was liable to lose my temper and start throwin' plates and glasses. Which didn't make me too popular with foster parents. I wasn't used to bein' treated like I had sense." She shrugged. "I guess I had a lot to prove. But Jupiter took an interest in me. He trusted me with the horses, started lettin' me feed and groom 'em. After a while, when I'd wake up early mornin's I could hear 'em callin' for me, wantin' me to hurry up. You know, all horses have got different personalities and different voices, not a one of 'em alike. Some of 'em come right out of the stall to meet you, others are shy and hang back. And when they look at you they don't care if you're ugly or deformed. They don't judge you by a mark on your face, like people do."

"Not all people," Dan said.

"Enough to hurt," she answered. She looked up at the stars for a moment, and Dan went to work with the paddle once more. "It was a good feelin', to wake up and hear the horses callin' you," she went on. "It was the first time I ever felt needed, or that I was worth a damn. After the work was done, Jupiter and I started havin' long talks. About life, and God, and stuff I'd never cared to think much about. He never mentioned my mark; he let me get to it in my own time. It took me a while to talk about it, and how I wished more than anything in the world I could be rid of it. Then he told me about the Bright Girl."

Dan said nothing; he was listening, but on this subject it was hard not to turn a deaf ear.

"I never really expected I'd ever be lookin' for her," Arden said. "But the way Jupiter talked about her . . . she seemed like some-body I'd know, if I ever found her. She seemed so real, and so alive. I mean, I know it sounds crazy for somebody to live so long and never get old. I know the faith healers on TV are frauds tryin' to squeeze out the bucks. But Jupiter would never have lied to me." She caught Dan's gaze and held it. "If he said there's a Bright Girl, there is. And if he said she can touch my mark and take it away, she can. He would never have lied. And he was right about *you*, too. If he said you're the man God sent to help me find her, then I be—"

"Stop it!" Dan interrupted sharply. "I told you I didn't want to hear that"—*bullshit*, he almost said, but he settled on—"junk."

She started to fire back a heated reply, but she closed her mouth. She just stared at him, her eyes fixed on his.

Dan said, "You're chasin' a fairy tale. Where it's gotten you? Do you think you're better off than before you left Fort Worth? No, you're worse off. At least you had some money in the bank. I don't want to hear any more about the Bright Girl, or what Jupiter told you, or any of that. Understand?"

"I wish *you* understood." Her voice was calm and controlled. "If—*when*—we find her, she can heal you, too."

"Oh, Christ!" He closed his eyes in exasperation for a few seconds. When he opened them, Arden was still glowering at him. "You could argue the horns off a billy goat, you know that? There is *no* Bright Girl, and there never was! It's a made-up story!"

"That's what you say."

He saw no point in going around in circles with her. "Right, that's what I say," he muttered, and then he concentrated on putting some elbow grease into the paddling. The current seemed to have gotten a little faster, which he thought must be a good sign. He was hungry and thirsty and his headache had returned, pounding with his heartbeat. Dried blood was in his nostrils, he'd lost his much-prized baseball cap and his muscles—what remained of them, that is—were rapidly wearing out. The water was rising in the bottom of the boat again, and Dan put aside the paddle for a few minutes while he and Arden cupped their hands and bailed. Then he shook off the sleep that was closing in on him and paddled them down the center of the bayou with slow, smooth strokes. He watched Arden's head droop as she fell asleep sitting up, and then he was alone with the noises of the swamp. After a while his eyelids became leaden and he couldn't keep them open. The heat pressed on him, lulling him to sleep. He fought it as hard as he could, but at last his weariness won the battle and his chin slumped.

He jerked his head up, his eyes opening.

They had drifted toward the left of the channel and were almost in the branches. Dan steered them toward the center again, and then he heard the sound that had awakened him: a muffled thudding like the heartbeats of a giant. Ahead and to the right, electric lights glinted through the thick woods. Dan looked at his wristwatch and saw that another hour had elapsed since they'd entered the wider channel.

"What's that noise?" Arden asked, waking up almost as quickly as he had.

"Machinery," he said. "I think we're comin' to somethin'."

Around the next curve the trees had been chopped away on the right to make room for a hodgepodge of weatherbeaten clapboard structures built on platforms over the water. Electric lights cast their glary circles on a dock where an assortment of motor skiffs and two houseboats were tied up. On the dock were gas pumps and an attendant's shack, also lit up with electricity supplied from a rumbling generator. Plank walkways connected the buildings, and Dan and Arden saw two men standing in conversation next to the gas pumps and a couple of other men on the walkways. A rusty barge loaded with sections of metal pipe, coils of wire, and other industrial items was anchored past the dock at a concrete pier where a long building with corrugated aluminum walls stood, the legend WAREHOUSE #1 painted in red across the building's doorway. Beyond the warehouse loomed oil storage tanks and twelve or more spidery derricks rising up from the swamp. The giant heartbeat— the sound of pumps at work—was coming from that direction.

The entire scene—a large, mechanized oil-pumping station, Dan had realized—was almost surrealistic, emerging as it had from the dark wilderness. As he steered them toward the dock, he saw a pole that held a tired-looking American flag and next to it was a sign on stilts that announced ST. NASTASE, LA. HOME SWEET HELLHOLE. On the supporting stilts were a number of other directional arrows with such things as NEW ORLEANS 52 MI., BATON ROUGE 76 MI., and

GALVESTON 208 MI. painted on them. One of the men on the dock picked up a line and tossed it to Arden as they approached, then he hauled them in. "Hey there, how you doin'?" the man asked in a thick Cajun patois. He was a husky, florid-faced gent with a red beard and a sweat-stained bandanna wrapped around his skull.

"Tired and hungry," Dan told him as he carefully stood up and helped Arden onto the dock. "Where are we?"

"Fella wanna know where he am," the Cajun said to the other man, and both of them laughed. "Friend, you *must* be in some sad shape!"

Dan stepped onto the timbers, his spine unkinking. "I mean how far from here to the Gulf?"

"Oh, blue water 'bout tree mile." He motioned south with a crusty thumb. His gaze lingered on Arden's birthmark for a few seconds, then he diverted his attention to the waterlogged skiff. "I seen some crackass boats before, but that'un done win the prize! Where ya'll come from?"

"North," Dan said. "Anyplace to get some food here?"

"Yeah, cafe's over there." The second man, who spoke with a flat midwestern accent, nodded in the direction of the clapboard buildings. He was slimmer than his companion, wore a grease-stained brown cap with a red GSP on the front—a company logo, Dan figured—and had tattoos intertwining all over his arms. "They got gumbo and hamburgers tonight. Ain't too bad if you wash 'em down with enough beer."

A door on one of the houseboats opened, and another man emerged, buckling the belt of his blue jeans. He wore a company cap turned backward. Behind him, tape-recorded rock music rumbled through the doorway and then a woman with bleached-blond hair and a hard, sunburned face peered out. "Okay!" she said with forced cheerfulness. "All-night party, boys! Who's next?"

"I believe I am." The man with tattooed arms sauntered toward the houseboat.

"*Non, mon ami.*" The Cajun stepped forward, seized his companion by shirt back and pants seat, and, pivoting, lifted him off his feet and flung him from the dock. With a curse and squall the unfortunate flyer hit the water and skimmed its surface like a powerboat before he went under. "I believe you *was!*" the Cajun hollered as his friend came up spitting. "Hey, Lorraine!" he greeted the bleached blonde. "You got sweets for me?"

"You know I do, Tully. Get your big ol' ass in here." She narrowed her eyes at Arden. "New chickie, huh?" She gave a throaty laugh. "You gonna need a little makeup, darlin'. Well, good luck to you." Tully lumbered into the houseboat, and Lorraine closed the door behind them.

It was time to move on. Dan ventured along one of the walkways, heading toward the buildings, and Arden followed close behind. The place made Dan think of a Wild West frontier town, except it had been built up from the muck instead of being carved from the desert. It was a carpenter's nightmare, the structures cobbled together with pressure-treated pineboards and capped by rusted tin roofs. Electrical cables snaked from building to building, carrying the juice from generators. The walkways were so close to the water that in some places reeds stuck up between the planks. There was a store whose sign announced it as R.J'S GROCERY and next to it was a little narrow structure marked ST. NASTASE POST OFFICE. A Laundromat with three washers and dryers and two pool tables was lit up and doing business. Dan noted that the men they saw gazed hungrily at Arden's body, but when they looked at her face they averted their eyes as quickly as Tully had.

St. Nastase, Dan had realized, most likely never closed down, to accommodate the crews who were off shift. Dan figured that the men here had signed on with the company for three or four months at a stretch, which meant prostitutes in houseboats could make some money plying their trade. It occurred to him that Lorraine had thought Arden was a "new chickie" because the only women who dared to go there were selling sex, and he was unaware of it but Arden had come to the same conclusions about ten seconds ahead of him.

In another moment they heard the mingled music of a fiddle and an accordion. The smell of food caught their nostrils. Ahead was a building with a sign that said simply CAFE. The place had a pair of batwing doors, like a western saloon. The music was coming from within, accompanied now by whoops and hollers. Dan figured this could be a hell of a rowdy joint, and again he wished Arden wasn't around because he was going to have to be responsible for her safety. He said, "Stick close to me," and then Arden followed him through the batwings, her right hand clenching the pink drawstring bag.

The cafe was dimly lit, blue-hazed with cigarette smoke, and at the ceiling a fan chugged around in a futile attempt to circulate the humid, sweat-smelling air. Hanging from the ceiling as well were maybe three hundred old, dirty brown caps with red GSP logos. At rough plank tables sat twenty or more men, a few of them clapping their hands in time with the jerky, raucous music, while four of their fellows danced with ladies of the evening. The fiddler and accordionist both wore company caps, and a thick-shouldered black man got up from his table, sat down at a battered old piano, and began to beat out a rhythm that added to the merry clamor. Some of the men glanced eagerly at Arden, but they looked away when Dan put his arm around her shoulders.

He guided her toward a bar where metal beer kegs, canned soft drinks, and bottles of water were on display. Behind it, a harried-looking man with glasses, a beard, and slicked-back dark hair was drawing beer into mugs, sweat stains on his red-checked shirt and a cigar stub gripped between his teeth. "Can we get somethin' to eat?" Dan asked over the noise, and the bartender said, "Burgers a buck apiece, gumbo two bucks a bowl. Take the gumbo, the burgers taste like dog meat."

They both decided on the gumbo, which the bartender ladled from a grease-filmed pot into plastic bowls. Arden asked for a bottle of water and Dan requested a beer, and as the bartender shoved trays and plastic spoons wrapped in cellophane at them, Dan said, "I'm tryin' to get this girl out of here. Is there a road anywhere nearby?"

"A *road*?" He snorted, and the tip of his cigar glowed red. "Ain't no roads outta St. Nasty. Just water and mud. She a workin' girl?"

"No. We're passin' through."

The bartender stared at Dan, his eyes slightly magnified by the glasses, and he removed the cigar from his mouth. "Passin' through," he repeated incredulously. "Now I've heard it all. Ain't no man comes here unless he's drawin' pay from Gulf States Petro, and no woman unless she's tryin' to get a man to spend it on her. Which insane asylum did ya'll get loose from?"

"We had an accident. Went off a bridge north of LaPierre. We got a boat, and—" Dan stopped, because the bartender's eyes had gotten larger. "Look, we're just tryin' to get out. Can you help us?"

"Supply boat from Grand Isle oughta be here tomorrow afternoon. I'd say you could hitch a ride with one of these ladies, but they'll be stayin' the weekend. Today was payday, see. Fridays and Saturdays, all these sumbitches wanna do is get drunk and screw when their shifts are over." He pushed the cigar stub back into his mouth. "You come all the way from *LaPierre*? Jesus, that's a hell of a hike!"

"Hey, Burt!" a man yelled. "Let's have our beers over here!"

"Your legs ain't broke!" Burt hollered back. "Get off your ass and come get 'em, I ain't no slave!" He returned his attention to Dan. "An accident, huh? You want to call somebody? I got a radio-telephone in the back."

"I'm lookin' for a woman," Arden said suddenly. "The Bright Girl. Have you ever heard of her?"

"Nope," Burt replied. A man with a prostitute in tow came up to get his beers. "Should I have?"

"The Bright Girl's a healer. She lives in the swamp somewhere, and I'm tryin' to—"

"Arden?" Dan caught hold of her elbow. "I told you to stop that, didn't I?"

She pulled loose. "I've come a long way to find her," she said to Burt, and she heard the sharp, rising edge of desperation in her voice. Burt's eyes were blank, no idea of what she was talking about at all. Arden felt panic building inside her like a dark wave. "The Bright Girl *is* here, somewhere," she said. "I'm gonna find her. I'm not leavin' here until I find her."

Burt took in the birthmark and looked at Dan. "Like I asked before, what asylum did ya'll bust out of?"

"I'm not crazy," Arden went on. "The Bright Girl's real. I know she is. Somebody here has to have heard of her."

"Sorry," Burt said. "I don't know who you're talkin' a—"

"I know that name."

Arden turned her head to the left. The prostitute who stood with the beer-swiller had spoken in a nasal drawl. She was a slight, rawboned girl wearing denim shorts and a faded orange blouse. Maybe she was in her early twenties, but her high-cheekboned, buck-toothed face had been prematurely aged by scorching sun and harsh salt wind. Lines were starting to deepen around her mouth and at the corners of her dull, chocolate-brown eyes, and her peroxided hair cut in bangs across her forehead hung lifelessly around her bony shoulders. She stared with genuine interest at Arden's birthmark as her escort paid for two beers. "Jeez," she said. "You got fucked up awful bad, didn't ya?"

"Yes." Arden's heart was pounding, and for a few seconds she felt on the verge of fainting. She grasped the edge of the bar with her free hand. "You've heard of the Bright Girl?"

"Uh-huh." The prostitute began to dig at a molar with a toothpick. "Woman who healed people. Used to hear 'bout her when I was a little girl."

"Do you know where she is?"

"Yeah," came the answer, "I do."

As Dan and Arden had been walking into the cafe, the man who'd just gone for an unwilling swim sat on the dock in a puddle of water, watching another boat approach. There were two men in the boat. He couldn't quite trust his eyes. The man who was paddling wore a dark suit and a white shirt, which was not quite the normal attire out here at St. Nasty. The second man—well, maybe it was time to swear off the beers, because that sonofabitch Burt must be mixing the brew with toxic waste.

When the boat bumped broadside against the dock, Flint stood up and stepped out. His mud-grimed suit jacket was buttoned up over his dirty shirt, the pale flesh of his face mottled with red mosquito bites, his eyes sunken in weary purple hollows. He stared at the battered and water-filled skiff tied up just beside them, a single broken paddle lying in it. Nobody would've traveled in that damn thing unless they'd been forced to, he reasoned. "How long have you been sittin' here?" he asked the drenched man, who was watching Pelvis clamber out of the boat with Mama.

"You gotta be *kiddin'!*" the man said, unable to take his eyes off Pelvis. "What is this, *Candid Camera?*"

"Hey, listen up!" Flint demanded, his patience at its bitter end. Clint—who was equally as tired and cranky jerked under his shirt, and Flint put an arm across his chest to hold his brother down. "I'm lookin' for a man and a woman. Shouldn't have been too long since they got here." He nodded at the sinking boat. "Did you see who that belongs to?"

"Yeah, they're here. Sent 'em over to the cafe." He couldn't help but stare at Pelvis. "I know we're hurtin' for entertainment 'round here, but please don't tell me you're on the payroll."

"Where's the cafe? Which direction?"

"Only one direction, unless you can walk on water. Scratch that," he decided, and he motioned at Pelvis with his thumb. "Maybe he *can* walk on water."

Flint started off toward the clapboard buildings, and Pelvis followed, leaving the man on the dock wondering what the next boat might bring. Others they passed stopped to gawk at Pelvis as well, and he started drawing catcalls and laughter. "Hey!" Flint called to two men standing in the shadows next to the Laundro-mat/poolroom. "The cafe around here?"

One of them pointed the way, and Flint and Pelvis went on. Flint reached into his pocket and put his hand on the derringer's grip.

"Who the hell are *they?*" the man who'd pointed asked his friend.

The second man, who had a long, vulpine face and close-cropped brown hair, ran his tongue across his lower lip. He wore faded jeans and a dirty yellow shirt with the tail flagging out, and the sweat on his flesh still smelled of swamp mud and alligators. "Friends of Doc's," he said quietly. "I believe he'd like to see 'em again. Here."

He slid a small packet of white powder into the other man's hand. "Keep your money. Just do me a favor and watch those two. All right?"

"Sure, Mitch. Whatever."

"Good boy." Mitch, who still had the pistol he'd fired at Flint in his waistband, turned away and hurried to his motorboat, his mouth split by a savage grin.

20

The King Bled Crimson

"**Y**eah," came the prostitute's answer. "I do." She continued to probe with the toothpick as Arden's nerves stretched. "Dead. Must be dead by now. She was old, lived in a church on Goat Island."

"That's bull!" Burt said. "Ain't nobody ever lived on Goat Island!"

"*Was* a church there!" the prostitute insisted. "Blew down in a hurricane, back fifteen or twenty years! The Bright Girl was a nun fell in love with a priest, so they threw her out of her convent and she come down here and built a church to repent! That's what my mama said!"

"Angie, you didn't have no mama!" Burt winked at the girl's customer. "She was hatched, wasn't she, Cal?"

"Right out of a buzzard's egg," Cal agreed, his voice slurred by one too many brews.

Angie jabbed an elbow into Cal's ribs. "You don't know nothin', fool!"

Arden tried to speak, but her throat had seized up. The word *dead* was still ringing in her head like a funeral bell. "Goat Island," she managed. "Where is it?"

"Don't do this," Dan warned, but he knew there was no stopping her.

"Way the hell out in Terrebonne Bay," Burt said. "Good ten miles from here. Got wild goats runnin' all over it, but there sure ain't never been no church out there."

"My mama wasn't no liar!" Angie snapped. "You wasn't even born 'round here, how do you know?"

"I been huntin' on Goat Island before! Walked the length and width of it! If there'd ever been a church there, I think I would've seen some ruins!"

"Miss?" Dan said to the prostitute. "You say the Bright Girl was an old woman?"

698

"Yeah. My mama said she seen her when she was a little girl. Came to Port Fourchon to see my mama's cousin. His name was Pearly, he was seven years old when he got burned up in a fire. Mama said the Bright Girl was crippled and walked with a white cane. I reckon that was"—she paused to calculate—"near thirty years ago."

"Uh-huh." Dan felt Arden's body tensing beside him. But he decided he had to go the next step, too. "What about Pearly? Did your mama say the Bright Girl healed him?"

"No, I recollect she said the Bright Girl took him with her in a boat."

"To where?"

"Goat Island, I reckon. She never saw Pearly no more, though. Mama said she figured he was too bad off for even the Bright Girl to heal. But that was all right, 'cause the Bright Girl made sure he wasn't scairt when he went to heaven."

"Come on, baby!" Cal grabbed Angie's thin arm and tugged at her. "Let's dance!"

"Wait! Please!" Arden's anguished voice cut to Dan's heart. "Is she buried out there? Have you seen her grave?"

"No, I ain't seen her grave. But she's dead. Got to be dead after all this time."

"But you don't know for sure, do you? You're not certain she's dead?"

The prostitute stared at Arden for a few seconds and then pulled free of Cal's hand. "I'm certain as I need to be," she said. "Ohhhhh." She nodded as things came clear to her. "Ohhhhh, I see. You was lookin' for the Bright Girl to heal your face. Is that right?"

"Yes."

"I'm sorry, then. Far as I know, she's dead. I don't know where she's buried. I can ask some of the other girls. Most of 'em were born 'round here, maybe they'd know."

"Let's *dance!*" Cal yawped. "Forget this shit!"

Both women ignored him. "I'd like to see the church," Arden said. "Can you take me?"

"No, I can't. See, I would, but I don't have my own boat. It's Lorraine's boat, and she don't take it nowhere but between here and Grand Isle."

"Hey, listen up, scarface!" Cal slurred at Arden, his voice turning nasty. "I'm rentin' this bitch by the fuckin' *hour*, understand? I don't have no time to waste—"

"Come over here a minute." Dan reached out, grasped Cal's

wrist, and drew him closer, beer slopping to the floor from the mug in the man's hand. Dan's face was strained with anger, his eyes hard and shiny. "The ladies are talkin'."

"Mister, you let go of me or I'm gonna have to knock the shit outta your ears!"

"No fightin' in here!" Burt warned. "You wanna fight, get out back!"

"You're drunk, friend." Dan kept his face close to Cal's, his arm low across the man's body so the beer mug wouldn't come up and smash him in the teeth. "Don't let your mouth get you in trouble."

"It's all right," Arden said. The remark wasn't anything she hadn't heard before. "Really it is."

She suddenly caught a strong whiff of body odor and swamp mud. Someone wearing a dark suit stepped between her and Dan. She thought of vulture wings sweeping onto a dying jackrabbit.

"Lambert?" A quiet voice spoke in Dan's ear. At the same time, Dan felt the little barrel of a gun press against his ribs. "The game's over."

Dan jerked his head around and looked into the pallid face he'd seen by the flashlight's glare in Basile Park, only now it was blotched with mosquito bites. His heart jumped and fluttered like a trapped bird.

Flint said, "Take it very, very easy. Nobody needs to get hurt. Okay?"

Beyond Murtaugh, Dan saw, stood the Elvis Presley impersonator holding his squirming bulldog. The music had faltered and ended on a squawked note from the squeezebox. The Presley clone was suddenly the center of attention, and he started drawing whistles and laughter.

Flint glanced quickly at the girl and saw that what he'd thought was a massive bruise was in fact a deep violet birthmark. "You all right, Miss Halliday?"

"I'm fine. Who are—" She realized then who it must be, and that he'd looked through her purse back where they'd gone off the bridge.

"My name is Flint Murtaugh. Fella," he said to Cal, "why don't you take your beer and move along?"

"I was fixin' to whip this bastard's ass," Cal answered, unsteady on his feet.

"I'll take care of him from here on out."

"Anytime, anywhere, anyplace!" Cal sneered in Dan's face, and then he grabbed Angie's arm again and jerked her onto the dance floor with him. "Well, shit a brick!" he hollered at the musicians. "How 'bout some goddamn *playin'*?"

The fiddler started up again, then the accordionist and the piano pounder joined in. Men were still laughing and gawking at Pelvis, who was trying his best to stand there and appear oblivious to the hilarity. His wig had started to slip, its glue weakened by the swamp water, and he reached up with a quick hand and straightened it.

"What the hell is *that?*" Burt grinned around his cigar stub. He hadn't seen the derringer Flint pressed against Dan's side, which was how Flint wanted it. "Is it animal, veg'table or mineral?" He spouted smoke and looked at Flint. "I swear to God, this is turnin' out to be a circus! Where'd ya'll come from?"

"We're with this fella here," Flint answered. "Just got left behind a little ways."

"Your friend's dressed up for Halloween early, ain't he?"

"He's a big Elvis fan. Don't worry about him, he's harmless."

"Maybe so, but these sumbitches in here sure smell blood. Listen to 'em howlin'!" He moved away down the bar to draw a beer for another customer.

"Hey, Elvis!" somebody yelled. "Get up there and shake that fat ass, man!"

"Give us a song, Elvis!" another one called.

Flint didn't have time to concern himself with Eisley's situation. He knew something like this was bound to happen sooner or later. But the important thing was that Daniel Lewis Lambert was standing right in front of him, and the derringer was loaded and cocked. "Did he hurt you, Miss Halliday?"

"No."

"You were lucky, then. You know he's murdered two people, don't you?"

"I know he killed a man at a bank in Shreveport. He told me about that. But he said he didn't kill the man in Alexandria, and I believe him."

"You *believe* him?" He darted another glance at her. "I thought he took you as a hostage."

"No," Arden said, "that's not how it was at all. I came with him of my own free will."

Either she was crazy, Flint figured, or somehow Lambert had brainwashed her. But she wasn't his concern, either. He kept the gun's barrel jammed into Lambert's ribs. "Well, you ran me a good chase, I'll give you that."

Dan didn't answer. His heart had stopped pounding, and now

there was ice in his blood. He was looking at a closed door about ten feet away. Maybe beyond it was a bathroom with a window, and if he could get in there and lock the door to buy himself a few seconds, he might still get away.

"Face the bar and put your hands flat on top of it."

Dan obeyed, but his attention was still fixed on the door. If he could get out a window into the swamp, then he could . . .

Could *what?* he asked himself. He was dead tired, hungry, and thirsty. His strength was gone. He doubted if he'd had the energy to trade a punch or two with Cal, much less swim through 'gator-infested water. As Flint quickly frisked him, wanting to attract as little notice as possible and helped in this regard by the loud and raucous attention being thrown at Pelvis, Dan realized that cold reality had just slapped him across the face. He had come to his senses as if awakening from a fever dream.

There was nowhere else to go. His run was over.

"You bring your pink Cadillac, Elvis?"

"Hell, get up there and sing somethin'!"

"Yeah, and it better be damn good, too!"

Pelvis had played rough rooms before, where the drunks with burning eyes would boil up out of their seats, wanting to either grab the microphone away from him or show their girlfriends that the King bled crimson. This room ranked right down there with the worst of them, and Pelvis tried to pay no mind to the jeering, but the shouts began stinging his pride.

"You ain't no Elvis, you fat shit!"

"What'cha got in your arms there, Elvis? Your girlfriend?" This was followed by a barrage of barking and laughter that drowned out the struggling musicians.

Flint saw the situation getting out of control, but any man who wanted to look and talk like a dead hillbilly had to take his licks. He kept his focus on Lambert, who—he was surprised to find—carried no weapons, not even a knife. "Empty your pockets."

"What're you gonna do?" Arden asked. "Rob him?"

"No. Lambert, you must have a way with the women. First your ex-wife stands up for you, now her. She doesn't know the real you, does she?"

Dan put his wallet on top of the bar, then a few soggy dollar bills and some change. He found the yearbook picture Chad had given him, wrinkled up by the swamp water. "How'd you find me?"

Flint flipped the wallet open and felt for hidden razor blades. "I heard your ex-wife tell you about the cabin. I've been waitin' for you all day." Flint picked up the damp picture and looked at it. "Your son?"

"Yeah."

"See, that's where you screwed up. You should never have gone to that park. If you'd steered clear of Alexandria, you wouldn't be lookin' at a double murder conviction." He slid Dan's wallet and the money into his coat, which was still buttoned to hide Clint's occasional muscle twitches under his shirt. "You can keep the picture."

Dan returned it to his pocket. "That man was alive when I left the motel. His wife killed him, and she's blamin' it on me."

"Nice try. Tell it to the police and see what they think."

"He already has," Arden spoke up. "He called the Alexandria police while we were in Lafayette. He told 'em to check the shotgun for his fingerprints."

"Uh-huh. He tell you he did that?"

"I saw him do it."

"And he was probably talkin' to a dial tone, or a recorded message, or he had his finger on the cutoff switch. Lambert, put your hands down in front of you and grip 'em together."

"You don't need to cuff me," Dan said flatly. "I'm not goin' anywhere."

"Just shut up and do it."

"I'd like to eat my gumbo and drink a beer. You want to feed me?" He turned around and stared into the bounty hunter's chilly blue eyes. Murtaugh looked as worn-out as Dan felt, his face gaunt, his dark hair with its lightning-white streak oily and uncombed. A dozen mosquito bites splotched his grizzled cheeks and chin, and he had to scratch two of them even as he kept the derringer pressed into Dan's side. "I won't run," Dan said. "I'm too tired, and there's no use in it." He read the distrust in the tight crimp of Murtaugh's thin-lipped mouth. "I give you my word. All I want to do is eat some dinner and rest."

"Yeah, I know what your word is worth." Flint started to reach into his pocket for the handcuffs, but he hesitated. Lambert had no weapon, and he did look exhausted. This time, at least, there was no woman between them who knew tae kwan do. Flint said, "I swear to God, if you try to get away, I'll put a bullet through your knee or elbow and let the lawyers sort it out. Understand?"

Dan nodded, convinced that Murtaugh would do as he promised.

"All right, then. Eat."

A skinny man in a GSP cap and greasy overalls plucked at Pelvis's arm. "Hey, you!" he said. Pelvis saw the man was missing most of his front teeth. His eyes were red and heavy-lidded, and the reek of beer and gumbo on his breath was enough to make Mama whimper. "I knew Elvis," the man wheezed. "Elvis was a fren' a mine. And you big ol' turd, you sure as hell *ain't* no Elvis!"

Pelvis felt the hot blood swelling his jowls. Hoots and laughter were flying at him like jagged spears. He walked to the blond woman with the birthmark on her face and said in an anger-tensed voice, "Excuse me, would you hold Mama?"

"What?"

"My dog," he said. "Would you hold her for just two or three minutes?" He pushed Mama into her arms.

"Eisley!" Flint snapped. "What're you doin'?"

"I've got my pride. They want a song, I'm gonna give 'em a song."

"No, you're not!" But Pelvis was already walking toward the musicians, braving the intoxicated jeers and insults. "Eisley!" Flint shouted. "Come back here!"

The musicians stopped playing their Cajun stomp as Pelvis approached, and then the whoops and hollers ricocheted off the tin roof. Burt had come back down the bar, and he yelled at Flint, "Your friend ain't gonna need a burial plot! Ain't gonna be nothin' left to bury!"

"He's a fool, is what he is!" Flint seethed, still holding the derringer low against Dan's ribs, but in the dim and smoky light Burt didn't see it. While Arden held on to the bulldog, the thoughts of what Angie had told her battering around in her mind, Dan took his first bite of gumbo and the hot spices and sausage in it almost set his tongue on fire.

"You fellas know 'Hound Dog'?" Pelvis asked the band. He got three heads to swivel. "How 'bout 'I Got a Woman'? 'Heartbreak Hotel'? 'A Big Hunk o' Love'?" There were negative reactions to all those. Pelvis felt sweat collecting around his collar. "Do you know *any* Elvis songs?"

"All we play is zydeco," the accordionist said. "You know. Like 'My Toot-Toot' and 'Diggy Liggy Lo.'"

"Oh, Lord," Pelvis breathed.

"Don't just stand there, Elvis!" a shout swelled up from the others. "You ain't dead, are you?"

Pelvis turned to face his audience. Sweat was running down under his arms, his heart starting to pound. He lifted his hands to quiet the jeering, and about half of it stopped. "I have to tell you fellas I usually accomp'ny myself on the git-tar. Anybody got a git-tar I can use?"

"This ain't fuckin' *Nashville*, you asshole!" came a reply. "Either start singin' or you're gonna go swimmin'!"

Pelvis looked over at Flint, who just shook his head with pity and averted his gaze. Then Pelvis stared out at the roughnecks, the butterflies of fear swarming in his stomach. "Start croakin', you big fat frog!" somebody else hollered. A drop of sweat rolled into Pelvis's left eye and burned it shut for a couple of seconds. Suddenly a bowl of gumbo came flying up from one of the tables and it splashed all over the front of his muddy trousers. A wave of laughter followed, then somebody began to bray like a donkey. Pelvis stared down at his mud-crusted brown suede shoes, and he thought of how those men in there didn't know the many hours he'd spent watching Elvis movies, learning the King's walk and talk and sneer; they didn't know how many nights he'd listened to Elvis records in a grubby little room, catching every phrase and nuance of that rich and glorious voice, that voice of the American soul. They didn't know how much he loved Elvis, how he worshipped at the shrine of Graceland and how his wife had called him a stupid fat loser and run off with all his money and a truck driver named Boomer. They didn't know how he had suffered for his art.

His public was calling for him. Ranting at him, to tell the truth. Pelvis squared his shoulders, tucked his chins, and turned away from the audience. He said to the piano pounder, "You mind if I sit there?" and he slid onto the chair when it was gladly vacated. Pelvis cracked his knuckles, looked at the dirty keyboard with its sad and broken ivories, and then he put his fingers down and began to play.

A strain of classical music came from the rickey-tick piano. The room was shocked silent, and no one was shocked more than Flint. But only Flint recognized the music: it was the stately opening chords of Chopin's Prelude Number Nine in E major, one of the soul-soothing pieces he listened to daily on his car's cassette player.

They let him play about ten seconds of it before they regained their senses. Then a second bowl of gumbo hit the piano and a half of a hamburger flew past Pelvis's head and a roar of dissatisfaction went up like a nuclear blast. "We don't want that damn shit!" yelled a man with a face as mean as a scarred fist. "Play us somethin' with a *tune!*"

"Hold your horses!" Pelvis shouted back. "I'm just limberin' up my fingers!" He was as ready as he would ever be. "All right, this here's called 'A Big Hunk o' Love'." And then his hands slammed down on the keyboard and the piano made a noise like a locomotive howling through a tunnel in red-hot, demon-infested, sex-dripping, and godforsaken Hades. His fingers skittered up and down the keys

705

in a blur of motion, the sound's power kicking all the jeers and hollers right out the swinging doors. Pelvis threw his head back, sweat shining on his face, his mouth opened, and he started bellowing about asking his baby for a bigga bigga bigga hunka love.

Flint's mouth was open, too; his jaw had dropped in amazement. Eisley's speaking voice might mimic Elvis, but his singing voice was something altogether different; though there were husky tones of the King's rockabilly Memphis in it, there was also the guttural moan of a rusty chain saw that suddenly broke into a startling, soaring, and unearthly high—*bigga hunka hunka luvvvvvvv*—more akin to the operatic wail of Roy Orbison. Watching Eisley beat that piano to pieces like a demented Jerry Lee Lewis and hearing his voice rattle the ceiling and then rumble the floorboards again, Flint realized the truth: onstage Eisley was a lousy Elvis, but that was like saying a ruby was a lousy diamond. Though Flint hated that kind of redneck thunder, though it made the skin crawl on the back of his neck and made him long for a good set of earplugs, it was clear that Pelvis Eisley was no imitator of a dead star. The man, whether he knew it or not, was an honest-to-God original fireball.

Dan followed a spoonful of the spicy gumbo with a drink of beer, and he regarded the Presley clone flailing at the piano. *Hunka hunka big olllll' love*, the man was growling. Murtaugh's gun had pulled a few inches away from Dan's ribs. The bounty hunter's focus was riveted on his companion. It flashed through Dan's mind that if he was quick enough, he could bring the beer mug down across the side of Murtaugh's head and run for the back door.

Do it, he told himself. Hit the bastard and run while there's still time.

He took another swallow of the bitter brew and held the mug ready to strike. On his forearm the ropy muscles tensed, making the tattooed snake undulate.

21

Silent Shadow

A second passed. Then another.

Do it! he thought, and he stared at the place on Murtaugh's skull that would bear the blow.

A third and fourth seconds went by.

No.

It was a strong voice. The voice of reason.

No, Dan decided. I gave my word, and I've caused enough misery. There'll be no more of it.

Murtaugh's head suddenly swiveled, and the pale blue eyes fixed on him.

Dan lifted the mug to his lips and drank the rest of his beer. "Your friend's not half bad."

Flint looked at the glass mug and then his gaze returned to Dan's eyes. He had the feeling that danger had just slid past like a silent shadow. "You're not thinkin' of doin' somethin' stupid, are you?"

"Nope."

"If you don't want to wear the bracelets, you'd better not be. I want to keep this as quiet and clean as I can."

Dan had wondered why Murtaugh was doing his best to hold the gun out of sight, and why he hadn't told the bartender who he was. "You afraid somebody else'll snatch me away from you if they find out about the money?"

"People hear what I do for a livin', they don't usually welcome me with hearts and flowers."

"Listen, I didn't mean to kill Blanchard," Dan said. "He drew a gun on me. I had the guard's pistol in my hand, and I—"

"Do us both a favor," Flint interrupted. "Save it for the judge."

Pelvis finished the song with a wail and a series of chords that threatened to demolish the piano. As the last notes were dying, another thunderous noise rose up: the whooping and applause of his audience. Pelvis blinked out at them, stunned by the response.

707

Though he used to play piano in a blues band when he was a lanky boy with a headful of wavy hair and big ideas, he was accustomed to standing behind an electric guitar, which he couldn't play very well but after all it was the King's instrument. He was used to hearing club managers telling him he needed to rein his voice in and keep it snarly because those high tenor notes didn't sound like Elvis at all, that's what the customers were paying for, and if he wanted to be a decent Elvis impersonator, he was way off the mark.

Here, though, it was obvious they were starved for entertainment and they didn't care that he wasn't twanging an electric guitar or that his voice wasn't as earthy as the King's. They started shouting for another song, some of them beating on their tables with their fists and beer mugs. "Thank you, thank you kindly!" Pelvis said. "Well, I'll do you another one, then. This here's 'It's Your Baby, You Rock It'." He launched off on another display of honky-tonkin' fireworks, and though his hands were stiff and he knew he was hitting a lot of clams, all his training was coming back to him. The fiddler picked up the chords and began sewing them together, and then the accordion player added a jumpy squeal and squawk.

"Hey!" Burt shouted at Flint over the music. "He done any records?"

"Not that I know of."

"Well, he ought to! He don't sound much like Elvis, but a fella plays a piano and sings like that, he oughta be doin' some records! Make hisself a lotta money that way!"

"Tell me," Flint said, "how do we get out of here? Back to a road, I mean?"

"Like I told him"—Burt nodded at Dan—"supply boat from Grand Isle'll be here tomorrow afternoon. That's the only way out."

"Tomorrow *afternoon?* I've got to get this man to—" He paused and tried it again. "We need to get to Shreveport as soon as we can."

"You'll have to wait for the supply boat. They'll take you to Grand Isle, but that's still a hell of a long way from Shreveport. See, there ain't no roads 'round here for miles."

"I can't stay here all night! Christ almighty! We've got to get back to—"*Civilization,* he almost said, but he decided it wouldn't be wise. "Shreveport," he finished.

"Sorry. I've got a radio-telephone in the back, if you need to let anybody know where you are."

Smoates needed to know, Flint thought. Smoates needed to hear that the skin was caught and on his way back. Smoates would be asleep right now, but he wouldn't mind being awakened to hear—

708

Hold it, he told himself. Just one damn minute. Why should he be in such a rush to call that freak-lovin' bastard? Right now he, Flint, was in control. He didn't have to run and call Smoates like some teenager afraid of his father's paddle. Anyway, if Smoates hadn't weighed him down with Eisley, he would have finished this thing yesterday. So to hell with him.

Flint said, "No, I don't need to call anybody. But what are we supposed to do? Stay here until the boat comes?" He didn't know if he could stand smelling his own body odor that long, and Lambert wasn't a sweet peach either. "Isn't there someplace I can get a shower and some sleep?"

"Well, this ain't exactly a tropical resort." Burt's cigar stub had gone cold, but he still kept it gripped between his teeth. Now he took it out and looked at the ashy tip, trying to decide if it was worth another match. "You talkin' about one place for all of you? Or you want somethin' separate for the lady?"

"I'm not sleepin' in a room with them!" Arden was still dazed and heartsick by what she'd heard about the Bright Girl. In her arms the little bulldog longingly watched Pelvis. "I'd rather sit in here all night!"

"How much money you got?" Burt asked Flint, and raised his eyebrows.

"Not much."

"You got a hundred dollars?"

"Maybe."

"Okay, here's the deal," Burt said. "The big boys—the execs—keep a couple of cabins to stay in when they come visit down here. They don't want to get dirty stayin' in the barracks with the workin' crews, see. I know who can pick the locks. Fifty dollars apiece, you can have 'em for the night. They ain't much, but they've got clean cots and they're private."

"There's fifty dollars in my wallet," Dan offered. Sleep on a cot—clean or dirty, he didn't care—sounded fine to him. It occurred to him that this was the last night he'd sleep without bars next to his mattress. "I'll pay for her cabin."

"Yeah, it's a deal." Flint brought out Dan's wallet and his own and paid the money.

"Fine. Wait a minute, lemme listen to this here song." Pelvis had started a slow country-western tearjerker called "Anything That's Part of You." His audience sat in rapt, respectful silence as the broody piano chords thumped and Pelvis's voice soared up in a lament that was painful enough to wet the eyes of hardcase roughnecks and bayou trash prostitutes. "I swear," Burt said, "that fella don't need to try to be Elvis. You his manager?" He looked at Flint.

"No."

"Hell, *I'll* be his manager, then. Get out of this damn swamp and get rich, I won't never look back."

"Arden?" Dan had seen the corners of her mouth quivering, her eyes glassy with shock. It was going to be tough on her, he knew. She'd put so much blind faith into finding the Bright Girl, she'd sacrificed everything, and now it was over. "You all right?"

She didn't answer. She couldn't.

"You mind steppin' aside?" he asked Flint, and the bounty hunter saw Arden's obvious distress and moved from between them. Dan stood close to her. His heart ached for her, and he started to put his arm around her shoulders but he didn't know what comfort he could give. "I'm sorry," he said. "I wish you could've found what you wanted."

"I—I can't believe she's dead. I just can't." Her eyes suddenly glistened with tears, but just as quickly she blinked them away. The bulldog licked her chin. "I can't believe it. Jupiter wouldn't have told me wrong."

"Listen to me," Dan said firmly. "Startin' from this minute, here and now, you're gonna have to go back to reality. That means back to Fort Worth and gettin' on with your life. However bad things look, they've got to get better."

"I don't think so."

"You don't know what tomorrow's gonna bring. Or next week, or next month. You've gotta go day by day, and that's how you get through the rough spots. Believe me, I've been there."

Arden nodded, but the Bright Girl was a candle she could not bear to extinguish. It struck her how selfish she'd been, consumed by her own wishes. From the moment the man in the dark suit had set foot into this cafe, Dan had been on his way to prison. "Are *you* all right?" she asked.

"I believe I am." He offered her a faint, brave smile when inside he felt as if he'd been hit by a tractor-trailer truck. "Yeah, I'm all right. This was gonna happen sooner or later." His smile faded. "I saw my son, I said what I needed to say without bars between us. That's the important thing." He shrugged. "At least where I'm goin' I'll have a roof over my head and hot food. Won't be much worse than the V.A. hospital, I guess. Anyhow—" His voice cracked, and he had to pause to summon the strength to continue. "Like I said, you go day by day. That's how you get through the rough spots."

"Miss?" Burt put his elbows on the bar and leaned toward her. Pelvis had finished the slow, sad number and was getting up from the piano to take his bows, sweat dripping from his chins. "I know who could tell you if there was ever anybody livin' on Goat Island or not. Cajun fella they call Little Train. He was born 'round here. Sometimes he takes the execs huntin' and fishin'. Sells us fish and game for the cafe, too, so he gets all 'round the swamp. If anybody would know, it'd be him."

"Arden?" Dan's voice was quiet. "Give it up. Please."

She wanted to. She really did. But she was desperate and afraid. This would be her final chance, and she would never come this way again. Even finding the Bright Girl's grave would be an answer, though not the one she wished for. She said, "Where is he?"

"Lives on a houseboat, anchored 'bout a mile south of here. Keeps to himself, mostly." He stared at her birthmark, his gaze following its ragged edges. "I've got a motorboat, and I'm off shift at six A.M. I need to run down there to see him anyhow, put in an order for some catfish and turtle meat. If you want to go, you're welcome. And I can carry two people, if *you* want to go along." He was speaking to Dan.

Dan saw the need in Arden's eyes; it was a painful thing to witness, because he knew she stood at the very edge of sanity. He had to turn away from her, and when he heard her say "I'll go alone," it was clear to him that she'd placed one foot over the precipice.

"Okay, then. Whatever suits you. Hey, fella!" He grinned at Pelvis, who was making his way to the bar through a knot of backslappers. "You 'bout knocked hell outta that piano, didn't you?"

Pelvis said, "Thank you, ma'am" as he took Mama back into his arms, and Mama trembled with love and attacked his face with her tongue. He was breathing hard, and he felt a little dizzy, but otherwise he was okay. Sweat was pouring off him in rivers. "Can I have some water, please?"

"Comin' right up!"

"Mr. Murtaugh?" Pelvis smiled broadly. "I think they like me."

"You were all right. If you care for that kind of music. Here, wipe your face." He pulled a handful of paper napkins out of a dispenser and gave it to him. "You're not gonna pass out on me again, are you?"

"Nosir. I'm just a bit winded." Pelvis took the bottle of water Burt gave him and guzzled it, then he poured some in his hand and let Mama lap it up. "Did'ja hear the way they were hollerin'?"

ROBERT R. McCAMMON

"Uh-huh. Well, step down off your pedestal and listen: we can't get out of here till tomorrow afternoon. We have to wait for a supply boat from Grand Isle. How the hell we're supposed to get back to the car I don't know, but that's how things are."

"At least we got him, didn't we?" Pelvis nodded toward Dan, who'd gone back to eating his gumbo.

We, my ass, Flint was about to say, but Burt stuck his bearded face over the bar again. "You play better'n you look, if you don't mind me sayin'."

"Sir?"

"You know. The Elvis thing, with the judo moves and all. That's what I expected."

"Well, all them songs I sang were ones Elvis done," Pelvis explained. "And I do them moves in my show, but I couldn't 'cause I was sittin' at the piana. Like I said, I usually play the git-tar."

"You want my advice? I'm gonna give it to you anyway. Don't hide behind Elvis. You don't need it, a fella can pound them keys and sing like you do. Hell, you oughta go to Nashville and show 'em what you can do."

"I been there. They told me I didn't sound enough like Elvis. Told me I couldn't play git-tar as good as him, neither."

"Well, hell! Don't *try* to sound like him! Don't try to look like him, or talk like him, or nothin'! Seems to me there was just one Elvis, and he's dead. Can't be another one. If I was you, I wouldn't touch a guitar again so long as I lived. I wouldn't wear my hair like that, either, and you oughta lose fifty or sixty pounds. Get yourself lean and mean, then go see them Nashville cats. You play for them like you did here, you're gonna be makin' yourself some money! Hey, do me a favor!" Burt reached for a napkin and pulled a pen out from beside the cash register. "Here. Sign me an autograph, just so I can say I spotted you first. Sign it To My Friend Burt Dunbro."

"You . . . want *my* autograph?" Pelvis asked, his cheeks reddening with embarrassment.

"Yep. Right there. To My Friend Burt Dunbro."

He put the pen to napkin and wrote what the man asked. Then he started *Pelv*—

He stopped.

"What's wrong? Pen jammed up?"

There was just one Elvis, he was thinking, *and he's dead. Can't be another one.*

Maybe there shouldn't be.

It had been fifteen years since he'd played piano in front of an audience. And that was before he'd dressed himself up as the King,

712

studied the records and movies and hip thrusts, bought the wig, the blue suede shoes, the regalia. It was before he'd let himself get fat on the Twinkies and peanut butter cookies and cornbread sopped in buttermilk. It was before he'd decided that who he was wasn't good enough, and that he needed something much larger to cling to and hide inside.

But what if . . . what if . . .

What if he'd given up on his own talent too early? What if he'd let it go in favor of the Elvis disguise because he wasn't sure he was worth a damn? What if . . . what if . . . ?

Oh, Lord, it would be so hard to give it up now and try to go back. It would be impossible to strike out on his own, without the King to help him. Wouldn't it?

But Elvis was dead. There couldn't be another one.

"Hold on, I'll find a pen that writes," Burt offered.

"No," Pelvis said. "This one's fine."

He was terrified.

But he got the pen moving, and with a hammering heart and a dry throat he scratched out *Pelv* and beneath it wrote *Cecil Eisley.*

It was one of the hardest things he'd ever done in his life, but when he was finished he felt something inside him start to unlock, just the slightest bit. Maybe in an hour he would regret signing his own name. Maybe tomorrow he would deny that he had. But right now—this strange and wonderful moment—he felt ten feet tall.

"Griff, come over here!" Burt called. The mean-faced man who didn't care for the classics came to the bar. Burt gave him twenty dollars and quietly told him what he wanted done. "Ya'll go on with Griff, he'll take care of you," Burt said to Flint, and to Arden he added, "Six o'clock. I'll see you here."

"Let's go, Lambert." Flint pushed the gun into Dan's side again. "Take it nice and easy."

The two cabins Griff led them to were about a hundred yards from the other structures of St. Nasty, up on a platform facing a cove of smooth black water. Griff produced a large penknife and pulled up its thin blade to slide into the first cabin's door lock. It took four seconds to open the door. "I better check for snakes," he said before he disappeared into the darkness within. Two minutes later a generator rumbled to life around back and then electric lights flickered on. "No snakes," he announced when he returned to the door. "Just a skin." He held the long gossamer thing up to show them. "Who's sleepin' in this one?"

When neither of the bounty hunters responded, Arden screwed up her courage and said, "I guess I am." She crossed the threshold.

The pine-paneled interior was hot, humid, and smelled of mold. There was a broken-down plaid sofa, a couple of standing lamps that appeared to have been purchased from a garage sale sometime in 1967, and a kitchen area with a rusty stove and sink. A hallway went back to what must be the sleeping area and—hopefully—an indoor bathroom. It would do for a few hours, until six o'clock.

"Shower and toilet's between the cabins," Griff said. "Pipes are hooked to a cistern, but I wouldn't drink the water. And you'd best keep the front and back doors locked. Lots of fellas 'round here can't be trusted."

Arden closed the door and locked it, then she pulled the sofa over in front of it. She found a switch that operated a ceiling fan, and turning it on helped cool the room some.

When the lights were on in the second cabin, Griff came out grinning. "Looky here!" He raised his right arm to show Dan, Flint, and Pelvis the thick brown snake his hand had seized, the head squeezed between his fingers and the coils twined around his wrist. "Big ol' sumbitch moccasin. Found him sleepin' under a cot. Ya'll step aside." He reared his arm back and flung the reptile past them into the water. It made a heavy splash. "Okay, you can go on in."

Flint guided Dan through the door first. The place was basically the same as the first cabin, a moldy-smelling assemblage of cheap furniture, pine-paneled walls, and a floor of rough planks. Pelvis entered last, his eyes peeled for creepy-crawlies. "Thing 'bout moccasins," Griff said, "is that for every one you see, there're three or four you don't. They'll keep to themselves if you don't step on 'em, but I wouldn't let that dog go nosin' 'round, hear?"

"I hear," Pelvis answered.

"Tough luck for that girl, huh? I mean, the way her face is. Awful hard to look at, but hard *not* to look at, too."

"Thanks for lettin' us in," Flint told him. "Good night."

"Allrighty. Don't let the bedbugs bite. Nor nothin' else." Griff chuckled a little to himself, slid his hands into the pockets of his blue jeans, and started walking back in the direction they'd come.

Flint closed the door and latched it. "Here, keep this on him." He gave Pelvis the derringer, then he took the cuffs and their key from his pocket and unlocked them. "Hands behind you."

"I'm gonna have to go pee in a minute," Dan said.

"Hands in front of you," Flint corrected him. "Grip 'em together."

"I gave you my word I wasn't gonna run. You don't have to—"

"Your word's not worth fifteen thousand dollars, so shut up." Flint snapped the cuffs around Dan's wrists and put the key inside his suit jacket. Dan saw a peculiar thing happen: the front of the man's shirt suddenly twitched, as if Murtaugh had just hiccupped. He recalled that he'd seen the same thing when Murtaugh was on the ground in Basile Park, just before the Elvis clone had started hollering. He had the bizarre sensation that there was more to Murtaugh than met the eye.

"Watch him for a minute," Flint told Pelvis, and he walked back through the hallway to find out what the rest of the cabin held.

"Don't try nothin', now," Pelvis said nervously, holding a sleepy Mama and aiming the derringer at Dan's belly. "I'll shoot if I have to."

"Just take it easy." Dan could tell that the man was uncomfortable holding the gun, and though it looked like a peashooter, it could still do a lot of damage at such close range. He decided silence would only increase the man's tension before Murtaugh returned. "What's your name?"

"Ce—" No, maybe he'd be ready to let go of it someday, but not yet. "Pelvis Eisley."

"Pelvis, huh?" Dan nodded; it figured. "Excuse me for sayin' this, but you and Murtaugh don't fit. You been partners long?"

"Two days. He's teachin' me the ropes."

An amateur, Dan thought. "This is your first bounty-huntin' job?"

"That's right. My very first."

"Seems to me you'd do better playin' piano in Nashville than doin' this kind of work."

"Eisley, don't talk to him." Flint came back in. What he'd found had been two grim rooms, each with two iron-framed, bare-mattressed cots. He hadn't failed to notice that the legs of the cots were standing in water-filled coffee cans to keep insects from climbing up them. If this was the executive quarters, he would have hated to see the work crew's barracks; then again, the cabin didn't look like anyone had been there in quite some time. But all he wanted was a few hours of sleep, and he didn't need a Hilton hotel pillow. Flint took the derringer back from Eisley. "Come on, Lambert. You want to do your business, let's get it done." Through a rear window he'd seen a tin-roofed shed that he figured must be where the shower and toilet were. The generator was sending juice to an electric bulb burning over the shed's door, but stepping in was going to be an act of either raw courage or sheer desperation.

Arden had already forced herself—out of desperation to walk into the shed. Fortunately, there was a light bulb inside as well as outside, but Arden approached the toilet with trepidation. There were no water moccasins coiled up inside, as she'd feared, but it wasn't the cleanest in the world. She did what she had to do, used a roll of tissue that could have scraped paint off metal, and got out as fast as she could.

In the room in which she'd chosen to sleep, she had put the pink drawstring bag atop a battered old pine chest of drawers. Now, under the single dirty light bulb that burned at the ceiling, she opened the bag and removed what was held within.

One after the other, she lined up five little horses side by side.

They had been bought at a dime store in Fort Worth. They weren't much, but they were everything. Five horses: two brown, one black, one gray. The paint was chipping off them, revealing the red plastic they were molded from. She knew their secret names, and they watched over her. They reminded her of a time when she'd been happy, when she could believe the future was wide-open spaces, even through the Texas dust and grit and the hard work that had to be done. They reminded her that once upon a time she had been needed.

She sat on the edge of a cot and stared at the small plastic figures, her eyes glazed and tired. She was wrecked, and she knew it. But her thoughts were still circling that flame, circling, circling. The Bright Girl. A touch from the Bright Girl, and she would be healed. Jupiter said so. Jupiter wouldn't have lied to her. No. A touch from the Bright Girl, and the mark—the ugly bad-luck mark that had tormented her all her life and caused her father to walk out the door and never come back and her mother to fall under the weight of the bottle—would be taken away. The Bright Girl wasn't dead. The Bright Girl was forever young and pretty, and she carried the lamp of God. Jupiter hadn't lied. He hadn't.

But what about Dan? He couldn't go any farther. If he was the man God had provided to take her to the Bright Girl, then why was he being wrenched away from her? She'd thought about trying somehow to get him away from the bounty hunters, but what could she do? And she'd seen it in his face, there in the cafe: he was sick and weary of running, and he could not go on. *You His hands*, she remembered Jupiter saying.

But what if Jupiter had been wrong?

Six o'clock, she thought. Six o'clock. She had to press that number into her mind so she could sleep for three or four hours and then get up in time. She had to forget about Dan, had to let him go. As much as she wanted, she couldn't help him. Now she had to help herself, and it seemed to her that the morning would be her last chance. Where she would go and what she would do if she found the Bright Girl's grave, she didn't know. She couldn't think about it, because that way led to black despair.

She lay down and stared at the ceiling. The five horses, her talisman, would watch over her during the night. She might dream of waking up, and hearing them pawing and snorting for her in the barn, saying *hurry come to us hurry we will never hurt you we will never hurt.*

At last, mercifully, her eyes closed. She listened to the rumble of the generator, the grump of frogs, and the chitterings of insects and night birds, the heavy thudding heartbeat of the oil-pumping machinery in the distance. She was afraid of what daylight might bring; she was equally afraid of knowing and of not knowing. A single tear trickled down the cheek on the deep-violet-birthmarked side of her face. Sleep came for her, and took her away.

Pelvis had gone outside to let Mama answer nature's call. While he was out there, he unzipped and added some water to the cove. After Mama was finished, he picked her up and started back inside, and that was when he saw a match flare on the plank walkway that led back over the swamp grass and rushes to the center of St. Nasty. He saw the orange-daubed face of a man as the match touched the tip of a cigarette, and then the match was flicked out into the water like a little comet.

He watched the cigarette's tip glow as the man inhaled. Then the glow vanished. Either the man was cupping the cigarette in his hand or he'd walked away, it was hard to tell in the dark. Pelvis stood there, stroking Mama for a moment, but when she let out a few exhausted yaps at something that rustled in the watery weeds under the platform, he decided it was time to get back inside. He wondered how many snakes must be watching him, and the thought made him shudder as if someone had just stepped on his grave.

22

The Sound of Scales

"I'm goin' to take a shower," Flint told Pelvis when he walked through the door. "I want you to sit in there and watch him, hear? Take the gun and just sit there. I'll be back in a few minutes." He'd taken Dan to the shed and found a grimy cake of soap in the cramped little shower stall. Though he had no towel, he couldn't bear his own body odor any longer. He started to turn away, but he had to ask a burning question. "Eisley, where'd you learn the Chopin piece?"

"Sir?"

"The Chopin piece. The classical music you played. Where'd you learn it?"

"Oh, that was somethin' my piana teacher taught me. Mrs. Fitch was her name. Said it was a good quick finger workout and 'cause you had to think about what you were doin' it calmed you down. I reckon it did the trick for my nerves."

"I never would've thought you could play classical music."

Pelvis shrugged. "No big thing. Them fellas pooted in their pants like everybody else. You go on and take your shower, don't worry 'bout Lambert."

Flint left the cabin, not quite sure he would ever again listen to his tape of Chopin preludes with quite the same reverence.

Pelvis went into the bedroom Flint had chosen for himself and found the killer lying on one of the cots, his right hand cuffed to the iron bed frame. Pelvis sat down on the other cot, laid Mama aside, and held the derringer aimed at Dan.

"I wish you wouldn't do that," Dan said twenty seconds later, when it was clear Eisley meant to point the gun at him until Murtaugh returned. "I'd hate for that to go off."

"Mr. Murtaugh told me to watch you."

"Can't you watch me and aim that gun somewhere else?"

"I could. I don't want to."

Dan grunted and allowed a slight smile. "You must think I'm a big bad sonofabitch, huh?"

"You killed two men. That don't make you an angel in my book."

Dan started to sit up, but he thought better of making any quick moves. "I didn't kill the man at that damn motel. His wife did it."

"His *wife*? Ha, that's a good one!"

"He was alive when I left there. His wife had already shot him in the gut with a shotgun, aimin' at me. She beat him to death after I was gone. Maybe she was mad at him because I got away."

"Uh-huh. I reckon somebody else popped up and killed that fella at the bank, too. And you just happened to be standin' there."

"No," Dan said, "That one I'll bear the blame for."

"Surprised to hear it."

Dan cupped his left hand under his head and stared up at the ceiling. A moth was going around and around up there, searching for a way out. "Blanchard had a family. It wasn't his fault things are how they are. There's no way on earth I can live with what I did, so I might as well die in prison."

Pelvis was silent for a moment. The derringer had wandered. He'd never met anybody who'd committed murder before, and he found his nervousness being replaced by curiosity. "What'd that fella do to you was so bad you had to kill him?" he asked quietly.

Dan was watching the trapped moth beating itself against the stark, bare light bulb. He was too tense to sleep yet, and the room was too hot. "I didn't go to that bank meanin' to do it," he answered. "Blanchard was takin' my pickup truck away from me. It was the last thing I had. I lost my temper, a guard came in, and we fought. Blanchard pulled a pistol on me. I had the guard's gun, and . . . I squeezed the trigger first. Didn't even aim. I knew Blanchard was finished when I saw all that blood. Then I got in my truck and ran."

Pelvis frowned. "You should've stayed there. Maybe pleaded self-defense or somethin'."

"I guess so. But all I could think about right then was gettin' away."

"How 'bout the girl? We thought you took her hostage. Is she . . . kinda off in the head?"

"No, she's just scared." Dan explained how he'd met Arden, and about her belief in the Bright Girl. "In the mornin' she wants to go find some Cajun fisherman called Little Train. He's supposed to live in a houseboat a mile or so south of here. That fella who runs the cafe's takin' her. I don't have the right to tell her not to go, and I don't think she'd listen to me, anyway." An idea struck him, and he angled his face toward Eisley. "*You* could go with her."

"*Me?*"

"Yeah. They're leavin' at six." He managed to twist his cuffed wrist around so he could see his watch. "Goin' on two-thirty. You could go with her, make sure she's all right. If the supply boat doesn't come till afternoon, you'll be back in plenty of time."

"Back from *where?*" Flint peered through the doorway, his hair still wet. He had carefully and methodically scrubbed the grime from his and his brother's flesh. It had been torment to buckle the sweat-stiff miniature shoulder holster against his skin and then put on his swamp-tainted clothes again. Under his once-white shirt Clint was sleeping, but Flint could feel the soft bones shift every so often deep in his constricted guts.

"He was askin' me to go with the girl," Pelvis said. "Burt—y'know, from the cafe—is gonna take her at six o'clock to see a Cajun fella lives a mile south. She's tryin' to find a—"

"Forget it." Flint took the derringer from him. "We're not nursemaids. I don't know what her story is, but we're leavin' here on that supply boat and she can go with us or not, it's up to her."

"Yes sir, but if it's just a mile off, I'll be back before—"

"Eisley?" Flint cut him off. "The girl's crazy. She'd have to be crazy to come down here knowin' who Lambert is. Get up off there, I've gotta lie down before I fall down."

Pelvis cradled Mama in his arms and stood up. Mama awakened and gave a cranky growl, then her bulbous eyes closed and she went limp again. Flint lay down on the cot. Springs jabbed his back through the thin mattress, but he was so tired, he could have slept on a bed of nails.

"Arden shouldn't go off in the swamp with somebody she doesn't know," Dan pressed on. "It doesn't matter what you think of her. She could still get in a lot of trouble."

"She's not our business. You are."

"Maybe that's so, but she needs help."

"Not from us."

"Not from *you*, I guess." Dan looked up at Pelvis. "How about it? Would you—"

"Hey!" Flint sat up again, his deep-sunken eyes red-rimmed and angry. "He doesn't have any say-so about this! I'm callin' the shots! Now, why don't you shut your mouth and get some sleep? Eisley, you go on, too!"

Pelvis hesitated. The electric lights, and their pools of shadow, gave him little comfort. Several times already he had imagined he'd caught a slow uncoiling from the corner of his eye. "How come Mama and me have to sleep in a room by ourselves?"

"Because there're only two cots in here, that's why. Now, go on!"

"That was an awful big snake that fella found. I wonder which cot it was under."

"Well, I'll tell you what," Flint said. "You and the mutt can sleep in here. Just curl up on the floor between us, maybe that'll make you feel safer."

"No, I don't think it would."

"The lights are on. All right? Nothin's gonna crawl out and get you with the lights on."

Pelvis started to retreat to the other room. It seemed a vast distance away from the protection of Flint's derringer. He paused again, his face furrowed in thought. "Mr. Murtaugh, don't you think it'd be wrong if we knew somethin' might happen to that girl and we didn't try to help her?"

"She can take care of herself."

"We don't know that for sure. Lambert says she's from Fort Worth, and she don't have any way to get home."

"It's *not* our problem, Eisley."

"Yeah, I know that and all, but . . . seems to me we oughta have a little feelin' for her situation."

Flint glared at Pelvis with a force that seemed to scorch the air between them. "You haven't learned a thing from me, have you?"

"Sir?"

"Bounty hunters don't *feel*. You start feelin', and you start gettin' interested. When you start gettin' interested, you start lettin' your guard down. Then you wind up with a knife in your back. If the girl wants to go see some Cajun swamp rat, it's her business. She knows the supply boat's leavin' in the afternoon. If she wants to be on it, she will be." He held Pelvis's gaze a few seconds longer, then he lay back down, the derringer in his right hand. "I've met all the swamp rats I care to, in case you've forgotten the marina."

"No, I ain't forgotten."

"I'd say we were lucky to get out of that alive. While you're with me, I'm responsible for you—much as I hate it—so you're not goin' off in the swamp with some crazy girl and end up gettin' your throat cut. Now go to sleep."

Pelvis chewed on Flint's logic, his brow still creased under his lopsided wig. Dan said, "She's not crazy. She's a decent person. I wish you'd help her."

"Lambert? One more word from you, and you're gonna spend the night with both arms between your legs and a sock stuffed in your damn mouth!"

"Sorry," Pelvis told Dan. "I can't." He summoned up his courage and went into the other room, where he laid Mama down on the cot and then settled himself beside her. He lay very still, listening for and dreading the sound of scales slithering across the planked floor.

Dan's head had been aching, a slow, insistent throb, for the past two hours. The pain kicked in again, getting between him and sleep. He would have given his left nut—whatever it was worth these days—for a bottle of Tylenol. Strangely, though, it was a relief his running was over. He didn't have to be afraid anymore of what might be coming up behind him. The idea of getting out of the country, he realized now, had always been an illusion. Sooner or later he would have wound up in handcuffs. He would learn to deal with prison in the time he had left. He was just sorry Arden had gotten mixed up in this.

Dan thought Murtaugh was asleep, but suddenly the bounty hunter shifted on his cot and said, "What the hell made that girl come down here with you, anyway?"

"She believes there's a faith healer livin' in here somewhere. Called the Bright Girl. She thinks that if she finds the Bright Girl, she can get that birthmark off her face."

"A faith healer? Like Oral Roberts?"

"A little quieter, I reckon. And poorer, too. I don't believe in such things, myself."

"I don't either. It's a shakedown for the rubes." Carnival talk, he realized as soon as he'd spoken.

"Arden's desperate," Dan said. "She found out who I was, but she still wanted me to bring her down here. She doesn't have any money, no car, nothin'. Lost her job. She's convinced herself that if she finds the Bright Girl and gets that mark off, her bad luck'll be gone, too, and her whole life'll change."

"To you, desperate," Flint said. "To me, that's crazy."

"I guess people have believed stranger things."

Flint was silent. He and Dan suddenly heard a noise like a buzz saw starting up, followed by a swarm of enraged bees trapped in a tin bucket. Pelvis was snoring.

"Yeah, I knew that was comin'," Flint sighed. He shifted again, trying to get comfortable. The heat was squeezing sweat from his pores, and his body was exhausted, but his mind wasn't ready to shut down and let him sleep. "Lambert, where'd you think you were gonna run to?"

"I don't know. Anywhere but prison."

"I'm surprised you got as far as you did. You've been all over the TV and newspapers. Is that why you killed the fella at the motel? Was he about to turn you in?"

"I told you I didn't do that. His wife did."

"Come on, now. You can level with me."

"I didn't kill him, I swear to God."

"Uh-huh," Flint said with a knowing half-smile. "I've heard that from a lot of guilty bastards." He recalled what Lambert's tae kwon do–loving ex-wife had said in the park: *It was self-defense, he's not a cold-blooded killer.* Another question came to him that he had to ask. "Why didn't you shoot me? When you had my gun, and I was on the ground. Why didn't you just blow my brains out? You didn't want to kill me in front of your family, right?"

"Wrong. I didn't want to kill you, period."

"You should have. If I'd had the gun and you'd been the bounty hunter after my ass, I would've shot you. At least blown away your knees. Didn't you think of that?"

"No."

Flint turned his head to look at Dan, who had his eyes closed. Of the twenty or so felons—mostly bail jumpers and small-time criminals, with a couple of real bad boys in the bunch—Flint had tracked over his seven years in the employ of Eddie Smoates, this one was different. There was something about Lambert he couldn't decipher, and this fact greatly agitated him. If Lambert had just finished killing the man at the motel before he'd come to Basile Park—if he was a "mad dog," as Smoates had said—then he would have had nothing to lose by putting a couple of bullets through Flint's knees, which was the fastest way to keep anybody from chasing after you. And why hadn't Lambert kept the gun? Why had he been carrying no weapons at all? Why had he brought the girl with him and not planned to use her as a hostage? It just didn't make sense.

It was self-defense, he's not a cold-blooded killer.

Cold-blooded or not, Flint thought, Lambert *was* a killer. Maybe Lambert had just snapped or something. Maybe he hadn't gone into that bank wanting to kill anybody, but the fact was that Lambert was worth fifteen thousand dollars and Flint wanted his share of it. Bottom line.

He listened to Lambert's deep and steady breathing. He thought the man was asleep, but he was going to keep the gun in his hand all night. Though Lambert couldn't get out of that cuff, he might go crazy, try to drag the cot across the space between them and attack

ROBERT R. McCAMMON

Flint. It had happened before. You never knew what set killers off, and the quiet ones were the most dangerous.

Flint closed his eyes. In the other room, Pelvis's snoring had taken on the sonic charm of a cement mixer, and now Mama gave a little *yip yip yip* in her sleep.

It was going to be pure pleasure to say good riddance to those two. He needed a fat hillbilly and a flea-bitten mutt hanging around him like he needed a fourth arm.

He thought of Pelvis's performance, which had been okay if you liked that kind of low-down caterwauling. He thought of the bartender saying *Hell, I'll be his manager, then! Get out of this damn swamp and get rich, I won't never look back.*

And then he knew he must be asleep, because he was looking at the clean white mansion of his dreams.

There it was: the beautiful rolling green lawn, the huge stained-glass window, the multiple chimneys. The sight of it thrilled his soul with majestic wonder. It was the mansion of his birth, the clean white mansion that existed somewhere in this land far from the dismal grime of his life. He began to walk across the lawn toward it, but as always he couldn't get any nearer. It always drew away from him no matter how fast or how long he walked. He could hear his shoes—his shining, polished black wingtips—pressing down the velvet blades of grass. He could feel the summer breeze on his face, and see his shadow walking ahead of him. He would have to walk faster. But again the white mansion receded, a beautiful taunt. Inside that mansion lived his mother and father, and if he could only get there, he could ask them to take him in, he could tell them he forgave them for giving him up when he was a three-armed baby with a fleshy knot on his side that had an extra mouth and set of nostrils in it. He could show them he'd grown up to be a man of taste, of manners and good breeding, and he could tell them he loved them and if they took him in he would promise—he would swear to God—that he would never cause them reason to be ashame—

BAM!

The explosion blasted Flint out of his dream. As the mansion was swept away in a heartbeat, he sat up with a jolt, his eyes bleary and the derringer held in a white-knuckled grip. His first thought was that Lambert had gone crazy and was trying to drag the cot over to flail at him with his free hand.

Dan was sitting up, too, his mind still shocked by the noise that had shattered his deep and dreamless sleep. The handcuff was cutting into his right wrist. He and Flint looked at each other, both

724

of them dazed. Mama had started barking, and Pelvis was making a sputtering noise as he struggled back to the land of the living.

Suddenly someone came into the room.

"They're in here! Got a gun!" a man shouted.

A figure lunged at Flint. He had no time to think to fire; his arm was seized, a hard blow hit him on the shoulder, and he cried out as pain streaked down to the tips of his fingers. The derringer was ripped from his hand, and a wiry arm went around his throat. He started thrashing, but the arm squeezed his larynx and took the fight out of him. Another man entered the room—a man in a dirty yellow shirt and blue jeans—and he said, "That's the bastard shot Virgil. Hey, Doc! In here he is!"

At the mention of those names Flint felt panic clutch his heart.

Doc walked in. Sauntered, actually. He was still wearing his Harvard T-shirt, but he had on chinos with patched knees. His round-lensed sunglasses had been exchanged for glasses with clear lenses. Doc grinned, showing his greenish teeth. His long gray-blond hair was pulled back into a ponytail and secured with a rubber band. "Gomer says hey," he said. "You sweet motherfucker, you." He reached out and clamped a hand onto Flint's chin. "Now, you didn't think we were gonna let you hit and run, did you?"

Flint didn't answer; he couldn't, because his lips were crushed together.

Doc's head swiveled. Still grinning widely, he looked at Dan and his gaze found the handcuff. "Well, what's this all about now, huh? Who're *you*, friend?"

"Dan Lambert." The haze of weariness hadn't quite cleared yet; everything was still weirdly dreamlike.

"I'm Doc. Pleased to meet ya. Monty, bring ol' Elvis in here with us!"

In another few seconds Pelvis was hurled through the doorway and he slammed down to the floor on his hands and knees. Behind him entered a heavyset man with narrowly slit eyes, crew-cut hair, and a bristly brown beard and mustache. The man was holding a snarling and kicking Mama by the scruff of her neck. "Look what I got me!" he announced.

"Please . . ." Pelvis's face was stricken with terror, his eyes sleep-swollen. "Please, that's my dog."

"No it ain't," Monty said petulantly. "It's *mine*."

"He ain't had a dog since last week, when he got hungry after midnight." Doc put a combat-booted foot on one of Pelvis's shoulders. "Down, boy!" he said, and he shoved Pelvis flat to the floor.

"My . . . throat," Flint gasped at the man who had an arm pressed into his larynx. "You're . . . crushin' my throat."

"Awwwwww, our man Flint can't hardly talk! Ain't that a bitch?" Doc shook his head with mock pity. "Best ease up on him."

The arm loosened.

"We wouldn't want to hurt either one of you fine fellas," Doc went on. "Not till we get a chance to boogaloo on your balls, I mean. Then we'll get down to some hurtin'."

"What's goin' on?" Dan asked. "Who are you?"

"I'm me. Who are *you?*"

"I told you. My name's—"

"No." Doc put a forefinger against Dan's mouth. "Who are you, as in why are you wearin' a handcuff?"

"Listen," Flint said, and he heard his voice tremble. "Listen, all right?"

Doc bent toward him and cupped his hands behind his ears.

"There's been a mistake," Flint said.

"Mistake, he says," Doc relayed to the others.

"Fuckin' *big* mistake!" the man in the yellow shirt said. "You shot a friend of ours. Crippled him. Ain't no good for nothin' now."

"Shhhhhh," Doc whispered. "Let the man weave his noose, Mitch."

If there was ever a time for the truth, this was it. Pinpricks of sweat glistened on Flint's face. He said, "I'm a bounty hunter. Workin' out of Shreveport. Both of us are." He nodded toward Pelvis. "The man in handcuff is a wanted killer. Fifteen-thousand-dollar bounty on his head. We followed him down here, and we're takin' him back."

"Oh, first you're an astronaut, now you're Mr. Wanted-Dead-or-Alive." Doc looked at Dan. "That the truth?"

Dan nodded.

"I can't hearrrrrr youuuuuuu!"

"It's true." Dan realized this man was two bricks shy of a load, but what had really set off his alarms was the fact that he'd seen a .45 automatic pushed down into the waistband of the man's chinos at the small of his back. The big bearded bastard named Monty had a holster on his hip with a pearl-handled .38 in it, and the man who gripped Flint's throat wore an honest-to-God Ingram submachine gun on a strap around his left shoulder, the derringer he'd wrenched away from Flint now held in his right hand.

"You killed somebody?" Doc's eyebrows went up.

"Two men," Flint answered. "When we were at the marina . . . I was callin' the man I work for. In Shreveport. Lettin' him know where we were."

"Where you were," Doc said quietly, "was on our territory." Pelvis had gotten up on his hands and knees once more, his eyes turned tearfully toward the man who held Mama. "Get *down*, I said!" Doc's gaunt cheeks burned red, and he jammed Pelvis to the floor with a boot again. "You stay down until I say you can move! Where's that fuckin' spray you shot me with, now, huh? I'll ram my fist up your fat ass and jerk your guts out, hear me? *Hear me?*"

"Ye-yes sir." Pelvis's body was starting to shake.

"Where you were," Doc repeated, speaking to Flint in a voice that was eerily calm after his outburst, "was in the wrong place at the wrong time. Okay, I admit it! I messed up! Okay? I thought you might've been somebody else. But when this bastard down here hurt me, and you crippled one of my friends, you crossed the line with me. I can't let that pass." He shrugged. "It's a hormone thing."

"I thought you were tryin' to kill me!" Flint said. "What was I supposed to do?"

"You were supposed to take what we gave you, Flinty. Anyhow, if you'd told us who you really were instead of pullin' that smart-ass bullshit, you wouldn't be hip-deep in hell, now, would you?" He held his palm out and wriggled his fingers. "The key."

"What key?"

"To the cuffs. Come on, give it up."

Flint hesitated. Doc smoothly pulled the automatic from his waistband, clicked the safety off, and pressed the barrel against Flint's forehead. On the floor Pelvis gave a muffled groan. "Give it up easy," Doc said, his eyes icy behind the glasses, "or I'll take it the hard way. Your choice."

Flint reached into his pocket—"Slowwwwwwly," Doc warned—and he put the key in the man's palm. Doc took two backward steps, turned toward Dan, and slid the key into the cuff's lock. He twisted it and Dan heard the mechanism click open. "Fly free, brother," Doc said.

Dan unlatched the cuff from his wrist. Flint's face had become a blood-drained study in anguish. "Listen . . . please . . . he's worth fifteen thousand dollars."

"Not to me, he's not. Not to any of us." Doc opened the other cuff and gave them and the key to Mitch. "See, man, we've all been there. There and back, on the long and twisty road. We don't give a shit for policemen, or jails. Least of all for bounty hunters. On your feet."

The man behind Flint hauled him off the cot. Again Doc placed the automatic's barrel to his forehead. "Mitch, shake him down."

"Wearin' an empty holster under his right arm," Mitch said as he frisked Flint. "And he's got somethin' . . . *holy Jesus!*" Mitch jumped aside as if his hands had been scorched, his eyes wide with shock. "*It moved!*" He fumbled under his shirt and pulled out a blue-steel revolver.

"It moved? *What* moved?" Doc tore the front of Flint's suit jacket open.

And they all saw it: a serpentine shape twisting and writhing beneath Flint's shirt.

Doc reached toward him, meaning to rip the shirt open, but before he could do it, Clint pushed free: first the small fingers and hand, followed by the slim, milky-white and hairless arm.

Doc stood very, very still. Everyone in the room was very, very still. Dan was starting to wonder what might've been in that gumbo he'd eaten.

Clint's hand clenched at the air. Flint knew what would happen next; his shirt would be torn right off his back. To prevent that indignity, he undid the rest of the buttons and opened his shirt for them all to have a good look, his face tightening with rage because their eyes had taken on that old familiar glint of ravening fascination he'd suffered so many times before.

"God*damn!*" Doc whispered. "He's a fuckin' freak!"

"My brother Clint." Flint's voice was toneless, dead. "Born this way. Here's his head. See?" He drew his shirt wider to show them the fist-size lump of Clint's eyeless face at his side. "I used to work the carnival circuit. Alive, alive, alive," Flint said, and a dark and terrible grin split his mouth.

"Ain't never seen nothin' like that before," Monty observed. He still held Mama—who'd given up on her snarling but was still kicking to get loose—by the scruff of the neck. "Seen a girl with three tits before, but nothin' like that."

"It ain't real!" The man who'd gripped Flint's throat and taken away the derringer had backed halfway across the room. "It's a trick!"

"You touch it and find out!" Mitch snapped.

Doc pushed Clint's hand with the automatic's barrel as Flint's insides trembled. Suddenly Clint's fingers closed around the barrel, and Doc gave a quiet laugh. "Farrrr out!" He carefully worked the pistol's barrel free. "He'd like to see this, wouldn't he? He'd get a rush out of it."

"Damn straight, he would," Monty agreed. "He'd laugh his ass off."

Doc finished the job of frisking Flint, then—satisfied the bounty hunter had no other weapons—he spun the .45 around a finger and pushed it back into his waistband. "Get up, Elvis. We're goin' for a boat ride. Mitch, cuff 'em together."

"Not me! I ain't touchin' that bastard!"

"You pussy." Doc took the handcuffs and snapped Pelvis's left wrist to Flint's right. The key went into a pocket of his chinos.

"Where are you takin' 'em?" Dan asked, standing up from the cot.

"Brother Dan, you really don't want to know. Just call this a gift and let it go at that. Now, if I were in your shoes—" He glanced down at them. "I'd steal some new ones. Those are about shot, kemo sabe. But if I were you, I wouldn't stick too long 'round here. Wouldn't be prudent."

"Can I have my dog, please?" Pelvis sounded close to sobbing. "Please, can I have her back?"

"I told you, it's *my* dog now!" Monty rumbled. He held Mama up and shook her. "Have it with some bacon and eggs come daylight."

One second Pelvis was a begging sack of sad flesh; the next second he was a juggernaut, leaping forward, his teeth gritted in a snarl, his unchained hand straining for Monty's throat.

Monty jerked Mama out of Pelvis's reach and hit him, hard and fast, with a scarred fist right in the mouth. Pelvis's head snapped back, his knees giving way, and as he fell he almost dragged Flint down with him. Mitch was laughing a high-pitched giggle, Mama was snarling again, and Doc said, "Get up, Elvis!" He grabbed a handful of pompadour, pulled, and wound up with a wig dangling from his fingers. "Shit!" he laughed. "This fucker's comin' apart!"

Pelvis was down on his knees, his head bent forward, and drops of blood were dripping on the planks. His back heaved, and now it was Dan's turn to be speared with anguish. He didn't know what to do; he didn't know if there was anything he *could* do. Flint shot a glare at Dan that said *Look what you got us into* and then he bent beside Pelvis and said, "Hang on. Just hang on."

"Stand him up, bounty hunter." Doc planted the wig backward on Pelvis's naked pate. "Let's go!"

"Why don't you leave him alone? He's not right in the head, can't you see that?"

"Ain't right in the teeth, ya mean," Monty said, and he grunted a laugh.

It was all Flint could do not to go for the bastard's throat himself,

but he knew it would do no good. "Come on, stand up," he said.
"I'll help you." He had to struggle with Pelvis's weight, but then
Pelvis was standing on his own. Flint didn't want to look at the
man's face. Some of the blood had dripped onto Clint's fingers and
Flint's shirt.

"Out," Doc told them, and Monty gave them a shove toward the
back door he'd kicked down. Dan stood, watching them go, the
wheels spinning and smoking in his brain. Doc lingered behind the
others. "Either of those men you killed a cop?" he asked.

It made no sense at this precarious point to tell Doc he'd killed
only one man, and that by sheer bad luck. "No."

"Next time try for a cop." Doc walked out of the cabin into the
dark, whistling a happy tune.

And Dan stood alone.

23

Crossbones

A pounding noise brought Arden up from the slow current of sleep. She looked out the window. Still dark. What was that noise? Louder, more insistent than the machinery. It took her another few seconds, her head still cloudy, to realize somebody was at the front door.

"Arden! Open up! It's me!"

Dan's voice. She stood up—slowly, a struggle against stiff muscles. When she was on her feet, she had to pause as dizziness made the room spin around her. "Wait!" she called. She limped to the door, then she had to use those same stiff muscles to push the sofa aside. Finally the latch was undone and Dan came in.

His face glistened with sweat, his eyes wild. "What is it?" she asked. "I thought the bounty hunters had you—"

"They're gone. Somebody came and took 'em away."

"Took 'em *away*? Where to?"

"I don't know. Takin' 'em by boat somewhere. Four men. I haven't seen so much firepower since 'Nam."

"What?"

"The four men. I thought they were gonna shoot 'em right there, but then they saw Murtaugh's arm . . . I mean, his brother's arm."

"What are you *talkin'* about?"

He knew he was sounding as crazy as a broken shutter in a windstorm. He had to calm down, take some deep breaths. He pressed his fingertips against his temples. "Four men broke into our cabin and took 'em away. To where, I don't know, but the one who was the boss said somethin' about a boat ride. They were all packin' guns." He started to tell her about Murtaugh's little secret, but he decided she wasn't ready for that yet. "They didn't want me, but they sure as hell marched Murtaugh and Eisley out of there." He looked at his watch. Five-thirty. "Come on, we've gotta tell somebody about this!"

"Wait a minute," she said. "Just a minute." She squeezed her eyes shut and then opened them again, trying to clear some of the cobwebs. Dan saw that sleep had lightened her eyes and that the birthmark had changed color again, like the rough skin of a chameleon, to a deep blue-tinged purple. "The bounty hunters are gone, right?"

"Right."

"Then . . . that means you're *free*, doesn't it?" She ran a hand through the unruly waves of her hair. Her fingers found the painful, blood-crusted knot where her head had been banged in the car. "They tried to break your neck, and mine, too. Why should you care about 'em?"

It was a good question. Maybe he shouldn't give a damn. Maybe he should go on as if Murtaugh and Eisley had never existed. He didn't know what he could do. Nothing, most likely. But at the very least he could tell somebody. Burt at the cafe had a radio-telephone. That was the place to go.

Dan said, "They were just doin' their job, the best they could. I've already caused two murders, I can't be quiet when I know there're gonna be two more." He turned toward the door. "I'm goin' to the cafe."

"Hold on," she said. He was right, and she was ashamed of her pettiness. The bounty hunters might have wanted to take Dan away from her before she found the Bright Girl, but the time had come to think clearly. "Give me a minute." She went into the room where she'd slept and put the five little plastic horses back into the pink drawstring bag. When she'd finished, she turned around and there Dan was, standing in the doorway. He'd seen what she kept in that bag, and he remembered her telling him about the horses she'd been responsible for at the ranch. It struck him what she'd said at the Rest Well Inn about her job with that band Joey the punk had been in, the Hanoi Janes. *Somebody had to be responsible.*

He thought he understood something more about her in that moment. It was at her core to be responsible, to feed and care for the old swaybacked and broken horses, to watch over a band of drunk hell-raisers, to offer a first-aid kit to a man she knew was a wanted killer. *Joey always said I missed my callin', that I should've been a nurse.*

The horses, he realized, must have reminded her of that time in her life when she had cared about something, and been cared for. His heart hurt, because it came clear to him how alone she must feel, and how desperate to find a place of belonging. He turned his face away.

"Don't laugh," Arden said as she drew the bag tight.

"I'm not laughin'. You ready?"

She said she was, and they left the cabin. Outside, in the stifling wet heat, the night's last stars glittered overhead, but to the east there was the faintest smudge of violet. It took Dan and Arden six or seven minutes to wend their path back across the walkways and through the sprawl of clapboard buildings to the cafe. Except for the noise of generators and the incessant pumping of machinery from the direction of the derricks, St. Nasty had quieted considerably. A few men were still in the poolroom, but the walkways were deserted. The cafe's dim lights remained lit, though, and when Dan pushed through the batwing doors, there was Burt, smoking another cigar stub as he swept the planked floor, the tables pushed back against the walls. Behind the bar a second man was scrubbing beer mugs in a metal sink full of soapy, steaming water.

"Mornin'," Burt said, but he kept to his task. "Ya'll want some breakfast, you'll need to go to the chow hall over by Barracks Number Two. Start servin' at five-thirty."

"Yeah, if you like them fake eggs and turkey-shit sausage," the man behind the bar said.

"These folks are with Cecil," Burt told his companion. "I swear, you should've heard him beatin' that—"

"Four men broke into our cabin," Dan interrupted. "Maybe twenty minutes ago. They all had guns, and they took Murtaugh and Eisley with 'em."

Burt stopped sweeping, and the other man stared at them through the steam.

"The one in charge called himself Doc. Wore his hair in a ponytail. I don't know what it was all about, but I think somebody needs to know."

Burt chewed thoughtfully on his cigar. "Can I ask you a question, mister? What the hell are ya'll mixed up in?" He held up his hand as if to ward off the answer. "Wait, forget it. Maybe I don't want to hear it."

"I thought you could call somebody on the radio-telephone. The law, I mean."

"Ha!" Burt glanced over at the other man. "The law he says, Jess! He ain't from around here, is he?"

"Must be from New York City," Jess said, and he returned to his scrubbing.

"Parish ranger used to check in on us every now and again." Burt leaned on his broom. "They found his boat over on Lake Tambour. Not a sign of him, though. They won't never find him."

"Yeah, he's gone south," Jess said.

733

Dan looked sharply at him. *"What?"*

"Gone south. That's Cajun talk for bein' dead."

"See—" Burt pulled the cigar from his mouth. "What'd you say your name was?"

"Dan."

"See, Dan, it's like this: you look on a map of the country, you see this swamp down here and it still looks like it's part of the United States, right? Well, the map lies. This down here is a world all to its ownself. It's got its own language, its own industries, its own . . . well, I wouldn't call 'em laws, exactly. Codes would be more like it. Yeah, codes. The first one is: you don't mess with me, I don't mess with you. Livin' and workin' down here ain't easy—"

"Tell me about it," Jess groused.

"—and so you do what you have to do to slide by. You don't stir up the water and get it all muddy. You don't throw over anybody else's boat, or spit your tabacca in their gumbo. You just live and let live. Get my drift, Dan?"

"I think so. You're sayin' you don't want to call the law."

"That's half of it. The other half is that by the time the law gets here—by boat from Grand Isle—those two fellas are gonna be dead. And that's a damn shame, too, 'cause Cecil had some talent." He pushed the cigar back into his mouth, drew on it, and returned to his sweeping.

"Isn't there somebody here who could help? Don't you have any police around here?"

"We've got what we call peacekeepers," Jess told him. "Company pays 'em extra. Five mean sonsofbitches who'll take you out behind a warehouse and whip your ass till there's nothin' left but a grease stain."

"Yeah." Burt nodded. "The peacekeepers make sure nobody robs anybody, or stuff like that. But I'll tell you, Dan, not even the peacekeepers would want to tangle with those fellas you just seen."

"You know who they were?"

"Uh-huh." He aimed a glance at Arden, who was standing behind Dan. "Still want to see Little Train?"

"Yes, I do."

"I'll be ready in a few minutes, then." He swept cigarette butts and other trash into a dustpan and dumped the debris into a garbage bag. "You decide to go along, too?" The question was directed to Dan.

He felt Arden staring at him. "Yeah," he answered. "I'll go, too."

"Ya'll don't want to eat breakfast first?"

"I'd like to go ahead as soon as we can," Arden said.

"Okay, then. Lemme see what I've got over here." Burt went behind the bar. "Some coffee left in the percolator, but I reckon it would strip the taste buds off your tongues. Oh, here you go. How about these?" He came up with two Moon Pies in their wrappers and two small bags of potato chips. "Want somethin' to drink? You paid for the cabins, I'll throw this in free."

"I'll try the coffee," Dan said, and Arden asked for a can of 7-Up. Burt brought them the Moon Pies and chips, then he went back to get the drinks. Dan still felt dazed by what he'd experienced, and he couldn't let it go. "Those men. Do you know who they are?"

"I know of 'em. Never seen 'em before, myself. Don't want to, either." Burt pushed a spigot and drew black, oily-looking coffee from a cold percolator into a brown clay cup.

"Who are they, then?"

"They're fellas you don't want to be talkin' about." Burt brought the coffee and the can of 7-Up.

"Damn straight." Jess had begun drying the beer mugs. "Plenty of ears in the walls 'round here."

Dan drank some of the coffee and wondered if a layer of swamp mud might not be at the bottom of the percolator; this stuff was even tougher than Donna Lee's high octane, but it gave him a needed kick in the brain pan. He remembered the smack of the big man's fist hitting Eisley in the mouth, a sickening sound. He remembered the drops of blood on the planks. *Nothin's gonna crawl out and get you with the lights on,* Murtaugh had told Eisley.

But Murtaugh had been wrong.

Dan found himself wondering what having an extra arm hanging from your chest and a baby-size head growing from your side would do to a man. It sure would twist you. Maybe make you mean and bitter. What kind of a life had Murtaugh led? That sight alone had been enough to knock Dan's eyes out. *He'd like to see this, wouldn't he?* Doc had said to Monty. *He'd get a rush out of it.*

Who had Doc been talking about?

He drank the coffee and ate the potato chips first, then he devoured the Moon Pie. His guts felt all knotted up. Eisley had seemed all right. A little strange, yes, but all right. Murtaugh was a professional doing a job. It was nothing personal. Fifteen thousand dollars was a lot of money. Hell, if he was a bounty hunter, he would've gone after it, too.

Dan had already caused the death of two innocent people. Now two more were going to die because of him. The torment of watching Emory Blanchard bleed to death, and knowing he was the one who'd pulled that trigger, came back to him full force. He couldn't stand the thought of Murtaugh and Eisley somewhere in the dark, destined to be either beaten or shot.

And what could he do about it?

Forget about them? Just let it go?

If he did, how in the name of God could he ever call himself a man again?

"I'm ready," Burt said. "My boat's at the dock."

The aluminum motor skiff had room for three people, a fourth would have had to straddle the Evinrude. "Throw the lines off!" Burt directed Dan as he got the engine cranked. Then Burt steered them away from the dock. They picked up speed and followed the bayou south past another warehouse and an area where several dredgers and floating cranes were tied up. The air smelled of petroleum and rust, the light turning lavender-gray as the sun began to rise. Arden sat at the front of the boat, her body bent slightly forward as if in anticipation, the warm wind blowing through her hair. Dan watched her hand kneading the drawstring bag. After a few minutes he looked back and saw the derricks of St. Nasty receding against the violet-streaked sky. Then he looked forward again, toward whatever lay ahead.

The boat growled on through the dark-brown foamy water. On either side of the bayou, half-submerged trees and vegetation boiled up in a wild variety of green fronds, lacy moss, spindly reeds, gold-veined fans, and razor-edged saw grass. Here and there flowers of startling red, yellow, or purple had opened their petals amid the tangle of thorns or rigid palmetto spikes. Burt tapped Dan's shoulder and pointed to the right, and Dan saw a four-foot-long alligator sitting on the decaying length of a fallen tree, a crumpled white heron in its jaws.

As they followed the bayou farther away from St. Nasty, the smell of crude oil and machinery was left behind as well. The sun had started throwing golden light across the water and through the thick boughs, and the cloudless sky was changing from gray to pale blue. Dan could feel the humid heat building, fresh sweat blotching his dirty T-shirt. Occasionally they passed the entrances to other, narrower channels, most of them choked up with swamp grass and duck weeds. Dan smelled sweet wild honeysuckle mingled with the earthier aroma of rotting vegetation. They rounded a bend in time to see a dozen white herons flying low across the water, then the birds disappeared amid the trees. The sunlight was strengthening, sparkling off the tea-colored surface, and the early heat promised misery by nine o'clock.

Burt turned them into a bayou that wound off to the left from the

736

main channel. They'd gone maybe fifty yards when Arden saw a piece of board with a skull and crossbones crudely painted on it in white nailed to a treetrunk. She got Burt's attention and motioned to the sign, but he only nodded. A second skull-and-crossbones sign was nailed to a tree farther up the bayou, this one in red.

"Little Train don't care much for people!" Burt told Dan over the motor's snarl. "It's okay, though! He trusts me, we get along all right!"

The bayou's green walls closed in. Thirty feet overhead the tree branches merged, breaking the light into yellow shards. Burt reduced their speed by half and steered the curve of another bend where the mossy tree trunks were as big around as tractor tires. And there, ahead of them in a still and silent cove, was Little Train's house.

Technically it was a houseboat, but from the looks of the vines and moss that had grown over its dark green sides, like fingers enfolding it into the wilderness, it hadn't been moved for many years. It had a screened-in porch that jutted out over the water, and up top was the hooded lid of a stovepipe chimney. Next to the houseboat was a short tin-roofed pier on which stood a half-dozen rusty oil drums, an old bathtub, a clothes wringer, and various other bits and pieces of unidentifiable machinery. On the other side of the pier was an enclosed floating structure fifty feet in length and fifteen feet high, also green-painted and its sides and roof overgrown with vines. Dan could see the crack between a pair of doors at the end of the structure and he figured another boat must be stored within.

"I'll drift up against the pier, if you'll jump out and tie us," Burt said as he switched the motor off, and Dan nodded. When they were close enough, Dan stood up, found his balance, and stepped to the pier. Burt threw him a rope secured to the skiff's stern and Dan tied it up to one of the wooden posts that supported the roof. When he grasped Arden's wrist in helping her out, Dan could feel her pulse racing. Her eyes had taken on that fervent shine again, and her birthmark had become almost bloodred.

"Hey, Little Train!" Burt shouted at the houseboat. "You got some visitors!"

There was no response. Up in the trees, birds were chirping and a fish suddenly jumped from the cove's water—a flash of silver—and splashed back again.

"Hey, Train!" Burt tried again. He stood on the pier, not daring to set foot without invitation on the Astroturfed walkway that connected it to Little Train's home. "It's Burt Dunbro! Come to talk to you!"

"Who you are I be seein', *fou*," rumbled a surly, heavily accented voice from a screened window. "Who *they* are?"

"Tell him," Burt urged quietly.

"My name's Dan Lambert." Dan could see a figure beyond the screen—the blur of a face—but nothing more. "This is Arden Halliday."

Silence. Dan had the feeling the man was studying Arden's birthmark.

Arden shared the same sensation. Her right hand had squeezed tightly around the drawstring bag, her heart slamming. "I need your help," she said.

"He'p," the man repeated. "What kinda he'p?"

"I'm . . . tryin' to find someone." Her mouth was so dry she could hardly speak. "A woman called the Bright Girl."

There was another stretch of silence for Dan and Burt, but Arden was almost deafened by her heartbeat.

Burt cleared his throat. "Ol' gal at the cafe told her this Bright Girl used to live in a church on Goat Island. Said she's in a grave out there. I said I been huntin' on Goat Island, and far as I know nobody ever lived on it."

Little Train did not speak.

"What do you say?" Burt asked. "Anybody ever lived on Goat Island?"

"*Non*," came the answer.

Arden winced.

"I told her that. Told her you'd know if anybody would. Hey, listen: I need to put in an order for a hundred pounds of cat and fifty pounds of turtle. What can you deliver by next Tuesday?"

"The Bright Girl," the man said, and hearing him say it sent a chill up Arden's spine. "For her you're lookin', ay?"

"That's right. I'm tryin' to find her, because—"

"My own two eyeballs broke, they ain't. Come from where?"

"Huh?"

"He wants to know where you're from," Burt interpreted.

"Texas. Fort Worth, I'm from," she said in unconscious emulation of Little Train's Cajun patois.

"Huuuuwheee!" he said. "That distance, you gotta believe mighty hard. Ay?"

"I do believe."

"This what you believin'," he said, "is wrong."

Arden flinched again. Her hand was white-knuckled around the bag.

"Bright Girl on Goat Island, *non*," Little Train continued. "Was a church out there, never. Who you think she may be, she ain't."

"Wait," Dan said. "Are you sayin' . . . there really *is* a Bright Girl?"

"Sayin' *oui*. Sayin' *non*, too. Not who this girl come from Tex-ay-ass to find."

"Where is she?" Arden's throat clutched. "Please. Can you take me to her?"

There was no answer. Both she and Dan realized the blurred face was gone from the window.

A door on the screened porch skreeked open, and Little Train stood before them.

24

Elephants and Tigers

His gravelly voice through the window screen had made him sound as if he might be a seven-foot-tall Goliath. Instead, Little Train stood barely five-six, only four inches taller than Arden. But maybe he had the strength of a giant, because Dan figured he carried at least a hundred and sixty pounds on his stocky, muscular frame. Little Train wore a faded khaki T-shirt over a barrel chest, and brown trousers whose cuffs had been scissored off above a well-worn pair of dark-blue laceless sneakers. His forearms appeared solid enough to pound nails. The bayou sun had burned Little Train's skin to the color of old brick, and it looked as rough. His jaw and cheeks were silvered with a three-day growth of beard, his hair a pale sandpaper dust across the brown skull. Beneath his deeply creased forehead his clear gray eyes were aimed at Arden with a power that almost knocked her back a step.

"Ya'll come on in," he offered.

Dan crossed the Astroturfed plank first, then Arden and Burt. Little Train went ahead into the houseboat, and they followed him across the porch into a room with oak-planked walls and oak beams that ran the length of the ceiling. On the floor was a threadbare red rug that instantly charged Dan's memory: it had a motif of fighting elephants and tigers, and it looked like one of a thousand the street-corner businessmen had hawked from rolling racks in Saigon. The furnishings also had an Oriental—Vietnamese? Dan wondered—influence: two intricately carved ashwood chairs; a bamboo table with a black metal tray atop it; an oil lamp with a rice-paper shade; and a woven tatami neatly rolled up in a corner. A shortwave radio and microphone stood on a second bamboo table next to a shelf of hardback and paperback books. Through another doorway was a small galley, pots and pans hanging from overhead hooks.

"My place," Little Train said. "Welcome to it."

Dan was struck by the cleanliness and order. There was the ever-present smell of the swamp, yes, but no moldy stench. In the black metal tray on the first bamboo table were three smooth white stones, some pieces of dried reeds, and a few fragile-looking bones that might have been fish, fowl, or reptile. Mounted on one wall was a variety of other objects: a huge round hornet's nest, wind-sculpted pieces of bleached driftwood, an amber-colored snakeskin, and the complete skeleton of a bird with its wings outspread. Then he knew for sure what he'd suspected, because he saw a group of framed photographs on the wall above the shortwave set. He walked across the Saigon-special rug for a closer inspection. They were snapshots of a boat's crew, bare-chested young men wearing steel helmets and grinning or firing upraised middle fingers from their stations behind .50-caliber machine guns and what looked to be an 81-millimeter mortar. There were pictures of a muddy brown river, of the garish nightlights of Saigon, of a cute Vietnamese girl who might have been sixteen or seventeen smiling and displaying the two-fingered V of a peace sign to the camera.

Dan said, "I was a leatherneck. Third Marine. Where'd you catch it?"

"Brown water Navy," Little Train replied without hesitation. "Radarman first class, Swift PCF."

"These pictures of your boat?" The Swift PCF patrol craft crews, Dan knew, had taken hell along the constricted waterways of 'Nam and Cambodia.

"The verra one."

"Your crew make it out?"

"Jus' me and the fella sittin' at the mortar. Night of May sixteen, 1970, we run into a chain stretched 'cross the river. Them black pajamas waitin' on the bank, ay? Hit us with rockets. I went swimmin', back fulla shrap."

"You never told me you were over there in Vet'nam, Little Train!" Burt said.

He burned his gaze at the other man. "Never you ask. And *bon ami*, I tell you plenty time: call me *Train*."

"Oh. Okay. Sure. Train it is." Burt shrugged and cast a nervous grin at Arden.

"Please," Arden said anxiously. "The Bright Girl. Do you know where she is?"

He nodded. "I do."

"Don't tell me you know where her grave is. Please tell me she's alive."

"For you, then: *oui*, alive she is."

"Oh, God." Tears sprang to her eyes. "Oh, God. You don't know how . . . you don't know how much I wanted to hear that."

"Who're you talkin' about, Train?" Burt frowned. "I never heard of any Bright Girl."

"Never you needed her," Train said.

"Can you take me to her?" Arden asked. "I've come such a long way. I don't have any money, but . . . I'll sign an IOU. I'll get the money. However much you want to take me, I swear I'll pay you. All right?"

"Your money, I don't want. Got ever'ting I need, I'm a rich man."

"You mean . . . you won't—"

"Won't take no money, *non*. Who tell you 'bout the Bright Girl way up there in Fort Worth Tex-ay-ass?"

"A friend who was born in LaPierre. He saw her when he was a little boy, and he told me all about her."

"Oh, them stories. That she's a young beautimous girl and she don't never get old or die. That she can touch you and heal any sickness, or cancer . . . or scar. Your friend tell you all that?"

"Yes."

"So you believe mighty hard, and you come all the way down here to ask her touch. 'Cause that mark, it hurt you inside?"

"Yes."

Train reached toward her face. Arden's first impulse was to pull away, but his gaze was powerful enough to hold her. His rough brown fingers gently grazed the birthmark and then drew back. "You strong-hearted?" he asked.

"I . . . think I am."

"Either am or not."

"I am," she said.

Train nodded. "Then I take you, no sweat."

Dan couldn't remain silent any longer. "Don't lie to her! There's no such person! There *can't* be! I don't care if she's supposed to be some great miracle worker, no woman can live a hundred years and still look like a young girl!"

"I say I take her to see the Bright Girl." Train's voice was calm. "I say, too, the Bright Girl ain't who she come to find."

"What?" Arden shook her head. "I'm not followin' you."

"When we get there, you see tings clear. Then we find out how strong you heart."

Dan didn't know what to say, or what kind of tricks this man was trying to pull. None of it made any sense to him. What had started to gnaw at him again was the fate of Murtaugh and Eisley. He couldn't stand the thought that his pulling the trigger in Shreveport had resulted in the death of Harmon DeCayne and now, most likely, the two bounty hunters. There would be four murders on his head, and how could he live with that and not go insane? He remembered what Burt had said about Train, back in the cafe: *He gets all 'round the swamp. If anybody would know, it'd be him.*

Dan had to ask. "There were two other men with us. We were at St. Nasty. Around five o'clock, four men with guns broke in our cabin and took 'em away. The one in charge was called Doc. Do you know—"

"Oh, shit!" Burt pressed his hands to his ears. "I don't wanna hear this! I don't wanna know nothin' about it!"

"Hush up!" Train's voice rattled the screens. "Let 'im talk!"

"I'm not stayin' around for this! No way! Ya'll have fun, I'm gettin' back up the bayou!" Burt started out but paused at the door. "Train, don't do nothin' stupid! Hear me? I'll be expectin' the cat and turtle by Tuesday. Hear?"

"Go home, *bon ami*," Train said. "And to you safe passage."

"Good luck," Burt told Dan, and he went out and crossed the gangplank. Train walked past Arden to a window and watched Burt untie his boat, climb in, and start the engine. "He's okay," Train said as Burt steered the motor skiff back up the narrow bayou the way they'd come. "Hard-workin' fella."

"He knows who Doc is, doesn't he?"

"Oh, *oui*. And so do I." He turned away from the window; his face seemed to have drawn tighter across the bones, his eyes cold. "Tell me the tale, ay?"

Dan told him, omitting the fact that he was wanted for murder and that Murtaugh and Eisley were bounty hunters. He omitted, as well, the fact of Murtaugh's freak-show background. "Doc said he was takin' 'em somewhere by boat. He had some kinda score to settle with 'em, but I'm not sure what it was."

Train leveled that hard, penetrating stare at Dan. "Friends of you, they is?"

"Not friends, exactly."

"Then who they is to you?"

"More like . . . fellow travelers."

"Where was they travelin' to?"

Dan looked at the elephants and tigers in the rug. He could feel Train watching him, and he knew there was no use in lying. Train was no fool. He sighed heavily; the only path to take was the straight one. "Flint Murtaugh and Pelvis Eisley are their names. They're bounty hunters. They tracked me down here. I met Arden in a truck stop north of Lafayette and brought her with me."

"I came because I wanted to," Arden said. "He didn't force me."

"Bounty hunters," Train repeated. "What crime you did?"

"I killed a man."

Train didn't move or speak.

"He worked at a bank in Shreveport. There was a fight. I lost my head and shot him. The bank's put fifteen thousand dollars reward on me. Murtaugh and Eisley wanted it."

"Huuuuwheeee," Train said softly.

"You can have the reward, I won't give you any trouble. Can you call the law or somebody on that shortwave set?"

"I a'ready tell you, I don't need no money. I'm rich, livin' as I do. I love this swamp, I grew up in it. I like to fish and hunt. What I don't eat, I sell. I boss myself. I get fifteen thousan' dollar in my pocket— *poof!* There go my riches. Then I want another fifteen thousan' dollar, but no more there is. No, I don't need but what I got." He frowned, the lines deepening around his eyes, and he rubbed his silvered chin. "If them bounty hunters after you, how come for you wanna he'p 'em? How come you even tellin' me this?"

"Because they don't deserve to be murdered, that's why! They haven't done anything wrong!"

"Hey, hey! Calm down. Flyin' you head off ain't gonna he'p nobody." He motioned toward the porch. "Ya'll go out there, set, and take the breeze. I'll be there direct."

"What about the shortwave?"

"Yeah, I could call the law way over to Gran' Isle. Only ting is, they ain't gonna find you . . . fella travelers," he decided to say. "Likely they dead a'ready. Now go on out and set y'self."

There wasn't much of a breeze on the porch, but it was a little cooler there than inside the boat. Dan was too jumpy to sit, though Arden settled in a wicker chair that faced the cove. "You're goin' with me, aren't you?" she asked him. "We're so close, you've got to go with me."

"I'll go. I still don't believe it, but I'll go." He stood at the screen, looking out at the water's still surface. "Damn," he said. "There's gotta be somethin' somebody can do!"

"*Oui*, you can take a swaller of this here." Train came onto the porch. He had uncapped a small metal flask, and he offered it to Dan. "Ain't 'shine," he said when Dan hesitated. "It's French brandy. Buy it in Grand Isle. Go ahead, ay?"

Dan accepted the flask and took a drink. The brandy burned its flaming trail down his throat. Train offered the flask to Arden, and when she shook her head he took a sip and sloshed it around in his mouth before swallowing. "Now I gonna tell you 'bout them men, so listen good. They got a place 'bout five mile southwest from here. Hid real fine. I ain't got an eye set for it, but I come up on it when I'm huntin' boar near Lake Calliou. They been there maybe t'ree month. Set up camp, brung in a prefab house, build a dock, swimmin' pool, and all whatcha like. Got a shrimp boat and two of them expenseeve cigarettes. You know, them fast speederboats. Then they put bob wire 'round ever'ting." He swigged from the flask and held it out to Dan again. "I hear from an ol' Cajun boy live on Calliou Bay them men be poachin' 'gator. Season don't start till September, see. Ain't no big ting, it happen. But I start to windin' in my head, how come they to poach 'gator? Somebody owns hisse'f two of them cigarettes, he got to poach 'gator? Why's that so, ay?" He took the flask back after Dan had had a drink. "Ol' boy says he seen lights at night, boats comin' and goin' all hours. So I go over there, hide my boat, and watch through my dark vision binocs 'cause I eat up with curious. Took me two night, then I see what they up to."

"What was it?" Arden asked, pulling her thoughts away from the Bright Girl for the moment.

"Freighter in the bay, unloadin' what look like grain sacks to the shrimp boat. All the time the two cigarettes they circlin' and circlin' 'round, throwin' spotlights. And huuuuwheee!—the men in them boats with the like of guns you never did saw! Shrimp boat brung the grain sacks back in, freighter up anchor and went." He had another swig of Napoleon's finest. "Now what kinda cargo unloaded by night and be that worth protection?"

"Drugs," Dan said.

"That's what I'm figurin'. Either the heroin or the cockaine. Maybe both. All them miles and miles of swamp coast, the law cain't hardly patrol a smidgen of it, and they boats in sorry shape. So these fellas bringin' in the dope and shippin' it north, likely takin' it up by Bayou du Large or Bayou Grand Calliou and unloadin' at a marina. Sellin' some of it at St. Nasty, too. Burt's the one found out fella named Doc Nyland was hangin' 'round the poolhall, givin' men free samples to get 'em interested. Peacekeeper tried to do somethin' about it, he went missin'. Only ting is, I cain't figure why they poachin' the 'gators. Then—boom!—it hit me like a brick upside my head." Train capped the flask. "They worry somebody gonna steal them drugs away from 'em. Worry so much they gonna be hijack they gotta figure a way to move 'em safe. So what they gonna do, ay? They gonna put them drugs somewhere they cain't be easy stole." His mouth crooked in a wicked smile. "Like inside live 'gators."

745

"Inside 'em?"

"*Sans doute!* You wrap that cockaine up in metal foil good and tight, then you jam it down in them bellies with a stick! How you gonna get it out unless you got a big knife and a lotta time to be cuttin'? That'd be the goddangest mess you never did saw!"

"I'll bet," Dan agreed. "So what are they doin'? Shippin' the 'gators north to be cut open?"

"*Oui*, puttin' 'em on a truck and takin' 'em to a safe place. Even if them 'gators die of bad digestion 'fore they get where they goin', the cockaine still protected in there."

"Maybe so, but I can't understand how Murtaugh and Eisley got mixed up with a gang of drug runners. Is Doc Nyland their leader?"

Train shook his head. "I seen somebody else over there, look like he was bossin'. Fella don't wear no shirt, showin' hisse'f off. Standin' by the pool, them irons and weight bars layin' ever'where. His girlfrien', all she do is lay there sunburnin'. I'm figurin' he's the honch."

Dan looked out through the screen at the water. The sun was up strong and hot now, golden light streaming through the trees. A movement caught his attention, and he saw a moccasin undulating smoothly across the surface. He watched it until it disappeared into the shadows. It seemed to Dan that in this swamp the human reptiles were the ones to be feared most of all. He lifted his forearm and stared at his snake tattoo. Once, a long time ago, he had been a brave man. He had done without hesitation what he'd thought was the right thing. He had walked the world like a giant himself, before time and fate had beaten him down. Now he was dying and he was a killer, sick at heart.

He felt as if he were peering into a snake hole, and if he reached into it to drag the thing out, he could be bitten to death. But if he turned his back on it like a coward, he was already dead.

An image came to him, unbidden: Farrow's face and voice, there on that terrible night the snipers' bullets had hissed out of the jungle.

Go, he'd said. It had not been a shout, but it was more powerful than a shout.

Go.

Dan remembered the glint of what might have been joy in Farrow's eyes as the man—a citizen of Hell, one of the walking damned—had turned and started slogging back through the mud toward the jungle, firing his M16 to give Dan and the others precious seconds in which to save their own lives.

Farrow could not live with himself because he'd gone south.

There in the village of Cho Yat, his simple mistake with the foil-wrapped chocolate bar had resulted in the death of innocents, and Farrow had decided—in the muddy stream, at that crisis of time—that he had found an escape.

Dan had once been a Snake Handler, a good soldier, a decent man. But he'd gone south, there in that Shreveport bank, and now *he* was a citizen of hell, one of the walking damned.

But he knew the right thing to do.

It was time to go.

"You braingears gettin' hot," Train said in a quiet voice.

"You have guns." It was a statement, not a question.

"Two rifles. Pistol."

"How many men?"

Train knew what he meant. "I count eight last time. Maybe more I don't see."

Dan turned to face him. "Will you take me?"

"No!" Arden stood up, her eyes wide. "Dan, no! You don't owe them anything!"

"I owe myself," he said.

"Listen to me!" She stepped close to him and grasped his arm. "You can still get away! You can find—"

"No," he interrupted gently, "I can't. Train, how about it?"

"They'll kill you!" Arden said, stricken with terror for him.

"*Oui,*" Train added. "That they'll try."

"Maybe Murtaugh and Eisley are already dead." Dan stared deeply into Arden's eyes. It was a strange thing, but now he could look at her face and not see the birthmark. "Maybe they're still alive, but they won't be for very long. If I don't go after 'em—if I don't at least try to get 'em out of there—what good am I? I don't want to die in prison. But I can't live in a prison, either. And if I don't do *somethin'*, I'll carry my own prison around with me every hour of every day I've got left. I have to do this. Train?" He directed his gaze to the Cajun. "I'm not askin' you to help me, just to get me close enough. I'll need to take one of the rifles, the pistol, and some ammo. You got a holster for the pistol?"

"I do."

"Then you'll take me?"

Train paused for a moment, thinking it over. He opened the flask again and took a long swig. "You a mighty strange killer, wantin' to get killed for somebody tryin' to slam you in prison." He licked his lips. "Huuuuwheeee! I didn't know I was gonna get dead today."

"I can go in alone."

"Well," Train said, "it's like this here: I knew a fella, name of Jack

Giradoux. Parish ranger, he was. He come by, we'd have a talk and eat some cat. I don't tell him about them men 'cause I know what he'll have to do. I figure not to rock the boat, ay?" He smiled; it was a painful sight. The smile quickly faded. "If he don't find 'em, I figure, he don't get killed. He was a good fella. Few days ago fisherman find Jack's boat on Lake Tambour. That's a long way from where them men are, but I know they must've got hold of him and then towed his boat up there. Find his body, nobody ever will. Now I gotta ask myself, did I done wrong? When they gonna find out I know about 'em and come for me, some night?" He closed the flask and held it down at his side. "Lived forty-five good year. To die in bed, *non*. Could be we get it done and get out. Could be you my death angel, and maybe I know sooner or later you was gonna swoop down on me. It's gonna be like puttin' you hand in a cottonmouth nest. You ready to get bit?"

"I'm ready to do some bitin'," Dan said.

"Okay, leatherneck. Okay. With you, I reckon. Got Baby to carry us, maybe we get real lucky."

"Baby?"

"She my girl. You meet her, direct."

"One more thing," Dan added. "I want to take Arden where she needs to go first."

"*Non*, impossible. Them men five miles southwest, the Bright Girl nine, ten mile southeast, down in the Casse-Tete Islands. We take her first, we gonna be losin' too much time."

Dan looked at Arden, who was staring fixedly at the floor. "I'll leave it up to you. I know how much this means. I never believed it . . . but maybe I should have. Maybe I was wrong, I don't know." Her chin came up, and her eyes found his. "What do you say?"

"I say—" She stopped, and took a deep breath to clear her head. So many things were tangled up inside her: fear and jubilation, pain and hope. She had come so far, with so much at stake. But now she knew what the important thing was. She said, "Help them."

He gave her a faint smile; he'd known what she was going to decide. "You need to stay here. We'll be back as soon as—"

"No." It was said with finality. "If you're goin', I am, too."

"Arden, it might be rougher'n hell out there. You could get yourself killed."

"I'm goin'. Don't try to talk me out of it, because you can't."

"Clock's tickin'," Train said.

"All right, then." Dan felt the urgency pulling at him. "I'm ready."

Train went into a back room and got the weapons: a Browning

automatic rifle with a four-bullet magazine, a Ruger rifle with a hunter's scope and a five-shell magazine, and in a waist holster a Smith & Wesson 9mm automatic that held an eight-bullet clip. He found extra magazines for the rifles and clips for the automatic and put them in a faded old backpack, which Arden was given charge of. Dan took the Browning and the pistol. Train got a plastic jug of filtered water from the galley, slung the Ruger's strap around his shoulder, and said, "We go."

They left the houseboat and Train led them to the vine-covered floating structure next to the pier. He slid open a door. "Here she sets."

"Jesus," Dan said, stunned by what he saw.

Sitting inside was Train's second boat. It was painted navy gray, the paint job relatively fresh except for patches of rust at the waterline. It resembled a smaller version of a commercial tug, but it was leaner and meaner, its squat pilothouse set closer to the prow. The craft was about fifty feet long, and thirteen feet high at its tallest point, a tight squeeze in the oil-smelling, musty boathouse. It had not the gentle charm of an infant, but the armor-plated threat of a brute.

Though the machine-gun mounts and the mortar had been removed and other civilian modifications made to the radar mast, Dan recognized it as a Swift-type river patrol boat, the same kind of vessel Train had crewed aboard on the deadly waterways of Vietnam.

"My baby," Train said with a sly grin. "Let the good times roll."

25

Reptilian

The sun had risen on a small aluminum rowboat in the middle of a muddy pond. In that rowboat Flint and Pelvis sat facing each other, linked by the short chain between their cuffed wrists.

At seven o'clock the temperature was approaching eighty-four degrees and the air steamed with humidity. Flint's shirt and suit jacket had been stripped off him, Clint's arm drooping lethargically from the pale, sweat-sparkling chest. Beads of moisture glistened on Flint's hollow-eyed face, his head bowed. Across from him, Pelvis still wore his wig backward, his clothes sweat-drenched, his eyes swollen and forlorn. Dried blood covered the split sausage of his bottom lip, one of his lower teeth gone and another knocked crooked, tendrils of crusty blood stuck to his chin. His breathing was slow and harsh, sweat dripping from the end of his nose into a puddle between his mud-bleached suedes.

Something brushed against the boat's hull and made the craft lazily turn around its anchor chain. Flint lifted his head to watch a five-foot-long alligator drift past, its snout pushing through the foul brown water. A second alligator, this one maybe three feet in length, cruised past the first. The cat-green eyes and ridged skull of a third had surfaced less than six feet from the rowboat. Two more, each four-footers, lay motionless side by side just beyond the silent watcher. Flint had counted nine alligators at any one time, but there might be others asleep on the bottom. He couldn't tell one from the other, except for their obvious size differences, so he really didn't know how many lurked in the sludgy pond. Still, they were quiet monsters. Occasionally two or three would bump together in their back-and-forth loglike driftings and there might be an instant's outburst of thrashing anger, but then everything would calm down again but for the rocking of the boat and the thudding hearts of the men in it. Flint figured the alligators were prisoners here just as he and Pelvis were.

The pond looked to be sixty-five feet across, from one side of a half-submerged, rusty barbed-wire fence to the other. Beyond the alligator corral's heavily bolted gate was a pier where two cigarette speedboats—both of them painted dark, nonreflective green—were secured, along with the larger workboat Flint had seen unloading the reptiles at the Vermilion marina. Eight feet of the pier was built out over the corral, and at its end stood a bolted-down electric winch Flint figured was used to hoist the alligators up onto the workboat's deck. During the thirty-minute journey to this place in one of the speedboats, Monty had gleefully ripped the jacket and shirt off Flint's back and taken the derringer's holster. Then, when they'd reached their destination, Doc and the others had debated for a few minutes what to do with them until "he"—whoever "he" was—woke up. Their current situation had been dreamed up by Doc, who got Mitch to row them in the aluminum skiff through the corral's gate while Monty had followed in a second rowboat. There had been much hilarity from a group of men watching on the pier as Mitch had thrown a concrete brick anchor over the side and then got into the boat with Monty, leaving Flint and Pelvis at the end of their chain.

The party had gone on for a while—"Hey, freak! Why don't you and Elvis get out of that boat and cool yourselves off?"—but the men had drifted away as the sun had come up. Flint understood why; the novelty had faded, and they'd known how hot it was going to get out here. Every so often Mitch, Monty, or some other bastard would stroll out to the pier's end to take a look and throw a remark at them that included the words "freak" or "motherfuckers," then they would go away again. Since Pelvis had been smashed in the mouth, he'd not spoken a single word. Flint realized he must be in shock. Monty had taken Mama with him, and the last time the bearded sonofabitch had come out to check on them, the little bulldog wasn't in his arms.

Flint could smell meat cooking.

Being burned was more like it.

The pier continued on past the boats to a bizarre sight: a large suburban ranch house with cream-colored walls, perched on wooden pilings over the water. The place looked as if it had been lifted up off the mowed green lawn of the perfect American town, helicoptered in, and set down to be the envy of the neighborhood. There was a circular swimming pool with its own redwood deck, one of those "above-ground" pools sold in kits; here the pool was not above ground, but on a platform above swamp. On the pool's deck was a rack of barbells, a weight bench, and a stationary bicycle.

Next to it was another large deck shaded by a blue-and-white-striped canvas awning, and on the far side of the house the platform supported a television satellite dish.

Other walkways went off from the main platform, connecting the house to three other smaller wooden structures. Cables snaked from one of them to the house and the satellite dish, so Flint reasoned it stored the power generator. Though the alligator corral, the pier, and the swimming pool were out under the full sun, most of the house was shaded by moss-draped trees. Around the house and the corral and everything else the swamp still held green dominion. Flint could see a bayou winding into the swamp beyond the farthermost of the three outbuildings, and there were red buoys floating in it to mark deeper passage for the workboat's hull.

His survey of the area had also found a wooden watchtower, about forty feet high, all but hidden amid the trees at the bayou's entrance. Up top, under a green-painted cupola, a man sat in a lawn chair reading a magazine, a rifle propped against the railing beside him. Every few minutes he would stand up and scan all directions through a pair of binoculars, then he would sit down again and return to his reading.

"We," Flint said hoarsely, "are in deep shit."

Pelvis didn't speak; he just sat there and kept sweating, his eyes unfocused.

"Eisley? Snap out of it, hear me?"

There was no answer. A little thread of saliva had spooled down over his wounded lip.

"How about sayin' somethin'?" Flint asked.

Pelvis lowered his head and stared at the boat's bottom.

Flint sniffed the air, catching the smell of burned meat. It struck him that that bastard Monty might be hungry again, and he realized Pelvis was probably thinking the same thing he was: Mama was on the breakfast grill.

"Hey, we're gonna get out of this," Flint tried again. He thought it was the most idiotic thing he'd ever said in his life. "You can't go off and leave me now, hear?"

Pelvis shook his head, and he swallowed with a little dry, clicking noise.

Flint watched another alligator gliding past, so close he could have reached out and poked it in the eye if he cared to lose a hand. Well, that'd be all right; he'd still have two. Hold on, he told himself. Hold on, now. Control yourself. It's not over yet, they haven't shoveled the dirt over you. Hold on. "I'll bet this is all a big mistake," he said. "I'll bet when that fella wakes up, he'll come see us and we'll tell him the story and he'll shoot us on out of here." His throat clenched up. "I mean, *scoot* us out of here." Eisley's silence was scaring the bejesus out of him, making him start to lose his own grip. He'd gotten so used to the man's prattling, the silence was driving him crazy. "Eisley, listen. We're not givin' up. Pelvis? Come on, talk to me."

No response.

Flint leaned forward, the sun beginning to scorch his back and sweat clinging to his eyebrows. "Cecil," he said, "I'm gonna slap the crap out of you if you don't look me in the face and say somethin'."

But it was no use. Flint closed his eyes and pressed his uncuffed hand against his forehead. At his chest Clint's arm suddenly twitched and the hand fluttered, then it fell motionless again.

"What'd you call me?"

Flint opened his eyes and looked into the other man's face.

"Did you call me Cecil?" Pelvis had lifted his head. His split lip had broken open again, a little bloody fluid oozing.

"Yeah, I guess I did." A rush of relief surged through him. "Well, thank God you're back! Now's not the time to crack up, lemme tell you! We've got to hang tough! Like I said, when that fella wakes up and we tell him what a big mistake all this is—"

"Cecil," Pelvis whispered, and a wan smile played across his crusty mouth. Then it passed. His eyes were very dark. "I think . . . they're cookin' Mama," he said.

"No, they're not!" Hold on to him! Flint thought in desperation. Don't let him slide away again! "That fella was just pullin' your chain! Listen now, get your mind off that. We've got other things to think about."

"Like what? Which one of us they're gonna kill first?" He squinted up at the sun. "I don't care. We ain't gettin' out of this."

"See? That's why you never would've made a good bounty hunter. *Never.* Because you're a quitter. By God, *I'm* not a quitter!" Flint felt the blood pounding in his face. He had to calm down before he had a heatstroke. "I said I was gonna get Lambert, and I got him, didn't I?"

"Yes sir, you did. I don't think neither one of us is gonna be spendin' much of that reward money, though."

"You just watch," Flint said. "You'll find out." He was aware of his own wheels starting to slip. Control! he thought. Control was the most important thing. He had to settle himself down before the pressure of this situation broke him. He enfolded Clint's clammy hand in his own, and he could feel their common pulse. "Self-discipline is what a bounty hunter needs. I've always had it. Ever since I was a little boy. I had to have it to keep Clint from jumpin' around when I didn't want him to. Jumpin' around and makin' everybody look at me like I was a freak. Self-discipline is what you need, and a whole lot of it."

"Mr. Murtaugh?" Pelvis said in a soft and agonized voice that had very little of Elvis in it. "We're gonna die today. Would you please shut up?"

Flint's brain was smoking. He was burning up. His pallid skin cringed from the raw sunlight, and there was water, water everywhere, but not enough to cool himself in. He licked his lips and tasted sweat. An alligator nudged alongside the boat, a long, scraping noise that made the flesh of Flint's spine ripple. He needed to get his mind fixed on something else—anything else. "You'd be worth a damn," he said, "if you had a manager."

Pelvis stared at him, and slowly blinked. *"What?"*

"A manager. Like that fella said. You need a manager. Somebody to teach you self-discipline, get you off that damn junk food. Get you to stop tryin' to play Elvis and be Cecil. I heard what he said, I was standin' right there."

"Are you . . . sayin' what I *think* you're sayin'?"

"Maybe I am. Maybe I'm not." Flint reached up, his fingers trembling, and wiped the beads of sweat from his eyebrows. "I'm just sayin' you've got a little talent to beat the piano, and a good manager could help you. A good *businessman.* Somebody to make sure you got paid when you were supposed to. You wouldn't have to be a headliner, you could be in somebody else's band, or play backup on records or whatever. There's money to be made in that line of work, isn't there?"

"Are you crazy, Mr. Murtaugh?" Pelvis asked. "Or am I?"

"Hell, we *both* are!" Flint had almost shouted it. Control, he thought. Control. God, the sun was getting fierce. A pungent, acidic reek—the smell of swamp mud and 'gator droppings—was steaming up off the water. "When we get out of here—which we *will*, after we talk to whoever's in charge around here—there's gonna be tomorrow to think about. You're not cut out to be a bounty hunter . . . and I've been lookin' for a way to quit it for a long time. I'm sick of the ugliness of it, and I was never gettin' anywhere. I was just goin' around and around, like . . . like a three-armed monkey in a cage," he said. "Now, it might not work. Probably won't. But it would be a new start, wouldn't—"

"Gettin' awful hot out here, ain't it?"

The voice caused both of them to jump. Monty was walking along the pier, splotches of sweat on his shirt. He was holding a plate of food, and he was chewing on some stringy meat attached to a small bone. "Ya'll ain't gone swimmin' yet?"

Neither Flint nor Pelvis spoke. They watched the big, brown-bearded man chewing on the bone in his greasy fingers.

"Don't feel much like talkin', do you?" Monty glanced quickly up at the sun. Then he threw the bone into the water beside their boat. The splash drew the attention of the alligators, and three or four of them quickly converged on the spot like scaly torpedoes. Water swirled, a tail rose up and smacked the surface, and suddenly an underwater disagreement boiled up, two reptilian bodies thrashing and the rowboat rocking back and forth on the muddy foam of combat.

"Them boys are hungry this mornin'." Monty started sucking the meat from another bone. "They'll eat anydamnthing, y'know. Got cast-iron stomachs. Bet they'd like to get their teeth in you, freak. Bet you'd be a real taste sensation."

The alligators, finding no food on their table, had stopped squabbling. Still, they crisscrossed the pond on all sides of the boat. "Don't you men think this has gone far enough?" Flint asked. "We've learned our lesson, we're not comin' back in here anymore."

Monty chewed and laughed. "Well, that's right. 'Course, you ain't leavin', either." He flung the second bone in, and again the reptiles darted for it. "Hey, Elvis! You want some breakfast?"

Pelvis didn't answer, and Flint saw his eyes glazing over again.

"It's realllll good. Lotta meat on them bones, I was surprised. Want to try a bite or two?" He held up a hunk of white meat, and he grinned through his beard. "Woof! Woof!" he said.

Pelvis shivered. A pulse had started beating hard at his temple.

"Hang on." Flint grasped Pelvis's arm. "Steady, now."

"I think he wants the rest of it, Mr. Freak. Here you go, Elvis! Arrrruuuuuu!" And as he howled like a dog, Monty tossed the rest of the plate's meat and bones up into the air over the corral.

Before the first piece of meat or bone splashed the surface, Pelvis went crazy.

He lunged over the rowboat's side. The chain of the handcuffs connecting their wrists jerked tight, and with a shout of terror Flint was pulled into the water with him.

For the last mile and a half Train had cut the Swift's husky double-diesels to one-fourth speed—about seven knots—to keep the noise down. Now he switched off the engines and let the Swift coast along the narrow bayou. "Gettin' close," he said behind the spoked wheel in the pilothouse. Dan stood at his side, and Arden had found a benchseat to park herself on toward the stern. "She gonna run minute or two, then we doin' some wadin'."

Dan nodded. The rifles, pistol, and the ammunition backpack had been stowed away in a locker at the rear of the pilothouse. After leaving the cove Train had brought them along a series of channels at speeds approaching twenty-eight knots, the Swift's upper limit. Before them, birds had flown and alligators had dived for safety. Train had told Dan his real name was Alain Chappelle, that he'd been born on a train between Mobile and New Orleans, but that he was raised in Grand Isle, where his father had been a charter fisherman. During his tour of duty in Vietnam his parents had moved to New Orleans, and his father had accepted a consulting job with a company that built fishing boats. Train had the swamp in his blood, he'd said. He had to live there, in all that beautiful wilderness, or he would perish. He'd known that the Swift boats—based on the design of tough little utility craft used to ferry supplies out to oil derricks in the Gulf of Mexico—were built by a contractor in the town of Berwick, which Dan and Arden had passed through forty miles north of Houma. In 1976 he'd bought the armor-plated hulk of a surplus Swift and started the three-year labor of restoring it to a worthy condition. Baby could be sweet as sugar one day and a raging foul-tempered bitch the next, he'd told Dan, but she was fast and nimble and her shallow draft was ideal for the bayous. Anyway, he loved her.

"Takin' us in there," Train said, motioning with a lift of his chin toward another channel that wound off to the left. "Gonna get tight, so tell the lady if she hear some thumps, we ain't gonna wind us up ass-deep and sinkin'."

Dan went back to relay the message. Train steered Baby into the channel with a steady hand and a sharp eye. Tree branches scraped along the sides and half-submerged reeds and swamp grass parted before the prow. Overhead the trees thickened, cutting the light to a dark green murk. The Swift was slowing down now to the speed of a man's walk, and Train came out of the pilothouse and picked up a rope with one end secured to the starboard deck and at the throwing end an iron grappling-hook. The boat shuddered, something bumping along the keel. Train threw the hook into the underbrush, pulled hard on the rope, and it went taut. In another few seconds Baby eased to a stop.

They got ready. Dan was sweating in the fierce wet heat, but he wasn't afraid. Maybe just a little. In any case, the job had to be done.

"Leave the pistol here," Train said as Dan took it from the locker. "She might be gonna need it."

"*Me?*" Arden stood up. "I've never fired a gun in my life!"

"Ever'ting got a number-one time." Train popped a clip into the automatic. "I'm gonna tell you 'bout this safety catch here, so you pay a mind. You get you'self a caller while we gone, only two fellas to save you neck be Mr. Smith and Mr. Wesson. Ay?"

Arden decided it would be very wise to pay close attention.

"Take t'ree reloads. We need more'n that, we gonna be haulin' butt," Train told Dan after Arden's quick lesson was done. Dan took three of the Browning's box magazines from the backpack, put one in each front pocket and the third in a back pocket. Train did the same with the Ruger's ammo, then he put on a gray-and-green camouflage-print cap. " 'Bout quarter-mile from here, them fellas be," he said as he slung the Ruger barrel-down to his right shoulder so water wouldn't foul the firing mechanism. "They got guns enough to blow the horns off Satan: rifle, shotgun, machine gun, ever' damn kinda gun. So from here on we mighty careful or we mighty dead."

While Dan strapped on the Browning rifle, also barrel-down, Train opened a jar of what looked like black grease and streaked some under his eyes. "Don't want no glare blindin' you when it come time to take a shot. You miss—*poof!* That's all she wrote." He handed the grease to Dan, who applied it in the same fashion. Then Train got his face right up in Dan's, his eyes piercing. "We get in a knock-ass firefight, am I gonna can count on you? You gonna stick it to 'em, no second thought? By the time you got second thought, you be twice dead. Ay?"

"I'll do what I have to," Dan said.

"They got a man spyin' for 'em in a tower, up where he can see the Gulf and the bayou one turn 'round. They got a big metal gate blockin' the bayou, and a bob wire fence 'round the whole place." He nodded toward the forbidding wilderness, thick with spiky palmettos, hanging vines, and cypress trees. "We gonna go through there. Ain't got no serpent-bite kit, so keep both them eyeballs lookin'."

"I will."

"If we see us two dead bodies layin' out, we comin' straight back quiet as sinners on Sunday. Then I make a radio call to Gran' Isle. Okay?"

"Yeah."

Train eased over the transom and lowered himself into the water. The swamp consumed him to the middle of his chest.

"Dan?" Arden said as he started to go over. Again her tangled emotions got in the way of her voice. "Please be careful," she managed to say.

"I was wrong to let you come. You should've stayed at Train's place."

She shook her head. "I'm where I need to be. You just worry about gettin' in and back."

Dan went into the water, his shoes sinking through three inches of mud.

"Listen up," Train told Arden. "You might gonna hear some shootin'. We don't come back half-hour after them shots, we ain't comin'. Radio's up on a shelf over the wheel. Got a fresh battery, you'll see the turn-on switch. We don't come back, you need to start callin' for he'p on the mike. Turn through them frequencies and keep callin'. That don't bring nobody, you got the water jug, the pistol, and you two legs. Ay?"

"Yes."

"Just so you know." Train turned away and started moving.

Dan paused, looking up at Arden's face. The deep-purple birthmark was no longer ugly, he thought. It was like the unique pattern of a butterfly's wings, or the color and markings of a seashell never to be exactly duplicated again in a thousand years.

"I'll be back," he said, and he followed Train through the morass.

When they'd gotten out of Arden's earshot, Train said quietly, "Them fellas kill us, they gonna find her, too, eventual. What they'll do I ain't gonna think on."

Dan didn't answer. He'd already thought of that.

"Just so you know," Train said.

They waded on, and in another moment the wilderness had closed between them and Baby.

Nasty brown water had flooded Flint's eyes and mouth, choking off his shout of terror. Pelvis was flailing beside him, insanely trying to get across the 'gator corral at the man who'd chewed Mama's flesh. Flint felt Clint's arm thrash, his brother's bones squirming violently inside his body. The thought of Clint's infant-size lungs drawing in water and drowning opened a nightmarish door on gruesome possibilities. He started fighting to get his balance as he'd never fought in his life. He got his legs under him, and his shoes found a bottom of mud and mess that could be described only as gooshy.

He stood up. His head and shoulders were out of the water. Still,

Clint was trapped below. Pelvis was standing up, too, his muddy wig hanging on by its last piece of flesh-colored tape, a strangled, enraged scream shredding his throat. With a surge of power that Flint had never dreamed the man possessed, Pelvis starting dragging him through the water to reach the pier.

Monty was laughing fit to bust a gut. "It's show time, boys!" he hollered toward the house.

Flint stepped on something that exploded to life under his feet and scared the pee out of him. A scaly form whipped past them, its tail thrashing. The tail of a second alligator slapped Pelvis's shoulder, and he grunted with pain but kept on going. All around them the pond was a maelstrom of reptiles fighting for the meat and bones Monty had just thrown in. Flint saw one of them coming from the left, its snout plowing through the foam and its catslit eyes fixed on him. Even as Pelvis kept hauling him, Flint struck out with his unhindered left arm at the thing, which looked large enough to make two suitcases and a handbag. He struck the surface in front of its snout, but the splash was enough to make it wheel away, its tail whacking muddy water into the air. Then Pelvis was hit at the knees by an underwater beast and he was knocked off his feet, the alligator's barklike flesh coming up from the depths for an instant, which was long enough for the crazed Pelvis to give a bellow and pound at it with his free fist. The startled reptile skittered away with a snort, pushing a small wave before it. With his feet under him again, Pelvis dragged Flint onward.

Two of the beasts were going at it fang to fang over a chunk of meat, their noisy combat drawing the attention of four or five others. A battle royal erupted, the monsters fighting on all sides of Pelvis and Flint. But more alligators were rising up from the bottom, and others were speeding in to graze past them as if to test how dangerous this particular food might be before they committed their jaws to a bite. Pelvis was single-mindedly pulling Flint toward the pier, while Flint was doing everything he could to keep the alligators away: kicking, slapping the water with the flat of his hand, and shouting gibberish.

But now the alligators were getting bolder. Flint managed to jerk the shoe from his right foot, and he used that to hammer the surface. And suddenly a horrible, thick body with gray mollusks clinging to its hide erupted from the water beside him, a pair of jaws wide open and hissing. Flint slammed his shoe down across the alligator's skull, going for an eye, and the jaws snapped shut. The head whipped to one side and its rough scales flayed the skin off his left arm from wrist to elbow. A mollusk's shell or some growth with a sharp edge did its work as well, and suddenly there was blood in the water.

"Get 'em out! Get 'em out, goddamn it!" somebody shouted.

They had reached the pier's end, which was three feet above the pond. Pelvis, his wig gone and his contorted face brown with mud, was trying to grip the timbers and pull himself up, but not even his maddened strength could do it with Flint on the other cuff. Blood floated on the surface around Flint's arm, and he saw at least four alligators coming across the corral after them, their tails sweeping back and forth with eager delight.

26

To the Edge

There was the racket of an electric motor and a chain rattling. "Grab it! Both of you, grab it!"

The winch's hook and chain had been lowered. Pelvis and Flint clung to its oversize links as a beggar might grasp hundred-dollar bills. The motor growled, and the chain began to hoist them up.

Hands caught them, pulling them onto the pier. Below Flint's muddy shoe and sock, three alligators slammed their snouts together. They started fighting in the blood-pink foam, and as their bodies hit the pilings the entire pier trembled and groaned.

But now Flint and Pelvis had solid wood under their feet. Flint could smell his blood; it was coming from a blue-edged gash across his left forearm and dripping from his hand to the planks. He staggered, about to pass out, and he found himself clutching Pelvis for support. Through a haze he looked at the choppy pond and saw two alligators battling for something between their jaws that appeared to be a mud-caked, scruffy bird. It took him a few seconds to realize it was Pelvis's wig. He watched with a kind of strange fascination as the two monsters ripped it apart and then each of them submerged with a souvenir of Memphis.

His chest heaving, Pelvis stared slack-jawed at the faces of Doc, Monty, Mitch, and two other men he didn't recognize. Doc was wearing his sunglasses again.

"Crazy as hell, man!" Doc was blasting Monty. "I don't want 'em dead till he sees 'em!"

"Well, shit!" Monty fired back. "How was I supposed to know they were fool enough to jump outta the—"

Flint had felt Pelvis's body tense. He thought of a hurricane about to wreak death and destruction.

Pelvis pulled back his right fist and then drove it forward like a fleshy piston into Monty's nose. With a gunshot *pop* of breaking

761

bones the blood spewed from Monty's nostrils all over Doc's Harvard T-shirt.

Monty staggered back, his eyes wide and amazed and the blood running into his beard as if from a faucet. One step. Two steps.

And into the corral, right on top of the reptiles fighting below the end of the pier.

"Oh, Jesus!" Doc shouted, blood on the lenses of his sunglasses and spotting his cheeks.

"Monty!" Mitch hollered, and he ran to operate the hook and chain.

But the sense had been knocked out of Monty, and maybe that was for the best because he might have been unaware exactly of his position. One of the other men Pelvis hadn't recognized drew a pistol and started shooting at the alligators, but they had already taken hold of Monty, one with jaws crunched into his left shoulder and another gripping his right leg. The winch's chain came down, but Monty didn't reach for it. The alligators started shaking him the way Pelvis had seen Mama shake one of her teddy bears. He recalled, in his dim cell of thinking at the moment, that the stuffing had come out everywhere.

So, too, it was with Monty.

Now Mitch had pulled his pistol and was firing, too, but the taste of blood and living meat had driven the creatures to a frenzy. More of them were racing over for a share. During the shooting, amid the thrashing bodies and the gory splashing, at least two bullets went into Monty. Maybe he was dead before his bones started to rip from their sockets. Maybe.

Doc didn't want to see any more. He'd known Monty was finished when he went in there, bleeding like that and with the 'gators already so riled up. He'd seen them go after the ranger, so he'd known. He turned away, removed his dark glasses, and slowly and methodically began to wipe the blood off the lenses with a clean part of his T-shirt. His fingers were trembling. Behind him Mitch threw up into the corral.

"Bummer," Doc said, mostly to himself.

He took the handcuff key from his pocket. He unlocked the cuffs and let them fall. Pelvis blinked at him, still dazed but his fury spent. Flint grasped his injured arm and then pitched to his knees, his head hanging.

Doc reached back, drew the .45 from his waistband, cocked it, and laid the barrel between Pelvis's eyes. "You're next," he said. "Walk to the edge."

Pelvis was already brain-blasted; seeing that man eat Mama for breakfast had done him in. He knew what was waiting for him, but without Mama—without his adored companion—life wasn't worth living. He walked to the edge.

Below him was something the alligators were still tearing at. It was getting smaller and smaller. It had a beard.

Doc stood behind him and put the automatic's barrel against the back of his naked head.

"Do it!" Mitch urged. "Put him down!"

Flint tried to stand, but he could not. He was near fainting, the smell of blood and mud and 'gator filth was making him sick, the harsh, hot sun had drained him. He said, "Eisley?" but that was all he could say. He hadn't felt Clint move since they'd come out of the water, but now the arm gave a feeble jerk and Clint's little lungs heaved like a hiccup deep in the folds and passages of Flint's intestines.

Doc put his other hand up to shield his face from flying bits of bone and brain matter. His finger tightened on the trigger.

He heard a gurgling noise.

He looked around, and saw brown water trickling from the mouth on the bizarre baby head that grew from the freak's side.

Flint heard boots clumping on the pier. There was the sound of bare feet on the planks as well.

Doc saw who was coming. He said, "Takin' care of business, Gault. Shondra don't need to see this."

"What's goin' on?" Flint heard a woman's irritated voice ask. A young woman, she sounded to be. "Noise woke us the fuck up. Who was hollerin' so much?"

"Shondra, you best stay put. Monty went in."

The slide of bare feet stopped, but the boots kept walking.

"Bastard here killed him!" Mitch said. "Doc was fixin' to blow his brains out!"

"These are the two from the marina." Doc was talking to whoever wore the boots. "This one got me in the eyes with the spray. One over there shot Virgil."

The boots approached Flint. They stopped beside him, and Flint lifted his head and saw they were made of bleached beige snakeskin.

"Dig that third arm, man. Got a little baby head growin' out his ribs, too. Gen-yoo-ine freak from freak city. I ain't seen nothin' like him since I ate a bag of magic mushrooms in Yuma, spring of 'sixty-eight. Damn, those were the days!"

763

Shondra gave an ugly snorting sound. "I wasn't even born then."

Doc might have laughed through clenched teeth.

With an effort Flint looked up at the man in the snakeskin boots. The individual was an exercise junkie. Or a steroid freak. Or maybe he just loved himself a whole lot. Because the muscles of his exposed chest, shoulders, and arms were massive swollen lumps that strained against the tanned flesh, the connecting veins standing out in blood-pumped relief, the visible ligaments as tight as bundles of piano wire. The man wore blue jeans with ripped-out knees, a piece of rope for a belt cinching his narrow waist, and he had a red neckerchief tied loosely around his throat. His face was a hard, chiseled slab of brown rock with a dagger-sharp chin and sunken cheeks, the facial flesh cracked with a hundred deep lines caused by what must have been years of serious sun-worship. The pure ebony of his commanding eyes, his thick black brows, and his curly black hair, the sides swirled with gray, gave him a distinctive Latin appearance. Flint guessed his age at late thirties or early forties, but it was difficult to tell since his body was young but his face was sun-wrinkled.

Standing several yards behind him was a blond girl who couldn't have been older than twenty. She was barefoot, wearing denim cutoffs and a black bra. She, too, appeared to be a slave to the sun, because she was burned a darker brown than the man. Her golden hair cascaded over her shoulders and she had icy blue eyes. Flint thought she was almost beautiful, as beautiful as any Hollywood starlet, but there was an ugly, twisted set to her collagen-plumped lips, and those eyes could burn a hole through metal.

And right now he felt like a little crumpled piece of tin.

The muscle man stared down at Flint with just a hint of interest, as if he might be viewing a particularly creepy insect, but no more than that. Shondra spoke first. "Damn, Gault! Look how *white* he is!"

Gault motioned at Doc with a twirling forefinger. Doc understood the command and lowered the automatic, then said, "Turn around!" to Pelvis.

Pelvis did, his eyes deep-socketed and his face and bald head still painted with ghastly mud.

"This is the fucker thought he was Elvis Presley," Doc said.

Gault's face remained impassive.

"You know who they are? Bounty hunters. Can you believe it? From Shreveport. They had a guy in cuffs back there at St. Nasty. Said at the marina they were callin' the man they work for. Anyway, they were takin' their prisoner in to get a reward. I set the guy loose, figured it was my good deed for the month."

Gault's eyes went to Flint and returned to Pelvis.

"I thought you'd want to see 'em, 'specially the freak. Do you want me to kill 'em now, or what?"

Gault's jaws tensed; muscles that seemed as big as lemons popped up on his face and then receded again. At last his mouth opened. His teeth were unnaturally white. "How much," he said in a voice that had no discernible accent but perfect diction, "were they planning on earning as their reward?"

"Fifteen thousand."

Gault's face settled into stone again. Then, very suddenly, he laughed without smiling. When he did smile, it was a scary thing. He laughed a little louder. "Fifteen thousand!" he said, obviously finding the figure an object of humor. "Fifteen thousand dollars, is that all?" He kept laughing, only it became a low and dangerous sound, like a knife being sharpened. He looked at Shondra and laughed, and she started laughing, then he looked at Doc and laughed and Doc started laughing. Pretty soon it was a real laff riot.

Flint, grasping his wounded forearm and blood still oozing through his fingers, said, "Mind tellin' us what the hell's so funny?"

Gault laughed on for a moment longer, then his smile was abruptly eclipsed. He said, "The pitiful amount of cash that a human being will throw his life away in pursuit of." He reached into a pocket of his jeans with his right hand. Flint heard something click like a trigger being cocked, and he steeled himself for the worst. Then Gault's hand emerged holding one of those spring-loaded wrist exercisers, which he began to squeeze over and over again. "If a man should die, he should die for riches, not petty change. Or for forbidden knowledge. That might be worth dying for. But fifteen thousand dollars? Ha." The laugh was very quiet. "I don't think so." *Click . . . click . . . click* went the springs.

"I don't know what's goin' on here. I don't *care*," Flint said. "Nobody would've gotten hurt if that goon hadn't tried to drown me in a toilet bowl."

Gault nodded thoughtfully. "Tell me," he said. "You were born the way you are, yes? You had no control over the way your chromosomes came together, or how the cells grew. You had no control over your genetics, or what quirk back in your family line caused your situation." He paused for emphasis. "No control," he repeated, as if seeing to the heart of Flint's pain. "You must know, better than anyone could, that God set up tides and winds, and sometimes they take you one way and then blow you the other, and you have no control. I think a tide took you to that marina, and a wind blew you here. What's your name again?"

"His name's Murtaugh," Doc said. "The other one's Eisley."

"I didn't ask you." Gault stared fixedly at the Harvard man. "I asked him. Didn't I?"

Doc said nothing, but he looked stung. He pushed the .45 back into his waistband with the air of a petulant child. "My shows are on. You want me, I'll be watchin' my shows." He trudged back along the pier toward the area that was shaded by the blue-and-white-striped awning. As Doc passed her, Shondra wrinkled her nose as if she smelled something bad.

Gault walked to the pier's edge, where Pelvis still stood. He looked down at what the alligators were whittling to the size of a wallet. His hand worked: *click . . . click . . . click.* Sinews were standing out in the wrist. "All the mysteries, spilled out," he said. His other hand pressed against Pelvis's chest. Pelvis flinched; the man's fingers seemed cold. "Monty always was a glutton. Now look how thin he is. You know, you could stand to lose some weight yourself."

"All right, that's enough." Flint clenched his teeth and tried to stand up. He couldn't make it the first time. He saw Gault grinning at him. Mitch stepped forward and aimed his pistol at Flint's head, but Gault said, "No, no! Let him alone!"

Flint stood up. Staggered, almost fell again. Then he had his balance. It was time to face ugly reality. "If you're gonna kill us—which I guess you are—then how about doin' it humanely?"

The clicking of the springs had ceased. "Are you begging, Mr. Murtaugh?"

"No. I'm askin'." He glanced distastefully at the corral. "A bullet in the head for both of us, how about that?"

"You mean you're not going to stall for time? Try to hold out false hope? Or tell me if I let you go you'll never, never, never speak of this to any soul on earth?"

"It's hot," Flint said. "I'm tired, and I'm about to fall down. I'm not gonna play games with you."

"Don't care to gamble that I might be in a lenient mood today?" Gault lifted his eyebrows.

Flint didn't answer. Don't bite! he told himself. He wants you to bite so he can kick you in the teeth.

"Maybe you're a New Ager?" Gault asked. "You believe in reincarnation, so your death today would be just another rung on the cosmic ladder?"

"I believe in re'carnation," Shondra said. "Gault and me were lovers in . . . you know, that old city that got swallowed up in the sea?"

"Atlantis," Gault supplied. He winked quickly at Flint. "Works every time."

Flint licked his parched lips. "How about some water for us?"

"Oh, I'm forgetting my manners. I was raised better than that. Come on, then. Time for my workout anyway. Shondra, go to the kitchen and get them a pitcher of ice water. Bring me a protein shake. Chop chop." She hurried off obediently, and then Gault motioned for them to follow and started walking toward the awning-shaded area. Flint was weak from his wound and the heat, but he took hold of Pelvis's elbow. "Hang on, all right?" Pelvis, in a state of shock, allowed Flint to guide him after the clumping snakeskin boots, and the other men, their pistols drawn, followed behind.

"Non," Train whispered as he lowered the Ruger, "can't get no clean shot off. Wouldn't he'p 'em none if I could. We gonna have to move in closer."

Dan's heart was slamming, but his mind was calm. He and Train were standing in the chest-deep water seventy yards from the fenced-in alligator corral, at the edge of where the swamp's vegetation had been hacked away. They had gotten over a barbed-wire fence in the water thirty yards behind them, and their hands were cut up some but they would heal. It had been a difficult slog from the Swift boat; Dan felt his strength ebbing fast, but he had to keep pushing himself onward. His father, the quitter, had not raised a quitter.

They'd come out of the underbrush in time to see Flint and Eisley standing on the pier with men holding guns and the muscular, shirtless "boss" Train had spotted on his last visit there. Dan had seen that both the bounty hunters were covered with mud, Eisley had lost his wig, and an aluminum rowboat floated at the center of the 'gator corral. No telling what they'd been through, but at least they were alive. How long that would be was uncertain. Flint and Eisley had just followed the muscle man toward the house, with the other men—the pistol-bearing "soldiers"—behind them.

"Fella up in that watchtower, leanin' back in his chair readin' a . . . ohhhhh, that naughty fella, him!" Train had aimed the Ruger and was looking through the 'scope. "Got a rifle to his side. Walk'em-talk'em on the floor. Pair of binocs." He took his eye away from the lens. "We gonna have to cross the open, get us around that 'gator pen."

767

"Right."

"Might try to circle 'round the house. Get up on the platform in back. You with me?"

"Yeah."

"Okay. We go, slow and quiet."

"Hey, Gault!" Doc called from his lounge chair in front of a large color television set on metal casters. "Look what's on Oprah today! Talkin' 'bout crack in the grade schools!"

"Chicago?" Gault didn't look at the screen. He was busy pumping iron: a thirty-pound barbell in each hand, his biceps swelling up, veins moving under the skin. A light sheen of sweat glistened on his chest and face.

"No, she's in Atlanta this week."

"The Samchuk brothers'll have that market cornered in three years." Gault kept lifting the barbells up and down with the precision of a machine. "If the Jamaicans don't kill them first."

Sitting a few feet away at a wrought-iron table with a blue glass top, a bloody towel pressed to his forearm wound, Flint had a flash of understanding. "Is that what this is about? Drugs?"

"My business," Gault said. "I supply a demand. It's no big thing."

They were on the platform under the striped awning. Pelvis was sitting across the table from Flint, his hands held to his face. In more chairs arranged around Flint and Pelvis sat Mitch and the two other men with pistols. A walkie-talkie and an Ingram machine gun sat on a white coffee table in front of a sand-colored sofa, along with copies of *House Beautiful*, *Vogue*, and *Soldier of Fortune* magazines. Flint had seen on closer inspection Gault's own house was not so beautiful; it was a prefab job, and the swamp's humidity had warped the walls like damp cardboard. Some of the joints were splitting apart and had been reinforced with strips of duct tape. *Click . . . click . . . click:* the sound wasn't coming from Gault's squeeze-grip, but from the remote control in Doc's hand. In the five minutes they'd been sitting here, Flint had watched Doc almost incessantly going through what must be hundreds of channels brought in by the satellite dish. Doc would pause to watch quick fragments of things like Mexican game shows, "F Troop," "The Outer Limits," professional wrestling, infomercials with a manic little Englishman running around a studio selling cleaning products, "The Flintstones," MTV videos, ranting, wild-eyed preachers, soap operas, and then the remote control would click rapidly again like the noise of a feeding locust. At the most, Doc had a seven-second attention span.

Flint eased the towel away from his wound and winced at the sight. The gash was four inches long, its ragged blue edges in need of fifty or sixty stitches. An inch and a half lower and an artery would have been nicked. Thick blood was still oozing, and he pressed the towel—which Gault had given him from a hamper beside a rack of free weights back against the wound.

Doc said, "Hey! It's your man, Flinty! Gault, that's the killer I let go!"

Flint looked at the television set. Doc had paused at CNN to watch gas bombs dispelling a prison riot, and on the screen was either a mug shot or driver's license photo of Dan Lambert. "That's him, right?" He turned the volume up with the remote.

". . . bizarre turn in the case of Daniel Lewis Lambert, who is being sought in the slaying of a Shreveport, Louisiana, bank loan manager and had also been wanted in connection with the death of an Alexandria motel owner. Under questioning by Alexandria police last night, the slain man's wife admitted it was actually *she* who had beaten her husband to death." A mug shot of a sullen-looking woman with wild red hair came up on the screen. "Hannah DeCayne told police—"

"*Boring!*" Doc changed the channel.

"Wait!" Flint said. "Turn it back!"

"Screw you." "Star Trek" was on now, Kirk and Spock speaking in dubbed Spanish. "Beam me up, Sccccottie!" Doc said excitedly, talking to the television set.

Flint figured the remote control in Doc's head never stopped clicking. He stared at the blue glass of the tabletop, this news another little ice pick from God in the back of his neck. If Lambert had been telling the truth about the motel owner, then was the murder at the bank an accident or an act of self-defense? If Lambert was such a mad-dog killer, why hadn't he picked up the pistol and used it at Basile Park? In spite of the situation, in spite of the fact that he knew he and Pelvis were going to die in some excruciating way after Gault finished his workout, Flint had to laugh. He was going to die because he'd gone south hunting a skin who was basically a decent man.

"Something's funny?" Gault asked, his labor ceasing for the moment.

"Yeah, it is." Flint laughed again; he felt on the verge of tears, but he laughed anyway. "I think the joke's on me, too."

"Who the *fuck* messed up the kitchen?" Shondra, looking both angry and more than a bit queasy, came through an open sliding glass door, carrying a tray with a plastic pitcher, two paper cups, and frothy brown liquid in a milk-shake glass. She set the tray down between Flint and Pelvis. "There's all kinda guts and hair in the garbage can, 'bout made me puke! Blood smeared all over the countertop, and somebody left the fryin' pan dirty! Who the hell did it?"

"Monty," Mitch said. Evidently Shondra's wrath was a thing to be feared.

"Well, what'd he fry? A fuckin' polecat?"

"Fella's dog there." Mitch pointed at Pelvis.

Another one?" Shondra made a disgusted face. "What's wrong with that fool, he's gotta be eatin' dogs and 'coons and polecats?"

"Go ask him, why don't you?" Doc had torn his eyes away from the television. "I'm tryin' to watch 'Dragnet,' if you'll keep it down!"

"You're not watchin' anything, you're just burnin' out that clicker! Gault, why don't you get rid of him? He makes me so nervous, I'm like to jump outta my skin every time he opens that dumb mouth!"

"Yeah?" Doc sneered. "Well, I know the only thing that has to get stuck in your dumb mouth to shut you up! I was with Gault long before you came along, girlie pearlie, and when he throws you out, I'm gonna kick your little ass back to your white-trash trailer!"

"You . . . you . . . you *old man!*" Shondra hollered, and she picked up the milk-shake glass and reared her arm back, froth flying.

"No," Gault said quietly, pumping iron again. "Not that."

She slammed the glass down on the tray, her face a pure image of hell, picked up the plastic pitcher, and flung it at Doc, water splashing everywhere.

"Look what she did!" Doc squalled. "She's tryin' to blow the TV out, Gault!"

"And I'm not cleanin' up that damn mess, neither!" she roared at all of them. "I'm not cartin' that damn stinkin' garbage out and gettin' that mess on me!" Tears of rage and frustration burst from her eyes. "You hear? I'm not doin' it!" She turned and, sobbing, fled back into the house.

"Your Academy Award's in the mail, baby!" Doc shouted after her.

Gault stopped lifting the barbells and put them on the floor. He looked at Flint, smiled wanly, and said with a shrug of his thick shoulders, "Trouble in paradise." Then he drank half of the protein shake, blotted the sweat from his face with the red neckerchief, and said, "Brian, go take the garbage out and clean the kitchen."

"Why do I have to do it?" Brian had neatly cut light brown hair, wore steel-rimmed glasses, and a chrome-plated revolver sat in a holster at his waist. He looked about as old as a college senior, wearing a sun-faded madras shirt and khaki shorts, black Nikes on his feet.

"Because you're the new boy, and because I say so."

"Heh-heh-heh," giggled the Latino man sitting next to him; he wore a Yosemite Sam T-shirt and dirty jeans, his blue-steel Colt automatic in a black shoulder holster.

"You want to laugh, Carlos, you go laugh while you're moppin' the kitchen floor," Gault said. Carlos started to protest, but Gault gave him a deadly stare. "Move *now*."

The two men went into the house without another word.

"I wouldn't let that bitch snow me," Doc said.

"Shut up about her." Gault finished his shake. "I wish you two would bury the hatchet."

"Yeah, she'll bury a hatchet in me if I don't bury one in her first."

"Children, children." Gault shook his head, then he crossed his swollen arms and stared at the two bounty hunters. "Well," he said, "I guess we need to take care of business. What would you think if I'd offer to cut your tongues out and chop your hands off? Would you rather be dead, or not?" He looked at Clint's arm. "In your case, it would be a triple amputation. How does that sound?"

"I think I might faint with excitement," Flint said. Pelvis was mute, his eyes shiny and unfocused.

"It's the best offer I can make. See, I told you I was in a lenient mood. Doc's the one who screwed things up."

"I'll be glad to cut his tongue out and chop off his hands," Flint said.

Gault didn't smile. "Forbidden-knowledge time: we've been having trouble from a competitor. His name is Victor Medina. We were trucking some merchandise in crates when we first moved our base here. He found out the route and took it away from us. So we had to come up with alternative packaging. The stomachs of live alligators do very well."

"I came up with that idea!" Doc announced.

"When Doc saw you making your phone call," Gault went on, "he—unfortunately—lost his composure. He thought you might've been working with Medina, setting up another hijack. Doc doesn't always reason things out. He was stupid, he was wrong, and I apologize. But you put a valuable man out of action. A knee injury like that . . . well, there's no health insurance in this business. A doctor would get very suspicious, and we would have a money leak. So Virgil, like a good horse, was laid to rest and you are to blame. Now Monty is gone. I have to hire new people, run them through security, train them . . . it's a pain. So." He walked to the coffee table and picked up the Ingram machine gun. "I *will* make it quick. Stand up."

"Stand us up yourself," Flint told him.

"No problem. Doc? Mitch?"

"Shit!" Doc whined. " 'The Flying Nun's just started!" But he got out of his chair, pulled his gun, and Mitch likewise stood up with a pistol in his hand. Doc hauled Flint to his feet but Mitch struggled with Pelvis and Gault had to help him.

There was fresh sweat on Gault's face. "End of the pier," he said.

27

Too Damn Hot

"There, we get up," Train said as he waded chest-deep toward a walkway at the rear of the prefabricated ranch house. Dan followed, not mired quite so deeply as Train because of their difference in heights, but he was giving out and he envied Train's rugged strength. Train slid his rifle up on the walkway, then grabbed the timbers and heaved himself out of the water. He took Dan's Browning and gave him a hand up.

"You all right?" Train had seen the dark circles under Dan's eyes, and he knew it had been a rough trek but the other man was fading fast.

"I'll make it."

"You sick, ain't you." Train wasn't asking a question.

"Leukemia," Dan said. "I can't do it like I used to."

"Hell, who can?" They were standing about eight feet from the rear entrance, which was a solid wooden door behind a screen door. The rear of the house was featureless except for a few small windows. Back here the platform was narrow, but it widened as it continued around the house. Train looked along the walkway they stood on. Behind them was more swamp and a large green metal incinerator on a platform fifty feet from the house. "Okay," Train said. "Look like this the way we go—"

He stopped abruptly. They heard voices from beyond the doors, getting closer. Someone was coming out. Train pressed his body against the wall ten feet away on the right of the door and Dan stood an equal distance away on the left, their rifles ready. Dan's heart pounded, all the saliva dried up in his mouth.

The inner door opened. "Yeah, but I'm not stayin' in the business that long." A young man wearing wire-rimmed glasses, a madras shirt, and khaki shorts emerged, both arms around a Rubbermaid garbage can. On the side of it were streaks of what looked like blood. "I'm gonna make my cash and get out while I can." He let the outer screen door slam shut at his back and he started walking toward the incinerator, a pistol in a holster at his waist.

Train was thinking whether to rush him and club at him with the rifle's butt or push through the screen door when the young man suddenly stopped.

He was looking down at the walkway. At the water and mud on the planks where they'd pulled themselves up. Then he saw the footprints.

And that, as Dan knew Train would've said, was all she wrote.

He spun around. Sunlight flared on his glasses for an instant. His mouth was opening, and then he was dropping the garbage can to go for his gun. "Carlos!" he yelled. "There's somebody out he—"

Train shot him before the pistol could clear leather. The bullet hit him in the center of his chest and he jerked like a marionette and was propelled off the walkway into the water.

A startled Latino face appeared at the screen. The inner door slammed shut. Then: *pop pop pop* went a pistol from inside, and three bullets punched holes through wood and screen. Train started shooting through the door, burning off four more shells. As Train wrenched the magazine out and pushed another one in, Dan fired twice more through the punctured doors, and then Train rushed in and with a kick knocked them both off their hinges.

"Gault! Gault!" the man named Carlos shouted. He had overthrown a kitchen table and was crouched behind it, his pistol aimed at the intruders. Train saw the table, and then a bullet knocked wood from the doorjamb beside his head and he twisted his body and threw himself against the outside wall again. A second shot cracked, the bullet tearing through the air where Train had stood an instant before. "Gault!" Carlos was screaming it now. "They're breakin' in!"

At the sound of the first shot Gault stopped in his snakeskin boots.

He knew what it had been. No doubt.

"Rifle!" Doc said. They were all standing about midway between the awning-shaded area and the alligator corral.

Pop pop pop went a pistol.

"It's Medina!" Mitch shouted. "The bastard's found us!"

"Shut up!" Gault heard more rifle shots. Carlos was shouting his name from the house. His face like a dark and wrinkled skull, Gault turned around and put the Ingram gun's barrel to Flint's throat.

"Gault!" Carlos screamed. "They're breakin' in!"

Two seconds passed. Gault blinked, and Flint saw him deciding to save his ammo for the big boys. "Mitch, stay here with them! Doc, let's go!" They turned and ran along the pier for the house. Mitch leveled his pistol at Flint's chest, just above Clint's arm.

Another pistol bullet thunked into the doorjamb. Train had sweat on his face. Dan shoved his rifle in and fired without aiming, the slug smashing glass. Carlos got off two more rapid-fire shots and then his nerve broke. He stood up and, howling in fear, left the relative safety of his makeshift shield to run for the kitchen door. He was almost there when he slipped on a smear of dog's blood on the linoleum tiles and at the same time Train shot at him. The bullet smacked into the wall as Carlos fell. Carlos twisted around, his gun coming up. Dan pulled the Browning's trigger, blood burst from Carlos's side, and he doubled up and writhed on the floor. As Train ran into the kitchen and kicked Carlos's pistol away, Dan pulled the empty magazine from his rifle and popped in another one.

The next room held a dining table and chairs, a jaguar's skin up as a wall decoration, and a small chandelier hanging from the ceiling over the table's center. A hallway went off to the left, and another room with a pool table and three pinball machines was on the right. Train and Dan started across the dining room, and suddenly Dan caught a movement and a dark-tanned blond girl wearing cutoffs and a black bra emerged from the hallway. Her icy blue eyes were puffy and furious. She lifted her right hand, and in it was gripped an automatic pistol. She let go an unintelligible, hair-raising screech and Train was swinging his rifle at her when the automatic fired twice, booming between the walls. The first bullet shattered glass in one of the pinball machines, but the second brought a cry from Train.

Train's rifle went off, the bullet breaking a window beside the blond girl. Dan had his finger on the trigger and the gun leveled at her, but the idea of killing a woman crippled him for the fastest of seconds. Then the girl scurried back into the hallway again, her hair streaming behind her.

Everything was moving in a blur, time jerking and stretching, the smell of burnt rounds and fear like bitter almonds in the smoky air. Train's cap had fallen off, and he staggered against the wall with his left hand clutched to his right side and blood between his fingers. There was a shout: "Jesus, it's that damn guy!"

Dan saw that two men had come into the game room through another doorway. One he recognized as the long-haired man named Doc, the other was a tanned bodybuilder who had a walkie-talkie in one hand and an Ingram machine gun in the other. Before the

muscle man could aim and fire, Dan sent two bullets at them but
Doc had already flung himself flat to the floor and at the sight of the
rifle the second man—the "boss," Dan remembered Train saying-
hurtled behind the pool table.

It was getting too damn hot.

"Go back!" Dan shouted to Train, but Train had seen the Ingram
gun and he was already retreating. They both scrambled through
the kitchen's entryway two heartbeats before the Ingram gun
chattered and the woodwork around the door exploded into flying
shards and splinters.

Mitch jumped when he heard the distinctive noise of Gault's gun.
He had moved Flint and Pelvis so they were between him and the
house, his back to the swamp and the bounty hunters facing him.
Flint had seen Gault snatch the walkie-talkie off the coffee table and
yell something into it, and then the man in the watchtower—the
same one, Flint realized, who'd half strangled him at St. Nasty and
had taken the derringer away—had strapped his rifle around his
shoulder and started descending a ladder. Now the man was just
reaching the walkway between the tower and the house.

Mitch was scared to death. Beads of sweat trickled down his face,
his hand with the revolver in it shaking. He kept glancing back and
forth from the bounty hunters to the house, wincing at the sounds
of shots.

Pelvis suddenly gasped harshly and put a hand to his chest.
Mitch's pistol trained on him.

Oh my God! Flint thought. He's havin' another attack!

But Pelvis was looking at something past Mitch's shoulder, his
eyes widening. He let out a bawling holler: *"Don't shoot us!"*

Even as Flint realized that was the oldest trick in the book and it
could never work in a million years, the terrified Mitch swung
around and fired a shot at brown water and moss-covered trees.

Pelvis slammed his fist into the side of Mitch's head and was
suddenly all over the man like black on tar. Stunned, Flint just stood
there, watching Pelvis beat on him with one flailing fist while the
other hand trapped Mitch's gun. Then the revolver went off again,
its barrel aimed downward, and Flint got his legs moving and his
fists, too. He attacked Mitch with grim fury. Mitch went down on
his knees, his facial features somewhat rearranged. Pelvis kept
hammering at the man like someone chopping firewood. Mitch's
fingers opened, and Flint took the pistol.

Footsteps on the planks. Someone running toward them.

Flint looked, his pulse racing, and there was the man from the watchtower unslinging his rifle. The man, a wiry little bastard in overalls, stopped thirty feet away and fired his rifle from the hip. Flint heard the sound of an angry hornet zip past him. Then it was Flint's turn.

The first bullet missed. The second struck the man in the left shoulder, and the third got him a few inches below the heart. The man's rifle had gotten crooked in his arms, and now his finger spasmed on the trigger and a slug smashed the windshield of one of the cigarette speedboats. Then the man went down on his back on the planks, his legs still moving as if trying to outdistance death. Flint didn't fire the last bullet in the gun. In his mouth was the sharp, acidic taste of corruption; he'd never killed a man before, and it was an awful thing.

Now, however, was not the time to fall on his knees and beg forgiveness. He saw that Pelvis's fists had made raw hamburger out of Mitch's mouth, and Flint seized his arm and said, "That's enough!"

Pelvis looked at him with a sneer curling his upper lip, but he stepped back from Mitch and the half-dead man fell forward to the pier.

They had to get out, and fast. But going through the swamp meant that Clint would surely drown. Flint wanted the derringer back. He ran to the dead man's side, knelt down, and started going through his pockets. His fingers found the derringer, and something else.

A small ring with two keys on it.

Keys? Flint thought. To what?

Flint remembered this man had been driving the cigarette boat that had brought them here. Which of the two boats had it been? The one on the right, not the one with the broken windshield. He didn't know a damn thing about driving a boat, but he was going to have to learn in a hurry. He pushed the derringer into his pocket and stood up. "Cecil!" he yelled. "Come on!"

In the kitchen, the doorway splintered to pieces and blood staining the side of Train's shirt, Dan knew what had to be done.

"Go!" he said. "I'll hold 'em off!"

"The hell with that! Runnin', I ain't!"

"You're dead if you don't. I'm dead anyway. Get out before they come around back."

An automatic fired, the bullet chewing away more of the door frame. The girl was at work again.

"Don't let them get to Arden," Dan said.

Train looked down at his bleeding side. Rib was busted, but he thought his guts were holding tight. It could've been a whole lot worse.

The Ingram gun chattered once more, slugs perforating the walls, forcing Dan and Train to crouch down. Dan leaned out, burned the other two shots in that magazine, and then popped his last four bullets into the Browning.

"Okay," Train said. He put his bloody hand on Dan's shoulder and squeezed. "Us two dinosaur, we fight the good fight, ay?"

"Yeah. Now get out."

"I'm gettin'. *Bonne chance!*" Train ran for the back door, and Dan heard him splash into the swamp.

He was in it for the long haul now. When the automatic fired again, the bullet shattered dishes stacked in a cupboard. Dan heard shots from out front, but surely Train hadn't had time yet to get around the house. Where the hell were Murtaugh and Eisley?

"Come outta there, man!" Doc shouted. "We'll tear down the wall to get you!"

Dan figured his voice was meant to hide the noise of someone— the muscle man, probably—either reloading or crawling across the floor. Dan gave Train six or seven more seconds, then he fired a wild shot through the doorway and took off for the rear. He jumped from the platform into water already chopped up by Train's departure. They'd hear the splash and be after him with a vengeance. He headed directly back into the swamp, through a tangle of vines and floating garbage spilled from the can the young man had dropped. Three steps, and on the fourth his shoe came down on the edge of a root or stump and his ankle twisted, pain knifing up his calf.

Gault had heard the second splash and had gotten up from the floor beside the pool table, ready to storm the kitchen, when there came another noise from out front. The flurry of gunshots had been enough to worry about, but now he heard the rumbling bass notes of one of the cigarette boat's engines trying to fire up. "Get back there after them!" he yelled to Doc. "Try to take one alive!" Then he sprinted for the living room and the sliding glass door that opened onto the platform.

"Can't you get it goin'?" Pelvis was sitting in the white vinyl seat beside Flint, who felt he could have used two more arms to operate the complicated instrument panel.

"Just hang on and be quiet!" The key was turned in the ignition switch, red lights were blinking on some of the gauges, and the engine growled as if it were about to catch, but then it would rattle

778

and die. They had untied the boat's lines, and were drifting from the pier.

Pelvis held the revolver they'd taken from Mitch. He'd seen one bullet remaining in the cylinder. His knuckles were scraped and bleeding; he'd been coming out of his stupor for several minutes before he'd attacked Mitch, the immediacy of their situation having cleared his head of despair for Mama, at least for right now. As Flint struggled to decipher the correct sequence of switches and throttles, Pelvis looked back over his shoulder and his stomach lurched with terror. Gault was coming.

The muscle man had just emerged from the house. He stopped, some of the tan draining from his face at the sight of his two downed associates and the bounty hunters trying to escape in a speedboat. "The Flying Nun" was still playing on the television screen. Gault staggered, as if he were beginning to realize his swamp empire was crumbling; then he came running along the pier, a rictus of rage distorting his face and his finger on the Ingram's trigger.

"Trouble!" Pelvis shouted, and he fired the revolver's last bullet, but it was a wild shot and Gault didn't slow down. Then Gault squeezed off a short burst as he ran, the slugs marching across the pier and chewing holes across the speedboat's stern. "Down!" Flint yelled, frantically trying to start the engine. "Get down!"

Crack, crack! another weapon spoke, and suddenly Gault was gripping his right leg and he stumbled and fell to the planks.

A man neither Flint nor Pelvis had ever seen before had come out from under the pier at the speedboat's bow, and he was standing in the chest-deep water, holding a rifle with a telescopic sight. He fired a third time, but Gault had already crawled over to the far side of the pier and the bullet penetrated wood but not flesh. Then the man shouted to Flint, "I'm drivin'!" and he threw the rifle in and pulled himself over the boat's side, his eyes squeezed shut with pain and effort.

Flint didn't know who the hell he was, but if he could operate this damn boat, he was welcome. He scrambled into the back and picked up the rifle as the man got behind the wheel. "Cover us, you better!" the man yelled; he pulled a chrome lever, hit a toggle switch, and twisted the key. The boat barked oily blue smoke from its exhausts, its engine damaged by the Ingram's bullets. Flint saw Gault getting up on one knee, lifting his weapon to shoot. There was no time to aim through the scope; he started firing and kept firing, and Gault flattened himself again.

The engine boomed, making the boat shake. The rifle in Flint's hands was empty. Gault raised his head. The man behind the wheel grabbed a throttle and wrenched it upward, and suddenly the boat's engine howled and the craft leapt forward with such power Flint was thrown across the stern and almost out of the boat before he could grab hold of a seat back. The man twisted the wheel, a mare's tail of foamy brown water kicking up in their wake. A burst of Ingram bullets pocked the churning surface behind them. The boat tore away toward the bayou, passing the vacant watchtower, as both Flint and Pelvis held on for dear life. Around a bend ahead, blocking the channel, stood a partly submerged pair of gates made of metal guardrails and topped with vicious coils of concertina wire.

Train chopped the throttle back. "Somebody get on the bow!"

Pelvis went, stepping over the windshield as the boat slowed. "You see a way to get that gate open?" Train asked. "Bolt on this side, oughta be!"

"I see it!" The boat's engine was muttering and coughing as Train worked the throttle and gear lever, cutting and giving power until the bow bumped the gate. The bolt, protected by a coating of black grease, was almost down at the waterline. Pelvis lay at the prow and leaned way over; he had to struggle with the bolt for a moment, but then it slid from its latch.

Train gave the engine power, and as Pelvis crawled back over the windshield, the bow shoved the gates apart through bottom mud. He smelled leaking gasoline. The oil gauges showed critical over-heating, red caution lights flashing on the instrument panel. "Hang you on!" Train shouted, and he kicked the throttle up to its limit.

Dan heard a pistol shot. Water splashed three feet from his right shoulder.

"Put the rifle down! Drop it or you get dropped!"

Dan hesitated. The next shot almost kissed his ear.

He let the rifle fall into the water.

"Hands up and behind your head! Do it! Turn around!"

Dan obeyed. Standing on the walkway that led between the house's rear entrance and the incinerator were Doc and the girl, both of them aiming their guns at him.

"I saw you on television!" Doc said. His face glistened with sweat, his hair damp with it. His sunglasses had a cracked lens. "Man, how come you want to fuck us up like this? Huh? After I turned you loose?" He was whining. "Is that how you reward a fuckin' good deed?"

"Get up here!" the girl snapped, motioning with her automatic. "Come on, you sonofabitch!"

Dan eased back through the vines, the pain of his injured ankle making him flinch. From the other side of the house there were more shots and the growl of a speedboat's engine. "Where're Murtaugh and Eisley?"

"Get your ass up here, I said!" The girl glanced at Doc. "You turned him loose?"

"Those two bounty hunters had him in handcuffs, back at St. Nasty. Takin' him to Shreveport. I let him go."

"You mean . . . it's 'cause of *you* all this happened?"

"Hey, don't gimme me any shit now, you hear? Come on, Lambert! Climb up!"

Dan tried. He was exhausted, and he couldn't make it.

"I'm not gonna tell you again," the girl warned. "You get up here or you're dead meat."

"I'm dead meat anyway," Dan answered.

"This is true," Doc said, "but you can sure lose a lot of body parts before you pass on from this vale of tears. I'd try to make it easy on myself if I were you."

Playing for time, Dan grasped the planks and tried once more. With an effort of will over muscle, he got his upper body out of the water and lay there, gasping, on the walkway.

"Shit!" the girl said angrily. "You're the damnedest fool in this *world!* How come you didn't kill him and forget about it? Your mind's gettin' senile, ain't it?"

"You'd better shut your mouth." Doc's voice was very quiet.

"Wait till this sinks in on Gault. You wait till he figures out it's your fault all this happened. Then we'll see whose ass gets kicked."

Doc sighed and looked up through the trees at the sun. "I knew this minute would come," he said. "Ever since you horned in, I did. Kinda glad it's here, really." He turned his pistol toward Shondra's head and with a twitch of his trigger finger put a bullet through the side of her skull. She gave a soft gasp, her golden hair streaked with red, and as her knees buckled she fell off the walkway into the swamp.

"I just took out the garbage," he told Dan. "Stand up."

Dan got his knees under him. Then he was able to stand, the sweat streaming off him and his head packed with pain. "Move," Doc said, motioning with the gun toward the house. "Gault!" he hollered. "I got one of 'em alive!"

They went through the destroyed kitchen, the shot-up dining room, and the bullet-pocked game room. Dan limped at gunpoint through a hallway and then entered a living room where there were a few pieces of wicker furniture, a zebra skin on the floor, and a ceiling fan turning. A sliding glass door opened onto the awning-covered platform, where the screen of a large television on wheels was showing a Pizza Hut commercial.

"Oh, Lord!" Doc said.

Gault was on the platform. He was lying propped up by an elbow on his side, a trail of blood between him and the place on the pier from where he'd crawled. The right leg of his jeans was soaked with gore, his hand pressed to a wound just above the knee. Next to him lay his Ingram gun. Sweat had pooled on the planks around his body, his face strained, his ebony eyes sunken with pain and shock.

"Don't touch me," he said when Doc started to reach down for him. "Where's Shondra?"

"He had a pistol hid! Pulled it out and shot her clean through the head! I knew you wanted him alive, that's why I didn't kill him! Gault, lemme help you up!"

"Stay away from me!" Gault shouted. "I don't need you or anybody!"

"Okay," Doc said. "Okay, that's all right. I'm here."

Gault gritted his teeth and pulled himself closer to Dan. The snakeskin boot on his right foot was smeared with crimson. "Yes," he said, his eyes aimed up at Dan with scorching hatred. "You're the man."

"How was I supposed to know he was gonna come here?" Doc squawked. "He's supposed to be a killer, killed two fuckin' men! I thought he'd be grateful!" He ran a trembling hand across his mouth. "We can start over, Gault. You know we can. It'll be like the old days, just us two against the world. We can build it all again. You know we can."

Gault was silent, staring at Dan.

Dan had seen the bodies lying on the pier. The one farther away was still twitching, the nearer one looked to be stone-cold. He saw that one of the speedboats was gone. "What happened to Murtaugh and Eisley?"

"You came here"—Gault was speaking slowly, as if trying to understand something that was beyond his comprehension—"to get two men who were taking you to prison?"

"He must be crazy!" Doc said. "They must've been takin' him to a loony prison!"

"You destroyed . . . no, no." Gault stopped. His tongue flicked out and wet his lips. "You damaged my business for that reason, and that reason alone?"

"I guess that's it," Dan said.

"Ohhhhh, are you going to suffer." Gault grinned, his eyes dead.

"Ohhhhh, there will be trials and tribulations for you. Who brought you here?"

Dan said nothing.

"Doc," Gault said, and Doc doubled his fist and hit Dan in the stomach, knocking him to his knees.

Dan gasped and coughed, his consciousness fading in and out. The next thing he knew, a bloody hand had gripped his jaw and he was face-to-face with Gault. "Who brought you here?"

Dan said nothing.

"Doc," Gault said, and Doc slammed his booted foot down across Dan's back. "I want you to hold him down," Gault ordered. Doc sat on Dan's shoulders, pinning him. Gault pressed his thumbs into Dan's eye sockets, the muscles of his forearms bunching and twisting under the flesh. "I will ask you once more. Then I'll tear your eyes from your head, and I'll make you swallow them. Who brought you here?"

Dan was too exhausted and in too much pain to even manufacture a lie. Maybe it was Train who'd gotten away in the speedboat, he hoped. Maybe Train had had time by now to put the fire to the Swift's furnace and get Arden far away from this hell. He said nothing.

"You poor, blind fool," Gault said almost gently. And then his thumbs began to push brutally into Dan's eye sockets, and Dan screamed and thrashed as Doc held him down.

Suddenly the pressure relaxed. Dan still had his eyes. "Listen!" Gault said. "What's that?"

There came the sound of rolling thunder.

Dan got his eyes open, tears running from them, and tried to blink away some of the haze. Doc stood up. The noise was getting steadily louder. "Engine," Doc said, his pistol at his side. "Comin' up the bayou, fast!"

"Get me another clip!" There was desperation in Gault's voice. "Doc, help me stand up!"

But Doc was backing away toward the television set, his face blanched as he watched the bayou's entrance. Behind him, the Flying Nun was airborne.

Gault struggled to stand, but his wounded leg—the thighbone broken—would not allow it.

With a full-throated snarl, all pistons pumping, Train's armor-plated Baby came tearing past the watchtower, veered, and headed directly at the platform.

Doc starting firing. Gault made a strangling, cursing noise. Dan grinned, and heaved himself up to his kneees.

The Swift boat did not slow a single knot, even as bullets pinged off the bow's armor. It hurtled toward the platform, a muddy wake shooting up behind its stern.

Dan saw what was going to happen, and he flung himself as hard and far as he could to one side, out of the Swift's path.

In the next instant Baby rammed the platform and the planks cracked with the noise of a hundred pistols going off. The pilings trembled and broke loose, the entire house shuddering from the blow. But Train kept his fist to the throttle and Baby kept surging forward, ripping through the platform, shattering the sliding glass doors, through the living room, through the prefab walls of Gault's dream house, and bursting out through the other side. Train jammed the engine into reverse and backed the Swift out between the two halves of the house, and as he cleared the broken walls the insides began to fall out: a hemorrhage of animal-skin-covered furniture, brass lamps, faux marble tables, pinball machines, exercise equipment, chairs, and even the kitchen sink.

Dan clung to one half of the platform as it groaned and shivered, the walls of the house starting to collapse into the water. On the other half Doc saw the television set rolling away from him, its plug still connected and the screen still showing the images to which he was addicted. He dropped his pistol, his sunglasses gone and his face stricken with crazed terror. He flung both arms around the television in a desperate embrace, but then the planks beneath his feet slanted as the foundation pilings gave way. The set rolled Doc right into the water, and there was a quick *snap, crackle* and *pop* and his body stiffened, smoke ringing his head like a dark halo before he went under.

"Dan! Dan! Grab my hand!"

It was Arden's voice. She was standing at the bow's railing, reaching for him as the boat began to back away from the splintered wreckage. Dan clenched his teeth, drawing up his last reserves of strength. He jumped off the platform, missing Arden's hand but grabbing hold of the railing, his legs dangling in the water.

"Pull him up! Pull him up!" Train shouted behind the pilot-house's bullet-starred glass.

Something seized Dan's legs and wrenched at him.

The fingers of one hand were pulled from the railing. He was hanging on with five digits, his shoulder about to come out of its socket. He looked back, and there was Gault beneath him, patches of the man's skin and face scorched in a gray, scaly pattern by the electrical shock, frozen nerves drawing his lips into a death's-head rictus, one eye rolled back and showing chalky yellow.

Gault made a hissing noise, the muscles twitching in his arms.

Another arm slid down past Dan's face.

In its hand was a derringer.

The little gun went off.

A hole opened in Gault's throat. Bright red blood fountained up from a severed artery.

Other arms caught Dan and held him. Gault's head rose, his mouth open. His hands loosened and slid down Dan's legs. The muddy, churning water flooded into his mouth and filled up his eyes, then his head disappeared beneath its weight.

Dan was pulled up over the railing. He saw the faces of Murtaugh and Eisley, and then Arden was beside him and there were tears in her beautiful eyes, her birthmark the color of summer twilight. Her arms went around him, and he could feel her heartbeat pounding against his chest.

He put his arms around her, too, and hung on.

Then the darkness swelled up around him. He felt himself falling, but it was all right because he knew someone was there to catch him.

28
Avrietta's Island

Dan opened his eyes. He was lying on the deck in the shadow of the pilothouse, the engine vibrating smoothly and powerfully beneath him, the blue sky above, the sound of the hull pushing deep water aside.

A wet rag was pressed to his forehead. Arden looked down at him.

"Where are we?" he whispered, hearing his own voice as if from a great distance.

"Train says we're in Timbalier Bay. We're goin' to a place called Avrietta's Island. Here." She'd poured some of the filtered water into the cup of her hand, and she supported his head while he drank.

Someone else—a man without a shirt—knelt beside him. "Hey, ol' dinosaur you. How you doin'?"

"All right. You?"

Train's face had paled, purplish hollows under his eyes. "Been better. Hurtin' a li'l bit. See, I knew bein' ugly as ten miles of bad road's gonna pay off for me someday. That ol' bullet, he say I gettin' in and out mighty quick, this fella so ugly."

"You need to get to a hospital."

"That's where we bound." Train leaned a little closer to him. "Listen, you gonna have to start associatin' with some more regular fellas, you know what I be sayin'? I take one look at that li'l bitty hand and arm movin' 'round on that fella's chest, my mouth did the open wide. Then I look at that li'l bitty head hangin' down, and I like to bust my teeth when I step on my jaw. And that other fella—the quiet one—he look in the face like somebody I seen, but no way can I figure where."

"It'll probably come to you," Dan said. He felt his consciousness—a fragile thing—fading away again. "How'd you get 'em out? The speedboat?"

786

"*Oui*. Skedaddled outta there, fired up Baby and *huuuuuwheeee!* she done some low-level flyin'."

"You didn't have to come back."

"For sure I did. You rest now, we gonna get where we goin' in twenty, thirty minute." He patted Dan's shoulder and then went away. Arden stayed beside Dan and took one of his hands in hers. His eyes closed again, his senses lulled by the throbbing of the engine, the languid heat, the aroma and caress of the saltwater breeze sweeping across the deck.

They passed through clouds of glistening mist. Sea gulls wheeled lazily above the boat and then flew onward.

"There she is!" Train called, and Arden looked along the line of the bow.

They had gone by several other small islands, sandy and flat and stubbled with prickly brush. This one was different. It was green and rolling, shaded by tall stands of water oaks. There were structures of some kind on it.

As the boat got nearer, Flint stood at the starboard siderail watching the island grow. He was wearing Train's T-shirt because he felt more comfortable with Clint undercover and because the sun had blistered his back and shoulders. Train had come up with a first-aid kit from a storage compartment and Flint's arm wound was bound up with gauze bandages. He had taken off his remaining shoe and his muddied socks and tossed those items overboard like a sacrifice to the swamp. Next to him stood Pelvis, his bald pate and face pink with sunburn. Pelvis hadn't spoken more than a few words since they'd gotten aboard; it was clear to Flint that there was a whole lotta thinkin' goin' on in Pelvis's head.

Train turned the wheel and guided them around to the island's eastern side. They passed spacious green meadows. A herd of goats was running free, doing duty as living lawn mowers. There was an orchard with fruit trees, and a few small whitewashed clapboard buildings that looked like utility sheds. And then they came around into a natural harbor with a pier, and there it was.

Flint heard himself gasp.

It stood on the green and rolling lawn, there on a rise that must have been the island's commanding point. It was a large, clean white mansion with multiple chimneys, a fieldstone path meandering between water oaks, and weeping willow trees from the harbor to the house. Flint's heart was racing. He gripped the rail, and tears burned his eyes.

It was. It was. Oh God, oh Jesus it was . . .

not.

He realized it in another moment, as they approached the pier. There was no stained-glass window in front. The house of his birth had four chimneys; this one had only three. And it wasn't made of white stone, either. It was clapboard, and the paint was peeling. It was an old antebellum mansion, a huge two-storied thing with columns and wide porches. The rolling emerald-green lawn was the same as in his dreams, yes. A few goats were munching the blades down. But the house . . . no.

He still had a star to follow.

"Mr. Murtaugh?" Pelvis said in a voice that was more Cecil's than Elvis's. "How come you're cryin'?"

"I'm not cryin'. My eyes are sunburned, that's all. Aren't yours?"

"No."

"Well," Flint said, and he rubbed the tears away. "Mine are."

Train had cut their speed back. The engine was rumbling quietly as they drew closer. So far they'd seen no one. Arden had left Dan to stand at the bow, the breeze blowing through her hair, her eyes ashine with hope. In her right hand was gripped the pink drawstring bag with her little plastic horses in it.

"I been wonderin'," Pelvis said. " 'Bout what you offered."

"And what was that?" Flint knew, but he'd been shrinking from the memory.

"You know. 'Bout you bein' my manager and all. I sure could use somebody to help me. I mean, I don't know how successful I could be, but—"

"Chopin you're not," Flint said.

"He's dead, ain't he? Both him and Elvis. Dead as doornails." He sighed heavily. "And Mama's dead, too. It's gonna take me awhile to get over that one. Maybe I never will, but . . . I figure maybe it's time for Pelvis to be put to rest, too."

Flint looked into the other man's face. It was amazing how much more intelligent he looked without that ridiculous wig. Dress him up in a nice suit, teach him how to talk without mangling English, teach him some refinements and manners, and maybe a human being of worth would come out of there. But then, it would be an almost impossible task, and he already had a job as a bounty hunter. "I don't know, Cecil," Flint said. "I really don't."

"Well, I was just askin'." Cecil watched the pier approach. "You gonna take Lambert back to Shreveport?"

"He's still a killer. Still worth fifteen thousand dollars."

"Yes sir, that might be true. 'Course, if you decided here pretty soon you wanted to like . . . give it a try at bein' my manager, helpin' me get on a diet and get some work and such, then you wouldn't be a bounty hunter anymore, would you?"

"No," Flint said softly. "I guess I wouldn't." A thought came to him, something the man at the cafe in St. Nasty had said, speaking about Cecil: *Hell, I'll be his manager, then. Get out of this damn swamp and get rich, I won't never look back.*

Maybe he could walk away, he thought. Just walk away. From Smoates, from the ugliness, from the degradation. He still had his gambling debts and his taste for gambling that had gotten him so deep in trouble over the years. He couldn't exactly walk away from those things—those faults—but if he had a purpose and a plan, he could work them out eventually, couldn't he?

Maybe. It would be the biggest gamble of his life.

He found himself stroking his brother's arm through the T-shirt. Clint was as famished as he was. As tired, too. He was going to sleep for a week.

Get out of this damn swamp and get rich, I won't never look back.

He had never been able to get out before, he realized, because he'd never had anything to go to. What if . . . ? he wondered.

What if?

Maybe those two words were the first steps out of any swamp.

"Comin' close!" Train called. "Jump over and tie us up, fellas!"

As Flint and Cecil secured the lines to cleats, Train stepped onto the pier and walked to an old bronze bell supported on a post ten feet high. He grasped the bell's rope and began to ring it, the notes rolling up over the green lawn and through the trees toward the white house on the hill.

In just a few seconds three figures came out of the house and began to hurry down the path.

They were nuns, wearing white habits.

"Sister Caroline, I sure'nuff got some hurt people here!" Train said to the one in the lead as they reached the pier. "Got a fella with a hurt leg, one with an arm needs lookin' at. And I *do* mean lookin' at. Believe I could use a Band-Aid or two myself, ay?"

"Oh, Train!" She was a sturdy woman with light brown eyes. "What's happened to you?"

"Gonna tell you all 'bout it later. Can you put us up?"

"We always have room. Sister Brenda, will you help Train to the house?"

"No, no, my legs ain't broke!" Train said. "Tend to that man lyin' there!"

Two of the nuns helped Arden get Dan up on his feet. Sister

Caroline rang the bell a few more times, and two more nuns emerged to answer the call.

"What is this place?" Arden asked Sister Caroline as Dan was taken off the boat.

The other woman paused, staring at the birthmark. Arden moved so their eyes met. "This island is the convent of the Order of the Shining Light," Sister Caroline answered. "And that"—and she nodded at the white mansion—"is the Avrietta Colbert Hospital. May I ask your name?"

"It's Arden Halliday."

"From?"

"Fort Worth, Texas." Arden turned to Train. "I thought you told me the Bright Girl lived here!"

"The Bright . . . oh, I see." Sister Caroline nodded, glancing from Arden to Train and back again. "Well, I prefer to think we are all bright . . . uh . . . women." She gave Train a hard stare. "Does she know?"

"*Non.*"

"Know what?" Arden asked. "What's goin' on?"

"We shall see," Sister Caroline said flatly, and she turned away to direct the others.

Dan was being walked up the path supported between two nuns, one a young girl maybe twenty-three, the other a woman in her fifties. The shadows of the oak and willow trees were deliciously cool, and a quartet of goats stood watching the group of pilgrims pass.

"Just a minute," someone said, beside Dan.

The nuns stopped. Dan turned his head and found himself face-to-face with Flint Murtaugh.

Flint cleared his throat. He had his arms crossed over his chest, in case Clint made a spectacle of himself. These fine ladies would get a shock soon enough. "I want to thank you," Flint said. "You saved our lives."

"You did the same for me."

"I did what I had to."

"So did I," Dan said.

They stared at each other, and Flint narrowed his eyes and looked away, then returned his cool blue gaze to Dan. "You know what I ought to do."

"Yeah." Dan nodded. Everything was still blurry around the edges; all of this—the morning's events, Gault's stronghold, the gun battle, the Swift severing of the house in two, this green and beautiful island—seemed like bits and pieces of a strange dream. "Tell me what you're *gonna* do."

"I think—" Flint paused. He had careful considerations to make. He held a man's future in the balance: his own. "I think . . . I'm gonna get out of this damn swamp," he said. "Pardon me, Sisters." He looked up the path at the man walking alone. "Cecil, can I talk to you, please?" He left Dan's side, and Dan saw Murtaugh put his hand on Eisley's shoulder as they began to walk together.

The closer they got to the house, the more in need of repair Dan saw it was. He counted a half-dozen places where rainwater must be leaking through loose boards. A section of porch railing on the first floor was rotten and sagging, and several of the columns were cracked. The place needed repainting, too, otherwise the salt breeze and the damp heat would combine to break down the wood in a very short time. He bet the old house had termites, too, chewing at the foundation.

They needed a carpenter around here, is what they needed.

Dan tried to put weight on his injured ankle, but the pain made him sick to his stomach. He was getting dizzy again, and his head was pounding. The blurred edges of things got still more blurry. He was about to give out, and though he fought it, he knew the sickness eventually had to win.

"Sisters?" he said. "I'm sorry . . . but I'm real near passin' out."

"Train!" the older one shouted. "Help us!"

As Dan's knees buckled and the darkness rushed up at him once more, he heard Train say, "Got him, ladies." Dan felt himself being lifted over Train's shoulder in a fireman's carry before he passed out completely, and Train—weak himself but unwilling to let Dan hit the ground—took him the last thirty yards to the house.

Late afternoon had come.

Arden was freshly showered and had slept for five solid hours in a four-poster bed in the room Sister Caroline had brought her to, on the antebellum mansion's first floor. Before her shower another nun about Arden's age had brought her a lunch of celery soup, a ham salad sandwich, and iced tea. When Arden had asked the young woman if the Bright Girl lived here, the nun had given her a tentative smile and left without a word.

On the way to this room they'd passed through a long ward of beds. Most of the beds were in use. Under ceiling fans and crisp white sheets lay some of the patients of the Avrietta Colbert Hospital: a mixture of men, women, and children, white, black, and

Latino. Arden had heard the rattling coughs of tuberculosis, the gasping of cancerous lungs, the slow, labored breathing of people who were dying. The nuns moved around, giving what comfort they could. Some patients were getting better, sitting up and talking; for others, though, it seemed the days were numbered. Arden heard a few Cajun accents, though certainly not all the patients were of that lineage. She was left with the impression that this might be a charity hospital for the poor, probably from the Gulf Delta area, and that the patients were there because no mainland hospital would accept them or—in the case of the elderly ones who lay dying—waste time on them.

The same young nun brought Arden a change of clothes: a green hospital gown and cotton slippers. Not long after she'd awakened there'd been a knock at the door, and when she'd opened it there stood a tall, slim man who was maybe in his mid-sixties, wearing a pair of seersucker trousers, a rumpled white short-sleeve shirt, and a dark blue tie. He'd introduced himself in a gentle Cajun accent as Dr. Felicien, and he'd sat down in an armchair and asked her how she was feeling, was she comfortable, did she have any aches or pains, things like that. Arden had said she was still tired but otherwise fine; she'd said she had come here to find the Bright Girl, and did he know who she meant?

"I most think I do," Dr. Felicien had said. "But I gonna have to beg off and leave that for later. You try to get yourself some more sleep now, heah?" He'd gone without answering any further questions.

A fan turned above her bed. Her window looked out toward the Gulf, and she could see waves rolling in. Shadows lay across the lawn. She had figured this room belonged to a doctor or someone else on the staff. When she went in the small but spotless bathroom to draw water from the faucet into a Dixie cup, she looked at her face in the mirror, studying her birthmark as she had a thousand times before.

She was very, very scared.

What if it had been a lie? All along, a lie? Maybe Jupiter hadn't been lying, but he'd just been plain wrong. Maybe he'd seen a young and pretty blond woman in LaPierre when he was a little boy, and maybe later on he'd heard the myths about a Bright Girl— a faith healer who could cheat time itself—and he'd mixed up one with the other? But if there *was* a Bright Girl, then who was she, *really?* Why had Train brought her here, and what was going on?

She lifted her hand and ran her fingers along the edges of her birthmark. What would she do, she asked herself, if this mark—this bad-luck stain that had ruined her life—had to remain on her face for the rest of her days? What if there was no magic healing touch? No ageless Bright Girl who carried a lamp from God inside her?

Closing her eyes, Arden leaned her face against the mirror. She'd felt she was so close. So very close. It was a cruel trick, this was. Nothing but a cruel, cruel trick.

Someone knocked at the door. Arden went to open it, thinking that it was probably Dr. Felicien with more questions or the young nun.

She opened the door and the face that looked at her both startled and horrified her.

It belonged to a man. He had neatly combed sandy-brown hair on the right side of his head, but on the left side there were just tufts of it. A terrible burn and the subsequent healing process had drawn the skin up into shiny parchment on that left side, his mouth twisted, the left eye sunken in folds of scar tissue. The left ear was a melted nub and the man's throat was mottled with burn scar. His nose, though scarred, had escaped the worst of the damage, and the right side of his face was almost untouched. Arden stepped back, her own face mirroring the shock she felt, but at once that feeling changed to shame. If anybody understood what it meant to look at someone shrink away from you in a display of ill manners and idiocy, it was she.

But if the man was bothered by her reaction, he didn't show it. He smiled. He was wearing dark blue pants, a blue-striped shirt, and a bow tie. "Miss Halliday?"

Arden remembered she'd told Dr. Felicien she was unmarried.

"She wants to see you," the burn-scarred man said.

"She? *Who?*"

"Oh, I'm sorry. I forget that everybody 'round here doesn't know her name. Miz Kathleen McKay. I believe she's who you've come to find."

"She's—" Arden's heart slammed. "She's the Bright Girl?"

"Some would call her that, I 'magine. If you'd like to come with me?"

"Yes! I would! Just a minute!" She crossed the room and got the little pink bag from atop a dresser.

On the way out they went through another ward toward the rear of the hospital, and in passing the man spoke to the patients, calling their names, giving some encouragement, throwing a joking remark here and there. Arden couldn't help but see how the patients—even the very, very sick ones—perked up at this man's presence. She saw their faces, and she saw that not one of them flinched or showed any degree of distaste. It dawned on her that they didn't see his scars.

Arden followed him away from the house and along another fieldstone path that led toward a grove of pecan trees. "I hear you had a time findin' us," the man said as they walked.

"Yes, I did." She figured Dr. Felicien or somebody had gotten the whole story from either Dan or Train.

"That's a good sign, I think."

"It is?"

"Surely," he said, and he smiled again. "It's not far, right through here." He led her under a canopy of interlocking tree branches, and just on the other side was a small but immaculately kept white clapboard house with a screened-in front porch. Off to one side was a flower garden, and a plot of vegetables as well. Arden felt faint as the man walked up the front steps and opened the door to the screened porch.

He must have noticed her condition, because he said, "Are you all right?"

"I'm fine. Just a little light-headed."

"Breathe deep a few times, that oughta help."

She did, standing at the threshold. And suddenly she realized who this fire-scarred man must be. "What's . . . what's your name?" she asked.

"Pearly Reese."

She had known it, but still it almost knocked her knees out from under her. She remembered the prostitute at the cafe in St. Nasty saying that the Bright Girl was an old woman who *came to Port Fourchon to see my mama's cousin. His name was Pearly, he was seven years old when he got burned up in a fire. Near thirty years ago*, she'd said. *The Bright Girl took him with her in a boat.*

"Do you know me?" Pearly asked.

"Yes I do," she said. "Your second cousin helped me get here."

"Oh." He nodded, even if he didn't quite understand. "I think that must be a good sign, too. You ready to meet her?"

"I am," Arden said.

He took her inside.

29

The Bright Girl

Once inside the door, Pearly called, "Miz McKay? I brought her!"

"Come on back, then! I know I look a fright, but come on back anyway!"

It had been the raspy voice of an old woman, yes. Dan had been right, Arden realized as the first hard punch of reality hit her. There was no such thing as a woman who could stay young forever. But even if Jupiter had been mistaken about that part of it, the Bright Girl could still have the healing touch in her hands. She was terrified as she followed Pearly through a sitting room, a short hallway, and then into a bedroom.

And there was the Bright Girl, propped up on peach-colored pillows in bed. Sunlight spilled through lace-curtained windows across the golden pine-plank floor, and above the bed a ceiling fan politely murmured.

"Oh," Arden whispered, and as tears came to her eyes her hand flew up to cover her mouth so she wouldn't say something stupid.

The Bright Girl was, indeed, an elderly woman. Maybe she was eighty-five, possibly older. If her hair had ever been blond, it was all snow now. Her face was heavily lined and age-spotted, but even so, Arden could tell that in her long-ago youth this woman had been lovely. She was wearing a white gown, and now she reached to a bedside table for a pair of wire-rimmed eyeglasses. The movement was slow, and her mouth tightened with pain. The fingers of her hand were all twisted and malformed, and she had difficulty picking the glasses up. At once Pearly was at her side, but he didn't put the glasses on her face for her. He steadied her hand so her gnarled fingers could do the work. Then she got the glasses on, and Arden saw that behind the lenses there was still fire in the Bright Girl's pale amber eyes. Like lamps, Arden thought. Like shining lamps.

"Sit." The Bright Girl lifted her other hand, the fingers just as twisted, and motioned toward a flower-print armchair that had been turned to face the bed. The elderly woman's voice trembled; either from palsy or being nervous, Arden didn't know. Arden sat down, her hands clutching the pink bag in her lap, her heart galloping.

"Lemonade," the Bright Girl said. Her breathing, too, looked painful. "Want a glass?"

"I . . . think I would."

"I can put a shot of vodka in it for you." The Bright Girl, surprisingly, had a midwestern accent.

"Uh . . . no. Just lemonade."

"Pearly, would you? And I *will* take a shot of vodka in mine."

The two women were silent. The Bright Girl stared at Arden, but Arden wasn't sure where to park her eyes. She was so glad to have found this person, so glad to finally be there, but she was feeling a crush of disappointment, too. The Bright Girl wasn't who Jupiter had said she was. The Bright Girl could not cheat time, and she wasn't a faith healer. If she had a healing touch, then why hadn't she been able to smooth the scars on Pearly's face? Tears burned Arden's eyes again; they were the bitter tears of knowing she had been wrong.

The Bright Girl—at least the time-cheating, never-aging, faith-healing part of her—was a myth. The truth was that the Bright Girl was a rather small, frail, white-haired eighty-five-year-old woman who had gnarled fingers and labored breathing.

"Don't cry," the Bright Girl said.

"I'm all right. Really." Arden wiped her eyes with the back of her hand. "I'm—" She stopped. The floodgates were about to burst. It had all been wrong. It had been a cruel, cruel trick.

"Go ahead if you want to cry. I cried my eyes out, too, that first day."

The tears had begun trickling down Arden's cheeks. She sniffled. "What do you mean . . . *you* cried, too?"

"When I came here and found out." She paused, her breathing strained. "Found out the Bright Girl couldn't just put her hands on me and take it all away."

Arden shook her head. "I'm not . . . I don't understand. Take what away?"

The old woman smiled slightly. "The pain. The Bright Girl couldn't heal me of the pain. That I had to do for myself."

"But . . . *you're* the Bright Girl, aren't you?"

"I'm *a* Bright Girl."

"Are you . . . are you a nun?"

"Me, a nun? Unh-unh! I raised too much hell when I was a young girl to be a nun now! The thing is, I enjoyed raising hell. Seeing my father"—again, she had to pause to regulate her breathing—"squirm when the police brought me home. We didn't get along so very well."

Pearly came in, bringing a plain plastic tray with two jelly-jar glasses of lemonade. "Take this one," he said, giving Arden a glass, "unless you want your head knocked off. Miz McKay likes the occasional libation."

"I wish you would *quit* that! Over thirty damn years," she said, speaking to Arden, "and he still calls me *Miz* McKay! Like I'm some weak little old flower that just slumps in the"—a breath, a breath—"slumps in the noonday sun! My name is *Kathleen!"*

"You know I was raised to respect my elders. Don't drink that down too fast, now."

"I'll gulp it in a second if I want to!" she snapped, but she didn't. "Let us be alone now, Pearly. We have to talk."

"Yes ma'am."

"There he goes with that southern-fried crap again! Go out and pee on the flowers or something!"

Pearly left the room. The Bright Girl gripped her glass with both hands, drew it to her wrinkled mouth, and sipped. "Ahhhh," she said. "That's better." She glanced up at the ceiling fan that turned above them. "I never could get used to this heat down here. For a time I thought I couldn't stand it, that I was going to have to get back"—a breath, then another—"to Indiana. That's where I'm from. Evansville, Indiana. You said you're from Fort Worth?"

"Yes."

"Well, that's good, then. Hot in Texas, too." She sipped her vodka-laced lemonade again. "That's some birthmark you've got there."

Arden nodded, not knowing how to respond.

"You came here to be healed, didn't you?"

"Yes."

"And now you're sitting there thinking you're the biggest. Biggest fool who ever put on panties. You came down here to be healed by a young, pretty girl who never ages. Who people say lives forever. You didn't come here to"—breathing again, her lungs making a soft hitching noise—"listen to an old woman spit and snort, did you?"

"No," Arden had to admit. "I didn't."

"I came to be healed, too. My 'condition,' as my father put it"—she nodded toward a walker by the bed—"used to be able to get around on a cane, but . . . I can hardly stand up on the walker now.

I've had severe arthritis since I was a young girl. About your age, maybe younger. My father was from old money. The family's in banking. Very social dogs, they are. So when the lovely daughter can't dance on her crippled"—a pause—"crippled legs at the social events, and when the white gloves won't slip over her twisted fingers, then. Then the specialists are called. But when the specialists can't do very much, then lovely daughter becomes a pariah. Lovely daughter spends more and more time alone, growing bitter. Drinking. Screwing any boy who. Boy who'll have her. Lovely daughter has several ugly public scenes. Then one day lovely daughter is told she will have a companion, to watch her and keep her out of trouble. Being enlightened bastards, we have hired a sturdy, nonthreatening woman of color who doesn't. Doesn't know what she ought to be being paid." Kathleen McKay drank from the glass once more, her gnarled fingers locked together. "That woman of color . . . was born in Thibodoux. That's about fifty miles up Highway One from Grand Isle. We used to share a bottle of Canadian Club, and she told me wonderful stories."

Arden said, "I still don't under—"

"Oh, yes, you do!" Kathleen interrupted. "You understand it all! You just don't want to let. Let go of the illusion. I've been sitting right where you are, talking to an old, used-up, and dying woman. In this very bed. Her name was Juliet Garrick, and she was from Mobile, Alabama. She had one leg three inches shorter than the other. The one before her . . . well, I don't remember. Some wicked deformity or another, I'm sure. Are you positive you don't want a shot of vodka?"

"I'm sure," Arden said. Her heart had stopped pounding, but her nerves were still raw. "How many . . . how many Bright Girls have there been?"

"Cemetery's not far. You can go count for yourself. But I think the first two were buried at sea."

Arden still felt like crying. She felt like having a cry that would break the heart of the world. Maybe she would, later. But not right now. "Who was the first one?"

"The woman who founded the hospital. Avrietta Colbert. Her journals and belongings and things are in a museum between the chapel and where the sisters live. Interesting, gutsy lady. Strong-willed. Before the Civil War she was on a ship with her husband, sailing from South America to New Orleans. He was a rancher. Wealthy people. Anyway, not far from here a storm blew up and smashed their ship. Smashed their ship in these barrier islands. She washed up here. The legend goes that she vowed to God she would build a church and hospital for the poor on the first island that would have her. This one did, and she did. There's a photograph of her over there. She was a beautiful young blond woman. But her eyes . . . you can tell she had fire in her."

Arden sighed. She lowered her head and put a hand to her face.

"The sisters came here sometime in the forties," Kathleen went on. "They manage the place, pay the staff, make sure all that work's done." She finished her lemonade and very carefully put the glass down on the bedside table. "All of us—the Bright Girls, I mean—came from different places, for different reasons. But we all have shared one very, very important thing."

Arden lifted her head, her eyes puffy and reddened. "What's that?"

"We believed," Kathleen said. "In miracles."

"But it was a lie. It was always a lie."

"No." Kathleen shook her white-crowned head. "It was an illusion, and there's a difference. What the Bright Girl could do— what she was—became what people wanted to believe. If there is no hope, what reason is there to live? A world without miracles . . . well, that would be a world I wouldn't care to live in."

"*What* miracles?" Arden asked, a little anger creeping in. "I don't see any miracles around here!"

Kathleen leaned forward, wincing with the effort. Her cheeks and forehead had become blushed with anger, too; she was a scrapper. She said three short, clipped words: "Open. Your. Eyes."

Arden blinked, surprised by the strength in the old woman's voice.

"No, you can't get your birthmark healed here! Just like I couldn't get my arthritis healed, or Juliet Garrick couldn't get her short leg lengthened! That's junk! But what's not junk"—a breath, a breath, a breath—"not junk is the fact that I can walk through those wards. Through those wards, hobbling on my walker. I can walk through them and people who are dying sit up they sit up in their beds and they smile to see me and for"—a gasp—"for a few minutes they have an escape. They smile and laugh as if they've touched the sun. For a few precious, precious minutes. And children with cancer, and tuberculosis, and AIDS, they come out of their darkness to reach for my hand, and they hold on to me. On to me like I am *somebody*, and they don't mind my ugly fingers. They don't see that Kathleen McKay of Evansville, Indiana, is old and crippled!" Her eyes were fierce behind the glasses. "No, they hold on to the Bright Girl."

She paused, getting her breath again. "I don't lie to them," she said after a moment or two. "I don't tell them they can beat their sicknesses, if Dr. Felicien or Dr. Walcott don't say so first. But I have tried—I have *tried*—to make them understand the miracle the way I and Sister Caroline see it. That flesh is going to die, yes. It's going to leave this world, and that's the way life is. But I believe in the miracle that though flesh dies, the spirit does not. It goes on, just like the Bright Girl goes on. Though the women who wear that title wither and pass away, the Bright Girl does not. She lives on and on, tending to her patients and her hospital. Walking the wards. Holding the hands. She lives on. So don't you *dare* sit there with your eyes closed and not look at what God is offering to *you!*"

Arden's mouth slowly opened. "To . . . me?"

"Yes, you! The hospital would survive without a Bright Girl—I guess it would, I don't know—but it would be. Be terribly changed. All the Bright Girls over the many years have held this place together. And it's not been easy, I'll tell you! Storms have torn the hospital half to pieces, there've been money problems, equipment problems, troubles keeping the. The old buildings from falling apart. It's far from perfect. If there wasn't a Bright Girl to solicit contributions, or fight the oil companies who want to start drilling. Drilling right offshore here and ruin our island. Keep our patients awake all night long, where would we be?"

She closed her eyes and leaned her head back against the pillow. "I don't know. I *do* know . . . I don't want to be the last one. No. I won't be the one who breaks the chain." She sighed, and was silent with her thoughts. When she spoke again, her voice was low and quiet. "The Bright Girl can't be any damn pushover. She's got to be a fighter, and she's got to do the hard work as best she can. Most of all"—Kathleen's eyes opened—"she can't be afraid to take responsibility."

Arden sat very still, her hands gripping the drawstring bag.

"Maybe you're not the one. I don't know. Damn, I'm tired. Those sisters over there, praying and praying at the chapel. I told them. I said if she's coming, she'll be here. But maybe you're not the one."

Arden didn't know what to say. She stood up from her chair, but she didn't know where to go, either.

"If you stayed," Kathleen said, "if you did what had to be done . . . I could promise you no one here would even see that birthmark. It would be gone. They'd see only the face behind it."

Arden stood in a spill of light, caught between what was and what could be.

"Go on, then." Kathleen's voice was weary. "There's a radio at the hospital. The ferry can get here from Grand Isle in half an hour. I know the man who owns the marina. He can find a ride out for you, take you up Highway One to Golden Meadow. Catch the bus from there. Do you have money?"

"No."

"Pearly!" Kathleen called. *"Pearly!"* There was no response. "If he's not outside, he's probably walked along the path to the barn. Go over there and tell him I said to give you fifty dollars and call the marina for you."

"The barn?" Arden's heart was pounding again. "What's . . . in the barn?"

"Horses, of course! Those things have always scared the skin off me, but Pearly loves them. I told him, when one of them kicks him in the head one day, he won't spend so much time over there."

"Horses," Arden whispered, and at last she smiled.

"Yes, horses. Avrietta Colbert's husband was a rancher. They were bringing horses back from South America on their ship. Some of the horses swam here, those started the herd. We raise and sell them, to make money for the hospital." Kathleen frowned. "What's wrong?"

Arden's eyes had filled with tears. She couldn't speak, her throat had clutched up. Then she got it out: "Nothing's wrong. I think . . . I think everything's right."

She was crying now, and she was half blind. But she realized at that moment that never before had she seen so much, or so clearly.

He was sitting in a chair on the upper porch, the blue shadows of twilight gathering on the emerald lawn. A crutch leaned against the railing beside him. He was watching the sun slide toward the Gulf, and he was thinking about what had happened an hour ago.

The ferryboat had come from Grand Isle. He'd been sitting right there, watching. Two men and Sister Caroline had left the hospital, walking down the path to the pier. One of the men was bald and fat, but he walked with his shoulders back as if he'd found something to be proud of about himself. The other man, tall and slim and wearing a dark suit and a new pair of black wingtips someone on the staff had brought him yesterday from the mainland, had stopped short of getting aboard the ferry and had looked back.

Dan had stared at Flint Murtaugh, across the distance.

Nothing had remained to be said. They'd still been cautious around each other during the last three days, both of them knowing how much he was worth as a wanted fugitive. Dan figured the idea of all that money still chewed at Murtaugh, but the fact that Dan had gone after them when he could have cut and run was worth much, much more.

Then Murtaugh had turned away and stepped onto the ferryboat. Sister Caroline had waved to them as the boat's lines were cast off. Dan had watched the boat get smaller and smaller as it carried Eisley and Murtaugh onward to the rest of their lives. He wished them well.

"Hey, ol' dinosaur, you. Mind if I plop?"

"Go ahead."

Train had walked out onto the porch. He drew a wicker chair up beside Dan and eased himself into it. He was still wearing a green hospital gown, much to his displeasure. His bullet wound—a grazed gash and a broken rib—was healing, but Dr. Walcott had insisted he stay for a while. It had been two days since Dan had seen Arden, whom he'd caught a glimpse of from the window beside his bed, walking around the grounds with Sister Caroline. Arden hadn't been at lunch in the hospital's small cafeteria, either. So something was definitely going on, and he didn't know if she'd found her Bright Girl or not. One thing was for sure: she still wore her birthmark.

"How the leg feel?"

"It's gettin' along. Dr. Felicien says I almost snapped my ankle."

"Hell, you coulda done worse, ay?"

"That's right." Dan had to laugh, though he would see Gault's mottled face in his nightmares for a long time to come.

"Yeah. You done good, leatherneck. I won't never say no more bad tings 'bout marines."

"I didn't know you ever said anything bad about marines."

"Well," Train said, "I was gettin' to it."

Dan folded his hands across his chest and watched the waves rolling in and out. When the breeze blew past, he saw some paint flake off the sun-warped railing. This was a peaceful place, and its quiet soothed his soul. There were no televisions, but there was a small library down on the first floor. He felt rested and renewed, though he couldn't help but notice there was a lot of carpentry work needed on the aging structure. "How long have you known about this place?"

"Years and years. I bring 'em cat and turtle. Who you tink carted the goats here from Goat Island?"

"Did you tell 'em about me?" he had to ask.

"Sure I did!" Train said. "I told 'em you was a fine ol' fella."

Dan turned his head and looked into Train's face.

"Ain't it true?" Train asked.

"I'm still a wanted killer. They're still lookin' for me."

"I know two men who ain't. They just got on the boat and gone."

Dan leaned forward and rested his chin on his hands. "I don't know what to do, Train. I don't know where to go."

"I could put you up for a while."

"In that houseboat? You need space just like I do. That wouldn't work."

"Maybe no." Both of them watched a freighter in the shimmering distance. It was heading south. Train said, "The steamers and workboats, they come in, unload, and load again at Port Sulphur. Ain't too very far ways from here. Some of them boats lookin' for crew. You up to workin'?"

"I think I could handle some jobs, if they weren't too tough."

"I tink you could, too. Maybe you take some time, decide for y'self. Couple a' day, I'm goin' back home. Maybe you stick 'round here week, two week, we gonna go do us some fishin', little dinosaur-talkin', ay?"

"Yeah," Dan said, and he smiled again. "That'd be great."

"I take you to a lake, fulla cat—huuuuwheeee!—big like you never did saw!"

"*Dan?*"

They looked to their left, toward the voice. Arden had come out on the porch. Her wavy blond hair shone in the late sunlight, and she was wearing a clean pair of khakis and a green-striped blouse. "Can I talk to you for a few minutes? Alone?"

"Oh, well, I gotta shake a tail feather anyhow." Train stood up. "I'll talk at you later, *bon ami.*"

"See you, Train," Dan said, and the Cajun walked back through a slatted door into the hospital. Arden took his chair. "What've you been up to?" Dan asked her. He saw she no longer carried her pink drawstring bag. "I haven't seen you for a while."

"I've been busy," she said. "Are you okay?"

"I believe I am."

She nodded. "It's a beautiful place, don't you think? A beautiful island. Of course . . . that's not sayin' it doesn't need work." She reached out to the railing and picked off some of the cracking paint. "Look there. The wood underneath that doesn't look too good either, does it?"

"No. That whole railin' oughta be replaced. I don't know who's in charge of the maintenance around here, but they're slippin'. Well"—he shrugged—"they're all old buildin's, I guess they're doin' the best they can."

"They could do better," Arden said, looking into his eyes.

He had to bring this up. Maybe he'd regret it, but he had to. "Tell me," he said, "did you ever find out who the Bright Girl is?"

"Yes," she answered, "I sure did."

Arden began to tell him the whole story. Dan listened, and as he listened he could not help but think back to his meeting with the Reverend Gwinn, and the man giving him the gift of time and saying *God can take a man along many roads and through many mansions. It's not where you are that's important; it's where you're goin' that counts. Hear what I'm sayin'?*

Dan thought he did. At last, he thought he did.

It occurred to him, as Arden told him her intention to stay on the island, that Jupiter had been right. He had a lot to think about in the time ahead, but it seemed that he had indeed been the man God had sent to take Arden to the Bright Girl. Maybe this whole thing had been about her and this hospital from the beginning, and he and Blanchard, Eisley and Murtaugh, Train and the drug runners, and all the rest of it had been cogs in a machine designed to draw Arden to this island for the work that had to be done.

Maybe. He could never know for sure. But she had found her Bright Girl and her purpose, and it seemed also that he had found his own refuge if he wanted it.

He could never go back. He didn't want to. There was nothing behind him now. There was only tomorrow and the day after that, and he would deal with them when they came.

Dan reached out and took Arden's hand.

Out in the distance, on the shining blue Gulf, there was a sailboat moving toward the far horizon. Its white sails filled with the winds of freedom, and it ventured off for a port unknown.